HEROES
AND
VILLAINS

HEROES AND VILLAINS

The True Story of the Beach Boys

Steven Gaines

NAL BOOKS

NEW AMERICAN LIBRARY

NEW YORK AND SCARBOROUGH, ONTARIO

Published simultaneously in Canada by The New American Library of Canada Limited

The author gratefully acknowledges permission to reprint the following song lyrics:

"California Girls." Lyrics and music by Brian Wilson, © 1965 & 1970, Irving Music, Inc. (BMI). All rights reserved. International copyright secured.

"Fun, Fun, Fun." Lyrics and music by Brian Wilson & Mike Love, © 1964, Irving Music, Inc. (BMI). All rights reserved. International copyright secured.

"God Only Knows." Lyrics by Brian Wilson and Tony Asher, Music by Brian Wilson, © 1966, Irving Music, Inc. (BMI). All rights reserved. International copyright secured.

"Heroes and Villains." Lyrics and music by Brian Wilson and Van Dyke Parks, © 1967, Irving Music, Inc. (BMI). All rights reserved. International copyright secured.

"I Get Around." Lyrics and music by Brian Wilson, © 1964, Irving Music, Inc. (BMI). All rights reserved. International copyright secured.

"In My Room." Lyrics and music by Brian Wilson and Gary Usher, © 1964, Irving Music, Inc. (BMI). All rights reserved. International copyright secured.

"Surfin' U.S.A." Copyright © 1958 & 1963 by ARC MUSIC CORPORATION. Reprinted by permission. All rights reserved.

 NAL BOOKS TRADEMARK REG. U.S. PAT. OFF. AND FOREIGN COUNTRIES
REGISTERED TRADEMARK—MARCA REGISTRADA
HECHO EN HARRISONBURG, VA., U.S.A.

SIGNET, SIGNET CLASSIC, MENTOR, ONYX, PLUME, MERIDIAN AND NAL BOOKS
are published in the United States by New American Library,
1633 Broadway, New York, New York 10019,
in Canada by The New American Library of Canada Limited,
81 Mack Avenue, Scarborough, Ontario M1L 1M8

Library of Congress Cataloging-in-Publication Data

Gaines, Steven S.
  Heroes and villains.

  1. Beach Boys. 2. Rock musicians—United
States—Biography. I. Title.
ML421.B38G3 1986   784.5'4'00922 [B]   86-12872
ISBN 0-453-00519-5

Designed by Fritz Metsch

First Printing, October, 1986

1 2 3 4 5 6 7 8 9

PRINTED IN THE UNITED STATES OF AMERICA

For Mom and Dad

Introduction

I was with Brian Wilson the first time he surfed.

It was Father's Day, June 20, 1976, a glorious summer Sunday on Trancas Beach, Malibu, half a mile from the Wilson clan's rented summer home. Standing by the edge of the ocean, Brian Wilson was a wondrous vision. Six feet three inches tall, weighing an imposing 240 pounds, he was dressed in a soft forest-green terry-cloth robe that flapped about his bare legs in the brisk June winds. His almost perfectly round belly— like a soft pink volleyball—swelled out from under the robe and was exposed to the chill late afternoon air. The wind blew his black hair away from a bearded, handsome, cherubic face. There was something mystical and childlike about him; he radiated an aura, a magnetic presence that drew people to him. He turned and looked out to the ocean, and the distance in his eyes made the expanse of the Pacific seem small.

But those eyes. Those cold blue eyes were terrified. Brian Wilson was somewhere else, struggling hard to be in touch with what was happening on the beach, but from the other side of a psychic glass wall. Brian Wilson is schizophrenic. As the producer-composer of the Beach Boys, Brian, along with his brothers Dennis and Carl Wilson, cousin Mike Love, and friend Al Jardine, had proselytized the legendary California good life around the world for fifteen years, but for twelve of those years Brian had been on a reclusive psychological odyssey.

That Sunday in June was not only Father's Day, it was also

Brian's thirty-fourth birthday and an unofficial celebration of his rebirth. Only eight months before, with the aid of Los Angeles therapist Eugene Landy, Brian had gotten out of bed in his $500,000 Bel Air home for the first time in four years and begun a daily routine of jogging, athletics, and sporadic trips to the recording studio.

Brian was on the beach that day, along with a few family members and his therapist, to film a segment of an upcoming NBC-TV special on the Beach Boys, "The Beach Boys: It's O.K." The show was part of the general excitement about Brian's recent steps back to reality. Produced by "Saturday Night Live" producer Lorne Michaels, the special was a celebration of Brian's rebirth. I was invited to the beach that day as a journalist writing a story about Brian for *New West* magazine.

To photograph Brian Wilson surfing was Lorne Michaels's *ne plus ultra* irony: Brian Wilson had never surfed. Although the Beach Boys had sold an estimated eighty million records—twenty million of them with surfing as a major theme—and Brian had splashed around in the water with his brothers for publicity photos, he had never mounted a surfboard before. Indeed, photographing Brian in the surf was almost a cruel joke, because Brian had a deep, abiding fear of the water, and in his childlike manner he would warble in a thin voice, "The ocean *scares* me!" Nevertheless, that day Brian would face the Pacific.

The segment of the show opened with Brian lying in the bed to which he had retreated for so many years, a four-poster adorned with a headboard of carved angels. He was a huge, whale-shaped figure under the blankets, with only his large bearded face visible, and those small, scared eyes blinking expectantly. Into the room, dressed in policemen's uniforms, strode two "Saturday Night Live" regulars, John Belushi and Dan Aykroyd. Belushi and Aykroyd presented Brian with a warrant for his arrest, charging him with never having surfed. They marched him down the curving staircase of the house, and brought him to the beach in a patrol car with a surfboard attached to the roof.

Now, with the cameras trained upon a terrified and wooden-looking Brian, the surfboard tucked under his arm, Belushi ordered, "Let's go, Wilson, here's your wave."

With his bathrobe still wrapped around him, Brian bolted into the water, the waves crashing around his corpulent body. For a fraction of a second he mounted the board on his huge belly, but the ocean quickly pulled him under, baptizing him. "I felt the power of the sea," he later told me. "It was cold and I felt the sea begin to grasp me." His wet terry robe clung to him as he regained his balance. With a stunned and questioning look, he turned toward the cameras, hoping his ordeal was over. But the people on the beach only laughed and cheered and shook hands, paying no attention to Brian at all, and the cameras rolled on. So Brian, ever the trouper, turned bravely back into the surf, his robe falling away from him as he played farther into the icy water after his drifting surfboard. When he finally emerged from the water, his wife, Marilyn, shielded him from ungracious photographers as she toweled and dried her shivering husband.

From that day on, my fascination with Brian Wilson and the Beach Boys grew to a passion. That summer I made three trips to California and spent nearly a month following the Beach Boys around, interviewing all of them at some length, including Dennis Wilson, Carl Wilson, Alan Jardine, and Mike Love. Mike Love not only consented to an interview, but even invited me to his apartment in Marina Del Rey for a lecture and meditation session. I also interviewed Beach Boys' mother Audree Wilson, and was invited into Brian's home by his wife, Marilyn Wilson, for a long and candid interview.

During those same weeks I spent several days and evenings with Brian's therapist, Dr. Eugene Landy, in direct interview. Dr. Landy invited me and my tape recorder to remain with him in his office during a therapy session with Brian Wilson. Thanks to Dr. Landy, I was also allowed to interview Brian extensively and observe him in his private life, which included going bowling with him at Pico Lanes, jogging in Rancho Park, and attending with him various public events for the taping of the NBC-TV show. The time I spent alone with Brian was the most exciting and valuable of all, and I am deeply grateful for this personal access. Brian is rawly honest and revealing, a child-man, terribly vulnerable to journalists and strangers, alternately frightened and eager to please. At the beginning of our first interview, he stopped after just two sentences. "I don't know why," he told me. "I'm just thinking of ending the interview here and letting you write the story." But he didn't stop there. He stayed for that interview and several more, all of which are included in this book.

Although in the preparation of *Heroes and Villains* I have depended heavily on those initial interviews and tapes with Brian Wilson and the Beach Boys and their families, over a hundred new interviews were conducted exclusively for this book. To my great regret, several sources with firsthand knowledge of the Beach Boys' personal and business lives refused to be identified, and would only agree to be interviewed anonymously. To these people I am indebted for their insight and for their massive contributions to this text. However, for this reason I must also caution the reader that a character's inclusion or exclusion in a scene or event does not necessarily indicate that that person has contributed to this book.

Fortunately, I am able to thank Brian Wilson's wife of nearly sixteen years, Marilyn Rovell Wilson, for her time and trust in me and her tremendous help with this book, which included many hours of interviews, as well as her endorsement of me to other participants. My thanks also to her sister, Diane Rovell, who worked and lived with the Beach Boys at Marilyn's side, as well as to their mother and father, May and Irving Rovell. Their exhaustive interviews and kindnesses—including May's delicious chicken soup—are greatly appreciated.

I am especially grateful to Karen Lamm, for sharing her life with Dennis Wilson in over twenty-five hours of interviews, including access to personal diaries she scrupulously kept over the last fifteen years; Carol Bloome, Dennis Wilson's first wife, for her long and candid interview; Barbara Charren Wilson, Dennis's second wife, for her exclusive interview and trust in me during the preparation of this book; Chris Kable, Dennis Wilson's personal assistant and dear friend, whose outspoken support has sustained me through many troubled times; Annie Hinsche Wilson, Carl Wilson's former wife of fourteen years, for her interview; Jerry Schilling, Carl's personal manager, for his interview; and Robert L. Levine, Dennis Wilson's personal and business manager, whose insights and information greatly enhanced the preparation of this book.

Rick Nelson, Brian Wilson's personal business manager, was instrumental in my gathering substantial information for this book, as was Janet Lent-Coop Nelson, former president of Brother Enterprises and Brian Wilson's co—business manager.

Stanley Love, brother of Mike and Stephen Love, also helped to inform this book substantially, as did his grandmother, Edith Clardy Love, and his father, Milton Love.

I am indebted to Eva Easton and David Leaf, for their support and kindness, and for putting up with my early morning phone calls. Without their help, and David's 1978 book on the Beach Boys, this book would have been a greater struggle. And to Peter Reum, whose Beach Boys archive is the finest in existence, and who supplied many of the exclusive photographs used in this book.

I would also like to thank, for their varied assistance and/ or interviews, many patient people, some of whom indulged me with two and three interviews, including Fred Vail, Van Dyke Parks, David Anderle, Gary Usher, Eddie Merado, David Marks, Nik Venet, Rich Sloane, Chuck Kaye, Tom Murphy, Curt Boetcher, Bob Merlis, Chris Clark, Steve Goldberg, Michael Moss, Coleen McGovern, Bill Oster, Bruce Morgan, Dorinda Morgan, Joel Moss, Carol Thompson, Joe Saraceno, Bud Cort, Ida Smith Kennedy, Bob Kennedy, Catherine Pace, Stephen Kalenich, Fred Morgan, Ben Edmonds, Gil Lindner, Maggie Montalbano, Michelle Meyers, Joanne Marks, Diane "Croxey" Adams, Rick Henn, Jeff Bolonski, George Hormel, Jr., Alice Fiondella, Carol Thompson, Mike Klenfner, Tony Martell, David Oppenheim, Chip Rachlin, Gail Buchalter, Andy Goldmark, Brenda Lewis, Michael Vosse, John Hanlon, Connie Pappas Hillman, David Elliot, Stephen W. Despar, Tony Asher, Nick Grillo, Stanley Shapiro, John Vincent, Gregg Jakobson, Ginger Blake Schackney, Tandyn Almer, James Reiley, Rene Pappas, Christine McVie, Richard Duryea, Rusty Ford, Peter Marshall, Keith Devoe, Brad Elliot, Steven Korthof, Charles Wilson, Jeanne Wilson Torbet, Rocky Pamplin, and Nancy Rosenthal.

My thanks to my attorney and friend, David Hollander, and to Bruce Roberts and his family, who gave me shelter and comfort during my long sojourns in Los Angeles, as did E. J. Oshins and Stephen Poe. My gratitude also to Bernie Berkowitz.

Finally, I would like to thank my agent, John Hawkins; my editor, Michaela Hamilton, for her encouragement and guidance; my wonderful publisher, Elaine Koster, for her faith in me; and Joseph Olshan, who put up with this all over again.

Steven Gaines
Wainscott, New York
1986

One

1

It was a surfer's dream. It was just after dawn on Santa Monica Beach, December 4, 1983, a magnificent clear and cool winter Sunday morning, the kind of day when the Pacific is cold but the surf is up and the waves sweep to the beach in perfect breakers and no intrepid surfer can see the ocean without a sigh. But on this day Dennis Wilson, a surfer since he was ten years old, hardly noticed the Pacific at all.

It was the morning of Dennis Wilson's thirty-ninth birthday. Dressed in green army pants, T-shirt, and flimsy jacket, he had just sleepily hitchhiked his way from a friend's house to the Santa Monica Bay Inn, a beachfront motel. Here his estranged nineteen-year-old wife, Shawn Love Wilson, lived with their fifteen-month-old son, Gage, in a $125-a-week kitchenette. Dennis intended to pay them a surprise visit, but it was he who was in for the surprise; he was about to find his wife asleep in bed—fully clothed—with two men.

The Bay Inn, as it is called, is a large three-story motel with a hundred units. Facing the beach, with a breathtaking view of the Pacific, it boasts a raised swimming-pool area fenced against the ocean winds by clear fiberglass. Located just two blocks south of the carny-like Santa Monica Pier, and not far north of the drug-ridden, artists' beach community of Venice, the Bay Inn, with its reasonable rates, drew a transient crowd of young residents, attracted as much to the area's drug activities as to the year-round beauty of Santa Monica Beach. The strip of motels and hotels, from the Sheraton on Wilshire Boulevard all the way south to Pico, was part of what the local hotel people called the Ho Chi Minh Trail, which ran all the way from Florida, fed by Interstate 10. If you were poor or drunk or drugged and hitchhiking across America looking for the Pacific, Ocean Boulevard in Santa Monica is where you'd come out.

It was not exactly where you would expect to find Dennis Wilson, a man known for his expensive taste and style, his Rodeo Drive wardrobes, his Ferraris and Rolls-Royces and his six-figure income. The drummer and middle brother of the Beach Boys, Dennis Wilson had for two decades been the personification of American virility and derring-do. It was Dennis who embodied the spirit of the Beach Boys to tens of millions of teenagers around the world; he was the epitome of the surfer playboy.

Over the years he had, much to his own pleasure, developed a reputation as one of California's most notorious symbols of wanton lust and overindulgence, the rock-and-roll James Dean of a generation raised on free love and fast cars. Mischievous and fun-loving, he was the group's sex symbol. A ruggedly good-looking man, he had been muscular and tanned year-round from surfing and working on his boat. His thick, brown, sun-crested hair, parted down the middle, framed a strong, bearded face. His blue eyes twinkled coyly, and his quick smile was not so much crooked as it was a devilish sneer. Men felt instant comradeship with him; women found him irresistible.

Dennis's ineluctable appeal had its spoils. From the time he was twelve years old, he bragged, girls were lining up to sleep with him, and he turned down not a single one. Indeed, Dennis was as addicted to women as he was to his other vices. He was obsessed with sex. Getting laid was a major preoccupation for him. He called himself "The Wood," because he was always hard and ready. Although he had been married five times previously and was father to five children, throughout all his marriages he had countless affairs—daily—including one with Patti Reagan, the president's daughter. He had recently ended a turbulent, three-year liaison with Christine McVie, the singer-composer of the English rock band Fleetwood Mac. His best-known—and most publicized—marriage was to the beautiful blond actress Karen Lamm, whom he married not once, but twice. It was a marriage straight out of the pages of *People* magazine. Together they were the perfect gleaming vision of a California couple, young, rich, and famous, whizzing down the coast highway in one of their matching Ferrari convertibles.

But if Dennis was every teenage Walter Mitty's fantasy of the California playboy surfer, the Dennis Wilson who hitch-hiked to his beloved beach on his thirty-ninth birthday was not the same young stud revered around the world as the essence of the California myth. He could have easily been mistaken for a man a decade older. Instead of the muscled and tanned athlete familiar to his fans, he was pudgy and over-weight, bloated with edema from drink and drugs. What had once been the brine and vigor of sailing and the outdoors was now the gray of heroin and cocaine. His bearded face was lined, his eyes puffy and bloodshot. He spoke in a roaring, rasping voice, worsened by several operations to remove polyps from his vocal cords and the consumption of at least two packs of Lark or unfiltered Camel cigarettes a day. Over the years, in various alcoholic accidents, he had cut or broken almost every appendage of his body, and everything ached. And if you looked carefully, in his eyes you could see a deeper damage than that self-inflicted by drugs or booze. Dennis was being *eaten away*.

His recent marriage to Shawn Love had only worsened his problems. Shawn was a round-faced, doe-eyed, blond teenager with a shag haircut and a pug nose. In a Byzantine twist, Shawn was the illegitimate daughter of Dennis's first cousin, the Beach Boys' Mike Love. She had been conceived in a one-night liaison with then-secretary Shannon Harris and subsequently born out of wedlock. Her mother had sued Mike Love for paternity in Santa Monica Superior Court two decades ago. Shawn reportedly won an award of $300 a year in child support and the right to use the name Love when she turned eighteen. Her father shunned her most of her life, and she and her mother appeared to remain very bitter toward him; some would say they harbored a vendetta against the Beach Boys.

To make this volatile situation even more explosive, Dennis Wilson and Mike Love despised each other. Since they were children, there had been a hostile and open rivalry between

Mike and Dennis that even led to public fisticuffs. Eventually, a mutual restraining order was obtained in court to keep them apart. Mike, it was said, resented Dennis's image as the group's sex symbol; he considered Dennis a child, overindulged and uncontrollable, yet adored by all the Beach Boys fans and always forgiven by an indulgent family. Mike, by contrast, was a hardworking, competitive man, a devout vegetarian and Transcendental Meditator who never drank or smoked. Dennis, naughty child that he was, goaded and provoked Mike at every turn. Once, on the Beach Boys' private plane, Dennis raced over to a small compartment where Mike was meditating, ripped open the curtain, and vomited in front of him. On another occasion, onstage at the Greek Theater in Los Angeles, Dennis flicked off Mike's omnipresent cap to uncover his balding pate in full view of the audience. Dennis also enjoyed taking various young women into the meditation room in the Beach Boys' privately owned recording studios and making love to them on the floor. Later, when Mike arrived to meditate, the room was often fragrant with spent passions.

Indeed, for Dennis to have married Mike's illegitimate daughter could be seen as nothing but the most bitter spite work. Yet few would deny that Dennis sincerely fell in love with and felt sorry for Shawn. She was only fifteen when she first started living with him in a small house on Wavecrest Avenue in Venice Beach. Dennis swore at first that the relationship was not sexual—that he was just helping straighten out a mixed-up kid by putting her up in a room in his large house—but soon they were sleeping together, and not long after she was pregnant. Dennis called two female friends to ask where Shawn could have an abortion, but reportedly she refused, and Gage was born on September 3, 1982. Dennis married her nearly a year later, on July 28, 1983.

From the start it was obvious that Dennis and Shawn had come from two different worlds and would have a hard time getting along. Shawn was used to scraping along with very little money, and she guarded every penny. Dennis, on the other hand, was famous for his prodigious spending. When she tried to instill her frugality in him, violent arguments ensued. One of the couple's close friends described the marriage as "one big fight." Screaming and punching matches were not unusual. The past November, one argument culminated with Shawn driving her silver BMW automobile right into the front door of their rented Trancas Beach house. On the wall of the house, scrawled in crayon, were the phrases "No love" and "No respect." Dennis would often call his friends or manager and complain, "What am I doing with her? She's such a kid." They had filed for divorce in November, not even four months married.

During the short time they were officially husband and wife, Dennis continued to see other women on the sly, but he remained sexually faithful to Shawn, as he saw it, by only allowing himself to get blow jobs, and thus avoiding the possibility of contracting a venereal disease. Such loosely defined fidelity did not work both ways in Dennis's chauvinistic rule book. The thought of Shawn with another man was something his fragile ego could little deal with, and of late Shawn had been friendly with a young man in his early twenties named Brant,* of whom Dennis highly disapproved and was violently jealous. Yet through all the torment of the relationship, and even with their divorce impending, Dennis could not bring himself to stay away from her. Their infant son, Gage, kept him coming back over and over again. Dennis loved and adored this towheaded, precocious little tot, whom he had come to visit that early December morning at the Santa Monica Bay Inn.

As he made his way up to room 353 of the motel's north wing, Dennis did not stop at the front office to phone ahead, because the management had already thrown him off the premises on several occasions; and anyway, most of the time when he called the room, Shawn wouldn't take his calls, and then he was left arguing with the operator. Already the switchboard had logged dozens of pleading phone calls to Shawn, which she had refused to answer. Yet Dennis needed to see Gage with an uncontrollable passion. Gage seemed the only constant in his life, the only living thing he could hold on to. Of course, Gage could hardly talk; but with him there was no hurt, just

*Not his real name.

simple, uncomplicated love. In a way very few people understood, Dennis needed the baby more than anyone in the world needed him.

Dennis would replay over and over again for friends the scene that greeted him that morning in Shawn's room. According to Dennis, when he entered the room, he found Shawn asleep on the bed with two young men—one of them her steady boyfriend, the other a relative stranger to Dennis. All three were fully clothed, and it appeared they had innocently fallen asleep together. Shawn's boyfriend, Dennis claimed, was a "heavy" drug user, and Dennis had complained many times to friends and business associates that Shawn was involved in the use of hard drugs. Gage, with his golden-white hair and angel's face, an active and inquisitive infant, was wandering around the room unattended.

"What the fuck is going on here?" Dennis rasped, rousing the threesome from sleep. When he screamed with his hoarse throat, it was like a great lion's roar. "What are you, fucking crazy?" he shouted to Shawn.

Before the occupants of the bed could compose an explanation, Dennis went berserk and began ripping apart the hotel room. He turned over furniture and punched holes in the door and walls. While all four screamed at the top of their lungs— Shawn with an incessant chorus of "Get out! Get out!"—a tug-of-war ensued over Gage. Dennis reportedly threatened to have Gage legally taken away from Shawn because she was consorting with drug users. The frightened child shrieked hysterically while Dennis threatened to call the police and have them all arrested for possession of narcotics. Then Dennis suddenly snatched Gage away from Shawn and raced out of the room with him.

With the child howling and squirming in his arms, Dennis flew down the three flights of steps, past the pool area, and out of the motel onto Ocean Park Avenue. Darting in and out of traffic, he ran pell-mell across the broad palm-lined boulevard, and took shelter in a cool, dark bar called Chez Jay's. Located almost directly across the street from the Bay Inn, at 1657 Ocean Park Avenue, Chez Jay's was one of Dennis's favorite hangouts. A small and quiet bar, its interior was lighted mainly by multicolored Christmas lights strung along the ceiling down the center of the room. The owners and employees all knew and liked Dennis, and Alice Fiondella, Jay's mother, who owned a small hotel next door, was there that morning with the clean-up crew when he came in. Dennis, who was frantic and near tears, told Alice he needed a taxi to take Gage to a friend's house. Alice called one for him while he tried to calm Gage. After a while he laid the infant down on a maroon Naugahyde banquette beneath a red-and-white-checkered tablecloth. It was cool in the dark bar. Dennis took off his jacket and wrapped it around his tiny son, who shortly fell asleep.

While Dennis waited for a taxi, he sat in the booth next to Gage and nursed his vodka and orange juice, which he often carried with him in a pint bottle. Ironically, this morning's events were no special trial for him. In fact, they seemed like just another thread in the incredible tapestry of his life. As he sat at the table, the past few months fell heavily on him, and he began to weep.

2

Since early November, when his household possessions were cleared out of a rented beach house in Trancas and put into storage, Dennis had had no real place to live, no special place to stay, and probably not more than ten dollars in his pocket at any one time, if that. It was impossible for him to have any money because he had virtually no control over his spending. He was nearly half a million dollars in debt, and the stories of his squandering were legion. Each friend had a favorite: Dennis orders a Rolls-Royce over the telephone and destroys it in a drunken traffic accident the same night; Dennis picks up the $600 restaurant tab of five virtual strangers; Dennis allows anyone who takes his fancy to move in with him, rent and telephone free—including, at one point, the entire Charles Manson family; Dennis pours a bottle of honey all over a table in a restaurant and then tips the waiter $100 to clean it up. "If he had a thousand dollars in his pocket," one of his ex-wives said, "he'd spend it." There was no way to impress Dennis with the stupidity of his largesse, even as he teetered on the edge of bankruptcy. He had borrowed so much money from his mother that even she was turning him down. "It's hard to imagine," Stephen Love, Dennis's cousin and one-time Beach Boys manager, told a reporter, "that anyone could just blow so much money, but Dennis did. He was totally unrestrained and undisciplined; he was foolishly, self-destructively generous."

His personal and business manager, Bob Levine, who had handled his finances since 1978, tried his best to rein Dennis in, but it was like trying to tame a bucking bronco. Levine, along with others, had begged him to stop spending and drinking, promising to guide him back to financial solvency if only he cleaned up his act. Levine diligently set up an extensive fiscal plan for Dennis, with a timetable and an arrangement for him to pay off his enormous debt, which included two years of back taxes and interest, numerous personal loans, unpaid insurance policies, and various child-support payments. But it was no use. Every time Dennis promised to control himself, the promise would be broken an hour later.

By that autumn, 1983, his drinking problem was threatening his health. He had tremors from the moment he woke up, and recently, in Malibu, where he had a charge at the local supermarket, he had had to go out into the parking lot and drink two cans of beer before he could stop shaking enough to sign his name to the charge slip. He had had dozens of alcoholic accidents, including one in which he dropped a glass bottle of Sparklett's water that sliced open his foot so deeply the tendons had to be sewn together; subsequently, all his toes moved in tandem. Dennis's driver's license had long since been revoked. All his friends assumed he had stopped driving because of his constant drunkenness, and Dennis let them think it; but the real cause was the alcoholic seizures and blackouts he had begun to suffer over the past year. That summer, while driving on Malibu Coast Highway with Gage in the car, he had blacked out, wrecking the car and nearly killing his son. After that, he swore never to drive again. But even the seizures and near-fatal accidents didn't seem to slow him down.

There was something so eminently likable about Dennis that

it was hard to be angry with him for long; he was a puppy who would not listen. But by now, the rest of the Beach Boys were exasperated with his behavior. Since they were a family unit first and a band second, they were especially close. As Dennis once put it in his inimitable way, "We've done everything together. Shit, eat, fart, cry, laugh. Everything." But as much as they cared for him, he was twice as incorrigible, and there was growing concern he would drag the band down with him into scandal. The situation had come to a head in front of a sold-out crowd at the Universal Amphitheater in June 1979, when Dennis mumbled something into the microphone about "cocaine and Quaaludes." In a backstage squabble with Mike Love about the comment, Dennis was kicked in the balls. When the group returned to the stage, Dennis lost his temper, knocked his drums off the risers, and leaped across the stage at Mike Love in full view of the audience. He was officially thrown out of the group—fired by telegram until he "obtain[ed] medical attention for [his] present condition"—to which Dennis replied that no one could stop him from showing up. He arrived uninvited at a concert in San Diego, and the security guards held him outside as he forlornly watched the Beach Boys drive into the stadium in a long caravan of limousines. Dennis eventually talked his way inside, but he was barred from going up on the stage.

When he was reinstated as a member of the touring group in the summer of 1981, the official dictum was that Dennis absolutely could not appear drunk onstage. To help him at least be sober for the shows, a team of bodyguard–baby-sitters was hired to keep him from hitting the bottle for at least two hours before the show, at a reported cost of $600 a day. "They were there to lock him in his room," said Levine, "beat him up if they had to, and physically restrain him." But Dennis always found a way to sneak the booze, usually aided by one of his alcoholic friends—the "loadies," they were derisively nicknamed—who were always around for the ride. One night Dennis simply turned to his "bodyguard–baby-sitters" and said, "Enough. I'm smart enough to hire you guys and I'm smart enough to fire you." Bob Levine took them off the job the next day.

Everybody who cared about Dennis had tried at one time or another to get him to go for professional help. He tried Alcoholics Anonymous but wouldn't go to regular meetings. He went to a few private therapists, including Don Juhl, who also worked with David Kennedy, Jr., but he always gave up after a few visits. Dr. Margaret Patterson, who had cured rock guitarist Eric Clapton of his heroin addiction, agreed to treat him, but Dennis never made an appointment. In one instance the other Beach Boys asked Dennis to come to a meeting with them in Dallas, where there was a program for athletes with drug and drinking problems. He brought Gage with him to the meeting and, holding the baby in his arms, he told them, "I appreciate what you guys are trying to do for me, but I have to do this myself. I will not talk about my personal life with a stranger."

The rest of the group, in a gesture of support, rented a private jet plane at a cost of $5,000 and put it at Dennis's disposal to take him off to whichever center he chose to enter, but he never got on the plane. The group also flew Dennis and Shawn to New York, all expenses paid, and put him up in the Parker Meridian Hotel in anticipation of his entering a clinic, but he never left the hotel. To make detoxifying even more attractive, they offered to pay him one-fifth of the touring money—even though he wasn't on tour with them—as long as he was in a clinic. Since the Beach Boys were commanding $50,000 a show, plus a percentage of the profits over that, it was a very attractive offer, but one that Dennis didn't take. Dennis would shake his head and smile sadly. "I really want to clean up my act, I really do," he'd say with that gorgeous earnestness, "and I'm going to do it this time." But "this time" never seemed to come.

With all this support and concern, and with so much at stake, Dennis still couldn't find the strength in himself to detox. There was a part of him so tormented, so helplessly frightened and childlike, that he could not be reached. He always had an excuse for himself, but the most recent—and heartfelt—excuse was that he didn't want to leave Gage, especially alone with Shawn. According to Bob Levine, "Shawn was an extreme detriment to these programs." That autumn, Dennis had tried to convince Shawn to let him take the baby with him to a detoxification center outside of Phoenix, Arizona, called Cottonwood. Levine had made arrangements for the baby to stay in a nearby home with round-the-clock nurses who would bring the little boy to visit Dennis every day. "Shawn put up a big stink about it," Levine said, "but then you could see her attempts [to stop it] were waning, she was going to let it happen, and then all of a sudden she got fired up again."

At one point, Dennis took Gage to the Los Angeles International Airport without Shawn's knowledge. When Shawn learned where Dennis had gone, she rushed to the airport and tried to get Gage back. A screaming fight over the child was conducted in the public terminal during which Shawn nearly bit off Dennis's thumb; the trip for rehabilitation was put off. The following month Dennis actually managed to get to Cottonwood for several weeks. "But he's the type who can't be alone," Levine said, "so he kept calling Shawn...she threw roadblock after roadblock." Shawn reportedly encouraged him to return to Los Angeles, but Dennis didn't even have the money for a plane ticket, and frantic to return, he convinced one of his "well-meaning" loadie friends in Venice to send him the fare.

When the lease was up at his Trancas house in November 1983, no substitute place was found for him to live. Levine says this was "basically by his own choosing," because Dennis had promised to enter a detox center. When he finished detoxification, it was decided, Dennis would be found a new house along with his new beginning. But that day never came, and by the morning of his thirty-ninth birthday, Dennis had grown resigned to drifting with no home, no money, and no transportation.

3

When a taxi arrived at Chez Jay's to pick him up that morning, Alice Fiondella thought she had seen the last of him. But over an hour later he was back again, the cab driver at his side. Dennis was frantic. He had been all over the area looking for shelter, but no one seemed to be at home or willing to take him in. "They had driven everywhere," Alice said. "The driver took him all over. The baby had messed in the backseat, and there was no money to pay the fare." The cab driver, who felt sorry for Dennis, shook his head sadly, and Alice agreed to pay the fare. Dennis finally managed to reach one of his closest cronies, Chris Clark, on the phone. Chris told him to wait in the bar until he could borrow a car to come get him. Dennis sat in a booth, rocking Gage in his arms, while he waited for Chris to arrive.

Dennis's "Little Buddy" Chris Clark was a Sancho Panza with whom Dennis could tilt at his alcoholic windmills. He was a pudgy, good-natured, loyal fellow, age thirty-two, who was struggling with his own alcoholic problems. For the most part unemployed, he had been friendly with Dennis for the past several years in Venice Beach. Chris Clark adored and looked up to "Denny" as a kid looks up to a big brother. In awe of Dennis's sexual prowess, his fame, and his capacity for alcohol, Chris was ready twenty-four hours a day to gallivant with him. At night they would often sit out on the beach together, getting drunk, staring up at the stars. "You know what, Little Buddy?" Dennis would tell Chris, pointing to the black sky littered with sequined stars. "I've been there and back again."

When Chris arrived at Chez Jay's shortly before noon, he was alarmed to find Dennis in tears. "It just tore me up," Dennis told Chris. "Shawn was in bed with *two* guys," he said, although, when pressed, Dennis admitted they were dressed and the situation did not seem of a sexual nature. Dennis thanked Alice and told her to call his business manager to get the taxi fare back. Then he and Chris went out of the dark bar onto the sunny boulevard and walked to the car Chris had borrowed. While Dennis was putting Gage in the backseat, he noticed that the 1982 Silver BMW he had bought for Shawn for $17,500 was parked in the lot next to Chez Jay's. Originally there were two BMWs, twins, but Dennis's had been stolen in a parking lot during a concert. The sight of the BMW seemed to enrage him. Poking around in the backseat of the borrowed car, he found a baseball bat. Before Chris could stop him, he raced to the BMW and smashed out the front windows. Chris yelled, "Whoa! Dennis, stop!," but at the same time he loved seeing him do it. Not surprisingly, nobody passing by on the street interrupted him at work with the baseball bat. When he was through, he seemed somehow relieved. "Now she won't be able to come after Gage," he told Chris, and ordered him to drive off.

After dropping Gage with friends in Venice who would look after him, Dennis spent the rest of his birthday cruising around with Chris in the borrowed car. At sundown, they drove to a palatial log-cabin-style house at 14400 Sunset Boulevard that had once belonged to humorist Will Rogers. Dennis had rented this house in the late sixties while he was divorcing his first wife and money was pouring in. It was a period of wild abandon for Dennis, but it was also in this house that he had lived with Charles Manson and the Family. It was an era of orgies and drugs, a time in his life he once said "destroyed" him. Yet he liked to return there; it was a way of revisiting some of his past glories, despite its associations, and it was with this idea that he directed his friend Chris Clark to drive there.

The beautiful, heavily landscaped house on Sunset Boulevard was then occupied by George Hormel, Jr., the fifty-six-year-old heir to the Hormel meat-packing fortune. Hormel had bought the house from its owner in 1968 for less than $500,000, and it was now worth nearly $3 million. The owner of a popular recording studio, Village Recorders, Hormel had been acquainted with Dennis for several years through the music business. They had first met many years before at Village Recorders, and then a few years later when Dennis brought Christine McVie over to show her the house. Hormel had grown fond of Dennis. "He was just a big puppy," he said. "Scratch him once behind the ears and he would follow you anywhere." Another year or so had gone by when, just that autumn, Dennis popped by unannounced and asked Hormel if he would work with him producing some tracks for an album. Dennis was very drunk and stoned, but after listening to the tracks Hormel agreed to work with him—"If you're straight," he admonished.

Dennis became a frequent visitor to the house, sleeping there when he had no other place to stay, and Hormel had become one of the latest of a long list of people whom Dennis had come to depend upon for support. During that November and

December, he and Dennis had exchanged nearly $5,000. "He had accumulated four or five thousand dollars' worth of debt for dope and I don't know what else—I didn't ask," Hormel said, "and I gave him the money. I made sure that it was to get people off his tail and not to buy more drugs." But by early December Hormel wouldn't give Dennis any more cash. "He wasn't getting it out of me. I was supporting him only as long as he was straight."

In the month and a half that Dennis stayed at Hormel's, they had long conversations about Dennis's addictions, and for a time Hormel believed Dennis was actually going to stop. Frequently they would stay up most of the night, talking into the early morning about Dennis's troubles. Hormel remembers that most of the conversations revolved around Dennis's personal problems with women and his family, and particularly his desire to end his alcohol and drug habits. Many times the conversations ended with Hormel convinced that Dennis was resolved to stop drinking. It was clear he couldn't go on as he was, Dennis's health had been deteriorating, and his epileptic-like seizures had increased. Hormel saw "several" of them during December. Dennis would suddenly fall to the floor, his eyes rolling back, and churn convulsively. "I witnessed a couple of real scary seizures," Hormel said. "He didn't remember a thing when he came to, but he knew something had happened." The next day another episode in the drama of his life would send him off-center and he would need another drink.

Hormel wasn't surprised to find Dennis ringing the bell at the gate that December night. Hormel's son John was there, along with several friends and musicians with whom Hormel worked. When Dennis bashfully admitted it was his birthday, everyone made a big fuss over him, and they all went to the kitchen and baked a cake to celebrate. That evening Dennis vacillated between bravado and sunken depression. At age thirty-nine, he saw the Big Forty and middle age coming up, and he knew he was getting too old to be a Beach Boy. But as soon as Dennis found himself becoming maudlin, he would catch himself and mask his mood with drunken gregariousness. He told several funny stories, acting them out dramatically in his big, rasping voice, and at one point Chris Clark said to him, "You know, your problem is you're just mad you

never made it as an actor. That's why you have to act everything
out."

Dennis grinned at him and said, "How did you know that?"

They all sang "Happy Birthday" and Dennis became a little
boy for a moment, embarrassed and pleased and flustered when
he blew out the candles. Later in the evening, they went to
the billiard room and played pool. Dennis suggested they make
the ante a thousand dollars a game, and everyone agreed, because it was play money anyway.

By the small hours of the morning, Dennis was blitzed on
every accommodation of the household. George Hormel
couldn't stand to see him that way, but instead of asking him
to leave on his birthday, Hormel just locked himself in his
study. In a few minutes Dennis was banging on the door, asking
to be let in, and the inevitable conversation followed: he loved
Shawn, but she was using drugs; he had to dry out, but he was
just so lonely; he loved her, he hated her, he couldn't live
without her; she was destroying him every minute they spent
together.

He stayed at Hormel's house that night and on and off for
the rest of December, sleeping off his binges or just hanging
out there during the day. It surprised Hormel that Dennis seemed
to have not one penny, but he took it for granted this lack of
funds was part of the pressure Dennis's family and management were putting on him to detoxify. As the weeks passed,
Dennis drank less, readying himself for another go at a detoxification clinic. But when Hormel returned home one night
around the twentieth of December, he found Dennis on a wild
drunken binge. Getting blotto seemed to make sense to Dennis.
"Everybody goes on a last binge," he said, and then poured
nearly an entire bottle of wine into the mixing console of Hormel's home studio. Hormel was exasperated. Ultimately the
truth hit home: if you gave Dennis shelter, you became part of
the problem. Unable in good conscience to give him a home
and booze to drink, Hormel had to ask him to leave, and by
Christmas, Dennis was homeless again.

4

The impending holidays loomed like some nightmare for Dennis. Without a home, without a cent in his pocket, he felt lost and afloat. He crashed in cheap motels along the Ho Chi Minh Trail or at the apartments of friends. He made several attempts to go to Alcoholics Anonymous, and the Beach Boys' manager, Tom Hulett, in a gesture of support, accompanied Dennis to one meeting. But outside the meeting, the two argued about money, and Hulett reportedly took a large roll of bills out of his pocket and offered Dennis fifteen dollars. Dennis was so insulted by the paltry amount, he refused to take it, and Hulett reportedly threw the money on the ground. Other reports say that the next day Hulett broke down and gave Dennis a hundred dollars; but the money quickly went for more booze and drugs. At this point Dennis was on the edge; he would either clean himself up and pull out of the nose dive, or else.

Dennis was finally able to steel himself for the ride to a detoxification ward two days before Christmas. He said it didn't make much difference to him to be in a detox ward of a hospital on Christmas; he had no other place to go, and perhaps it was the best Christmas present he could give himself. On Friday morning, December 23, Bob Levine drove Dennis to St. John's Hospital and Health Center in Santa Monica, only a mile from the Santa Monica Bay Inn.

He was checked into the detox unit by Dr. Joseph Takamine, who headed the twenty-one-day detox program. According to Dr. Takamine, Dennis was serious about the program and determined to stick it through this time. His blood test on admittance showed a .28 alcohol level and traces of cocaine. Dennis told the doctor he had been drinking about a fifth of vodka a day and using what he called "a little coke." The doctor prescribed 100 mg. of Librium every two hours "so he could come down slowly and maybe start the program in five days." Takamine and Dennis talked extensively on Saturday, and the doctor told him their discussions would resume on Monday morning when the doctor returned to the hospital following a one-day Christmas break.

All Christmas Eve day Dennis suffered tormenting physical and psychological withdrawal symptoms cloaked by the 100 mg. doses of Librium. Itching to walk out, he spent the day obsessively making phone calls to friends, all of whom encouraged him to stick it out, promising to visit or call him whenever they were allowed. He reportedly called his brother Carl, vacationing in Colorado, several times, his mother, Audree, and his brother Brian, but could not reach them. Only Bob Levine came by to see him that day. "I brought him some presents, some necessities, toiletries, cigarettes, things to make the guy feel respectable. He was trying again. And then the siren called."

The "siren" was Shawn. Dennis had placed dozens of phone calls to Shawn at the Bay Inn. She refused most of them until Christmas Eve, when she told Dennis that she and Gage were being thrown out of the Bay Inn for nonpayment of rent. The manager said he had been given the runaround about payment for too long. Dennis would say Shawn would take care of the bill, Shawn would say Dennis would be by later to pay it. The physical damage Dennis had caused to the room was also a factor. Dennis became determined to leave the hospital and see Shawn and Gage.

Shortly after Shawn's phone call, Dennis's friends Steve Goldberg and Denice Graves visited him in his room and encouraged him to stay, promising him that Shawn and Gage would be all right. But by 3:30 Dennis was on the phone to his "Little Buddy" Chris Clark, telling him he was about to walk out of the hospital. He asked Chris to pick him up and take him out for a drink.

Chris Clark was disgusted. He had no idea what to say to keep Dennis in the detox ward, so he hurried over to the hospital and offered to stay with him overnight. Dennis calmed down somewhat, and Chris slept on the floor next to Dennis's bed, talking him through the night. On Christmas morning, about 8:30 A.M., the hospital staff insisted that Chris leave. "If I leave, he's not going to stay," Chris warned the nurses in the hallway outside of Dennis's room. But they insisted Dennis could not go through the therapy with a friend. Chris reluctantly went back inside the room to say good-bye.

Immediately after Chris Clark left, Dennis called Steve Goldberg at least six times, demanding to be picked up at the hospital. Goldberg refused to be an accomplice in this self-destructive act. By noon, Dennis had walked out himself. From St. John's, he hitchhiked his way to his friend Nick's liquor store in Venice, where he begged a bottle and some cash. Then he went to Shawn's mother's house on Twelfth Street in Santa Monica, where Shawn and Gage were paying a Christmas visit. Reportedly, everything there was copacetic. "He said he was really lonely and that he wanted to be with us on Christmas," Shawn said. After an hour, he left to hitchhike his way to the nearest bar.

Later Christmas night, John Hanlon, a recording engineer and one of Dennis's longtime friends, received a panicky phone call from one of Dennis's loadie friends who said that Dennis was making a commotion at a club called At My Place in Santa Monica. Would Hanlon come by and help get him out of there? Hanlon, twenty-seven, loved Dennis. Dennis had given him his first break as an engineer at the Beach Boys' Brothers studios and had comforted him through many difficult personal times. He knew in what condition he would probably find Dennis, but went to get him nevertheless. Dennis was in the worst shape Hanlon had ever seen him. "He was a total drunk," Hanlon said, "disrupting business, yelling at patrons, screaming at the barmaids, trying to get up on stage, making a general mess of things." Hanlon managed to coax Dennis out of the club and drove him back to the Santa Monica Bay Inn, although Dennis kept insisting he be driven to George Hormel's house. "I didn't know where to take him. I made a phone call to George, who said, 'It's not a good time right now because I'm with family.' Dennis was sitting in my car throwing booze all over and he was making a mess and I was getting real uptight. I said, 'Look, I called Geordie for you, and there's nothing else I can do. I can't deal with this anymore, you've got to help yourself.'"

Dennis said, "Nobody loves me, John. Nobody."

"That's not true, Dennis," Hanlon told him softly, helping him out of the car. "Everybody loves you, man. Too many people love you, that's your problem."

"I don't want to live another couple of weeks," Dennis said.

"That's stupid talk," Hanlon answered.

Dennis shouted, *"I'm not leaving. You're taking me over to Geordie's!"* He began to break the antennae off the car's hood and then tried to tear the door off the hinges. Hanlon screamed at him to stop. Seeing his words had no effect, he jumped behind the wheel and sped off, leaving Dennis standing on the street. Dennis stumbled across the road to Chez Jay's, and at about midnight he set out for the Santa Monica Bay Inn.

When he arrived unannounced at Shawn's room, she was there with her male friend. Dennis later told Chris Clark, Bob Levine, and others that he demanded to use the telephone and Shawn's friend wouldn't let him. A shoving match quickly escalated into a fistfight. Now came one of the craziest moments of the past few weeks: Dennis decided not to fight back. He simply made fists at his side to withstand the pain. He was so doped up from his hospital treatment, he felt very little of the serious damage being done to him by the repeated blows. Dennis said, "I just stood there and let him hit me. I didn't do a thing."

Severely beaten, he stumbled out of the motel room and walked down to Ocean Boulevard. He called Chris Clark from a phone booth and convinced him and Steve Goldberg to come get him in Goldberg's pickup truck. His friends found him bleeding from bruises on his face, with scrapes on his forehead and one black eye, holding his ribs, drunk and sick. They took him back to St. John's, the hospital he had walked out of several hours earlier. On the way there, his complexion gray, Dennis told Chris Clark about letting Shawn's boyfriend hit him. Chris couldn't help but laugh. "That's the most destructive thing you've ever done," Chris told him.

But Dennis was in no shape to laugh. "I just want to go down there and kick his ass," he kept repeating. "I'm gonna call the cops. Close the place down. Bust everyone." That was Dennis's ultimate revenge, to call the police. But he could not bring himself to do it. Dennis had stopped hitting back.

Inside the hospital Chris Clark got Dr. Michael Gales on the phone and tried to convince him to readmit Dennis to the program. But Gales said he couldn't. "He's just too much trouble," Dr. Gales reportedly told Clark.

"He might die, you know," Chris Clark said earnestly. "He just stood there and got the shit beat out of him."

"He may have to die," the doctor allegedly replied.

Chris Clark knew another doctor, Christopher Bador, at the Daniel Freeman Marina Hospital, who worked with drug and alcohol abusers, and called him to get Dennis admitted. Dr. Bador reportedly suggested that, in order to restrain Dennis, the police lock him up, but Chris couldn't bring himself to call the police on his friend. By now it was 2:00 A.M. on December 26.

Dennis was eventually admitted to the Marina Hospital that morning, and again Chris Clark convinced the hospital staff that he would have to spend the night with Dennis in order for him to stay in the hospital. Chris slept on the floor until Dennis went off into a fitful sleep. But in the morning came the same hospital rules: Dennis had to see this through alone, and despite his repeated warnings that if Dennis was left alone he'd walk out, Chris Clark was made to leave the hospital.

It wasn't forty-five minutes later that Dennis started calling him. "Where am I going to meet you, Little Buddy?" he asked. Chris was adamant this time; he would not see Dennis anymore if he walked out of the hospital. Next Dennis called Steve Goldberg to pick him up, and Goldberg also refused. And sometime within the next hour, Dennis walked out yet again.

He wound up at another favorite haunt in Venice—Hinanos, a dark bar with sawdust on the floor, at the end of Washington Boulevard near the beach. There he got steadily drunk until 1:00 P.M., when again he called and asked Steve Goldberg to pick him up. Goldberg was busy tinkering with his van, and anyway, Hinanos was only a few blocks from where Goldberg lived. "Why don't you just walk over here?" he said. But Dennis was cantankerous and stubborn. He called Goldberg several more times that afternoon as he got drunker, demanding money and a lift. When it became clear that Goldberg wouldn't budge,

Dennis got angry, ending the phone call with the word *termination.*

Said Goldberg, "I don't know if he was referring to the conversation, our friendship, or his life."

5

Later that afternoon, Dennis got in touch with a sometime girl friend of his called Crystal, who had just returned from her Christmas vacation, and she arranged to pick him up. Born Coleen McGovern in Wisconsin, she claimed she was nicknamed "Crystal" when she worked as a Playboy bunny at the Lake Geneva Playboy Club. Dark-haired and pretty, she was full of the same kind of fidgety nervous energy as Dennis. At the time she lived in a furnished two-bedroom apartment in the Fox Hills apartment complex in Culver City with a female roommate and two pet birds. She had only recently taken a position of prominence in Dennis's life, as a last resort for comfort, shelter, and a beer.

She first met Dennis the Thanksgiving of 1981 at a party in Venice across the alley from a rented house where Dennis was living. Dennis was shyly sitting outside on the steps, drinking, and she asked him to come in and have a plate of food. "I asked someone who he was, and when I found out I said, 'Oh, OK, forget about him.' I didn't want to have anything to do with him at first. Too heavy for me." Yet in the coming weeks she kept running into him, and eventually they struck up a friendship. "We just hit it off, but I still kept my distance. He had Shawn and I had this boyfriend, so I didn't want to mess things up." But as time passed and his marriage to Shawn dissolved, his relationship with Crystal blossomed into a romance of convenience, and Dennis spent many nights at her apartment in Fox Hills. Crystal picked him up at Hinanos and took him to a pay phone at the Fox Hills shopping mall.

Realizing that all of his pals were burned out on his broken promises, aborted detox attempts, and drunken scenes, Dennis phoned an old friend from better times, Bill Oster. Oster, forty-four, was a moustachioed, weathered, outdoorsman who owned a fifty-two-foot yawl, the *Emerald*. The *Emerald* was kept in a berth at the Villa Del Mar, a three-story white-stucco apartment building and "rudder and racquet" club at 13999 Marquesa Way, Marina Del Rey, where Dennis had once berthed his favorite possession, the sixty-two-foot, sleek sailing boat he called the *Harmony*. The last time Oster had seen Dennis was fourteen months earlier, backstage at the Greek Theater, where the Beach Boys were performing. Oster was surprised to hear from him after so long, but unpredictability was part of Dennis's charm, so when Oster heard his voice on the phone, now hoarser and scratchier than ever, he took it in stride. "Pick me up at the Fox Hills Mall," Dennis ordered him, without saying hello.

Just like Dennis, Oster thought. "After all these months, he couldn't even ask, just kind of demanded."

Oster first met Dennis in 1978, just as Dennis's second marriage to Karen Lamm was breaking up and he was beginning to miss many tour dates. Dennis was living full-time on the boat, and he and Oster became close friends. Living on his boat was one of the best times for Dennis. He keenly loved the *Harmony*, with its flashy, hand-carved teak fittings and a beautiful carved golden teak pelican on the prow. Purchased years before in Japan, it had once been sunk and submerged, and Dennis had painstakingly refurbished it to its original beauty. But Dennis loved the *Harmony* not so much for its physical beauty as for the total freedom it represented. Only the open sea was fierce and strong and unrelenting enough to be his full-time companion. The *Harmony* became Dennis's chief means of escape; over the past few years it was only on the *Harmony* that he was not in pain. He sailed it up and down the coast, or to Catalina or to Hawaii, but mostly he just kept it berthed at the Villa Del Mar so he could stay close to his beloved ocean. Oster had gone on several trips with Dennis on the *Harmony*, and once, sailing up from San Diego, Dennis discovered a huge school of porpoises swimming and playing next to the boat. Exhilarated by the beautiful mammals, Dennis wrapped one hand in the mastings and hung over the side of the boat in the ocean breeze, serenading the dolphins with his harmonica as they popped up and down like corks in the rush of the wind and waves.

But by the summer of 1981, the always-erratic installment payments to American City Bank hadn't been made in several months, and one day, while Dennis was walking down the long wooden boat slip, he discovered a city marshal on board. Dennis didn't tell the marshal who he was. Instead, he got on Oster's boat across the dock and stood there, his heart breaking, as the marshal posted repossession signs, locked the door, and chained the *Harmony* to the dock. For a while, a marshal's representative lived on the *Harmony* until it was auctioned off for $53,000—half its worth. It tore Dennis up so much to lose his boat that Oster offered him the *Emerald* to live on, and Dennis stayed there for a while, greeted with the empty slip of the *Harmony* when he got up each morning. The slip remained empty to that very day.

The Fox Hills Mall was a large shopping mall near the end of the Marina Freeway, about a mile from where Crystal lived. Around 7:30 P.M. on Tuesday, December 27, Oster and his fiancé, Brenda, found Dennis, dressed in army fatigues and T-shirt, waiting for him near a pay phone with Crystal at his side. He looked pretty beaten up; there was dried blood on his ear, and he had scabs on his nose and forehead. His ribs ached terribly, he said. It seemed to Oster that Dennis already had quite a few drinks in him, but the first thing he asked for was to be driven to a liquor store. Oster tried to dissuade him, but Dennis complained about the pain in his ribs and said the liquor would be good for him. Oster relented. On the way to the dock, they stopped at Marina Liquors, where Dennis bought a bottle of the house-brand vodka, Delray.

When Crystal and Dennis arrived at the *Emerald*, Dennis began drinking in earnest. None of the others drank, hoping to slow him down. They stayed up talking until midnight, trading stories about old times. Oster told Dennis, "It wasn't six months ago that I said to Brenda, 'I hope the next time we see Dennis it's not at his funeral.'"

Dennis looked Oster in the eye and said, "Don't you worry about that."

Later, Oster told Dennis that by ironic coincidence the *Har-*

mony, after it had been repossessed and purchased at auction, had been berthed by its new owner just the second dock down from where they sat. The boat had been for sale about six months ago for $180,000, but now, Oster heard, it could be bought for $115,000. Dennis thought the price was inflated—the boat needed a lot of work—but he would love to have it back. About midnight, Oster and Brenda went into the forecabin and fell asleep.

In the middle of the night Dennis woke up and talked with Crystal about getting the *Harmony* back; he decided that was what he wanted more than anything just then. He told Crystal he intended to call Bob Levine in the morning and promise to present himself at any rehabilitation clinic the Beach Boys named, if they would only help finance buying the *Harmony* back. This time, he swore, he was going to stop drinking. It was just that it was so damn *lonely* in those places and the shakes were so bad. Dennis talked about a crazy scheme of having Gage live with Crystal in an apartment near the detox clinic so he could see them on visiting days. "He wanted to be able to take someone with him that he loved and to be with them through this whole thing," Crystal said. "He knew he needed it, and he wanted to do it for his son and for the band." Most important to him, Dennis knew that in his impending divorce from Shawn there would probably be a custody battle for Gage, and he needed to be sober to prove he was a fit parent.

Never needing much sleep, Dennis got up at 9:00 A.M. and looked around for his bottle of Delray vodka. The night before, Crystal had hidden it behind the trash bin in the galley so Dennis wouldn't find it, but he complained and moaned and searched all over the boat until he discovered it. "He knew we were going to make it difficult for him," Oster said, "but he also knew that we most likely wouldn't pour it down the drain on him because we did have some concern that if we completely dried him out he would have a seizure."

Oster and the women had coffee while Dennis fixed himself the first screwdriver of the day. Then the women went out for a shower in the dock facilities. By the time they got back to the *Emerald*, Dennis was excited and flying high. He said he had called Bob Levine to say he wanted the boat back, *had* to have the boat back, and that he was determined to sober up. He and Levine discussed a thirty-day detoxification program in New Mexico, and the possibility of his going back to Cottonwood in Phoenix.

"He made me a deal," Dennis said of Bob Levine. "Thirty days' detox and he'll buy the boat back for me!" He hugged Crystal and asked, "Do you want to live on the boat with me?"

Crystal, taken by surprise, said, "What about Gage?" And Dennis said, "No problem, no problem. Gage too." This time, he swore over and over again, he would complete the program. He knew how important it was—Gage was at stake—and he sat around the floor of Oster's boat for the rest of the morning, talking about detoxing and pulling his life together and how much he loved Gage.

Oster suggested that he and Dennis put together a new rowing rig that Oster had purchased but never used. This project caught Dennis's attention for a while, and the two men assembled the small boat and went rowing around the marina. Dennis wanted to row across the marina to Aggy's Chris Craft, a large boat sales and repair shop whose owner he knew. When Dennis owned the *Harmony*, he loved to hang out at Aggy's and frequently offered to buy the place from him.

"How much do you want for it?" he bellowed to Aggy that morning. "How much? Just tell me how much and it's yours!"

"A million dollars," Aggy said, smiling.

And Dennis said, "Just call up my business manager and he'll send it to you!" They soon left Aggy's and by noon were back at the *Emerald*.

This time the bottle had been hidden better. Dennis went through an elaborate search until he found it. He fixed himself another drink, and they all settled down to have lunch. Brenda made turkey sandwiches from Christmas leftovers, and Dennis talked again of getting the *Harmony* back. After lunch, Dennis spilled his drink all over his pants. Oster loaned him a pair of cutoff jeans that were slightly too baggy for him. Dennis rinsed out his stained pants and laid them on the deck in the sun to dry.

Suddenly, Dennis said he was going swimming.

"You're crazy," Oster said to him, and Crystal chimed in

with, "Dennis, it's too cold!" But Dennis went up on deck, and in another moment there was the sound of a splash as he jumped into the water. Oster decided he should go up on the dock to watch him. He found Dennis swimming around in the murky water of the empty berth once filled by the *Harmony*. The water was thirteen feet deep and hovering at an icy fifty-eight degrees. The most hardy swimmer would have needed a wet suit, but Dennis just took a few deep breaths of air and then disappeared below the surface for what seemed like a long time. Oster grew worried, but in another moment he heard Dennis surface on the far side of the dock, laughing at having tricked him. Oster again tried to cajole Dennis out of the water, but Dennis only swam back over to the spot where the *Harmony* had been berthed, and began diving in earnest. On each trip to the bottom, he found another piece of the *Harmony*, sometimes only a small piece of junk, pieces of metal fittings and battery parts, and an old rotted piece of rope.

After about twenty minutes, he got out of the water to have another turkey sandwich. Inside the boat, as he started to eat his sandwich, he got the shivers. They put a towel on the floor for him so he could sit in front of the heater, but his teeth wouldn't stop chattering. He sat there sipping vodka and orange juice, trying to warm up, and whenever his back was turned Oster would try to water down his drink. When Dennis caught on to what Oster was doing, he complained loudly and, sitting there on the floor, practically finished off the fifth. The whole time, he was talking about the "big box" he had seen on the floor of the marina where the *Harmony* had been docked. "I betcha it's a treasure chest. I know it is! It's a treasure chest with a bag of silver dollars." He entertained Oster, Brenda, and Crystal with the story of a submerged treasure, some of it a bag filled with silver dollars he had allegedly thrown overboard himself. None of them really wanted Dennis to go back in the water, but Dennis was intent on finding it. Oster complied by going to get a line of rope so Dennis could take it down with him and tie it to the "big box" he had seen.

But meanwhile, Dennis, annoyed that the bottle had run out, had wandered off to find more booze. He walked a few berths down to the houseboat on which Lathiel Morris lived.

Dennis seemed very excited, according to Morris. "I'm getting my boat back," he bragged. Morris had his pretty sixteen-year-old granddaughter on board, and Dennis smiled and flirted with her. Dennis talked about his impending divorce from Shawn, and Morris asked how many times he had been married. Dennis told him six. "I'm lonesome," Dennis told Morris. "I'm lonesome all the time."

And Morris said, "Ahhh, baloney," gesturing toward Crystal across the way on Oster's boat.

Soon Oster went out looking for Dennis and caught up with him talking to yet another boat owner he knew from the marina, asking if there was any vodka to spare. Just as the man was about to hand over a half-filled bottle of vodka, Oster signaled frantically behind Dennis's back not to give it to him. The boat owner caught on right away and said, "Wait a minute, Dennis!" He whisked the bottle back into the galley. A moment later he brought the same bottle back with much less vodka in it. Dennis thanked him and took it back to the *Emerald*. Then he swigged it right down, not even mixing it with his usual orange juice.

Almost immediately Dennis insisted on diving again. Despite everyone's protestations, he jumped back in at the outward end of the dock and dived under the surface once or twice before disappearing for what seemed like a long time. Eventually, he surfaced close to the dock and handed Oster a rectangular object about the size of a book, coated in mud. Dennis held on to the side of the dock with both hands while Oster rubbed off some of the muck. It was a wedding picture of Dennis and Karen Lamm in a sterling-silver frame that rock manager–producer James Guercio had given to them the first time they got married. Dennis had thrown it overboard in a fit of anger during their divorce. The glass was shattered, but in the faded, water-bleached photo Dennis was still tanned and handsome and young, and Karen was laughing, her baby-blue eyes sparkling, and they were such a perfect couple, it took your breath away.

Oster called to his girl friend. "Brenda, come over here and see this," and then Dennis went back down again, down into the dark waters of the marina.

*If there wasn't the Beach Boys
and there wasn't music, I would
not even know them. I would not
even talk to them. But through the
music I fell in love with my brothers.*
                                    —DENNIS WILSON

Two

1

"Hey, Dennis! Play it again!" Murry Wilson roared from his bed. A great big bear of a man under the sheets, Murry loved bed. For Murry, bed was like a throne for a potentate. He would lie there for hours in the mornings, reading the papers, talking on the phone, watching TV, the bedsheets pulled halfway up his huge, rotund belly.

He was a big man, with a meaty face and a double chin. His thick brown hair was carefully combed back from a high forehead, and his half-framed mock tortoiseshell glasses sat across the bridge of his small, wide nose. His left eye—which he had lost in a freak industrial accident when he was twenty-five— had been replaced by a glass prosthetic eye that he kept in a container on the dresser at night. Even in bed he smoked his omnipresent pipe. It jutted out from between his teeth, the bowl blackened and charred by the double kitchen matches he used to continuously light it. The smoke filled the room with a pungent sweetness that his family and friends associated with him; occasionally an ember would billow from the bowl and land on his chest, singeing the gray hair.

"Hey, Dennis!" Murry bellowed again in his deep, sonorous voice, like the giant's voice in "Jack and the Beanstalk." "Put it on again!"

Murry had just listened, for the tenth time that morning, to "Two Step Side Step," a composition he had written a few years before. By occupation Murry owned the ABLE machine shop—Always Better Lasting Equipment—a small company that imported lathes and drills from England. But in his heart he considered himself a songwriter. He had been writing songs since he was a teenager, and after many years of dogged pursuit, one or two of his songs had actually been recorded. But, according to his wife, Audree, his songs "just died. They never did anything." Yet Murry's love for music was still his abiding passion. The very sound of music soothed him; he would close his eyes and tilt his head back, losing himself in the melody and chord changes, which seemed to transport him someplace joyous and peaceful. He especially liked to hear one of his own compositions playing on the hi-fi as he lay in the small, dark bedroom of his modest Hawthorne, Los Angeles, bungalow. "Dennis!" His voice boomed through the house. "Put it on again!"

In the modern pink kitchen at the rear of the house, Murry's thirteen-year-old middle son, Dennis, sat stubbornly at the dinette table, his face knotted in pure resentment. He was a thin, wiry adolescent, athletically built, his sun-bleached, blond hair electric-razored into a flattop crew cut. He remained at the table, purposely ignoring his father. Dennis and his father were the family antagonists—although Murry was often at odds with all three of his sons. In many ways, Dennis and Murry were the most alike. Fiercely loyal and devoted to each other, they were totally unable to express their feelings. Instead, they seemed to be locked into some terrible competitive duel. On the surface it appeared to be a typical generation gap of the late fifties, with Murry's tough, Depression mentality and hard-work ethics pitted against Dennis's casual, California teen sensibility; but the passions between this father and son went well beyond any ordinary generation gap.

Audree Wilson gingerly turned the bacon strips in a frying pan at the stove. A pleasant and cheerful young housewife, she was in the pressure spot of mediating the daily turmoil between her husband and three sons. Looking anxiously at Dennis, she said to him, "Go ahead, Dennis, put it on for him." Slightly plump, with blond hair and a warm smile, Audree made the kitchen her domain and salvation. Food was a major preoccupation in the Wilson household—for everyone but Dennis—and the kitchen was the center of household activity.

It was also by far the most modern room in the simply appointed bungalow. Facing the rear of the house, with a small garden beyond, the kitchen had been remodeled by Murry on several occasions. It now sported new cabinets and appliances, including a dishwasher and a two-door refrigerator, making it look like the kitchen of a much larger, more expensive house, like the set from a suburban TV sitcom.

Dennis looked at his mother and groaned. "Oh, Ma, do I have to?" he asked. He went to the small monophonic record player in the music room and put the stylus back to the beginning of the spinning 78 disc. Dennis thought all this music-writing stuff was stupid. Just one listen and you could tell Murry "couldn't write a fucking good tune"; that he was a "frustrated piece of shit writer." Murry couldn't even play an instrument.

But Murry could pick out chords on the piano, and despite Dennis's critical opinion of him, many people thought he wrote beautiful melodies. His musical ideas did seem a bit corny, if not downright anachronistic. Murry first took song writing seriously as a teenager when he entered one of his compositions in a New York radio contest that was aired in Los Angeles. Over the years his songs were turned down hundreds of times, and on occasion he was cheated outright by unethical publishers, as when he wrote the lyrics to an obscure single for which he claimed he was never paid. But the small group of Murry's tunes that were published and recorded gave him supreme pleasure. One of Murry's favorites was Jimmy Haskell singing Murry's "Hide My Tears" on Palace Records; another was the "Fiesta Day Polka."

Perhaps Murry's all-time favorite was the record on the phonograph in the family room, "Two Step Side Step," which was recorded by a group called the Bachelors on Palace records. It was an upbeat, hillbilly tune that Lawrence Welk, then at the height of his fame, once played on live radio. There was even sheet music for it, and Murry was so certain the song would sweep the nation he invented a little side-stepping dance that went with it. But the cha-cha and the merengue were the big popular dances at the time, and "Two Step Side Step" was hardly noticed. When the record ended this time, Murry called out to Dennis once more, "Play it again! Play it again," and Dennis, a little more resentfully, put the needle back to the start.

2

Murry had something of a hyperactive personality. He had a commanding voice and spoke so forcefully that he was at once galvanizing and irritating. His speech cadence had all the energy of a tough football coach cussing out his team. Five feet ten inches tall, balding, overweight, he had the air of a desperate salesman. Actually, "Murry was a very good salesman," one of his neighbors, Joanne Marks, remembered. "The only trouble was he oversold everything and then ruined it." Said another neighbor, Ida Kennedy, "He was a loudmouth."

Yet at heart, Murry was nothing more than the average American who believed in the American Dream and achievement through hard work. Although raised as a Lutheran, he wasn't a frequent churchgoer; but he was a religious man who believed in God and heaven and hell, and he worked hard for his living. He was born Murry Gage Wilson on July 2, 1917, in Hutchinson, Kansas, on the Arkansas River, smack-dab in the middle of the middlemost state. The son of William Coral Wilson and Edith Sthole, he was third oldest of four brothers and four sisters. His father, nicknamed "Bud," was a land enthusiast—not that he ever had enough money to buy any. A plumber by trade, like his father before him, Murry's father traveled first to Montana, then to Texas, looking for a new homestead for the family, before finally moving to Escondido, California, along with the tens of thousands of other dustbowl families in search of the California dream. In Escondido, Bud Wilson played semiprofessional baseball before the lure of better employment brought him and his large family to Los Angeles in 1922. They rented a big farmhouse at 9722 South Figueroa on the corner of Ninety-eighth Street.

"He was very strict and struggled hard to feed eight kids during the Depression," remembered Bud's youngest son, Charles. "I don't know how he survived." While Bud took whatever plumbing work he could find, including long stints in the desert helping to build the Los Angeles aqueduct, his wife, Edith, worked a steam press, ironing clothes for a garment manufacturer. Most of the family's clothing was handmade by Edith, a formidable figure five feet eight inches and weighing over two hundred pounds. "Nobody got sassy with her," said Charles.

Nor with Bud. He was a hard drinker with an explosive temper who often wreaked havoc on his large family, beating the kids and his wife. "He was an ornery son of a bitch," remembered one of his sons-in-law. "He punched around and beat up his wife and kids—until the kids were big enough to beat him up back." On one occasion, Bud beat Charles so badly for breaking his eyeglasses that the entire family was up in arms against him. Another time he punched Murry so sadistically that Murry finally hauled off and smacked him back. There was so much bitterness that after Edith Wilson passed away, Murry and his younger sister Emily never saw their father again, although he lived to be ninety-two. Emily hated her father in particular for the way he treated her mother. But the other children had fonder memories of Bud Wilson, including the nightly family sing-alongs around the old upright piano Bud and Edith had saved up to buy secondhand. Often the younger kids would fall asleep listening to their parents singing in the living room.

Murry was an active, curious child, always into some mischief, but good-natured, with a soft side. He was so sensitive that he would cry if someone was mean to him. He met Audree Korthof at Washington High School in Los Angeles. Born in Minneapolis, Minnesota, Audree came to California in 1928 with her mother and father, Betty and Carl Korthof when she was ten years old. Her family settled in downtown Los Angeles, where her grandfather and father were both bakers. Eventually her father opened his own bakeshop, the Mary Jane Bakery, in central Los Angeles. Audree was a pretty girl, already a bit overweight, but cheerful and warm. Murry fell for her instantly. They had in common a great love of music. Audree belonged to the school glee club, and had a beautiful singing voice, an attribute that was of no small importance to Murry Wilson.

They were married on March 26, 1938, and moved to a small apartment at 8012 South Harvard Boulevard, where they were living when Audree gave birth to their first son, Brian Douglas Wilson, on June 20, 1942, at Centinela Hospital in Inglewood. "When Brian was born, I was one of those young, frightened fathers," Murry Wilson once said, "but I just fell in love with him, and in three weeks he cooed back at me." Their second son, Dennis Carl, was born December 4, 1944, and a third son, Carl Dean, was born on December 21, 1946.

Three months after Dennis's birth, the family moved to the south bay community of Hawthorne. With a hard-earned and harder-saved $2,300 down payment, they bought a small, neat, two-bedroom house at 3701 West 119th Street on the corner of Kornblum Avenue. Located just three blocks north of the Hawthorne Airport, where light planes would land and take off, the community was a barren tract, with no trees for shade. There weren't even any sidewalks; the front lawns just tapered off into the street, where the newly dug sewer lines had been put in. Because the house had only two bedrooms, all three boys slept in the same twelve-by-ten-foot room, with one small window overlooking Kornblum Avenue.

The Wilsons were hardly out of place in Hawthorne, the "City of Good Neighbors." It was one of the many new and burgeoning communities of young marrieds and new families that had sprung up throughout the south bay area just after the war. Twelve miles southeast of central Los Angeles, the small community didn't have electrical power until 1910 or even a police department until 1922. Nearly half of the population was on relief during the thirties and the working-class residents almost all declared bankruptcy; almost three thousand parcels of property were sold off for delinquent taxes, some at one dollar each. The community was virtually saved in 1939 by the Northrop Aircraft Company, which opened offices there and brought with it dozens of contractors and twenty thousand jobs.

By the time the Wilsons arrived in Hawthorne, during the postwar urban sprawl, it was still a predominantly white, working-class community. Flat, bleak, hot, it comprised seemingly endless patches of development homes laid end to end, street after street—row after row of duplicate tract houses, available for under $10,000 each. It was a community of Mah-Jongg and checkers, Foster Freeze, supermarkets, churches, Little League, and cookouts on Sundays. It was the essence of heartland Los Angeles, and if there was anything unusual about Hawthorne, it was that it was the most benignly typical Los Angeles suburb you could find.

Murry worked as a clerk for the Southern California Gas Company, and later at the Goodyear Tire and Rubber Company. One day at the plant, when he was working near a high-power machine that conditioned rubber with acid, one of the swabs of acid flew across the room and hit him in the face. It splintered his glasses and completely burned out his left eye. Murry spent two weeks in the hospital, followed by long months despairing at home. He was fitted with a glass eye, but the scarred socket was too sensitive at first for him to be able to wear it, and Murry sported an eyepatch for a time. "When I was twenty-five, I thought the world owed me a living," Murry said. "When I lost my eye, I tried harder, drove harder, and did the work of two men in the company and got more raises." After leaving Goodyear he worked for Air Research Industries, and then for his brothers, who were in the machinery business. After some time he borrowed against his home to open ABLE Machinery in Southgate. Murry was especially proud of the fact that his company imported the Binns and Berry's lathe. According to Murry, the business "succeeded against million-aire dealers. Now you figure it out. Guts." But in truth, the business wasn't all that successful. According to Dennis, Murry never brought home more than $15,000 a year, although in those days that might have meant he was doing much better than most of his struggling neighbors.

3

All three Wilson boys went to nearby York Elementary School, and later to Hawthorne High School, on the corner of El Segundo and Inglewood. Hawthorne High was a large school of two thousand students, a compound of long, low, turquoise buildings built of cinder blocks and Quonset huts, bounded on one end by railroad tracks, the town swimming pool, and a large athletic field. Since the city of Hawthorne was just a few miles from the Los Angeles International Airport, jet planes passed over the school at regular intervals, like spaceships gleaming in the hot afternoon sun. The Wilson brothers were fair-to-middling students at best; Dennis being the worst and Carl a chronic hookey player.

Brian was the best-looking of the Wilson sons, a handsome youngster with a sweet smile, gorgeous hazel-blue eyes, and dark hair. By his teens he had grown into a gangling, six-foot three-inch smirking teenager with a crew cut. He was a gentle soul, a polite and caring young man, always eager to please and to be accepted by his peers. Around Hawthorne High he was considered a "regular guy." He loved sports, cars, junk food (meals and snacks were a major event for him, and only his youthful metabolism kept him slim)—and girls. The girls didn't take him very seriously, though, despite his appealing, dreamlike qualities. But perhaps he was a trifle too romantic for the other teens at Hawthorne High. For years he worshiped a girl named Carol Mountain from afar. He was crazy about her and talked to his friends about her all the time, but she wouldn't give him a second look.

Like many teenagers in Hawthorne, where a small-town mentality pervaded, Brian was remarkably unsophisticated. He was a fun-loving, immature kid, a real "locker-room cutup." He developed a penchant that he would never outgrow for practical jokes, along with a huge, deep laugh: "Har! Har! Har!" His sophomoric pranks were fairly typical. Once, on the way to school in his beat-up two-tone '57 Chevy, he stopped his car at a light. To the astonishment of the driver behind him, he threw up what seemed like a river of milk by hiding the carton next to his mouth. During some horseplay in the school locker room, he once pretended to be knocked unconscious by a wet, knotted towel. While he lay on the floor of the shower, refusing to get up, one of the other guys urinated on him, which brought him to his feet quickly enough. Some of his other pranks were less inspired, such as cursing at the passengers of other automobiles and then hiding on the floor of his car;

wrapping toilet paper around his head like a bandage while visiting a friend in the hospital; and introducing his mother to friends by saying they thought she was overweight and needed to diet. Even Murry was not exempt from his pranks. He once filled Murry's favorite pipe with grass from the lawn and laughed till tears rolled down his cheeks when Murry tried to light it.

But pranks on Murry were rare events indeed. As the oldest son, Brian had the gravest responsibility to please his father, and wholeheartedly tried to live up to Murry's expectations of him—never an easy task. Murry was impossibly hard on Brian, with rarely a kind word. One close neighborhood observer said, "Brian had a tremendous capacity for love, and he wasn't able to express it around his family. He got no love from his father, and his mother was always balanced between them. Murry would say, 'Audree, if you love me, you will see my point, and don't give in.' Audree was always being put in the middle. If she agreed with the kids, then she deserted Murry, and he'd throw a tantrum and there'd be hell to pay. If she agreed with Murry, then the kids lost their mother and their father."

Brian played left field for the Little League "Seven Up" baseball team. Murry was always at the sidelines, coaching and complaining about Brian's performance. Later, in high school, Brian played center field for the varsity baseball team and quarterback for the Cougars, the school football team. A dead shot at practice, Brian would clench up and fumble balls as soon as he was in a game. And Murry never let him forget it. As Brian recalled: "I had him come to my football games, and I'd say, 'What did you think of me?' And he'd say, 'You sloughed off! You're lazy!' I used to catch it from him all the time over that stuff. 'Don't slough off, get in there and fight!'"

Although Brian got along with almost everybody, the one person he didn't get along with was his middle brother, Dennis. "We were very competitive because Brian was the oldest and the most important," Dennis said. "I spent more time with Carl because I could beat Carl up." Indeed, Dennis not only swatted Carl around unmercifully, calling him a "pussy" at every turn; he also had trouble getting along with most other people.

Dennis looked the least like the Wilsons, with his blond hair and slim, athletic body. "I felt guilty because I wasn't fat," Dennis said. "I felt out of place. I couldn't stay at the dinner table, I'd have to run out." And yet, Dennis was the most like his father. Strong-willed, arrogant, fearless, with no sense of physical danger, he was filled with nervous energy. Even when he was too small to go out alone, he would spend hours standing by the screen door, staring out into the street and the world beyond. Athletics became a natural release for him, and the beach held a special lure. When Dennis was old enough, Murry bought him a blue nine-foot two-inch surfboard. Although he never mastered surfing completely, he had such perfect coordination that he could wiggle each toe independently and entertained the girls on the beach by picking up dimes with his toes. On weekends, when the family would drive toward the beach, Dennis would stand up in the backseat of the car, waiting breathlessly until the ocean appeared over the last rise.

A typical middle child, without the authority of his older brother or the sympathy of the baby of the family, Dennis never got enough attention. So he developed some specific ways of attracting it. "My brothers both had a bed-wetting problem, until they were thirteen or fourteen," Dennis said. "I hated those motherfuckers for that—they got all the attention. You know what I'd fucking do? I'd pee in their fucking beds in the middle of the night, once in a while, just so they'd get into trouble. I was the wild boy in the family."

By the time he was a young teen, Dennis was smoking cigarettes, the pack rolled up in the sleeve of his dirty white T-shirt. Anytime something was wrong in the neighborhood—broken windows or air let out of car tires—Dennis was likely to have had something to do with it. The neighbors called him "Dennis the Menace." Ida Kennedy, who lived a few doors down from the Wilsons, could not keep Dennis from climbing the telephone pole in her backyard until she put him in charge of keeping the other children off of it, a duty he performed with relish. Once, he tried to purchase a gallon of gasoline at Lindner's Grocery Store. Gil Lindner quickly discovered that Dennis intended to concoct a bomb to throw down the sewage ravine and blow it up. When he was a little older, Dennis arrived at a neighbor's house crying real tears, carrying a Mason jar filled with ashes. "It's Brian," he told the neighbors. "He was trying to light the gas heater and it exploded."

Murry was not exempt from Dennis's mischief either. "I was very proud of my dad's glass eye," Dennis said. "It was the only one on the block. When I was very young, I took it off the dresser while he was asleep and took it to school for 'show and tell.' I was very proud of it. Of course, when my dad woke up, he couldn't leave the house without it, and he was pretty pissed off."

As Dennis got older, his pranks got him into more trouble. When he was fourteen he hot-wired Murry's car and drove it around the neighborhood with friends, stripping all the gears. On a nearby street he offered a little girl a nickel to get into the car with him. It was a joke to Dennis, but not to the little girl's parents, who called the police and had Dennis hauled off to the local station.

"I grew up beating up every guy in sight," Dennis said. "I was the fighter. I was always slugging away. I'd be set off like that [snap], I'd go, 'Oh, yeeeah?' I walked around with a chip on my shoulder. I was happy but I wasn't."

Carl, a pudgy, square-faced little boy with a chip-toothed grin, looked the most like his father. The baby of the family, he was by far the most spoiled—although none of the Wilson children was spared the rod. While his bad case of adolescent acne cleared up as he grew older, his weight problem only got worse. He was terribly self-conscious about it, even as an adult. Dennis taunted him with the nickname "Porky." Carl was a quiet, fairly withdrawn boy who idolized his brother Brian. Said Audree, "Carl ... was always sitting, watching the parade go by, very calm." His mother's favorite, Carl was able to develop a more sensitive side that Murry would not allow Brian. He was not exactly a momma's boy—the Wilson kids were much too tough for that appellation—but he developed a closeness and empathy with Audree that Brian would always resent.

Carl has sweet memories of his childhood. "We'd all sleep in the same room," Carl remembered, "and after we went to bed, Brian would sit there trying to make us laugh. First, my mother would come in and warn us. If our father came in, then it was curtains. So we'd be trying not to laugh, covering our mouths, hiding under the sheets, and Brian would keep cracking us up." They would often fall asleep harmonizing with each other on a hymn called "Come Down, Come Down from the Ivory Tower." But Carl still remembered Murry with the same respectful awe as his brothers. "When my dad walked through the house, it would shake," he said. "It sounded like a giant."

The Wilson house on the corner of 119th Street and Kornblum was a vortex of neighborhood activity. With three growing boys, each with his own group of friends, there were always bikes lying on the lawn, a game of catch, or touch football in the yard, often with Murry at the helm, coaching, directing, putting in his two cents. On Saturdays the boys would have to go down to Murry's shop in east L.A. and help him clean the machines, a chore they all dreaded. Murry saw himself as the perfect all-around dad; as far as he was concerned, he and the boys were buddy-buddy, and nothing was wrong. In fact, he bragged to friends that he had told his sons all about sex one night, "eyeball to eyeball," all in bed together, kind of like a pajama party. Some nights, Murry would invite the boys into his bedroom and make them massage his back to relax his muscles.

To the outside world, the Wilson boys seemed to be well-behaved children who toed the line for a strict father. But something more was going on behind the doors of the Wilson household. In a neighborhood of simple values, where a swift crack for a misbehaving child was thought to be a good thing, a disciplinarian father was not out of the ordinary. But Murry's discipline went beyond any swift crack. Twenty years later, when it would become a national issue, it would be called child abuse.

4

"My father resented the fucking kids to death," was Dennis's explanation for it. "The motherfucker hated us, or he would have loved the shit out of us. It's that fucking simple. That asshole beat the shit out of us." Then Dennis grinned sardonically. "He just had a very unique way of expressing himself physically with his kids," he said. "Instead of saying, 'Son, you shouldn't shoot a beebee gun at the streetlight,' he'd go *boooom!!!* I got the blunt end of the broom. *Crack!* One minute late! Just one minute late! *Boom!* And that's it. Brian and Carl would hide in the bathroom, 'Oh God! He's getting it!' Later they'd ask, 'Did it hurt, Dennis?'"

Murry's father beat him; Murry beat his children. Audree watched helplessly from the sidelines, according to Dennis, frightened of Murry herself. "Ohh, please, Murry, no, don't do that."

According to Audree, "He was a taskmaster. He really was. He was tough. And I used to think he was too tough. But, it was a very hard job for him having three teenage boys. He used to call them 'young stallions.'"

"Denny did [get] some pretty hard spankings..." Audree said. "Dennis reminds me very much of his father. Sometimes I think, I don't believe this, it's like Murry revisited. Dennis got the worst of it. Because he was more aggressive. But what constitutes a beating, I don't know."

Indeed, if beating the boys had been all Murry did, it would have been one thing. But Murry had red-faced, screaming, roaring tantrums. On many occasions his punishments went beyond simple beatings into the realm of the sadistic. Dennis spoke of Murry beating him up in the bathtub so he couldn't break anything by kicking. Once, to humiliate a preteen Brian, Murry reportedly forced him to defecate on a newspaper or plate in front of the family. (This story has many versions. Another popular one is that Brian and his brothers served up a portion of rubber "doggie-do" to Murry on a plate, which was taken as a good-natured prank. Both versions of the story are sworn to.) Another time, Murry reportedly tied Brian to a

tree for punishment, and once, when he caught Brian mastur-
bating, he made him go without dinner for two nights. Dennis
was summarily punched, kicked, and beaten with a two-by-
four. At a family Christmas gathering, when Murry noticed
Dennis sneaking drinks, he actually picked him up and tossed
him across the room, where Dennis crashed against the wall
and collapsed in a pile on the floor. Once, Dennis refused to
eat the tomatoes on his plate. Thereafter, Murry forced him to
eat one every time they were served until he vomited at the
sight of them. Throughout his adult life, Dennis was never able
to eat another raw tomato. In another incident, Dennis remembered, "I almost burned the house down a couple of times. I
was four or five or six, and I was playing with matches on the
curtain, the little balls of lint...and they'd go *fooom*. The
punishment for that was he burned my hands with the matches.
He was brutal." Murry also used his prosthetic eye—which
he could pop out to reveal the gnarled and scarred socket—
to punish the boys. At the dinner table, he would sometimes
roll the glass eyeball next to his plate while winking the empty
socket at them. While the socket frightened and horrified Brian
and Carl, it fascinated and amused Dennis, with his macabre
sense of humor.*

In some ways, Brian got the worst of it, if not in terms of
physical punishment, then in terms of psychological torment.
Brian was a nervous wreck as a teenager, and the slightest
challenge made him extremely anxious; he had to take a tranquilizer to go through with his driver's test. Brian found it next
to impossible to satisfy Murry. He claimed the only reason he
got B's and A's in school was so he could come home and say,
"Hey, look, Dad," but the grades were never good enough.
Indeed, Murry seemed to have a special way of attacking Brian.
In later years, a project called the High Risk Consortium, com-
prising fifteen major research centers around the world, was
formed to study schizophrenic children. As reported in the

---

*In 1971, when some of Murry's bizarre punishments came to public light for the
first time in a *Rolling Stone* article by Tom Nolan, Murry vehemently denied them.
Reportedly, Murry phoned Brian and accused him of spreading vicious rumors, particularly about defecating on a plate. Brian was supposed to have responded, "Let's
tell them that I shit in your ear and you hit me in the head with a plate."

New York Times, the findings of the consortium indicated that "specifically, when showing disapproval... parents tended to attack the child himself rather than to criticize things he had done; they habitually told the child what the child's feelings and thoughts were rather than listening to what the child had to say...." Said Dr. Michael J. Goldstein, the director of a study at the University of California at Los Angeles, "The parents of these kids engaged in character assassinations. Instead of criticizing what the child had done, they would make a personal attack, saying, 'You're no good,' which damages the child's self-esteem." Brian once described Murry's criticism of him after school football games in this way. "It bothered me because it made me feel like I was goofing up, that I was inferior. It made me feel worthless."

When Brian was only six or seven years old, the family noticed that he had a peculiar way of turning his head to listen. According to Audree, Dennis and Carl had frequent ear infections, but not Brian. A doctor suggested that all three boys should have their tonsils out. Audree related, "The doctor said that Brian's tonsil on the right side was so huge that if we had his tonsils taken out... that [it] would stop blocking... his eustachian tube—he said after three months he should be okay. But it wasn't okay. They say it's a nerve deafness... it could be congenital or it could have been caused by an injury. We had a neighbor who he got into a fight with one time. He hit him really hard on his ear..."

What is really important is that Brian believed that Murry was responsible—a belief that he was only able to admit much later in his adult life. In Brian's mind, his deafness was possibly the result of Murry smacking him on the side of the head when he was only two years old.* Incredibly, this hearing defect—only 6 percent of normal hearing in his right ear—meant that Brian, who was to become one of the great innovative producers of modern music, would never hear stereo. The irony of this loss would plague him for life.

---

*This story has been embellished with time until some witnesses, including Brian's high-school music teacher, Fred Morgan, claim they saw Murry hit Brian in the head with a baseball bat at Little League. If this is the case, it is unlikely it caused Brian's nerve damage, which occurred before he was old enough to play baseball.

"My dad was an asshole," Dennis said, "and he treated us like shit, and his punishments were sick. But you played a tune for him and he was a marshmallow. This mean motherfucker would cry with bliss, like the lion in *The Wizard of Oz*, when he heard the music."

5

If music can soothe the savage breast, the Wilson children learned to make music at an early age.

Brian's musical accomplishments were prodigious, embellished by family pride and media legend over the years. At the age of eleven months, Brian allegedly was able to hum the entire "Marine Corps Hymn." Murry would sing "do, do, do, do, do do" and Brian would repeat the sequence of notes exactly. According to his proud daddy, before he was a year old he was able to say "Mi-sez-zip-py." Brian said his earliest musical memory was of listening to "Rhapsody in Blue" at his grandmother's house when he was two. This Gershwin piece, he said, became his "general life theme." When the boys were still toddlers, Murry did an extensive renovation on the garage and built a music room where he and Audree would harmonize at night on a Hammond organ, just as his own mother and father had.

"Brian took six weeks of accordion lessons when he was very young on a little, almost toy accordion," Audree said. "He excelled, he just flew through it, but we couldn't afford to buy the big accordion."

Brian started to sing at age three. He was able to pick out chords and "he'd sing right on key," according to Audree. Later, Brian joined the church choir, where he was asked to be a soloist, and would often sing for school functions. One Christmas he and three other students dressed up as clowns and did a satire on "Jingle Bells" that Brian wrote. He had a pure and beautiful alto voice, almost like a *castrato*, and the children in school laughed and made fun of him, calling him a sissy. Dennis remembered Brian running home from school in tears. "It broke my heart to see him emotionally involved in the

music at such an early age and have his friends laugh at him."
He learned to sing in a deeper voice, saving the falsetto he was
developing for when he was alone.

Fascinated by harmonies, Brian would come home from
school and go directly to the music room. "There were many
years of his life when he did nothing but play piano," Carl
said. The Four Freshmen became something of an obsession
for him. "Months at a time. Days on end. He'd listen to Four
Freshmen records." He would sit next to the hi-fi, his head
cocked, carefully picking out the different harmonies and
studying how they wove into the melody line.

"When Brian was fourteen, the Four Freshmen were playing
someplace in Hollywood," Audree said. "We couldn't afford
to take [everyone]—we didn't have very much money—so
Murry took Brian this Sunday night just in the hopes he could
meet them because he was so thrilled with their music. He
was already writing vocal arrangements, even though he hadn't
had any musical training. Years later, when they were the Beach
Boys, the Four Freshmen remembered meeting Murry and
Brian."

For his sixteenth birthday Murry and Audree gave Brian a
Wollensak tape recorder. For the first time he could record the
harmonies himself. First he taught Audree the simplest part
and sang harmony with her into the tape recorder. Then he
would play it back and he and Audree would sing live to it,
creating four parts. Later he would expand the parts to include
Murry, with the bass line, and eventually Carl.

While Brian was into classical music, Gershwin, and harmonies, Carl was into rock-and-roll, particularly Chuck Berry
and Little Richard, whom he listened to on the radio. "Carl
was the second one to show interest," Audree said. When Carl
was three years old, "he was really into the cowboy music and
Spade Coolie. He would stand with his foot on a stool pretending he was playing the violin. Carl was twelve when he
decided he wanted to play the guitar, so we bought him an
inexpensive one, and he took a few lessons from a neighbor.
One day he came home and he was playing an old standard,
and one of the chords was way off, and I was appalled. And
Brian said, 'How can you let him take lessons when he's learn-

ing wrong chords?' Well, that didn't last long; Carl began to play on his own and he loved it."

Dennis was the last to participate—reluctantly; he stubbornly refused to join in on the family sing-alongs. But he started playing the piano on his own when he was fourteen. He never had any formal musical training, but he played well enough to hack out a mean boogie-woogie.

On Friday nights the whole family would go down to ABLE Machinery and pick up Murry in his 1950 "Henry J," which Dennis thought was "the ugliest car in the world." "My dad would take us out to dinner and we used to write tunes," Dennis said. "The three of us would sing three-part harmony every Friday night in the backseat."

6

Every Christmas, the Wilson family would attend elaborate holiday parties at the home of Murry's younger sister, Emily "Glee" Love. Glee and her husband, Milton Love, lived with their five children in a large, imposing home on the corner of Mt. Vernon and Fairway, in the Baldwin Hills section of Los Angeles. The house was not a mansion, but in contrast to brother Murry's Hawthorne bungalow, it was quite impressive: a five-thousand-square-foot Mediterranean villa on three levels, situated atop a sloping lot. At Christmas, the house would accommodate as many as sixty family members and friends. After a huge traditional feast of turkey and hams and puddings, which Glee would spend all week preparing, there might be a small musicale in which the family members would perform. Sometimes the guests would put on their winter coats and go out into the chill Los Angeles night air to stroll from house to house, singing carols for the neighbors.

"Glee would teach us the carols, and we'd harmonize," Brian remembered. Often, when the caroling was over, Brian and his eldest cousin, Michael, would go off by themselves to a quiet room and sing their own harmonies, usually to "Happy, happy birthday, baby...." "Mike would add a few little bass lines, and I used to recognize that he had a great bass voice," Brian said. "I started teaching him Four Freshmen parts...."

Michael Edward Love, born March 15, 1941, was nine months older than Brian. Tall and skinny, with reddish-blond hair that began irrevocably to thin from the time he was a teenager, he had piercing, cold blue eyes. The oldest child, with two brothers and two sisters, Michael was looked up to by his siblings and was the favorite of his grandmother, Edith. A bright, quick-witted young man, he inherited the Wilson family's musical interests. When he was only four years old, he sang "That Old Black Magic" in perfect pitch, remembering the lyrics from beginning to end. For one of the musical shows at his mother's Christmas galas, he wrote a song called "The Old Soldier," which so impressed Murry that he felt compelled to write new lyrics for it. Brian dutifully performed the number at the next family gathering, wearing his first set of long pants, and, according to Murry, "He brought the house down."

Michael was never very interested in school. He started out with fair grades, but he got bored easily and his marks fell as he went into high school. The teachers complained that he disrupted classes with his wisecracks and that he would read his own books under the desk when he was supposed to be studying. At Dorsey High, where he graduated in 1958, he was an extremely well liked student who distinguished himself as a cross-country runner. Much was expected of Mike, and his mother was quite demanding of him. He was expected to baby-sit for his brothers and sisters whenever needed, and once when he forgot to close the lower casement windows so his siblings wouldn't fall out, Glee threatened to throw him out of the house and took all of his clothing and put it on the front porch.

All kinds of achievement in music, arts, and athletics were encouraged in the Love household. Any music lessons the children wanted were supplied. Mike's younger sisters, Maureen and Stephanie, were talented harpists and singers; younger brothers were both outstanding athletes, Stanley an exceptional basketball player and brother Stephen a surfer, as well as a promising student. Maureen was the first female student-body president at Western High School, and Stephen was student-body president at Morningside High.

The children's interest in music was inherited from their mother, Glee, who loved music as much as her brother Murry did. Glee had a beautiful, clear soprano voice, and would sing along to the recordings of operas. As the hi-fi blared away, she would study the librettos and learn the words. A supporter of local L.A. opera, she attended all the new productions. Milt would go along with her bravely, but he didn't care for opera very much. Though proud of their mother's pretty voice and impressed with her interest, the children too, found opera stuffy, and much preferred listening to rock-and-roll. However, rock-and-roll had to be played very quietly in the Love household, and sometimes at night the boys would sneak a transistor radio—a new invention —under the covers to listen to their favorite tunes. In fact, when Brian slept over, he and Mike would often fall asleep outside in the family's Nash Rambler, listening to the radio.

As a young girl at George Washington High School, Glee was considered one of the prettiest in school. She was in all the school plays (where her future sister-in-law, Audree, was in the chorus), and starred in a production of The Red Mill in her senior year. She was just a pretty girl of fifteen when she was introduced to Milton Love, seventeen, also a student at George Washington High School, where he graduated in 1935. They dated for three years and, despite the objections of her parents, ran away and got married in Ventura, California.

Milton Love's family was of English-Irish descent. Grandpa Edward Love was born near Shreveport, Louisiana, and came to Los Angeles with his family in 1905. They were so poor they pitched a tent on Huntington Beach and lived there until Edward could find a job and rent a house on Thirty-first Street in downtown Los Angeles. There Edward met a neighbor, Edith Clardy, who was born in Glendora, California, on an orange ranch. They were married on January 4, 1917. Edward went to night school and later into the sheet-metal business. When their two sons, Milt and Stanley, were old enough, they joined their father in the growing family-run concern, the Love Sheet

Metal Company. Theirs was a fortuitous situation; Los Angeles in the forties and fifties was experiencing an unprecedented building surge. The Love Sheet Metal Company got many of the major fabrication contracts to install new stainless-steel kitchens for hospitals and schools. They made a great deal of money, and in the late forties Milt and Glee moved to their handsome View Park home.

But by the end of the fifties, things started to change drastically for the Love family. First, their golden boy, Mike, didn't seem to have much direction in his life. "I was in the oil business for a while," Mike said. "Gas and oil, check the tires." He worked the night shift at a Standard Oil station at Washington and La Brea. He hated it, particularly after he was held up at gunpoint. During the days, he was an apprentice at his father's sheet-metal factory. It was around then that he found out that his high-school sweetheart, Francine St. Martin, was pregnant. He wanted to take her to Tijuana for an abortion, but his mother wouldn't hear of it, and they married soon after. The wedding was a small affair at Franny's mother's house. A daughter, Melinda, was born in 1959. Although the Loves liked Franny, the family couldn't help feeling that perhaps Mike had ruined his life. The young couple took a small apartment on Eighth Avenue in Inglewood.

In the late fifties the recession began to hit the building industry hard, and the sheet-metal fabricating business, particularly that part of it where Milt Love and his brother were making most of their money, was soon wiped out. "It happened before we realized it," Milton said. "There was much more money owed out than coming in." They struggled to keep the business together for a few years, but by 1959 it was clear the bottom had fallen out. The bankruptcy laws were stringent at the time, and not only was it considered the utmost shame to have to declare bankruptcy, it cleaned the Loves out financially. Everything they owned was gone in a year: the house on the corner, the cars, all of it. For the children, especially the younger ones, it was a great trauma. The family moved to a much smaller, three-bedroom house, at 10212 Sixth Avenue in Inglewood. "It was two miles from Hollywood Park race-track," remembered Stanley Love, "two miles from Morningside High School, where I attended, as did my brother Stephen, and three miles from Hawthorne, where the Wilson family lived." On Wednesday nights Brian and Mike and Maureen would walk home together from the Angela Mesa Presbyterian Church Sing Night, singing "In the Still of the Night" at fever pitch.

When Brian and Mike were nineteen, Dennis seventeen, and Carl fifteen, they were asked to sing at an evening talent show at Hawthorne High School. Although Brian had already graduated from Hawthorne High the year before and was now attending El Camino Junior College, hoping to become a psychologist, he thought it would be fun to go back to the old school and perform. For some reason, Carl didn't want to do it and Audree insisted. To coax Carl along, Brian named the impromptu group Carl and the Passions. They intended to sing only for this one high-school assembly. Dennis suggested they write a song about the surfing craze, and Mike came up with a "bob-bob-dit-dop" scat for the middle. The act was great fun, but nobody took it very seriously.

> *You know, few families are*
> *together spiritually and emotionally*
> *over a piece of art.*
>
> —DENNIS WILSON

Three

1

"It was a dreary afternoon in 1961," Dorinda Morgan wrote years later. "My husband Hite and I were in our office on Melrose Avenue in Hollywood. We were just about ready to call it a day when Alan Jardine came in." The Morgans were old-time Los Angeles music publishers, Alan Jardine an aspiring folk singer.

At the time, the Morgans owned Guild Music, a small, storefront recording and publishing firm located in a one-story building just across the street from KHJ Studios in the old Capitol Building. A large plate-glass window faced the street, with a sign that read STEREO MASTERS. The front part of the store was the office. In the rear was a small monophonic recording and mastering facility. Through the doors of this small store had passed scores of beginning groups, singers, and songwriters auditioning for Hite and Dorinda Morgan. Kindhearted, open, and encouraging, the Morgans had seen practically everything the business had to offer during their long careers in music publishing, which they had begun in New York with offices on Tin Pan Alley before they moved to Los Angeles in the late forties.

Alan Jardine was one of the many hopefuls who came to the Morgans' offices. Nineteen years old, only five feet four inches tall, with blue eyes and brown hair, he had a ready smile that showed slightly buck teeth. Immaculately clean and neat, Alan had an elflike quality that made him "cute." A second-year student at El Camino College, he was a sedate, conservative folk-song aficionado. He had first called the Morgans for an appointment several months earlier to arrange an audition with a group of friends, doing a song about the Rio Grande. The Morgans were unimpressed. "Professional, but not original," Dorinda Morgan said. "We turned them down. They were imitators, not innovators."

A few months later, Alan Jardine was back with a new folk group called the Pendletones. One of the boys innocently explained that they had named the group after the manufacturer of the wide-striped shirts that were fashionable at the time, hoping they might get free clothing that way. The Morgans thought it was a silly, but cute name, and didn't bother to tell the boys they had already auditioned another group using it.

"The tallest boy in this group said, 'Mrs. Morgan, I bet you don't remember me,'" Dorinda Morgan said. "He was right." But Brian Wilson certainly knew who the Morgans were; they had known his father since the early 1950s. Not only had they published several of his songs, including "Two Step Side Step," but Murry had brought Brian to the Morgans' home several years earlier to audition to record a song called "Chapel of Love" (not the Dixie Cups hit of 1964) when they were looking for a "young voice." Brian, twelve or thirteen years old at the time, was rejected. Over the years the Morgans had become social friends of the Wilsons, and the two couples dined together occasionally. It was Murry who had originally recommended the Morgans to Alan Jardine, when Al asked him how to get started in the music business. Murry gave Al the Morgans' phone number, then called Hite Morgan himself and said, "See if you can do anything for him."

Alan had known Brian from Hawthorne High, where both boys had been on the football team and in rival singing groups. But they had only recently become friendly and started singing together. Born Alan Charles Jardine on September 3, 1942, in Lima, Ohio, he was the second child of Charles Jardine and Virginia Louise Loxley. His mother was a housewife, his father a plant photographer for the Lima Locomotive Company. The Jardines lived outside of Lima on Rural Route #5, where Alan's grandfather first taught him to play clarinet. When Charles Jardine moved to California to manage a blueprinting plant for the Scott Railroad Company, Alan wound up at Hawthorne High, where he joined a folk group called the Islanders. He had been singing and harmonizing with various groups ever since.

During the summer of 1961 Alan had run into Brian Wilson on the El Camino campus. Alan had once suggested nonchalantly to Brian that they form a singing group. "I said, 'Let's do it, let's get together.'" They met the next day in the nurse's room in the college medical center. Alan brought along "a football player, a deep bass singer who couldn't carry a tune," he said. "So Brian said, 'Hey, my little brother Carl can sing." And I said, 'Him?' I remembered him from high school, when he was about three feet tall...twelve years old. And Brian said, 'He's young but he's really talented and so is my cousin Mike....'" Alan gave it a shot and came over to the Wilsons' house to harmonize. Eventually the boys called themselves the Pendletones.

The Pendletones intended to audition for the Morgans with some old favorites that Alan had dug up, but the Morgans told them that they needed original music to get recorded. "You've got to have an angle," Mrs. Morgan told them. "Something to set you apart from the others." Suddenly, the boy with the blond crew cut and the devilish twinkle in his blue eyes piped up, "Have you heard about the new surfing craze?" The other kids in the group looked at Dennis as if they wanted to shoot him.

"I honestly have not," Mr. Morgan said. "What's that?" Dennis described the floating slab of wood the size and shape of an ironing board, on which you stood while being hurled toward the shore by a wave. "It's the biggest thing happening at the beach," Dennis assured the Morgans. "Everybody's got a surfboard. They even give surf reports every morning on the radio."

The boys pointed out that there were already scores of musical surfing groups throughout southern California. Every beach community along the coast had a surfing band with a local following, and many of the kids in the groups were avid surfers themselves. The better groups, like the Surftones, had already broken through and recorded on small labels. The boys confessed they had recently started writing a song called "Surfin'," and the Morgans agreed to hear it when it was finished. Dorinda Morgan in particular liked the idea—she told the boys to write down all the surfing phrases they knew, add them to the lyrics, and polish the melody. She sent them home to work on it. If she liked what she heard when they came back, they could record it.

Audree and Murry were not at home. They had gone off to Mexico City for a long weekend with a business associate of Murry's, Barry Haven, who was visiting from England with his wife. Before leaving, Audree had stocked up on coldcuts for the boys, and had left some money in case they wanted to eat out. The boys took the food money and rented instruments to work on the song about surfing for the Morgans.

2

It was quite remarkable that the Morgans had never even heard about surfing; it was already one of the biggest recreational crazes ever to hit California. Hollywood had begun to exploit the California beach scene in 1959, with Columbia Pictures's release of the first "beach" picture, Gidget, which included an early surf song, "Lonely Surfer." Based on the real-life adventures of a petite surfer girl named Kathy Kohner, nicknamed "Gidget," shorthand for "girl-midget," the story came from a best-seller written by Gidget's father, Frederick Kohner. This vanilla classic of the innocent teenager in a bikini, tempted with sex, love, and the ultimate virginal romance, was high teen fantasy. It immortalized Sandra Dee as Gidget, and included James Darren and Cliff Robertson in the co-starring roles. But most important, it romanticized surfers and surfing for the first time; the Boy on the Board was on his way to becoming a sturdy part of California folklore.

Yet what was happening along the beaches was no plastic Hollywood product—it sprang out of the real California postwar life-style. The baby boom's millions of first-generation Angelinos were coming into adolescence; the first modern generation of southern Californians was developing its own culture. For most young natives—whose life was literally bordered by the Pacific—surfing was more than just a sport. It was a part of their natural environment. Surfing was almost addictive; it had a hypnotic effect. Many said surfing was like sex— it felt good every time you did it. The surfing craze had spread as far inland as San Bernardino and up and down the coast in a crowded arc from Malibu to Redondo Beach, where there were already about two hundred well-known surfing beaches. By 1961, when the boys first told the Morgans about surfing, there were an estimated thirty thousand regular surfers on the beaches each weekend; by 1968 there would be one million.

The California surfing craze came as no surprise to the people of Australia, where, since 1954, there were so many surfers that surfboards were registered like automobiles. The Polynesian "sport of kings" had been discovered by westerners when Captain James Cook visited the Hawaiian Islands in 1778. But surfing wasn't popular in America until the 1920s, when the Hawaiian surfing champion, Duke Hahanamoku, who had broken the hundred-meter swimming freestyle record in the Olympics in Stockholm in 1912, gave a surfing demonstration in Atlantic City. It wasn't until the fifties that the sport reached mass public interest among the war babies coming of age along the California coastline.

The surf music being produced at the time was supposed to duplicate the feeling of surfing. It was a musical brew specific to beach and surf that was best appreciated live, but it had become big radio business too—KFWB, called "Color Radio," was the "surfer's choice." There were dancing clubs and "surf groups" all over the south bay area—the Chantays, the Pyramids, the Rumblers, the Challengers, and the Marquettes, whose most popular number, the "Surfer's Stomp," had its own dance that was supposed to simulate the movements of riding a board. The best-known group was Dick Dale and the Deltones, who used to pack the Rendezvous Ballroom in Balboa every weekend. Born in Beirut but raised in California, Dale was nicknamed "The Pied Piper of Balboa," and at Friday-night dances at the Rendezvous the Deltones would draw four thousand kids. Dale claimed he invented his staccato guitar style to simulate riding a wave. The Deltones' repertoire included "Miserlou," "Surfing Drums," "Death of a Gremmie," and the famous "Let's Go Tripping" and "Surf Beat." Although Dale was a popular live performer, his songs never recorded well. His tunes were raunchy, chord-throbbing instrumentals that all sounded as if they were recorded live including the hoots and hollers of surfers.

The surfing culture had already developed its own etiquette, dress code, and language: "outside" meant "in the fast-breaking waves"; the "boneyard" was the area between the breaking waves and the beach; "cutting back," "climbing," and "dropping" meant "hotdogging," or making moves that the better surfers made; trunks were called "baggies"; to "hang ten" meant to run up to the end of the board and hang your toes over the end (boards are now usually too small for this to be possible). Using bits and pieces of this slang, Brian and Mike Love sat down in the music room of the Wilson bungalow and wrote a version of a song called "Surfin'."

They had the song completed when Audree and Murry returned home from Mexico with Barry Haven and his wife. The two couples walked in the door to find the den full of equipment, including amplifiers and microphones. "We saw all this stuff," Audree said. "They had used all of the grocery money. They had borrowed some from Mike Love, and they rented the mikes and the bass. I'm not sure about the drums—I think they bought them."

Murry's face turned deep red as he exploded in full fury. How dare they spend all the grocery money on equipment!

The boys knew how to diffuse Murry's anger immediately. They rushed to the instruments, warmed up the amps, and started to play. Murry grew calmer with each note. "His attitude changed pretty fast after he heard the song," Barry Haven said. "Oh, they had the teen beat and all that, but also some pretty melodies and chords that really made you feel like relaxayvooing."

The boys had something there, Murry decided. And of course, he wouldn't mind giving them a few pointers.

3

The Morgans liked the surfing song and booked time for the boys at a small, privately owned studio in Beverly Hills called Keen Studios. During the rehearsing and preparation of the song, there were major blowouts with Dennis, and by the time of the recording date, Brian and the others had decided he wasn't good enough to play with them. Audree finally insisted the boys let Dennis stay in the group. However, on the night of the session the boys arrived with another drummer, whom Brian had heard play in a country-western band at a club called the Shed House. Dennis put on a brave face, standing on the sidelines when the replacement drummer set up. Brian and Mike teased Dennis, while Carl tried to act as mediator. Dennis glowered in the background as the boys started to warm up.

"This other drummer was a hillbilly Gene Krupa," Dorinda Morgan said, "a real hotshot. I let them do one set with him and I said, 'No way, this guy has got to go.' We paid him and sent him home." Dennis took over on drums—but not that night. According to Carl's version of the session, "I played basic chords on the guitar, Al thrummed bass, Brian took off his jacket, laid it across the drum, and beat it with his hand, while we all sang into one microphone." Although Carl remembered that there was a drum, Brian probably only played the top of a plastic trash-can cover. In most future sessions Dennis was the official drummer, but he never learned to hold his drumsticks in the "approved" manner. As he was to admit years later, "I'm not an artist; I'm a clubber."

The finished song was no knockout. Produced by Hite Morgan, with assistance from studio engineer Dino Lappas, it took all of an hour to record. Nasal, whining, and childlike, the two-minute-and-ten-second song was hardly a hint of what would become the Beach Boys' warm layers of bell-like harmonies. But it was certainly an authentic-sounding surf song, and different. When the track was finished, the boys were surprised to learn that the Morgans insisted the "B" side of the single be a composition by their own son, Bruce, who was nineteen at the time. Bruce had been writing songs since he was eleven, and the Morgans felt his one-minute-and-forty-three-second "Luau" was right for the other side. Grudgingly, the boys laid down the track.

A standard songwriter's contract dated September 15, 1961, was signed between Guild Music Publishing and Michael Love and Brian Wilson for the song "Surfin'." They were to receive 28.5 percent of the wholesale royalty on sheet music, and 50 percent of the publishing, as well as six cents a copy—a typical low-end contract. The Morgans also agreed to get the boys into the musicians' union.

When the session was over, the Morgans took the boys out to one of the nearby chain restaurants. After wolfing down burgers and fries, the boys politely thanked the Morgans and left, ditching Dennis, who was driven home by the Morgans. Over apple pie à la mode, Dennis pretended not to mind that the others had left him behind. "I really want to be a screenwriter," he confided to Hite and Dorinda, "or maybe write short stories." He admitted that he was earning pocket money by sweeping out a local laundromat for a dollar a day and didn't have high expectations for his brothers' musical career.

4

Although record sales had tripled in the last half of the fifties, from $60 million to $205 million (and would triple again to an astounding $600 million by 1965), the Los Angeles music business in the late fifties and early sixties was a far cry from the multimillion-dollar industry it would soon become. The centers of musical growth were still Manhattan, where the Brill Building saw the height of songwriting activity; Detroit, where Berry Gordy had started Motown; and Nashville, the home of the country-music sound. The major record companies in existence—Capitol, RCA Victor, MGM, Decca, Mercury, and Columbia—were only signing "star" quality singers; that meant mostly white, middle-class Americans, with a big-band sound. The airwaves were full of such artists as Connie Francis, Percy

Faith, Bert Kaempfert, and Brenda Lee. The teen market, which consisted of a host of young vocalists like Fabian, Shelley Fabares, Del Shannon, and Frankie Avalon, was considered a passing phase. Only Elvis Presley had crossed over to an adult audience in a big way. Gimmick records were quite popular: Sheb Wooley's "Purple People Eater," David Seville's Chipmunk songs, and Chubby Checker's twist records, to which Jackie Kennedy was dancing at the Peppermint Lounge in New York—were all on the hit parade.

In the west it seemed the only way to be discovered was by small, independently owned companies, who could take the time and effort—but often did not have the money—to seek out unknown groups and record them. The problems of distribution were much tougher for independent labels. Their only route was to wholesale the record to "one-stops"—large clearing houses with warehouses full of every possible record. The records would then be distributed nationally to the thousands of "Mom and Pop" record stores all over the country. Since accounting malpractices were common, many of the "indies" worked on a "two-record payment system," in which they took it for granted that the Mom and Pop stores would cheat them on the revenues from a hit record. The only way a new group could collect its just royalties was to have a second hit and then withhold the second record from the one-stops until the Mom and Pop stores paid up. The most cutthroat part of this struggle was that often the major record companies would quickly cover hit records put out by the independent labels—that is, record a duplicate version of the song with one of their own stars. Under this system, the original artists would remain relatively unknown.

Yet hitting it big held a special lure for an independent label. There was a gold fever mentality. Los Angeles in the late fifties and early sixties had hundreds of independents, publishers, and mastering companies all over Hollywood in hot little offices on back streets. Some, like the Guild Music Company, listened keenly to whatever might be the next big thing to come along. "Surfin'," the Morgans hoped, was that next big thing.

The Morgans knew Joe Saraceno, the artists-and-repertoire

man at a small label called Candix Records. They played "Sur-fin'" for Saraceno, and he in turn called Russ Regen,* a one-time recording artist who worked at Buckeye Record Distrib-utors, which distributed Candix, among many others. Saraceno played "Surfin'" over the phone to him. Regen thought the boys sounded like another local group, Jan and Dean, who already had a hit with a single called "Linda." He thought "Surfin'" had a shot, but the name of the group—at that point Saraceno was calling them the Surfers—just wasn't right: "There's already a group on Hi-Fi Records called the Surfers." Laughingly, Regen added, "Why don't you call them the Life-guards or the Beach Bums...something to do with the beach? I got it! Why don't you name them the Beach Boys?"

The newly christened group was released on a small sub-sidiary called X Records on December 8, 1961.† Hopeful and excited, the boys waited for reaction. Meanwhile, the Morgans got to work. Along with Saraceno and several others connected with the deal, they started calling programmers at local radio stations. The Morgans knew Bill Angel, the record librarian at KFWB—the station that gave surfing reports and was on the air twenty-four hours a day. KFWB claimed to have introduced the "Surfer's Stomp," Connie Francis's "When the Boy in Your Arms," and Frank Sinatra's "Pocketful of Miracles" in the Los Angeles area. Bill Angel listened to "Surfin'," liked it, and decided to play it. At the same time, a disc jockey named Sam Riddle introduced the song on KDAY.

A few days later, the boys were cruising around Hawthorne in Brian's 1957 Ford listening to the radio when the disc jockey announced a contest. Three songs would be played, and the one that drew the most phone calls would be added to the playlist. One of the three songs was "Surfin'."

The boys went berserk in the car. "Nothing will ever top the expression on Brian's face," Dennis said. "Ever.... *That* is the all-time moment." Carl got so excited he celebrated by drinking

---

*Russ Regen went on to an illustrious career in the music business, and eventually became president of 20th Century Records.

†"Surfin'"/"Luau" was first on the X label. The name of the label was changed to Candix reportedly because of the threat of legal action by an RCA subsidiary with the same name.

as many milkshakes as he could before throwing up. Dennis ran up and down the street screaming, "Listen! We're on the radio."

On December 29 "Surfin'" officially debuted on the KFWB playlist at number 33. "So this record was out and going strong and we booked them at the Rendezvous Ballroom," Dorinda said. They took the boys to a small tailor shop in Glendale and bought them cheap gold jackets to wear for the performance. The boys didn't get paid to play, but the Morgans thought it was good exposure; Dick Dale was headlining, and the Challengers and Surfaris were also on the bill. But the inexperienced Beach Boys could hardly hold the crowd's attention. They were only allowed to play during the intermission, and the audience quickly grew restless and bored before the Beach Boys even finished their two songs. The performance was clearly a bomb. Although they were all disappointed, the group seemed undaunted—except for Brian. "He was really humiliated," Dorinda Morgan remembered. But in Brian's humiliation, a spark of competitive determination was lit.

On New Year's Eve that same year the group appeared for a second time, at a Richie Valens Memorial dance. They were paid what seemed like a shockingly large sum at the time— $300. By January 13, 1962, "Surfin'" on the Candix label was number 118 in *Billboard*. Thrilled with their success, the boys signed contracts to publish and record several more surfing songs with the Morgans. On February 8, 1962, the Morgans recorded four more songs with the group at Keen Studio: "Surfer Girl," "Surfin' Safari," "Judy," and "Karate." Before the session, Murry insisted the boys record one or two of his own songs. When they refused, Murry considered it an insurrection, but Brian held firm. No Murry Wilson compositions were to be recorded by the Beach Boys that night.

Meanwhile, "Surfin'" ate its way slowly up the charts, each week the song's progress seeming more incredible. The excitement at the Wilson household grew into a frenzy. From 118 "Surfin'" went to 112, the first week of February to 105, the next 101, the next 93, and then 90. By March 24 "Surfin'" had sold fifty thousand copies and reached number 75 in the *Billboard* charts. The Wilsons were in heaven.

Murry was so pleased with the Morgans for their overnight magic that he practically gave the group to them in a grand, sweeping gesture that he would soon regret. On newly printed Beach Boy stationery ("Teenage Dances, Recording Artists, Television and Radio and Stage Appearances, Brian Wilson leader, M. Wilson Manager") that he had quickly printed up, Murry sent the Morgans an unsolicited letter of "Intent and Agreement," dated March 29, 1962. It said (in part) that the Morgans would be expected to "perform the duties of producing, recording and promotion, any or all songs written. It is also hoped that you will obtain major recording contracts, to distribute the group's releases and that as producers can make decisions pertaining to the leasing of the Beach Boy tapes, masters and songs... and will protect the rights of the Beach Boys in matters of contracts."*

According to Dorinda Morgan, "Murry was so ecstatic he just handed them to us on a silver platter."

5

Now that "Surfin'" was a hit, Mike Love didn't want to keep working at his father's sheet-metal factory, and told him so.

"Well, what if this doesn't work out?" Milton asked him.

Mike shrugged. "So if it doesn't, I'll be back scraping shit off metal."

The success of "Surfin'" caused a change in Brian that no one expected. To say that it went to his head is no understatement—even his hair changed one day when he arrived home with bleached-blond locks. He said he felt his "public" needed to see his hair the sun-bleached color of the surfers he wrote about. When Audree saw it, she howled, "Oh my God!" and took him right into the bathroom to see how much of it she could wash out. She finally made him dye it back to its original color, and it wound up with a greenish tinge.

---

*Murry added a paragraph that read, "It is understood that Brian Wilson, leader of the Beach Boys, may hire or fire anyone of the Beach Boys from time to time at his discretion, to keep the group together or to improve same...." This, presumably, to keep Dennis in line.

Brian was suddenly very much aware that he was a *star*, of sorts, and his public—the people in the neighborhood—received kind but condescending treatment. Brian started getting "pushy," according to the Morgans. A competitive streak a mile wide suddenly emerged in him. It wasn't so much that he wanted to further his own self-esteem—he seemed to want to beat out the other surfing groups. He kept asking the Morgans what kinds of awards and accolades the group could win. "What do you care?" Dorinda Morgan said. "Here's this kid— a month ago he didn't have anything and now he's Paul Anka. He got so 'up the neck,' my husband and I started to get a little fed up with him."

Murry, of course, had his own characteristic reaction to the success of "Surfin'." Having a national hit, even at number 75, was a feat of which any family would have been proud. But when Murry Wilson heard the record "Surfin'," he hated it. It was amateurish—bush-league. Everything was wrong with the record; it was put down live and had all been done in one take on one track. It was mixed terribly, with a disappearing bass line and buried vocals.

Brian's heart sank like a stone. "My father was critical of the first thing we did," he remembered.

"It's crude," Murry Wilson said. "It's rude. Well look, you don't hear the guitar, you don't hear this, what is going on here? Listen, I'm going to have to take over as producer."

"Which he did," Brian said. "He took over as producer."

One of Murry's first ideas was, of course, to have the group record and sing some of his *own* songs. Good old-fashioned songs, with his boys' pipe-organ harmony. Suddenly Brian found himself with Murry as a songwriting partner, ready to live out his own aspirations through his sons.

Oh man, he fought for his kids,
he got them a contract at Capitol.
                          —AUDREE WILSON

Four

1

Diagonally across from the Wilsons' house on 119th Street lived the family of Benny Jones. Mr. Jones knew that the Wilson children were local celebrities, and he mentioned them to his sister's son, Gary Usher. A handsome, lanky twenty-four-year-old, Gary Usher had a small claim in the music business—he had recorded two singles on the small, independent Titan label when he first moved to California from Massachusetts after high school. While nothing had happened to the obscure songs, Usher had a cursory knowledge of the Los Angeles recording scene and more than a passing interest in it. By day he worked as a teller at the City National Bank in Los Angeles, and at night he took courses at El Camino Junior College. In Hawthorne he lived with his grandmother, but spent much of his time at his Uncle Benny's house, where he could see Carl and Dennis racing up and down the street on their bicycles.

One Sunday in January 1962, just as "Surfin'" was hitting the *Billboard* charts at 118, Gary Usher heard the Wilson family practicing in their converted garage. With his Uncle Benny's encouragement, he followed the music across the street and sheepishly introduced himself. Usher said, "Maybe I inflated my two credits more than they were worth," but he must have seemed very expert to Brian. The five-year age gap—Brian was only nineteen at the time—seemed to melt in their mutual interest, and the young men took to each other instantly. "What happened in those days was something I've never experienced since. There was a spirit going down between us. It was actually magical. There was a freshness, a naïveté."

That evening Usher played guitar and bass while Brian picked out some melodies with him on the organ. Within twenty minutes they had written their first song together, "The Lonely Sea," which would later appear on a Beach Boys' album and in the surf movie *The Girls on the Beach*. Brian and Usher became inseparable friends. During the next several months they wrote over thirty songs together, twelve of which would be recorded, among them several Beach Boys classics.

The alliance with Gary Usher would mark the first of many times that Brian looked outside of his immediate family for a collaborator. Although he continued to write music with his cousin Mike, for the rest of his career he would generally be aided by a New Best Friend—an adjunct personality for which Brian had a strong need. In part, these friendships happened because Brian didn't think of himself as a competent lyricist. But in his own peculiar way, Brian fell in love with his song writing collaborators—he would develop an intense, psychological bond. "We became almost platonic lovers," Usher said. "Brian isn't gay, and neither am I, but there was a really deep attraction."

While they were making a demonstration tape of their first song, Usher was introduced to Brian's whimsical side. For "The Lonely Sea," Brian wanted to record the actual sound of the ocean as background, and since they had no means of overdubbing sound effects, he insisted on lugging his huge, forty-pound monophonic tape recorder to Manhattan Beach to record the surf live. Because the recorder was electrically powered, Brian brought a hundred-foot extension cord with him to the beach. "I'll never forget walking up to somebody's house at one o'clock in the morning and asking if I could plug in a line..." Usher said.

A few days later, Brian had an idea for a song in the tradition of New York song writers Jerry Goffin and Carole King, whose smash hit "Locomotion" had been recorded by their maid, rechristened "Little Eva." Brian's West Coast version was called "Revolution"—but since the Wilsons had no maid, Brian decided they should go out and look for one. Brian told Usher,

"Oh, you just go down to the black part of the city and get a singer. Let's go in the car."

Usher said, "Shit, we'll get killed for sure. You don't walk up to some black girl and proposition her to sing." But Brian insisted it would be safe. Shoeless, in bleached chinos and T-shirts, the two of them drove to Watts in Usher's car. They parked the car on a busy street, and Brian blithely walked up to the first stranger he saw and asked, "Do you know a girl who sings?"

"It turned out a lot of guys knew girls who sang," Usher said. "I can remember knocking on a guy's door at five o'clock in the afternoon and saying, 'Does your daughter sing?' We actually found a girl singer and we tried her out, but she was bad. Even so, that led us to another singer, and she was good." This girl's name was Betty Willis, but they credited the record to Rachel and the Revolvers for commercial purposes. The song was later released on Dot records, backed with another tune Brian and Usher wrote together called "Number One." It was one of Brian's first productions outside of the Beach Boys.

Some of Brian's ideas went beyond the whimsical. As Usher describes this side of Brian, "He was sensitive to the point of being unbalanced. He was esoteric and very eccentric. If it was two in the morning and Brian had an urge for a milkshake, he couldn't go to bed unless he had a milkshake. If he wanted to play Ping-Pong at eleven-thirty at night, he'd knock on the neighbors' door and get them out of bed to play Ping-Pong." One night, in the music room, they got into a discussion about parallel dimensions and of the possibility of life existing on another time plane. In the middle of the conversation Brian was suddenly petrified. He insisted that a being from another dimension had appeared outside the window. For Brian this was no joke—he became so frightened that he scared Usher, who fled the Wilson house.

Gary Usher's greatest musical contribution was that he helped Brian inaugurate a new Beach Boys specialty—the automotive song. Cars were not merely a teenage obsession in California in the sixties—they were a necessity. Usher owned his own car, a 1961 248 white Chevrolet that he had bought with money he earned at the bank. His dream was to own a 409 Chevrolet, one of the fastest cars on the market. Brian and Gary were driving on Western Boulevard, headed for an auto-supply store, when Usher started talking about saving up for his dream car. "Save my pennies, save my dimes," Usher said, and Brian started to hum a tune. "I need more horses," Usher said of his 248 Chevy. "This dog's not going quick enough." Suddenly Brian said, "That's it! We gotta write a song about the hottest car on the road." That night they wrote "409," which added to Brian's growing stockpile of tunes.

Brian often discussed his problems at home with Usher, but his fierce loyalty to Murry prevented him from completely opening up. The Wilsons' was a household where everyone's emotions—except Murry's—were kept inside, and there was really no one for Brian to confide in. Brian had only one place where he could retreat from the tension that pervaded his life—the music room, where he now slept. "Brian was always saying that his room was his whole world," Usher said. One day they decided to write a song about it called "In My Room." Although Usher wrote the lyrics, they were all based on Brian's sentiment. "In My Room" not only turned out to be one of the most hauntingly beautiful of Brian's early compositions, but also one of the most telling—and one of the most prophetic.

> There's a place where I can go,
> to tell my troubles to,
> In my room, in my room....

Of course, Murry was at once suspicious and jealous of Usher. He was alarmed to see that Usher and Brian took to each other so quickly, and he was wary of Usher's influence on Brian. Usher not only ran with what Murry presumed was a fast Hollywood crowd, but he would frequently take Brian with him into Hollywood and introduce him to the other people he had met in the record business. Usher's greatest crime, however, was that he was an outsider collaborating musically with Brian. When Murry learned how many songs Brian and Usher were writing together, he practically insisted that Brian write songs with him. Usher once attended one of these father—

son songwriting sessions. It began with Murry saying, "Let's write a song about yellow roses."

Usher couldn't believe what he was hearing. "That's really old-fashioned," Usher told Murry, not realizing what he was daring.

"It is not old-fashioned..." Murry began to sputter.

"Oh come on, Brian," Usher said. "You don't have to write with him. He's doing Lawrence Welk stuff, let's do Goffin and King."

Murry flew into a rage and threw Usher out of the house.

Usher was upset. He could hear Murry screaming at Brian all the way down the street as he walked back to his Uncle Benny's house. "Walking into the Wilsons' house was like walking into twelve soap operas in one day. You never knew what was going to happen. It was always some scene...." Indeed, Usher walked into the house one day to find Murry lying on the floor in his bedroom, beating his fists with rage. The next time Usher came over, Brian apologized profusely for his father's behavior.

Before long, Usher decided he wanted a fair share of the publishing ownership for the songs he and Brian wrote together. He suggested a fifty-fifty deal. Brian said he'd have to talk to Murry about it, and any further discussion was put off for several weeks. Then Brian apologetically gave Usher the verdict. Murry wouldn't hear of any deals. Brian wasn't twenty-one and couldn't enter a deal on his own. Brian said Murry thought Usher was trying to drive a wedge between him and his brothers. Murry believed Usher was only thinking of his own concerns and not thinking about what was best for the brothers—which would be to have their own publishing company.

And so Murry formed his own publishing company, Sea of Tunes, to handle Brian's songs. If Usher was going to write songs with Brian, Murry would split the publishing three ways: Usher would receive one-third of the profits, Brian one-third, and Murry one-third for administering the growing catalog. The proposed split in itself was not particularly unfair—often the publisher gets 50 percent in return for a cash advance—

only there was no cash advance and the publisher is not often your father. "When the deal was made," Usher said, "if I wanted my money, I had to sign a contract," which limited his royalties as a writer. Moreover, Murry wrote the contracts so that he owned controlling interest in Sea of Tunes, giving him an enormous influence over the Beach Boys' career.

2

Murry's bedroom—more specifically, Murry's bed—soon became command central for the Beach Boys' activities. Murry's next move was to take over the boys' personal appearances; he began to manage them, with Audree doing the bookkeeping. However, in the beginning there wasn't very much bookkeeping. It was Murry's idea that exposure was more important than salary. According to Audree, "My husband used to say they did forty freebies . . . we used to drive to San Bernardino, to Fresno, to many other cities [and give free concerts] . . . it was actually a smart move. . . ." The station manager of KMEN in San Bernardino remembers that Murry "literally begged" him to let the Beach Boys play a teenage fashion show in a local department store, and that they looked and played very badly.

"The DJs were all putting on their own dances at the time," Audree said. "They called and asked [for the Beach Boys to perform for nothing], and we'd say yes. At that time, my husband and I were doing everything . . . wild days. . . ." So wild, in fact, that some of Murry's practices verged on payola, which included giving gifts of cheap necklaces to radio-station managers, encouraging them to play the boys' recordings.

His approach with the people at the boys' record company and distributor was more direct. Murry would attend meetings with the record-company people without the Morgans' knowledge, and they hated it. "He was very aggressive, very pushy," Dorinda Morgan said. "He was a born high-pressure salesman. It put almost everybody off. So he sold and then he unsold."

Murry's relations with Candix grew worse when the royalty check came in for "Surfin'" and turned out to be less than

$1,000. "He always said they really got cheated," Audree said, "because that record went to number seventy-five in the nation, it was a big hit on the West Coast. At that point Hite was their publisher, and Brian said to his dad, 'Would you please help us?...'" Murry took the difference out of his own pocket so each of the boys would earn an even $200. Murry became even more suspicious and unhappy when he learned that Candix Records was reportedly having financial troubles. They had spent so much money pressing copies of "Surfin'" that the company funds were depleted before they could get their money back from the slow-paying distributor. In the interim, Hite Morgan tried to make arrangements with Era Records to pick up the distribution of the boys' records. Allegedly that gave Murry the right to terminate the contracts and go elsewhere.

Although only months before, he had signed an exclusive management contract for the boys with the Morgans, Murry booked time at Western Studio without telling them. On a Sunday, with a talented engineer named Chuck Britz at the controls, Murry had the boys rerecord several of the songs owned by the Morgans—"Surfin' Safari," which Brian had written with Mike Love; Brian's solo compositions, "Judy" and "The Surfer Moon"; and the Gary Usher collaboration, "409."

Murry set out with these demos under his arm and made the rounds of the record companies one by one. Dot, Decca, and Liberty passed.* It seemed that with the current popularity of white solo singers, the major record companies weren't interested in a vocal group. They were on automatic pilot, so blithely indifferent to discovering new talent, that if the switchboard of a recording company got a call from someone who had a new group, the operators were instructed to say they weren't signing anybody for six months. Murry and his sons were lost.

Murry had a different tactic for approaching Capitol Records, the next company on his list. Some years before, Murry had submitted a few of his own songs to Capitol's country-

---

*Audree remembers that these demos were done with Hite Morgan's knowledge, and that both Murry and Hite "cooled their heels at Decca and at Dot and someplace else." Dorinda Morgan disputes this.

western A&R man, Ken Nelson, who had passed on them. But Murry thought Nelson might like the Beach Boys' old-fashioned harmonies and called his office several times asking for an appointment. Nelson was much too busy to hear Murry's sons' songs and was hardly the right man at Capitol to champion a surfing group. Instead, he referred Murry to a colleague in pop A&R who could relate to the idea of a surfing group a little better.

Twenty-one-year-old Nikolas Venet was Capitol's youngest executive and probably the only one to have a surfboard on the top of his car, which in his case wasn't a car at all, but a Leland Land-Rover jeep. A first-generation Greek-American born in Baltimore, Venet had moved to Los Angeles in the late fifties and started working for a jukebox company. Savvy, glib, and charming, Venet was considered Capitol's "street connection," and was by the older men esteemed because he was in touch with the "youth market." Venet already had an impressive track record. At the age of nineteen he had produced several hits for the Lettermen, including "When I Fall in Love," "The Way You Look Tonight," and the number-one hit song "Tom Dooley." Ken Nelson's secretary called Venet's office and asked him to please see Murry because he was driving Nelson crazy.

Venet's connection to the Lettermen made him the perfect contact for Murry, who called him shortly before Venet was to take a two-week vacation in Baja, California. Murry waited impatiently until Venet got back and then went to see him in his twelfth-floor office in the famous circular Capitol Building in Hollywood. Murry blustered and raved, making his usual indelible impression on Venet. After telling Venet at length how wonderful his sons were, he finally put the demo of "Surfin' Safari" on a turntable in the office.

"Before eight bars had spun around, I knew it was a hit record," Venet said. "I wasn't one to hide my feelings. I got all excited, and of course [Murry] got all excited, because he wasn't one to hide his feelings either. I knew the song was going to change West Coast music." Venet promised he would recommend that Voyle Gilmour, a Capitol executive, purchase the masters, and Murry asked for a three-hundred-dollar advance per song.

The story of what happened next differs according to who tells it. Murry's version, which is firmly part of the Beach Boys legend, has it that Murry, Brian, and Gary Usher waited in a nearby coffee shop for only an hour before going back to hear Voyle Gilmour's decision. According to Venet and Usher, Gilmour was busy, and it took a few days for Venet to pressure Gilmour into making an offer. Gilmour said $300 for the masters was too much money, and suggested offering Murry $100. Venet wouldn't hear of it. "Voyle, you gotta give them three hundred dollars," Venet said. "It would cost that much to make it here." Venet eventually went over Gilmour's head to chief executive Lee Gilette and was able to pay Murry his asking price.

In the days when record albums sold for $2 each, $300 for the outright purchase of a master, plus 2.5 percent royalties, wasn't as poor an offer as it sounds. At the next meeting, Murry accepted the offer. According to Usher, when Venet asked about buying the publishing rights, he quickly said, "It's already taken." Venet paused for a moment, as if this might queer the deal. Usher had his heart in his mouth until Venet finally said, "Okay," and called the contract department to draw up an agreement.

In the elevator, going down from Venet's office, Murry cornered Usher, putting his bright red face up close to his, and said in his most menacing tone, "You do that one more time and you're finished!"

"He made mincemeat, he decimated me in front of Brian on the way down," Usher said. Ironically, not turning the publishing rights over to Capitol was one of the best things that could have happened to Murry. Within a few years, those rights would be worth millions of dollars.

3

Meanwhile, the Morgans got wind of the impending Capitol release of the rerecorded tracks they already owned. "We found out through the grapevine," Dorinda Morgan said. "We were a little angry, but we weren't surprised; this is a dog-eat-dog business, and you're not surprised at anything. They started to make it—it was very simple."

To soften hard feelings, as a sort of farewell present, a few members of the Wilson family showed up at the Morgans' studio and put some vocals on prerecorded instrumental tracks of two songs written by their son Bruce. Alan and Carl were on the tracks, but not Dennis or Mike Love. Even Audree sang along. The tracks were attributed to a group the Morgans called Kenny and the Kadets.

Hite and Dorinda Morgan discussed what to do about Murry's recutting the songs they clearly owned and selling them to Capitol. With the signed contracts and management agreement, they had enough ammunition to win a lawsuit, but neither of them could bear the thought. Murry was too overpowering to drag through a suit; if he wanted his boys that badly, he should have them. In the long run, in terms of aggravation, the Morgans thought they were better rid of him. Hite Morgan's farewell statement to Murry was "Rots of ruck to you!"

"Can you imagine that?" Audree said. "That's what the man said. 'Lots of luck to you.'"

"That statement cost him two million seven hundred thousand dollars," Murry gloated. "Two million seven hundred thousand dollars."

Hite and Dorinda Morgan had some legal recourse, however. The Morgans sued Capitol for the use of the songs they owned. The suit was resolved, after many years, with a reported cash settlement to the Morgans of $80,000. The Morgans' small part in the Beach Boys' history was over.

Now came a strange twist of fate. Just as the Capitol contracts were about to be signed, Al Jardine left the group. He was discouraged by the small amount of money they had made through Candix. "I made the decision I didn't really want to put a big investment into the group, and at the same time I wanted to finish dental school...so there was David Marks for a year...."

David Marks was a bratty thirteen-year-old neighborhood kid who lived across the street from the Wilsons. David and his mother and father, Joanne and Elmer Marks, were from a small town south of Newcastle, Pennsylvania. They had moved to California when David was seven. After renting for a time, the Markses bought a house at 11901 Almertons Place in Inglewood. David met Dennis Wilson the day they moved in. He was eight, Dennis was ten. Dennis Wilson, as usual, was up to no good. The Marks' home was just on the other side of the sewage lines that divided Hawthorne and Inglewood, and according to neighborhood status, it was better to live on the Hawthorne side. While the Markses were moving in, Dennis was busy throwing bags of garbage across the street to the Inglewood side. David Marks threw it right back, and he and Dennis became fast friends. David would often play with the Wilson boys at their house, and Murry used to love to roughhouse with the kids. David remembers Murry getting him into a headhold and giving him a "noogie," a hard pinch in the back of the neck. "They hurt like hell," David said.

The Wilsons' offer to David to become a replacement for Alan Jardine wasn't given much thought; that he played rudimentary guitar was enough of a qualification. The boys and Murry showed up at the Marks house one night while David was watching "Bonanza" and asked him to join the group. David was thrilled, but his parents weren't sure it would be a good thing for him. There was school to think about, and the group traveled constantly on "personal appearances." The Wilsons and David spent an hour cajoling and begging, until Joanne and Elmer finally consented.

"So when they signed their first contract with Capitol," Audree said, "David was one of the original Beach Boys. He was at our house all the time. David was so young—I always liked him and felt sorry for him. He was a pain in the neck, he really was, he drove everybody crazy. Brian would not allow him to sing on the records, because he *couldn't* sing...."

And now, with a new lineup, a contract from one of the majors, and complete control, Murry set out to make his boys *stars.*

4

At the time, Brian was deeply in love with a girl he knew from school called Judy Bowles. She was pretty, with azure eyes and reddish-brown hair that she wore in the bangs and French roll that were fashionable at the time. She dressed like a proper young lady, in skirts and white blouses. Judy was Brian's first "true love." In Hawthorne, and in Brian's simplistic, romantic conception of things, the girl you pinned and went steady with, the girl you made love to, was the girl you were going to marry. There was never any doubt in Brian's mind that Judy Bowles would be the mother of his children and his partner for life. She became the inspiration for many of his early songs, including "Judy." When Brian started to attend El Camino College, he proposed and gave Judy an engagement ring.

Brian and Judy frequently double-dated with Gary Usher and his fifteen-year-old girl friend, Bonnie Deleplain. Brian, Gary, and the girls would spend evenings driving around Hawthorne and Inglewood, visiting the Fosters' Freeze or buying a couple of six-packs. A typical date included a drive-in movie and a visit to the neighborhood haunt, the 'Which Stand, where Brian would order his usual vanilla Coke and fries drenched in ketchup. "I can distinctly remember being half drunk with Brian and singing 'Sherry' in the car at the top of our lungs with the windows rolled up," Usher said.

Usher and Brian's major concern at the time was birth control. The only available method was condoms. Buying them would have been a near-impossible hassle; hiding them in the house from Murry was unthinkable. Instead, they practiced the birth control of the fifties—"pulling out." "I'm surprised she didn't get pregnant," Usher said.

Brian's need for privacy with Judy instigated his decision to move out of the Wilson home for the first time when he was nearly twenty years old. Life at the Wilsons' hadn't changed much, even though "Surfin'" was a hit. Dennis and Carl were both under eighteen and treated like children. Murry still made them go to the shop on Saturdays and clean the lathes. Brian's purchase of a red-and-cream-colored 1960 Impala gave him more mobility, but he remained very much under Murry's thumb, and the pressure was unrelenting. Brian would sit in the music room composing, and if Murry heard a chord change he didn't like, he would come barreling out of his bedroom to criticize Brian's work. "I remember one incident," Audree said. "Brian was in the music room writing and Murry was in the bedroom watching television, and Murry came rushing down and criticized Brian's rhythm. Brian was furious, just furious. He said, 'Fuck you!' which was horrible. I said, 'Brian!' And Carl was there too and he said, 'Brian!' Murry never got over that. He used to bring it up all the time. I was supposed to go over and hit Brian with a board, or clobber him or do something horrible." The arguments became more frequent as Brian's creative ego expanded, and soon it become untenable for him to live at home.

Brian met his first roommate while playing at a Sigma Chi fraternity party at the University of Southern California. Murry had booked the date for them while "Surfin'" was still on the charts. Bob Norberg was a twenty-three-year-old USC alumnus, a part-time salesman of copying machines who also taught swimming, and on the side had toyed with a career in music. At the same fraternity party, during the Beach Boys' intermission, he performed with his girl friend, Cheryl Pomeroy. The friendship that developed between Brian and Norberg echoed Gary Usher's friendship. For a time, Norberg was to become Brian's New Best Friend.

Soon after the fraternity party, Brian brought Norberg home and introduced him to the family. Norberg passed muster at the Wilson household as an "okay guy," although Murry was still suspicious of outsiders. But Norberg didn't seem to be one of those "Hollywood phonies" Murry hated so much, and finally Brian was given tacit permission to move out. "He was ready to be on his own a bit more, get more independence," Norberg said.

Brian moved into Norberg's hundred-and-fifty-dollar-a-month, one-bedroom apartment at the Crenshaw Park Apartments at 10800 Crenshaw Boulevard in Inglewood, not far from where the Wilsons lived. It was furnished cheaply—wall-to-wall carpeting littered with Norberg's barbells and surfboards, and two mattresses on which Brian and Norberg slept. There was a huge, antique mirror that Norberg had bought to work out dance steps for his act with Cheryl.

Norberg had a good understanding of electronics, and he pieced together a crude recording system with a quarter-inch, seven ips monophonic Wollensak tape recorder, along with a second tape deck, hooked together with kits for pre-amps and amplifiers. This system enabled Brian to record overdubs for the first time, and the process would become integral to all Beach Boys recordings. Brian even began to record guitars this way, sometimes detuning them to create a clashing sound. Many of the rudimentary Beach Boys sounds were developed in that apartment on Crenshaw. Norberg played guitar, and Brian bass, using Dennis's drumsticks and a "block," with a TV-dinner aluminum container for a cymbal sound—all recorded over and over many times.

Before long, Brian wrote a song for Norberg and his girl friend Cheryl called "The Surfer Moon." Again, Brian wanted realistic sound effects on the record, so he and Norberg dragged the Wollensak outdoors at night to record the sound of real crickets. Murry took the demo of "The Surfer Moon," backed with a song Norberg had written called "Humpty Dumpty," and sold it almost immediately to Safari Records. Curiously, Bob Norberg's name appears on the credits as Bob Norman. Norberg says he was "swayed" into it because Murry claimed Norman was a more commercial-sounding name; others said it was because Murry thought the name Norberg sounded too Jewish. The record was a flop, but marked the second time Brian composed and produced outside of the Beach Boys.

Norberg later recorded his own song, "1204," which was arranged by Murry, for Tower Records, but his recording career was short-lived, as was his New Best Friend status with Brian. Norberg had started to fly planes privately, and he wanted to do it full-time. Within a few years he was hired by TWA and has worked for them ever since.

5

On June 4, 1962, Capitol released its first Beach Boys single, "409," backed by "Surfin' Safari." Initially there was some discussion at Capitol about what song to put out first. Although "Surfin' Safari" was a likely follow-up to their first hit, Nik Venet was concerned that the surfing theme would confine sales to the West Coast and decided to put it on the "B" side of the single, releasing the automotive song "409" first. But when "409" didn't attract much airplay in its first few weeks of release, Capitol changed tactics and started to push "Surfin' Safari" instead.

"That record was a hit in a matter of hours," Nik Venet said. "Eight hours after it was in the field, we were getting isolated reports from places like Phoenix, Arizona. The biggest order Capitol had from a single market all year was from New York City—where there was no surfing. It sold approximately nine hundred thousand records, but not enough for a gold." The record appeared first on the national *Billboard* charts on August 11 at number 85. Throughout the summer and into the fall, it made a slow but steady ascent up five or ten positions each week. From the thirteenth through the twenty-seventh of October, it clung to its best position, number 14.

In the interim, Capitol rushed the Beach Boys into the studios, and in one twelve-hour session they recorded an entire album of songs, *Surfin' Safari*. It was an adolescent mishmash—including a hymn to root beer, "Chug a Lug"—produced by Nik Venet (except for "409" and "Surfin'," which were the masters Murry had produced). For the album cover, Venet snuck the boys away from Murry and out to Malibu, where for $50 they rented a truck from a local beach contractor named Calypso Joe. Photographer George German airbrushed Calypso Joe's name from the door, and Venet and the boys decorated it with palm fronds. Dennis proudly held a surfboard. The album didn't do as well as the singles, however. Over the next three months it straggled up the charts to number 32—a fair but unspectacular showing. But it was good enough for Capitol's enthusiasm about the Beach Boys to continue.

"409" got massive airplay in Los Angeles, particularly at KFWB, which was known as "Channel 98." KFWB's most popular disc jockey was Roger Christian, a short, handsome young man with wavy hair who worked the night shift. One night Christian was on the air discussing what the lyrics to "409" meant. "A 327 was really better," he later recalled. "...But the 409 was the big number they were pushing back then. Everybody who got one thought it was just the biggest thing around....So I was playing the record, and I said it was a good song about a bad car." Christian went on at length to discuss some of the technical details of the 409 that he thought were deficient.

In his bedroom in Hawthorne, Murry Wilson was listening to Roger Christian's erudite explanation of positraction and four-barrel carburetors, and decided this was the man to write more car lyrics with Brian. And it would be a good way to get Gary Usher out of the picture. He picked up the phone and called KFWB, announcing that he was the father of the Beach Boys, and demanded to be put through to Roger Christian.

"Say, you're really into cars," he told Christian.

"We got to talking," said Christian, "and he asked me if I wrote songs. I said I'd written a couple of things."

Murry suggested he try writing with his son Brian and arranged for the two of them to meet. Often Brian would go over to KFWB when Christian got off from the nine-to-midnight shift, and go out and have hot-fudge sundaes with him at a place called Otto's. "We'd be writing lyrics...and all of a sudden we'd realize we wrote fifteen songs." Christian would come up with a lyric and Brian would produce a melody instantly. Over the course of their collaboration they wrote more than fifty songs, sixteen of which would appear as Beach Boys records. Now Roger Christian was Brian's New Best Friend.

Gary Usher was crushed by Brian's new friendship. "When Roger Christian really came in heavy, frankly, I felt a little hurt," Gary Usher said. "Roger was Brian's new love...love in the sense of attention, and I wasn't....I no longer enjoyed Brian's company. It was a great relationship and it slowly drifted apart for no reason...."

The coup de grace that Gary Usher received from Murry began with a violent family argument that caused Dennis to move out. Murry had promised some business friends from Europe that Dennis would make them a hand-carved cigar box. At sixteen, Dennis greatly resented being forced into fulfilling this promise. One Saturday afternoon Murry came out to the garage, where Dennis was working, and examined the cigar box. "It's not good enough," he said, tossing it down on the workbench in disgust. "It's lousy." One word led to another and suddenly Dennis punched Murry in the face. It was the first time that Dennis had actually lifted a hand to Murry, and the incident turned into an all-out brawl. The racket that came out of the garage could be heard all over the neighborhood. David Marks and his father rushed across the street to help separate the two. "They would have killed each other," David remembered.

Murry banished Dennis from the house, and for several days he slept in the backseat of his friend Louie Marado's car. After a week or so, Dennis caught a bad cold and Audree insisted he come back to live with them. But Murry was still angry, and shortly after Dennis felt better, he moved back to Louie Marado's car. One morning Gary Usher ran into him—he looked exhausted and unwashed. Dennis told Usher what had happened, and Usher, who had recently rented his own apartment on Eucalyptus Avenue, invited Dennis to stay there. Dennis happily accepted the invitation. Usher remembered that Dennis's first activity was to line up some girls. "Dennis had an incredible knack for picking up girls," Usher said, "as well as a strange drive. Often he would have twelve girls in a week."

"When Murry found out [that Dennis was my roommate]," Usher said, "I might as well have been dead." Under Murry's orders, Usher was pushed out of the Beach Boys' professional circle forever. To seal his fate, Capitol next released one of

Usher's collaborations with Brian titled "10 Little Indians," a lame vocal rendition of the famous nursery rhyme, backed with another Usher song, "County Fair." Both of these songs were unqualified failures and the only real out-and-out flops of the Beach Boys' early career.

6

Capitalizing on the success of "Surfin' Safari," the Beach Boys launched into their first professional tour in the summer of 1962. The forty-day midwestern trek marked the beginning of the prolonged road trips that would characterize the rest of their career. With Mike Love and Brian the oldest at twenty-two and twenty-one respectively, Dennis nineteen, Carl seventeen, and David Marks fourteen, they were too young to go out on the road alone. Much to the boys' relief, Murry had no time to go with them, since he was still running ABLE Machinery. Instead, he hired a professional road manager, John Hamilton, who had once road-managed the Ventures.

"The first tour, we went out in a station wagon," Mike Love said, "and we got so crazy in that station wagon it was ridiculous. There were five of us and the driver, and we all lugged our own instruments. We'd drive sometimes five hundred miles to the next date...Fargo, North Dakota, and then to Minneapolis, Minnesota, and then over to northern Michigan...we drove like eight hundred miles from one place to the next. We set up our own equipment and played on existing P.A. systems, which were really horrible."

Dennis remembered that they "played at halls for men who were all over sixty. It went down all right. When you're playing, you think it's fantastic. I don't know whether the people liked it, because they'd never seen anything like it before. They all walked out, all twelve of them. But we kept on playing and we got ten dollars between us."

For Mike, the first impact of the group's success came one night at a concert in Hatfield, Minnesota, shortly after "Surfin' Safari" had come out. "It was literally a barn, converted into a dance hall, and there was a stage that was so narrow....A drunk sat down on my foot." The boys had just finished their second set and had gone outside through the employees' door to get some fresh air. They were stunned at what they saw. There was a line of cars, pairs of headlights stretching a mile and a half into the distance, waiting to pull into the club's parking lot to see them. "So," said Mike, "I knew something was happening."

Those first road tours were fondly remembered by the boys as a wonderland of sex and freedom during which they indulged in as much debauchery as any teenager might dream about. At one hotel Dennis painted his penis green, hung it out of his fly, and went downstairs to the lobby for a Coke. In another hotel they paraded around naked in front of their window. "There were a bunch of old ladies sitting around in the street in front of the hotel," David Marks said, "and we were scratching our nuts from the second floor and jumping up and down in front of an air-conditioner. From the street they saw five guys jumping up and down and they didn't know why."

The boys had lots of petty quarrels on the road, especially Dennis and Mike, who got into an occasional fistfight. "Dennis usually instigated stuff," David remembered. "Once we went into the bathroom and peed in these squirt guns and put soap in them. Al Jardine was sitting on a couch reading *Reader's Digest*, and Dennis and I came in and squirted him. Al just levitated three feet off the chair."

Naturally, girls were a major preoccupation on the road. "On my fifteenth birthday we played an amusement park in West Virginia," David Marks said. "A multimillionaire owned the park. He was a fun-loving guy who wore khakis and drove a jeep. After we played the show, he took us in his yacht club, which was a converted underground speakeasy. He got me some scotch and took me upstairs with some twenty-one-year-old whore that was sitting on a chair. I remember washing my cock off in a pan with soap and water—I don't know why—and she said, 'Don't come in the pan, now.'"

When David left the room, Dennis was waiting in the hallway to go next. "Was it nice and warm in there?" Dennis asked with a dirty smirk on his face.

"Oh yeah," David answered naïvely, "I think the heat was on."

Carl also lost his virginity to a hooker on one of their early tours. More sensitive and serious than his brothers, he found the experience depressing. When Dennis congratulated him afterward, he shook his head sadly and said, "She didn't even care."

John Hamilton's employment ended when David Marks got the clap on the road and told his dad, who told his mother. She went straight over to Murry's house and complained. Murry fired Hamilton and went on the road himself for one week, determined the boys would be as decorous as a group of nuns. He made them absolutely miserable, trying at first to be reasonable. He lectured the boys, "Now, this is a business we're involved in, and you have to act right. You can't just smile when you feel like it; you *have* to smile onstage, it's part of the performance." At times they would be in the middle of a show and Murry would come running up the aisle screaming, "Treble up! Treble up!" But he couldn't stop them from having egg fights in hotel rooms, and he quickly turned into a tyrannical taskmaster.

"One time Murry was sitting in the backseat," David remembered, "and I just leaned up and farted in his face. Murry turned around and said, 'Well, that's OK, Dave, now just don't show me any disrespect, that's all.'" Murry would regularly call Joanne Marks to complain about David. "He doesn't smile onstage and he doesn't carry his own amp," Murry would tell her. "He takes girls to the motel...."

When Murry decided that he wasn't cut out for the road, David Marks's father, Elmer, was elected for the job. "It was just him and the boys," Joanne Marks said. "He hadn't been working—he was ill with a back problem—and Murry said, 'OK, you can be the road manager. Go with the boys and watch them....'" Murry then suggested that perhaps Audree should go on the road with Elmer Marks to help keep an eye on the youngsters. "Audree didn't really want to go," Joanne said, "and there was no sense in her going. When everyone was away, Murry asked me to dinner. He thought he was going to strike up a rélationship with me," she said. Joanne Marks refused the dinner invitation, but the next Saturday morning she looked out the back door of her house and saw Murry crossing the street. Frightened, she locked the door before he could get there and refused to let him into the house. Joanne felt it was "punishment" when Murry subsequently fired Elmer. David Marks claimed he never saw a penny from the road because Murry always said all the money went toward expenses. This was just the beginning of many quarrels between the Marks family and Murry. Said David Marks, "Murry talked to me like he was dealing with a man, and I was just a kid, just out of the dirt with my cars and trucks...and all of a sudden here I was copping whores and drinking whiskey."

If everybody had an ocean,
across the U.S.A.
Then everybody'd be surfin'
like Californiyay!
—"Surfin' U.S.A."

Five

1

By mid-October of 1962, "Surfin' Safari" had hit number 14 on the national record charts, and in Los Angeles, where the Beach Boys were local celebrities, it was number 1. His boys were riding high, and Murry booked them at one of the hottest clubs on Sunset Boulevard, Pandora's Box. Sunset Boulevard was undergoing a transformation. Once a more expensive preserve of nightclubs and restaurants, it was now becoming the mecca of teen nightlife in Los Angeles. The area between Highland Avenue and Doheny Drive was turning into a turbulent strip, populated by swarms of teenagers and college students cruising up and down the street in expensive cars. The exclusive restaurants and chic beauty salons were being replaced by scores of trendy clothing boutiques, coffeehouses, and teen discos. Pandora's Box was one of the better-known teen clubs, a tiny place built on a small triangular island in the middle of the strip. No liquor was served, and the oversized hand-scripted menus boasted cappuccino, iced tea, and hot chocolate—which is what Ginger Blake and her cousins, The Rovell sisters, were drinking the night the Beach Boys took the stage.

Ginger Blake and the Rovell sisters were friends of Gary Usher. Although Usher had been relegated to a bench position on the Wilsons' team, he still kept in touch with Brian at the apartment Wilson shared with Bob Norberg. Usher was busy promoting his own career with appearances at high-school proms and record hops, many of them emceed by Brian's new collaborator, Roger Christian. It was at one of these hops that Usher met Ginger Blake, a teenage singer promoting "Dry Tears," which she had recorded on the Titan label. Ginger Blake was an adorable, petite Jewish girl whose real name was Sandra Glantz, and Gary started dating her although she was only fifteen. It turned out that Ginger had three cousins around her own age who also sang semiprofessionally—Diane, sixteen; Marilyn, fourteen; and Barbara Rovell, thirteen. One day Ginger invited Usher over to the Rovells' house on Sierra Bonita Drive to meet her cousins. Usher boasted to the young girls about his association with the Beach Boys, and the next weekend, when they were appearing at Pandora's Box, he invited Ginger and her cousins to see them.

The Rovell sisters were what the decidedly anti-Semitic Hawthorne crowd considered "Fairfax Jews"—they had grown up in the ethnic stronghold south of Fairfax Avenue in L.A. The three sisters looked remarkably alike, with beautiful dark skin and large brown eyes. All three had deep, distinctively froggy voices. Barbara was cute and quiet. Marilyn was the charmer; easy to laugh, vivacious, and bright, she was the leader, her moody older sister, Diane, the follower.

The first night at Pandora's Box, only Ginger and Diane went to see the Beach Boys, and they instantly fell in love. "They were these darling little surfer boys in their Pendleton shirts," Ginger said. She was so taken with them that the next night she came back with her cousin Marilyn in tow. The Beach Boys ran through their set while Brian smiled down at the sweet, suntanned young girls sitting at stageside. Between songs, Brian asked Marilyn if he could have a sip of her hot chocolate, and as he handed it back, he spilled it all over her. But she didn't mind at all. "He was so gorgeous," Marilyn said. "He had a perfect nose and he was very good-looking."

Later, backstage in the crowded, dimly lighted dressing area, Ginger and Marilyn chatted with the boys and were introduced to Murry and Audree, who attended every show. Murry was very stern with the boys after the show, criticizing their performances, berating them for mistakes. "You can't sit there and tune your instruments," he told them. "You have to play." Then he turned to the girls and said, "You know, girls, I'm only doing this for their own good." Then he made a little wisecrack and softened up for a moment before abruptly becoming stern again.

The girls came back every night of the Beach Boys' week-long engagement, and on the last night Brian invited them out to visit his parents' house in Hawthorne. Marilyn enthusiastically agreed to come. But it wasn't Brian Wilson, who seemed much too old and sophisticated, that Marilyn had her eye on—it was his chunky, fifteen-year-old brother, Carl. "You know, when you're young," Marilyn said, "everyone chooses to have a crush on someone, and I chose Carl." Diane says she chose Dennis for herself, and set out to pursue him; but most observers at the time distinctly remember that Diane had a crush on Brian.

Marilyn was infatuated with Carl only for a few days, but a strong bond formed between them that would last a lifetime. "One time we both ran to the park...I kind of chased him," Marilyn said, "and we fell all over each other and were cracking up....I remember I wanted to kiss him and I don't think he had kissed a girl yet, and we just kind of looked at each other and laughed." When they got back to the house, flushed and out of breath, Audree gave them a suspicious look. "Then we just got to be friends with him and Dennis," Marilyn said, "and we went over to their house a few times. Then Brian moved out of the house and moved into the apartment with Bob Norberg."

One night Marilyn and Diane brought the boys back to the house on Sierra Bonita Drive to meet their parents, May and Irving Rovell. Irving was a tall, reserved man with an aristocratic Jewish nose and a large moustache; May a short, round-faced, warm, Jewish mother. The Rovells and their three daughters had come to Los Angeles in 1955 from Chicago, where Irving owned a hand laundry. In Chicago the family had lived in a damp basement apartment, and every winter the girls used to come down with chronic tonsillitis. When the children's health could no longer withstand another bleak Chicago winter, Irving's mother loaned him $6,000 and they loaded up their old Buick, setting out for Los Angeles. Shortly after they arrived, they purchased a two-bedroom house with white stucco walls on Sierra Bonita Drive for $16,000, an unheard-of sum in those days. To make ends meet, Irving held down two jobs, one at the Lockheed Precision Factory, as a sheet-metal worker, and the other a weekend position as a clothing salesman.

With their first savings, May and Irving bought an upright piano for the small living room. May was the musical one in the family, having studied piano as a young girl. She could listen to a song just once on the radio and pick out all the chords. All three of her daughters had strong, harmonious voices and loved to sing. May entered them in various local talent contests, including the "Yeakles Amateur Hour," which was broadcast on a local television station throughout the night. May sat up with the girls until three in the morning for their chance to sing "Sugar in the Morning." Their heart's desire was to sing professionally.

For Brian Wilson, the warm, loving Rovell household was an exotic change from the tension-charged atmosphere in Hawthorne. The Rovells were so giving and generous that he was not only fascinated with them but found their house a refuge. The Rovells, particularly Irving, enjoyed Brian a great deal; used to living in a house with four women, Irving took to Brian at once. "Brian made him laugh," Marilyn said. "I never saw my father laugh so much. And my mother loved him."

Brian quickly became a fixture at the Rovells' house. May's unfailing generosity and open kitchen—no matter how tight her budget—enthralled him. It was literally impossible to enter the Rovells' house, no matter what time of the day or night, and not have May prepare a meal for you. If Brian was hungry at three in the morning, May would organize a feast without hesitating. The Rovells opened their home not only to Brian, but to his brothers and all their friends and business associates. They entertained what seemed like every Los Angeles disc jockey and session musician in the business. Since many recording studios were located near their house, May was not surprised to get a phone call at 5:00 A.M. alerting her that the boys and their friends would be over at 7:00 A.M., when she would happily prepare breakfast for fourteen. Although May's food budget was only $30 a week, the boys left so much money lying around, some of which fell into the cracks of the sofa, that she started a fund from lost cash and added treats to the revolving menu. Often the street in front of the Rovells' house would be filled with teenagers drag-racing their automobiles, while Carl and Brian were in the backyard testing a new amplifier. Suddenly the small, happy home on Sierra Bonita Drive became the center of the Beach Boys' social scene. Everyone was allowed to sleep over if the hour grew late. David Marks remembers, "I would go over there and get drunk and pass out on the couch. I would kind of open one eye and Marilyn's little sister Barbara would be covering me up."

One discordant moment so stung Irving Rovell that the incident remained with him for years. Of all the Beach Boys' entourage, only Dennis was seldom a visitor to the Rovell household. On one of his rare appearances, he was bragging to Irving about how much money the Beach Boys were making and how little it meant to him. To illustrate his point, he took out a dollar bill and tore it up. Irving, who worked seven days a week at two jobs, was heartsick. After Dennis left, he saved the pieces of the dollar bill and taped them together. He keeps the dollar in his wallet to this day.

By now Carl and Dennis were objects of great resentment at Hawthorne High School. Dennis had already been suspended for throwing a screwdriver at another boy in his shop class. Soon after he turned sixteen, he was expelled. The way Dennis told it, "There was this tall guy...who had ten all-day suckers—you call them lollipops. I didn't have a nickel to buy one, so I took one of his. He said, 'Meet me in the boys' bathroom.' We had this fight and I didn't mean to hit him in the head— he had braces on his teeth—but I did." Dennis went to school with his father the next day, and the school administrators suggested that perhaps Dennis would be better off out of school. Dennis spent his nonworking hours speeding around in his newly acquired XKE automobile. Carl, who was still under sixteen, was required by law to stay in school. But he hadn't been attending many classes, and with his newfound celebrity he received either inordinate attention or cruel and derisive teasing. It was mutually decided by the school and his parents that he would leave Hawthorne High and attend the Hollywood Professional School, along with David Marks. It wasn't long before Marilyn and Diane Rovell joined them there.

"We were both at Fairfax High at the time," Marilyn said, "when Carl and David found out about Hollywood Professional School." It let out at 12:30, and some of the younger Hollywood stars went there—along with a lot of kids who couldn't handle regular school. Every morning Diane and Marilyn would walk to the corner of La Brea and Hollywood. Carl and David Marks would pick them up and take them to school.

On Thanksgiving of 1962, May Rovell prepared a giant spread for her extended family. Brian, Carl, and Dennis showed up for dinner, along with several friends. It is still fondly remembered as one of their happiest meals together. After dinner and a good deal of wine, they all started to tell their favorite jokes, each one getting more risqué. May and Irving, who never cursed, couldn't help roaring with laughter. When it came time for May to tell a joke, she couldn't bear to curse, and instead she came up with a new word, "fick." This convulsed everyone at the table even more—they begged her to say the real word. But May held firm. She did make a promise, though; when the girls' recording career got under way, and they had a hit record, she would say the word the real way.

Brian was determined to promote the Rovells. By now he had enough clout with Capitol and Nik Venet to record and release practically any single he wanted. When Marilyn, Diane, and Ginger came up with the idea for an all-girl version of a surfing group, called the Honeys (surfing terminology for "female surfers"), Brian brought up the idea to Nik Venet. At first Venet wanted just Ginger to join the Beach Boys as a Beach Girl, but when Brian insisted that all the girls be included, Capitol agreed to pay for studio time and give it a try. Brian and the girls chose to record an old Stephen Foster favorite, "Way Down Upon the Swanee River," and turning it into a surfing tune called "Surfing Down the Swanee River." Another surfing tune, "Shoot the Curl," composed by Sandra Glantz and Diane, would go on the "B" side. Produced by Brian and Nik Venet and released on Capitol later that winter, the record never made it onto the charts. Two more Honeys singles fol-

lowed and met the same fate as the first. Finally, Brian suggested to Venet that the Honeys record an entire album, but
Nik rejected the idea gently. May continued to say "fick," but
the girls' desire to become recording stars remained very much
alive.

In January 1963 Brian moved into a three-bedroom apartment with friends in Inglewood, but went back there less and
less. He soon became a regular overnight guest on the Rovells'
living-room sofa, and after a few months, it appeared he had
permanently moved in. May was doing his laundry, and often
his brothers' laundry as well. Brian reveled in his relationship
with May, and they frequently spent late nights having intimate
conversations about his life. After a month or two of sleeping
on the sofa, Brian moved into a small rear bedroom, furnished
with two little dressers and twin beds, which Marilyn shared
with her younger sister, Barbara. The two girls slept in one
bed together and Brian slept in the other. This arrangement
didn't seem to raise any eyebrows at the Rovell household,
although May and Irving were particularly moral and conservative. May seemed to have wisely decided that whatever was
going to happen, it would be better happening in her home
than in the backseat of an automobile. Anyway, Diane was
considered to be Brian's girl, and she wasn't in the room. Some
visitors at the Rovells' remember that May and Irving were
extremely encouraging over Brian's relationship with their
daughters and would have liked to have him as a son-in-law.

"One day," Marilyn remembers, "I spent the afternoon with
Brian together, alone. And then we wound up spending days
together. I was crazy about him but I was so young.... Once
he came into my life I was immediately...fascinated." Marilyn
admits, "I did have a little bit of a sexual fantasy. One time I
saw him in his underwear, and I went, 'Wow.'"

But Brian was still engaged to Judy Bowles, whom Marilyn
saw when Brian took Marilyn to the studio for a recording
session. Marilyn remembers Judy as being sweet and naïve,
and that she and Brian fought all the time. Brian would often
complain to Gary Usher that Judy wanted to break off with
him, and several times Gary had to comfort a weeping, distraught Brian after a turbulent argument with Judy.

"I do know he really cared for her," Marilyn said, "and I never ever tried to take Brian away from Judy...no one did ...it just happened. He came into the room one night and said, 'That's it. I can't deal with her anymore. Our relationship is never going to work.'

"All of a sudden," said Marilyn, "before you knew it, Brian and I were kissing, out of nowhere. I don't even know how it happened."

For a short time, no one in the family knew about Brian and Marilyn's budding romance—not even Diane. It was often unclear to outsiders exactly which sister Brian loved best. He seemed to have crushes on all the girls, including Barbara. Brian later wrote one of his most telling songs about this era, the title a phrase uttered to him by Diane, "Don't Hurt My Little Sister"—perhaps referring to Barbara. But there was no curtailing Brian's ambiguous romantic interests in the sisters. Diane and Marilyn found themselves caught up in a benign competition that would last for many years.

2

In March 1963 the Beach Boys broke through to national prominence and success with a force that staggered everyone at Capitol. "Surfin' U.S.A.," Brian's most recent single, written in collaboration with Mike Love, was one of his cleverest ideas to date. The song not only avoided alienating the vast sections of the country where there was no surfing, but united a nation of teenagers in the California dream. Its lyric, beginning "If everybody had an ocean," brought the entire nation to California shores. Ironically, this first giant hit did not even have an original melody. The tune derived from a Chuck Berry song called "Sweet Little Sixteen," combined with the idea of Chubby Checker's lyrical theme from "Twistin' U.S.A.," in which the names of many U.S. cities are mentioned.* Brian and Michael wrote a vibrant arrangement for the song, with a heavy surf-

---

*Naturally, Chuck Berry's music publishers, Arc Music, sued for this uncredited use of his melody. The case was settled out of court by Capitol, which gave Berry an undisclosed sum and writer's credit on the song.

guitar sound and an instrumental break. "Surfin' U.S.A." spent seventeen weeks on the national charts, topping out at the number 3 position. It was an unqualified smash hit, in which the Beach Boys came into their own with their characteristic harmonies, falsettos, and production style.

The flip side of "Surfin' U.S.A.," "Shut Down," was a short, catchy automotive song about a drag race between a Corvette Sting Ray and a 413 Dodge. It featured Mike Love's nasal vocals and was the first song released from Brian's collaborations with Roger Christian. "Shut Down" hit the charts for thirteen weeks and climbed as high as number 23. In response to the two hits, Capitol rushed Brian and the boys into the studio and quickly released an album late in March, also entitled *Surfin' U.S.A.* This album was undistinguished except for the hit singles— it included five instrumentals—but nevertheless *Surfin' U.S.A.* spent seventy-eight weeks on the charts, hitting the number 2 position by the Fourth of July weekend.

Capitol took notice of the Beach Boys now, but not in the way Brian or Murry had expected. The company was indeed impressed with the group's success, but primarily as a sales vehicle for what they considered fad-oriented teen music, rather than as an emerging, creative sound in the music business. Capitol shifted into an unprecedented, intensive release schedule of Beach Boys songs that was to continue unabated for the next three years, in an attempt to milk Brian and the group before their popularity died. The ferocity of the scheduling, and the enormous amount of material Brian was asked to produce, would have depleted a lesser composer and producer. "There was a compulsion involved [in pouring out singles]," Brian said later. "We did it out of compulsive drive. You see so many pressures happening at once, and you grit your teeth...." As Brian saw it, he was "in a state of creative panic...." To complicate matters, Brian refused to record any more songs at Capitol's cavernous studios, which he claimed were giving a hollow ring to his productions. At the time, it was unheard of for an act to take its sessions elsewhere, since all recording artists were summarily charged for their studio time. But Brian put his foot down and Murry was sent up to Capitol to work it out. Finally Brian was allowed to record where he wanted—with Chuck Britz as engineer at Western's number 3 studio.

The next single, "Surfer Girl," clearly showed the difference the new studio made. "Surfer Girl" was the first Beach Boys ballad, intended to broaden the group's appeal. It was one of the original tunes Murry had first brought to Capitol. Rerecorded for this release, it was a sweet, dreamy tune about a little surfer girl that "made my heart come all undone," written about Judy Bowles. This was also the first Beach Boys tune that Brian recorded without the other members of the group, using studio musicians and his friends on the vocals. Yet the finished song sounded just like the group—which certainly gave all the other members pause; Brian could do it without them, without Capitol, and certainly without Murry. Significantly, it was also the last Beach Boys single about surfing. Brian was moving on. "Surfer Girl" hurtled up the charts to the number 7 position, while the flip side, another automotive song, called "Little Deuce Coupe," managed eleven weeks on the charts, hitting number 15 at its best.

Less than a month later, another Capitol album appeared, *Surfer Girl*, which stayed on the charts for well over a year, hitting the number 7 position. This album's most notable inclusion was Brian's moody—and unexpected—"In My Room." The rest of the cuts were forgettable mediocre songs about surf and cars, with titles like "Catch a Wave" and "Surfer's Rule." And yet, just two months later, Capitol sent a third LP, entitled *Little Deuce Coupe*, out on the market. Although it was unashamedly stuffed with four reissued songs ("Little Deuce Coupe," "409," "Our Car Club," and "Shut Down"), it rode the charts for a staggering forty-six weeks, hitting number 4 on the *Billboard* listing. The *Little Deuce Coupe* album contained Brian's most crystalline teenage effort yet, "Be True to Your School." An anthem for high schoolers, the song was recorded with the aid of fifteen sidemen (borrowed from top producer Phil Spector) and rerecorded as a single with an opening chorus of cheerleaders sung by the Rovell sisters, billed as the Honeys. "Be True to Your School" spent twelve weeks on the charts, hitting the number 6 position. To polish off this remarkable year, on December 9 Capitol released a Beach Boys

Christmas single, "Little St. Nick," backed with a lovely version of "The Lord's Prayer."

Ironically, the first number-1 single that Brian ever wrote was given away to another California group. Jan and Dean had already had several hit songs, dating back to their 1958 debut single, "Jennie Lee." After a few flop records they had returned to school, but had been drawn into the music industry again when a single, "Linda," reached 28 on the national charts. The singing duo, whose vocals many people mistook for those of the Beach Boys, met the group at a concert early in their career, when the Beach Boys were the opening act. After the Beach Boys sang their two or three hit songs, Jan and Dean took the stage and sang theirs. When the audience wanted more, they asked the Beach Boys to come back on stage on the spot and play their few songs over again, to which Jan and Dean jammed. They added some highs and lows to Brian's precision parts, and sang "Surfin'" and "Surfin' Safari" with them.

Soon afterward, Jan and Dean, under the guidance of their manager, Lou Adler, decided to do a surfing album and capitalize on the success of "Linda." At Adler's suggestion, they called the album *Jan and Dean Take Linda Surfing*. Jan and Dean told Brian they wanted to record "Surfin'" and "Surfin' Safari" for their album, and asked if he and the guys would do backup. Thrilled that Jan and Dean would think to cover his songs, Brian rounded up the group and brought them into the studio, where they graciously sang the same arrangement they had sung on stage. Brian further obliged Jan and Dean by showing them the rudimentary studio techniques of doubling parts he was developing. After the session was over, Brian played some of his new tunes, and Jan and Dean picked out songs to record as though choosing breakfast cereal from a supermarket shelf. One of the songs, which they eventually co-wrote, was called "Surf City." It was about a mythical kingdom—California—where there were "two girls for every boy." Brian agreed to sing at the recording session of "Surf City." By midsummer of 1963 it was number 1 on the national charts.

Brian was thrilled, Murry infuriated. Murry felt, with some justification, that Brian had given away the group's first number one single to competitors. Murry called Jan and Dean "pirates," and when Jan heard how enraged Murry was, he arrived at a Beach Boys session at Western Studios dressed in an elaborate pirate's costume, complete with eye patch. Murry was not amused; from now on, all of Brian's hit songs would be kept in the family.

3

Meanwhile, back on the twelfth floor of the Capitol Tower, Venet had his hands full with Murry and the boys. Capitol wasn't too pleased about the financial settlement it had to make with Hite and Dorinda Morgan, and because of it regarded Murry's business practices as forever suspect. Murry had recently borrowed from the company $17,000 against the Beach Boys' next advance, to buy a piece of equipment for ABLE Machinery, which he was still running part-time. It was anybody's guess whether the Beach Boys would ever see that money again. Capitol soon learned that Murry had his own conception of what show business was like, and strong ideas about the Beach Boys' promotion. The trouble started in December 1963, a few weeks after they signed their Capitol contracts. Murry arrived at Venet's office with all the boys in tow and a photographer, saying they wanted to take a picture of the contract signing. Venet was not enthusiastic. "Nobody takes pictures of kids signing contracts," Venet told him. "That's union stuff." But Murry blustered on about what a good idea it was. Finally all the boys were huddled into a conference room and a photograph was taken of them holding a piece of paper. "The pictures always looked like something you would see at the A&P," Venet said. Another of Murry's promotional ideas was to print five thousand buttons that said, "I Know Brian's Dad." Murry was an admirer of the Kingston Trio—a group produced by Voyle Gilmour—and of their "clean" image. He immediately found out where they bought their short-sleeved striped shirts and bought a dozen for the Beach Boys, and several dozen more to give away to disc jockeys. These were the shirts the Beach Boys wore in their earliest Capitol publicity pictures.

Venet was often forced to spend hours listening to Murry's own songs, and he had to pay attention, because somewhere in the conversation Murry would slip in what Brian's next single would be or when it might be available. Venet was reluctant to give Murry trouble—though it happened all the time; Murry soon discovered that it was easy to go over Venet's head within the company. Venet claims he once looked out of his office window and saw Murry with the "president of the company," whom he had "cornered in the parking lot." Venet rushed down to the lot to create a diversion, getting Murry away from the executive by pretending he had new photographs of the boys to show him.

On another occasion Murry stormed into Venet's office, insisting the legal department fire Mike Love on the grounds that he breached the morals clause in his contract. (It seems he said the word *fuck* several times backstage.) "There were reporters present," Murry told Venet, "as well as disc jockeys. If the disc jockeys heard him use the work *fuck*, they might take the Beach Boys off the air."

Venet said, "Fuck, you're kidding," and Murry stormed around the office biting on his pipe.

"One of the major problems I had with Brian and Murry," Venet said, "was that Brian would often look at me and say, 'Why is this man sitting where my father usually sits?' or 'Why does this man tell me things my father tries to tell me?' Brian would confuse things he felt about me with disloyalty to his father. There was a constant struggle with disloyalty, and Murry—I must tell you—played it to the hilt."

Murry remembered the situation very differently. As he saw it, the boys didn't really know what they were doing in the studio, and it was Murry's expertise that saved them. He would browbeat Brian mercilessly, telling him all his songs were rotten. In 1971, Murry told *Rolling Stones*, "Truthfully—I'm not beating myself on the back, but knowing them as a father, I knew their voices, right? And I'm musical, my wife is, we knew how to sing on key and when they were flat and sharp and how they should sound good in song. I'd surge on the power to keep the level of their musical tone the same. Or if they were singing a phrase weak, when Mike was singing 'She's fine, that 409,' we'd surge on the part. [I did this] Without their knowledge at first." However, "surging" the volume and speeding up the recording to make the boys sound younger, along with putting echo on, was virtually the extent of Murry's production expertise. In desperation, Chuck Britz rigged up a fake control panel for Murry to fiddle with during recording sessions.

Anything was bound to happen in the studio, where family fights ensued with no more restraint than in the living room in Hawthorne. Venet says he witnessed instances when Murry hauled off and smacked the boys, particularly Dennis, who once jumped out from behind his drum set to tackle Murry but was held back by his brothers. On another occasion Dennis actually took a swing at Murry, who stepped aside and let Dennis punch the wall instead. Chuck Britz put a picture frame around the broken plaster to commemorate the event. "If you run out of dialogue with your manager or attorney, you walk out," Venet said. "But we had a father-and-son relationship here, and Murry would not let them separate. When you disagreed with Murry, it wasn't a manager you were talking to, it was your father." Yet the group was hot, and Capitol was willing to put up with a lot from Murry to keep those teen songs coming in. "I would tell Voyle Gilmour, 'That man is a maniac,' and Voyle would say, 'Don't talk like that where anybody can hear you.'"

Venet remembers the last time he was in the studio with the Beach Boys. Earlier that day Brian had dropped by his office and said, "Please don't invite my father to the session tonight. We don't want him at the studio." Later on, Dennis called him and said that the boys had had a huge blowup with Murry that morning and didn't want him around. "If my father shows up tonight, I'm going to freak out. I'm going to punch him in the mouth and I'm going to punch you in the mouth. I want that session closed and I don't want my father in that studio."

Venet was more than happy to comply, but later in the afternoon he got a phone call from Murry. Murry told Venet that he and the boys had "patched it up" and that it was all right for him to attend the session. "What time is it?" Murry asked.

"Well, Mr. Wilson, it's starting at seven, but are you sure—"

"Yes, yes," Murry told him, "it's all patched up. I won't be staying. I'm only going to drop in."

That night Venet and the engineer, Peter Abbott, were sitting in the booth while the boys were doing vocals in the studio on the other side of a huge glass window. The door opened, and Venet could see Murry's figure, pipe in mouth, reflected in the window. "I turned around and the music stopped and everything stopped," Venet said. "Murry was standing there doing the championship handclasp above his head." Murry proceeded to loosen his tie and take off his jacket, sitting down between Venet and the engineer. All hell broke loose. Accusations flew from both sides, and in another five minutes the session was canceled. In the long run, however, the kids took Murry's side. Venet stopped producing, remaining merely the liaison at Capitol, coordinator between the company and the group.

4

By now the Beach Boys had become a major concert attraction, and the complications of booking tours grew to be too much for Murry. Although he once swore he would never do it, Murry signed the boys up with the William Morris Agency. Comedian Milton Berle's young son, Marshall Berle, was their responsible agent. Ira Okun, who was head of the concert department, remembers, "Those early days were not difficult because they seemed to catch on all over the country. On the first tour that I booked for them, they did major business. It was incredible, we didn't believe the numbers they did. We were booking them a guarantee against a percentage, and they were taking in triple and quadruple the money...that's how hot they were."

But Brian clearly hated being out on the road. Before one performance in northern California, he drank an entire bottle of wine to give himself the courage to go on. He complained about his hearing problem, and that the amplification of the stage speakers created a painful buzzing sound. As the Beach Boys' touring schedule grew heavier, they were out on the road for weeks and then months at a time and there was little time for Brian to compose and meet Capitol's heavy production schedule. Day by day Brian grew more resentful about being forced to go on the road. Promoter Irving Granz remembered, "The William Morris Agency had booked them on a big tour and Brian Wilson...refused to go because there was a two- or three-day drive before they came to Oklahoma City, which is where the tour began. Ira Okun, the agent, asked me to fill in dates or cities before the first one so they could play their way through. He said, 'Just book them, no matter what. Just get them in there.' Because they had all the money in for the tour, and the rest would have been profit, I thought there was nothing to lose and I booked them at a college—the University of Arizona at Tucson—which thought they were a folk act, because I'd booked folk groups there before....The ceiling fell down from the vibrations of the guitar—they'd never had anything like that before."

Eventually, Brian began to miss so many dates that Murry invited Alan Jardine back into the group. Jardine had since married a pretty young girl named Lynda, and was back studying at El Camino Junior College. Since the group was obviously in a good financial position, Jardine agreed to go out on the road with them. Both Alan Jardine and David Marks toured with the group, but not for long. Having Jardine back was just what Murry was waiting for, as a way of getting rid of David Marks. David made that easy. Hurt because Jardine was suddenly playing on sessions, and cocky because the young girls in the audience liked him so much, Marks said to Murry, "You'd be happy if I quit, wouldn't you?" When Murry remained sullenly silent, David said, "Okay, I quit. Happy now?"

"You heard him!" Murry bellowed. "He quit! You heard him, he's out!"

Although the rest of the group tried to get both Murry and David to reconsider, David stuck to his word. Within a few months he had formed his own group, David Marks and the

Marksmen, one of the first groups to sign with the newly formed A&M Records. When Murry heard this, he started a campaign against Marks among the local disc jockeys, telling them not to play any of his records. David Marks's new group lasted only a year, after which he joined Casey Kasem's group, Band Without a Name. Later came a stint as a session musician with the Turtles, and soon after that, an early retirement. According to Marks, he spent several years, "lying on my back on LSD in Venice." Eventually, he went to the Berkley School of Music in Boston, and later to the New England Conservatory of Music. As of this writing, David Marks is reliving his past glories and living off his royalties from the early Beach Boys albums—an estimated $300,000.

The rubber band had stretched
as far as it would go.
                    —BRIAN WILSON

Six

1

January 1964 greeted the Beach Boys with exciting news. They were about to embark on their first foreign tour, a week-long trip to Australia, with a stop for a concert in Hawaii on the way back. The bad news—Murry insisted on going along.

Naturally the boys did not want Murry on this trip, but they had little choice. Murry wanted to oversee the business and practical end of the tour, and he intended to curtail one of the boys' expanding extracurricular interests—girls—as well. With the Beach Boys' newfound fame came the spoils of teenage groupies, a bonus that particularly distressed Murry. He was not only morally opposed to the boys' sexual adventures, but saw them as a potential route to easy scandal. A competition was raging between Dennis and Michael as to who could have the most beautiful girl on his arm, and Michael seemed to be winning. This was one contest Murry was determined to end.

The tour had hardly gotten under way in Sydney when Murry invoked some of his most stringent rules about the road. There was to be absolutely no fraternization with members of the opposite sex, and anyone caught cussing or drinking in public was to be fined—not a $100 fine as had been established in the past—but $1,000, which Murry would subtract from the touring proceeds. Murry even sat in the hotel hallways outside the boys' rooms to make sure they couldn't sneak a girl up the back stairs. At one concert, Murry slapped Dennis's face for cursing in front of some fans. Dennis was so shocked and mortified, he burst into tears and ran away. These incidents, compounded by Murry's constant criticism and bad-gering, were finally too much for them to bear. By the end of the tour, the boys agreed that in the near future Murry would have to get the ax. "There was too much tension in the family," said Carl. "It was difficult separating the family thing from the group thing."

The cataclysmic moment occurred in Brian's exclusive do-main—the studios. Earlier in the year Murry had canceled a session for one of Brian's new songs called, "Fun, Fun, Fun" because he "wasn't happy with the material." In fact, "Fun, Fun, Fun" was one of Brian Wilson's best songs. It was written in a car while he and Mike Love were discussing Dennis's obsession with young girls. Dennis had told Mike about a girl who borrowed her father's Thunderbird, allegedly to go to the library, when in reality she was going to meet Dennis at his apartment. Brian and Mike liked the idea so much, they easily turned it into a classic of teenage rebellion. The lyric, "She'll have fun, fun, fun till her daddy takes her T-Bird away" was soon to become a catchphrase in American culture—but not for Murry, who thought the song was "weak" and called Chuck Britz at Western Studios to cancel the session. When Brian found out, he angrily rescheduled the recording date and called Murry to give him hell.

Several months later, while "Fun, Fun, Fun" was sitting near the top of the charts at number 5, Brian and the group went back into Western's number 3 studio to record a clever follow-up, titled "I Get Around." This catchy, fast-paced song was by far the best-crafted, best-produced tune of Brian's career to date. With its soaring vocals and breezy lyrics about a group of guys who cruise around in their cars, who have "never been beat," and who "never miss yet with the girls we meet," "I Get Around" was soon to become the most identifiable Beach Boys song Brian had written. But that April, sitting in the control room while they were recording it, Murry would not stop crit-icizing the song and Brian's production techniques. Murry rambled on about what a loser Brian was, how poor the music was, and how only Murry had the real talent in the family. At one point he insisted that Brian end the session because some-

thing was wrong with the bass line. Murry kept poking Brian
with his finger as he challenged him.

"You don't know what you're talking about, Dad," Brian
finally told him.

Murry flew off the handle. "Don't ever speak to me that
way!" he screamed at Brian. "I *made* you and the Beach Boys!
Hear me? You'd be *nothing* without me!"

Brian tore off his headset, rushed over to where Murry was
sitting, tore him out of his chair, and physically threw him up
against the wall, ripping his shirt. "Get out of here!" Brian
screamed. "You're *fired!* Do you understand? You're *fired!*"
For a moment there was an agonized silence in the control
booth. Then Murry adjusted his clothing and left.

In retrospect, Audree defends Murry's fanaticism about the
boys. "He did about seven jobs, without experience, just native
intelligence. Always do better, always be stronger, always be
honest. They heard that so much.... The boys just weren't
happy, they really weren't. At that time they were having growing pains, and they thought they really knew.... Murry wasn't
happy either, he was miserable most of the time...so it was
just a natural thing.... It happened right after they came home
from their first trip to Australia where they had lots of strife
and problems...and they fired him. I know he was devastated.
The funny part was he said he wouldn't work for them anymore anyway, he said he couldn't stand it. But it really crushed
him. He went to bed for about five weeks...he really did, just
totally stayed in bed."

Shortly afterward, Brian and the boys hired an accounting
firm, Cummings and Currant, in Torrance—the same people
who did Murry's taxes—to oversee their finances. But Murry
was far from finished. He still held sway over the boys activities, and let Brian know exactly what he thought of each
decision that the group made. A few months after he recovered
from the shock of being fired, Murry was ready to get even.

2

That same winter of 1964, a cruel fate awaited Brian Wilson—the Beatles. First in Liverpool, then throughout Great Britain, the Beatles had swept the population into frenzied ecstasy. With their long hair, collarless jackets, and simplistic love songs, the Beatles seemed as gimmicky as the Beach Boys with their surf and automobile songs. Yet the Beatles' music was much more widely received than that of the Beach Boys; Brian immediately perceived the group as a threat. Worse, he was distressed to discover that his own record company, Capitol, was about to launch for the Beatles one of the biggest publicity blitzes ever attempted in the recording industry.

"The Beatles Are Coming"—a promotional campaign including posters, bumper stickers, hundreds of radio spots and clever "talking head" commericals—made it seem as though the Beatles were arriving in every city across America. The airwaves were full of the Beatles, as were newspapers and TV news reports. Their widespread publicity certainly made Murry's "I Know Brian's Dad" buttons seem pathetic. As an extra little jab to Brian's fragile ego, both groups began with the letters *Bea*, and they were listed right next to each other on every company roster and in every record-store rack. Even Carl Wilson had a picture of the Beatles on his wall. ("He's a traitor," was Murry's comment.)

The day before Brian's latest masterpiece of abandon, "Fun, Fun, Fun," first appeared on the *Billboard* record charts at number 116, the Beatles appeared on "The Ed Sullivan Show." Now began a blatant competition for consumer dollars. Already the Beatles' new single, "I Want to Hold Your Hand," had far surpassed "Fun, Fun, Fun" by leaping onto the charts at number 45. The single sold half a million copies in ten days, obliterating the record previously held by the Beach Boys for "Surfin' U.S.A."

To Brian's ego, the Beatles' challenge represented a fight to the death. "When I hear really fabulous material by other groups, I feel as small as the dot over the *i* in 'nit,'" Brian told a journalist at the time. "Then I just have to create a new song to bring me up on top.... That's probably my most compelling motive for writing new songs—the urge to overcome an inferiority feeling.... I've never written one note or word of music simply because it will make money...and I do my best work when I am trying to top other songwriters and music makers."

Even Phil Spector remembered, "When 'Fun, Fun, Fun,' came out, [Brian] wasn't interested in the money, but wanted a top-ten record. He wanted to know how the song would do against the Beatles and if KFWB would play it."

During the coming year in the studio, Brian turned out a prodigious amount of hit songs, one after another, with an album every three months, and numerous singles. Indeed, Brian rose to the Beatles' challenge so admirably throughout the summer and fall of 1964 that the Beach Boys had seven singles on the charts at one time. For a brief period, the Beach Boys were clearly the most important and popular group in America. "Fun, Fun, Fun," leaped its way up the charts to 69, then made a huge jump to 27, and finally, four weeks later, to its peak at number 5 in *Billboard* on March 21. Not a bad position, but Brian couldn't break into the top four because those positions were being held by the Beatles. It wasn't until July 4 of that year that Brian was able to overtake the Beatles, with the Beach Boys' first number 1 single, "I Get Around."

The success of "I Get Around" was quickly followed by the release of an album, *All Summer Long*, which shot up to number 4 on the album charts. By the end of August, "When I Grow Up," another single, was released, and that fall, it too would be at the top of the charts, reaching number 9 by October 17.

This enormous recording popularity spurred a national public-appearance schedule that was staggering. The group was getting $20,000 a night, plus percentages, selling out wherever they appeared. As *Billboard* reported, "The Capitol artists have never been able to make extensive [public-appearance] tours in the past because one or more of the group were still in school. Last June, Carl Wilson, the youngest member of the group, was the last Beach Boy to graduate." In September 1964, they began to tour heavily, hopscotching across

America traveling to Buffalo, Syracuse, Boston, Hartford, Salt Lake City, Boise, Miami, Montgomery, Nashville, Providence, and Oklahoma City, all topped by the Beach Boys' first appearance on "The Ed Sullivan Show" on September 17—which, for them, certainly signified their "arrival." Their last date of this tour was in Worcester, Massachusetts, where the group quite literally brought down the house—the *Worcester Telegram* reported that "officials termed it the most damage done to the auditorium in thirty-one years." Finally, in October, the Beach Boys' touring party set out for its most exciting journey yet—a twenty-three-day performance and promotional tour of Europe. The best part about it: no Murry.

3

The Beach Boys' first major European tour was well documented by a middle-aged, goateed hipster named Earl Leaf. Leaf, a former photographer for *National Geographic*, a world traveler, and a Hollywood sharpie, in the early sixties was the editor and chief writer of an in-house Capitol publication called *Teen Scene*. A glossy magazine with flattering pictures of Capitol recording artists, *Teen Scene* was used to tout the company's popular singers. Leaf's column, "My Fair and Frantic Hollywood," gave him the best access of any journalist to the Beach Boys in their early years, and he became the primary source for much of the early information and many of the photographs available on the group.

Aside from Earl Leaf and the new road manager, Don Rice, there were eight members of the Beach Boys' touring party. An interesting coincidence occurred on the way to England. The group was grounded at Shannon Airport in Ireland for several hours while waiting for the weather to clear at Heathrow. Also stranded in the VIP lounge with the Beach Boys was Brian Epstein, the Beatles impresario, who at this point was nearly as famous as his wards. Brian Wilson was eager to meet and speak to Epstein, and his primary concern was finding out when the Beatles would next be arriving in America. Epstein assured Brian that he was safe for almost a whole year; the

Beatles couldn't make it back there until the next American swing of their world tour—in August 1965.

Perhaps the greatest reassurance to Brian's competitive spirit was the frenzied, enthusiastic reception the Beach Boys received in England. Their music, perceived as the encapsulation of the American dream, was in some ways more popular in England than in the United States. Heathrow was filled with young girls waiting for them despite the wet, cold weather, and an even larger crowd had assembled at their hotel, the London Hilton. The trip to England was a purely promotional eight-day whirlwind of interviews, TV shows, and press conferences to plug "I Get Around." Capitol's parent company, Great Britain's EMI, held a high-powered reception at the headquarters, causing such a sensation in the building that all work came to a halt. In the Beach Boys' first English appearance, for the BBC, they gave a short performance at the Playhouse Theater, followed by a spot on the "Top Gear" television program on October 24.

In Paris, where the boys were terrified of the French audiences, they learned they had sold out the prestigious Olympia theater after only a few radio advertisements. They headlined a show there, singing for an hour and a half and thoroughly captivating their listeners. From Paris they went on to Sweden, Rome, Berlin, Munich, Frankfurt, and Copenhagen, stopping at each place for just a few TV and radio appearances to promote their new songs.

Earl Leaf had some hotly disputed memories about the tour. About Mike Love, Leaf said, "He was awfully wild ... girlwise, he'd fuck anybody ... " Then Leaf reconsidered. "Dennis was the worst. Dennis was an animal." Leaf claimed that Mike was naïvely taken in by professional women in Paris, where they "pumped" him with champagne at "about four thousand francs a bottle" until about 4:00 A.M., closing time, when the young women disappeared into the night and left Mike with the bar bill. Leaf also claimed a girl took money from Mike in London, promising to have sex with him and never showing up.

In Munich, Mike and Don Rice had just left a club on their way back to their hotel when, in the parking lot, they saw a young woman being dragged into a Mercedes 300 SL. Mike intervened, only to find himself staring down the muzzle of a Luger pistol. "Three hours in the clink, a bruised hand and a $250 fine taught Mike a lesson," Leaf wrote in *Teen Scene*. Later, Leaf claimed that Mike hadn't gone to the aid of a damsel in distress at all. Instead, "He went and found a girl and started feelin' her up and her pimp came and got a gun and held him until the police came. He spent the night in jail."

"Earl's a lecherous old man," Mike contended in response. "He's just jealous. Anything Earl Leaf says must be sifted through a sieve. He elaborates in his senility." Mike claimed he only had trouble once on that tour, in Germany. "I was going to go to this girl's house for a drink. I found her outside with some other fellow in a Mercedes. I was pretty drunk. I had on these black gloves. I smashed his window in. The only minor problem was, he had a gun. That was in my wild youth. I don't do that, anymore. I never did make a habit of it."

But of all the Beach Boys, perhaps Brian's behavior could be considered the most notable on this trip. In Copenhagen, the three Wilson brothers were walking through a red-light district call the Nieu Haven when Brian got an inspiration to write a song. He dashed into the nearest restaurant, a "dance hall—opium den—chop-suey joint," according to Leaf, where he ordered a meal and tried to take possession of the piano from the piano player. A struggle ensued between the restaurant's keyboardist and Brian over the piano stool, and Brian ran from the restaurant just before the bouncer could throw him out. He raced back to the Royal Hotel and spent the night locked away at a piano in the hotel café, composing "Kiss Me Baby" (which would appear as the flip side of "Help Me, Rhonda" the following year) into the early hours of the morning. Equally childish but less troublesome was his sudden impulse to kiss a statue in the Palais de Chaillot in Paris. He climbed a huge column and began to kiss the statue on the mouth when Alan Jardine yelled, "Cheese it, the police," and scared Brian into coming down. Another peculiar moment occurred in a Munich beer hall. The boys were getting pleasantly drunk when Brian, who was particularly smashed, started talking about Audree. "She's such a wonderful woman," Brian kept saying. Then he suddenly started crying uncontrollably.

"Isn't she wonderful?" he kept asking his brothers, sobbing. "Isn't mother a wonderful woman?" Finally, they took Brian back to the hotel and put him to bed.

Al Jardine, characteristically, remained separate from the rest of the group, spending his early mornings touring the various cities, visiting museums and shops. He also spent hours on the phone with his wife, Lynda, and reportedly ran up several thousand dollars' worth of phone bills.

4

In the autumn of 1964 Brian finally moved out of the Rovells' house to his own one-bedroom apartment at 7235 Hollywood Boulevard. It was in a large, anonymous building and Brian was lonely there. From the day he moved in, he was constantly on the phone with Marilyn. "Please come over," he'd say, "I can't stand it. I can't stand to be without you... please come over."

Marilyn would say, "Oh Brian, it's too *cold* to go out," and he would keep her on the phone for two hours. Then Marilyn would catch a few hours' sleep before the phone rang again. It would be Brian begging her to come by. When she turned fifteen and a half, she was of legal age to drive a motor scooter, and Brian bought her one. Now there was no excuse for her not to come over. "It was freezing out, and I would bundle up—I mean gloves, hats, you name it—and at two in the morning I would get on my little motor scooter. His apartment was about two miles away and I would go and be with him."

The nighttime visits soon extended into protracted mornings, until Marilyn finally wound up spending the entire day with him, accompanying him from appointment to appointment. "Somehow he felt really comfortable with me, and we were the best of friends. I was in awe, he was so different. I would do everything for him just out of caring. So I had started falling in love with him. I knew he really liked me and I knew that he cared for me, but I didn't think he was in love with me."

Everything changed one day in November when the group was about to leave for their second trip to Australia, where their popularity had reached the same proportions it had in England. Marilyn and the other girl friends and wives went to Los Angeles International Airport to say good-bye. While waiting in the lounge for the group to board the plane, Marilyn and Brian sat next to each other—but didn't hold hands. "I'm sure Brian hadn't told everybody that he was in love with me. I think the rest of the guys knew that we had started sleeping together. I was very young...."

While waiting for final boarding to be called, Mike Love turned to Brian and said, "Hey, Brian, we're really going to have a blast [in Australia]... we're just going to have a ball, you and me."

Marilyn sat there listening to them talk about all the conquests they would have in Australia, growing more annoyed by the minute. Finally she remarked pointedly, "I hope you guys enjoy yourselves, because I'm going to have a good time too."

For the first time Brian seemed to snap to attention. According to Marilyn, his mouth dropped open in surprise. "What did you say?" he asked her.

"I said that I was going to have a good time while you're gone, too."

A few hours later a telegram for Marilyn arrived at the Rovells' house that amazed them all. Brian had it sent from the plane, insisting the pilot wire it. The telegram read, PLEASE WAIT FOR MY CALL. I LOVE YOU. BRIAN.

"I just couldn't believe it," Marilyn said. "I almost fainted. It was just unreal."

Early the following morning, Marilyn was awakened by the telephone. It was Brian in Australia. "That was the most painful trip I have ever taken on an airplane in my life," he told her. "Just to think of losing you, all of a sudden it was like a arrow shooting straight through my heart... all of a sudden I realized how much I love you."

"Oh Brian," Marilyn said, swooning.

"We've got to get married," he said. "We've got to make plans when I get back."

Marilyn said she would have to discuss it with her parents. After all, she was only fifteen years old. But Brian insisted, and throughout the entire Australian tour the phone would ring day and night with long-distance calls from Brian, proposing marriage. At the time, Marilyn was working at a doughnut shop trying to earn back the money that her father had loaned her to buy costumes for the Honeys, and sometimes May Rovell would speak to Brian on the phone. Brian begged May to arrange for the wedding, but May refused. "I'm not going to arrange your wedding, honey," May told him. "You do it yourself when you get back." And then she added, "You better take it easy with these long-distance phone calls, Brian. I can imagine what this phone bill is going to be like!"

When Brian returned to Los Angeles, he was as certain as ever that he wanted to marry Marilyn, although his family had some reservations about her age. There was also the problem that Marilyn was Jewish. According to Ginger Blake, "Murry was not too happy about it at first. But then he got to know May. Can anybody not like May?"*

The very day that Brian returned from Australia, he insisted on marrying Marilyn, right then. "When I say that day," Ginger says, "I mean that day." Because California law required that the couple wait, they decided to fly to Las Vegas and be married there by a justice of the peace. Brian called his friend Lou Adler, manager of Jan and Dean, and said, "I want to marry Marilyn. We've got to set everything up."

"Don't worry about it," Adler said. "You get Marilyn and I'll get the room together."

Marilyn, May, Diane, and Ginger rushed out to the airport with Brian and caught the next flight to Vegas. Lou Adler arranged accommodations for them at the Sands Hotel. May, Diane, and Ginger had a large room, while Brian and Marilyn had the bridal suite, which Adler had filled with flowers and champagne.

The next stop was the marriage-license bureau, where officials asked for Marilyn and Brian's birth certificates. Marilyn

---

*Some sources say that the Wilson family, as well as Brian's friends, were strongly against Brian's involvement with a Jewish girl, and it took them years to appreciate Marilyn and her family.

had hers, but it had never occurred to Brian to bring one. Brian produced his driver's license with his picture on it, but it wasn't good enough. He held up the license to the clerk and said, "Can't you tell that's me? That's me and this is the date I was born." Then he looked at the license carefully and said, "Yeah, that's me. Look!" But it wasn't acceptable, and everybody rushed outside to a pay telephone booth, where Brian called home. Murry and Audree weren't home at the time, but Carl and Dennis were. Brian asked them to find his birth certificate and get on the next plane with it. After a lot of hemming and hawing, they said they couldn't find it.* Brian got so upset he kicked the phone booth and smashed the glass. Marilyn stood nearby crying.

That night they went back to the hotel. Marilyn cried herself to sleep in the bridal suite, while Diane and Ginger drove around Vegas in a rented car. The next morning they all returned to Los Angeles, where Brian found his birth certificate. At this point May took over and found a judge at the city courthouse. Brian and Marilyn were married in a municipal ceremony on December 7, 1964.

The personal lives of the other Beach Boys were also changing with their newfound fame and fortune. Mike had left his wife and children and filed for divorce, settling on a reported $200-a-month support payment for the children. Carl and Dennis had moved to their own apartments in the same complex in Inglewood. Dennis had fallen in love, but he wisely hid his new relationship completely from Murry. Coincidentally, the girl he loved, like Marilyn, was Jewish, but she was regarded as a pleasant change from his previous girl friend, a Mexican biker with a tattoo on one arm.

Dennis met his new love at the Carolina Pines, a hamburger-and-fries hangout on Highland and Sunset. Dennis liked to go there late at night after work in the studio, and word always

---

*There is some dispute over whether or not Carl and Dennis willfully withheld Brian's birth certificate so he wouldn't be able to marry Marilyn. Audree claims this is not so, but many familiar with the situation at the time claim that the two brothers, knowing Brian's sudden whims, wanted to give him more of a chance to think about it.

Brian Wilson in grade school, age
12 (*right*), and in junior high
school (*below*).
PETER REUM COLLECTION

Brian (*center*) was
an all-around
athlete in high
school, but never
good enough to
satisfy his father.
PETER REUM
COLLECTION

Above: Brian in a dramatic slide to base. Unfortunately, he's "out." The ball is already in the catcher's mitt.
PETER REUM
COLLECTION

Right: Carl and his date at his high school prom.
PETER REUM
COLLECTION

Left: Dennis (*center*) in a school photo taken in spring of 1960. Dennis preferred surfing to school.
PETER REUM COLLECTION

Right: Alan Jardine as he looked in spring of 1960. He first approached the Morgans to record a folk song.
PETER REUM COLLECTION

Alan Jardine, a high school shot-putter.   PETER REUM COLLECTION

The graduates: Brian and Carl Wilson; Diane and Marilyn Rovell.

Audree and Murray Wilson arrive at the airport in
Sacramento, where the Beach Boys experienced
their earliest popularity. Audree is carrying a carton
of promotional records to give to local disc jockeys.
PETER REUM COLLECTION

One of the earliest photographs of the Beach Boys, taken at Capitol
Records soon after signing the first contract. *Left to right:* Mike Love,
Dennis Wilson, David Marks, Carl Wilson, Brian Wilson.
MAGGIE MONTALBANO

Right: Dennis helps with the roast in the kitchen of the Wilsons' Hawthorne house. PETER REUM COLLECTION

Below: Mike, Brian, and Carl stand next to a paneled wall covered with album covers and photographs in the Wilsons' den. PETER REUM COLLECTION

Brian poses with Capitol Records' in-store display of Beach Boys records.
PETER REUM COLLECTION

Young, debonair Mike Love, with most of his hair still on his head. The competition for girls was between him and Dennis.

Above; Suzanne and Mike Love, February 1967. PETER REUM COLLECTION

Left: Mike Love in his 1890's look. The photo was taken by Debbie Keil at a Beach Boys rehearsal. PETER REUM COLLECTION

The Honeys in the mid-sixties. PETER REUM COLLECTION

Above: The Honeys today. From left to right: Diane, Ginger, and Marilyn. THE HONEYS

Left: May and Irving Rovell. They turned their home over to the Beach Boys. May was on 24-hour kitchen duty— and loved it. MAY AND IRVING ROVELL

Above: On their first trip to London, the Beach Boys, holding a few slats of wood in parody of their original surfboard photo, pose outside the EMI offices.
PETER REUM COLLECTION

Right: Brian and Roger Christian, who wrote the lyrics to some of the Beach Boys' best automotive songs. PETER REUM COLLECTION

Left: Brian onstage at the Hollywood Bowl, 1963. The next year he would quit touring.
CAPITOL RECORDS

Below: The Beach Boys' first film appearance, in Paramount's *The Girls on the Beach.* The 1965 film also featured The Crickets and Lesley Gore.
PARAMOUNT PICTURES CORP.

Right: Dennis Wilson and his first wife, Carol. PETER REUM COLLECTION

Below; Linda and Alan Jardine with Mike Love. MAGGIE MONTALBANO

Above: Brian gives Dennis and Al the pitch for their harmonies in the studio. PETER REUM COLLECTION

Left: Brian, Dennis, Mike, and Carl arrive at the Honolulu airport in July 1963. FUDGIE

Above: At Western Studios, 1967. *From left:* Carl and Annie Wilson, Annie's brother Billy Hinsche, and cousin Steve Korthof. PETER REUM COLLECTION

Right: Bruce Johnston first joined the Beach Boys in April of 1965. A falling-out with manager Jack Rieley caused him to leave in 1972, but he was back for good in 1978. PETER REUM COLLECTION.

spread quickly that a Beach Boy was present. There wasn't a girl in the place who didn't want to meet Dennis, and he shortly picked up one named Ellen Brown, who happily went back to his apartment with him. By this time Dennis had moved to a relatively expensive apartment building on Hollywood and Sycamore that had its own swimming pool. After spending a few days with Dennis, Ellen Brown called her girl friend, Carol Freedman, who had also been in the Carolina Pines that night, and asked her to visit. It was the last time Ellen Brown would see Dennis.

Carol Freedman was sixteen, already married, and the mother of a one-year-old named Scott. Born November 10, 1946, in Michigan, she had moved to the Los Angeles area with her parents when she was an infant, and had grown up in Hollywood. The rumor was that her infant son had been fathered by rock star Jim Morrison, although Carol says this is not so. Carol was pleased to be invited to Dennis Wilson's apartment and was impressed with the apartment building and pool. But she was confused by Dennis. "I couldn't figure out what he was doing," she said. "He was hugging Ellen Brown and holding two fingers up behind her and mouthing 'Two o'clock.'" Carol was quite shocked when, at two o'clock in the morning, Dennis showed up at her parents' house in West Hollywood. Her parents weren't too happy with this nocturnal visit either. But Dennis was so charming, Carol said, "that even when you were angry he could make you laugh." He smiled and they had to smile.

Dennis came back the next day because he wanted to meet Scott. "He literally fell in love with Scotty," Carol said. "He really did love children. And within a few weeks, Scott and I were living with him."

Audree knew about Dennis's relationship with Carol, but it had to be kept a secret from Murry, who disapproved of unmarried couples living together. In the beginning it hurt Carol to have to hide the truth, but she soon learned that Dennis was desperate to please and appease his father, so she stayed out of the way. "No matter how hard Dennis tried," Carol said, "no matter how perfect he was, no matter how hard he tried to emulate Murry, he could never win Murry's outward love."

5

Living with Marilyn in his own apartment, Brian had total freedom from family restraints for the first time. A little like Alice let loose in a Hollywood Wonderland, he was finally able to make a new set of friends without parental interference. This wasn't too difficult, since Brian now enjoyed a certain prominence in the Los Angeles music-business scene and all the cognoscenti wanted to meet him. A whole new cast of characters began to emerge in Brian's life. Some were other musicians he had met through business contacts, some were just high-level groupies—what Marilyn Wilson would come to call the "drainers." As Brian saw it, all these people were hipper, smarter, and more clever than he. According to Marilyn, "They had the gift of gab.... Brian came from Inglewood, Squaresville.... All of a sudden he was in Hollywood—these people talk a language that was fascinating to him. Anybody that was different and talked cosmic or whatever...he liked it."

The New Best Friend in Brian's life from this period, and the one who would leave the deepest and most lasting mark on him, was a young man in his twenties named Loren Schwartz. He was a small, good-looking guy a few years older than Brian, married to a pretty girl named Linda. An aspiring music-business agent, Loren met Brian at one of the many Hollywood studios where Brian recorded. Loren had gone to Santa Monica City College and lived in a small apartment at the back of a building on Harper between Hollywood and Santa Monica boulevards. One of his school chums described him as a "new-wave Jewish intellectual. He was very skillful at asking people what 'the sound of one hand clapping' was. You'd think this guy was really *out there*. He could impress people with his intellect, which was genuine, but wasted. Loren was something of a social manipulator. He turned Brian on to all this literature. Well, Brian just got overawed by it." Loren's literature included *The Little Prince*, by Antoine de Saint-

Exupéry, the poetry of Kahlil Gibran, the collected works of Hermann Hesse, and the writings of Krishna. At the time these were trendy works, widely read by college kids, but a far cry from anything Brian had ever read in Hawthorne. It all seemed deeply mystical and terribly important to him.

At a time when the drug culture would soon flourish into everyday prominence, there was already a plentiful supply of grass and hashish at Loren Schwartz's apartment. Four or five nights a week, a circle of friends would meet there, with candles and incense, the latest and hippest music, a kilo or so of marijuana, and a Sara Lee cake to satisfy the munchies. According to Loren, the drugs always had some special cachet about them, such as marijuana allegedly given to him by George Harrison, or hashish Jim Morrison had sent back from a monk in the Himalayas. The scene at Loren's, according to one of the participants, "was a little like Paris in the days when the impressionist painters met at coffeehouses." Among the players were David Crosby, shortly to become famous as part of Crosby, Stills, Nash and Young; Jim McGuinn and Chris Hillman of the Byrds; a session musician named Van Dyke Parks; and Tony Asher, an aspiring songwriter and bright young advertising jingle writer with the Carson/Roberts agency.

It was early winter of 1964, and under Loren's auspices, Brian smoked marijuana for the first time. One night, when he and Marilyn had been married only a short while, she was waiting for him at her mother's house on Sierra Bonita Drive. Brian arrived late, as usual. But there was nothing usual about the way he looked. "His eyes were all glassy and he was acting real funny, like real spacy," Marilyn said.

"What's wrong with you?" she asked him. "What is it?"

"Oh, I tried this marijuana cigarette and it got me really... high."

Marilyn rolled her eyes and her heart sank. "Who had ever heard of a marijuana cigarette?" she later said. At the time, Marilyn put grass in the same category as heroin. "The most I'd ever heard of in my life was taking aspirin. All I knew was that suddenly Brian was not himself."

"Who gave you that?" Marilyn demanded angrily. "Who gave you that cigarette?"

When Brian told her it was his new friend Loren Schwartz, she demanded he never see him again. But her pleas were useless. Brian looked forward to the gatherings at Loren's house, and continued to smoke pot—a deep, dark secret that was kept from the rest of the band and his family, but one that would have a radical effect on him within the next few weeks.

6

The pressure from Capitol for more Beach Boys product was unrelenting. With the exception of the Beatles, the Beach Boys were Capitol's highest-grossing act. In just two years, their first six albums had sold nearly six million copies. As the calendar year of 1964 ended, their seventh album, *The Beach Boys*, hurtled almost straight to the number 1 position. Their sixteenth single, "Dance, Dance, Dance," was also headed for the top ten of the singles charts. As far as Capitol was concerned, Brian Wilson was the horn of plenty. They continued to "encourage" him to produce and record as many songs as he wanted.

But the pressure was clearly taking its toll. Toward the end of 1964, while sustaining a hectic composing and recording schedule, newly married, Brian hit the road for what would be his last tour for over a decade. Said Brian, "I was run-down mentally and emotionally because I was running around, jumping on jets from one city to another, on one-night stands, also producing, writing, arranging, singing, planning, teaching—to the point where I had no peace of mind and no chance to actually sit down and think or even rest. I was so mixed up and so overworked."

On December 23, 1964, at the start of a small western tour to promote "Dance, Dance, Dance," Brian Wilson had his first publicly acknowledged psychological episode. Things had been going badly for weeks. He hated going out on the road. Brian was especially reluctant to go away at this time because he and Marilyn hadn't been getting along, after only three weeks and two days of marriage. They were having the typical squabbles that many young marrieds endure; but to Brian they seemed tragic. Marilyn accompanied the boys to the Los Angeles International Airport to say good-bye. It was two days before Christmas and the airport was a madhouse, filled with tens of thousands of passengers traveling before the holidays. The sound of Christmas carols piped over the public-address system was drowned out by the noise of the crowds. The atmosphere was hectic and tense. Brian later claimed that as the group huddled together in the airport waiting room, just before boarding the plane, he saw something that drove him over the edge. "I saw Marilyn staring at Michael," he said. "So I assumed she loved Michael. I wasn't hallucinating, I was seeing what I was seeing. I saw them stare. Oh boy, I didn't like that at all. I don't like someone liking Michael and not me. My ego gets real crushed and then I get real juiced up."

Marilyn laughs nervously at this accusation, but asserts, "Brian was very jealous at the time. But if I was looking at anyone, it would definitely not have been Mike Love."

The plane had only been airborne for five minutes when Brian turned to Al Jardine in the seat next to him. Eyes glazed with terror, Brian said in a small, strangled voice, "I'm going to crack up any minute!" Al told him to "cool it" and tried to calm him down.

"Then I started crying," Brian said. He put a pillow over his face and began screaming and yelling, alarming everyone on the plane. "I just let myself go completely," Brian said. "I dumped myself out of the seat and all over the plane. I let myself go emotionally." Some would say Brian purposely let himself lose control so he would never have to go out on tour again. Regardless of his reasons, Brian put on a harrowing display.

When the stewardess came over to see what was wrong, Brian started screaming, "She doesn't love me! She doesn't love me!"

After a while, the group managed to calm him down, but he spent the rest of the ride white-knuckled and teary. He even refused his meal, which confirmed to the rest of the group that Brian was seriously ill. When the plane finally landed in Houston, Brian didn't want to get off and begged to be taken right back to L.A.

They checked into their hotel, and in the solitude of his room Brian was able to regain some composure. "That night I cooled off and played the show. The next morning I woke up with the biggest knot in my stomach and I felt like I was going out of my mind. In other words, it was a breakdown period. I must have cried about fifteen times [that] day. Every half-hour I'd start crying. Carl came to my hotel room. I saw him and I just slammed the door in his face. I didn't want to see him or anybody because I was flipping out. Nobody knew what was going on. I wouldn't talk. I just put my head down and wouldn't even look at anyone. That night the road manager took me back to L.A."

In her new house in Whittier, Audree Wilson received a phone call from accountant Dick Cummings, who was on the road with them. "He said Brian was coming home and that he had been crying and breaking down and just couldn't carry on." Cummings said that Brian wanted her to pick him up at the airport, but "he made it very clear that only I was to meet Brian, not his father." Audree was waiting at the terminal when Brian got off the plane. "He was a total wreck," she said. "He got in the car and I said, 'Where do you want to go? Do you want to go to our house or to your apartment?'"

Brian refused to be taken either place. Instead, he wanted to go back to the house in Hawthorne where he had grown up, which they still owned and kept vacant. Audree drove him there and they let themselves in. There was something dark and eerie about the deserted house now. They went to Brian's old bedroom and sat down and talked. "He was in a bad state, crying; then he stopped and he talked a lot...." For the first time, Brian was able to unleash all his inner terrors to his mother, and nothing was ever the same for him afterward.

For the next week Brian relaxed at home while Marilyn pampered and reassured him. After he felt a bit more collected, he went to the studio to meet with the rest of the band. The boys had been waiting patiently for him to start work on their eighth LP, *The Beach Boys Today*. "We were about halfway through the album," Brian said, "and one night I told the guys I wasn't going to perform on stage anymore, that I can't travel."

Here Brian's narrative becomes slightly hysterical. What follows is a transcript of a tape he made with Earl Leaf at the time. When he told the group of his decision, Brian claimed, "They all broke down. I'd already gone through my breakdown, and now it was their turn. When I told them, they were shook. Mike had a couple of tears in his eyes. He couldn't take the reality that their big brother wasn't ever going to be on the stage with them again. It was a blow to their sense of security, of course.

"Mike lost his cool and felt like there was no reason to go on. Dennis picked up a big ashtray and told some people to get out of there or he'd hit them in the head with it. He kind of blew it, you know. In fact, the guy he threatened to hit with the ashtray was Terry Sachem, who became our road manager within two weeks.

"Al Jardine broke out in tears and broke out in stomach cramps. He was all goofed up, and my mother, who was there, had to take care of him.

"And good old Carl was the only guy who never got into a bad emotional scene. He just sat there and didn't get uptight about it. He always kept a cool head. If it weren't for Carl, it's hard to say where we'd be. He was the greatest stabilizing influence in the group.... He cooled Dennis, Mike, and Al down.

"I told them I foresaw a beautiful future for the Beach Boys, but the only way we could achieve it was if they did their job and I did mine. They would have to get a replacement for me"—Brian corrected himself—"I didn't say 'they,' I said 'we,' because it isn't them and me, it's 'us.'"

Brian's sweet magnanimity aside, this was the beginning of the attitude that what was best for Brian wasn't necessarily best for the rest of the group, a position that would become increasingly threatening to the rest of the members as time went on.

Of course, Murry had no sympathy at all for Brian and let him know it. Al Jardine remembered, "It affected his father very intensely. His dad was really uptight about it. He felt that Brian was copping out or...that he was dodging responsibilities and gave him a pretty rough time."

Privately, Marilyn was happy that Brian would not be going

out on tour anymore. He was away from the groupies and the temptation of other women on the road, and she enjoyed having more time to spend with him at home. Said Marilyn, "Onstage it was just too painful for him; it really hurt his ear. That was one factor, but the main reason at the beginning was that he couldn't tour and write at the same time."

Brian's first replacement on the road was a session guitarist named Glenn Campbell, who had worked with the Beach Boys in the studio and who could sing Brian's high parts on stage. In February 1965, with Glenn Campbell on the road with them, the Beach Boys netted $98,414 for fourteen one-nighters— quite a sum—but Campbell was reportedly paid a straight salary and only stayed with the group about three months. "I'm too much of an individual," he later said, when he went on to become famous in his own right. "I didn't like being responsible for something done by a group. That's the way I felt being with the Beach Boys. If the Beach Boys did something, then I did it [too], and I didn't like that at all. I wanted to do what I wanted to do."

Campbell was replaced by Bruce Johnston, a handsome young man who would eventually be incorporated into the Beach Boys lineup as a permanent member. A native of Los Angeles, Johnston was an orphan whose real name was Billy Baldwin. He had been adopted by a wealthy vice-president of the Rexall drug chain and grew up in Beverly Hills and Bel Air. In high school he had been in a band with Phil Spector, who asked him to play with the Teddy Bears on a session that turned out to be his first hit, "To Know Him Is to Love Him." Later, Bruce was in a group called the Rip Chords, who had a minor hit with the song "Hey Little Cobra." More recently, he had been making records with Terry Melcher, Doris Day's son, under the name Bruce and Terry.

"In 1963 I was working at Columbia Records, across the street from where [the Beach Boys] were recording...and I kind of met them through making similar records.... A couple of years passed and I was asked by Mike Love to find somebody to replace Brian...on a tour. So I called a few people and they wanted someone yesterday. I said, 'Look, Mike. I'll come. I don't play bass, I play piano, but I suppose I could sing all the parts if you show me what to do.' So an hour later I was on my way down to New Orleans. That was in April [on the 9th] of 1965—I performed with the group, completed the tour, and came home. They asked me to go on another tour, so I said, 'Well, all right.' I was still working for Columbia Records as a record manager, and I was kind of reluctant to leave because I felt that Bri would come back into the group. But when I came home from the second tour, they asked me to sing on the next album, *Summer Days (And Summer Nights!!)*. The first song that I sang on was 'California Girls.'"

The Beach Boys' concert booklet later read, "Bruce Johnston is very clever, very healthy, very ambitious, and very rich...."

A genius musician,
but an amateur human being.
TONY ASHER
on Brian Wilson

Seven

1

Early in 1965 Brian and Marilyn moved into a new apartment together on Gardner Street, just two blocks from her parents' home on Sierra Bonita. It was a two-bedroom duplex, which Marilyn furnished modestly. Several weeks after they moved in, Brian arrived home one day and said, "Guess what? Loren's got some of this LSD and he wants me to take it with him."

"Don't you dare!" Marilyn screamed, though she hardly knew what LSD was—except that it was bad.

"He said that I have a very bright mind and this LSD will really expand my mind and make me write better."

"Don't you dare!" Marilyn insisted, near tears.

"I really have to do it," Brian said. "I have to do it, I have to try it."

Despite Marilyn's fierce objections, Brian made plans to take his first trip with Loren. They set aside a special day for the event, and Brian told Marilyn not to expect him home. At the time, LSD was not a widely used drug. Most of the supplies available in California were made by the famous San Francisco psychedelic chemist called "Owsley," whose laboratories were turning out a full-strength, powerful acid—so strong that in later years the dosage would be cut in tenths. But this was the acid that Brian ended up taking with Loren Schwartz.

When Marilyn saw Brian the day after his first trip, he looked drained and exhausted. "I'll never do it again," he swore.

"But what happened?" she asked him. "What was it like?"

Tears welled in his eyes, and suddenly he was crying and

133

hugging her. "I saw God," Brian told her. "I saw God and it just blew my mind." Over and over again Brian repeated the phrase "my mind was blown," but Marilyn had no idea what that really meant, or even harbored the suspicion that perhaps something had actually happened to his mind. As far as Marilyn knew, he only took the drug one more time with Loren. But she later realized that over the next few years, Brian took LSD many more times—perhaps dozens—when it was slipped to him by a variety of people who became his New Best Friend.

Within a fortnight after his first LSD trip, Brian seemed to be stoned on marijuana all the time. "He was just not the same person I fell in love with. He had started changing little by little. He was not the same Brian that he was before the drugs. . . . These people were very hurtful, and I tried to get that through to Brian, but he was like a kid. You tell him 'no,' and he's going to do it. More and more Loren had a hold over him."

According to Marilyn Wilson, Loren Schwartz began to rule Brian's life. "Brian was just completely taken with him," she said. Feisty and dedicated, Marilyn kept up an active campaign for Brian to end their friendship. "He would always want me to go over to Loren's house, and I would say, 'No, I'm not comfortable with those people.'"

When the fighting over Loren became explosive, Marilyn threw up her hands. "I decided he was acting too weird for me to deal with. I said, 'I've had it.' I decided we should have a little separation. So I went out on my own and found a small apartment on Detroit Street." The first day she lived there, Carl came to see her. "He begged me, 'Please Mare, I don't want you and Brian to break up.'"

But it didn't seem as though Brian cared at all about this separation. "I think he was too involved with the drug thing," Marilyn said. "He wasn't devastated at all." They were separated for a full month before Marilyn heard from him. "One night there was a loud banging on the door. It was Brian, and he was crying, 'Please, Marilyn, let me in! Let me in!' I had never given him my address and somehow he had found it out—Carl probably gave it to him." Marilyn felt sorry for him and let him in. For once he didn't appear to be stoned.

"Please, honey," he begged her. "I'm sorry, really I am, Mare.

I miss you terribly. Let's go find a house together and buy it. I know you want a house, and I can afford it now. We can become a happy family and have children and we'll live just like regular people...."

But Marilyn wasn't ready to go back with him so easily. She said she wanted some time to think about it, and several weeks went by before she consented to give the marriage another try. One morning Brian picked her up at her Detroit Street apartment and they went to meet a Beverly Hills real-estate agent. They bought one of the first houses they saw. "It was way on top of Beverly Hills on Laurel Way," Marilyn said. "Half of it looked down on the valley and half over Beverly Hills and L.A." They paid $185,000, and moved in a few weeks later, in late summer of 1965. The house on Laurel Way became Marilyn and Brian's first real home together, and for a while at least, things seemed to go well.

While Brian busied himself composing new Beach Boys material, Marilyn set about fixing up the house with the help of decorator Lee Polk (wife of director Martin Polk)—and Brian's overriding advice. The master bedroom had flocked red wallpaper. A huge four-poster bed, with a headboard of carved angels, was blanketed in a leopard-print spread. In the bathroom hung a plastic picture of Jesus, whose eyes opened and closed when you moved. In the shag-carpeted living room several "Lava Lamps" slowly undulated, while nearby, inexplicably, was a display rack of children's dolls in their plastic shipping tubes. On the walls were Kean prints of dark-eyed children, along with cheap prints of the Mona Lisa and Blueboy. The large dining room was furnished with an immense, Spanish-style table covered in a dark blue cloth and surrounded by high-backed chairs. The kitchen had black-and-white houndstooth-check wallpaper and striped window shades, like an "Op-art painting," according to one visitor. The den was a small room prepared in a bright orange, blue, yellow, and red wall fabric, with a jukebox loaded with Beach Boys singles and Phil Spector tunes. A pair of mechanical parrots, dyed fluorescent colors, sat in a huge cage. Two dogs, Louie (named after Brian's pal, Lou Adler), a dark brown Weimaraner, and Banana, a beagle, completed the scene.

But their home was far from the perfect picture of domesticity. Brian's fascination with Loren Schwartz and drugs did not end, and soon Loren was a daily visitor to Laurel Way, where the air was always permeated with the scent of marijuana.

2

Meanwhile, Murry knew nothing of his son's drug use. He was living in Whittier in a new, expensively decorated house with a circular driveway and an expansive view of the valley, purchased with the enormous publishing royalties that continued to flow in. The new house had a large music room, with an organ and piano, and a huge stained-glass window with a visual depiction of a "Sea of Tunes." Renovations on different areas of the house were continuous, just as they had been in Hawthorne. Curiously, Murry had bought Audree her own home just around the corner from his. This was a kind of stalemate separation; Audree and Murry loved each other, but they could no longer live together. Even after spending the day with Murry, Audree would go to her own house to sleep. After a trip to Japan, Murry hired a Japanese secretary, which raised a few eyebrows—friends referred to her as his "geisha."

After recovering from the blow of being fired, Murry decided the ultimate proof that he had "made" the Beach Boys would be to do it again without them. "Those ungrateful little bastards," he told friends. "I'll start a group that will be bigger and better than the Beach Boys." That group was a bunch of teenage musicians who had gone to Hollywood Professional School with Carl—Eddie Madora and Marty DiGiovanni, and their friend Rick Henn, who went to Uni High. Murry named them the Sunrays and taught them how to harmonize by giving each a tone to sing and making them practice vocalizing it for hours. He hired professional song arranger Don Ralke to arrange songs for them, and he pulled strings to obtain a recording contract, which enabled the Sunrays to be distributed on Capitol's subsidiary label, Tower Records. "Murry wanted us to be a Beach Boys clone group," Henn said. He even wanted the Sunrays to tour with the Beach Boys and be their exclusive opening act, but the Beach Boys objected so vociferously that Murry dropped the idea. He told them, "Hey, after all I did for your careers you're going to shit on me like that?"

Murry took his new band on a "station tour" to introduce them to all the disc jockeys he had met through the Beach Boys. At each station he gave the disc jockey a little present of costume jewelry. He made the Sunrays rehearse a few bars from the classic song "Still," and insisted they sing at every station, changing the lyrics to include the station's call letters: "We love you KBOZ." When the Sunrays objected to this corny approach, Murry returned gruffly, "You boys are getting very big-headed."

The Sunrays' first singles, released in March 1965, were straight rip-offs of the Beach Boys popular car songs. "Car Party" and "Outta Gas" had music and lyrics written by Murry, of course. The songs got little local airplay and were generally ignored, but the next single, "I Live for the Sun," released in June 1965, took off and made the charts. Written by Murry and produced by Ralke and Murry, "I Live for the Sun" was a local top-ten hit. But the Sunrays' next song, "Andrea," made a weak showing. Murry and the Sunrays put out four more, increasingly obscure singles into 1966.

Murry wouldn't let the group play in Los Angeles proper because he claimed they would become "jaded by the Hollywood scene" that he hated so much. "The only time we ever performed in Hollywood," said Rick Henn, "was at the Hollywood Bowl with the Beach Boys, and they resented the shit out of that." According to Henn, "Somebody sabotaged the gig." There was a circular stage, and after the previous group, the Lovin' Spoonful, finished playing, the Sunrays began to set up their equipment. Suddenly, the huge circular stage began to revolve. One of the guitar players got his leg caught, and it was almost cut off. The rest of the group jumped off the stage just in time. They did a forty-five-minute gig with only fifteen minutes' worth of songs. "It was a real nightmare."

"Still," released in January 1966, became the Sunrays' last record. By then they were perceived as a dying group, and were relegated to tours of roller rinks that Murry booked for them in the northwest. "It was embarrassing as hell," Henn said. "The tours were happening less and less, and everybody looked down on us as Beach Boys clones."

One day, when things looked particularly bad, Murry ditched the Sunrays. He said, "That's it, boys. I can't help you any more, you're on your own."

"I think he just abandoned us because he knew that it was a sinking ship," Henn said.

Not long after Murry left the Sunrays, they were booked into one of the Hollywood clubs Murry despised. Murry heard about the booking and called Henn on the phone. "I knew as soon as I left you, you would go Hollywood," he said.

3

The Beach Boys' first single of 1965, "Do You Wanna Dance?," performed admirably on the charts, reaching number 12 in its eight-week run, although it broke no new ground musically. The album it came from, *The Beach Boys Today!*, was the first album Brian was able to produce without any road activity. The increased polish and depth of his production techniques showed clearly. However, the album was not one of Brian's best works, consisting mostly of a mélange of uninspired car tunes and even a comedy cut with the voice of Earl Leaf discussing kosher pickles. Good times for the group would not return until April, when Capitol released the single "Help Me, Rhonda" (featured on *The Beach Boys Today!* in a longer, sloppier version). This song was a wonderful Brian Wilson composition, an irresistible sing-along in which a spurned young man beseeches his new girl, Rhonda, to "help me get her out of my heart." Complemented by Brian's falsettos and Mike's "wop-wop-wop" bass line, the song was a smash hit, logging fourteen weeks on the chart, and becoming the Beach Boys' second number 1 single.

On July 5, 1965, Capitol released the Beach Boys' *Summer Days (And Summer Nights!!)* album. This so-called "quickie" album, which Capitol pressured them into as a follow-up to the smash hit "Help Me, Rhonda," was recorded in April through June of that year. A single from this LP, "California Girls," became one of the more remarkable and enduring hits of Brian's career and a solid, number 3 chartbuster. Throughout the next several decades this musical ode to California beauty was used as the background for countless TV commercials and jingles, and became a major hit for David Lee Roth in 1985.

> Well, East Coast girls are hip
> I really dig those styles they wear
> And the Southern girls with the way they talk
> They knock me out when I'm down there
> The Midwest farmers' daughters really make you
>   feel all right
> And the Northern girls with the way they kiss
> They keep their boyfriends warm at night
> I wish they all could be California
> Wish they all could be California
> I wish they all could be California girls

Despite Brian's tremendous musical accomplishments, the shadow of the Beatles had fallen across him, obscuring any pleasure he may have felt. To make it worse, Brian loved the Beatles' music and was in awe of their musical progression. The Beatles were now on Brian Epstein's promised summer assault, playing sellout shows as they toured the country. On the liner notes of the *Summer Days (And Summer Nights!!)* album, Brian mentions that he's writing at a coffee table in the living room, while his friends are sitting around singing Beatles songs.

Brian was to include three Beatles songs ("I Should Have Known Better," "You've Got to Hide Your Love Away," and "Tell Me Why") on the next LP, *Beach Boys Party!*, which Brian decided should be recorded live. So as not to make the album just another concert LP, they recorded it at a "party" that the Beach Boys conducted in the studio.

This superb album was recorded in several different sessions. It included background sounds recorded at an actual party held at Mike's house, and later, freewheeling vocal sessions at Western's studio 2, where the Beach Boys' wives, girl friends, and friends were present. Down the hall at another studio, Jan and Dean were having their own recording session, and stopped in to say hello. "They were all sitting around trying to think of another song to do," reported Dean Torrance. "So they asked me what I wanted to sing. I said 'Barbara Ann' [a song written by Fred Fassert that Jan and Dean had done on one of their own albums a few years before], for what reason I don't remember." Although Jan and Dean had been forbidden by their own company to perform on other records, with the threat of having their royalties held up, Dean helped out on the session anyway. At the end of "Barbara Ann" Carl's voice can be heard saying, "Thank you, Dean"; and indeed, Dean's suggestion turned into a tremendous international hit. As Dean said, it took just "three minutes to cut a huge, best-selling record." Released in November of that year, "Barbara Ann" reached number 2 on the American charts. The *Beach Boys Party!* album reached number 6 and spent a well-deserved six months on the charts, boosted in small part by Capitol's promotional ploy of preparing one million bags of potato chips with reproductions of the cover of *The Beach Boys Party!* on them, which they supplied to record dealers, to be given away with the purchase of an album.

The *Beach Boys Party!* album spawned another new beginning. Mike Love met his second wife at the session. Mike had been seeing a girl named Pam Rexroad, who invited a girl friend, Suzanne Belcher, to the session. Suzanne was a stunning young woman—a seventeen-year-old San Fernando Valley College student with dark hair and eyes, and a gorgeous figure. The girls had been promised a real party, but when they got to the studios, they were surprised to find a rather sterile atmosphere. Mike went across the street and came back with a couple of cases of beer and wine and some potato chips. By the time the session was over, Mike had asked Suzanne for her phone number. At the time, Suzanne had a steady boyfriend in the National Guard and she refused Mike's requests to date her. She finally accepted when Mike asked her to join him for lunch with the Beach Boys' booking agent, Irving Granz, who would allegedly help Suzanne get a job at the William Morris Agency. No job was ever offered during lunch, but Suzanne was hooked. Mike was charming, funny, and attentive. On the way back from lunch, they drove to Malibu to look for a piece of property for Mike to buy. At the end of the date, Mike bought Suzanne a carton of cigarettes as a gift—a gesture that would soon take on ironic significance.

Some thought it was a little soon for Mike to find a new love. Only recently divorced, he was still involved in a messy paternity suit that had come to public light a few months earlier. On March 25, 1965, the story had hit the front page of section D of the Los Angeles *Herald Examiner*. A pathetic photograph showed a twenty-two-year-old secretary, Shannon Harris, holding her three-month-old daughter, Shawn. That day Miss Harris had charged in a paternity action before Superior Court Commissioner Frank B. Stoddard that Mike Love had fathered her child. Harris, with long dark hair down to her shoulders and dressed in a herringbone suit, held the little baby in her arms as she told the commissioner that she had first met Mike two years before, on March 25, 1963, and they celebrated their meeting exactly one year later by "engaging in a romantic interlude," according to the published report.

Mike reportedly admitted he had made love to Shannon Harris, and that he sent her certain love letters (which were not produced in court), but he denied that he was the father. Shannon Harris's attorney, Jack Ritter, asked for temporary child support and medical expenses pending the paternity trial. But Mike Love and his attorney, George E. Wise, alleged that there were other men in Harris's life and that Mike's relationship with her had ended before he could have fathered the child. After the initial publicity, the case died down, and Mike reportedly settled the suit by giving the child a few hundred dollars a year in support plus the right to use the name Love when she was eighteen. The paternity suit was eventually forgotten, and none of the group ever expected the subject to come up again.

The incident didn't slow down Mike's new relationship with Suzanne Belcher. After only two dates and ten days of knowing each other—with Mike bragging he had $70,000 in the bank— he asked Suzanne to marry him. They flew to Las Vegas on October 15, 1965, where they were quietly married. Then Mike had to rush home for a Beach Boys appearance on "The Andy Williams Show." Mike took his new bride with him and the rest of the Beach Boys on a long Asian tour, which included Japan, Hong Kong, and Honolulu.

With the other Beach Boys gone, Brian started work on a new album, which would turn out to be the watershed of his career.

4

Late in 1965 Brian Wilson heard the newest Beatles album, *Rubber Soul*. "I was sitting around a table with friends, smoking a joint," Brian said, "when we heard *Rubber Soul* for the very first time, and I'm smoking and I'm getting high, and the album blew my mind because it was a whole album with all good stuff! It flipped me out so much I said, 'I'm gonna try that, where a whole album becomes a *gas*.'"

Brian went into the kitchen and told Marilyn, "I'm going to make the greatest rock-and-roll album ever made."

Almost immediately Brian began composing small fragments of mood music, which he called "feelings." As the bits and pieces began to fit together, he thought about finding a lyricist for the new album. One thing was certain—he didn't want to use Mike Love. Since retiring from the road, Brian had begun to put more distance between himself and the rest of the group. Once again, Brian found an outside lyricist. His choice this time was as peculiar as it was fortunate. He called on one of the bright young men he had met at Loren Schwartz's house, Tony Asher. When they first met, Asher had been a fledgling songwriter trying to peddle his songs. "In those days," Asher said, "everybody would play their songs at the piano. For some reason, I played a couple of tunes for Brian." Brian must have been very impressed, because now, a year and a half later, he tracked Asher down by getting his number from Loren Schwartz. By this time Asher had given up the music business and was writing copy for an advertising company, Carson/Roberts, whose clients included Gallo wines. "I was really just interested in a regular income," he said. "I am a pretty conservative guy."

At first Asher thought it was a joke when somebody told him Brian Wilson was on the phone for him. Brian was in something of a panic; the pressure was on from Capitol, which was eager for a new album. There had been no new material since the *Beach Boys Party!* LP, and Capitol was anxious to keep the flow going. There was reportedly the threat of a lawsuit if Brian didn't produce another album soon. "We were supposed to have done it months ago," he told Asher, "and I haven't even started it. I've done only one or two tunes and I hate them. How would you like to write some tunes for me?"

"You could have knocked me over with a feather," Asher said later. "That was like saying, 'How'd you like twenty-five thousand dollars?'" Asher managed to wrangle a three-week leave of absence from his advertising agency, and began the task of writing the lyrics for what would become one of the greatest albums in pop-music history.

The next Monday morning Asher drove his 356 Porsche up to Laurel Way, expecting Brian to be ready to go to work. Instead, Brian was in bed. It took most of the day to get Brian up and at the piano, with Marilyn supplying a steady flow of food from the kitchen. Asher realized the album was going to take longer than three weeks. He thought Brian was a nice guy, but something of a Hawthorne hick, who found it next to impossible to express himself verbally. Sometimes Brian's lack of sophistication manifested itself in small ways, such as ordering only shrimp cocktail and steak no matter where they ate, for fear of experimenting with other foods. Other times, his childishness was more pronounced, as when he halted work to watch "Flipper" on TV and wept at the tender moments. Asher found Brian's life-style—in bed till noon, then kibitzing around the house for hours—extremely difficult to take. "The only times I actually enjoyed myself or even got comfortable with Brian was when I was standing by the piano working with him. Otherwise I felt hideous!

"I wish I could say he was totally committed. Let's say he was...um, very *concerned*. But the thing was, Brian Wilson has to be the single most irresponsible person I've ever met in my life." Asher remembers uncashed royalty checks totaling over $100,000 lying around the house. When word got out that Asher was working with Brian, he began to receive phone calls from frantic attorneys and from Broadcast Music Industries (which collected Brian's royalties) begging him to get Brian to sign papers or return phone calls.

Brian's increasing use of drugs compounded his erratic behavior. Asher remembers that he would often lose control while listening to playbacks of his own music, and would go from hysterical laughter to crying jags. "He had fits of this just uncontrollable anger. Then he'd fall apart and start crying during playbacks of certain tracks. ... What I saw appalled me," Asher said. "I remember how he interacted with women, the kinds of sexual fantasies he would talk about, and his apparent need to get involved with Marilyn's sister, Diane. He openly discussed the conflicts he was feeling ... not knowing whether he loved Diane more than Marilyn ... could it be possible he loved them both, could it be possible that he had married the wrong one. ... "

One day Loren Schwartz brought some hashish to Brian's house and they decided to make hash brownies. "We got this brownie mix and put the hash in," Asher said. "Loren was in charge. The question was, 'How much do we put in?' We had been smoking some and our judgment was already off. We put half in and then we put some more in, and then we ended up putting it all in. We cooked it up and put them on a tray, and in the meanwhile we smoked more dope and ate three brownies each. They tasted great—when you're stoned brownies are hard to resist. Forty-five seconds later we said, 'It's not working yet,' so we each had four more. ... We started to get so stoned it was terrifying. I really thought we were going to die. There was a tapestry above the fireplace with a medieval embroidered bird and the bird just took right off and started flying across the room. I was hallucinating and I was petrified. I was on an elevator going up fast, and I had the sense that I was only a fourth of the way up. We all piled into a car and drove to a Mexican restaurant. How we got there alive, I don't know. ... "

Asher wrote most of the actual lyrics for the new album, called *Pet Sounds*, although all of the songs were based on Brian's concepts. During work sessions Asher would make up "dummy" words while they were composing, and rewrite real lyrics on his own at night. The next day he would come in and Brian would decide whether he liked them or not. In a few instances, Asher contributed to the music too, as in "Caroline No," "I Just Wasn't Made for These Times," and "That's Not Me."

Although the songs Asher wrote on *Pet Sounds* are credited equally, Asher hardly got equal compensation for his efforts. When Brian first asked Asher to help him with the album, Asher didn't bother to ask about royalties. After all, it was a great honor to be asked to collaborate with Brian no matter what the royalty arrangement was. Asher was well aware that royalties between lyricist and composer were split fifty-fifty; at that time the standard royalty rate was two cents to the publishers and one cent split between lyricist and composer. But when the album was finished and Asher discussed the matter with Brian, he was surprised to hear Brian claim, "I wrote all the music." Asher was sent to Murry to work out the details. Tony Asher's summation of Murry was this: "I've got to say that he came across to me as a really sick man. Pathetically so, in fact." Asher wasn't going to argue, and simply agreed to one-quarter of a percent. Over the years, he earned an estimated $60,000 from his work on the album.

Pet Sounds is the first album on which none of the Beach Boys played instruments. Diane Rovell was hired to be Brian's production secretary, and set about hiring the finest session musicians in the industry to play on the album. Brian would write the musical arrangements himself, and start each song with the basic tracks. Most of the recording for *Pet Sounds* was done "live"—that is, the instruments and musicians were assembled at one time in a studio where the music was played in ensemble, instead of having each instrument on a single track to be mixed together later. "Brian was producer, writer, and arranger," engineer Jim Lockert said.

Brian would occasionally play tracks over the long-distance phone lines for Michael in Japan, and when the other members

of the group returned to L.A., they found that most of the tracks
were complete. Brian was ready for them to plug in their vocals—and they didn't like it. They objected to Brian's precon-
ceived notion of what the vocals should sound like. Mike Love
reportedly considered this Brian's "ego" music. But Brian held
firm; *Pet Sounds* was *his* masterpiece. "It took some getting
used to," Alan Jardine admitted. "When we left the country,
we were just a surfing group. This was a whole new thing."
The vocal tracks were arduous to lay down, and Brian made
them work harder than ever to perfect them. Mike hated Brian's
role as taskmaster. "Who's gonna hear this?" he asked. "The
ears of a dog? But Brian had those kind of ears, so I said, 'Okay,
we'll do it another time.' Every voice in its resonance and
tonality and timbre had to be right. Then the next day he might
throw it out and have us do it over again." Brian even brought
in outside singers, including Terry Melcher, to work on some
of the tracks. He would sometimes let the group do the vocals
the way they wanted, then, after they left the studio, he would
wipe the vocals off completely and finish the track himself,
since he could sing all the parts.

At the unheard-of cost of $70,000 for production, *Pet Sounds*
was brilliant—not only for its innovation, but for its melancholy innocence. A searching album about growing up and
the pain involved in the realities of adulthood, *Pet Sounds* is
introverted, thoughtful, and childishly curious. There is something odd about the album, lonely and alienated. The tone of
the album went beyond sensitive into a realm of something
nearly pathetic—the whimper of a tortured young mind. *Pet
Sounds* caused critic Nik Cohn to write years later that Brian
wrote "sad songs about loneliness and heartache. Sad songs
even about happiness." Critic Richard Goldstein later noted,
"Everyone sang about loneliness as though it came from disappointment in love. But Brian sang about it as an active pursuit."

The titles alone could be woven into a psychodrama about
Brian's state of mind at the time: "Don't Talk (Put Your Head
on My Shoulder)," "Let's Go Away for Awhile," "God Only
Knows," "I Just Wasn't Made for These Times," and "That's
Not Me." The songs for the most part were under three minutes.

Many remain classics of their kind. "Wouldn't It Be Nice," in particular, is a song expressing the longing for the age when one could do what one wanted, get married, have children—and stay overnight together. "God Only Knows,"* was perhaps the most beautiful, a song about the love felt for someone who transforms life for you. ("God only knows where I'd be without you....") There was also "Caroline No," a song about a young girl who personifies Brian's loss of innocence.† The album ends with a remarkably forlorn and melancholy sound effect, Brian's two dogs barking in the faraway distance and the fading sound of a lonely railroad train. The title *Pet Sounds* was Mike's contribution, suggested in the hallway of Western Records while they were adding the vocals.

This was Brian's first fully realized album. When it was finished, he brought it home, put it on the stereo, and lay down with Marilyn in bed. "Oh boy, he was just so proud of it," Marilyn recalled. "People weren't ready for it—it was too much of a shock, but a lot of people who understood it really loved it."

5

Before they even heard *Pet Sounds*, the older, conservative executives at Capitol were becoming increasingly worried about Brian's erratic behavior and the apparent dissension within the group. Nik Venet, who was still Capitol's liaison to the Beach Boys, found Brian's behavior extraordinarily vexing. At one Capitol meeting, Brian arrived with a set of eight cassette tapes made in loops. Each tape repeated a simple phrase over and over again, like, "No comment," or "I like that idea." Venet also remembers running into Marilyn and Diane at a music-business party on the lawn of a producer in Beverly Hills. Brian was sequestered somewhere inside the house, and Marilyn kept saying, "Brian really wants to speak to you. Don't leave without seeing him." Venet waited half an hour. Brian

---

*At first Brian was nervous about including the word God in the title, which had never been done in a pop song before.

†Obviously written for Carol Mountain, although Marilyn claims it was written for her.

came out and said, "Don't go yet, I want to talk to you," and then disappeared back inside the house. Half an hour later Brian came out of the house again and said, "Don't go yet, I want to see you," and disappeared a second time. Venet eventually gave up and left.

One day Brian called the executives at Capitol and told them he had a new single for immediate release, a brilliant single they would love. He showed up at the offices with a tape of "Caroline No," the song that would close the *Pet Sounds* album, just before the barking dogs and fading sound of the train. Although "Caroline No" was a beautiful song, the people at Capitol knew it was not a hit. Yet, hoping to encourage Brian to complete his forthcoming album, they released the song on March 7, while "Barbara Ann" was still on the top of the charts. As they expected, "Caroline No" peaked at 32 on April 30.*

After nearly ten months of preparation on *Pet Sounds*, the executives at Capitol were unsure whether Brian would finish his new album on time for a scheduled release—or finish it at all. They prepared a "best of" compilation package for release instead. According to Nik Venet, the schedule of this album had absolutely nothing to do with whether or not they would like the forthcoming *Pet Sounds*. Capitol's only concern was to keep up the flow of Beach Boys product. When the chief executives at Capitol finally heard *Pet Sounds*, they didn't like it at all. There were no cars, no blondes in bikinis, no beach. They heard no single, no commercial hits. Their first reaction was to refuse to release it. "I thought Brian was screwing up," Venet said. "He was no longer looking to make records, he was looking for attention from the business." Most of all, Venet saw *Pet Sounds* as a very specific way of getting back at Murry. "He was trying to torment his father with songs his father couldn't relate to and melody structures his father couldn't understand."

On March 23, 1966, just two weeks after the release of the unsuccessful "Caroline No," Capitol chose to release the song "Sloop John B.," from the *Pet Sounds* album, as a single. Although Brian and the Beach Boys liked the song, they had little

---

*This is the only Beach Boys song released credited as a "Brian Wilson Single."

faith that it would become a major hit. "Sloop John B." was a traditional folk song arranged by Brian, and the only song on the album suggested by another member of the group—Al Jardine. Much to everyone's surprise, the single shot up the charts, making giant leaps from 112, to 68, to 38, to 13, 8, 4, and finally on May 7, to number 3. Luckily for Brian, this was a month-long period when not one Beatles single appeared on the charts.

The entire *Pet Sounds* album was unveiled to the world on May 16. It was the first Beach Boys album without striped shirts and surfing or automobiles on the cover. On the front were photographs, taken at the San Diego Zoo, of the boys dressed in cardigan sweaters and feeding goats. The back showed them dressed in traditional Japanese regalia in pictures taken on their recent Asian tour. Statistically, *Pet Sounds* didn't do too badly—it spent a total of thirty-nine weeks on the charts, peaking at number 11 only five weeks after its release, with well over half a million units sold. Although the musical cognoscenti, including important disc jockeys, felt that *Pet Sounds* was a masterpiece, for the most part the public was confused and disappointed in it except for "Sloop John B." The Capitol executives were right about one thing—the public expected a particular kind of song from the Beach Boys, and none of those songs were present on the album. However, *Pet Sounds* found its own special audience—a growing number of disenfranchised, lost, and sensitive people throughout America. To them the album became the theme music for a time of painful transition. In England the reviews and reception for *Pet Sounds* were nearly ecstatic. But at home, *Pet Sounds* was considered a loser.

Capitol didn't even bother to promote *Pet Sounds*. Instead, the advertising thrust and sales force went into the "best of" compilation package. "[*Pet Sounds*] was probably ahead of its time," said Al Couri, head of promotion, "and yet it didn't sell. The retail activity was not as good as previous Beach Boys albums." Only eight weeks after the release of Brian's precious *Pet Sounds* LP, Capitol released *The Best of the Beach Boys*, which quickly went gold. "You've got to understand that Brian was so impulsive, compulsive, you never knew what was coming next," Venet said. "The 'Best of' package was put together while Brian was working on *Pet Sounds*. There was a great love at the time of Beach Boys product.... There were [salesmen] out there that could sell Beach Boys product and the [customers] were asking for it. The *Pet Sounds* album was supposed to be ready a long time before, and it wasn't going to be ready. The whole company was geared up to the 'best of' package. Everything had been locked in, magazine advertising, the separations for the cover had been printed and stacked in a warehouse." *The Best of the Beach Boys* compilation far outshone *Pet Sounds* in terms of sales, with a total of seventy-nine weeks on the charts, topping out at number 8 on October 24, 1966.

6

By this time the Beach Boys had already left the accounting firm of Cummings and Currant and had signed with one of the big powerhouse business-management companies in Los Angeles, Julius Lefkowitz and Company, whose offices were located in the CEIR Building at 9171 Wilshire Boulevard. Lefkowitz's brother Nat was president of the William Morris Agency in New York, and the Lefkowitz company in Los Angeles handled many elite literary and show-business clients, including James Michener, Gregory Peck, Danny Thomas, and Danny Kaye, as well as several music groups, such as Buffalo Springfield and Sonny and Cher, giving the company access to approximately $500 million in funds. Lefkowitz, around fifty at the time, was a smart and savvy businessman, whose approach with the Beach Boys was to make long-term investments with the short-term spurts of income they were experiencing. But the Beach Boys were hard personalities to deal with, and spent their money as they pleased, accumulating an array of expensive cars and homes. In fact, Lefkowitz assigned a full-time employee in the accounting department, Stanley Shapiro, to keep track of his clients' "rolling stock," or automobiles, of which the Beach Boys collectively owned twenty-six at this point. "People like the Beach Boys were a pain in the ass," Shapiro said, "because no matter what they had, they didn't want to give up dollars and cents for investments. They preferred to spend it on toys." According to Catherine Pace, who worked as the Beach Boys' bookkeeper during that period, "The boys were like children... and they would do crazy things," including never being on time for meetings with Julius Lefkowitz. "You can't be Beach Boys all your lives," Lefkowitz told them, but they didn't want to hear that.

The accountant in charge of their portfolio at Lefkowitz was Nick Grillo, a young, industrious fellow in his late twenties. Grillo was a clever businessman who had an easygoing rapport with the Beach Boys and a tremendous appreciation of their music. He was more interested in personal management than in straight investment, and early in 1966 Mike Love suggested that Grillo leave Lefkowitz and become their personal business manager. "As part of the deal," Grillo said, "they would fund whatever the costs were in terms of personnel, and I would have a staff composed of an accounting side and a personal-management side. I would oversee their entire operation. For this I would get X number of dollars a year, plus a percentage of the override, but they would be responsible for funding the day-to-day activity." The Beach Boys were already dealing with a concert-promotion company called American Productions. Retaining the name, Grillo took charge of concert promotion, as well as of all the Beach Boys' business finances. Grillo and the Beach Boys opened up spanking-new offices on the eighth floor of a new tower at 9000 Sunset Boulevard.

The 9000 building was seething with rock and show-business management firms, representing groups such as Paul Revere and the Raiders and the Byrds. Directly across the hall from the Beach Boys' new offices, Derek Taylor, one of the most famous publicists in the business, moved in. Taylor was famous for one act, and one act only—the Beatles. He had met them early in his career as a journalist from a Manchester newspaper, wrote about them often, and was finally signed on by their manager, Brian Epstein, as press officer. He had left the Beatles the previous year, and set up his own publicity company in Los Angeles. Taylor had a great capacity for alcohol and marijuana, as well as a reputation as a kind of psychedelic visionary. In a world where publicity was considered so much hot air, Taylor was extraordinarily talented. He was blessed with charm, wit, and intelligence. Journalists loved him, and the feeling was mutual. Taylor was able to convey a message about the groups he handled better than anyone else. The Beach Boys quickly became his clients. Ironically, Taylor's famed connection to the Beatles was most important to the Beach Boys.

Taylor first got to know Brian and the Beach Boys during the preparation of *Pet Sounds*, and many consider Derek Taylor's influential word in England to be the cornerstone for the album's success there. "I lived in Hollywood then," Derek said, "but my British links were strong, and with *Pet Sounds* out and the Beatles increasingly flattering about the Beach Boys ... and with [a new single] on the way, we started to pump information into England about this tremendous band, with their new plateau. Soon everyone was saying 'genius,' and the beauty of it, as with the beauty of anything, was that it was true."

"Genius" thus became the adjective now constantly applied to Brian Wilson, a tag he began to carry with great weight. Throughout the Los Angeles music-business community, Brian was suddenly considered a "genius," despite the failure of *Pet Sounds* on his home turf. Brian became determined to prove the appellation accurate. His next single, he felt, would vindicate the failure of *Pet Sounds*. It was a single he was especially enthusiastic about. Truly the work of a "genius," it was a song he called a "pocket symphony." Its title: "Good Vibrations."

> *The smile that you send*
> *out returns to you.*
>   Indian wisdom

> *I think it's a real tragedy.*
>   DAVID ANDERLE
>   *on* Smile

Eight

1

The Age of Aquarius had come to Los Angeles.

Everywhere you turned was a new breed of teenager collectively known as hippies. Bearded, barefoot, bedecked in bells and beads and bell-bottom trousers, they were as ubiquitous as they were hairy. In San Francisco the hippies had settled mainly in the Haight-Ashbury district; in Los Angeles they had invaded the Sunset Strip directly below Beverly Hills, and *Time* magazine reported "Hippiedom has transplanted Shangri-La a go-go."

Indeed, the former teen mecca of Sunset Strip had become a hippie haven. Good-bye prosperity; hello peace, flowers, and LSD. The stores up and down the Strip that had catered just a few years before to affluent young teenagers were now replaced with "head shops," dimly lit, incense-scented stores that sold drug paraphernalia, day-glo posters, and hand-strung beaded necklaces. Expensive clothing boutiques gave way to shops filled with tie-dyed T-shirts, bell-bottom pants, and wide-ribbed corduroys. There was a surfeit of all-night health-food restaurants, motels with hour-long rates for swingers—called "hot-sheet" motels—and a new dance club, the Trip, where the glowing dance floor was called an "infinity space." Signs in the windows of more establishment restaurants implored NO BARE FEET. Along the strip, on the concrete median that separated east and west traffic, the hippies sold their wares: necklaces, incense, and a radical "underground" newspaper called the *L.A. Free Press*. Love was free too, as a new era of

153

promiscuity was ushered in, with sex becoming a gesture of friendliness. Vocabulary changed drastically. The exclamantion "Wow!" became an all-purpose word, and everyone was called "man." Hippies no longer slept, they "crashed," usually coming down from drugs. People didn't get nervous, they were "uptight," and when the "narcs" arrested you, you were "busted." Soon the freewheeling bikers joined the hippies on the strip, with their Harley-Davidson motorcycles, Nazi regalia, and cutoff denim jackets.

Here was the rub for the Beach Boys: The new hippie movement was almost exclusively white; the blacks were already disenchanted, remaining outside of society. *Time* had only a year before reported that the Beach Boys were the only "white" (-sounding) pop band—almost all others were a blend of R&B, or English with R&B roots. Simply put, Brian Wilson's entire audience of affluent white middle-class kids had been swept away in a wave of change. Gone completely were the trappings of the classic California life-style, the sun-bleached surfers and expensive cars. Now the badge of honor was awarded to the poor, to those living in socialist communes. Overnight, surf and car music was dead, and *Pet Sounds*'s gloomy introversion was of little help. Overnight, the Beach Boys were suddenly the epitome of square.

The new social wave was galvanized into a cohesive force by opposition to the growing war in Vietnam. Moreover, rock music was now being written as much for content as for entertainment. A new magazine published in San Francisco, *Rolling Stone* (whose first issue included a free roach clip), coalesced the idea that rock musicians were modern-day minstrels, responsible for delivering socially relevant messages. They wrote anti-establishment, antiwar, pro-love songs, and songs that spoke of the magic of drugs. San Francisco was a hot bed of this kind of music, and a local promoter named Bill Graham had converted an old dance hall called the Fillmore into a showplace for groups with strange and alluring names: the Grateful Dead, Big Brother and the Holding Company, the Jefferson Airplane, Iron Butterfly. On glorious sunny Sundays, Golden Gate Park was the site of free concerts and mass love gatherings called "be-ins."

By mid-1966 the hippies of Sunset Boulevard had formed an alliance against what seemed an obvious enemy—the Los Angeles Police Department. In their leather boots and military-like uniforms the police were formidable opponents. At the behest of a local councilman, who claimed the strip was "a dangerous powder keg, ready to explode," a 10:00 P.M. curfew was issued for anyone under eighteen. Each night the LAPD cruisers would roll down the broad boulevard with loudspeakers, announcing, "Attention, it is now past ten P.M. and anyone under eighteen years of age will be arrested." American International Pictures began production on a film called *Riot on Sunset Strip*. But the confrontations on Sunset Boulevard were no joke, aggravating the growing youth unrest. When real-estate developers announced plans to tear down Pandora's Box, which had become a symbol of the hippie culture, the tension brimmed over. Led by Chief William Parker and Sheriff Peter Pitchess, the leather-booted, jodhpur-clad police formed a "flying wedge" on Sunset Boulevard and mowed down the hippies, who were armed only with flowers and beads.

In response, Jim Dickson, manager of the Byrds, formed an organization called Community Action for Fact and Freedom, or CAFF. Backed by some of the major recording artists of the day, CAFF took space for its headquarters in the office of the Beach Boys' publicist, Derek Taylor. But the Beach Boys were not drawn into the fray, perhaps because the group at this time was almost continuously on tour, away from Los Angeles. More important, they were locked in a time warp—1959 in 1966. Still wearing striped shirts, indulging in expensive cars, clothes, and the joys of young women on the road, the Beach Boys had no social consciousness. Only Brian was provoked and fascinated by what was happening around him, and actively sought to include himself in the "scene."

One prominent member of CAFF was David Anderle, a tall, handsome young man whom the underground papers referred to as "the Mayor of Hip." Twenty-eight years old, Anderle was clever and industrious, with a superior business sense. Born in east L.A. and raised in Inglewood, he attended the University of Southern California drama school and then went to work at MGM records, where he signed the handsome singer

Danny Hutton as well as Frank Zappa and The Mothers of Invention. By 1966, Anderle had left MGM and was managing Danny Hutton. Meanwhile, Hutton had met Brian in the studios, and together they had produced a single called "The Farmer's Daughter" for a quickly forgotten group called Basil Swift and the Seegrams. Brian remained a lifelong fan of Hutton's, and the two became close friends.

Coincidentally, David Anderle had met the Wilson family years before, when his cousin, Bill Bloom, became friendly with the younger Wilson boys in Hawthorne. Anderle met Brian again around the time of *The Beach Boys Today!* album, when someone brought him up to the house on Laurel Way. "It was very groovy," Anderle said. "I really liked Brian right away... because there was something there that I had not seen in many people in my lifetime. And [then] I was out again." A year later, Danny Hutton took Anderle to Brian's house, where Brian had finally finished his forthcoming masterpiece, "Good Vibrations."

At a reported cost of more than $50,000, this three-minute-and-thirty-five-second song was recorded over a period of six months, using ninety hours of tape in nearly twenty different sessions at four different studios: Western, RCA, Gold Star, and Columbia. There was a host of new sounds on the recordings: cello, fuzz bass, clarinet, harp, and a strange new instrument called the Theramin, which made an eerie, wailing sound and was traditionally used in horror films. "We had a slew of musicians working on it," remembered Chuck Britz, who engineered the song. There were still no lyrics, although Tony Asher had written several verses for it while working on *Pet Sounds* with Brian.

Brian had long been concerned about "vibrations" of different sorts. He first heard the word from his mother, who tried to explain why dogs bark at certain people and feel comfortable with others. "My mother used to tell me about vibrations, and I didn't really understand too much of what she meant when I was a boy. It scared me to death.... So we talked about good vibrations with the song and the idea, and we decided that on the one hand you could say... those are sensual things. And then you'd say, 'I'm picking up good vibrations,' which is a contrast against the sensual, the extrasensory perception that we have. That's what we're really talking about."

According to Chuck Britz, "Good Vibrations" virtually jelled in the first session, but as soon as the other Beach Boys heard it, they had suggestions and changes. Eventually, Mike Love was elected to write new lyrics. Unsure of himself, Brian listened to suggestions from every quarter and tinkered with the song. "There was a lot of 'Oh you can't do this, that's too modern' or 'That's going to be too long a record,'" said one observer. Under pressure from the rest of the group, Brian was never really happy with "Good Vibrations." When Mike Love first heard the song, he described it as "very heavy R&B...it sounded like Wilson Pickett would be recording it." At one point Brian gave a version to Capitol Records for release, then changed his mind the next day and took it back. Eventually, the song seemed like a problem with no answer. Discouraged and beleaguered, Brian put the track aside for a while and considered selling it to Warner Brothers as an R&B single.

When he played the song for David Anderle one night at Laurel Way, Anderle thought it was so beautiful, "it destroyed me." Later, on the way home in his car, Anderle couldn't get the song out of his mind. When he got home, he called Danny Hutton. He suggested to Danny that the track might be right for him. The next day Anderle called Brian and asked him to sell the track for Hutton to record. Anderle's enthusiasm for the cut changed Brian's mind and made him decide to finish it, and also cemented one of Brian's most important friendships—Anderle was now his New Best Friend.

"Good Vibrations" became the Beach Boys' biggest hit to date, selling over 100,000 copies each day in its first week of release. In England it was an immediate smash, appearing on the charts at number 6 and leaping to number 1 a week later. A London *Sunday Express* headline proclaimed, THEY'VE FOUND A NEW SOUND AT LAST! Within a few weeks, the Beach Boys topped the *New Musical Express* readers' poll as the most popular group in England, one place ahead of the Beatles. In America, the reaction was less certain, but almost as good. "Good Vibrations" appeared on the charts at 81 on October 22, a week after its release, then jumped to 38, 17, 4 on November 12, and hung in at number 2 for three weeks. On December 10, like a giant Christmas gift, the song hit number 1.

Yet from then on in, it was all downhill.

2

David Anderle, Brian's New Best Friend, was a conduit to the new hip society emerging in the L.A. recording business. Brian's circle of friends enlarged to encompass a whole new crowd. Some of these people were "drainers," whom a close observer at the time remembers as "the usual trailings of sycophants trying to get close to power. Like white on rice, like a cheap suit, they were all over the place." But some of these followers were talented and industrious and a few truly loved Brian, not just for his talent, but for his naïveté and warm generosity. Among these people were Brian's longtime friend Lou Adler, who had recently produced the Mamas and the Papas; Terry Melcher—the blond, moustachioed son of Doris Day and boyfriend of ingenue Candice Bergen—who was a record producer for the Byrds and Paul Revere and the Raiders; Jules Siegel, a gifted writer covering the music business for the *Saturday Evening Post*, who had written a well-received piece on Bob Dylan; Michael Vosse, a warm, articulate friend of Anderle's from the USC drama school, and a part-time stringer for Jules Siegel; and Paul J. Robbins, who wrote free-lance pieces for the *Los Angeles Free Press*. With this new cast of characters, the scene at Laurel Way turned into a creative caldron of ideas, drugs, and activity.

During this period Brian decided to redecorate his house. His new decorating ideas were in keeping with the time—at least the times of a rock star. He placed a call to Nick Grillo at the office and insisted that the den—where his grand piano now sat—be filled with several tons of sand, so that he could feel the sand under his feet as he composed. The next day carpenters arrived and built what amounted to a giant sandbox around the piano. Then a truck hauled several tons of sand up to the house and dumped it in. Soon afterward, the office got a call from a harried saleswoman in the children's department of a large store in Century City. The woman got the Beach Boys' bookkeeper, Catherine Pace, on the line and said, "I have a young man here who's crawling through our tree house. He wants to buy it and he says you will send me the money." The young man turned out to be Brian. Catherine Pace said she would send the money right away, and when the tree house was delivered to Laurel Way, Brian put it in the entryway of the house. You had to crawl through it to get inside.

Physical health took on sudden importance, and for the next week Brian decided that all the furniture should be moved out of the living room, and the floors lined with gym mats. An assortment of gym equipment was moved in, only to sit unused and dusty for months. Next, a portable, enclosed sauna was installed in the hallway just outside the living room. There was a small ventilation hole in the wall, and every now and then Brian would thump on the wall. Marilyn, who sat outside waiting for his signal, would blow marijuana smoke through the hole into Brian's mouth. Finally, in the room with the beautiful view of the city, a tent was erected consisting of nearly $30,000 worth of fabric. It had velvet floors, huge cushions, and an assortment of hookahs. The first time Brian went into the tent with his friends, they realized there was no ventilation, and it was so hot and stuffy they never used it again. Vegetables, too, were in vogue at Laurel Way—Brian wanted Marilyn to start a garden of organic vegetables and sell them to motorists through a window in the kitchen.

Brian's friend Terry Melcher lived in Beverly Hills at 10050 Cielo Drive in a huge, rented house with a beautiful manicured lawn where he often gave parties for the crème de la crème of the L.A. hip. On this emerald lawn, David Anderle and Terry Melcher introduced Brian to his next collaborator, Van Dyke Parks. Van Dyke had first met Terry Melcher at a recording session where he was hired to play the piano. Van Dyke was a short, elfin, young man with a brilliant mind and an unfailingly sarcastic sense of humor. He spoke in a torrent of punning, polysyllabic words, in sentences so melodious they were almost a musical leitmotif. The youngest of four sons of a Jungian psychiatrist from Pennsylvania, Van Dyke had originally come west as a child actor. After attending Carnegie Tech, he returned to California, where he lived at Seal Beach and occasionally worked at the Balboa Ballroom, a "folkie playing guitar in coffeehouses up and down the coast" as he put it. In the early sixties he met David Anderle at MGM, where he made an obscure record called "Sunshine." When Brian met Van Dyke at Terry Melcher's house, he was instantly fascinated by Van Dyke's golden tongue and sense of style.

"He called me up out of a clear blue sky and said, 'Let's write a tune together,'" Van Dyke said. Although flattered, Van Dyke was concerned. He had heard that Tony Asher had disassociated himself from Brian and the Beach Boys despite the critical praise he received for the *Pet Sounds* lyrics. "I think Tony Asher was a foil to Brian and that Brian wanted another foil when he asked me to write with him." At first Brian asked Van Dyke to finish the lyrics of the still incomplete "Good Vibrations," but Van Dyke didn't want to step into a muddled situation, and suggested they start afresh on Brian's next project. Brian explained that his next project, tentatively entitled *Dumb Angel*, was going to be a recording of such magnitude and encompassing vision that it would be bigger and better than *Pet Sounds*. It would be greater in scope than anything the public had ever heard—including the Beatles' latest LP, *Rubber Soul*, which had taken the recording industry by storm. Brian's new album would have threads of music interwined from song to song to fill a vast tapestry. The album would establish a new arena of accomplishment in the recording industry, or, as Brian put it, "I'm writing a teenage symphony to God." If Van Dyke decided to help, the lyrics could express the interests both of them had in American history, which the music would complement in a variety of forms, from campfire music to labor songs to western folk music and Latin jazz. Van Dyke couldn't resist.

The first time Van Dyke went to Laurel Way, he rode a small motorcycle he had managed to buy secondhand. He had no driver's license because he couldn't afford the fee. Indeed, the day Van Dyke and Brian had met at Terry Melcher's house, Van Dyke was penniless. "I was living in a garage apartment on Melrose near La Brea. I had no bathroom at the time, and I was vaulting the pay toilet at a Standard station around the corner. I was also using the bathroom of a hardware store." Van Dyke was the only one of Brian's acquaintances who was personally insulted by Brian's monetary indulgences. He was horrified by the piano in the sandbox. "It wasn't funny, a grand piano set in a sandbox. I found it offensive. Absolutely repugnant." As for the tent, "I didn't understand how so much farbic could be spent like that. My father was a heavy Calvinist, and economic propriety and frugality never left me."

When Brian learned how poor Van Dyke was he immediately got on the phone with Murry, who was still handling the Beach Boys' publishing. "I've got a guy here named Van Dyke Parks who's a wonderful worker and he needs a car. Let's buy him one." Van Dyke was amazed. "And he'll need some money," Brian told Murry, "about five thousand dollars." Brian turned to Van Dyke. "Would that be all right?" he asked.

Stupefied, Van Dyke said, "Yes, that would be fine." The check arrived later that day while Van Dyke was working on one of the songs. "There were no stipulations about what the five thousand dollars represented," Van Dyke said, "but what it meant was my undying loyalty to Brian Wilson."

In some ways Van Dyke Parks was the most brilliant lyricist Brian ever chose, and in some ways he was the worst. Van Dyke wrote in an impressionistic stream that was far too complex for the average listener to comprehend easily. Even with a lyric sheet his writing was obscure. Although Van Dyke's lyrics were evocative and beautiful, they were eons beyond anything the Beach Boys' fans could appreciate. While in another short year many rock groups would be experimenting lyrically, this unexpected jump from the car and surf lyrics— or even the melancholy, but simple lyrics of Pet Sounds—was most perplexing to all who heard them. Still, Van Dyke was determined to aid Brian, as foil or friend, in producing his incredible new album.

The first order of business was the purchase of the necessary drugs. Brian arranged for and bought over $2,000 worth of the finest Afghani hashish. "We smoked a lot of it and got into a good place with the black hash," Brian said. "We went ahead and lay on the floor recording with the microphones about a foot from the ground. We were so stoned we had to lie down.

We got to the point where we thought this was the way to record. We got halfway through the album before we decided to stand up because we got sleepy."

Over twenty songs were prepared for the new album, some comprised of several musical fragments strung together, with passages repeating and echoing each other. According to David Anderle, they recorded enough songs for three albums, but the material changed continually, and the events surrounding the album differed so much according to each person's point of view, that no one can be certain. Van Dyke and Brian started with a song called "Heroes and Villains," first written in fragments and then strung together into one song. Those who heard the original version thought it was stronger and even more important than "Good Vibrations," but as with all the cuts, the original version was never to be heard by the public. There was "Barnyard," about a farm in the Old West, and "Cabinessence," about a log cabin in the woods. There was also a beautiful a cappella song called "Our Prayer." Another, "Do You Like Worms?," featured the lyrics "Rock, rock, roll, Plymouth rock roll over, roll over," ending in a music-box version of the "Heroes and Villains" theme.

The album cover prepared by Capitol included names of tunes called "Wonderful," "I'm In Great Shape," "Child Is Father of the Man," and "The Elements," which was an entire suite consisting of segments titled, "Fire," "Air," "Water," and "Earth." In yet another song, according to Van Dyke, "we were trying to write a song that would end on a freeze frame of the Union Pacific Railroad—the guys come together and they turn around to have their picture taken."

But perhaps the most beautiful and important song of all was "Surf's Up." Composed in a single evening, "Surf's Up" is as obscure as it is poignant. It had a lilting, rolling melody, and its lyrics were a phantasmagoria of images. Brian once tried to explain the song's meaning: "It's a man at a concert," Brian said. "All around him there's the audience, playing their roles, dressed up in fancy clothes. . . . The music begins to take over. 'Columnated ruins domino.' Empires, ideas, lives, institutions—everything has to fall, tumbling like dominoes. . . . 'Canvas the town and brush the backdrop.' He's off in his vision, on a trip. Reality is gone....'A choke of grief.' At his own sorrow and the emptiness of his life, because he can't even cry for the suffering in the world, for his own suffering. And then, hope. 'Surf's Up!'..."

During the preparation of *Dumb Angel*, Brian's creativity was fueled with not only hashish but also a prescription amphetamine called Desbutol, which was reportedly purchased in the black market, and—although never in the presence of David Anderle or Van Dyke Parks—occasional psychedelics. Under this barrage of drugs, Brian's state of mind became fragmented and out of control. Ideas for new projects came in powerful spurts, distracting him for long periods from *Dumb Angel*. These myriad concepts soon began to overtake work on the album itself, as even the album's name changed to, simply, *Smile*. Other new distractions that kept him away from the piano and the studios were health foods; a preoccupation with his swimming pool—Brian installed a sliding pond leading from the roof of the house into the pool; whipped-cream fights during which Brian would get high by breathing the empty aerosol cans into his mouth; and chants—meaningless sounds repeated *ad nauseam* until, to the stoned mind, they sounded like music. Said Derek Taylor, "[Brian] used to talk a lot of totter about health food [while he was] digging into a big, fat hamburger. And gymnasiums! I was fitter than he was. ...Going on about vitamins. I thought maybe he was just being amusing, you see. Having a meal with him was like the Mad Hatter's tea party: 'Have some tea, there isn't any.'"

One night, while Marilyn prepared dinner for Brian's new group of friends, he sat at the dining table with his guests, idly tapping utensils on a white china plate. "Listen to that!" he suddenly said. "Come on, let's get something going here!" He encouraged his dinner companions to take their utensils and bang on the table, plates, and glasses. "That's absolutely unbelievable!" Brian exclaimed. "Isn't it unbelievable? That's so unbelievable I'm going to put it on the album." It was forgotten the next day. On another occasion, Loren Schwartz, who was still very much a part of Brian's inner circle, told Brian about the caftans everyone was wearing. Brian was so taken with the idea that he immediately stopped working on *Smile* and spent the afternoon with Loren looking for an available store where he could open up a robe shop.

Brian and David Anderle would often pop five Desbutols and sit up all night looking at the stars. One night Brian decided they needed a telescope. When Anderle said that no telescope store would be open so late, Brian told him they would have to buy a telescope store so they could have one whenever they wanted. On another occasion Brian embarked on a hunt to purchase a Ping-Pong table in the middle of the night.

Soon to be abandoned was an idea for an album of just sound effects, which Michael Vosse was put on the payroll to record. These sounds would include the gurgling of water, from fountains, taps, and the ocean; the crunching of gravel; the sounds of animals, and sounds of chewing and swallowing—all cut together to form an entire album based on water. There was also an entire album devoted to humor, which Brian actually recorded with photographer Jasper Dailey, and which was rejected by A&M Records. "Brian was consumed with humor at the time and the importance of humor," Anderle said. "He was fascinated with the idea of getting humor onto a disc and hot to get that disc out to the people." But there wasn't very much interest in this project at Capitol Records, and this fact led to one of the grandest, albeit most intelligent ideas, of the era: the formation of the Beach Boys' own record company, Brother Records.

Brother Records was already a major topic of discussion between the Beach Boys and Nick Grillo. Grillo was involved in intensive negotiations with Capitol to upgrade the Beach Boys' royalty before their old contract lapsed. He was not thrilled to learn in October 1966 that Brian wanted David Anderle to be put on the payroll, forming Brother Records. "Anderle came out of the thin air for me," Grillo said. "He didn't have the credentials that would warrant making him the head of a record company." Of all the Beach Boys, Mike Love was the most receptive to the idea of a separate record company. Mike wanted the Beach Boys to have more control, and his support for Anderle, whom he respected as a businessman, lent the idea weight. The others were also enthusiastic, seeing

Brother Records as an opportunity for each of them to discover and record their own artists and thereby emerge from Brian's shadow.

One of the first things Anderle did in conjunction with Nick Grillo was to hire Abe Somers, a top Los Angeles lawyer who was well known in the record business. Checking through old royalty statements from Capitol, Anderle discovered that "at that point Brian had never been paid a producer's royalty," which he claimed "was bizarre. Everything was changing then. Artists were now starting to be treated a lot differently, and it was my feeling that Brian should be treated right." A lawsuit was threatened, but Capitol did not seem cowed at first; their agreement with the Beach Boys had another two years to run, and they saw no reason to pay additional funds, particularly without any new hit material forthcoming. So the Beach Boys took Capitol to court. The suit, filed in Los Angeles Superior Court, alleged "withholding of royalties due" totaling $275,000.

Meanwhile, Anderle held meetings with several other record companies to try to get a distribution deal for Brother Records. He even met with Atlantic Records's president, Ahmet Ertegun, but there were no takers in sight.

3

As summer drifted into fall, and then into winter, *Smile* was still not finished. It became apparent to Capitol, which had already printed 468,000 album covers, which were sitting in a Scranton plant, that *Smile* would not be available for Christmas release. Brian's behavior continued to grow more peculiar, although none of his intimate circle seemed concerned. This was a time when outlandish behavior was not only accepted, but lauded. No matter how far-out Brian got, his actions were never considered signs of a deteriorating mental state, but just symptoms of drug use or general eccentricity. After all, Brian had been declared a "genius," and geniuses were *supposed* to be eccentric. "Thinking back," Anderle said, "there was so much weirdness going on that was whimsical and humorous, those signs certainly didn't alarm me. Brian wasn't the only one. We were all strange, doing strange things."

During that fateful autumn, Brian became obsessively concerned that Murry was planting eavesdropping devices in his home and automobile, ostensibly to find out not only what Brian was doing in his personal life, but what his new music would be like. Instead of suggesting to Brian that this was an irrational fear, and that not even Murry was capable of doing such a thing, the people around him took Brian's suspicions seriously. Indeed, Murry seemed to have such an adverse affect on Brian that when he called ahead to say he intended to visit the house on Laurel Way, Brian would vomit in fear. Brian was so convinced that Murry was "bugging" the house that he began to insist on having all important business meetings held in the swimming pool. A stock of bathing suits was kept in the pool house, where harried associates and business executives would have to change before climbing into large rubber rafts to discuss important matters with Brian. Eventually, he hired a professional detective agency to "debug" his house and car. "Magically," said Michael Vosse, "they found a bug in Brian's car. To this day I think they brought it with them to get the job." The detectives were placed on the payroll for a while, and insisted that all of Brian's close friends change their phones to unlisted numbers.

One evening Brian was sitting in his living room with Stanley Shapiro from Jules Lefkowitz' office, discussing old relationships, when the topic of Carol Mountain, his high-school flame, came up. Brian had recently heard that she was married to a physical-education teacher and still lived in Hawthorne. "Why don't you call her up?" Shapiro suggested. Brian got on the telephone at once and started calling every Mountain listed in the Inglewood-Hawthorne area, until he finally located Carol's parents. He hurriedly explained who he was, and asked for Carol's address, which the girl's mother trustingly gave him. Two minutes later Brian was out of the house, driving to Hawthorne in his Rolls-Royce, intending to get Carol Mountain to come back to Laurel Way with him. "It was the funniest thing I had ever seen in my life," Shapiro said. "The two of us were bombed out of our minds. He's standing on the doorstep ringing her doorbell and Carol Mountain opened the door with rollers in her hair. Brian explained to her who he was, and when she heard that he was Brian Wilson of the Beach Boys she was really surprised—she never knew." Brian tried to convince the surprised woman to come back to the house with them, but naturally she didn't want to go. "In the middle of all this, her husband showed up," Shapiro said. "Brian said a few things that didn't sit right with the guy, and before you knew it there was an altercation and the guy started yelling, 'I'm going to get my gun.' Brian took off running and came back to the car, and the two of us tore out of there."

That same autumn, Brian's deep, paranoid obsession with Phil Spector began in earnest. While Brian's competition with the Beatles was heartfelt, it had always been a friendly one. Now suddenly Brian thought Phil Spector was out to control or destroy him in some way. Brian would go to the record store and buy ten copies of Spector's hit song "Be My Baby" and literally wear out the grooves playing them, listening for hidden meanings and messages. Spector was having his own problems by this time. He had become a virtual recluse. Surrounded by bodyguards, he hid behind the gates of his Beverly Hills mansion, venturing outside only when shielded by the dark-tinted windows of a limousine.

The situation came to a head one night when the usual group of Brian's friends, including David Anderle and Jules Siegel, was at the house waiting for him to come home. Marilyn was painting her fingernails when Brian arrived at the house, shaking and upset. Everyone asked what was wrong.

"It's Spector, man. He's really after me," Brian said.

"Why? What happened?" Marilyn asked.

Brian said he had walked into a movie theater where *Seconds*, a new film starring Rock Hudson, was playing. The movie was about an older man who undergoes head-to-toe plastic surgery and has a second chance at life. As the movie starts, Brian explained, "The first thing that happened was a voice from the screen that said, 'Hello, Mr. Wilson.'"

"So what?" Anderle said.

"*So what?*" Brian repeated, wide-eyed. "It completely blew my mind! Don't you see how weird it was?"

"But wasn't that the name of the character in the movie?" someone asked.

"That's not all," Brian went on, his agitation growing. "Then the whole thing was there. I mean my whole life. Birth and death and rebirth. The whole thing. Even the beach was in it, a whole thing about the beach. It was my whole life right there on the screen." Brian also noticed that the street number of the house where the movie character lived was the same as the number of his house in Hawthorne.

"It's just coincidence," Anderle offered.

"No it wasn't. It was mind-fuck. Spector's mind-fuck. Haven't you heard of 'mind gangsters'? It was Spector who set it up. It was a Columbia movie and Spector records for Columbia."

"Brian," Marilyn said calmly. "You don't think that Spector made them write the movie that way just to frighten you."

But that was exactly what Brian thought.

David Anderle tried another tack. "Listen, Brian, why would John Frankenheimer [the director of the film] make a movie just to terrify you?" he asked.

Brian said, "Think about this. John Frankenheimer is Jewish. Phil Spector is Jewish. If Phil Spector went to a fellow Jew and appealed to him on a fellow-Jew level to help him destroy Brian Wilson, don't you think he'd do it?"

Anderle, himself a Jew, was so insulted he couldn't speak. The veins stood out on his forehead, and it was all he could do to control himself. It took him several days to forgive Brian.

Brian then walked briskly into the den and went over to his jukebox. He punched a few buttons and the sound of Spector's "Be My Baby" came blaring out into the room. He played the song over and over again, at least twenty times. As the song played, he sat down at his desk and began to draw diagrams with a felt-tipped pen. "Spector started the whole thing," he said. "He was the first one to use the studio. But I've gone beyond him now. I'm doing spiritual sound, a white spiritual sound. Religious music. Did you hear the Beatles album? Religious, right?"

Everyone looked at each other in amazement.

"That's the whole movement. That's where I'm going. It's

going to scare a lot of people. Yeah." Brian hit his desk. "Yeah," he said again, and smiled.

4

There was one other crucial moment that some believe helped tip Brian over into a netherworld. It was the outcome of the Derek Taylor "Brian is a genius" campaign. CBS television was doing a prime-time documentary series called "Inside Pop: The Rock Revolution," and had assigned David Oppenheim, a young producer from their New York office, to assemble an hour-long show, hosted by conductor Leonard Bernstein, about the important new voices in the world of rock-and-roll. "Some person in New York was very high on Brian Wilson," Oppenheim said. "I was very curious about him and his music."

Oppenheim set off for Los Angeles, and soon after arriving drove up the hill to the house on Laurel Way. He just walked in and said who he was. "It was a kind of informal drop-in place," Oppenheim said. "There were always people around.... Brian at the time had his piano put in the sand, and in the back there was a tent. I was invited into the tent. I went in once or twice but never understood what it was about. Brian was looking at the TV set with the volume off and just the color, detuned, and lots of vegetables around. Marilyn was nice, receptive and warm, and made sure I had a drink. I never understood Brian and her together. It was a stange, insulated household, insulated from the world by money.... A playpen of irresponsible people. If they'd had to feel the road and the gravel under their feet, they would have had to behave in a very different way, but this wasn't necessary.

"A film crew and I went to Columbia Records's studios with Brian and his friends, and they were doing tiny little pieces that made no sense in and of themselves...just a few notes ...also the sessions didn't make a scene that was at all interesting.... I had hoped to get Brian masterminding a recording session, but instead it was terribly spread out.... Brian was a little spacy, but he didn't seem drugged. We filmed a piece called 'Surf's Up,' and he accompanied himself at the piano.

After that we tried to talk with him but didn't get much out of him. Some guy said, 'He's not verbal.' He was odd and he seemed odder. I had heard the stories before we got there about how crazy he was. Van Dyke seemed brilliant, intelligent, off-the-wall, and smashed."

Later, they filmed a sequence in the pool. "We got an underwater camera and they went down that slide into the pool and the camera went down underneath with them. The camera crew was in the swimming pool."

The completed show aired soon afterward. It began with Leonard Bernstein talking about the discoveries that rock musicians were making both musically and in lyrics, mentioning Tandyn Almer, Janis Ian, and Brian among others. Bernstein did not call him a genius—Oppenheim used the word in the introduction to Brian's number—but Bernstein said "Surf's Up" was "too complex to get all of it the first time around." However, it was perceived that Leonard Bernstein had called Brian a "genius," and for Brian this was a proclamation, an investiture as king of the heap. Now Brian was under tremendous pressure to live up to his reputation.

In autumn 1966, with "Good Vibrations" high on the charts, the touring revenues of the Beach Boys were quickly approaching $2 million annually. To cash in on the Beach Boys' sudden renewed popularity, the touring segment of the group—Carl, Mike, Dennis, Alan, and Bruce Johnston—embarked on a worldwide tour through the Midwest of the United States, then on to Sweden, middle Europe, and Great Britain. Early one morning, shortly after the tour had begun, Michael Vosse received a phone call from Brian. "I'm worried about the tour," he said. "I think the boys need more rehearsing." In particular, Brian was concerned about the way his masterpiece, "Good Vibrations," would sound when played live in concert. Brian asked Vosse to pick him up and drive him out to the Los Angeles airport, where they would catch a plane for Chicago and then drive to Ann Arbor, Michigan, where the group was rehearsing for a concert the following night.

When Vosse and Brian arrived in Chicago, they spent the first hour riding around in a taxi cab while Brian interviewed the driver about rock-and-roll and his various thoughts about youth. The driver, although perplexed, was happy to get the large fare and spent the time talking into Brian's Nagra recorder. After spending the night in a Chicago hotel, Vosse and Brian drove to Ann Arbor the next morning. It was a pretty autumn day, but Brian had no time to enjoy the weather. He put the boys through a grueling rehearsal, stopping them every few seconds to make recommendations. The concert that night went off splendidly—the boys gave a spirited, almost perfect performance. Brian watched from backstage, and when the last encore had been played, the rest of the group literally dragged him out on the stage for a bow. Brian was both upset and tickled—he had not wanted to break his vow of never appearing onstage again. When the spotlight picked him out and the audience realized who he was, a high-pitched frenzy erupted. As Brian stood frozen, the audience leaped to their feet and gave him a standing ovation.

On the way back to Chicago's O'Hare Airport, Brian got stoned on grass, and by the time they boarded the plane he was very high. Sitting in the first-class compartment next to Mike Vosse, Brian was upset and quiet. Something was obviously on his mind. When the stewardess offered him a menu for dinner, Brian decided he wanted *all* the entrées on it. The stewardess tried to explain politely that he could only choose one, but Brian made such a fuss she finally consented, giving him what he wanted. Only an hour into the flight he had another idea: he wanted to call Marilyn. He summoned the stewardess and told her he had to make an emergency phone call. The stewardess explained that it was impossible; there were no phones on the plane. But Brian insisted, relentlessly, and after much consultation with the chief flight attendant as well as the pilot, it was agreed Brian's message would be radioed to the nearest airport on the ground, where an airline official would make the phone call for him. The message was this: Call Marilyn at home and have her assemble as many of Brian's friends as she could in the next several hours and have them waiting at the airport, along with Guy Webster, a photographer who had photographed the Beach Boys many times.

When the plane landed, nearly twenty of Brian's friends were waiting at the terminal. Guy Webster lined the large group up against the white-tile wall of the terminal, and photographed them with a wide-angle lens, like an eerie graduation photograph. For the next few months a giant blowup of the photograph hung on Brian's living room wall. In just as much time, all of the people in the photograph would become strangers.

5

Meanwhile, word from Great Britain was thrilling. The Beach Boys arrived to find Heathrow Airport swamped with fans, and Capitol's EMI headquarters was besieged with reporters waiting for a press conference. Throngs of teenage girls appeared wherever the group went, tearing at their clothes. Paul McCartney phoned, John Lennon and George Harrison came to visit them at the Hilton, and they were introduced to the Rolling Stones. Mike Love called Brian in Los Angeles to tell him that the same kind of frenzy that greeted the Beatles was happening to them. In celebration, four Rolls-Royce Phantom VII limousines were purchased in a London showroom, one for Dennis, Carl, and Mike Love, and a fourth for Brian at home, at a cost of $32,000 each.

In Los Angeles, Brian was finishing work on *Smile*.

One of the most peculiar incidents involving the production of *Smile* occurred on November 10 at the Gold Star Studios on Santa Monica Boulevard. It happened during the final session for "Fire," which was to be included in "The Elements." Brian had assembled, at great cost, an enormous string session to help record the "Fire" segments. He had already sent the violinists home once because, while sitting outside the studio in his Rolls-Royce, he had decided the "vibrations" weren't right for that night's session. Van Dyke Parks, who was with him in the limousine, was so dismayed by this decision that "I avoided the 'Fire' sessions like the plague. I didn't want to embarrass myself. I thought it was regressive behavior."

When the string session was reassembled, Brian insisted that everyone in the studio wear a fire helmet, including all the middle-aged violinists, the engineers, Marilyn and Diane, and

anyone else who happened to walk into the studio. Brian sent
a roadie, Arnie Geller, to a toy store to buy them. When Arnie
returned, producing the red helmets from the trunk of Brian's
Rolls-Royce, the session musicans all donned them and began
to play.

Brian remembered, "I walked in [to the studios], and there
was a janitor named Brother Julius who lived in a little bungalow in the backyard. Before I walked in, I said, 'Brother
Julius, could you start a little fire in the bucket and bring it in
the studio?' Well, he hit the ceiling. He said, 'What do you
want me to do that for?' I said, 'I want these guys to smell
smoke.' You see, I was flipping. I wanted to smell smoke.

"So there were the musicians smelling smoke with fire hats
on. They were all firemen. *Rooooar, rooar.* The violins were
screeching up, reaching upward, rolling down...*Whoooorrr*..."

Those who were there say the track was a terrifying internal
whine. Jules Siegel, in his article "Goodbye Surfing, Hello
God!," said the music summoned up "visions of roaring, wind-
storm flames, falling timbers, mournful sirens and sweating
firemen, building into a peak and crackling off into fading
embers as a single drum turned into a collapsing wall...."

"It was sick," Brian said. "I mean, it was sick. Weird chords,
it wasn't the straight eight and all that. I started thinking, Oh
God, I'm flipping here. But I liked it." After twenty-four takes
Brian was satisfied. Carrying the tapes out of the studio, still
wearing his fire hat, he said, "I'm going to call this 'Mrs.
O'Leary's Fire,' and I think it might just scare a whole lot of
people."

According to Brian, later that night, "We got the news that
a place nearby burned down. Well, I thought I started the fire.
I thought that for some magical reason what we were doing in
the Gold Star [started fires]." Brian had his staff of cronies
research the number of fires in and around Los Angeles that
week. Discovering that there was an "unusual" number of fires,
he decided it was his music that had caused them. Brian then
tried to destroy the "Fire" tapes by burning them, but when
the tapes would not ignite, they were locked away in a vault,
where they reportedly remain to this day.

"I don't have to do a big scary fire like that," he said. "I can do a candle and it's still fire. That would have been a really bad vibration to let out on the world, that Chicago fire. The next one is going to be a candle."

One day Jules Siegel and his girl friend arrived at the recording studio to visit a session and found their way barred by a security guard. Michael Vosse was sent out to explain the exclusion to Jules. "It's not you," Vosse said. "It's your chick. Brian says she's a witch and she's messing with his brain so bad by ESP that he can't work. I'm really sorry." Jules Siegel never came by again.

6

The touring segment of the Beach Boys knew nothing of Brian's strange behavior. When they returned to California to put the vocals on the new record, the scene they found waiting infuriated them. It was as if a whole group of strangers had infiltrated and were taking over the Beach Boys. Anderle, whom they had trusted to start Brother Records for them, seemed to be the leader of the pack. They now began to deeply resent him, suspecting him of encouraging Brian to leave the Beach Boys and go out on his own. "Sure I was an interloper," Anderle said, "and I'm sure they saw me as somebody who was taking Brian away from them. And somebody who was fueling Brian's weirdness. And I stand guilty on those counts ...I was an interloper and I was definitely fueling his creativity. No holds barred. No rules." And when the others heard the music, they were furious. Mike Love was the most vocal and vehement. "You're going to blow it, Brian," he said. "Stick to the old stuff. Don't fuck with the formula."

Facing the other Beach Boys, Brian felt a sense of tremendous responsibility. "I think he was pressured by the group," said one close observer of that period. "And by knowing that everyone in that group was married, and had children and a house. I think he felt like more of a *benefactor* than an artist....He was a creative force and there were five other people—five other families—relying on his creativity." The

Beach Boys had seen infiltrators before—Gary Usher, Tony Asher, Loren Schwartz.

Not long after the Beach Boys returned from Europe, Van Dyke Parks got a phone call from Brian inviting him to a session. He knew something was up. "I was stunned. Usually I did not go to sessions...but Brian called and said would I come to the session and help Mike with the lyrics...there was some question about them. Well, I was frightened for a second. I realized that Brian wasn't anything more than a one-man Trojan horse."

Van Dyke got into his car and drove warily down to the studios, where Mike Love and Brian were waiting for him. The problem seemed to be that the lyrics were too abstract and obscure. Mike began to grill Van Dyke on what each individual lyric meant. Reportedly, the line "Columnated ruins domino" was particularly vexing—though no more vexing than most of the rest.

"I have no excuse, sir," Van Dyke told Mike sarcastically. Insulted and hurt, he refused to explain what any of the words meant, or claimed he didn't understand them himself. "I remember leaving with the sensation that I wouldn't be asked back. Yet I somehow thought that *Smile* would be finished, and I didn't want to do anything that would contravene it. It was like watching a balloon let loose from a child's hand...."

David Anderle was the last to go. As Brian's behavior grew more peculiar and childish, so did Anderle's frustration. Anderle was trying to make Brother Records a reality, a task that necessitated a stronger sense of day-to-day responsibility and punctuality than Brian was able to muster. Perhaps the most wrenching moment of all came one night at Anderle's apartment. As a surprise, David had been working on an oil portrait of Brian. Because he couldn't ask him to pose, Anderle had painted it from memory. One night he invited Brian to the small, one-room apartment he rented above a garage on Twenty-eighth Street near the University of Southern California. It was nearly two in the morning when Anderle, his wife Sheryl, and Brian arrived there. The painting stood in a corner, covered with an old bedspread. David announced a surprise and uncovered it. He remembered, "The room got very quiet. There was a definite feeling that came over us. I walked away from Brian and sat down on the bed with my wife. Brian stood in front of the painting for a long time, perhaps for as long as an hour. He examined every inch of it. When he finally spoke, his reaction wasn't what I expected."

"You captured my soul," Brian said. "It's like the American Indians who have their soul captured." Brian grew increasingly distressed, claiming that the number of objects in the painting, the circles and designs placed in the background for decorative relief, were numerologically important, relating to different stages in Brian's life. He became so upset that eventually Anderle called Michael Vosse to pick Brian up and take him home.

In the car with Vosse, Brian was even more upset. "This painting business has been going on for thousands of years, huh?" he asked. Vosse didn't know what to say. He too was fired a few weeks later.

A final incident involving Brian and Anderle took place several days later. The lawsuit Anderle had helped implement against Capitol Records was coming to a head—depositions were being taken and it was a time of serious tension. "I brought an attorney up to Brian's house," Anderle said, "and Brian would not come out of the bedroom." Anderle tried to get Marilyn to bring him down, but he would not come. Anderle told Marilyn, "I will not do business this way. I will not be one of those guys in Brian's life who is treated this way." But Marilyn was helpless, and eventually Anderle went up to the bedroom door himself and knocked. "Brian?" he called out. "Listen, Brian, if you don't come out of this room, I'm gone. This isn't kid time anymore. Do you hear me, Brian?" But there was no answer.

Anderle never saw Brian again on a professional level. The painting of Brian to this day hangs in Anderle's living room, but he has never painted again.

I'm not a genius.
I'm just a hard-working guy.
—BRIAN WILSON

I think it was the drugs.
—DENNIS WILSON

Nine

1

Capitol Records didn't officially announce that Smile had been abandoned until May 2, 1967. Many things dealt the final blow to Smile—Brian's inability to finish the album, the drugs, the lyrics, the family squabbles—and finally, the release of two new Beatles singles, "Penny Lane" and "Strawberry Fields," so wondrous and different-sounding that Brian was crushed. He was still recording on April 10 when Paul McCartney, on a surprise visit to Los Angeles to see his girl friend, Jane Asher, stopped in to one of Brian's sessions. Within a few hours they had co-produced a song called "Vegetables."* At that session Paul spoke enthusiastically about a new Beatles album to be released the following month—*Sergeant Pepper's Lonely Hearts Club Band.* When Brian finally heard that album, he was shattered. The greatest album in the history of rock-and-roll had already been recorded.

Derek Taylor, writing for *Disc and Music Echo* magazine in England, broke the news of Smile's cancellation overseas: "In truth, every beautifully designed, finely wrought, inspirationally welded piece of music made these last months by Brian ...has been SCRAPPED. Not destroyed, but scrapped. For what Wilson seals in a can and destroys is scrapped." Music critic Greil Marcus was later to point out that the Beach Boys' artistic reputation would be forever based on unheard, unreleased music.

---

*Some claim Paul only observed the session and did not co-produce it.

Brian's confidence was severely shaken, as was evidenced by his next, disastrous decision. That June a massive festival was to be held at the Monterey Fairgrounds, to celebrate the new music and new philosophy that gripped the nation's young people. The idea for the nonprofit festival came early in April from Los Angeles promoter Ben Shapiro, Los Angeles scene maker Alan Pariser, and Derek Taylor. The three set up an office on Sunset Boulevard to coordinate local acts and sell advertising space in a concert booklet. Soon the original organizing committee expanded to include Terry Melcher, Johnny Rivers, John Phillips of the Mamas and Papas, and Lou Adler. With the help of San Francisco promoter Bill Graham, a number of popular groups was enlisted to perform, and TV rights were sold to ABC to help finance the festival. The San Francisco hippie commune known as the Diggers volunteered to help feed concertgoers and arrange for Free Clinic doctors to treat the expected acid casualties. The list of acts included Janis Joplin, Otis Redding, Ravi Shankar, The Who, Laura Nyro, Buffalo Springfield, and the Byrds, among many others.

Naturally, California's native sons, the Beach Boys, were asked to perform. Although they readily accepted—and even loaned the festival the use of their sound system—they were secretly gripped by fear at the thought of appearing—fear they would be laughed off the stage by the young audience, fear that their growing musical anachronisms would show. "You know," Brian told Michael Vosse, who was working on the Monterey committee while acting as an informal liaison for the Beach Boys, "the idea of a show with the Beach Boys and the Mamas and Papas is okay. But all those people from England who play acid rock—if the audience is coming to the concert to see them, they're going to hate us."

Brian's final decision not to show up at Monterey may have been made one night about two weeks before the festival, at Alan Pariser's house. Vosse had brought Brian there to meet Pariser for the first time, and Brian seemed distant and uncomfortable from the start. After some small talk, Pariser said casually to Brian, "I don't even know what you guys are doing. I haven't heard from you in a while."

"Brian's mouth flew open," Mike Vosse said. "He was so

insulted. Just at the climax of all this tension, the door flew open and in came ... a guy who was a chiropractor ... a pushy hippie-type. He took one look at Brian and said, 'Terrible back, we're going to have to do something about that.' Before Brian knew it, he was on the floor on his stomach, screaming in agony as the chiropractor worked him over.

"He was absolutely terrified," Vosse said, "but too scared to tell him not to do it. ... He was totally humiliated and in pain."

When Brian left that night, Pariser said, "If I don't see you before then, I'll see you at Monterey."

And Brian said, "I doubt it."

The Monterey Pop Festival turned into the most important rock-music event prior to Woodstock. Fifteen thousand people were expected at Monterey; 50,000 showed up. The feeling was celebratory, and the event would long be remembered as the dawn of the age of rock festivals. The Beach Boys were scheduled to close the show on Saturday night, a plum position in the lineup. Their decision not to play was announced only at the last minute, infuriating many of those who had worked so hard to make the festival happen. The official story was that their inability to play had to do with Carl's personal problems, but everyone involved thought the same thing—they were scared. At the last minute, Otis Redding took their spot, and the Beach Boys' no-show became the talk of the festival. On Sunday night, during his spectacular performance, Jimmi Hendrix told the audience, "You heard the last of surfing music...."

The decision not to appear at Monterey had a snowballing effect. The Beach Boys' self-exclusion from the festival was seen as a damning admission that they were washed up, unable to compete with the "new music." On December 14, an article in *Rolling Stone*—which at the time was considered a kind of bible—truly sealed their doom. Written by *Rolling Stone* publisher Jann Wenner, the article tore into the Beach Boys— their image as well as their music. Extolling the virtues of the Beatles, and their amazing leap from *Rubber Soul* to *Sergeant Pepper*, Wenner explained how the British fans only two years before had placed the Beach Boys ahead of the Beatles in popularity polls. Wenner pointed out that Brian's publicity people compared him to Lennon and McCartney. "Except," wrote Wenner, "no one is John Lennon except John Lennon and no one is Paul McCartney except Paul McCartney and the Beach Boys...are not the Beatles." Wenner went on to say that the label "genius" was "essentially a promotional shuck" that Brian himself believed. He gave faint praise to "Good Vibrations," which he said was not really rock-and-roll. Wenner called the group "totally disappointing" live, and concluded, "The Beach Boys are just one prominent example of a group that has gotten hung up in trying to catch the Beatles."

2

Brian sold the house on Laurel Way. "He wanted a bigger home," Marilyn said. "You know, he was making a lot of money, and we started looking for a real house." The tent was disassembled, the recording equipment moved out. A contractor was hired to haul out the several tons of sand from the den, where it had been irretrievably soiled by the dogs. An era was over.

That April Brian and Marilyn moved into a four-bedroom home on Bellagio Road in Bel Air. They paid $320,000 for the mansion, which had once belonged to Edgar Rice Burroughs. "We bought the house without even looking at the upstairs," Marilyn said. "We saw the whole downstairs and the yard, but the people who owned it didn't want us to go upstairs because something was going on up there that day. I said to Brian, 'I can't buy a house without looking at the bedrooms. I've got to see my closets, I've got to see the bathrooms.' But Brian said, 'Oh, don't worry about it, it will be fine.' I trusted Brian, and what Brian said went—that was it."

The house boasted a large living room, a formal den with a fireplace, and a hidden study that could be entered through a secret door behind a bookcase. There was a fountain in the inner courtyard and a spiral staircase in the entrance foyer. Marilyn and Brian had some minimal construction done— they removed the old flagstone from around the swimming pool, replacing it with mosaic tiles, and built a tall brick wall around the perimeter of the acre-and-a-half grounds. The psychedelic and hippie paraphernalia from Laurel Way was thrown out, and Marilyn decorated the new house in tasteful pastels and with fashionable furniture. All that remained from before was the grand piano on which Brian had composed "Pet Sounds," and the four-poster bed with its headboard of carved angels. To keep strangers away, a new electric gate was installed with an intercom and a sign that read STAND BACK— SPEAK NORMALLY. At first Brian wanted to repaint the house a bright magenta; the painting was only half finished when the Bel Air Residents Tenants Committee started a suit to stop him. The house was painted a simple beige.

With the Beach Boys now in a weakened position, the lawsuit against Capitol was quietly dropped, and an arrangement was made for Capitol to distribute Brother Records. Meanwhile, hurried recording began on a replacement album for *Smile*, which would be titled *Smiley Smile*. But Brian was no longer interested in leaving the house on Bellagio Road to go to the studios—so the mountain was brought to Mohammed. A makeshift studio with remote equipment was constructed at Bellagio Road. Engineer Jim Lockhart remembered, "They had one large room which had been a music room for the former owner and there was a hallway and an office. All the consoles and tape machines were set up in the office. There was a closed-circuit television so you could see what was going on." Because there was no soundproofed studio *per se*, the recording took place all over the house, including the tiled showers and the bottom of the swimming pool, which had been drained for repair.

This time, the other Beach Boys were never far away, and they showed up at the house almost every day to assist with the recording. Compared to the grand vision Brian had for *Smile*, *Smiley Smile* was a throwaway album. A few cuts were salvaged from *Smile*: "Vegetables"; "Earth," from "The Elements"; and "Wonderful." "*Smiley Smile* was a very simple album to make," Carl said. "It took a couple of weeks at Brian's house. Tops, two weeks." The entire album was mixed in one overnight session at the Wally Heider studios, and it was the first LP to bear the words, "Produced by the Beach Boys" instead of "by Brian Wilson." "It was a bunt instead of a grand slam," said Carl.

Of all the songs Brian prepared for *Smiley Smile*, the only one he really cared about was "Heroes and Villains," which he had written earlier with Van Dyke Parks. The song now opened the album—side one, first cut. There were already several versions of this song, one of them almost seven minutes long. Yet it was obvious to everyone who heard it that "Heroes and Villains" was more than salvageable. It had the quality and inventiveness that marked "Good Vibrations." Although the song described the Old West, its lyrics reflected many of Brian's feelings about his past year in Los Angeles.

> *I've been in this town so long,*
> *that back in the city*
> *I've been taken for lost and gone*
> *and unknown for a long, long time*

When an abbreviated three-minute-and-thirty-six-second version of "Heroes and Villains" was finished, Brian held on to it for a long time, afraid to release it. He had been consulting with a female psychic-astrologer named Genevelyn, who came up to the house frequently. By that June she felt the time was right to present the new song to the world. Terry Melcher remembers Brian clutching the single in his hand and calling all the members of the group to ask them to assemble for the world premiere of the record. By 11:00 P.M. that night, Brian was ready. An incredible procession of Rolls-Royces and limousines set out from Bellagio Road to KHJ-Radio in Hollywood. But when the cortege of automobiles reached the studio gate, the security guard refused to let them in. Finally, after a long argument with the guard, who called his superiors, the five cars were allowed inside the gates. Brian and the Beach Boys found their way down the long fluorescent-lighted hallways to the small soundproofed booth where the disc jockey was broadcasting live out over Los Angeles.

Brian made a simple speech. "I'm Brian Wilson and I'm

holding the new Beach Boys single, 'Heroes and Villains.' I'd like to give you and KHJ an exclusive on it."

The disc jockey looked at Brian and the small, seven-inch disc he was holding, and shrugged his shoulders. "Sorry," he said. "I can't play anything that isn't on the play list."

"It really killed Brian," Melcher said. A fierce debate ensued. The rest of the group forced the reticent disc jockey to call the station manager, who screamed at him, "Put it on, you idiot!" The disc jockey put the song on, and "Heroes and Villains" was released to the world.

"Heroes and Villains" was the first Beach Boys single released since "Good Vibrations" the previous October. It was also the first piece of the extraordinary new music that everyone in the Los Angeles music business had been waiting to hear since the *Smile* project was announced ten months before. The reaction was decidedly mixed. It was special, yes, and different—but was it commercial? That question could be answered only by the public. "Heroes and Villains" first appeared on the *Billboard* charts on August 5 at number 61, leapfrogged to number 33 on the twelfth, reached its pinnacle of number 12 for two weeks around Labor Day, and then one week later, fell off the charts forever, its novelty gone. "Heroes and Villains" was, by everyone's estimation, a failure. It was the last Beach Boys single to break below the top twenty for nearly a decade.

In July, Capitol released a compilation album of old tunes called *Best of the Beach Boys—Volume 2*, and although it was on the charts for twenty-two weeks, it only broke 50. It seemed even repackaging was no longer working for the group. On September 18, 1967, *Smiley Smile* became the first official release of Brother Records, distributed by Capitol. Although it was on the *Billboard* charts for twenty-one weeks, it never broke into the top forty, and the album spent the majority of its chart time wavering between 100 and 197. Just two months later, the Beach Boys quickly released another album, *Wild Honey*, although pointedly on the Capitol label and not on Brother Records. This album was to become a favorite for hardcore Beach Boys fans, considered by many to be a "soul album," lauded for its simplicity and rawness (the longest cut on it was only 2:42). But it too was a commercial failure. It was most notable for Carl's increased role as producer. Carl passed the album off as "music for Brian to cool out by. He was still very spaced." After a fifteen-week run on the charts, *Wild Honey* reached only number 24. Word was out—the Beach Boys were in serious trouble.

3

Marilyn Wilson was pregnant. That August the Beach Boys and their wives had gone to Hawaii for three weeks, to shoot a promotional film to be released in conjunction with the upcoming *Smiley Smile* album. The child was conceived in tropical, romantic surroundings, and was due in spring of 1968. Marilyn was hoping for a girl, but Brian didn't seem to care. While Marilyn contentedly redecorated one of the many rooms to create a nursery, Brian retreated into the master bedroom, where he slept all day. Soon he had a refrigerator installed in there, and rarely came downstairs at all. Sometimes, because the "vibrations" weren't right in the master bedroom, he would sleep in one of the other rooms, frequently switching from one to the other several times in a night. Ironically, with the remote studio downstairs in the music room, the recording sounds easily penetrated the floorboards, making the Beach Boys' presence inescapable. Brian began to feel, more than ever, that the Beach Boys were a monster of his own making—there was no escape from them. He worried about money, and wanted to go out on his own, but he felt it was too late. He still wanted to work, and when Danny Hutton formed a group called Redwood, Brian managed to produce a tune for them called "Darlin'." But when the Beach Boys heard the song, they took it for themselves.

Brian was worn and devastated. On April 29, 1968, his first child, a girl named Carnie, was born. "It was around then that I started really getting worried about Brian," Marilyn said. "There was suddenly a difference between having fun and having sick fun. I don't think I really saw, or let myself see that, until after Carnie was born. I remember her lying in the crib and Brian being weepy. I was worried before that, but once you have a child you look at things differently."

Retreating further and further, less and less interested in friends and going out, Brian stayed in bed later into the day, until he finally took to bed altogether. He would stay there for many years.

Carl was now emerging as the level-headed, dependable Wilson brother, growing calmer and fatter with the passing years. Professionally, he was esteemed as a first-rate live guitarist, though the confines of playing Beach Boys songs rarely gave him a chance to display his talent. Carl was the last of the Beach Boys to fall in love and marry. Annie Hinsche was a sweet, dark-haired, fifteen-year-old with a round face and a bright smile. The daughter of a well-to-do casino owner from the Philippines, Annie had been born in Manila and moved to Los Angeles with her family when she was five. She grew up in Beverly Hills and was no stranger to the show-business world—her brother Billy was already on the record charts as part of the rock group Dino, Desi, and Billy. Annie met Carl at the Los Angeles airport, where she had gone to accompany a girl friend who was dating Bruce Johnston. Carl was only eighteen at the time.

"He had a great sense of humor, and we hit it off," she said. "He was also very sensitive and perceptive. It was really love at first sight." In Salt Lake City, where the Beach Boys had gone to perform that weekend, Carl asked Bruce to call his girl friend and ask if she could bring Annie to meet him at the airport on his return. Annie was waiting at the gate when the plane landed, and Carl drove her home in his brand-new Astin Martin. He gave her an engagement ring two months after meeting her on her sixteenth birthday, December 27. When she wore the ring to the Marymount School in Beverly Hills, where she was a sophomore, the nuns told her she either had to leave school or give back the ring. Annie discussed it with her parents and they decided she should choose Carl over school. They were married just two months later, on February 3, 1966. By the time he was married, Carl had already bought his first

big house at 1902 Coldwater Canyon, for a modest $100,000.
It was a contemporary, U-shaped house, with a patio in the
center and a swimming pool in back. It too was decorated by
Lee Polk.

At the time, Carl was involved in a protracted legal battle
with the government over his draft status. The problem came
to a head in 1967 when he was arrested in New York for refusing to be inducted, claiming to be a conscientious objector.
Carl said the arrest was "a hype," and insisted that the authorities had forewarned him of it. "They called me a few days
before and said, 'Okay, listen, there's a warrant for your arrest.
You just come in to the office in New York and we'll arrest
you. Then we'll release you on a personal-recognizance bond,
and you'll go back to L.A. and take care of it.'" According to
Carl, when he presented himself to the authorities, they "really
wanted to do a news thing" and had a photographer waiting.
They "actually arrested me and did a hoked-up trick, held me
in jail for a few hours.... It's cost me thirty thousand dollars
to fight this thing so far. Imagine what it would be like for
somebody who didn't have the money."

Of all the Beach Boys, Mike Love had perhaps changed the
most. Professionally, his nasal vocals had turned into something of a trademark, and he had become the consummate stage
frontman. Perhaps because he was self-conscious about not
playing an instrument, he would prance, jump, and dance
across the stage, giving the audience something to look at. More
than anyone else in the group, Mike clearly enjoyed performing
live and touring. Mike's vision of himself as a celebrity included his personal life. In the summer of 1967, after living
in a small house in Manhattan Beach for a year, he and Suzanne
moved to a house at 1215 Coldwater Canyon in Bel Air, which,
Mike bragged, "cost about three number-one records." For-
merly owned by internationally known auctioneer Milton
Wershow, the house was handsome and imposing, with a large
tiled pool surrounded by gardens of lemon and tangerine trees.
From the living room, which one visitor described as "the
width of an airplane hangar," there was a breathtaking view
of the twinkling city below. For a few months before the fur-

niture arrived, the living room was bare except for the lavish lemon-yellow carpeting that Suzanne had installed as soon as they moved in—they called it the "Yellow Valley." To make this picture of seeming domestic tranquillity complete, on December 27, 1966, their daughter, Hayleigh, was born; and two years later, on May 23, 1968, a son, Christian. By this time Mike owned a vintage yellow MG convertible and a large white Jaguar, in which he would tool down the hill to the Daisy, a celebrity disco in Beverly Hills, where he danced all night and rubbed elbows with Barbra Streisand.

But within Mike's marriage things were not so glamorous. The couple hadn't been together very long before Suzanne discovered that Mike was given to violent fits of temper, sparked by what he saw as her transgressions, such as cigarette smoking. His reaction must have seemed particularly ironic to Suzanne, since Michael had given her a carton of cigarettes on their first date. Suzanne quickly realized that Mike's temper tantrums went beyond the momentary flare-up of a man under pressure from a demanding career. Once, when she was pregnant with Hayleigh, Mike hit her. They had just checked into the Fountainbleau Hotel in Miami after a concert in Memphis. In the room above them, Dennis started throwing chairs out of his window onto the roof below to let off steam, incensing Michael. Suzanne went downstairs to the pharmacy, and when she came back to the room, Mike had discovered a pack of cigarettes hidden in her suitcase. After the beating, Mike was apologetic and charming, but Suzanne lived in increasing fear. On a trip to England, Mike hit her so hard she sported a black eye for a week.

Dennis's wife Carol remembers one incident when Christian and Hayleigh were little. "They were disturbing this man who claimed to be all peace and love. He came down and hit [Christian] so hard that he flew across the room. I actually went after Mike with a frying pan, I was so outraged that a person could get that violent."

Al Jardine, the stable, quiet—some say boring—mainstay of the group was happily married, living with his wife, Lynda in a beautiful house and small ranch in the Mandeville Canyon area at 1820 Westridge Road. They had dogs, horses, and even a pet monkey—and "Monkey" became Alan's nickname around the office. On the road he worked hard, was prompt for concerts, and read books on ecology. He eschewed drugs and drink. Dennis once described Alan as "a man waiting for a bus." Throughout the Beach Boys' early fame, Alan had been an employee of the group; now he was finally made a full financial partner in the firm.

Dennis was having the best time of all—or at least the wildest. Rock stardom agreed with his personality, his ego, his foolish generosity, and his lust. He did not care much for the hard work of recording, and session drummer Hal Blaine had long been handling most of the chores involved. But Dennis did like the glamour of touring, the jet planes, limousines, and adoring crowds. At home he had attracted his own circle of admirers. Some, as in Brian's life, were drainers while others appreciated Dennis, bringing excitement and vitality. Brian's friend Terry Melcher had become part of Dennis's circle. Dennis had also befriended a former employee of Julius Lefkowitz, Stanley Shapiro, whom he had nearly run over one day while driving in Century City. After Shapiro bawled him out about his recklessness, the two became fast friends. Shapiro quit his job at the Lefkowitz office, and came to work for Dennis. One of Dennis's first gestures was to buy Shapiro a new wardrobe in one of L.A.'s most expensive clothing stores.* But Dennis's closest friendship was with a self-styled talent scout and sometime actor named Gregg Jakobson. Jakobson was born in Los Angeles and had gone to Venice High School (with photographer Guy Webster). He had met Dennis in Hawaii through Bruce Johnston and Terry Melcher, who were still performing together. Jakobson married Carol Costello, daughter of comedian Lou Costello, and lived not far from Dennis, just over the hill in Benedict Canyon.

Dennis's wild side was growing even wilder. His newest love was dirt bikes. "He had a feeling about himself that he was invulnerable, and nothing could hurt him," said Shapiro.

---

*Stanley Shapiro's father was Bernie Shapiro, the investment counselor for Lefkowitz.

On one occasion, Dennis decided to ride his bike up to and inside Brian's Bellagio Road house. "There were tufts of carpeting shooting out from behind him as he rode up the stairs," Jakobson said. "We'd be riding on motorcycles and he would buy out all the whipped cream in the supermarket, literally all of it, hitting the nitrous oxide gas and throwing the cans over his shoulder," said Jakobson.

Dennis had adopted Carol's son, Scott, when the child was eighteen months old; a daughter, Jennifer, was born around the same time, in 1967. He was a wonderful father, when he had the time or interest. In 1965 they had moved to a large tan house with white trim at 2600 Benedict Canyon Drive on two and a half acres of land. They gutted the house and renovated it completely. The living-room ceiling was lifted to a towering thirty feet, and one of the four bedrooms was transformed into a music room for Dennis. Lee Polk also decorated this house, except for the red velvet bed and matching headboard Murry gave the couple as a gift the first Christmas they lived there. Murry also donated the quartz rock, taken from outside his house in Whittier, that was installed around the fireplace. In the backyard was a stable with a pony named Skipper for Scott, and horses for both Carol and Dennis—Rusty and The Big Black. Cars came and went with spendthrift speed—an XKE; a Ferrari that had once belonged to murdered singer Sam Cook; another Ferrari, this one red; a British racing-green Austin Healy followed by a green Corvette convertible and a bright yellow Cobra that Dennis sometimes raced.

The first two years of the marriage, according to Carol, were wonderful. "I had a blast. He was terrific," she said. But soon the day-to-day reality set in. Some of Dennis's behavior, though not malicious, was difficult to take, such as his foolhardy generosity. "I once came home and our washer and dryer were gone." When she questioned Dennis, he told her he had met a man who lost his job and had five kids. Dennis decided to give the washer and dryer to them.

By the end of 1967 it was clear to Carol that their marriage was in serious trouble. "For me it was the drugs," Carol said. "I was not into drugs, and with two little children, that was really hard for me. The drugs started right after Jennifer was born, maybe while I was pregnant. Murry was really against drugs, and at first so was Dennis. This was one way Dennis could be separate from everybody else and get the love he wanted from Murry. I would say a big part of Dennis's problem was that he could never connect with his father or please Murry."

But of all the problems Carol had with Dennis, his extramarital affairs hurt the most. While Dennis was extremely prim and moral about Carol—she joked that she was the only woman on the beach in a turtleneck bathing suit—he had another standard for himself. Dennis cheated on Carol without apologies or apprehensions. He bragged to his friends that the night his daughter was born, he made love to another woman on the lawn of his house. Frequently he would come home from touring with a case of gonorrhea, contracted from a groupie on the road. He and Terry Melcher and Gregg Jakobson formed a club called the Golden Penetrators. "They considered themselves roving cocksmen," Carol said. "It was mostly guys hanging out and getting stoned." Gregg Jakobson donated his old car. "They even painted this old car gold, drove it up our driveway, and parked it on the side of our hill. It hurt, of course. You don't like thinking of your husband belonging to a club called the Golden Penetrators. It was tough."

When the fights with Carol became onerous, Dennis would disappear for days, usually sleeping at Gregg Jakobson's house. The marriage took a disastrous turn with the death of one of the horses. Dennis claimed that Carol had starved it to death; Carol said it had gotten pneumonia and had to be put to sleep. The horse's death caused an irreparable rift. Much to Carol's relief, early in 1968 Dennis finally rented his own place, an enormous house at 14400 Sunset Boulevard. Once a hunting lodge owned by Will Rogers, it had vast, manicured grounds with trees so rare they were registered. The house was woodpaneled, with handmade furniture, and out in back was a swimming pool the shape of the state of California.

Murry and Audree's marriage continued to have its ups and downs. Audree loved Murry, and could see the misguided but well-meaning man so often hidden from strangers by his gruff exterior. But even for Audree, Murry was often difficult to take, and she spent much of her time at her favorite son Carl's house before Murry bought a second house for her to live in. Still, Murry and Audree were extremely dedicated to one another.

One major breach occurred when Murry discovered that his sons were smoking marijuana. "I remember Carl and Brian telling me," Audree said, "we were walking through the airport—they had just come back to Los Angeles from someplace—and [they told me about smoking pot]. I just choked because at that time it was such a new thing to me. . . . I knew nothing about it except, 'Oh, stay away! Dangerous! Bad!' And of course, their father, oh Jesus, he just went wild cause they all told him—they were very honest. I wished they had never told us." Murry forbade Audree to have anything to do with them. "It was a terrible time in my life," she said. "He wouldn't allow them to come over until they would say, 'I'll never touch another marijuana cigarette again.' I only got to see them sort of sneakily because he didn't want me to go to their houses. Instead of asserting myself and saying, 'Go to hell, they're my sons,' I did what he told me." Murry finally relented on Christmas Day of 1967. "All of a sudden," Audree related, "he said, 'You can have the family for Christmas,' and I was ecstatic. I was so thrilled—they all came and had a wonderful day. But the important thing that I remember was the pain of the months he wouldn't allow them to come to my house."

The worst was to come in January 1967, when Audree went on a short vacation to Las Vegas with her brother, Carl Korthof. Carl, who had been trying to cut down on his drinking because of a serious heart condition, had been introduced by his nephews to a much less lethal high—marijuana—and had brought some with him to Las Vegas. By this time Audree was no stranger to marijuana. One morning while her brother was in the other room, he had a sudden and fatal heart attack. In a panic, Audree called for an ambulance. When the police and paramedics arrived, the first thing they saw was the marijuana on the living-room coffee table. Already beside herself with shock at her brother's death, poor Audree was now arrested and "put behind bars," according to Carl's son, Steve Korthof.

Said Steve, "I flew to Vegas with my mom and Murry, and Murry didn't know anything about [Audree's arrest]. They were going to Vegas to identify my dad, and when they got to the hotel I already knew. I didn't say a word. They were told that Audree was at the police station. So Murry says, 'Police station? I guess she went to file a report.' When he got down to the station and went to the normal department where she should have been, he found out she was [being held] in the narcotics division. 'What?' he said. When he found out what happened, he totally flipped out...oh Jesus, when he found out..." It took a long time for him to forgive Audree for that one.

During this period Murry was still promoting various new ventures in the music business. He had recently re-teamed with Rick Henn, of the Sunrays, who said he "sort of became Murry's Brian." One of Murry's projects was to write unsolicited jingles for television commercials, "because he felt the sponsors needed his help," according to Rick Henn. "Little did Murry know that no advertising agency takes outside input." Murry wrote and recorded a Kentucky Fried Chicken commercial and a Taco Bell commercial, among others—all were politely turned down. The only song of Murry's to be heard by the general public was one he wrote with Brian under the pseudonym Reggie Dunbar, called "Break Away." The Beach Boys released the song as a single in June 1969, without much success.

But to Murry, his most important project was the LP entitled, *The Many Moods of Murry Wilson*. Murry wrote and produced most of this album, with Don Ralke doing arrangements. However, Murry still fancied himself a talent scout and showcased a new discovery on the LP—a forty-year-old plumber named Eck Kynor who had helped with the renovations on Murry's Whittier house. Kynor was represented on the album by tunes called "The Plumber's Tune" and "The Happy Song." Also included on the LP were tunes entitled "Leaves" and "Betty's Waltz" (with an assist from Audree). Capitol released the album in October 1967.*

---

*Allegedly, Murry arranged for Capitol to have the cost of his album charged back to the Beach Boys' account.

That December Murry took Audree to England, where the album was also released, and embarked on his own self-styled one-month promotional tour. Interviewed in a luxurious suite at the London Hilton, Murry told a reporter from *Disc and Music Echo* that "after 'Good Vibrations' Brian lost a lot of confidence. He didn't think he could ever write anything as good as that again.... With [my] LP I'm going to nudge my boys' competitive spirit. Show them that the Beach Boys don't have all the talent in the family. Brian may find new rejuvenation in his confidence as a result. They may all find new spirit to stay at the top.

"I call them my 'Monsters,'" Murry laughed. "But they've never let me down. How could I be anything other than proud of them?"

4

While Murry was in England promoting his own album, the Beach Boys were rehearsing for a UNICEF benefit to be held in Paris on December 15 and rebroadcast on TV to 250 million people around the world. The benefit boasted a program of international stars, including Marlon Brando, Richard Burton, Elizabeth Taylor, Burt Lancaster, and Lena Horne. On the first day of rehearsals, John Lennon and George Harrison accompanied their recently acquired guru, the Maharishi Mahesh Yogi, to hear Ravi Shankar play. The Maharishi was sitting cross-legged in the audience with the two Beatles when Dennis Wilson wandered in and made a beeline for them. Dennis shook the Maharishi's hand. "All of a sudden," Dennis said, "I felt this weirdness, this presence this guy had. Like out of left field. First thing he ever said to me [was] 'Live your life to the fullest.' So the next day I went over to his room, and he said, 'Tell me some words of your songs.' So we told him the lyrics to 'God Only Knows' [which Tony Asher wrote] and he goes, 'That's the sun rising and the stars and the planets and it connects with...' So I said, 'God, this is great!' And he said, 'We'd like to initiate you into the program.' I said, 'What does that mean, how much?' And he said, 'We'll just do it to you tomorrow morning.'"

The rest of the Beach Boys had already flown on to London. "So I called Michael and all the guys in London. 'C'mon down here to Paris. We're all gonna meditate.'" And then I got my mantra, and as the Maharishi was giving them to us he said, 'What do you want?' I said, 'I want everything. Everything.' And he laughed and we meditated together. It was so wild."

The Maharishi Mahesh Yogi was a small, brown-skinned man who seemed to offer instant spiritual relief and salvation, a modern-day psychic Band-Aid with fast results that appealed not only to Dennis but to Mike Love and the other members of the group. The Maharishi spoke of Jesus, of God, of eternal happiness and peace—he seemed for all the world a mystical, Eastern sage. But the Maharishi was far from an unsophisticated hick from the Himalayas. College-educated, with a degree in physics, he had studied Sanskrit and learned the scriptures with a well-known Indian sage named Guru Dev. Reportedly, the title "Maharashi" was self-adopted. Sometime in the late fifties he began to preach his brand of mystic salvation to sold-out audiences in various Western countries.

Most of the world learned of the Maharishi through the Beatles. Leaders of the burgeoning youth movement, the Beatles were under enormous pressure to find the "truth" and the "meaning of life." When the Beatles first went to hear the Maharishi lecture at the London Hilton, they were fascinated. They promised to travel to the Maharishi's Himalayan ashram as soon as possible. The trip took place early in February 1968, when Mike Love also went to India. Of all the Beach Boys, Mike Love was the most influenced by the Maharishi. "When I heard about TM," Mike said, "I consciously took steps to expand my awareness.... I didn't want to live life at the same level twenty years from now.... And one of the greatest things that interested me was that [the Maharishi] said, 'You don't have to give up your Rolls-Royce...and forsake all your pursuits of material pleasures...to develop inner spiritual qualities.' That sounded real good to me." Indeed, Mike Love looked at meditation as a way to wash his spiritual laundry; he could "clean up" the bad karma from his other deeds.

For Mike Love, the trip to India marked the start of a lifelong passion for meditation. For the Beatles, it was the beginning of the end of their interest in Eastern mysticism. While the Beatles were in India at Rishikesh, the Maharishi suggested they tithe 10 to 25 percent of their income into a Swiss account in his name. At the time the Beatles were considering starring in a film about TM to promote the Maharishi's university, and when a Beatles aide arrived in Rishikesh to negotiate the deal, he found that the Maharishi not only had a full-time accountant, but was also haggling with him about points in the profit structure. Moreover, the Maharishi had announced that the Beatles would appear with him on an ABC television special in America to help publicize his movement. Although the Beatles management told ABC this was not true, the Maharishi insisted it was. Eventually the Beatles had to insist he stop using their name for his benefit. When the Maharishi persisted, George Harrison shrugged it off, saying that since the Maharishi was not a worldly man, he could not understand the ramifications.

Mike Love was so taken with not only Maharishi, but the celebrity-studded scene in Rishikesh, that he was determined to make a movie about it. He called Nick Grillo several times in Los Angeles, demanding that Grillo advance him a considerable sum of money to rent or purchase film equipment, as well as a helicopter. "He was driving us nuts," Grillo said. For Grillo, the idea was out of the question; money was tight, and the boys weren't touring. But Mike was so determined that he demanded Grillo get an advance from the next Capitol royalty check. When Grillo refused to comply, Mike wrote a "threatening" letter to Alan Livingstone, then president of Capitol Records, insisting he get the money. "We all said no," Grillo explained, "and Mike was very upset about it—there were a lot of harsh words, to say the least."

While Mike was at the ashram in Rishikesh, a scandal erupted that is still a highly contested incident to this day. Allegedly, the Maharishi had made advances to an American nurse who was also studying with them, and to whom he had served the forbidden meal of chicken. By this time Ringo and Paul had begun to doubt the usefulness of Transcendental Meditation and had already left the ashram—only George and John were left there with their wives. The scandal about the nurse and the Maharishi destroyed John's belief, and the next morning he and George left the ashram for good. The Beatles were through with the Maharishi, but Mike Love's faith was not shaken. When he returned from the ashram to Los Angeles late in the spring of 1968, he was still a firm believer and prosyletizer, encouraging everyone in the office to meditate and join the TM movement. Mike managed to convince the rest of the group that it would be a good move for the Beach Boys to tour America with the Maharishi—a kind of spiritual California rock-and-roll package to be booked into large college auditoriums.

5

While discussion about a tour with the Maharishi continued, the Beach Boys needed desperately to replenish their quickly dwindling company funds. In April 1968 they set out on the road, with funds advanced to them by banker Joe Lipsher. "It was the answer to all our dreams," Grillo said. Although it was a small tour of primarily the Southeast, with only seventeen dates, "we would see net big bucks," Grillo said. This was because the Beach Boys were basically promoting the tour themselves. Said the road manager, Richard Duryea, "At that point we were hiring the halls and paying for the newspaper ads, paying for the radio spots, fronting the whole tour." In an attempt to spark audience interest, the Strawberry Alarm Clock and the Buffalo Springfield were added to make the bill more eclectic. The Beach Boys were on a plane to Memphis, Tennessee, at the beginning of the tour, when they learned of a national tragedy: Martin Luther King, Jr., had been assassinated. Later in the day, when the Beach Boys were setting up their equipment, the National Guard arrived, informing them that no audience was expected at the concert, and that there was a curfew in effect to curtail expected racial violence. "We flew on to the next city," Duryea said, "Greenville, North Carolina, and we ended up waiting in a Holiday Inn for a couple of days while all the other cities that we scheduled went dead because no one wanted to go. We had to wait until it blew over, and we finished the tour as best we could. Even then people didn't come because they were concerned about violence."

"Some dates we played to half-houses," Grillo says. "Some dates only twenty-five people showed up." Eventually, the remainder of the tour was cancelled, after only four performances, and every penny the Beach Boys had borrowed went down the drain. "Devastating," Grillo said, "a fucking nightmare."

The Maharishi tour was supposed to remedy all that. "We were licking our wounds from the other tour," Grillo said, when just a month later, on May 3, the Beach Boys set out on a seventeen-day tour with the Maharishi in a private rented plane. The Maharishi had certain demands, including elaborate flower settings wherever he went, as well as fresh fruit and other dietary needs that the Beach Boys were obligated to fulfill. Billed as "The Most Exciting Event of the Decade" by the New York promoters, the shows took place in huge concert halls and stadiums, instead of college auditoriums as originally planned. On opening night, at the Singer Bowl in New York, "more police showed up than audience," according to Richard Duryea. The fans were completely uninterested in hearing the Maharishi, and those who might have turned out for the Beach Boys alone, stayed away. "There was a date at the Spectrum in Philadelphia where quite a few people showed up to see the Beach Boys, but when the Maharishi came on, they all left. No one cared, which is what everybody told Mike would happen. You can't slug your audience around like that and ask them to pay a high-priced ticket to hear this guy talk." On a typical tour date, the Maharishi opened with a long, boring, unintelligible lecture while the audience booed and yelled for the Beach Boys. "The Maharishi laughed," said Duryea. "He was laughing all the time. He got his money."

Grillo called it "another disaster." Quoted in an article by Carl Fleming in *Newsweek*, Jardine summed it up: "The only people that are going to make money on this tour are the florists." The tour was cancelled halfway through, at a loss approaching half a million dollars.

The culmination of the Beach Boys' official business relationship with the Maharishi was an album, called *Friends*, released that June after the miserable tour. Known as the "TM album" by fans, it was one of their worst-selling albums by far—a boring, emotionless LP. This low-key album was, according to Al Jardine, "just a collection of cuts. It was done in Brian's house." Beach Boys biographer David Leaf called the album, "so laid back as to be almost soporific, which gives an accurate insight into what Brian Wilson was up to...." Indeed, Brian's solo contribution to the album was called "Busy Doin' Nothin'."

On June 15, in London, the Beatles formally renounced their association with the Maharishi as a "public mistake." Mike Love would continue to be a lifelong follower.

6

Across the nation the Beach Boys' concert grosses plummeted. Promoters were reluctant to book them, considering them passé. In an effort to keep more of their proceeds, the Beach Boys had changed their arrangement with Irving Granz at William Morris. At the end of 1967, they formed their own promotion entity, called American Productions, but would look to Granz to fill in dates they could not book. "I was under pressure," said Grillo, "because the guys would not go on the road. They were spending money, Brian was in the bedroom locked up, and their wives wouldn't go on the road because they were fucking other women.... How do you go on? It was difficult."

Yet they still made other investments. One of them was a major real-estate deal in the Simi Valley, north of Los Angeles. It was a good guess that the Simi Valley would soon become one of the next major development properties around the city, and under Grillo's direction the Beach Boys purchased over six hundred acres of income-producing farmland at between $6,000 and $8,000 an acre, with orange and lemon groves that would cover the cost of the real-estate taxes. Brian, who had the largest, most stable income of all the Beach Boys because of his publishing revenues, invested the lion's share of approximately $250,000 in the Simi Valley, owning 62 percent of the deal. "It was a brilliant investment," Grillo said, "that would make the guys into multimillionaires.... The balloon payment was down the road...."*

At the same time, the group gave up the lease at 9000 Sunset Boulevard and worked out a favorable deal with Bernie Shapiro, the real-estate investment counselor for Julius Lefkowitz and Company, for a lease-option agreement on the Mannis Fur Building at 1654 North Ivar Street in Hollywood. "The deal was very favorable," Grillo said. "We were paying a monthly fee [of only $1,500] against the purchase price of the building ...[Shapiro] agreed to put together the upstairs the way we wanted it, renovating it to suit us...he paid for all that.... It was based on the premise that we would eventually buy the building. We were expecting X number of dollars coming in from various deals." The two-story building offered six thousand square feet of office space upstairs, and the downstairs tenants were Albert Hosiery and Sir George Smorgasbord. Grillo's office, which had previously been a humidified fur vault, now had an electric sliding door. The new place included a small rehearsal studio, accounting offices, room for the fan club, and even a sauna. The only drawback was there were no windows. "It was a tomb in more ways than one," said their old friend Fred Vail—and a tomb it would soon become.

---

*At the time, tax laws allowed an immediate five years of "pre-paid interest" on property purchases to be deducted from income taxes. The idea was to purchase property and use the prepaid interest as a down payment. The property would then immediately be put on the market, and hopefully sold at a vast profit before the five years' interest was due to the government. Many Hollywood stars became wealthy from this tax loophole.

He was really dirty and stinky . . .
this awful person in the lobby hanging
out and playing his songs.
His music sucked too.

—RICHARD DURYEA

Ten

1

It was nearly three o'clock one morning in late spring of 1968
when Dennis returned from a recording session to his newly
rented home at 14400 Sunset Boulevard. He had not left the
outside spotlights turned on, and as he pulled his silver Ferrari
GTB down the long, curving driveway, he was surprised to see
that the house was well lit inside, seemingly full of activity.
He stopped the car near the rear of the house. As he got out,
the back door swung open and a small man emerged. He was
a remarkable vision, like a hippie from a gothic horror movie.
He was a slight fellow, scarcely more than five feet tall, and a
bit hunchbacked. He wore a work shirt, jeans, and fringed
buckskin shoes. His dark, shaggy hair was shoulder-length,
and even in the shadows Dennis could detect a strange, almost
crazed look in his dark eyes. Dennis instinctively felt a chill;
something told him this was no ordinary housebreaker, and
no ordinary hippie. Without even knowing why, he heard himself ask, "Are you going to hurt me?"

The man looked wounded. "Do I look like I'm going to hurt
you, brother?" he asked. Before Dennis could answer, the man
dropped to his knees. Dennis stood there, frozen, as the man
leaned forward and kissed his sneakers reverently.

"Who are you?" Dennis asked in wonder.

"I'm a friend," the man said, and invited Dennis into his
own house. As they went in the back door, Dennis noticed a
black school bus hidden by the trees. The words *Hollywood
Productions* had been painted sloppily on its side.

Dennis was shocked—but not unhappy—to find the house occupied by a dozen or so young girls. They were smoking pot and had helped themselves to liquor and whatever food was in the refrigerator. A few of the girls were topless. The stereo was on, blasting Beatles songs.

Dennis immediately recognized two of the girls—one who said her nickname was "Yellerstone," and another who called herself Marnie Reeves and had long brown hair and beautiful blue eyes. He had twice picked them up hitchhiking in Malibu—the first time a month before, the second earlier that day. Marnie had told him that she had been born and raised in Inglewood, virtually Dennis's childhood backyard. Earlier that day he had driven them to 14400 Sunset Boulevard to show them his gold records. As he hoped, he ended up having sex with both of them, and he had bragged about the incident that same evening in the studio. He would soon find out the experience had given him gonorrhea. Much later, he would find out that "Yellerstone"'s real name was Ella Jo Bailey, and that Marnie Reeves's real name was Patricia Krenwinkle.

Patricia Krenwinkle came forward when she saw Dennis and said, "This is the guy we were telling you about. This is Charlie Manson."

Charlie Manson, as the girls had told Dennis earlier that day, was a musician of great power and talent. He was also a philosopher, a leader and prophet. As it turned out, the two men had a lot in common. Manson was a musician; so was Dennis. Manson hated the blacks; Dennis didn't care much for them either. Manson liked young, innocent-looking girls; they were Dennis's favorites, too. Manson spun a vivid and convincing scenario about the apocalypse that was soon to come. In the near future, Manson told Dennis, there would be a worldwide race war—black, red, and yellow against white. Manson had formed a "family"—a loving army for security and protection against the coming war. Manson and his followers would arm themselves and live safely in the desert until the wars passed. Said one of Dennis's friends later, "If you didn't have a basis for reasoning, if you were not a very deep-thinking person, you could really be taken in by this guy because what he said was a lot of half-truths." Manson lived on other people's fears, and he sensed fear in Dennis. Confused, depressed about his impending divorce, and very stoned, Dennis was the perfect prey for Charlie. Not only that, Charlie held the strongest lure of all for Dennis: wild, free, orgiastic sex. That very night, the orgies started. Charlie's dictum was sex seven times a day—before and after each meal and once in the middle of the night.

Manson orgies were a very organized affair. "It was more like a business transaction," said Stanley Shapiro. Manson himself handed out the drugs, usually psychedelics—LSD, STP, mushrooms, or whatever was handy—and made sure that he took a much smaller dose than anyone else so he could remain in charge. According to Paul ("Tex") Watkins, Manson's second-in-command and procurer of young girls, "Everything was done at Charlie's direction." As Charlie began to strip, so did the girls. Then everyone would lie down on the floor and, under Charlie's directions, take twelve deep breaths with their eyes closed, rubbing up against each other until everyone was touching. Charlie would proceed to literally direct the orgy, suggesting positions and sexual acts. "He would say, 'You take off your blouse,'" said one of Dennis's friends who was brought over to 14400 Sunset to participate, "'and now spread your legs.'" Watkins told police, "He'd set it all up in a beautiful way like he was creating a masterpiece in sculpture."

At the moment Charles Manson met Dennis, he was thirty-three, an illiterate burglar, car thief, forger, and pimp; a drifter and ex-con who had spent seventeen years—half of his life—in various prisons. He had last been released from Terminal Island prison in the spring of 1967. The morning of his release he begged the prison officials to let him stay, afraid he could not adjust to the outside world. But they forced him to leave, and he roamed the streets of San Francisco, sleeping in doorways, until a friend got him a room in a transient hotel. He spent his days wandering Telegraph Avenue, playing his guitar, and eventually met a girl named Mary Brunner, then twenty-three. He moved in with her and they had a child.* It was the San Francisco peace-and-love-movement that helped Manson

---

*Manson's children, as well as other Family children, were placed in foster homes by the courts, and their real identities and locations are sealed in court records.

coalesce his free-love Family philosophy. Dr. David Smith, who had worked with the Family at the Free Clinic in San Francisco, said, "Sex, not drugs, was the common denominator." During the summer of 1967 Manson procured a school bus, piled into it his expanding Family—which now included Mary Brunner, Ella Jo Bailey, Lynette "Squeaky" Fromme, Patricia Krenwinkle and three or four young boys—and started wandering for a year. They lived in Mendocino, Big Sur, Mexico, Nevada, Los Angeles, Topanga Canyon, Malibu, and Venice. Shortly before meeting Dennis, Manson and his Family had been living in a deserted ranch once used as a movie location, the Spahn Movie Ranch in Chatsworth, in the Simi Valley.

Dennis was sufficiently impressed by Charlie and his girls to ask them to move in with him, thus beginning what the media would later call Manson's "Sunset Boulevard" period. Living with Dennis was paradise for Charlie and his band of locusts. Dennis's self-styled brand of generosity was just what Charlie needed. Charlie helped himself to anything that belonged to Dennis: cars, clothing, money, food, and a couple of gold records—the latter Charlie gave away as gifts. Yet, although they were living in high style, some aspects of the Family's behavior remained the same, such as their food-collection activities. Despite the enormous deliveries to the house every day by the Alta Dena Dairy, of parcels including yogurts and ice cream, and generous cash supplements from Dennis to buy food, Manson still sent the girls on nightly "food runs." On these scavenging hunts, the girls would pile into Dennis's Rolls-Royce in the middle of the night and visit a selection of closed supermarkets, where they would search the garbage dumpsters for decaying foods that were waiting to be picked up by private sanitation companies. Dennis thought these food runs were a lot of fun and made some of them himself, sometimes driving the girls a hundred miles an hour up and down Sunset Boulevard in his Ferrari.

That summer Dennis began an affair with a beautiful fifteen-year-old girl named Diane Adams, who was on vacation from boarding school. One weekend, while staying with her father in Encino, she heard that Dennis Wilson, the Beach Boy, was living in a house on Sunset Boulevard and went there to find him. Diane, whose nickname was "Croxey," drove her Nassau-blue 1965 Stingray into the driveway of 14400 Sunset and found Dennis running across the lawn dressed in silk lounging pants. For the rest of the time that Dennis lived with Charles Manson and the Family, Croxey Adams was his girl friend.

"It was very bizarre," Croxey said. "They were sleeping all over the house. Charlie had these girls providing for him—sewing, cooking, doing anything he wanted...." According to Croxey, daily life with the Family was calmer than anyone would have expected. The girls would lounge around the pool, dividing up the household chores. A group of them worked in the kitchen and baked bread for the evening meals, while others took turns watching the children. Croxey didn't fit in with this group from the start, and although Manson made a persistent effort to have her join the Family, she resisted him. Her only interest was in being with Dennis, whom she remembered as "the greatest stud at twenty-three." Because of her separateness from the Family, Charlie and the other girls mistrusted her greatly. Croxey wouldn't take orders from Charlie, and she couldn't take the group sex seriously. When Manson started to choreograph, Croxey would find herself giggling and trying to hold it in, which interrupted the flow. Manson would get furious with her and throw her out. "I would try to stop [the orgies]. I would start cracking up. I would get out of those things and say this is not for me.

"Charlie had a passion for me," Croxey said, but she refused to sleep with him. "I slept every night on a little antique love seat, my legs and head up so that Charlie couldn't sleep next to me. I wouldn't sleep anywhere where he could crawl next to me. He was such a creep, and I would say, 'Would you get away!' I said, 'I'm here because I like Dennis,' and Charlie would say, 'You're not allowed to have crushes. Everybody is supposed to love everybody.' Sometimes it would get so intense I would leave and go home. It's not very complimentary to know that Charlie Manson has a crush on you. I told Dennis, 'You better get these people out of here, because I have a feeling you're going to get busted.'"

But Dennis wasn't afraid of getting busted. He liked Manson

and the Family so much that he bragged about his friendship with them in a 1968 issue of an English music magazine called *Rave*. "Fear is nothing but awareness," he told the writer, mimicking Manson's mumbo jumbo. "Sometimes the Wizard frightens me—Charlie Manson, who is another friend of mine, says he is God and the devil! He sings, plays, and writes poetry...." Moreover, Dennis thought he had made a great musical discovery in Manson, and wanted him to record for Brother Records. Although he was later to claim that "Charlie didn't have a musical bone in his whole body," Dennis was quite impressed with Charlie's song-writing ability at the time, and tried to help Charlie's musical career get off the ground. One of the first people he introduced Manson to was Gregg Jakobson. "One day Dennis called me up," Jakobson recounted, "and said, 'Hey Gregg, you should have been down here. Some guy pulled in with a big black bus ... and he's got about thirty girls.' Charlie later told me that the only reason why he used to travel with all those girls was to attract guys. He was always recruiting." The following night Jakobson went to Dennis's house and was overwhelmed by the scene—a host of subservient, half-naked young women, catering to Dennis's and Manson's every whim. Jakobson's first impression of Manson was that he was "intellectually stimulating." "He had a very powerful intellect," Jakobson said. "He could discuss almost any subject, just like he said [later, in court] he had a 'thousand hats' and he could put on any hat at any time. In another situation he would have been capable of being president of a university...." Over the next year, Jakobson had more than a hundred philosophical conversations with Manson, and got to know him as well as anyone outside of the Family.

One night Dennis and Gregg took Manson and some of the girls to the Whiskey A Go Go on Sunset Boulevard. "Charlie started dancing, and I swear to God, within a matter of minutes the dance floor would be empty and Charlie would be dancing by himself. It was almost as if sparks were flying off the guy."

Jakobson was so taken with him that along with Dennis, he touted Manson to others—such as Rudy Altobelli, a business manager for show-business personalities. Altobelli owned several properties in Los Angeles, including an enormous mansion at 10050 Cielo Drive. Altobelli lived in the guest house behind the mansion, and rented the main house to Terry Melcher and his girl friend, Candice Bergen. Altobelli met Manson at a party at Dennis's house that summer, and listened to a tape of Charlie's music. "They were telling me about his philosophy and his way of living and how groovy he was." But Altobelli had no interest in Manson, and declined to help Manson's career, as did John Phillips, of the Mamas and Pappas. The only one of Jakobson's friends to show any real interest in the man was Terry Melcher. Jakobson was convinced that Melcher's production company should record Manson, and brought Melcher to meet Charlie at Dennis's house several times. On one occasion Dennis drove Melcher home to 10050 Cielo Drive, while Charlie sat in the backseat, softly strumming his guitar. Eventually, on August 9 of that summer, Jakobson arranged for Manson to have a preliminary recording session at a Van Nuys studio, but not much was accomplished.

2

It wasn't long before Dennis started to bring Charlie up to the Beach Boys' offices and introduce him to everyone. After all, the philosophy of Brother Records was supposedly that each member of the group should be allowed to discover new acts and record them, and Dennis had found one. He didn't find much support for Manson at the office, however. "He just gave us all the creeps. He was very sullen," said bookkeeper Catherine Pace. "He would hang around and plunk away on the guitar, just one tune—*plank, plank, plank*—one string he would plank away, this mastermind...." Manson was so filthy they called him "Pig Pen"—but not to his face.

Nick Grillo was obligated to take Manson more seriously than the rest, because Dennis insisted. "Charlie was a very bright guy, and his major concern was public acceptance of his music," Grillo said. "Dennis was enamored with Charlie, and the other members of the [Beach Boys] were enamored with the fact that he had twelve or thirteen women. The other guys were looking to get laid...." Indeed, Croxey Adams remembered, "They would come over to the house because they were all eyeing the situation. The Beach Boys loved it." Grillo, however, suspected the worst about Charlie, and asked a friend of his at the district attorney's office to check Manson out for him. Grillo was told only a limited amount of information: that Charlie had robbed a supermarket with a gun, had served some time, and was on probation. "He was looking to connect with something to fulfill the probationary situation [to have a job]...it was important to Charlie...it would give him some credibility and relieve him of the probationary responsibility...." Finally, after much urging on Dennis's part, Grillo called Stephen Despar, the new engineer at Brian's house on Bellagio Road, and said, "Crazy Dennis has some friend he wants to record. You can work at night. Dennis will bring him in and they'll work till two or three in the morning, and it shouldn't take too long."

Stephen Despar was a twenty-four-year-old electronics wizard who had built the Beach Boys' traveling sound system. At that time there were three fully equipped systems, which the Beach Boys had hoped to lease out to other touring rock groups at a profit. One of these systems had been sent to Monterey for the festival before the Beach Boys decided not to show up, and Despar served as one of the main sound technicians for the concert. Recently, he had been elected to build "a full-fledged recording studio with the capacity of any other" at Brian's house, as an improvement over the mobile equipment that had been installed previously. "This studio was supposed to be available so whenever Brian wanted to come down and record, it would be there," Despar said. Despar designed the recording system, and the Beach Boys hired a studio builder named Henry Mancini to construct it. Mancini arrived one morning with nine carpenters and finished the job that night. "It was a temporary kind of construction," Despar said. "The big window that overlooked the fountain in the courtyard was covered, a hole was opened in the wall above the fireplace so you could see out of the control room, and the final revision was the installation of a thirty-cubic-foot speaker encloser and custom-made monitors." Despar estimated the total cost at nearly $150,000.

At first Brian didn't even come down to see the new studio, but he could still hear all the sessions through the floorboards in his bedroom above. "Eventually it got the better of him, and he came down," Despar said. "He was in his pajama bottoms and must have weighed about two hundred pounds. He said, 'Hi, Steve. I thought I'd come down and look at this place.'" Despar gave him a tour and showed him how the new board worked. "Then he noticed there were coffee stains on the rug, and he didn't like that. The next day some carpet installers came and replaced the carpet with another rug of the same color." Soon afterward Brian said he wanted to paint the walls. "I want red and green and orange and pink and blue," he said. Despar purchased acoustical paint and Brian painted the panels himself. His final decorating touch was the purchase of a $1,500 alabaster lamp.

According to Despar, Brian would come down to the studio "in waves." All of a sudden the door would fly open and Brian would be standing there in his bathrobe and say, "Hey guys, I've got an idea! Listen to this line." He'd play a little tune on the organ and then disappear into his bedroom again. One night Despar and Brian discussed Brian's deafness and his subsequent inability to record in stereo. Despar had a suggestion: when Brian was in the studio, they would pipe the sessions over the speakers in mono while recording in stereo. After this, all the Beach Boys records would be produced in stereo.*

It was to this new studio—while Brian was upstairs in his bedroom—that Dennis brought Charles Manson. According to Despar, a demonstration tape would be recorded "that would be shopped around by American Productions." It was also assumed—at least by Manson—that Terry Melcher would help him get a contract with a major label.

"Dennis was really taken in by Manson," Despar said. "He went on for days about how much he loved Manson and how he wanted to help him out, saying that he really had talent, and that he was terribly misunderstood." When Manson finally

---

*Brian did manage to produce several songs in the studio that summer—but not for the Beach Boys. Instead, he recorded a double-sided single for Marilyn and Diane and their cousin Ginger.

showed up at Brian's house for his first professional recording session, he was completely unprepared. "He brought nothing," Despar said, "except half a dozen girls, and they stayed in the studio with him and smoked dope. I guess I got on Charlie's good side, because the first thing that happened was he pulled out a cigarette and didn't have a match, so I went to the kitchen and got a match for him. He was very impressed that someone would actually go to the trouble just for him. He made a big thing about that."

Charlie had just one caveat about his music. He used to say, "I don't care what you do with the music. Just don't let anybody change any of the lyrics." Between six and eight songs were recorded, some of which were "pretty good," according to Despar. "He had musical talent. . . . Dennis really should have been producing him, but he only came in a couple of times, and then he would leave."

Eventually, Manson's true nature started to come across, and Despar got nervous. "What struck me odd was the stare he gave you. It was scary. We were in there two or three nights, and then he got pretty weird. [He] pulled a knife on me, just for no reason really, just pulled a knife out and would flash it around while he was talking. I called Grillo and said, 'Look, this guy is psychotic, I don't think without a producer you're going to get anything on him. And the guy is just too weird for me. I don't know if I'm going to say something and that's going to tick him off and he's going to pull a switchblade on me." Grillo told Despar that the six or eight songs they had already recorded were enough, and called off any further recording sessions.

According to Gregg Jakobson, "Charlie couldn't make it with those people [at Brian's house]. They were too stiff for him." "Stiff" was an understatement—they were frightened to death of him. Marilyn in particular hated Charlie and the girls he brought around, especially one girl called "Sadie Glutz" (Susan Atkins). Marilyn once called the office and told Catherine Pace, "Kathy, please, I want you to buy us an ultraviolet toilet seat for the bathroom." When Catherine questioned her further, she said, "Dennis is bringing those crummy girls up here with Charles Manson, and I'm afraid they're going to give us or the children some diseases." But there was no such thing as an ultraviolet toilet seat, and Marilyn had to make do with thorough washings with disinfectant when they left. Once, Tex Watson "borrowed" one of Brian's sports cars without telling them. Marilyn, furious, had Diane track them down, give them hell, and get the car back.

Dennis's estranged wife, Carol, had meanwhile noticed an extreme change in Dennis. He seemed to be continuously in a drugged stupor, as though completely overwhelmed by his new friends. "He invited me [there] a lot and I never went, and I think the reason I didn't go is because I knew what was going on," Carol said. "I didn't want to walk around where there were naked girls and sex happening at all hours of the day and night and stuff like that." Carol had several conversations with Manson on the phone. "He would call and say, 'Come on, we want you to be here,'" but she always made some excuse. Carol did, however, go to the house on a few occasions to pick up her children, Scott and Jennifer, who visited their father on the weekends. One weekend Carol arrived at the house to discover that all the water had been drained from the California-shaped swimming pool, and that there were several young girls sitting at the bottom of the empty pool with an elderly, white-haired man. (This was Family member Ruth Moorehouse's father, himself a nonviolent sometime member of the Family.) After that, Carol never let the children go back to visit with Dennis.

Before long Dennis's wardrobe, including all his flashy Rodeo Drive outfits, was added to the communal Manson Family clothing pile. Manson ordered the girls to cut up all the clothing into large swatches and sew them into robes for everyone to wear. "One day Dennis walked into our house in Benedict Canyon," Carol said. "I'll never forget him coming down the dark hallway. He was barefoot and wearing a robe they had made for him out of patches of clothing. I just looked at him and said, 'If you will pack all your things right now and move out of here, I'll file for divorce tomorrow.'" Dennis packed and Carol filed for divorce soon afterward.

Dennis did manage to get his mother to visit the house. "Dennis was at the recording studio in Brian's house," Audree said, "and he said, 'Will you take me home?' I was very hesitant because I thought, Oh God, Murry's not going to like this. But I took him home and he said, 'Will you just come in and meet them? Come on, they're nice.' And I said, 'Dennis, promise me you won't tell Dad.'

"So I went in, and Charlie Manson was walking through this big yard with a long robe on, and Dennis introduced me. We went into the house, and I think three girls were in the house, just darling young girls, I thought. I zipped through the house, got back in my car, and left. And wouldn't you know that Dennis told his Dad?...Murry didn't like it. He was pissed....I did think [Manson and the Family] were a bunch of leeches. Dennis...could never stand to see anyone who needed anything or anybody who had any kind of problem. He was right there."

Manson and the Family drained Dennis of over $100,000 that summer. This included money spent on food and clothing, bills for wrecking Dennis's uninsured $21,000 Mercedes-Benz, and constant bills for doctors' visits to cure the Family of gonorrhea, which kept reinfecting Dennis. The doctor bills were sent to Catherine Pace at the North Ivar Street office, and she summarily paid them from Dennis's account. Dennis also picked up the bill to fix Susan Atkins's teeth.

As the summer progressed, Dennis began to grow disillusioned with Manson. As Gregg Jakobson described the situation, "Ultimately Dennis and Charlie went head-on, because they both had the same energy. Only, Dennis was more heart-cultured. They attracted each other immediately and then immediately repelled." The turning point may have come one day when Charlie pulled a hunting knife on Dennis, put it to his throat, and said, "What would you do if I killed you?" Dennis just shrugged and said, "Do it!" Manson lowered the knife.

The Beach Boys toured heavily throughout the late summer and early autumn of 1968, and Dennis was in and out of Los Angeles. He never really had the courage to tell Manson and the Family to leave his house. Instead, early in August, three weeks before his lease expired, he moved to a small rented house on the hillside just above the Pacific Coast Highway in the Palisades, leaving the big house at 14400 Sunset to the Family. The rent was not paid, and eventually the Family was thrown out.* The maid who worked there sued Dennis for back pay. Charlie was not particularly upset by Dennis's actions—he simply moved back to the Spahn ranch, where he had been before. However, he did show up at Dennis's new house in the Palisades whenever he needed something. Fred Vail remembers Manson arriving one day and saying, "We're getting low on food and we need stuff for the Family." Dennis told him to help himself. Charlie proceeded to empty out the refrigerator, and then Dennis's clothing closet. "He took out every shirt and pair of pants that Dennis had," Vail said, "bundled them up and threw them in the back of a jeep. He left one shirt hanging on a hanger in the corner." He also appropriated the jeep, which belonged to Gregg Jakobson. Jakobson's wife, Carol, wanted to report it stolen, but instead Dennis and Jakobson simply drove out to the desert and got it back. On this trip Jakobson ran over a scorpion on the road, infuriating Charlie, who began a lecture that the life of the scorpion was more important than a human life.

On another occasion, Charlie arrived at the house looking for Dennis and found Croxey Adams instead. He demanded she have sex with him, and she refused. "I said, 'Get out of here and leave me alone,'" Croxey said. "He pulled out a knife and said, 'You know I could cut you up in little pieces....'" Croxey ran out of the house and down the road to the Coast Highway before she gathered the courage to go back and confront Manson. "I belittled him so much that he left," she said. "I told him, 'Go ahead! Go ahead, you wimp! Try and get it up, you motherfucker! You're a punk peon! You got me in a spot, so go for it, buddy! Get out that knife and kill me! Slice my throat! Slice it!'" Faced with the challenge, Manson seemed cowed. He put the knife down and left. It was nearly a year before Croxey would realize how lucky she had been.

In September, Manson paid another visit to Dennis and Gregg and demanded they join the Family full-time, but both demurred. It mollified Manson somewhat when Dennis played

*Some say Nick Grillo hired plainclothes detectives to do the job.

one of Manson's songs, "Cease to Exist," for the Beach Boys, and they recorded it for inclusion on their next album, *20/20*, their last album with Capitol Records. The Beach Boys' twentieth album, it was a disparate collection of tunes, mostly leftovers from recent records, and almost completely devoid of Brian's production input. "It was recorded all over the world," said Despar, "on both sides of the U.S., in England, France, and Germany." *20/20* became an opportunity for each group member to contribute his own music. Bruce Johnston called it "a very un-Brian album." The album was most notable for the inclusion of Carl Wilson's first major production, the beautiful song "I Can Hear Music" (written by Jeff Barry, Phil Spector, and Ellie Greenwich); the "Cabinessence" track left over from the *Smile* album; a telling Brian Wilson composition entitled "I Went to Sleep"; and the Manson song. Reportedly, Manson was aware of the strife within the group, and wrote "Cease to Exist" as a tonic. The lyric was easily changed to "cease to resist," and the title to "Never Learn Not to Love." Charlie was furious that his lyrics had been changed. Even so, on December 8, 1968, the song was released by Capitol Records on the "B" side of the first single from the soon-to-be-released *20/20* album, backing "Bluebirds over the Mountain." The single never got past number 61, but the Beach Boys had put Charles Manson on the charts.

3

That winter, Dennis moved into a small, one-room garage apartment below Gregg Jakobson's house in Benedict Canyon. When it got too cold at the unheated Spahn Ranch, Manson and the Family moved, too—to a two-story house on Gresham Street in Canoga Park, where they would prepare for Helter-Skelter.* This was the term Manson now used to describe his race wars, having heard the phrase on the newly released Beatles record, the so-called *White Album*, which now played

---

*Dennis later told friends he visited Tex Watson in this apartment and smelled a terrible stench. When he asked Watkins what it was, Watkins told him there was a "dead body" in the closet." Dennis thought he was joking.

incessantly at Gresham Street. During this winter, Manson's anger with Terry Melcher was ignited. According to accounts given by Family members (but denied by Melcher and Jakobson), Melcher had promised to listen to Manson's new songs at the Gresham Street house. The girls even baked cookies for him one night, but Melcher didn't show up. Manson never forgave him.

In March 1969, Manson went to 10050 Cielo Drive to find Melcher, and learned from Rudy Altobelli—who was then occupying the guest house in the back—that Melcher had moved out. Although Altobelli knew that Melcher had gone to his mother Doris Day's house in Malibu, he told Manson he did not know where to find him. On the way out, Altobelli asked Manson why he hadn't stopped at the main house. Manson said he had, but the new occupants, who had moved in on February 15, had sent him back to the guest house. The new tenants were movie star Sharon Tate, pregnant with her husband Roman Polanski's child; Jay Sebring, a successful hairstylist and one-time boyfriend of Sharon's; Abigail Folger, heiress to the Folger coffee fortune; and Folger's boyfriend, Voytek Frykowsky, who had been introduced to her by Polish novelist Jerzy Kosinski.

Jakobson finally convinced Melcher to see Manson that spring, when Manson had moved back to the Spahn ranch. "My idea," said Jakobson, "was for a film, not just a record. I said to Terry, 'This guy should be captured on film. You're never gonna capture this guy on tape.' It'd be like having footage on Castro while he was still in the mountains or something. This guy was a real rebel—it had to be movie footage. This crazy guy with all his girls and music, but his music was visual, too. You had to see the guy sing his songs, not just hear him on a tape. I wanted to do a documentary, at least...it would be like a B movie."

Jakobson brought Terry Melcher to the Spahn ranch on April 18, 1969, to hear Charlie sing in his natural setting. Charlie sat on a rock and sang while the girls, all naked, sat around him humming a background chorus. After the performance, Melcher gave Manson $50 to buy some feed for the horses on the ranch, but "wasn't impressed enough to allot the time necessary" to Manson's career. Family members, however, claimed that Melcher discussed a recording contract with Charlie, but that Charlie refused to sign any papers, since he thought his word was good enough. Melcher later denied ever discussing a formalized recording situation with Manson. Melcher did, however, come back to the Spahn ranch again on June 6, this time with recording engineer Micheal Deasy, who had a mobile recording unit. According to Jakobson (who later wrote about the experience under the pseudonym of Lance Fairweather for *Rolling Stone*), Melcher *was* "impressed the first time he went to the ranch." However, on Melcher's second trip an ugly scene took place. They were all sitting by a stream where Charlie was singing when a drunken old Hollywood stunt man who lived on the ranch began waving a gun. Charlie yelled, "Don't draw on me, motherfucker!" and "beat the shit" out of the man in front of Melcher and Jakobson. That incident completely put Melcher off.

4

On August 9, 1969, the occupants of 10050 Cielo Drive were massacred in one of the most sadistic and terrifying crimes committed in this century. On the very next day, Leno and Rosemary LaBianca of 3301 Waverly Drive, near Griffith Park, were slaughtered in a similar manner. While the identity of the murderers still remained a mystery to the police, Dennis and his friends hoped fervently that their most frightening assumptions would not turn out to be true. But one thing was undeniably clear—the Tate murders had been committed in the very house where Melcher had lived. Their fears may have seemed farfetched; in any event, they decided not to come forward and contact the police.

A few days after the Tate murders, Manson and twenty-six members of his Family were arrested in a daybreak raid on the Spahn ranch. They were charged with auto theft—they had been stealing Volkswagens and turning them into dune buggies. The police had no idea who they had arrested or that there was any connection between Manson and the Tate murders. Almost all those arrested in the raid gave false names, and to make matters worse, the warrant had been misdated. A day later all the suspects were released to roam free.

Manson appeared at Dennis's apartment at Gregg Jakobson's house not long afterward. Dennis was playing the piano when the door flew open—and Manson was standing there, looking like a crazed wildman. He demanded $1,500 in cash from Dennis so he and the Family could move farther into the desert, this time to the Barker ranch, in the rugged area south of the Death Valley Monument. When Dennis nonchalantly asked Manson where he had just been, Manson told him, "I been to the moon." Dennis gave Manson all the money he had on him and Manson left, disgruntled. By this time Manson had apparently learned that Melcher was living in Malibu in his mother's beach house. One morning, Melcher awoke to find that the telescope kept outside the house had been moved to the far side of the deck in the dark of the night. Presumably, this was on one of the Family's "creepy crawly" expeditions, in which they went to the homes of sleeping people and silently moved the furniture around to show they were ubiquitous. In fact, Manson called Jakobson one day and asked if Melcher had a green telescope on the deck at Malibu. When Jakobson said he did, Manson replied, "Not anymore, he doesn't."

While the police investigation continued into the Tate–LaBianca murders, Dennis and his friends lived in constant fear. "One evening," related Stanley Shapiro, "I was in Gregg Jakobson's house, within a day of the Tate murders, and Gregg was not home. Dennis was scared to death and had to go to Canada to play a concert with the Beach Boys. While he was gone, Charlie Manson called numerous times to talk to him, and he was pissed [that Dennis wasn't in]. Later, there was a knock at the door and it was Manson. He had a .45-caliber automatic pistol stuck in his waistband and he said, 'Where's Dennis?'"

Manson was told that Dennis was out of town and could not be reached.

"Oh yeah?" he raged. "Well, you tell Dennis I've got something for him." Then Manson pulled the .45 out of his waistband and took out the magazine. He popped a bullet out of it and threw it on the floor. "When you see Dennis, tell him this is for him. And I've got one for [his son] Scott, too."

Fred Vail remembered, "We were in Canada, and after the show we went back to the hotel, and there was a message from Carol: Scott was missing! They were up in the mountains, looking in ditches for him, and Carol was getting frightened. Scott was gone for six or eight hours and Dennis was really worried. He said, 'I want a jet right now. I'm going home.'" But not only were there no private planes available, the group had no money to pay for one, and Dennis was booked instead on the next commercial flight. Just before he boarded the plane, they received another call from Carol: Scott was safe. He had gone to a friend's house to spend the night and had forgotten to call.

It wasn't until November 19 that the police tracked down Manson and the Family at the Barker ranch, and in a dawn raid arrested him and the entire Family for car theft. This time the arrest warrants were in order, but the police still did not connect Manson and the Family to the Tate–LaBianca murders. It was only after Susan Atkins bragged to her roommate in jail about the murders that the police realized the murderers were already in custody. Within a few days, the entire story came spilling out on TV.

"Right after that, the district attorney wanted to see Dennis," Shapiro said. "In fact, they waited for him at the airport [returning from a tour], and took him into custody. He was pissed off and blamed me for telling the D.A. where he had gone."

Dennis told the D.A. nothing that day. He was afraid for his family's safety as well as his own, knowing that, although Manson was in jail, there were still many Family members out on the street. "The next day was [Dennis's] birthday," Audree recalled, "and he was at Carl and Annie's. I went there and we had dinner. And we were all very quiet. And somebody said something and Carl said, 'I don't think we should talk about it.' So we just watched television and had a very quiet evening. We were totally terrified. I remember Carl saying, 'Mom, let's all go back and stay at your house.' And I said, 'Carl, everybody knows where I live. What good would that do?' So I stayed at their house for a couple of nights."

Several nights later, at Gregg Jakobson's house, Dennis was paid a visit by Family member Squeaky Fromme, who told Dennis that if he didn't give up the tapes Manson had made at Brian's house, she was going to kill him. According to Stanley Shapiro, "Dennis just scoffed at the whole idea. I said, 'Dennis, do you have those tapes?' And he said he had already turned them over to the D.A., which was bullshit." In fact, when Nick Grillo had heard the news on TV, he locked the tapes in a vault, where they remain to this day.

Susan Atkins later admitted that although the Family knew Melcher had moved out, the "reason Charlie picked that house was to instill fear into Terry Melcher, because Terry had given us his word on a few things and never came through with them." Atkins also told the police that the "only reason why we were going to that house was because Tex knew the outline of the house."

Terry Melcher testified at the Manson trial. He told prosecuting attorney Vincent Bugliosi that he was so terrified of Manson, he had been under psychiatric treatment and was constantly accompanied by a bodyguard since December 1969. Melcher had to be given a tranquilizer before taking the stand, and was reportedly relieved when Manson smiled at him after he testified.

Gregg Jakobson was a key witness at the trial, bravely coming forward to tell the whole story, explaining what at first seemed to be incomprehensible motives for the murders. Later, during Jakobson's custody battle with his wife, Carol, Bugliosi wrote a letter in his behalf.

Dennis never testified at the Manson trial, pretending to remember little of what had happened. He was interviewed by the district attorney, and did explain how he had met Manson, and some of the subsequent events. Dennis lived in fear of Manson and the Family for years afterward, but for some reason, although reporters always questioned him about this period, he never discussed it. During an interview in 1976, Dennis said, "I don't talk about Manson. I think he's a sick fuck. I think of Roman and those wonderful people who had a beautiful family and they fucking had their tits cut off. I want to benefit from that?"

*The public thinks of us as
surfing Doris Days.*
—BRUCE JOHNSTON

*The Beach Boys, unfortunately,
had become dinosaurs.*
—DAVID LEAF
*The Beach Boys and
the California Myth*

Eleven

1

The Beach Boys sued Capitol Records on April 12, 1969, formally severing their seven-year relationship with the company. According to the group, the audit of Capitol's books, begun in 1967, had disclosed an alleged underpayment of royalties of over $622,000, based on an outdated "breakage" clause,* as well as $1,418,827.92 in producer's fees for Brian Wilson. In a peculiar move, penalizing both sides, Capitol *deleted* the Beach Boys catalog, making it next to impossible to buy any of their old records, and completely cutting off the flow of royalties. The Beach Boys were now adrift without a recording contract.

Nick Grillo, under enormous pressure to keep the group going, scrambled to find another recording company, but none of the majors was interested. According to Grillo, "Brian was notorious at this point," and record-company executives were afraid to take a chance with him. Grillo felt it was unfair to base the entire value of the Beach Boys on Brian—there was enough talent in the rest of the group, especially Mike and Carl, to produce commercial albums without him. But Brian was the legendary "genius," and the legend now had it that he was also a reclusive drug casualty. Because the Beach Boys' popularity remained consistently high in Europe—particularly in Great Britain—and Brian's reputation was less blem-

---

*The recording industry traditionally based payment on revenues less 10 percent. This automatic 10 percent deduction began when records were breakable and many were destroyed in shipping.

221

ished overseas, Grillo tried to land a foreign, worldwide deal with a European company before attempting to convince a U.S. company to take a chance with them. The boys went off to tour Europe, where they were still selling concert tickets and where the revenues would keep them from bankruptcy. As a business ploy, their tour was to end in Germany—the Deutsche Grammophon company was sincerely interested in giving them a contract, and the chief executives would be attending the final concert. Grillo, who had already traveled with attorney Abe Somers to see the Grammophon executives, hoped to close the deal after their triumphant concert in Germany. A major contract was outlined, "but the trigger," according to Grillo, "was that we had to have an American distributor for our records." There was a long shot that Polygram would sign them in the U.S., but they were "trepidatious about the Beach Boys delivering product, and the domestic side of the deal was falling apart."

However, when Grillo and Abe Somers arrived in England, they were greeted with the terrible news. Brian had given an interview to an English rock newspaper, confessing that the group was teetering on the edge of bankruptcy. "If we don't pick ourselves off our backsides and have a hit record soon, we will be in [even] worse trouble," he was quoted as having said. He went on to say that Grillo had predicted the Beach Boys would soon have to file a chapter 11 proceedings in Los Angeles. "We all know that if we don't watch it and do something drastic, inside a few months, we won't have a penny in the bank," Brian concluded.

"It was devastating," Grillo said. "Here we were going to meet with the Germans, and that information was released to the press. The whole deal fell apart."

Back in Los Angeles, various bankers became "angels" to the group, loaning money to keep them afloat, holding checks instead of bouncing them, and generally giving Grillo and the boys time to land a new record deal. Whenever possible, the group was booked on the road for concerts, where the revenues would repay their bank loans, but traveling expenses were high and concert prices were low. Things got so bad that road manager Richard Duryea and Fred Vail, now their promotion man, began to charge the group's plane tickets on their personal credit cards.* To make matters worse, the Beach Boys' wives didn't want them on the road all the time.

Somehow, the group members themselves didn't take their predicament seriously enough. They continued to spend—"prolifigate" Grillo called them—and to expand. That year a new group called Flame was signed as an act for Brother Records. Flame was a black South African group from Durban consisting of three brothers—Ricky, "Brother," and Steve Fataar—and their friend, Blondie Chaplin. Mike and Carl had discovered them one night playing at a club in London, and everyone thought the addition of black members would increase the Beach Boys' cachet. Plans were immediately set in motion for Flame to record an album for Brother Records, and they were signed up as the Beach Boys' opening act. Later, they would play with the Beach Boys as sidemen. Meanwhile, Mike's middle brother, Stephen, a recent graduate of the University of Southern California with a master's degree in business administration, was hired to assist Nick Grillo in the office. Finally, Rene Pappas, a young, attractive, former booking agent at the Ashley Famous Agency, was hired as "director of personal appearances."

With all these additional expenses, Grillo was constantly searching for ways to shore up the boys' sagging finances. A newly formed entertainment company called Filmways, with ready investment capital, was looking for projects, and Grillo was able to negotiate a clever deal with Filmways president Dick St. John. Grillo had already discussed the possibility of the Beach Boys going into business with Wally Heider, who owned a successful recording studio on Selma and Cahuenga avenues in Hollywood. Heider intended to open a second studio in Los Angeles, as well as a third in San Francisco, and Grillo convinced Filmways to put up all the capital to buy the Heider studios. Thereafter the Beach Boys would record all

---

*Vail was fired with thousands of dollars' worth of charges still left on his credit cards. The Beach Boys were "unable" to pay him at the time, and his credit was ruined. It took an obligatory seven years to get his credit rating in order. Dick Duryea had a similar problem; however, he took the money owed him out of proceeds from concerts while on the road. The Beach Boys then told everyone he was a thief.

their records with Wally Heider. In return the group would own 25 percent of the studios. Not long after the deal was closed, Brian decided he didn't like the sound at Heider's, and within two years they were "bumped out of the deal" by Film-ways. "They paid us off," Grillo said, "for about three hundred thousand dollars net for our twenty five percent."

However, Filmways was also interested in building a library of music-publishing rights—considered one of the soundest show-business investments—and Grillo went to speak to Murry about selling a piece of Bri-Mur publishing, which owned Sea of Tunes, the complete catalog of Beach Boys songs. "Filmways wanted to buy out the catalog," Grillo said, "but the group would still retain a fifty percent interest in perpetuity in the publishing, and that would revert to the guys after Filmways recouped the entire amount of money they paid."

But at the moment, Murry Wilson wasn't interested in Film-ways's offer—although he had been seriously contemplating selling Sea of Tunes himself. Murry had already decided that Brian and the Beach Boys were finished. Some would say he reveled in the idea. As far as Murry was concerned, Brian's songs were so specific to the Beach Boys that they would be next to worthless to anyone else. More important, Murry had a basic, jealous distrust of anyone involved with the Beach Boys, including Nick Grillo, and he was shopping around to find his own deal. Murry's deal, not surprisingly, turned out to be one that would completely devastate Brian. According to Chuck Kaye, then vice-president of Irving Almo Music, the publishing arm of A&M Records, "It was a wonderful deal"— for Irving Almo. "Seven hundred thousand dollars for one hundred percent of the songs," Kaye said. "At the time every-body thought I was crazy. The trend in music was English rock, like Black Sabbath and Led Zeppelin. The Beach Boys were history, the squarest music." But Kaye had absolute faith in Brian's music. "He was a musical genius with a sense of pop music behind him better than anybody I had ever come in contact with." As for Murry, "He was a sick fuck, that's who that guy was. He reared a brilliant genius of a son, raised him as a total neurotic. Look what could have been and what is."

When Murry told Brian that he had negotiated a deal with

Irving Almo to sell 100 percent control of every song he had ever written—Brian was distraught. He begged Murry not to sell the catalog, but Murry insisted it was a good deal at a good price. "Murry wanted to be mean," Grillo said. "Murry was Murry. He acted like a total prick." The rest of the band was just as upset as Brian—they appealed to Murry, begging him to accept the Filmways deal instead. Mike Love even called Chuck Kaye at Irving Almo to somehow scotch the deal, but Kaye held firm, as did Murry. "The cash deal was equal [to the Filmways deal]," Grillo said, "but there was something about Murry, in that mean state. He told the boys that Filmways would screw them down the road and he had to go with Irving Almo, that they were more reputable, that Filmways was a new company and they might never pay. He came up with a zillion excuses."

In November 1969, Sea of Tunes and all of Brian's compositions—his children and his spirit—were sold. Murry was paid, according to Chuck Kaye, in a single cash payment. "The guys didn't see one dime," Grillo said. "I never forgave Murry for that. Brian was heartbroken."

"It killed him," Marilyn said. "*Killed* him. I don't think he talked for days. He was tortured, he couldn't believe his father had done that to his songs. That's like saying to Brian, 'Your songs aren't going to become anything any more than they ever were, and therefore I'm going to get the money out of them now.' Brian took it as a personal thing, Murry not believing in him anymore. That's what destroyed him."

As it turned out, selling Sea of Tunes was Murry's single worst business move. Sea of Tunes would become one of the most valuable music catalogs in existence, generating millions of dollars of income over the years. The total worth of the catalog is now estimated at $20 million. Brian's songs have become advertising staples, used to sell everything from soft drinks to shampoos, breakfast cereals, granola snack bars, and automobiles. Every day dozens of Beach Boys songs accompany commercials played on TV and radio, accruing huge sums of royalties that Brian would never see.

Around that time drummer Hal Blaine received an unusual call from Brian, who wanted to come by to see him. Brian arrived with a carton "filled with [his gold] records," said Blaine, "and wanted me to have 'em all." Brian had given up.

Now came an even crueller twist of fate. Once Irving Almo owned the catalog, they naturally wanted to generate some recording activity with it. One of the more blatant attempts to have one of the tunes "covered" was the Carpenters' version of "Don't Worry Baby," which met with little chart success. While it was generally agreed that the Beach Boys melodies were timeless, Chuck Kaye had the idea that perhaps if the lyrics were updated—changed from car and surf themes— other artists would be more likely to record "cover" versions of them. At that point, it didn't seem at all sacrilegious to change the lyrics of these songs; no one guessed that in a short time they would be considered classics. When Dennis Wilson heard about this, he suggested that his friend Stanley Shapiro write the new lyrics. Although Shapiro had absolutely no previous experience as a lyricist, he was hired for the job by the A&M artists and repertoire department. Shapiro went through the catalog and made a curious discovery: the "lead sheets"— printed music of the songs—were almost all incorrect. "Every time someone tried to play the music, it didn't come out right," he said. It seemed the problem had developed because Brian didn't write music—early versions of his instrumental recordings had been submitted to freelance copyright music writers to be transposed onto paper. The music that had been filed for copyright was only a rudimentary facsimile of Brian's original music.

Shapiro took this problem directly to Brian. Brian seemed pleased that someone cared enough to get his old songs covered—even if he would only share in "mechanical" composer's royalties and not the more lucrative publishing rights. Brian told Shapiro that he had his own tapes of just the instrumental tracks of the songs, and that Shapiro could use those to facilitate the rewrites.* Brian had recently become friendly with Tandyn Almer, a songwriter who was highly regarded for the complicated and beautiful lyrics that he had

---

*An LP of these tracks called Stack of Tracks was released in December 1976 on Capitol Records. This rare album has since become a collector's item.

written for the song "Along Comes Mary," a hit for the Association. Brian suggested that he, Tandyn Almer, and Stanley Shapiro all collaborate on new lyrics. After several weeks of writing and rerecording, Shapiro took the songs, fully recorded with new lyrics and vocals by the three of them, back to David Bayard Nelson, the A&M executive in charge of the project. Nelson loved the tapes. "Damn, this is great stuff," Shapiro claimed he said. "Who are those voices? Who's that at the piano?"

Shapiro said, "This is the problem," and told him about going back to Brian and getting Tandyn Almer to help rewrite the lyrics. Shapiro explained that the credit for the new lyrics would have to be split three ways. According to Shapiro, Nelson was furious. "What the heck do I want to cut them in for?" Nelson asked him. Nelson reportedly worked himself into a rage, telling Shapiro that they had once thrown Tandyn Almer off the A&M lot for being disruptive, and that "they wouldn't have Brian Wilson walk in their lot in a million years." According to Shapiro, "They were afraid he'd want to throw up circus tents and have parades running through the place." Shapiro walked out of Nelson's office, and the lyrics were never rewritten.

2

In recent years Dennis's wild behavior increasingly rankled Mike's quiet, meditative pose, while Mike's "holier than thou" attitude irritated Dennis immeasurably. Mike, the hardworking frontman, was more than a little aggravated by the screams and cheers Dennis would get simply from appearing on stage. The lowest blow was served when Mike discovered through office gossip that Suzanne—whom he was divorcing—was reportedly having an affair with Dennis.* Suzanne and Mike were legally separated, and Mike had promised a bitter custody battle over their two children. Suzanne was so afraid of Mike

*By this time, office gossip was rife with intramarital affairs, so much so that a weekly "newsletter" was circulated among the office staff—a satiric scoresheet of who was doing what with whom. Although most of the information in this newsletter was a joke, there was more than an element of truth to some of the allegations.

that she had a restraining order put against him so he could not come to their house and harass her.

One day Suzanne got a phone call from Dennis, who was temporarily staying at the Beverly Hills Hotel during the period after Manson. Dennis invited Suzanne over for a drink, and later in the evening they were lying on the sofa together, kissing, when the door opened suddenly and Bruce Johnston was standing there. He said, "Aha!" and left almost immediately. Mike counterfiled against Suzanne, alleging adultery, and hired a private detective to follow her. When the divorce trial started, Bruce Johnston testified in Mike Love's behalf. According to one close member of the Beach Boys family, Suzanne was painted as a "drug-addict hippie" who took LSD and writhed on the floor while having conversations with the devil. (Suzanne passed that incident off as a stomachache.) Other evidence introduced in court alleged that Suzanne had endangered the lives of their children by driving through a red light while under the influence of drugs. Mike was summarily awarded custody of the children. The large house in Benedict Canyon was sold and the proceeds were reportedly donated to the Maharishi. All Suzanne received was a $15,000 settlement. She never remarried and was rarely allowed to see her children until they were teenagers.

Mike was going through some rather difficult personal times of his own. In early spring of 1970 he embarked on a strenuous fast, and everyone in the office noticed he had begun to act strangely. "People kept telling us, 'Keep your eye on Mike! Keep your eye on Mike!'" said Fred Vail. During that period the rock performer Little Richard was appearing at the Coconut Grove in Los Angeles, and a contingent of the Beach Boys went to see him. After the show they went backstage and invited Little Richard up to Brian's house, where Bruce and Carl joined them for a pleasant evening spent in the music room. The next day they received a strange phone call in the office. Reportedly, Mike Love had gone to Little Richard's room at the Ambassador Hotel and accidentally exposed himself. Everyone wrote the incident off as some whimsy on Mike's part, but Rene Pappas's sister Connie, who was going out with Mike, remembers that Mike's behavior at the time was indeed bizarre. He appeared on a local TV show and "he was an embarrassment," she said. "He was taking his clothes off on the show, really getting out there, and they pulled the cameras off him." Connie also recalled that Mike was seeing a chiropractor at the time who he said would "take the demons out of his solar plexus."

One day Mike came up to the office on North Ivar and explained that he was feeling okay, but everyone said, "Mike, do us a favor, you might be fine, but let's just go see a doctor. We'll set up an appointment after office hours and no one will know." According to Fred Vail, Mike abruptly said, "Okay, let's go." He got into his rented car, and Vail followed in his Thunderbird. They drove to a doctor's office on Hollywood Boulevard near La Brea.

"Mike was carrying around a two-gallon glass jug of apple juice everywhere he went," said Vail, "kind of like a security blanket. Apparently the doctor realized Mike was right on the edge, and he was about to give him a sedative when Mike saw what was coming and became very neurotic. He jumped up and fled the room." When he came out into the reception room, where Vail was waiting, he threw the jug of apple juice at him, and it smashed against the wall. A second later Mike was gone. He leaped into his car and took off with Fred Vail following him. "He was flipping out, and we went everywhere; it was like the Steve McQueen chase in *Bullitt*. We're going up and down hills and around corners and through red lights in Hollywood, and we ended up somewhere near Venice where Mike pulled into a gas station to get gas." While he was filling up, Vail called Mike's brother Stephen and told him what was happening.

Stephen and his father, Milton, were waiting at Mike's house in Manhattan Beach when Mike and Vail arrived. Everyone insisted Mike go for medical treatment, and when he refused they tried to force him physically into a car. Mike became violent and nearly bit a chunk out of his brother's shoulder. Eventually they managed to restrain him and forcibly put him into the back of Fred Vail's car. The three men drove Mike to the Edgemont Hospital in Hollywood. The orderlies and the nurses helped him out of the car and got him inside, but Mike was fighting and they had to use a straitjacket. Vail wrote out a $350 check to get him admitted. He remained there "about a week" under observation, then was moved to a convalescent home for another week until he recovered. Connie Pappas went to see him at the Edgemont Hospital. "I vividly remember him being in a straitjacket," said Pappas. "It was pretty, pretty scary." Connie Pappas broke up with Mike soon afterward. In later years Mike would explain away the incident, saying he had been "tainted by the Wilson blood."

3

In the late summer of 1969, Dennis was waiting in line at the Bruin Theater in Westwood to see *Midnight Cowboy* with his friends John Vincent and Stanley Shapiro. The line snaked around the corner, past the windows of the local branch of a popular restaurant chain, the Hamburger Hamlet. Dennis happened to glance in the window. Not more than ten feet away, behind the cashier's counter, stood one of the prettiest women he had ever seen. He mentioned the girl at the cash register several times to his friends until the line started to move. No one thought anything about it until a few nights later, when Dennis was out cavorting with Stanley Shapiro and asked if they could go to the Hamburger Hamlet for dinner.

While they ate, Dennis could not take his eyes off the girl behind the cash register. "She's beautiful, huh, don't you think?" Dennis kept asking Stanley, who was by now accustomed to Dennis's sudden infatuations with women. "I'm going to go up there and talk to her," he said. Dennis left the table and went to the cashier's desk to ask for change.

The girl behind the desk was twenty-three-year-old Barbara Charren. Born and raised in Indiana, she had moved to Los Angeles with her parents when she was ten years old. She had long dark hair, beautiful blue-gray eyes, and a sweet, Mona Lisa–like smile. There was a warm, charming quality about her, as well as an intelligence that intimidated Dennis. Barbara Charren well remembers Dennis coming up to the cashier's desk that night. "He acted like a three-year-old kid with a crush," she said, "fumbling for his money and staring, acting nervous. I had no idea who he was, but I thought he was real cute."

The Hamburger Hamlet in Westwood quickly became Dennis's favorite place to eat dinner. He would come by with a friend as often as three times a week and try to make conversation with her. "I didn't take him seriously at all," Barbara remembered, "and then all of a sudden he stopped coming in, and that's when I paid attention." A few weeks later Dennis showed up again and Barbara asked him where he'd been.

"Have you ever heard of a group called the Beach Boys?" Dennis asked her.

"Sure," Barbara said. "Everybody knows who the Beach Boys are."

"Well, I'm with the Beach Boys and we were just on tour. I'm the drummer," he said.

By the end of that conversation, Dennis had enough confidence to ask her out on a date, and Barbara liked him enough to accept. It was the beginning of the soundest, most heartfelt relationship of Dennis's life. The night of their first date Dennis borrowed Brian's Rolls-Royce and asked a friend to pick up Barbara (since he had recently lost his driver's license for various driving offenses). Barbara was driven to Dennis's tiny apartment below Gregg Jakobson's house on Beverly Glen, where she found Dennis at the piano, working with Jakobson on a new song called "Forever." It was a beautiful love song, about a love that would last an eternity, and it became the song of their relationship. Later that night they went to Pink's Hot Dog Stand for dinner, and Barbara was completely charmed.

Barbara Charren quickly became the center of Dennis's world, stabilizing his life after his traumatic divorce from Carol and the ugliness of his relationship with Manson. They showered each other with attention and affection, and the two could not bear to be apart. For Barbara, Dennis was a fascinating combination of lost little boy and sexy young man. A night out with him was a whirlwind of activity and excitement. He was funny, unpredictable, and full of boundless energy. They called each other "Big Poop" and "Little Poop." "Dennis made you feel alive in a way not many people do," Barbara remembered. "Dennis impacts on your life. There's the other side of it too—

the crash landing. But in the beginning he's always there and it's exciting, something most people never got to feel in their lives, and it really shakes you." Less than four months after they started going out, Dennis asked Barbara to marry him as soon as his divorce from Carol was final. They planned the wedding for April 1970, and made reservations at the Hana Lei Plantation Hotel in Hawaii. However, when the date rolled around, the divorce from Carol wasn't yet legal—there was a sixty-day waiting period till he was free to marry—so they decided to go to Hawaii anyway and pretend it was their wedding. In Hawaii Barbara became pregnant with their first child, and they were married when Barbara was four months pregnant, on August 4, 1970. A son, Michael, was born on February 19, 1971.

About this time, a new movie was being cast—*Two-Lane Blacktop*, directed by Monte Hellman. Singer James Taylor was to star, along with another, as yet unnamed male. The producers hoped to snag another big name from the recording industry for this "road movie" about a cross-country race between a gray 1955 Chevrolet and a GTO. When Dennis heard about the film, he asked Nick Grillo to arrange an interview for him and Fred Vail drove him to the audition. During the ride over, Dennis got cold feet. "Maybe I shouldn't even audition," he said, but Vail encouraged him to go in. Dennis's audition left much to be desired as far as acting ability was concerned, but his personal appeal was evident, as was his physical attractiveness. Two weeks later, Dennis was astonished to learn that he had gotten the part. The rest of the Beach Boys, more than a little jealous, heard the news within an hour. Dennis was going to be a movie star.

4

By January of 1970 Nick Grillo had been able to set up a recording contract with Warner Brothers Records to distribute Beach Boys products on the Reprise label. Other Beach Boys products would be distributed by Starday-King out of Nashville, Tennessee. The Warner Brothers deal was for only two albums, to be delivered eighteen months apart, with a handsome advance of $205,000 per album. The cornerstone of the deal was Mo Ostin, the venerable president of Warner Brothers Records and a long-standing Beach Boys fan who had been convinced by Grillo that Brian would be able to produce and write. According to David Berson, Ostin's executive assistant at the time, "Mo loved them." Moreover, Ostin believed that the Beach Boys held a special place in American musical history—they were too important, both to American culture and the music business in general, to be abandoned because of a losing streak. Naturally, on the business side, it was important to Warner Brothers that Brian become an integral part of the recording process. Brian's services as producer and composer were written into the contract, although curiously, he never got around to signing the contract himself.* But around the Burbank offices of Warner Brothers, few people actually believed that Brian would be able to pull it together, and the deal was commonly known as "Mo's Folly."

Sure enough, the first album the group submitted to Warner Brothers was rejected. Originally titled *Add Some Music*, from the single titled "Add Some Music to Your Day," the album didn't have an all-important hit single and was thought to be weak by Warner executives. "It seemed like an amazing thing to do," said Berson, "to say to the Beach Boys, 'This is not the kind of an album we want to pay for.' Contractually we didn't have any right to reject albums." Now, feeling more insulted and disgruntled than they had with Capitol, the Beach Boys edited out five songs from the album and replaced them, retitled the album *Sunflower*, and convinced Warner Brothers to take a chance with it. The single "Add Some Music to Your Day" was bought by wholesalers at a promising rate—one of the highest-selling orders that Warner had ever received. But the song received little or no radio airplay, and sat in record bins gathering dust until it was returned. The album, released August 31, fared no better—it turned out to be the worst-selling album to that point in the Beach Boys' career. As usual,

---

*In the Beach Boys' corporate structure, three out of five votes was legally binding for the group. David Berson made sure Brian's signature was obtained when the contract was renewed.

England had the opposite reaction—the public loved the album, and *Sunflower* was acclaimed in the British press as "the Beach Boys' *Sergeant Pepper*." The group hurriedly left for Great Britain to perform at sell-out concerts, where they were mobbed by fans. At home, however, their reputation as has-beens solidified.

Although Brian spent most of his time in bed, he ventured out occasionally, sometimes to visit his friend Danny Hutton, or to shop at the Radiant Radish, a health-food store in which he had invested during the summer of 1969, with his cousin Steve Korthof and road manager Arnie Geller. An offshoot of Brian's preoccupation with vegetables, and financed for only $15,000, the Radiant Radish was located in West Hollywood across from the Black Rabbit Inn. Occasionally, late at night, dressed only in pajamas and bathrobe, Brian would go to the store and raid the vitamin supplies, making off with as much as a thousand dollars' worth of stock. At other times he would wait on surprised customers. One night *Rolling Stone* writer Tom Nolan stumbled in after a late movie to discover the store deserted, except for Brian. When Nolan tried to buy a bottle of vitamin B-12, Brian refused to sell it to him unless it had been prescribed by a doctor. Fred Vail remembers Brian going to the store one night to count the day's grosses. They were just a few dollars shy of $600—the best tally so far—and Vail bought a bottle of vitamin C to push them over. "Here was this genius songwriter," said Vail, "a real spokesman for the sixties, and the six hundred dollars was the only thing that mattered to Brian for the day." But the store was poorly run and undercapitalized, and when Brian grew bored with it he closed the shop on July 29, 1970.

The same night the Radiant Radish closed, Brian was scheduled to help promote the *Sunflower* album with his first full-length radio interview in months. Along with Mike Love and Bruce Johnston, Brian went over to Pacifica Radio, KPFK, where they were interviewed by Jack Rieley, a tall, rotund, deep-voiced announcer with long dark hair. Brian had first met Jack Rieley at the Radiant Radish when he walked in one night and introduced himself: "Hi, I'm Jack Rieley from NBC News." Rieley said he was a former Peabody Award—winning journalist and Brian was struck by Rieley's gift of gab. "We took a liking to the guy," Brian said, and agreed to do the interview. They covered the usual topics: why Brian recorded only in monophonic and what unreleased tracks still remained from the *Smile* album. Brian also discussed the Beach Boys' current business and recording problems. But more important than the interview itself was the impression the interviewer made on Brian.

A little over a week later, on August 8, Jack Rieley wrote the Beach Boys a six-page memo about their career dilemma. Divided into three sections, the memo's main points were "(1) What are the causes of the problem; (2) What have been the effects of the problem; and (3) What is the solution to the problem." The ego-pumping, soothing memo, which encapsulated the Beach Boys' well-known struggle for public acceptance and relevance in an era of hip rock-and-roll, was full of references to "heavy, trippy" music, "funky" music, and "lack of recognition of your profound creativity." Rieley recommended a publicity-promotion campaign to educate the public, which included a promotional mail-out to disc jockeys. The memo ended with the sentence, "The creativity of the communications man has to match the creativity of the musicians and the producer in order to meet with the success you guys deserve and must have."

There was really nothing new in the memo, nor any bright ideas, and it was not even written in the style of a Peabody Award—winning journalist. But it was clear that Rieley had tremendous clarity of thought and that he wanted to be involved with the Beach Boys in an important way. Mike Love and Carl liked what Rieley said, and although they hardly knew what a Peabody Award was, Rieley's credentials seemed impressive. The Beach Boys trusted and believed in Jack, and suddenly, before anyone else could voice an objection, Jack Rieley was in charge of public relations and general direction of the Beach Boys at a reported salary of $600 a week.

John Frank Rieley III was born in Milwaukee on November 24, 1942, and was the elder of two sons. He grew up in the community of Bayside with his brother James and graduated from Nicolet High School in the suburb of Glendale. After attending Beloit College in Wisconsin for a short time, he got a job in the news department at a local Beloit radio station. Bright, a smooth talker, and a good salesperson, Jack grew bored quickly and liked to keep on the move. He worked at another radio station in Wilmington, Delaware, and then moved to San Juan, Puerto Rico, where, he told the Beach Boys, he had been news director for NBC. At one point he returned to Milwaukee, and then went to New York to form his own company, Hand Music, and recorded a group called Space. He also said he had once been executive administrator to the Democratic party of the state of Delaware and that he was a personal friend of Robert Kennedy. He moved to Los Angeles in the late sixties and wound up at KPFK, where he was a disc jockey and announcer when he met the Beach Boys.

"Jack Rieley did not amuse me," Nick Grillo said grimly. "I think we might have worked well together, but it became a situation in which the more power the guys gave him, the more he abused it. There were a number of things that were happening at the time, the most important of which was that the Beach Boys and I were falling out of love. Nothing was happening in their careers, and they refused to listen to career guidance. They were just sitting back and waiting for a new voice, and Jack Rieley was that voice."

5

On Labor Day weekend of 1970 a telegram arrived at the Beach Boys' offices from Van Dyke Parks. Van Dyke had been working on the board of the upcoming Big Sur Folk Festival, which was being organized by Joan Baez. That year the festival would take place at the Monterey fairgrounds—the same location as the festival the Beach Boys had decided not to play, with such disastrous results. Many connected with the group felt that now the Beach Boys had a chance to make it up. But not everyone was for it. Mike Love was especially worried about Joan Baez's prominent sponsorship of the festival. "Oh my God," he said in all seriousness when he heard about it. "How can we play up there? I think she's a commie." A tug-of-war quickly ensued over whether or not the group should play Big Sur. One of the stumbling blocks, as far as the Beach Boys were concerned, was that A&M Records intended to make a live recording of the festival. Some group members thought they should only play if the recording could be released on Brother Records. This was a ludicrous demand, considering the state of the Beach Boys' recording careers, yet they insisted Grillo make the proposal. As a result, they were practically uninvited to the festival and only Rene Pappas's gentle diplomacy ensured them a spot on the bill.

Jack Rieley was all for having the Beach Boys play at Big Sur. He knew the festival would receive media attention and hoped the rock world would discover that the Beach Boys were not just a good, enjoyable live act, but a terrific one. While audiences expected a nostalgia act, the Beach Boys were indeed much more. Alive and vibrant onstage with a tight, solid sound, their show was near-dazzling.

As Rieley hoped, the Beach Boys received rave reviews at the festival, and almost immediately afterward Jack encouraged them to book themselves into a four-night appearance at the Whiskey A Go Go, the small but venerable rock club on Sunset Boulevard. Although the Whiskey's fame had decreased since its heyday in the sixties, it still provided an excellent local showcase for the Beach Boys to prove their stuff. This was their first Los Angeles performance in four years and much to the surprise and delight of everyone involved, the Beach Boys packed the house all four nights. According to Bruce Johnston, "the line went three blocks up [around the corner]." The group even managed to get Brian onstage for one set, but his appearance lasted no more than a few minutes. Stoned and spiraling into his increasing paranoia, Brian claimed the sound of the giant speakers caused a painful buzzing in his ear. He disappeared backstage, halfway through the performance.

As the months went by, Jack Rieley's control over the group began to solidify, while the antagonism between him and Nick Grillo came to a head. Grillo ran the office with businesslike precision—some might say military precision—and Rieley was the antithesis of Grillo. Hypochondriacal and frequently sick, Jack Rieley would often not show up for work at all, missing meetings and sometimes disappearing for days at a time. Such behavior was more than Grillo could tolerate, and the battle lines were clearly drawn. Yet Grillo was not able to fire Rieley, and indeed, Rieley was so manipulative that Grillo seemed as much in danger of being fired as Rieley did. Said one observer, "The situation in the office made Justinian's court seem like a kindergarten."

Whenever Rieley's position needed some shoring up, some remarkable occurrence would take place. Ricky Fataar needed immigration papers to work in the United States and Rieley produced a personal letter from Robert Kennedy welcoming him to the country. But the most remarkable of these incidents took place in Laguna Beach, a lovely community some ninety miles south of Los Angeles. One summer Sunday a group consisting of Bruce Johnston, Connie Pappas, her sister Rene, and Jack piled into Mike Love's Rolls-Royce and went to Laguna to have lunch. Although no one had decided in advance where they were going to eat, Rieley was paged to the telephone while they were having lunch. He came back to the table a few minutes later, flushed and excited. "I've won the Pulitzer Prize!" he exclaimed. Congratulations went up all around, and a bottle of celebratory champagne was ordered. The next day in the office it was all anyone could talk about: Jack Rieley had won the Pulitzer Prize for journalism for his work as bureau chief of NBC-TV in Puerto Rico.

*"When you love someone
as much as I loved Brian,
you begin to accept more and more.
Maybe more than you should."*
—MARILYN WILSON

Twelve

1

The four nights the Beach Boys played the Whiskey A Go Go in November 1970 had one other, far-reaching repercussion, aside from raising the value of their stock among the L.A. cognoscenti. In the audience one night, a young man named Michael Klenfner was fascinated and delighted by the group's performance. Klenfner had been listening to the Beach Boys' music ever since he was a kid growing up in Brighton Beach, Brooklyn. From the time he was a teenager, Klenfner had been in the music business, beginning as a candy seller and security guard at the Fillmore East and working his way up to various administrative positions for promoter Bill Graham. A tall, burly man with a warm outgoing personality, Klenfner was on a working vacation in Los Angeles the night he caught the Beach Boys at the Whiskey A Go Go. After returning to New York, he approached Graham about booking the Beach Boys at the Fillmore East, but Graham was not interested. Graham considered the group passé, yesterday's music, and in the vernacular of the music business, a "stiff" for ticket sales. Graham said that he had once booked the Beach Boys, and after the concert they had demanded a stub count, impugning his honesty.

But Klenfner didn't stop with Graham. Convinced the Beach Boys were too good a live act to pass up—even if they might not be a big money-maker initially—Klenfner decided the public would have to be educated. He next approached his good friend Chip Rachlin, then a twenty-one-year-old junior agent at the Millard Agency, which was the booking arm of Graham's organization. Himself a Beach Boys fan, Rachlin was intrigued with the idea of bringing the group to New York. He asked if Graham would mind if he and Klenfner, along with two partners, were to book the Beach Boys into a local hall and promote their own concert. Graham was convinced they would "stiff," but wished them luck anyway. Rachlin called Carnegie Hall and found an open night on February 24. Then he called American Productions and spoke to Rene Pappas, who convinced Jack Rieley of the importance of trying to break New York. The agreed guarantee was $9,000 for two shows, with a top ticket price of only $5.50. If the two shows sold out, the total take would be $28,000.

As Graham had predicted, the ticket sales were slow and painful. The second show hardly sold at all and had to be cancelled, but by the evening of the performance, only thirty tickets were left unsold for the first one. Pete Fornatele, a respected local disc jockey on WNEW-FM radio, who had remained a loyal Beach Boys fan and continued to air their music over the years, was asked to emcee the show. Fornatele walked out on stage with a surfboard, and gave a simple and eloquent introduction: "Growing up wouldn't have been half as much fun without these guys: the Beach Boys." The two-hour show, simply put, brought down the house.

Rachlin followed the Beach Boys to Boston, where they played Symphony Hall to a meager crowd, and tried to convince the group to let him continue to book them. With aggression and fresh blood, he argued, he could help turn their career around. Rachlin suggested they do a series of two-hour shows as they had at Carnegie Hall, covering their whole career and including their latest music. Rachlin promised no glamorous fees—in most places they would see no more than a $1,000 guarantee until the ball got rolling. He asked for a two-year contract. What he got was a telegram, a week later, which confirmed that he had ninety days to prove himself. Rachlin would stay on for seven years and some six hundred shows.

The group rented a Trailways bus and set out on a three-week tour, which in seventeen dates would gross $50,000—if they were lucky. "They still had the headline mentality," Rachlin said, "and they were uncomfortable with the bus." But they were all ready for hard work, especially Mike Love, who was willing to do two shows a day if possible. Rachlin booked them on a northeastern tour of colleges, where they had a better chance of selling tickets than in big cities. The highest-paying date that first tour was a $5,000 guarantee at a thousand-seat movie theater in Worcester, Massachusetts, for three shows in a day. Rachlin didn't bother to tell the group that it was a porno theater, but when the boys found out they played anyway. At Bucknell University they sold only eleven hundred seats in a three-thousand-seat gym at only $3 a seat. Rachlin was so depressed he sat under the bleachers during the concert. At a hockey rink in a college in Manchester, New Hampshire, the box office told them they had sold out. When Rachlin spied a shoe box sitting on a shelf in the office containing tickets to two thousand unsold seats that had been overlooked, he didn't mention it. In Portland, Maine, the group played to a half-filled movie theater whose owner couldn't even pay the $1,000 guarantee. They had to leave immediately after the performance because the janitor had to sweep up the popcorn left on the floor of the theater from the show before.

Mike tried to talk Michael Klenfner into meditating with him every day, but Klenfner refused unless Mike told him his mantra, which he knew Mike couldn't do. "I would constantly ask him if his mantra was 'cash,'" Klenfner said. "Mike would say, 'Oh you Jew boys!' and laugh." Klenfner would answer, "I'm Jewish? I'm going to change your name to Loveinsky." Klenfner, who basically did not like Mike Love, thought he "was a pretty evil guy, kind of like a secret-service agent, with a real military attitude."

The most important date of the tour was April 27, 1971. The Grateful Dead were playing several nights at the Fillmore in New York, and because of Klenfner and Rachlin's entrée there, they were able to convince the Dead's leader, Jerry Garcia, to jam with the Beach Boys at the end of one show. Klenfner saw the potential of exposing the Beach Boys to the Dead's "hip" kind of audience, and he was instrumental in getting Mike, Carl, and Jerry Garcia to sit down and talk. Rieley was dead-set against the idea, and thought Mike Love was scared the kids would laugh at them. "It took an hour of yelling at Jack Rieley to convince him it was an important move," Klenfner said. "Mike Love would put up a fight about everything and then claim it was his idea." It was finally agreed that the Beach Boys would appear on the final night of the Dead's venue, after the last encore.

"The Dead had been playing for three hours that night," Rachlin remembered, and by now it was eleven o'clock. A heavy stench of pot hung over the auditorium, and it was a good guess that of the twenty-seven hundred members of the audience, twenty-seven hundred of them were tripping—as was *de rigueur* for a Grateful Dead concert. "The audience was so stoned that nothing could have taken them higher," Rachlin said. After the Dead's last encore, Garcia said into the microphone, "Now we'd like you to welcome some fellow Californians." Pause. "The Beach Boys."

There was dead silence from the audience, at which point the group walked timidly onto the stage and took up their instruments. The Fillmore was suddenly hushed. Then unexpectedly from the back of the auditorium, someone started to applaud, and slowly, like a wave, row after row began clapping, clapping, until the wave hit the stage and the audience was on its feet cheering. Absolute pandemonium rang through the auditorium. The Beach Boys launched into "Heroes and Villains," "Help Me, Rhonda," and all their greatest hits, and the audience loved it. The bootlegged tape of that concert became legendary in the rock-and-roll business. *Billboard* wrote of their performance, "From their opening 'Heroes and Villains' to the closing of 'Good Vibrations,' the Beach Boys combined the best of their many standards with different material and treatment, producing a contemporary feel." The rock critic for *Crawdaddy* wrote, "They were brilliant ... their excellence that night equaled any rock performance I have ever seen."

Word spread through the music industry. The Beach Boys were coming back. On May 1, with Jack Rieley's prodding, they played the May Day antiwar demonstration in Washington, D.C., and on June 22, two days after Brian's twenty-ninth birthday, they played the closing of the Fillmore. Rachlin and

Klenfner were having less and less trouble booking them. "That first year they worked about seventy-five dates and grossed about $300,000 which is not a whole lot, but it started," Rachlin said.

By July 25 of that year, when the Beach Boys released their next Warner Brothers album, *Surf's Up*, their resurgence was in full swing. *Rolling Stone's* review of the album said, "The Beach Boys are back. After suffering several years of snubbing, both by rock critics and the public, the Beach Boys stage a remarkable comeback beginning with the release of *Surf's Up*, an LP that weds their choral harmonies to progressive pop and which shows youngest Wilson brother Carl stepping into the fore of the venerable outfit." Although Brian had relatively little to do with *Surf's Up*, with the exception of his tragically beautiful contribution of "'Til I Die," the album was more cohesive and better produced than the recent few before it. Influenced by Jack Rieley, the album contained several ecological ("Don't Go Near the Water") and student-revolution songs, including an old Jerry Lieber–Mike Stoller tune called "Riot in Cell Block Number Nine," transformed into "Student Demonstration Time" with new lyrics by Mike Love. Bruce Johnston contributed the second best composition of his career, a love song entitled "Disney Girls" that was a lush evocation of a simpler, sweeter time.* "Feel Flows," an airy mixture of jazz and Moog synthesizer by Carl, was another outstanding cut. But perhaps the most special was the title song, written by Brian and Van Dyke Parks for the long-lost *Smile* album. The strangest contribution was without doubt "A Day in the Life of a Tree", featuring Jack Rieley as lead singer, which many suspected was one of Brian's devilish put-ons. *Surf's Up* hit number 29 on the charts at its peak, making it the Beach Boys' best selling LP in years and renewing Warner Brothers' faith in them. The release of the album was followed on August 19 by a live broadcast on ABC-TV of a Central Park concert that nearly filled Sheep Meadow, and then on September 24 a triumphant return to Carnegie Hall.

---

*Bruce Johnston's most memorable song is "I Write the Songs" which was recorded by Barry Manilow and has since become a pop-music classic.

2

Despite the Beach Boys' newfound popularity, road expenses continued to be enormous, and profits small. Back in the offices on North Ivar in Hollywood, tension was running high. The vortex of the inner-office problems seemed to be Jack Rieley. Rieley was suspected of troublemaking, setting the group members against each other in petty arguments, and interfering in crucial Beach Boys business. The worst example of this kind of behavior involved the group's relationship with Warner Brothers, which had agreed to renew their initial contract for several more albums. Warner Brothers had learned that as part of the group's settlement with Capitol Records, the Beach Boys had retained complete ownership of the last five albums they recorded for the company—everything from *Pet Sounds* on. Warner wanted to distribute these albums as part of the new deal. Another important element in the deal became the *Smile* album. It had become legendary at this point, and Warner Brothers wanted to put it out. "After literally months of negotiations with Nick Grillo," said David Berson at Warner, "Jack Rieley called me up one day and said, 'Look, I now manage the Beach Boys and I've been managing them quite sometime, in fact. They're totally unaware that negotiations have taken place with you.'"

Rieley naturally wanted to jack up the price for the new deal Grillo had set up—$90,000 for the five Capitol LPs and $300,000 per new album (according to Grillo). When confronted with Rieley's allegations that Grillo was no longer managing the Beach Boys, Berson said he "yelled and screamed and said they had a deal and a moral committment and I was going to sue them. The result was they signed the agreement. Even Brian." According to Grillo, Rieley had actually been negotiating the price *down*, but this was a hotly contested allegation.

The office back-stabbing was heightened when a member of the staff found a stack of stationery from Robert Kennedy in Jack Rieley's desk drawer. Thinking now that perhaps the letter welcoming Ricky Fataar had been a fake, Grillo and Rene Pappas decided to look further into Rieley's credentials. Rene Pappas still had connections through her previous job at the Ashley Famous Agency in Beverly Hills, where she worked with several newscasters as clients. She asked a close friend at NBC to check the personnel files and find out exactly what Rieley had done at the Puerto Rican bureau and how he had won his Pulitzer Prize. Rene said, "I got a call back from [my friend] who said, 'a) We have no Puerto Rican bureau, and b) this Jack Rieley has never worked for NBC in any capacity.'"

With this shred of deception to work from, the same private detective that had trailed Suzanne Love during her custody battle with Mike Love was hired to investigate Rieley. Although Grillo claims Rene hired the investigator, Rene denies this. "I could much less afford to pay my own rent," she said. "This was all paid for by Nick Grillo. What I did was I was the liaison between the [office and the] detective, because Nick was afraid that even his secretary wasn't loyal and it would get out that this was happening."

Several weeks later, a six-page report was delivered to Rene Pappas. According to the report, Jack Rieley had not won a Pulitzer nor a Peabody Award and had never worked for NBC News. However, the report claimed that Jack was in the employ of a Washington, D.C., right-wing conservative organization called the Stern Concern. Reportedly the Stern Concern was hoping that Rieley would infiltrate rock-and-roll groups that might have subversive intent. This report was photocopied and summarily hand-delivered to each of the Beach Boys' homes the next day.

"I will never forget that day," Rene said. "I was sitting with Nick Grillo in his office when Jack Rieley walked in. He was green, red, and purple. He said, in effect, 'Since Rene has done this terrible thing, it was decided among the boys that Rene must be fired.'"

Rene turned to Nick Grillo who was sitting behind his desk, for a response. "Wonderful gentleman that he was," Rene said, "he sat there quietly and didn't say a word. Eventually he said, 'Yes, Jack, you're right.'" And Rene was fired the next day.

Despite the revelations in the report, Jack Rieley's control

over the group continued to solidify throughout the year. Rieley was able to take credit for every success, carefully sharing
the credit with others as necessary. For every failure, Rieley
was able to assign blame elsewhere. Ultimately, he stayed on
the good side of Brian, who had the final say, and Carl and
Mike Love, who were his supporters. But from the start Bruce
Johnston, more sophisticated and less guillible than the rest,
mistrusted Rieley and his intentions, and as the year progressed Johnston and Rieley began to openly dislike each other.
Said one observer, "Bruce was definitely the one who most
clearly saw what Jack Rieley was up to." Said another, "Bruce
was raising the flag early about Rieley and felt he should have
been fired." The turning point came when Bruce was reportedly shown a letter that Rieley had written to a drummer (not
Dennis), which Bruce termed "a love letter."

When push came to shove, Bruce Johnston left the group
after seven years with them, allegedly by the unanimous vote
of the rest of the group, instigated by Rieley. Johnston claims
he wasn't fired, but left by a mutual decision. He didn't seem
to take it too personally, however, telling one reporter, "I don't
know if he was trying to get rid of me; I think he was just
trying to redirect the band."

In the office on Ivar in Los Angeles, the animosity was even
stronger. According to Grillo, "The Beach Boys were beginning
to fall out of love with Nick Grillo." For one thing, the payments on the huge Simi Valley deal that Grillo had secured
for them were falling far behind. Brian even took out a second
mortgage on his home to help out financially, but nothing
seemed to stem the tide. According to Grillo, "The problem
was that they could not keep up with that portion of the annual
payment to the principals, and they thought that I was getting
a kickback. They all thought I was making out like a bandit.
...I must say that the one person that I think instigates a lot
of this...is Mike Love." Grillo met with the Simi Valley owners, who were waiting for their annual payment, and tried to
buy time, but to no avail. The entire investment had been lost
by the end of 1970. To make matters worse, Grillo and his
brother, Frank Roy Grillo, tried to take the Beach Boys "public"
by floating a company called the American Recreation Cor-

poration. "We were never able to generate the activity only because like all the Beach Boys' deals...they sat back and said, 'Okay, why do you have so much?,'" Grillo said. Once, Grillo nearly had a fistfight with Dennis in a men's room in New York. The last straw was when Stanley Shapiro claimed he saw documents that showed Grillo was getting a share of the proceeds on a sale of property the Beach Boys owned for some time in Beaumont, California, to two doctors in Florida whom Mike Love had met while on tour. Grillo vigorously denied this. In a complicated tax-shelter scheme, the two doctors were to donate medical equipment to a foundation and buy the property.

The corporation had paid Grillo's fees and salaries fairly regularly during the previous year, and was only one tour or so behind, according to Grillo. But before the group went out on the road in April 1972, Grillo put approximately $40,000 of his own money into the corporation to cover expenses. On a Friday afternoon Grillo got a phone call from Stephen Love on the road. He was fired. Grillo hung up and made some fast decisions. "Knowing how they operated, I felt I could deal with fighting with them...in terms of a fee, but I wanted what I'd advanced them in the form of a loan [back right away]." Grillo sat down with the corporate checkbook—which he had power of attorney to sign—and wrote himself a check for the money owed to him. "It was specifically for that amount of money, and nothing more. I don't give a fuck what anybody says. Whatever I advanced to them for the tour, I wanted back. I felt I would have to go head-to-head with them for my fee."

Over the weekend, someone in the office called Stephen Love on the road and told him about the check Grillo had written to himself. By Monday morning, the bank had been notified and the check stopped. "When the tour was over," Grillo said, "I said to Stephen Love, 'I don't want to go to litigation over this situation. You guys made a decision. I think you buried me, Rieley buried me. What I want back is what I loaned the group and what is owed to me to date in terms of my fee.'" Grillo claims that Stephen Love offered him fifty cents on the dollar. "I did not loan them fifty cents on a dollar," Grillo said. "I did not work fifty cents on a dollar and I want a hundred cents on a dollar. I told him, 'I'll give you thirty days, and if I don't get a favorable response I'm going to sue.'"

Grillo took the matter to court, as did his brother. In court papers he alleged breach-of-contract, specifically naming Rieley and Stephen Love, as well as the Beach Boys' lawyer, Abe Somers. Grillo asked for $35,000 out-of-pocket reimbursement, $182,000 for payment of services, and $10 million in damages. According to Grillo, he realized his money in litigation, except for the damages. The Beach Boys have continued to bad-mouth him for years, blaming Grillo for the loss of the Simi Valley property, for their bad touring times, and for just about every other financial woe they ever had. Grillo now lives in Los Angeles, where he is a movie producer.

Jack Rieley was now managing the Beach Boys.

3

Brian's psychological state had deteriorated further into what was unmistakably mental illness. However, it was hard to tell how much of his behavior was out of true craziness and how much was Brian's clever faking to control the band and keep them away from him. He had periods of deep depression when he became suicidal. One day he dug a grave in his backyard and fantasized about jumping off the roof into it. On another occasion he threatened to drive his Rolls-Royce off the Santa Monica Pier, and once he actually did jump off the pier—but luckily Dennis was nearby and pulled him to safety. He said that killing himself was the best way to kill off the Beach Boys, for by now he hated the idea of the group—it was a monster he had created, and the unrelenting symbol of the demands and pressures weighing on him. He was stoned most, if not all of the time, and now weighed over 210 pounds. His friends Tandyn Almer and Danny Hutton were not much help in encouraging his mental health, as they still found Brian's behavior amusing. Brian spent many days by himself sleeping in the tiny chauffeur's quarters at the back of the house. Some nights he frequented the massage parlors along Santa Monica Boulevard and even wrote a song, "Marcella," for one of the girls.

Marilyn Wilson tried to keep the household going, maintain her sanity, and raise her children. Although a second child, Wendy, had been born on October 16, 1969, Marilyn's romantic and sexual life with Brian had virtually ended, and their personal difficulties were compounded by Brian's increasing fascination with her sister Diane. Diane had never worked, except for her sporadic career as a member of the Honeys and as a studio assistant to Brian, hiring musicians for sessions. Her entire life was spent as an adjunct to her younger sister Marilyn, who had authority and power as Mrs. Brian Wilson. Still, Marilyn was more than generous with and loyal to Diane, sharing everything with her, including the love of her husband.

Yet another love interest developed in Brian's life—a young girl named Deborah Keil. Debbie Keil was pretty and winsome, with long blond hair and huge blue eyes. A telephone operator, born in Kansas, she had been a longtime, hardcore Brian Wilson fan who had first met the Beach Boys in Atlantic City after traveling there to attend one of their concerts. When she was nineteen, she moved to Los Angeles to be close to Brian, and got a nonpaying job working for the fan club. Marilyn highly disapproved of Debbie's presence—once the girl was forced to hide in the office sauna when Marilyn came to visit. She was fired after Marilyn discovered that Brian had driven her home one day from the office. But that didn't keep Debbie away. She worshiped Brian and was there for him, whenever he needed her, with no complications or demands. She was brazen in her affection for Brian, and mistakenly saw Marilyn as a competitor instead of the long-suffering wife at the end of her rope. Debbie's relentless pursuit of Brian was terribly distressing to Marilyn, and she tried to keep Debbie a respectable distance from the household, often to no avail. Brian would call Debbie whenever he was lonely and invite her over.

Even more bizarre was Brian's desire for Marilyn to have an affair with another man. He chose Tandyn Almer for this role, and encouraged Tandyn to make love to Marilyn. "Brian spent months at Tandyn's place, day and night," Marilyn said. "In fact, I remember sleeping at Tandyn's house for two or three nights in a row." During one summer Tandyn stayed at Brian's house for a month, and Tandyn once went to bed with both of them. "It's just funny," Marilyn said. "It's no big deal." This relationship came to a bad end one day when Brian went shopping at Tower Records on Sunset Boulevard with Stanley Shapiro and arrived home to find Tandyn and Marilyn romantically involved by the swimming pool. Brian complained bitterly about this incident, but almost immediately forgave Tandyn and took him back into the circle. But not for long. "We had a giant fight and he was gone," Marilyn said. Marilyn accused Tandyn of taking a piece of recording equipment out of the house on Bellagio Road without permission and sent "two guys to get it back. They kicked doors in and they took guns and they broke open the door and smashed it in and they said, 'Give us the stuff back,' and he gave it back quick." (Actually, Brian would have given away anything he was asked for, and this piece of equipment had been sold, not to Tandyn, but to someone who lived in Tandyn's house.)

4

At this time, a new album, *Carl and the Passions—So Tough*, was released by Warner Brothers. Brian had practically no involvement in the album, except for the donation of the song "Marcella" and a song he had written with Tandyn Almer called "You Need a Mess of Help to Stand Alone." Curiously, Warner Brothers turned *Carl and the Passions* into a double-album set by packaging it with *Pet Sounds*, one of the albums the group got back in the settlement with Capitol. *Carl and the Passions* made a dismal showing on the *Billboard* charts, peaking at number 50.

On February 24, 1972, the Beach Boys were scheduled to play at the Grand Gala du Disque in Holland, an event broadcast on Dutch television. The Beach Boys had been to Holland before—in December 1970—and had pleasant memories of the trip. On their way to Amsterdam, they had found themselves fogged in at Heathrow and had to take a jet from Gatwick to Brussels. They were then driven by a fleet of Mercedes-Benz automobiles to Amsterdam. Meanwhile, their audience had assembled in the auditorium and was waiting patiently, hear-

Right: Marilyn Wilson at the dinner table on Laurel Way, 1967.
PETER REUM COLLECTION

Left: An Earl Leaf photo of Brian taken at one of the many dinner parties at the Laurel Way house.
PETER REUM COLLECTION

Below: Brian at the electric organ in the house on Laurel Way. Behind him is a store display of dolls enclosed in plastic bubbles.
PETER REUM COLLECTION

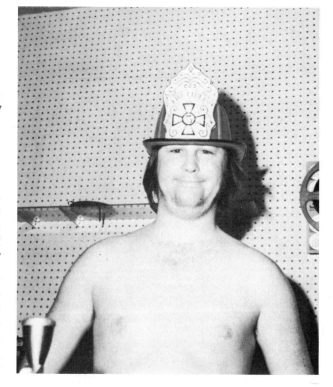

Above: Brian directing musicians at United Studios A control room, December 9, 1968, in a photo taken by Jasper Dailey. PETER REUM COLLECTION.

Right: Brian donned a fire chief's hat for the "Fire" segment of the "Elements," from the ill-fated *Smile* album. Brian believed the music started fires around Los Angeles. PETER REUM COLLECTION

Left: Van Dyke Parks
at a recording
session. He met
Brian at Terry
Melcher's house.
PETER REUM
COLLECTION

Below: January 25,
1967. A string
section was hired to
record the "Fire"
segment of *Smile*.
The musicians were
later sent home
because the
"vibrations" weren't
right. PETER REUM
COLLECTION

Right: A Capitol publicity photo from the late sixties when the Beach Boys were desperately trying to look hip. MAGGIE MONTALBANO

Below: Sheryl and David Anderle relax late at night in the studios during a *Smile* session. PETER REUM COLLECTION

Published here for the first time, the infamous group photo taken at Los Angeles Airport just before Brian's total retreat from the world. Within a few months he would stop speaking to almost everyone in the picture. Standing: Danny Hutton, Mark Volman, Dean Torrance, Diane Rovell, Annie Hinsche Wilson, Brian and Marilyn Wilson, Mike Vosse, David and Sheryl Anderle, Gene and Barbara Rovell Gaddy, Dick and Carol Maier. On floor: June Fairchild, Van Dyke and Durry Parks. GUY WEBSTER

Right: Brian, Nick Grillo, and Mike Love proudly show off their new Warner Brothers contract. The photo was taken July 27, 1970. PETER REUM COLLECTION

Below: Dennis, Laurie Bird, and James Taylor on the set of *Two-Lane Blacktop*. The movie was Dennis's big shot at an acting career. UNIVERSAL PICTURES, PETER REUM COLLECTION

Above: Barbara Charren and Dennis Wilson in the early bloom of love. Friends said she was the best thing that ever happened to him.
PETER REUM COLLECTION

Left: Tandyn Almer at the keyboard in Western Studios, circa 1970.
PETER REUM COLLECTION

Right: Terry Melcher, son of Doris Day, was Manson's real target. The Tate–La Bianca murders were meant only as a warning.
CONNIE PAPPAS

Below: Charles Manson (*right*) and his "family" were Dennis Wilson's long-term house guests. Dennis later told the District Attorney that he didn't remember anything significant about their time together. UPI/
BETTMANN NEWSPHOTOS

Above: The Love Brothers: Stephen, Mike, and Stanley. PETER REUM COLLECTION

Left: Mike Love meditates live onstage. PETER REUM COLLECTION

Right: Brian stands in front of the house on Bellagio Drive on his way to the Grammy awards in 1977. FUDGIE

Below, left: Rocky Pamplin in Australia. FUDGIE

Right: Debbie Keil gave Brian refuge from business and family, much to Marilyn Wilson's chagrin.
CAROLYN W. POULIN

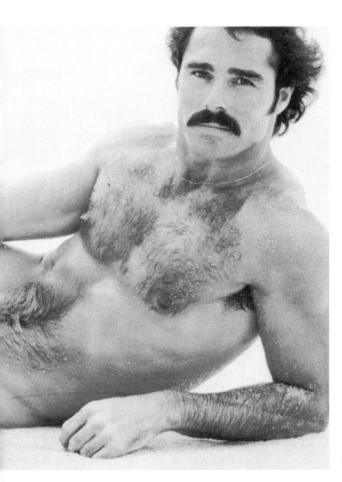

Left: Rocky Pamplin's *Playgirl* centerfold.
PLAYGIRL MAGAZINE

Below: Fred Vail and Dennis in 1977 at Dennis's house in Venice, California.
FRED VAIL

Right: Mike Love, the consummate showman, took the Beach Boys look into new dimensions. FUDGIE

Below: Brian and his mother, Audree. PETER REUM COLLECTION

Right: Stephen Love rides the waves in Hawaii in 1980. LEE LUCAS

Above: Dr. Eugene Landy and Brian backstage at the Washington, D.C., concert on July 4, 1984. FUDGIE

Left: Brian at almost 300 pounds in the parking lot behind Brothers Studio in Santa Monica.
FUDGIE

Top: Carnie, age 17, and Wendy, age 15. MARILYN WILSON

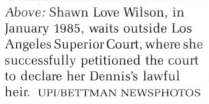

Above: Shawn Love Wilson, in January 1985, waits outside Los Angeles Superior Court, where she successfully petitioned the court to declare her Dennis's lawful heir. UPI/BETTMAN NEWSPHOTOS

Right: A recent photo of Marilyn Wilson, who lives in a large home in Encino, California, with the children, Carnie and Wendy. MARILYN WILSON

Dennis Wilson and Karen Lamm on the beach in Malibu. Together they were the perfect young California couple.
GUY WEBSTER

Karen Lamm in a recent photo. She forgave Dennis too many times for her own good. GUY WEBSTER

ing the step-by-step account of the group's progress. The Dutch audience was worked up into a frenzy by 5:15 A.M. when the Beach Boys finally reached the hall, and the crowd went berserk. Although the Beach Boys were exhausted, nevertheless this was one of the band's best concerts and most appreciative audiences. Now they were looking forward to going back to Holland. Before Rieley worked with the Beach Boys, he had never been to Europe. After their arrival, he fell in love with Holland and was determined that they should all move to Amsterdam to live and record. Thus started the Great Holland Fiasco.

Actually, while Jack Rieley has been blamed for the decision to move to Holland, it was the group's general consensus that a change, a move from Los Angeles, would be refreshing and creative. In Holland, there was no traffic, less drugs, and a place where the most exciting entertainment was a choice of "Flipper," "Zorro," or Rod McKuen on television at night. However, brother Brian said he didn't want to go. Brian had not gone far from home for more than a day in many years.

The wives and children of the rest of the Beach Boys were more than happy to be off to Holland, where the surf was never up. The move began early in spring. Eventually the entourage included Dennis Wilson, Barbara, and their son; Carl and Annie and their two sons; Audree Wilson; Annie's brother Billy Hinsche; Carl's housekeeper and his two dogs; Mike Love and his third wife, Tamara, and their maid; Al Jardine, his wife, and their maid; Ricky Fataar with his wife and her parents; Blondie Chaplin and his girl friend; engineer Steve Moffit, Moffit's secretary, and her son; engineer Gordon Rudd and his wife; friend and road manager John Parks and his girl friend; Tom Gellert; Rieley's friend Russ Mackie, who was being billed as photographer and traveling attaché; Rieley's secretary, Carole Hayes, and her husband; and a PR man from Hollywood, Bill de Simone.

Marilyn tried to get Brian on the same plane with her, but realizing this might be a long, drawn-out chore, she went over first with Wendy and Carnie and the housekeeper. The office staff twice managed to get Brian as far as the Los Angeles Airport, but he insisted on turning back, claiming he had forgotten things. The third time he was brought to the airport, his escorts thought he was safely on the plane and called ahead for Marilyn to collect him in Amsterdam. But when the plane landed, he was not in his seat; they found only his passport and plane ticket, as if he had vanished in midair. Now nearly hysterical, Marilyn called Los Angeles. Friends were sent to Los Angeles Airport where they discovered Brian sleeping deeply in an airport waiting room. He had boarded the plane, found an excuse to get off at the last moment, and it had left without him. Brian was put on the next plane.

The group started out living in hotels until more permanent accommodations could be found. In all, eleven houses were rented within a thirty-mile radius of central Amsterdam. Brian and Marilyn moved to Laren; Carl was in Hilversum; Mike and Al in Bloemandaal. Once settled the group rented nine Mercedes, one Audi, purchased three Volkswagens and one van. Offices were set up at Jack Rieley's duplex apartment in the children's room, which was filled with stuffed animals on the tables not more than a foot and a half high. A Telex clattered away in the corner. Phone calls had to be placed through an international operator in the United States, located, oddly enough, in Pittsburgh, Pennsylvania. So many calls were placed from Holland daily that the international operators knew the number by heart.

The Beach Boys originally hoped to use Dutch recording facilities but either they were all booked or there were none that they liked. Instead, they decided to build their own studio in a converted barn in Baambrugge. This was sheer folly—a nearly impossible, incredibly expensive idea; but the group rushed into it with total enthusiasm. Steve Moffit, the engineer of *Carl and the Passions—So Tough* was alerted in mid-March to break down the studio at Bellagio Road and ship over the twenty-four-track quadrophonic console. Moffit was given a deadline of June 1 to assemble the studio in Baambrugge. Since none of the manufacturers in the United States could supply him with additional consoles and equipment in time, he decided to try to create his own studio from scratch. The idea was to fashion a modern studio in Los Angeles, disassemble it, ship it, then reassemble the studio in Holland. Moffit constructed the new studio in the back of a two-hundred-square-foot warehouse in Santa Monica, where assemblers worked in shifts around the clock. Then each component was shipped to Amsterdam in crates which cost $5,000 each to ship. The crates filled almost every one of the four flights a day from L.A. to Amsterdam. Every time a piece broke down, they had to ship it back again. The racks for the limiters, Kepexes and Dolbys were so heavy, they cracked the tarmac in Amsterdam, and the gross weight of all the shipped parts was 7,300 pounds.

When the studio was finally reassembled, nothing worked. Moffit then flew to Holland, where he spent eighteen hours a day for the next four and a half weeks trying to get the equipment running. This ruined the touring schedule the Beach Boys expected to keep in Europe, severely limiting the needed income to cover the expense of living in Holland. In the interim, the group tried to mix down a live tape from their recent European dates by having Moffit detach a 3M sixteen-track mixer from their new equipment and move it to a studio in Amsterdam. It immediately blew up, smoke pouring out, and finally a representative from the Minnesota Mining and Manufacturing Company, which had made the machine, was flown to Amsterdam from London to repair it.

Brian Wilson celebrated his thirtieth birthday in Holland. He was melancholy and morose most of the time, spending every day in the house, listening continuously to Randy Newman's new album *Sail Away*. Somehow the sound and feel of this album inspired Brian, and he wrote a strange "fairy tale" called "Mount Vernon and Fairway" to contribute to the upcoming *Holland* LP. The story derived from the nights he spent at the Loves' when they still lived in the big house on Mt. Vernon and Fairway. As Brian explained it, late at night in Mike's bedroom, when the rest of the household was asleep, "I'd have a transistor radio under the covers so we could listen to the late-night R&B on KGFJ and KDAY. You [know the] part in the fairy tale about the prince's 'magic transistor radio'? Well, that came from *that*."

Brian explained the rest of the story line in his own inimitable fashion: "The fairy tale? Okay, lemme tell you. Well, we were in another country; we were in Holland, and I just sat around and drank apple sap—that's like apple cider—and just sat around and dreamed. And one night I was listening to that Randy Newman album called *Sail Away*. So I started playing the album and I was sitting there with a pencil and I started writing. And I found that if I kept playing the Randy Newman album, I could still stay in that mood. It was the weirdest thing; I wrote the whole fairy tale while listening to that album. It was the weirdest little mood I created. I was thinking about Mike Love's house, and I just wrote, 'There was a mansion on a hill,' and then later on, in my head, I created a fairy tale."

Predictably, nobody in the group appreciated this bit of whimsy, however brilliant it might have been; "*Nobody* was ready for that," Brian said. "*Nobody*. I remember, Carl said, 'WHAT?'"

Brian quickly hurtled back into a depressed state. Carl, realizing how hurt Brian was, took the bits and pieces of the song to the studio and put it together while Brian lay in bed. When Brian heard the finished product, he was overjoyed. "It was really a thrill; the first time we'd ever done anything that creative." However, the group thought the piece was too long for the album, and their opinion depressed Brian further. In the end, the group convinced Warner Brothers to include the song as an additional record the size of a single to be included with the album as a special "bonus."

When the *Holland* album was finally submitted to Warner Brothes for release, the company hated it. In reality, the album was not very good. There was an especially long and pretentious three-part song written by Mike Love, and Alan and Lynda Jardine called "California Saga: Big Sur; The Beak of Eagles; California" that took up most of side one. Side two was equally disappointing, including "The Trader," written by Carl Wilson with lyrics by Jack Rieley; "Leavin' This Town," composed by Ricky Fataar, Carl Wilson, and Blondie Chaplin; and a forgettable tune called "Funky Pretty," composed with a little help from Brian, with lyrics by Mike Love and "additional lyrics by Jack Rieley." The only outstanding part of the album was a small segment of the "California Saga" and a pretty song called "Clear Cool Water." Warner Brothers immediately rejected the LP for lack of a single. "It was bloodshed," said a Warner executive. "Everybody went wild." The Beach Boys had just spent eight months in Holland, gambling every penny they had, and each member of the group thought he had contributed a small masterpiece. Now Warner thought the album was "soft."

"When it was delivered, it didn't seem that it was...well, it seemed like a pretty weak album," said David Berson. In fact, having heard what *Holland* sounded like, Warners realized that perhaps they shouldn't have accepted *Carl and the Passions—So Tough* either. "*Carl and the Passions* was a real disappointment, maybe because it was released in tow with *Pet Sounds*; but for whatever reason, it didn't do very well." Then came *Holland* and the Warner executives thought, "Gee, two weak albums in a row—it's going to be very bad," Berson said.

Mo Ostin suggested to Berson that perhaps they could turn to Van Dyke Parks for help. At that time, Van Dyke was working for Warner Brothers in a staff position as director of audio visual services, making $350 week. Mo contacted him and told him he was thinking about dropping the Beach Boys from the label altogether. Van Dyke said, "'But Mo, you can't do that. These boys have spanned presidencies. They're an important American institution.' So David [Berson] came down to my office to play the record to prove it was no damn good."

According to Berson, Van Dyke immediately said, "I have the answer to your problems." It seemed that Van Dyke had in his possession a cassette of a song he had written with Brian on a recent visit to his house on Bellagio Road. "It was a rare visit. In a five-day rush at that house, I came out with one song. I called him up out of the clear blue sky and at some point he said, 'Let's write a tune.' It was better than having him stare at the angels on his headboard and write tunes about them." Van Dyke said this was the single that would save the *Holland* album. He loaded the cassette on his office stereo equipment and Berson sat in a chair while an amazing dialogue came out of the speakers.

First Brian's voice, plaintive, low: "Hypnotize me, Van Dyke."

Van Dyke: "Cut the shit, Brian. You're a songwriter, that's what you do, and I want you to sit down and write a song for me."

"Hypnotize me, Van Dyke, and make me believe I'm not crazy," Brian pleaded. "Convince me I'm not crazy."

"Cut the shit, Brian, and play the tune," Van Dyke said.

"What's the name of the tune?" Brian asked.

And Van Dyke said, "Sail on Sailor."

What followed was a small masterpiece, in league with "Heroes and Villains" and "Good Vibrations." They sang the entire tune together, with only Brian accompanying on the piano. "Sail on Sailor" was the last masterpiece to come out of Brian and the Beach Boys. Ironically, when Mo Ostin and David Berson told the group they wanted to put "Sail on Sailor" on the *Holland* album and release it as a single, it became impossible for them to get Brian into the studio. When Brian finally got around to working, he started his usual procrastination, tinkering with the song, trying to make it perfect, as he had with "Good Vibrations" and *Smile*. Finally, the rest of the group did not allow Brian into the studio to work on it at all. The finished song credits Brian, Tandyn Almer, and Van Dyke Parks as "composers," with lyrics by Jack Rieley and Ray Kennedy. Blondie Chaplin sings the lead. Berson remembers that the initial tape of "Sail on Sailor" that Van Dyke played for him in his office was much better.

Even so, "Sail on Sailor" got the most airplay of any Beach Boys song in years, and helped to sell the *Holland* album, which got mixed reviews. It entered the album charts on January 20, 1973, and made a steady climb, hitting 37 at its height and logging twenty-six weeks on the charts—although most of that time it remained high above the number 100. "Sail on Sailor" hit a tepid 79 at its best. Curiously, the song reappeared on the charts in April, May, and June of 1974 and reached number 49 its second time around.

When the group packed to return to the United States after spending eight months in Holland, Jack Rieley refused to go with them, saying he had decided to run the Beach Boys' careers from Amsterdam. This naturally infuriated the group, and the problem was compounded by another situation that had arisen during their stay. It was reportedly noticed by members of the group that Jack's young male assistant seemed to be living with him. Whether the relationship was sexual or not was never determined, but in the homophobic enclave of the Beach Boys, enough of a shadow had been cast. Chip Rachlin, Michael Klenfner, Nick Grillo, and others had suggested to the group that Jack Rieley might be gay.

Carl made the trip back to Holland and fired Rieley. For some time now, Stephen Love, Mike's younger brother, had been waiting in the wings to take over as manager.

Jack Rieley was heard from again five years later, when he contacted David Berson, Chip Rachlin, various Warner Brothers employees, and members of the Beach Boys to tell them he was dying of cancer. He asked everyone for a loan, and his impending death was so "heavy" that most people sent him whatever they could afford. This became a hotly discussed situation, and for several years people wondered what actually happened to Jack Rieley. He turned up again in Los Angeles in 1982 and spent some time with Dennis Wilson. Rieley claimed he had been miraculously cured of his cancer by a Laetril treatment he could get only in West Germany. As of this writing, he is living in Amsterdam, Holland.

I was his lover,
she was a best friend
I mean, if I couldn't trust
my own sister, who could I trust?
—MARILYN WILSON

Thirteen

1

Dennis Wilson did not become a movie star. *Two-Lane Black-top* opened to less than respectable reviews, and neither James Taylor nor Dennis was acclaimed for his acting ability. Dennis wound up hating the experience—the subtle ego competition with Taylor and the demanding schedule that required him to get up at six in the morning to face a long, boring day on the set. Besides, rock drumming paid better than acting. The $25,000 Dennis received for his role in the film was gone within a month.

Back with the Beach Boys, Dennis felt continually thwarted in his role as a musician. The tension between him and the other members of the group, especially Mike Love, had reached a new peak. Little if any song-writing material that Dennis submitted for inclusion on the new Beach Boys albums was considered seriously. This attitude was truly unfortunate, because Dennis was now blossoming into an accomplished song-writer. But he was brash and abrasive on a personal level, and it was difficult to take him seriously. When Dennis was out on the road, he indulged in all manner of childish behavior, smashing rental cars as though they were amusement-park bumper cars, dropping the complimentary fruit from hotel windows to watch it splatter on the sidewalk below. In every bar and restaurant, he would buy a round of drinks for all the patrons. Dennis was ever the foolish, big-time spender looking to be loved.

Dennis's marriage to Barbara had long since gone awry. Barbara was more than most men could have hoped for in a wife and friend. Their second son, Carl, had been born on New Year's Eve of 1972. But there was no stability in the relationship, and no promise of improvement. They had already moved fourteen times since they were married, and the frequent relocations had naturally unnerved Barbara and the children. When Dennis lost his temper, anything was liable to happen. During one argument, he punched his fist through a plate-glass window and cut his hand so severely he was unable to play the drums. Ricky Fataar had to take over onstage drumming tours for him for nearly a year. Being replaced on tour depressed and angered Dennis even further. One night, while driving to a restaurant with Barbara and some friends in his latest Rolls-Royce, Dennis was stopped by the police for a traffic infringement. He was so obstreperous (and licenseless) that they hauled him down to the station house and kept him in the clinker overnight.*

"Dennis was impossible to live with by now," Barbara said. "He was having an affair . . . at the time, and it was very painful; but somehow I was able to swallow it and think somehow it's going to get better. It was awful, just awful." Barbara convinced Dennis to see a female psychiatrist, and Dennis went for several sessions. The doctor reported that Dennis was suffering from tremendous guilt because of his fame and money, and that he felt he didn't deserve his riches and feared he would always live in the shadow of his brothers. After he terminated therapy, Dennis told Stanley Shapiro that the only reason he went every week was to see if he could talk the doctor into sleeping with him.

"I was graced with the knowledge there was nothing I could do," Barbara said, "nothing I had to take personally anymore. The illusion was gone, and I got to see Dennis for who he was and me for who I was. I either had to accept it the way it was

---

*Dennis later told friends that he was raped by a black man while in jail that night. He also told friends that he had once stopped to help a stranded motorist and was dragged into an alley by three black men and raped. And on another occasion, he claimed he was raped by a black handyman on his boat, the *Harmony*. He would also later claim to be raped by a black man in the alley behind his first wife Carol's house in 1982. Obviously, this was a recurring fantasy, and whether or not any of these stories is true remains unknown.

or move on." Within a year, Barbara would decide to move on.

One of the few positive things Dennis had done in recent years was to try to grow closer to his father. Although Murry loved Dennis in his own way, he continued to criticize the way Dennis led his life. It was important to Dennis to come to terms somehow with Murry—this man he loved so much and was never able to touch, this man who had hurt him so deeply and never seemed to give him a modicum of respect. Through Dennis's efforts, they had become friends over the last year. There were now brief periods when the two got along well. "Every Thursday night," Barbara related, "Murry and Dennis would be on the phone together throughout the boxing matches on TV. It was like a connection they had together, talking on the phone like two guys about the fights. That was a highlight of their relationship, that they connected during those couple of hours the fights were on."

After speaking to Audree at her house on Mother's Day of 1973, Dennis called his father. Murry had been seriously ill for over a year with a stomach ailment called diverticulitis, and just two weeks before had suffered a serious heart attack. Murry was mainly confined to bed, although he had recently been able to attend a Beach Boys concert, where he announced backstage that he was finishing an opera that he intended to have the boys perform. On Mother's Day, however, Murry was singing quite a different tune. "I'm just going to live about a month," he told Dennis, to which Dennis replied, "Aw, Pa, cut it out."

A few days later they were on the phone again, Dennis complaining that he had nothing to show for years of being a Beach Boy, not even a car "worth having."

"I'll give you my Thunderbird," Murry told him gruffly. Murry loved his Thunderbird like a loyal old mistress.

"Yeah, and what are you going to drive?" Dennis asked him.

"I don't need a car," Murry said. "I'm dying."

"Yeah, I'm sure you're going to die," Dennis said sarcastically. "You're always dying."

Later that evening, Stanley Shapiro picked Dennis up and took him to Will Wright's Ice Cream Parlor in Westwood. They were in the midst of devouring huge sundaes when Dennis started to cry. Tears rolled down his cheeks. Shapiro said, "What the fuck's the matter with you?"

"I think my dad is going to die. I think he's dying," Dennis said.

"But your old man's always talking about dying," Shapiro said.

Dennis just shook his head. "Somehow this time I think it's real."

Murry also spoke to Brian occasionally on the phone. Murry told him he had written a new song, "Lazzaloo," which he wanted the boys to record. According to Brian, the song was five and a half minutes long, about a "guy who goes to Turkey and meets a Turkish girl." Murry had some great ideas for sound effects. "When we [sing] 'we made love all night long,' you go 'aaah,'" Murry said. Brian played along and said they would record the song.

On the morning of Monday, June 4, 1973, six weeks after Murry's near-fatal heart attack, ever-loyal Audree Wilson was in the kitchen of Murry's house, waiting for her husband to wake up. She sat at the table drinking coffee, watching the hands of the clock. I wish he'd wake up, she thought. I wonder if he's really okay.

Finally, she heard Murry stirring, and went into the bedroom. "We had a great talk," she said. "He was in a good mood. We talked for quite a while, about so many things. He said to me, 'I'm so glad I've never had to take nitroglycerin.' And I was glad too, because I knew that would be frightening. That's for the pain."

Murry was feeling so good that day he decided he wanted to take a walk. Although he had been out of bed several times and had walked around the house, he hadn't been outside since his heart attack. Audree suggested she make cereal for breakfast, and then they would drive down to Whittier Boulevard and Murry could stroll with her. She was in the kitchen when she heard him yelling for her. "I started dashing down this long hallway. He was in the bathroom sitting on the toilet and he said, 'Nitroglycerin,' so I grabbed it and said, 'Put it under your tongue.' But he just sat there, very pale. And he said,

'Cold water.' So I got a cloth with real cold water on it and kept touching his forehead. Then I held it on the back of his neck and he still just sat there. I said, 'Are you okay?' And he said, 'I don't know.'"

Audree stood up to hold him, but Murry just toppled over, facedown. Using all her strength, she managed to turn him over, but somehow she knew he was already gone. She patted his cheek and said, "Baby, baby," but she could tell he couldn't hear her. "All I said to him was, 'Baby, baby, I love you.'"

Audree went into the bedroom, called the fire department, walked out of the house, locked the door, and waited in her car for the ambulance to come. Later, in the hospital waiting room, a doctor came out and said, "We're doing everything we can."

Audree said, "I'm sure you are."

Audree called Carl when it was all over. Carl had gone up to the family cabin at Big Bear Lake, and she reached him there. Carl left immediately for Audree's house, but not before calling Brian. Marilyn answered the phone. "Mare, Dad is gone," Carl told her. "You have to tell Brian."

Marilyn composed herself and went up to the bedroom, where Brian was sleeping. She sat on the side of the bed and shook him gently. "Brian, I have to tell you something that you're not ready for. It's really going to hurt, but your father's gone."

"My father is gone?" Brian said, trying to make sense of the words. "My dad is...My dad died?" He laid his head back and broke into tears. "My dad...my dad..." he sobbed.

"We all went to his mother's house," Marilyn said. "I said to Brian, 'Come on, we have to go,' and he said, 'Okay.' He immediately got up and we got in the car and went to Whittier. They were all there. Dennis, Carl, all of them." Eventually the family retired to the Big Bear Lake cabin and spent a few days there together.

For Dennis, the only way to know that Murry was really gone was to see him in death. He took Barbara to the morgue with him. "He wanted to see Murry dead," Barbara said. "Dennis needed to see Murry that way to somehow digest the fact that he was gone. He couldn't get over the fact. Murry was just lying on a table in the morgue but they hadn't fixed him up or anything. He was still all cut up from the autopsy."

Dennis did not go to the funeral. According to Barbara, "He was having an affair with one of his best friend's wife at the time and he took her to Europe with him."*

Brian, too, fled Los Angeles. "Going to the funeral would have been a reality," Marilyn said, "but Brian didn't live in reality. Brian lived in fantasy." It made Carl furious; he didn't expect any better from Dennis, but he thought Brian owed it to Murry to stick it out. For Audree, however, it made perfect sense that Brian had to go away, and she forgave him immediately. Marilyn stayed in Los Angeles to attend the funeral, and Brian went to New York with Diane, ostensibly to promote a new Honeys single he had produced called "Shyin' Away." "I couldn't go," Marilyn said. "I knew I had to be there with the family. So Diane was his sidekick sometimes. Honestly, honestly, there is no way that I thought they were doing anything. When he was with Diane, I knew he was safe. I know it's peculiar, and I felt funny about it, but I felt if he's going to go off with anybody, let him go with someone I trust. I knew that my sister was not going to take my husband away from me."

In New York, Brian did several interviews with Diane at his side. He told *Record World* magazine, "The real reason that we're here is that my father died. . . . I went through a little bit of a change. . . . I haven't been feeling too good because he died, you know. I went through a shock and I wanted to leave town. I said, 'Come on, Diane. Let's go to New York and promote.'"

The interviewer tried to move Brian away from the subject of his father, but he kept coming right back to it. "You know, since my father died, it's been a lot different. You know, I feel a lot more ambitious. It really does something to you when your father passes away. Takes a while to get over it, too. I got a new perspective on life. I'm gonna try a little harder now. . . . It's makin' a man outta me."

---

*Typically, Dennis would forever remain irreverent about Murry's death, telling all his friends that when Murry died, his head landed in the toilet bowl.

But Murry's death did not make a man out of Brian. Brian retreated even further, and did not return to the studio to produce more material as promised. Tired of the hordes of strangers and drainers who showed up at her house at all hours of the day and night, Marilyn had the studio dismantled and removed. From the release of the *Holland* album in January of that year Brian would contribute no new Beach Boys material for the next three years. Instead, he became even more self-obsessed. His fondness for cocaine grew to prodigious proportions, as did his intensely close relationship with Danny Hutton. When asked in later years what he did exactly during that period, Brian answered, "Drugs and hanging out with Danny Hutton." Indeed, Brian would spend much of his time at Danny Hutton's small, "gingerbread" cottage in Laurel Canyon, and on several occasions Marilyn had to send friends there to climb the fence that surrounded Hutton's house and bring Brian home forcibly. "He would get *real fried*," said one observer at Hutton's house. Yet no professional help was sought for Brian—his problem was perceived as drug abuse, not mental illness. Audree Wilson told one reporter, "It would get to the point where Marilyn really thought Brian needed help; then he seemed okay, and she'd sort of forget about it, not necessarily talking to him about it at all."

Eventually, in September 1973, Marilyn's frustration culminated in a cataclysmic argument with Diane, who was banished from Bellagio Road. At the same time, Debbie Keil maintained her friendship with Brian as quietly as possible. By the end of 1973, Brian had moved to the chauffeur's quarters in the back of the house, where he spent most of his days in an escapist's sleep.

2

When the Beach Boys delivered their next album to Warner Brothers, it was again "rejected." It was a live album that "didn't make sense to me," according to David Berson. "They took the album back and made a whole new album," Berson said. The second album, too, was almost rejected, but Warners and the Beach Boys fiddled with it until it was acceptable. "It was a two-record set and it was a much better album," David Berson said. "When I played the album track-by-track some of the tracks on the first album were stronger, but it was a single record instead of a double record. I frankly thought it was something they threw together to deliver." When *The Beach Boys in Concert* LP was finally released, it turned out to be the only Warner Brothers Beach Boys album that went gold— technically. "It did not go gold because it sold enough copies to push a single-record package into the realm of a gold record," Berson explained, "but because it was a double-record set and had a great retail price. It went gold if you prorate the sales via the price...."

As part of the Beach Boys' settlement with Capitol, the group had retained the rights to the unfinished *Smile* album. These tapes were expected to be delivered to Warner Brothers no later than January 1973, or $50,000 would be deducted from the next advance to the group. Stephen Love sent a memo to the group members to this effect; but *Smile* was not forthcoming, and the $50,000 was subtracted from the next check. With no new product in sight, Warner Brothers released a series of reissues. In May 1974, they reissued *Pet Sounds*. On July 15, *Wild Honey* backed with *20/20* was put on the market, and on October 5, 1974, *Friends* and *Smiley Smile* were re-released, all greeted by minor sales. In a move that would have seemed to flood the market even more with unwanted Beach Boys product, Capitol Records decided to reissue their own compilation of favorite Beach Boys songs. Mike Love willingly consulted with Capitol on this album, helping them choose the songs and even suggesting the title *Endless Summer* to take the curse off the image of a "best of" package.

Astonishingly, when the album was released on June 24, it went hurtling to the top of the record charts. Capitol, wisely, put together a strong television promotion and advertising campaign for *Endless Summer*. Backed by the Beach Boys' constant touring and their rediscovery by a new generation of music listeners, this campaign gave the album tremendous impact. *Endless Summer* hit the number-one position on October 5, 1974. It stayed on the charts for an astounding seventy-one weeks, dropped off, and had a second wind the following summer as it went back up the charts to reach as high as number 20. After falling off the charts during the winter months of 1975, it was back yet again for another breathtaking sixty-seven weeks. *Endless Summer* became the talk of the recording industry as it went double platinum. Its success drove the Warner Brothers executives crazy, and even "freaked Brian out." As Brian told a Los Angeles disc jockey, who showed a copy of the record charts to him with *Endless Summer* in the number-one position, "It's going to be a little freaky for me to see that, but nevertheless, I can accept [it]. It seems weird. It gives me a shock...." Capitol had the good sense to package quickly another "best of" album entitled *Spirit of America*, released in April 1975. This record leaped to number 8 on the charts that summer, and logged an impressive forty-three weeks on the *Billboard* charts.

With Stephen Love now at the group's financial helm as business manager, the Beach Boys entered a new era of financial prosperity, not experienced since their earliest years. Janet Lent-Coop, a one-time secretary and bookkeeper who had been with the boys for five years, was named administrative assistant.

Stephen Love seemed in many ways the antithesis of his brother Mike. He was a quiet, introverted, well-educated man whose primary interest was in figures. "He worked very hard for the Beach Boys," Janet Lent-Coop says. "His whole heart and soul was in what they did." First, he fired the bookkeepers, and managed to bring the accounts payable as up to date as possible. Stephen hated the Ivar Street offices—they were impractical, claustrophobic, and dark because there were no windows. He moved the Beach Boys' offices to 3621 Rosecrans Avenue in Manhattan Beach, a small, two-story building behind a gas station, not far from where Stephen himself lived at 4201 Ocean Avenue. Although the offices were hardly glamorous, the rent was right. Since the studios had been moved out of Brian's house, new facilities called Brother Studios were opened in a leased building at 1454 Fifth Street in Santa Monica. Initially, Brother Studios was owned by all the Beach Boys, but it was later sold to Dennis and Carl, who ran the business for many years at a deficit.

The Beach Boys' resurgence in popularity was augmented by twenty-nine-year-old James William Guercio, who had been the guiding force behind the group Chicago and a successful record producer for several groups including Blood, Sweat, and Tears. A former guitarist for Frank Zappa's group, The Mothers of Invention, Guercio had become a millionaire moviemaker with the film *Electra Glide in Blue*. Guercio ostensibly joined the Beach Boys on tour as a bass player to replace Blondie Chaplin, who had reportedly been fired after "onstage inebriation,"* but it quickly became evident that Guercio would play a much more important role in their careers. Guercio was a friend of Dennis, who suggested that perhaps Guercio could make some suggestions and changes to improve their stage performances. More important, Guercio became a stabilizing force, almost a "Dutch uncle" to whom the individual members of the group could go with their problems. Guercio resolved conflicts with what seemed a Solomon-like wisdom. He quickly moved up the ranks into a full managerial position and his company, Caribou, was officially named as the Beach Boys management arm. With Stephen Love in the office as business manager and Guercio out on the road, the Beach Boys suddenly experienced a reincarnation, selling out even the largest halls. Their nightly guarantee leaped to the $25,000 range and then even higher. Perhaps the crowning touch was when *Rolling Stone* voted the Beach Boys "Band of the Year."

In May 1975, under Guercio's direction, the Beach Boys teamed up with Chicago in one of the most successful tours in rock-and-roll history. It was a twelve-city odyssey that would gross $7.5 million and play to a total of over 700,000 people, despite a general recession, which had hit the rest of the music business hard. It seemed almost miraculous that within a year

---

*Chaplin also had a near swing-out with Stephen Love at a Madison Square Garden concert after Stephen refused to allow Chaplin's wife and girl friends up on the stage at the end of the concert. When Chaplin said, "Fuck you" to Stephen, Love threw Chaplin against a wall, took his gum out of his mouth, wadded it up, and threw it in Chaplin's face.

the Beach Boys were back on top, grossing as much money without any new recorded product as they had in their best days with Capitol Records.

But James Guercio and Caribou Management didn't stay with them for long. The following spring Guercio was relieved of his business responsibilities with the Beach Boys. An intimate member of the Beach Boys family claims Caribou was fired because it was getting 10 percent of the gross of both tour and record income, while the ICM talent agency was receiving another 10 percent to book the group. Various group members felt Caribou was being overpaid on the concert end of things because the group was already on its way up from the end of 1973 and Guercio didn't have anything to do with their renewed popularity. Initially, it was claimed, the disparity would balance out in the end because it was alleged that James Guercio promised he would get more productivity out of Brian. When this didn't happen, Stephen Love reluctantly fired him. However, many observers suggest the Beach Boys followed an old pattern of jettisoning personnel when their financial situation improved. Now Stephen Love took over as de facto business manager.

3

By this time Dennis Wilson had found the new love of his life, the *Harmony*. A sleek, impressive sailing vessel, built by the Azuma boat company in Japan in 1950, the *Harmony* was originally christened the *Watadori*, which means "bird of passage." The boat was constructed with materials from all over the world, including teak from Burma, mahogany from the Philippines, and brass fittings made in Scotland. With a sixteen-foot beam and four large plate-glass windows, the boat had an air of spaciousness below deck. Dennis needed $50,000 to buy it, and Stephen Love helped him get 100 percent financing through a local bank. Dennis put the boat in drydock and began to pour tens of thousands of dollars into its renovation.

On Saturday night, October 5, 1974, after working on the

boat all day, Dennis went for dinner to Mr. Chow, a chic Chinese restaurant in Beverly Hills. As he sat with his friend Steve Kalenich, Dennis noticed, at a large round table across the room, one of the most beautiful girls he had ever set his eyes on. Yes, for Dennis there were lots of beautiful girls, and each of them was more beautiful than the last, but this girl was different. It wasn't simply that she was blond and had blue eyes so electric they shone across the restaurant; it wasn't simply that her figure was provocative and she radiated an animal sexuality (like his own). This girl had poise, a worldly, aloof sophistication that was rare, particularly in the world of Hollywood starlets. His hair streaked from the sun, dressed in jeans and a baby-blue tanktop that said "France" across the front, Dennis stared at her. Occasionally, but not often, he caught her staring back.

The girl was Karen Lamm, Dennis was told, a twenty-two-year-old model and actress. Karen, who was dining with her girl friend, actress Candy Clark, wondered who the handsome, wild-looking guy in the "France" T-shirt was and learned he was Dennis Wilson of the Beach Boys. But neither had the courage to say hello that night. Karen and her friend had just come from a screening of *Vrooder's Hooch*, which starred one of Karen's boyfriends, Timothy Bottoms. At one point Dennis walked across the room in his tight Levi's and Karen turned to Candy Clark and said, "Hmmm, real cute. I want to go out with that guy." And Candy said, "Me too. Well, all's fair in love and war. Let's see who dates him first."

And Karen said, "I'll top you. I'll marry him."

Later that night Dennis was joined at his table by agent John Burnham, whom Karen coincidentally also knew. When she got home she phoned Burnham and asked, "What do you know about Dennis Wilson?"

Burnham said, "I know that Dennis didn't shut up about you all night long."

Burnham arranged a double date for them for two weeks later, after Karen finished shooting a "Manhunters" TV episode. On Friday, October 18, Dennis arrived at Karen's house on his newly purchased Harley-Davidson motorcycle. He came in, bashfully put his head on her shoulder, and Karen immediately smelled a couple of beers on his breath and didn't like it. "Back off," she said.

The couple met Burnham and his girl friend Heidi at Mr. Chow's for dinner. Dennis was nervous. He got the sense that Karen was making a large amount of money from modeling and acting and wasn't the least bit impressed that he was a rock star. During dinner he began to drink to get up his courage, switching from margaritas to straight tequilas. Eventually he got pretty loose, and at one point he reached across the table and grabbed Karen's right breast. "Great tits!" he exclaimed, like a little boy. Quickly glancing around the room, Karen could tell many people in the restaurant were staring, and she nearly fell to the floor trying to shove his hand away.

Flushed with embarrassment, Karen let out a little cry as she stood up and ran into the bathroom. What am I going to do with this fool? she thought. For a moment she considered looking for the rear exit to the restaurant and leaving him there, but eventually she regained her composure and went back to the table. Dennis was sincerely apologetic and spent the rest of the meal pouring on the charm.

Later, when he dropped her off at home, Dennis asked if he could come in. She said yes. For the first time that evening, Karen felt she was getting to see the real Dennis Wilson. "He didn't make a big play," she said. "He was just low-key and charming. We sat around and talked about music, his life, the entertainment business. We took out all my old family albums and photographs of me through the years and went through them." Dennis told Karen that money was tight within the Beach Boys' organization,* and that he was living in a $160-a-month apartment at 3109 Ocean Front Walk in Venice. He seemed reluctant to go back there that night, but Karen "wouldn't let him stay," she said, "although I was very attracted to him."

In her diary that night, she wrote, "Dennis changes under pressure. Hah, nobody laughs when you're alone...and an ass. Very sexy, boyish grin."

Two days later Dennis came by Karen's house while she was rehearsing a scene with a girl from her acting class. Saying he

---

*It really wasn't, but he was spending it as fast as he made it.

would amuse himself in the music room until she was through, he began to play the piano. "This amazing sensitivity came through, this sober, sensitive feeling that was romantic," Karen said. "I stopped rehearsing and went back and sat down next to the piano. Dennis played for a long, long time." Later they went out for dinner, and on the way home Dennis bought her a Halloween pumpkin as a gift. Dennis said to her, "I'd like to stay tonight," and Karen smiled.

"You can stay," she said, "but you'll have to stay in the guest room." She made up a bed for him and went into her own room, but she couldn't sleep. Later, she went to the guest room and knocked on the door, where Dennis, too, lay awake. She said to him, "I've changed my mind."

He never left. "It was magic," Karen Lamm said. "He spun my head around. I was in a trance after that."

Karen Lamm was born Barbara Karen Perk on June 21, 1952, in Indianapolis, Indiana. When she was five years old, she was adopted by her stepfather, James Sullivan. By the age of fifteen she had blossomed into an extraordinary beauty, dropped out of high school (to finish at night), and started a modeling career in Indianapolis and Chicago that was almost instantly successful. At seventeen she met composer-pianist Bobby Lamm of the rock group Chicago at the Whiskey A Go Go. She married him a year later on December 18, 1970, at the Self-Realization Fellowship Center on Sunset Boulevard in Los Angeles. They moved to a rented house in Studio City, where Karen discovered she had a lot to learn about being a rock star's wife.

"We were on the road three hundred days a year," Karen said, "which was a strain. Besides, I was too young to be married. To live with a musician you've got to have a certain confidence in yourself and a strong bond with the man. I didn't have an understanding of what life was about." While Lamm was touring Germany with Chicago, Karen found his datebook and realized he was seeing other girls. In May 1971, after only five months of marriage, she filed for divorce.

She moved into her own small rented house and started diligently studying acting with Lee Strasberg. She quickly became one of his favorite students, and her beauty, combined with raw talent, started to land her acting jobs. Her first movie role was in the 1973 film *Scarecrow*, which was quickly followed by two starring parts in national commercials for Ford Pinto and Royal Crown Cola. Major advertising campaigns for Clairol and Maybelline came next, and in 1975 she was put under contract by Benson and Hedges. A famous photograph of her holding a broken extra-length cigarette appeared in magazines and on billboards around the world. With her career well under way, Karen moved to a larger house at 1850 Beverly Drive, which she decorated beautifully with art nouveau lamps and furniture and a large brass bed in the bedroom. It was here that Dennis eventually moved in with her.

For Dennis, Karen Lamm was quite a girl to reckon with. She was no pushover and was not at all in awe of him. She had her own successful career and depended on him for nothing. He was hardly the first famous man she had gone out with. Not only had she already been married to a rock star, but Dennis knew she had dated many celebrities, including Tim Matheson and Jan-Michael Vincent. Yet Dennis's double standards didn't cease in his relationship with Karen. Although he was head-over-heels in love with her, that wasn't going to stop him from sleeping with any pretty little thing he laid his eyes on. But if he thought for one second that Karen was fooling around with anyone else, Dennis became irrationally jealous. Karen was to discover the extent of Dennis's wrath only a few months into their relationship.

One day in January 1975, Dennis returned to Karen's house from a Beach Boys tour to find Elliott Gould stretched out on the sofa watching TV, the straps to his overalls hanging around his waist, and Karen in a nearby chair in her bathrobe. Although this was in reality an innocent situation, Dennis was infuriated, his rage compounded by the fact that Gould was wearing a T-shirt Dennis had recently given Karen that said, "I am a Blond Bombshell." Gould, sensing the explosive tension in the air, made some polite conversation and quickly excused himself. Dennis and Karen had it out after he left, and Karen thought the subject had been laid to rest for good. But a few days later Gould and a friend of Karen, actress Patti D'Arbanville (the recent girl friend of "Miami Vice" star Don Johnson), asked Karen to meet them at the Bistro, one of Beverly Hills's most exclusive restaurants. Karen left a message for Dennis saying that if he was interested he should meet them there for dinner. Dennis arrived at the restaurant in a snit. "He reached across the table at the Bistro," Karen remembered with a shudder, "grabbed Elliott by the jacket and tie, and said, 'You stay away from Karen, she's *mine.*'"

Karen raced out the door in tears.

But for Karen and Dennis, passion and heat were the perfect formula for love. Their relationship seemed only to strengthen through each tumultuous event. "We were so in love with each other," Karen said, "when everything is so intense, one little thing just triggers you off and you go off the deep end. When you put two dynamos together, you are going to get a dynamo."

Indeed, each fight was like an episode from a gothic soap opera. After one lovers' spat, Dennis had begun moving his clothing out of Karen's house when she decided to help him. Outside in the driveway Dennis became so enraged that he punched her in the stomach, ripped off her diamond earrings, and stepped on them. Karen ran inside and locked the door. Dennis stood in front of the house taunting her. "What are you going to do now, honey? Get your gun?"

"I said, 'That's a fucking good idea!' I thought, I'm going to scare the shit out of this guy." Karen went to the bedroom and got the licensed .38 revolver she kept next to her bed, for personal protection, opened up the front door, and assumed a combat stance.

"Don't you think this crazy little girl won't do it!" she shouted. "I'm tired of your bullshit! You get your goddamn butt off my property."

Dennis said, "You're crazy. That gun doesn't scare me. And you know the Mercedes I gave you? A tow truck will be here to get it!"

Karen aimed the gun at the Mercedes 450 SL that Dennis had given her and said, "You know what I think of that car?" and pulled the trigger. She put a hole in the car a half-inch from the gas tank, shattering the rear lights and nearly blowing it up.

Dennis left on tour the next day. He called every day from the road, apologizing for what had happened. When he returned, he phoned her and asked, "Do you want to see our new home?"

"What new home?" Karen asked.

Dennis told her he had rented a two-story, five-bedroom house for them at the Malibu beachfront community of Trancas, at 32184 Broad Beach for nearly $3,000 a month. Karen packed her belongings and moved in with him there. For a while, their life together was dreamlike. They bought two Irish setters, Christian and Wagner, and that Christmas, under the tree, Karen found four boxes of Chloe outfits. Later that day, Dennis gave her a necklace of pear-shaped diamonds, and before they went to sleep that night, she found a heart-shaped diamond ring sitting on the marble commode in the bathroom. Karen bought Dennis a telescope, and a little catamaran. Later, he anchored the *Harmony* just off shore, and they swam out to it every morning and ate breakfast. Sometimes Dennis would put on his wet suit and spear fresh halibut for lunch. Their photographs started to appear in the papers as they became rock-and-roll's favorite twosome. "We were unmistakably the perfect couple," Karen said. "It was an extraordinary relationship."

Of course, the rest of the Beach Boys didn't think so. Not one of them liked Karen or the influence she exerted over Dennis. She was as headstrong and tough as any of them, and did not show the kind of deference the group members had come to expect of their women. She could drink as hard as the best of them, and when she wanted, could cuss as well too. Once, at a concert in Oakland, she even managed to insult promoter Bill Graham. By then Karen was singing backup harmonies with the Beach Boys for fun. Between the last number and the encore, she had gone off stage and given one of her friends her backstage pass. When she tried to get back on stage, a black security guard roughly grabbed her and said, "Where do you think you're going?"

Karen lost her temper for a moment and said, "Get your hands off me, nigger!"

Graham, incensed, insisted Karen apologize for what he termed her "bigotry." Karen looked Graham straight in the eye and said, "I'm no bigot, I had lunch with Huey Newton!" The humor of the remark was lost on Graham.

Later, for having insulted Karen, Dennis told Graham, "Go fuck yourself!" Graham refused to allow him on stage until both he and Karen apologized. After that incident, Graham refused to book the Beach Boys ever again.

Dennis did not have many intelligent, understanding friends with whom he could discuss his problems. Since Murry's death he had become especially close to Carl's wife Annie's father, "Pop" Hinsche. "Pop," who was pushing eighty by this time, was a wise and warm father figure to Dennis. But by mid-1976 "Pop" Hinsche was fatally ill, and when he died of cancer on May 7, Dennis took the news hard. It seemed there was no anchor in his life, that he was drifting. Dennis decided it was time he and Karen married. "He wanted to marry me about two weeks after we met," Karen said. "But I knew better. He loved the romance of being married but hated the confinement. We were supposed to get married many times, but I would always pull out at the last minute. The idea scared me. I didn't want to get married to get divorced. But after 'Pop' died, he seemed lost. So I said, 'OK, let's get married.'"

On May 21, Dennis and Karen, along with Audree, her sister Gwenn Korthof, and Karen's brother Jeff, flew to Hawaii and took a boat trip down the Fern Grotto River on Kauai where they were married. This time, Dennis said, the marriage would last forever. For a short time everything seemed perfect. Although they had no children, Dennis's relationship with Karen was the most important one of his life. No other woman galvanized Dennis the way Karen did—or incensed him. Their relationship burned with such intensity and heat that it nearly incinerated them both.

> *They killed the Golden Goose.*
> —STANLEY LOVE

> *I never considered him sick.*
> *Because what is sick to most people*
> *is they just don't know how*
> *to accept the unusual, the eccentric.*
> —MARILYN WILSON,
> 1976

Fourteen

1

Brian was a very sick man by the beginning of 1975, and he had long passed the point where even his most loyal supporters could dismiss his behavior as either eccentricity or the effects of simple drug addiction. Brian now weighed 240 pounds. He did not shower or shave. He seldom went out, and would appear in public in his pajamas and bathrobe. Once he even climbed onto the stage of the Whiskey A Go Go, uninvited by the group who was playing. His preferred drug was cocaine, and his access to it seemed uncontrollable, even though all his money had been cut off and he had no checkbook. His well-meaning friends were not much help in this matter. In order to alleviate Brian's cash-flow problems, Terry Melcher and former Beach Boy Bruce Johnston, who now ran an RCA-funded production company called Equinox Records, gave Brian a contract to produce thirty-six sides with an advance of $23,000.* But Brian refused to finish any of the tracks—the studio seemed to scare him—and his access to the $23,000 was wisely cut off by the Beach Boys.

More than occasionally, Brian found a way to purchase and snort heroin, after which he would be "nearly catatonic" for

---

*Carl Wilson wrote a letter to *Crawdaddy* magazine in 1976 in which he said, "While people were saying they're trying to look out for Brian, [and] he didn't have any money, [and] he didn't have any control—well, the fucking truth was that Sly Stone and Terry Melcher and all those people were hitting on him for like $1,500 a week so they could score coke, okay? That is the fucking reason why [Brian's] name was taken off the checks...." Carl later apologized to Sly Stone and Melcher in a follow-up letter to *Crawdaddy*.

days. Reportedly, the children found his drug stash, but Brian was not concerned. Marilyn, already pushed past the breaking point, was desperate for help. She finally decided to consult a psychiatrist herself, but after only a few sessions the doctor told her that Brian was clearly the person in need of treatment. Yet Brian refused to get counseling of any kind. One morning in the spring of 1975 Marilyn called Stephen Love at his office and told him that she was going to put Brian in a psychiatric hospital and divorce him if he didn't voluntarily get medical treatment. Some believed that the best possible thing for Brian would have been for him to receive intensive psychiatric care in a hospital setting. But in some ignorant, convoluted way, that idea seemed to be an admission of defeat and an embarrassment to the Beach Boys. Stephen Love suggested that instead of taking any drastic action, they hire his younger brother, Stanley, to assist Marilyn in trying to straighten Brian out at home.

Stan Love was twenty-six and a professional basketball player. Six feet four inches tall, macho and tough, Stanley nevertheless had a good-natured, almost sweet quality about him. In 1961 he had graduated from the University of Oregon, where he was a leading scorer in the Pacific Eight conference and was named an All-American in his senior year. After college he was chosen in the first round of the NBA draft by the Baltimore Bullets, and his contract was negotiated by Nick Grillo and Stan's brother Stephen. Later he played for the Los Angeles Lakers, but was laid off early in 1975, when Stephen called him to ask if he wanted to take on the chore of rehabilitating Brian. Although Stanley had no experience with this kind of situation, he had always idolized his cousin Brian. He said he would do whatever he could to help. An extra incentive was the salary Stephen negotiated for him with Marilyn: $50,000 a year, plus perks, half paid by the Beach Boys, half by Marilyn and Brian personally.

Stanley arrived at the house on Bellagio Way one day in April 1975. "It was the first time I had seen Brian in years," Stanley said. "He was lying curled up in a ball on the floor, shaking and crying, because he and Marilyn had just had a tremendous blowout, a yelling contest. I knew that little kids were usually intimidated by my height, so when I walked in I immediately sat down on the floor with him for about an hour, to make him feel a little more comfortable. Brian was right on the verge of a nervous breakdown—drug saturation, everything. It was dangerous, really. I mean, you push that guy much further and he would have freaked out."

Stanley's priority, aside from keeping Brian away from drugs, was to get him to wash. "He was gross. He wouldn't take showers because he was afraid of what would come out of the shower head. He didn't know what would happen, and that scared him. 'Could be too cold, could be too hot, could be *gas!*' is what he thought. Then he said, 'Maybe *nothing* will come out. Oh no! What does that mean? *Nothing!*'"

After convincing Brian it would be safe to bathe and coaxing him into the shower, Stanley next tried to get him to lose some weight. A huge padlock was installed on the refrigerator. Then the coffeepots were thrown away. "He'd go down and fill a coffee cup halfway up and then put in five tablespoons of instant coffee and stir that sucker up and fill the rest with hot water and then try to drink it as fast as he could to get the [caffeine] rush," Stanley said. "Everything he did was to orchestrate a rush, a high, a kick."

Cigarettes were another high for Brian, literally as many as he could smoke, sometimes five packs a day. Marilyn, who also smoked at the time, would safely lock hers away, but Brian would either take the car keys and drive to the market (licenseless) to buy a carton or wander out on Bellagio Road to flag down passing cars and bum smokes. A guard was hired for the front gate to keep Brian from wandering out. Then Stanley and Marilyn walked up and down Bellagio Road and rang the doorbells of the neighboring houses. "Brian Wilson is not feeling well," Stanley explained, "and we're involved in a program for his rehabilitation. In case you see him wandering down the street, or he comes by asking for money or cigarettes, would you kindly call us so we can come and get him?"

But it wasn't long before Brian discovered a new method of obtaining controlled substances. Stanley claims Brian was privy to what he called the "Beverly Hills Home Delivery Service."

According to Stanley, Brian only had to leave cash in the mailbox, and whatever drug he wanted would appear in exchange during the night. Marilyn fiercely denies even the possibility that this was true, as Brian had no money of his own.

Finally, a psychiatrist was found, and Brian embarked on a three-day-a-week appointment schedule. The treatment turned out to be a total farce, since Brian frequently refused to go to appointments, and when he did attend sessions he was less than cooperative. According to Stanley Love, this first psychiatrist soon refused to treat Brian, and recommended him to a "meditating" therapist in San Diego. Again, Brian refused to be driven to sessions, and therapy soon ended.

Throughout this period, Debbie Keil continued to visit Brian at the house, steering as clear of Marilyn as possible. Her visits were often solicited by nocturnal calls from the phone Brian had installed in the chauffeur's quarters. Brian used to refer to her as his "golden-haired angel coming in at night." She spent hours talking with him, consoling him, careful never to make any demands. Brian was truly fond of her, and even wrote a song for her called "The Night Was So Young."* But Debbie was soon to learn that she was competing with someone for Brian's attention—Diane. Diane had made up with her sister and was now allowed back into the house. One night, Brian called Debbie in her apartment and invited her over. Debbie was getting dressed when she received a second phone call from Brian telling her not to come. Now determined to find out what was going on, Debbie drove to Bellagio Way at about 1:00 A.M. and let herself into the open house to discover Brian, shirtless, talking with Diane. Marilyn was asleep in the master bedroom. Diane disappeared downstairs while Brian locked himself in a bedroom. Debbie stood in the hallway knocking on the door, calling to Brian. The noise awakened Marilyn. "There was Debbie Keil in my hallway. God knows how she got in my house. She was knocking on the door saying, 'Let me in, Brian. Let me in!' Brian was saying, 'Go away! Let me alone! I don't want to see you!' I went up to her and said, 'Get the fuck out of here ... before I kill you!' That's when I realized

---

*The song later appeared on the Beach Boys' *Love You* album.

something else had been going on." When she escorted Debbie downstairs, Marilyn was even more surprised to discover her sister Diane in the kitchen.

Stanley Love was asked how a two-hundred-and-forty-pound, unwashed, emotionally disturbed man could wind up with three women fighting over him. He replied, "These weren't your average surfer chicks. And anyway, you're talking about Brian Wilson, a symbol of talent and wealth."

At the end of the summer, Stanley got an offer to play basketball for the Atlanta Hawks and left his job in the Wilson household. Brian quickly retreated to his room, where he lay in bed stuffing himself with food and drugs, beating his toes against the headboard of carved angels and humming his own songs, California dreaming.

2

Eugene Landy is also the stuff of California dreams. Within a month of Stanley Love's leaving, Marilyn began to search around again for a therapist who could deal with Brian. Through the cousin of a friend she was told about Eugene Landy, a psychologist who had experience working with drug problems. Marilyn first went to consult with Landy in his offices in a two-story mocha-colored building on South Robertson Boulevard, directly across the street from Pips, a private backgammon club. Although the wooden sign above the doorway to the building proclaimed FREE (The Foundation for Rechanneling Emotion Through Education), an hour with foundation president Landy—$90—was no more free than a session at the backgammon boards across the street.

Landy was a short, smiling man, with dark, unkempt hair. Warm and likable, he spoke with a heavy cadence akin to that of comedian Jackie Mason. His office had grass-cloth covered walls; a low, square orange coffee table; and two brown lumpy sofas. As soon as Marilyn laid eyes on Landy, she liked him. "I got semi—dressed up, and when I walked into his office there was this guy in jeans and boots and I loved it. I said,

'This guy is great! He's as eccentric in his world as Brian is in his own.' I knew that it would click, that I was talking with somebody who was well known for working with people who had taken drugs."

Eugene Landy was born November 26, 1934, in Pittsburgh, Pennsylvania. A self-described "sixth-grade drop-out," he attended night school and earned a high-school diploma. Landy told *Rolling Stone*, as well as this author, that he had worked for a circus, produced a radio show, and worked as a promotional man for RCA, Coral, Decca, and Mercury records, and also at Republic Pictures for a time. Landy also told *Rolling Stone* he had worked for the Peace Corps, Job Corps, and VISTA before becoming a pyschologist. But jazz guitarist George Benson sheds further light on Landy's background.

George Benson also grew up in Pittsburgh, one of six children in a family so poor they had no electricity. He was first "discovered" at the age of seven while playing the ukulele in the street for change. "When I was ten years old," Benson said, "a guy came to my house and convinced my mother to let him manage me...this guy...was a very zealous young person. Man, he could sell anything. My people developed a distrust for him when he made them sign a power of attorney that they didn't understand and he got all my mail and all my checks. He dressed things up a bit. He was a guy that people hated to see coming, but once he got to talk to you, you were done. I didn't like his style, but I always liked his go-getterness....He was a very good-looking young kid, girls were all he would talk about.

"He finally introduced me to this very wealthy woman who managed an apartment building...and lived in the penthouse. It was fantastic. This woman bought me a new guitar and a new outfit. Well, at the time I didn't understand the whole thing, but later I began to understand. They wanted me to go to New York to cut a record. To get permission to go to New York, they had to convince my principal at school that they were going to send a tutor along with me—a very attractive nineteen- or twenty-year-old girl. Now, the other woman was middle-aged, and had money, and that's why he had her. This agent of mine was a very handsome person....She and this [agent] were very good friends, and I assumed later that was the relationship. I was just a kid, I knew nothing. We stayed at one of New York's most famous hotels, the Savoy Plaza. She rented a suite and we went to these fantastic dinners, and I got very ill. The evening I got sick, we had been to the Copa and had a big dinner there, and I ate steak and lobster or crab and they had to rush me back to the hotel. They had a doctor come up, and they had this violent argument that woke me up. I remember this woman coming in and saying, 'George, I don't expect you to understand anything I'm going to say, but something has happened ... and I'm getting ready to go to Pittsburgh. You can come with me, and when I bring you back I promise you'll cut a record; but if you say no, I'll understand.' And I said my mother had entrusted me to [my agent]. After she left, we moved from that fantastic hotel into a [bad one]. We ended up going back to Pittsburgh, but a few months later we went back to New York and cut a record for RCA Victor. He got me a single deal. The single didn't make it, and very soon after that he took off. He did what he said he was going to do. The last thing he told my mother before he left was, 'I'm going to be a *millionaire*, and George is going to be rich too, if you put him in my hands.' He was moving from Pittsburgh to Hollywood. He was setting up what he called 'Landy Productions.' That was his big thing, 'Landy Productions.' 'It's gonna be big,' he'd say. 'I'm gonna be rich.' That's all he talked about. That was my manager. We called him Eugene Landy."

In a way, Landy did set up "Landy Productions." At age thirty, according to Landy, he returned to school. He attended Los Angeles State College, where he majored in psychology and received a bachelor-of-arts degree in 1964. Afterward he attended the University of Oklahoma, where he received a master-of-science degree on June 4, 1967, and the following year a Ph.D. In 1970 he received a California license for private practice. Landy became a "director" of the "young people's" adolescent program at Gateways Psychiatric Hospital and Community Health Center and a senior lecturer in psychology at the University of Southern California. In 1971 Simon and Schuster published his book *The Underground Dictionary*, which contained phrases of drug abuse and street language such as "roach position," "kick ass," and "knock up." According to Landy, "My background is basically that of a hyperkinetic, perceptually disoriented, brain-damaged person. I'm also very bright, very intuitive, very sensitive, and I'm quite capable of reading what most people are thinking or doing." At various points in his career Landy treated Alice Cooper, Rod Steiger, and Gig Young.*

According to Landy, from Marilyn's first description he felt that Brian might be a paranoid schizophrenic. Landy told Marilyn that in order for treatment to work, Brian would have to want to have therapy, so he devised a plan. Landy arrived at the plush beige house on Bellagio Road one day in October 1975. Marilyn took him up to the bedroom where Brian, a huge bulge under the sheets, lay on his back with a pillow over his head. Marilyn introduced Landy, and when Brian tried to sneak a peek at Landy from under the pillow, Landy spun around like the Phantom of the Opera unmasked, so Brian couldn't see his face.

During the following three weeks Landy made two trips a week to the house and met with Marilyn, hoping to get Brian interested. Each day before the session, Marilyn would write Landy's name and her appointment time on a large red chalkboard next to the refrigerator. Then they would lock themselves in the den and talk. Landy's initial drama had provoked the right mechanism in Brian. After the eighth visit, Brian himself answered the front door when Landy arrived.

Landy said to him, "Who are you?" and pushed past him. Marilyn and Landy locked themselves in the study. Five minutes later Brian was pounding on the door, according to Landy, begging for his own appointment.

Landy swiftly took almost total control of Brian's life. Scott Steinberg, a young aide whose mother was Landy's office bookkeeper, was hired to keep watch over all of Brian's activities. A list was made of "banned" individuals who might have had a negative influence on Brian. The list included some of Brian's closest friends. "One night," Landy said, "Brian called me

*Gig Young later shot himself to death in his New York apartment.

about going out to coffee with Terry Melcher and I said no, because of [Brian eating too many pancakes with Terry in the past], but I also said Terry Melcher was *persona non grata*, and I told Terry to get the hell out of the house because when I spoke to him I could tell he was ripped out of his fucking head...." Then a rigid schedule of exercise and productive activity was designed. The only trouble was, Brian wasn't interested in following a schedule, and quickly returned to his bed.

"I had to be crazier than Brian," Landy explained. "There is only room enough for one crazy person in Brian's head, and that's got to be me. I have to be the ultimate power in this situation. That's how I got into this dance. Brian said, 'Make me.' I said he had to get out of bed and start living a normal life, and he said, 'Make me.' How do you make a guy get out of bed after so long? Explain it to him first? No. You throw water on him first. That's just what I did. I warned him, and then threw water on him and he got up."

This was just the beginning of Brian's rude awakening. He had met his match. Landy was not about to sit back idly and allow him to be "eccentric" as his friends and family had done for years. "Look," Landy said, "I can't let Brian blackmail me. He's manipulated everybody for a long time, and I have to confront him at every turn." At one point Brian threatened to beat Landy up if he didn't "get off his back," Landy said. Landy took off his shirt and told Brian to hit him. "I'm forty-two years old, and I said to this big guy, 'Do it! Take your best shot if you're gonna do it!' [Brian] said he couldn't hurt me."

Landy supervised every aspect of Brian's daily life. In the morning, Brian was brought to Rancho Park to jog. Later he was made to bowl at lanes on Pico Boulevard. Often, Brian would refuse to pick up the bowling ball. "If he doesn't do the bowling, then he continues to bowl," Landy said. "If he just sets the ball down and won't do it, then I'll hire three heavy-duty dudes—the big ones (hah!) who will stand there and say, 'You may not bowl, but we're renting this alley by the minute and we're gonna stay here until you do.' And we'll stay there! I give you my word that within a period of time he will decide

that it is easier to bowl than to sit there. *And I give you my
word: Brian Wilson will bowl over a hundred!* and he'll compose again!...

"It doesn't matter who he is," Landy went on. "I don't give
a fuck whether he's a Beach Boy or a beach bum.... I'll make
him go to work as a welder, if he has to. We'll see how many
crazy people there are in Brian's head!"

The rest of the group, including members of the Warner
Brothers publicity department, got a chance to see firsthand
what *New Musical Express* journalist Nick Kent would call
Landy's "bullying tactics."* The group attended a $5,000 steak
dinner at Ernie's restaurant in San Francisco to celebrate the
Joffrey Ballet's having choreographed Brian's music of "Little
Deuce Coupe" at the War Memorial Opera House. At first, Brian
didn't want to go to the performance at all, telling Landy he
was afraid the audience would boo his music. Later, at the
party, with a hundred people in attendance, Brian had only
been in the restaurant five minutes when he told Landy he
wanted to leave. "We were all sitting around a long, elegantly
set table, and Brian said he was sick and had to go to bed, that
he would throw up if I didn't let him go," Landy said.

Landy stood up and pointed to the table in front of Brian.
"Throw up!" he screamed. *"Throw up!"*

Brian sat at his place and sheepishly went on with dinner.
"But I had to be ready to get the table the hell out of there if
he threw up on it!" Landy said.

According to Arnold Horowitz, one of Landy's assistants at
the time, Landy's methods were based "upon very very heavy
reality confrontation on a very consistent basis.... Gene, in
addition to being eloquent at times...is...*dramatic.*"

At first, the treatment was perfectly all right with Marilyn,
although the rest of the group, formally introduced to Landy
at a meeting at Brian's house, had reservations. Brian was indeed up and around. Brian was losing weight. Brian was composing, daily, during ninety-minute work sessions that Landy

---

*Kent wrote: "He forced Wilson to act the role of the responsible member of society;
bullied him into writing songs; bullied him into going onstage with the group...and
bullied him into performing humiliating solo performances.... To get full mileage out
of this specious ploy, Brian was made to do interviews, most of them farcical.

insisted he adhere to. Although Landy's fees for his "twenty-four-hour therapy" began to increase each month, everyone involved thought he was worth it, considering Brian's progress. "I thought it was *cheap*," Marilyn said. But then, something strange began to happen.

The problem became obvious to the other group members when they agreed to deliver to Warner Brothers their first album of new material in nearly four years—a "comeback" album. Thus began the ill-fated "Brian Is Back!" campaign. The "Brian Is Back!" campaign was Stephen Love's brainchild—he felt that a publicity campaign highlighting Brian's recovery and ability to contribute to the group, especially as writer and producer, would increase their financial value, and facilitate negotiating a new recording contract when their existing one expired. Stephen designed the entire "Brian Is Back!" campaign and hired publicists Rogers and Cowan at $3,500 a month to implement it. The media coverage was enormous, resulting in a *People* cover, as well as major feature pieces in *Newsweek*, *New West*, *Rolling Stone*, and *Crawdaddy*.

Under Brian's fragile, distracted guidance, the Beach Boys returned to the Brother Studios in Santa Monica and began recording a new album. Dennis suggested calling the LP *Group Therapy*, but eventually the title *15 Big Ones* was agreed upon—the album would contain fifteen songs and would come out during the Beach Boys' fifteenth year of existence. At first, Mike Love deeply resented Brian's control over the album. *Newsweek* reported, "Jardine and Love were all for letting Brian take full charge, even though Love makes no secret of resenting him. Love, who jumped rope to get in shape for the tour, recently declared, 'I'm not going out on the road like some broken-down rock star.'" In the end, only half the songs on *15 Big Ones* were new material.

The Warner Brothers publicity department soon learned that the only way to contact Brian was through Gene Landy's office, and didn't like the idea. Warners publicity director Bob Merlis immediately had a falling-out with Landy. He told reporters interested in writing about the Beach Boys that he found the doctor "repugnant." Several journalists covering the story of Brian's reemergence were directed to Landy for consultation, including this author. When one reporter asked Landy how much he, as a doctor, could talk about his patient, Landy immediately phoned a member of the California State Psychological Association's ethics committee for direction. Landy was told it was up to the patient, and he then phoned Brian, who told him to say whatever he pleased. Landy said, "Brian would probably give me permission to say anything."

At the same time, Dennis Wilson had been harping on the idea that the Beach Boys should be featured in a national television special. Stephen Love asked the ICM agency to find a sponsor and help them locate a producer and director. Dr. Pepper, the soft-drink company, agreed to fund the production, and Lorne Michaels of "Saturday Night Live" agreed to produce it for NBC-TV. The special, to be called "The Beach Boys: It's O.K.", co-starring Dan Akroyd and John Belushi, was scheduled to air on NBC on August 5 of that year. It was to be directed by "Saturday Night Live" contributor Gary Weis.

When Lorne Michaels started dealing with the Beach Boys on the special, he found the project next to impossible as he discovered they were "five people who couldn't make up their minds. It was unlike most situations, where there is one central figure or manager or agent. In our first meeting somebody would suggest something and someone else in the group would knock it down." When Michaels first heard that in order to get Brian's cooperation on the special he had to give Landy control over Brian's segments, he was affronted, and refused. After much discussion, Landy agreed to allow Brian to attend a production meeting without him at Michaels' production offices on Sunset Boulevard. Landy waited outside the conference room, while inside Brian pleasantly agreed to whatever was said to him and excused himself in eight minutes, begging off for an imaginary luncheon appointment although it was late afternoon. Landy had made his point, but the incident only increased Michaels's fascination with the project. Michaels agreed to sign a quasi-censorship agreement giving Landy approval on segments that either he was involved in or might be detrimental to Brian's psychological welfare. In return, Brian would be available for filming—with Landy at his side.

At the first production meeting held at Brian's house, with

Michaels, Weis, Dan Aykroyd, and John Belushi in attendance among others, several pizzas and bottles of beer were brought in. Brian quickly drank five beers, got sleepy, and excused himself. Soon after he left, Landy, who had been sitting in the corner, scolded the group for bringing beer and pizza. "Now, when you come back next Monday," Landy told the group sternly, "no beer, no food, no anything. Today somebody was very naughty and brought beer. Brian's on a diet."

An uncomfortable silence followed, broken by John Belushi's half-apology: "It was just a friendly gesture."

It was exactly this kind of Svengali-Trilby relationship that observers found so uncomfortable in the Landy-Wilson pact. In recognition of Landy's unique methods, the production crew facetiously taped to the door of the editing room a sign reading, WELCOME DR. LANDY—FREUD WAS NO SCHMUCK.

Lorne Michaels in particular found Landy difficult to deal with. His own staff members suggested that Landy could come off looking not his best in the special; but Michaels had other ideas. "I am committed to not making Landy look bad in this, out of a sense of personal morality," he said at the time. "If somebody's putting out a fire with a Dixie cup, running back and forth to the room, it doesn't make any difference to me because at least their intentions are honorable. Whether or not I like the method they're using or whatever, to go in there and rupture that relationship in front of forty or fifty million people [on TV] would be rather stupid and gratuitously unkind." Lorne Michaels held to his promise, and the TV show aired to excellent reviews later that summer. A few months afterward, Brian would also appear as the host of "Saturday Night Live" in a poignant, frightened performance during which Landy stood behind the cameras holding up cue cards that said "Smile," and "Relax."

On July 4, 1976, Brian Wilson played at a concert in Anaheim, just as Landy had promised, appearing onstage for the first time in seven years. The new Warner Brothers release, 15 Big Ones, fared better than any new Beach Boys album in years, although not as well as they had hoped. The only hit generated by the album was a cover version of "Rock and Roll Music," which reached a more-than-respectable number 5 on the sin-

gles charts that August, propelling the album into the top ten
a few weeks later. But the reviews were less than favorable.
The *Village Voice* review was especially disturbing, calling the
album "the kind of music one might expect to find at a rock
star's funeral."

By December the Beach Boys were quickly growing disenchanted with Gene Landy. Reportedly, the most disenchanted
of all was Stephen Love. There were several reasons for Stephen's mistrust of the psychologist. Some who were closely
involved say that Stephen disliked Landy right from the start,
when Landy proposed that he receive a percentage of Brian's
income. According to sources, Landy felt that the further Brian's
recovery progressed, the more songs he would be able to produce and write. Because Landy would in effect be responsible
for Brian's increased productivity, he felt he should participate
in the increased earnings. Stephen Love reportedly thought
this proposition "stunk to high heaven." Also, Landy would
reportedly charge his hourly fee while on tour with Brian,
which meant a twenty-four-hour-a-day charge, plus billing for
expenses for himself and his lady friend, Alexandra. Stephen
Love's strict policy had always been that any touring member
who brought a wife or girl friend with him did so at his own
expense. Moreover, Landy tried to control what times Brian
would be available to work at the studio as well as what songs
he would work on. There was even talk of Landy's collaborating with Brian on song writing. Stephen felt this would
interfere with Brian's creativity far too much. There was a final
argument at Brother Studios in which Landy's aide, Scott
Steinberg, wanted to take Brian away from the studio to keep
him on Landy's prearranged schedule, while Stephen wanted
Brian to finish working on the song he was producing. Stephen
lost his temper and had Steinberg removed from the studio.
Brian stayed behind.

But the deciding factor occurred when Landy's monthly fee,
including charges for the twenty-four-hour staff, which began
at a reported $10,000, escalated to $12,000, then $15,000, then
$18,000, and finally to $20,000. Stephen tried to persuade
Marilyn to let him fire Landy, which by then wasn't too difficult. Marilyn was disgusted with the control Landy was ex-

erting over her personal life as well as Brian's career. "What psychologist or therapist writes songs?" Marilyn asked. "So when it came to the point where it was costing around twenty thousand a month, I said, 'Brian, Jesus Christ, it's costing twenty thousand a month.' And Brian said, 'What!?'

"So we went to Landy's office, and Brian confronted Landy, and Brian said, 'You son of a bitch!' You have to understand that I have never seen Brian get physical, ever, ever. I saw him take his fist and start to punch this man, and I started screaming. Landy said, 'No, no, no, let him do it, let him do it!' Landy thought it was the greatest thing. He was saying, 'Come on, you motherfucker, hit me, hit me!' And then finally Brian just did it, he made Brian do it. Landy was pushing me away, saying, 'No, he needs to hit me, he needs to do it, he needs to take his anger out on me...' That was a therapeutic session, if you can believe it."

Reportedly, Stephen Love was not concerned that Brian would regress without Gene Landy. He had made tremendous gains and even managed to go out on the Christmas tour of 1976 without the psychologist. After Landy was fired, Brian was immediately brought to a new psychiatrist, whom he saw for several sessions. Said Brian at the time, "Now I'm seeing someone else twice a week, Dr. Steve Schwartz; he's a very mild man, doesn't have much to say, just listens." Then a tragic event occurred. One day the phone rang and a strange doctor asked Brian to come see him; when Brian arrived at the office, he was told that Dr. Schwartz had been in a terrible camping accident and had fallen off the side of a mountain to his death. "It scared Brian so bad," Marilyn said, "I don't think he could believe it. He didn't talk for days after that."

Brian was clearly in need of round-the-clock supervision, and Stanley Love, whose career with the Atlanta Hawks had been short-lived, was asked to come back to work at Bellagio Road. In addition, Brian's first cousin and former Beach Boys roadie, Steven Korthof, was hired to assist them. Korthof was a short, heavyset, good-natured man in his early thirties who had grown up with Brian. Like many members of the family, he had a special respect and love for Brian. Several months later, Stanley told Marilyn that they needed yet another man to assist them, and he suggested Rushton Pamplin, an old college chum of his.

Six feet three inches tall, handsome and muscular, "Rocky" Pamplin was a professional model. He was an expansive, volatile young man with a big temper and a short fuse. Born in Minnesota, he grew up in Florida and moved to California when he was ten years old. He attended the University of Oregon for three years, where he met Stanley Love. For several years he played professional football with the Saints and the Alouettes. When his athletic career petered out, he became a model. Two of his more prominent modeling jobs were the well-known Times Square billboard for Winston cigarettes and a nude centerfold for *Playgirl*, whose readers voted him both "Man of the Year" and "Man of Five Years."

The first time Rocky walked into Brian's house to play basketball with Stanley, Marilyn took Stanley aside and said, *"Where did you find this guy?"* A few weeks later, Rocky was put on the payroll to assist Stanley at the handsome fee of $40,000 a year. Three weeks later, Marilyn and Rocky were having an affair. "He was an attractive guy," Marilyn said, "and I had a sexless marriage. He was a gorgeous man." He was also available. "If you put Bo Derek in front of any guy, do you think they are going to turn her down? It was easy for me to fall into the trap." Marilyn's major concern about the affair was that Brian should never find out, for his welfare was still uppermost in her mind. She loved Brian deeply, but her love was now more that of a sister for a brother, and Rocky was impossible to resist.

According to Rocky, his affair with Marilyn was "hard in the first place, but the money made it easier. I made myself do it, day by day, month by month, I made myself do it."

If Marilyn suspected she was being used by Rocky, she pushed the thought to the farthest corners of her mind. She needed to feel attractive and sexy again, and Rocky made her believe that she was. Marilyn felt that after a time Rocky began to fall in love with her, and even Rocky admits there was real affection between them. "She was real spontaneous, a great person in some ways. But the one thing about Jewish people is sometimes they think the worst about people." At one point, he even brought her home to meet his parents and said he was going to marry her if she divorced Brian. When asked why he did this, Rocky said, "A fifty-thousand-dollar-a-year job, traveling around the world in Lear jets...."

Rocky, Stan, and Steve Korthof were dedicated to Brian, and managed for the most part to keep him away from drugs and to keep track of his whereabouts, although the job was sometimes nearly impossible. Brian could be clever and wily, and anything was liable to happen if they took their eyes off him for one minute. Once, in Chicago in 1978, they were all staying at a hotel near the airport. Brian met a stranger in the bar, had a few drinks with him, and made an appointment to meet the man the next morning at 8:30 and go off with him to Minnesota. When Stan and Rocky awoke the next morning and found Brian missing, Rocky ran down to the lobby in his pajamas and asked, "Did you see a guy with a beard?" He was told that Brian, barefooted, had left shortly before. Rocky raced to the airport and learned that the next departing plane was going to Minnesota. Making the logical guess that Brian would be on that plane, he convinced them to stop the plane and boarded it with a security guard. "I walked on, and there's Brian sitting with some guy, and he says, 'Rocky, what are you doing here?'"

Rocky said, "Get off the plane, Brian."

"No. I'm going to Minnesota with my friend," Brian said, gesturing to the man in the seat next to him.

"*Brian, get off the plane!*" Rocky shouted.

"Okay," Brian said quietly, and followed Rocky back to the hotel.

Other examples of Brian's drifting mental state are even more poignant. One day Paul McCartney came to visit Brian, and when Brian heard he was at the house, he became petrified, although he had met McCartney several times before. He raced outside to the chauffeur's quarters and locked himself inside. McCartney knocked on the door for twenty minutes, but Brian would not come out. All he could hear were the gentle sounds of Brian weeping.

3

With only one more album due to Warner Brothers and their contract scheduled to expire on July 1, 1977, it was now Stephen Love's responsibility to negotiate a new recording contract for the group. Stephen hired crack music-business attorneys Mike Lorimer and John Frankenheimer to help with the negotiations. At Warner, interest in the group was understandably sagging. They had not made tremendous profits from the record sales, and Warner Brothers was all too familiar with the group's internal struggles. At the same time, CBS Records was showing keen interest in signing the group, not only because the company felt the Beach Boys were prestigious, but also because of the close relationship with James Guercio and Caribou Records, which CBS distributed. Although Guercio had been fired, he still admired the Beach Boys' music and believed in their commercial potential. With Guercio's encouragement, CBS became determined to sign them. A bidding war ensued between Warner Brothers and CBS, which CBS easily won with a bid of $1 million per album, including bonus provisions. As a special sweetener, the CBS deal included a $2 million advance to the group upon signing the contracts, $1.8 million to Brother Records Inc. and $200,000 to pay off working capital loans at the Wells Fargo Bank. The total worth of the deal was a handsome $8 million.

Warner Brothers knew of the CBS deal by January 1977, when the Beach Boys' final Warner album, *The Beach Boys Love You*, was submitted. Once again, the Warner Brothers executives were none too happy with the product, although the material included twelve new Brian Wilson compositions written under Gene Landy's aegis. To make matters worse, Warner had just shipped *The Beach Boys Love You* to the record stores when the CBS deal was announced on April 1. Warner was so disgusted with the Beach Boys at this point that the group members were convinced the company was doing very little to promote the album. In truth, the best promotional campaign in the world couldn't have helped *The Beach Boys Love You*, which made a feeble showing of seven weeks at the top end of the charts.

On March 1, 1977, the Beach Boys officially entered into a recording agreement with CBS, with the first album expected by January 1, 1978. In addition to the $2 million advance upon signing, the group would receive $667,667 upon the delivery of each album, shooting up to a bonus $1,167,000 if the preceding album sold more than 1.5 million copies. The basic royalty rate was a dollar per album and fifteen cents a single. In return, the CBS contracts placed many demands on the group, as was only fair. Brian was required to compose at least four songs on each album, and co-write at least 70 percent of all the material, acting as producer or co-producer with Dennis or Carl. Although it wasn't necessary for Brian to tour, the group was required to play thirty dates a year in the United States in large arenas to back up the albums, in addition to two tours within four years in at least seven European cities, and one tour in Australia and Japan. When Brian signed the contract, he cried, knowing he would now have to go back to the studio full-time.

Suddenly, Mike Love took off for Leysin, Switzerland, where the Maharishi was running a study center. Mike believed the Maharishi was going to teach him how to levitate. But it was a most inopportune time for Mike to learn how to float, not only because of the group's pressing recording obligations, but because the trip meant that he would not be present for the negotiations with CBS on the new contract. A hotly contested incident then took place. Mike was reportedly unhappy with the "outside projects provision," which would not allow him to work on solo projects for the benefit of the Maharishi. But Stephen thought it ill-advised to ask CBS for clauses allowing such projects, fearing the company would be concerned that the provision would dilute the strength of the group. While Mike was in Switzerland, Mike Lorimer reportedly initiated a phone call to him to confirm that Stephen Love had his permission to sign the contracts for him. Stephen Love listened in on the extension, with Mike's knowledge, as Mike gave his permission for Stephen to sign his name, *in absentia*, to the CBS contracts. Reportedly, the contract was signed "Michael Love by Stephen Love, as his attorney-in-fact."

With the first CBS album due and Mike Love nowhere in sight to begin work on it, Stephen fired off a telegram to Mike, which advised, "NOW IS NOT THE TIME IN YOUR LIFE TO BE SELF-INDULGENT AND STUPID...." Stephen also sent a letter to the rest of the group warning them to shape up or he would leave. The letter included the phrase "I no longer choose to render my services to punks or incompetents...."

> *Sleep well, everybody.*
> *Pleasant dreams.*
> —DAVID FROST
> *to the Beach Boys*

Fifteen

1

There are as many different versions of the firing of Stephen Love as there were participants.* Stephen Love was perhaps the finest business and personal manager the group ever had, but he was also the most didactic and controlling. Stephen's rigid, albeit intelligent, approach to organizing the group and its finances was too stringent for the Beach Boys. "They said he was too arrogant," one observer recalled. He was also a firm opponent of drug use, as were Michael and Al Jardine, and could not tolerate any group member or associate partaking of illicit substances. He was outspoken in his criticism of personal behavior. Stephen did not appreciate Karen Lamm or the influence she had on Dennis's life—when Dennis asked him to be best man at their wedding, Stephen refused.

By letting Stephen Love go, the Beach Boys were repeating the same innuendo that Nick Grillo had decried years before: "Why do you have so much and I have so little?" Nineteen seventy-seven had turned out to be the biggest year in Beach Boys history. The total group gross was running upward of $8 million, including the nearly $2 million advance from CBS on the signing of the new contracts (which was quickly put into an interest-bearing account until the first album could be delivered). Brian's income from his songwriting royalties neared the $1 million mark. Mike, Carl, Dennis, and Alan were earning

---

*Technically, Stephen Love was not fired; he was relieved of his managerial responsibilities and his contract simply wasn't renewed.

close to $600,000 each. What troubled them was that Stephen Love's income was almost $300,000 for the year, before office overhead expenses. Indeed, Stephen had watched his money and made investments judiciously, and this fact alone aggravated some group members who felt he hadn't served them as well personally.

Stephen had fallen into disfavor with Carl for giving what he perceived to be poor real-estate advice. Since Annie's father, "Pop" Hinsche, had died, Annie and Carl had been paying $6,000 a month to rent a luxurious house at Trancas Beach from the widow of Las Vegas hotel owner Del Webb. Carl now wanted to sell his Coldwater Canyon house and buy his own place at the beach. Stephen suggested that Carl set a limit on what he would pay for his new house and stick to it. When Carl made a bid on a house he and Annie especially liked, the seller turned them down, and Stephen insisted he not go any higher. A short time later the house was sold to another buyer for only $20,000 more, and Carl was reportedly furious with Stephen.

But perhaps Stephen's greatest offense was that he was entitled to 5 percent of the CBS Records deal. On March 17, two weeks before Stephen Love's contract expired, the Beach Boys received their first check from CBS for $1,800,000. Then the real trouble started. According to Stanley Love, "The Beach Boys have a history of not paying people, that's why a lot of their deals fall apart. If your five percent of an eight-million-dollar contract is four hundred thousand—that's too much money for you. They figured they could save that four hundred thousand for themselves." Mike Love now contended that he never gave Stephen permission to sign his name to the CBS contracts, which drove Stephen wild with anger. Insiders say this change in Mike's attitude occurred when he realized that the CBS contract did not have the special riders he wanted that would have allowed him to record solo albums under their label. Meanwhile, Dennis, through his friend James Guercio, was getting a $100,000 advance from CBS to record his own solo album.

The group expected to negotiate a settlement that would allow Stephen to continue working as a consultant until his contract officially expired on March 31. In the interim, the Beach Boys needed a new, full-time manager, and Carl thought he knew just the right guy. Henry Lazarus, thirty-five, claims to have met Carl "through friends" in Los Angeles. They had been discussing the Beach Boys' management problems for several months, and Lazarus, a loquacious, quick-thinking man, had many suggestions. Carl called Lazarus and said, "Listen, you've been giving us the best advice of anybody," and asked if he would take over the management post—at a reported $75,000 a year.

Born in New York, Lazarus had sold his family business, Lazarus Fabrics, a commercial drapery-fabric company, in 1974. He had moved to Los Angeles, where he purchased, coincidentally, the same Coldwater Canyon house in which Mike Love had lived with his second wife, Suzanne. He started a new company, World Wide Artists, that dabbled in the entertainment business. He then changed the name of this company to the Alchemy Company, with the slogan "We Turn Shit into Gold," but had toned it down to "...Ideas into Gold" by the time he started managing the Beach Boys. Although Lazarus had no previous experience in the music business, Carl thought he was just what the group needed.

One of Lazarus's first jobs was to settle the matter of whether or not Stephen Love had signed the CBS contracts with Mike's permission. According to Lazarus, CBS Records President Walter Yetnikoff, "asked me to get Mike's signature." Mike was still in Leysin, Switzerland, studying with the Maharishi, and Lazarus flew there to see him. At the Grand Hotel, Lazarus entered two giant rooms "the size of basketball courts, filled with mattresses on the floor." According to Lazarus, this was the room where the Maharishi's students were learning to levitate, and the mattresses were there to break their falls. Lazarus and Mike met for the first time there, and according to Lazarus they got along very well. Mike even took him to meet the Maharishi, who also approved of Lazarus. Mike told Lazarus to write down his home address so he could send the newly executed contracts to him, and when he noticed the address he said, "Why are you writing down my old home address?" Lazarus told him he now lived there, and Mike was ecstatic.

"It's written in the heavens and stars that you should be our manager," Mike told him.

Lazarus moved the group's management headquarters into his own offices at 1888 Century Park East and started going over their books. Lazarus claimed "there was a lot of money being stolen from the Beach Boys" at the time but declined to say by whom. He apparently found discrepancies in the group's withholding statements.* Lazarus brought the Beach Boys to a new law firm, Fierstein and Sturman, who began by issuing a subpoena to get the accounting books from Stephen Love. That April, Stephen's loyal associate, Janet Lent-Coop, arrived early at Stephen's Manhattan Beach offices and found an "odd-looking person" sitting behind the wheel of a car outside the gas station. This was a process server who was trying to seize the books. Stephen and Janet managed to protect Love's personal records, but everything else was turned over to the accounting firm of S. D. Leitersdorf, where several accountants looked for some irregularity in Stephen's financial management of the group. When the results came in several months later, they could find nothing wrong.

Lazarus's next task was to set up a giant European tour for the Beach Boys, which would include Germany, Switzerland, and France, both to satisfy the terms of the CBS contracts pertaining to tour commitments and to generate income. This tour was to be kicked off by a live performance at the CBS Records international convention being held in London on July 30. Attended by hundreds of CBS affiliates from different countries, the concert would solidify the record company's worldwide support of the Beach Boys. CBS even rented a private plane to fly the group to London. Although the Beach Boys were an enormous hit at the convention, an unpleasant surprise awaited them. The entire European tour was in disarray. The proper tax documents and working papers had not been obtained from the foreign governments; travel arrangements

---

*Indeed, during the dark financial days of the early seventies, Stephen Love intentionally claimed as many deductions as possible in the Beach Boys' withholding statements to give them as much free cash flow as he could. Because he knew this might cause a potential tax problem later, he had the Beach Boys sign statements indemnifying him against any future action by the IRS.

and hotel reservations had not been confirmed; the contracts had not been fully signed by promoters. It was obvious the tour could not take place. By July 21, before the Beach Boys had even played the CBS convention, Lazarus was gone. The tour was canceled, and many of its promoters sued the Beach Boys.

Later, Lazarus was formally fired. The blame for the lawsuits and enormous monetary loss was placed squarely on Henry Lazarus—and the blame for Henry Lazarus was placed squarely on Carl. A Beach Boys' employee called it the "second Jack Rieley affair." The estimated loss to the Beach Boys was $200,000 in out-of-pocket expenses, and an additional $550,000 in potential revenues.

The group did manage to play one concert in England that July, at Wembley Stadium, where one of the ugliest public displays to date occurred. In the middle of the concert, before an enormous audience of over fifteen thousand, Mike Love lost his temper, picked up a piano bench, and threw it at Brian. It bounced off the stage and nearly hit his own children, Christian and Hayleigh, who were sitting in the front row.

If anything could further exacerbate the growing bad feelings among the group members, it was the release of Dennis's solo album, *Pacific Ocean Blue*, on September 16, 1977. This first solo album by any Beach Boy came as a mighty shock to the rest of the group—not only because Dennis had managed to pull it off, but because the album was a small masterpiece. Dennis's years in the studio watching brother Brian had paid off handsomely. Co-produced and co-written by Gregg Jakobson, *Pacific Ocean Blue* received excellent reviews. The album sold over 200,000 copies, although it only broke the top one hundred on the charts. However, it was clearly a *succès d'estime* of which any performer could be proud, and Dennis wouldn't let any of the Beach Boys forget it. Mike Love was especially infuriated that Dennis was the first to go solo, and get such glowing reviews. According to Stanley Love, "The Beach Boys were scared. Intimidated by it." And some of them wanted to top it.

2

To Michael and Alan Jardine, one thing was clear: they needed Stephen Love back. Alan flew down from his Big Sur ranch that August to ask Stephen if he would consider coming back to work for them full-time, but Stephen was understandably wary. He knew that Carl and Dennis were still strongly opposed to him, and that the tension and animosity within the group were so explosive that Mike and Alan were hardly talking to Dennis and Carl. They traveled separately and even stayed at different hotels. Among the Beach Boys' staff, the two contingents were known as the "meditators" and the "free-livers." Stephen did agree to discuss returning to the group at a meeting to be held in New York over Labor Day weekend at the end of a northeastern tour. A day earlier, the Beach Boys had bowled the city over with a free concert in Central Park, attended by over 150,000 people, according to police estimates.

The meeting with Stephen was held at the Sherry Netherlands hotel, where the free-livers were staying (the meditators were at the Plaza). Stephen brought with him a "memorandum agreement" stating the terms he wanted. These were basically the same terms he had tendered to them that January, three months before his employment contract was to expire. He proposed a sliding scale of 5 percent of the first $5 million and 7.5 percent over that, net of his overhead expenses.

But Mike Love had a different proposal for his brother. Stephen would be employed not by the Beach Boys, but by a corporation called All American Management Organization, of which Mike Love and Alan Jardine were officers. AAMO would be compensated 2.5 percent of the gross of the Beach Boys' touring revenues for providing tour management and promotional services for the group. Stephen Love would be guaranteed a minimum annual salary of $250,000 against 5 percent of the first $5 million gross income received by the Beach Boys, and 7.5 percent thereafter, aside from business and travel expenses. Reportedly, Stephen was not happy about being piggybacked on AAMO, but he had little choice. Stephen also wanted a $70,000 bonus for management services he had performed for the group after Caribou was fired and before he was officially named manager. When Carl and Dennis heard about AAMO and the terms of Stephen's employment, they were outraged—they would not have Stephen back under any circumstances, especially if he was to be employed by AAMO. They made it known that they were prepared to walk out of the group if Stephen was forced on them. Yet Stephen left the meeting with his employment memorandum, signed by three-fifths of the group—Mike, Al, and Brian Wilson—enough signatures to ratify it.

The next afternoon the group piled into two different limousines and headed to Newark Airport to fly to a concert in Providence, Rhode Island, on two separate planes—a prop rented from singer Ray Charles for the free-livers and a sleek private jet for the meditators. On the way to the airport, Dennis told a *Rolling Stone* reporter, "This could be the last Beach Boys concert tonight. I see the Beach Boys coming to a close, and there's a lot of backstabbing and maliciousness going on." According to Carl, there was even talk of "replacements" for him and Dennis.

After the Providence concert, at a stopover at Newark Airport on the way back to Los Angeles, Dennis and Karen joined the meditators on the faster jet for the flight home, but Carl still refused to be on the same plane with them. During the long wait for maintenance and refueling, Dennis and Karen decided to spend the night in New York and take a commercial flight back to L.A. in the morning. When Brian heard this, he decided to stay over with them and help paint the town, but the meditating contingent forbade him to remain behind. This infuriated Dennis, and when he saw Carl standing outside the plane, he told him they wouldn't let Brian get off. Tempers erupted and Dennis raced back on the plane to tell them the group was finished.

Now everybody poured out of the two planes for a confrontation on the tarmac. The reporter from *Rolling Stone* called it "a scene right out of [the movie] *Casablanca*." Both planes stood waiting, engines running, for their passengers while Mike, Stephen, and Stanley Love formed a tight circle around Dennis and his bodyguard. They stood there screaming at each other over the roar of the engines. Stanley kept repeating that Dennis "got into this band on Brian Wilson's coattails! ... I'm the one that's brought [Brian] around. I'm the one that keeps him from walking out in front of buses. And you're gonna quit on us after all that?"

Later, riding in a limousine back to Manhattan, Dennis said to Karen, "What's today's date? September third? I'll remember it. The Beach Boys broke up on Al Jardine's birthday."

But the Beach Boys did not break up. Two weeks later, on September 17, 1977, an extraordinary meeting was held at Brian and Marilyn's house on Bellagio Road to discuss the future of the group. Each contingent was accompanied by a high-powered, high-priced attorney. Those attending were Brian, Carl, Mike, Alan, Dennis, Stephen, Marilyn, along with attorneys Harvey Fierstein, Skip Brittenham, Jeff Ingberg, Michael Allen, and David Braun (who was hired as "special counsel" to the Beach Boys acting in Brian's behalf). Several motions were brought up to be voted on, including securing the management of All American Management Organization to engage Stephen Love as manager; securing proper recording facilities and equipment; auditing the books; and getting new office facilities. It was also suggested that Stephen Love purchase equipment not to exceed $200,000 to be installed at the Maharishi International University in Iowa, where the next album would be recorded. The meeting began on a calm note, but quickly became a shouting match as it became apparent that Mike, Al, and Brian—who fell asleep on the floor during the meeting—would vote down any of Dennis and Carl's objections.

Carl and Dennis, as well as their attorney, were hotly opposed to Mike's commissioning 2.5 percent from the top for AAMO. They wanted the gross income "split at the source" before anybody else got their hands on it. Mike accused Carl: "You have lost us four million dollars over the last couple of years. Carl, you're a big-time bullshit. Nick Grillo, Jack Rieley. Hang on to Jimmy Guercio and not let him perform, and then Henry Lazarus. Wonderful." But Carl also objected to the fact that while he had in effect produced the last three Beach Boys albums, he had received no special credit or compensation. Accusations flew back and forth for nearly an hour.

Stephen Love was quietly fuming about a remark made by Carl and Dennis's attorney Harvey Fierstein, who had called the compensation for his work with the Beach Boys "atrocious." Finally Stephen turned on Fierstein, who had a hunchback and was less than five feet tall, calling him a "hideous little creature."

With that, Carl and Dennis stormed out of the room, followed by their lawyer. But the group had been officially reunited. Stephen Love was back, and the Beach Boys would soon leave to spend the winter recording their next album at the Maharishi University in Iowa.

Going to the Maharishi University to record was a little like going to Holland, only worse. Ostensibly, it was another out-of-the-way location where there would be few distractions. It was hoped that two albums could be recorded. One album would satisfy the terms of the Warner Brothers contracts, the second would become the album due soon to CBS. As it turned out, only one album was forthcoming, and not a very good one at that. The entire group, and most of their family members, set up house in the circular dorm rooms of the university. Stanley Love described the situation as "torture. Agony. Like being put right in the middle of nowhere, frozen and cold and small, with only one decent restaurant in town. Brian was putting in his time, but he wasn't too happy. He was depressed and on medication. We passed the time playing Ping-Pong." The resulting album reflected the mood of the group. Released on September 25, 1978, the MIU album was on the record charts for only four weeks, never reaching higher than 151. Nick Kent, of New Musical Express, called the effort "dreadful" and said, "Both critics and pundits ignored the product's pitiful contents."

3

Mike Love and his wife, Tamara, a pretty, dark young woman he met through his endeavors in Transcendental Meditation, had a baby girl named Summer (Love). But their marriage was falling apart and a divorce suit was filed. Carl's seemingly solid marriage to Annie was also in trouble, and Carl began to flirt with cocaine and alcohol. Said Annie, "Carl had been flirting with drugs" out of a sense of profound unhappiness with the group and the managerial morass he found himself in. Naturally, Dennis was blamed for much of Carl's indulgence, as he was considered a "bad influence."

Indeed, Dennis seemed incorrigible. His drinking had increased along with his tolerance to it, and his philandering had grown to satyric proportions. Even the lovely Karen Lamm couldn't keep Dennis from fooling around, and within a few months of their marriage he was having an affair with a local beauty queen. Yet he was still insanely jealous of any man that Karen so much as talked to, including important business associates. Dennis once warned her that if she did a commercial with a handsome man, he would walk out on her.

The Beach Boys had already lost a prized employee as a result of a squabble between Dennis and Karen. Road manager Rick Nelson (not the performer) had been with the group in various capacities since the early seventies. Nelson had met Mike and Alan at a Transcendental Meditation center in Los Angeles and had been quickly taken into the fold. He was an easygoing road manager, although not a baby-sitter by temperament, and he usually called things as he saw them. While the group was on tour in Houston, Texas, Karen Lamm called Rick Nelson's room looking for Dennis. She had been calling Dennis's room through the night, and suspected that he was shacked up elsewhere with another girl. Nelson simply told her the truth—she was correct. Dennis was off with some girl he'd picked up and Nelson couldn't reach him. When Dennis learned that Nelson had "turned him in" to Karen, he insisted that Nelson be fired, and Carl backed him up. Stephen Love thought this was a terrible move; Nelson was one of the best and most loyal employees the group had. Stephen even wrote a letter imploring Dennis and Carl to reconsider, but their decision stuck and Nelson was gone.* In his place, Jerry Schilling, a former member of Elvis Presley's "Memphis Mafia," was asked to take over road-management chores. Schilling would later be promoted to become Carl Wilson's personal manager.

But Karen was more concerned about Dennis's drug intake than she was jealous of his infidelities. On one occasion she found a huge bottle of cocaine on the console at Brother Studios and got so angry she threw it all over the carpet of the control booth. When she returned the next night, the locks on the front door had been changed and the group would not let her in. She found a brick in a nearby lot and threw it through the front window. The brick was thereafter used as a doorstop, referred to as "The Karen Lamm Memorial Brick."

On December 30, 1976, Dennis woke up one morning and turned to Karen in bed next to him. He said, "Honey, I don't want you to take this personally, but I don't want to be married anymore."

Karen said, "Go for it, Dennis, if that's what you really want." Then she rolled over in bed and went back to sleep. "I thought he was kidding," she said. But Dennis was serious. He picked up the phone at his bedside and called his lawyer. Later that day he left for Florida, where the Beach Boys were performing.

"New Year's Day," Karen remembered, "I found a house at 9747 Yokum Drive in Beverly Hills and moved out of the Broad Beach house. When Dennis returned to Los Angeles and discovered I wasn't there anymore, he moved into a trailer that was sitting on blocks behind Gregg Jakobson's house." When Dennis filed for divorce, Karen hired well-known divorce attorney Marvin Mitchelson to represent her. She was worried about the $70,000 she had loaned Dennis to get him out of various financial pinches and wanted the money back. Two weeks went by before Dennis called, sheepishly asking to see her again. "For months it went back and forth," she said. "Are

*Rick Nelson later married Janet Lent-Coop and became Brian Wilson's personal business manager.

you going to drop this divorce or what?" Eventually, he moved into her house on Yokum Drive with her. "Mind you," she said. "we had a great time. It wasn't like anything was different except that he was divorcing me. Then one morning he woke up and said, 'Okay, let's get married again and stop all this boloney.'" The two of them went straight to the Santa Monica courthouse and tried to file the proper papers to get remarried. They were consulting with the clerk when he said, "I'm sorry, we can't marry you. You're already married." Dennis was so frustrated he threw the papers up in the air.

On the ride back to the house, he and Karen had a huge fight. By the time they were at the house, Dennis was furious. He took all his clothes and threw them in the back of his Ferrari. As a farewell gesture, Karen overturned a twenty-five-pound planter on the car, smashing the hood. A few minutes later Marvin Mitchelson called her. He had received a phone call from the Santa Monica city clerk saying she and Dennis wanted to get married again and now Dennis's lawyer was on the phone saying that Dennis wanted to have her arrested.

"He left for a tour that day," Karen said. "He thought I was insane, but I joined him on tour two days later. It was a wild relationship. We were both so strong, we were both like fire, extremists, so that everything we did was done really big. When we were together we were so powerful that nothing could stop us. But when we were at each other's throats, nothing could stop us either. The love was intense, the craziness was intense, and the productiveness was intense."

On New Year's Eve of 1977 Dennis and Karen tried heroin together for the first time. "Dennis was saying I will never do that drug, and I said, 'Come on, what are you, chicken?' Dennis tried it on my account, and I always felt deeply guilty about that. He got violently sick and so did I. We spent New Year's with our heads in the toilet and vowed never to do it again."

But Dennis never lost his urge for heroin and began a lifelong struggle to avoid its lure. He snorted it on several occasions, only to awaken so depressed the next day that he resolved never to try it again. His resistance to heroin took strange forms. "One night he was at a restaurant in Venice," Karen said, "and this surge of destruction comes over him and he wanted to try heroin again. Instead he got very drunk. Later, he told me, 'Either I did heroin or I went out and burned down the car.' So he chose to burn the car." The car was a $70,000 1976 GTB baby-blue Ferrari with a tan interior. He asked a friend to drive him to where the car was parked and then drove it to a parking lot in Venice, covered the inside with charcoal lighter fluid, and torched it. The vagrants who had been sleeping in the parking lot danced around the car with him as it burned.

But that was not the end of Dennis's experience with hard drugs. Heroin would play a prominent part in the Beach Boys' winter tour of New Zealand and Australia in 1978.

4

One of Stephen Love's first responsibilities in his renewed role as manager was to arrange a three-week tour of New Zealand and Australia to comply with the terms of the CBS contract. The tour was to be promoted by David Frost's Australian entertainment company, Paradigm Productions, and road-managed by Richard Duryea, who was now working for Caribou. One of Frost's most important demands was that Brian Wilson appear on tour, and he insisted on a contractual letter guaranteeing Brian was well enough to work.

Everything about this tour seemed destined for trouble from the start. Allegedly, Dennis had brought heroin with him into New Zealand at the start of the trip. When Karen saw him in terrible shape, she thought he was just drunk and left him in the hotel bar. He came back to their room in the small hours of the morning and she refused to let him in, telling him to "go sleep it off in Carl's room." The next morning, when she opened the door for him, he smacked her across the face, punched her in the chest, threw her down on the bed, and sat on her. He left her behind at the hotel, taking her money and passport with him. Karen talked two groupies who were hanging around the hotel lobby into driving her to the airport, where she found Dennis in the lounge, barefoot. She took his shoes and beat him over the head with them, demanding he hand over her passport and airplane ticket so she could get back to

Los Angeles. She eventually went to Auckland, where the concert promoter loaned her $500 and drove her to the local hospital. Karen's X rays revealed that Dennis had broken her sternum in three places. She immediately left for Hawaii, where she was treated at the Kaiser Hospital.

But this incident was minor compared to the trouble that started in Melbourne. Allegedly both Dennis and Carl purchased $100 worth of heroin from a Paradigm employee. The rest of the Beach Boys might never have learned about this had the heroin not reached Brian. At this point Brian was doing quite well under the auspices of Stan, Rocky, and Steve Korthof. He had been away from most drugs for months and was functioning without prescribed medications. Still, it took a great deal of effort to make sure that no drugs were around, and each night, in each hotel room, Stan and Rocky made a careful sweep of drawers and closets, checking under furniture and behind pictures to make sure Brian hadn't procured some drug while they weren't watching and stashed it for when he was alone.

One night, according to Steve Korthof, "Brian wanted to do a live radio broadcast from a station in downtown Melbourne, and a woman publicist said she'd take him to the station and watch him carefully." Korthof let Brian go unescorted, not knowing that Dennis, in his own room, was snorting heroin. When Brian returned from the radio broadcast, he went directly to Dennis's room, where he snorted some himself. "When Brian came back to his room, he started throwing up," Korthof said. "I had no idea, I thought he had been drinking. I said, 'Brian, did you have a drink at the bar?' And Brian lied to me and said, 'Yeah, I had a drink.' He went to sleep and it was over."

The next day Stan and Rocky did a little investigating and found out about the heroin. According to Rocky, a guilty production assistant employed by David Frost told the whole story. As unlikely as this story seems, the following tale was related. The production assistant had apparently been approached by Dennis to purchase him heroin, but he wanted to give it to someone more responsible than Dennis, and sold it instead to

Carl for $100 in the hotel bar. When Rocky related the story to the rest of the Beach Boys, they were understandably furious, and threated to call off the remainder of the tour unless Dennis was sent home immediately. Naturally, David Frost was against taking any radical action, lest it erupt in ugly publicity. Late that night, after the show, the group insisted on meeting with David Frost and his partner Pat Condon in Stephen's hotel suite. Carl—evidently a little drunk—Mike, Al Jardine, Richard Duryea, Rocky, and Stan attended. Dennis was unaware of the meeting, and Brian was kept in his room with Steve Korthof.

David Frost tried to be reasonable and low-key. "First off," he began in measured tones, "I thought the show was terrific and I was ecstatic as everyone else in the audience. A breathtaking experience.... The only two points I wanted to make are that we're in the middle of a tour that's on the verge of being the most successful tour in Australia ever, record-breaking, a stunning success, due to all of you. The realities of the situation are that the fees that we pay are the result of the backing of AGC, the biggest financing company in Australia, and we would seek that they not know of any problems that are going on.... Obviously, they've got two billion in assets, they might sue us...they would certainly sue you for fifty million dollars, because if anything goes wrong...What I'm really saying is that without wishing to interfere in any way ...we have a kamikaze pact...please delay any explosions until the tour is over because otherwise AGC...would just go berserk.... If Dennis left the tour, all hell would break loose, on our heads too."

"This is a veiled kind of threat," Stephen Love said. "You're threatening us with a potential lawsuit of fifty million dollars if we send the drummer home for buying heroin...."

A shouting match followed. "I see this as condoning fucking bullshit!" Mike yelled. "I'm not in the fucking Rolling Stones, goddamn it!"

Rocky told Frost, "If I employed somebody who procured heroin for the Beach Boys, I'd be worried about a lawsuit!"

Rocky started screaming at Carl to admit that he had personally paid $100 for the heroin, but Carl denied it. "You know what happened?" he slurred. "*I flushed it down the toilet!* I didn't buy Brian shit or spend a penny on shit."

Rocky yelled, "Then you didn't flush it soon enough!"

Stan turned to Frost and said, "You wanted a piece of paper saying Brian was in good enough health to attend this tour, then your man turns around and buys heroin? How would that look?"

"Okay," Carl said. "It's a possibility I was drunk and gave him one hundred dollars, but I really don't think I did."

"And one hundred per cent went down the toilet?" Frost asked.

"Yeah," Carl said, and continued to deny that he had bought it.

After prolonged screaming and threats of taking Frost and his organization to court, Frost interjected, "Let's stop the insults and look at the future for a minute. The point is that to try and send Dennis home causes problems. I think that he should have one last chance. I think that your moral stance is absolutely correct, but I think that this [tour] should not be destroyed because it probably would be the destruction of the Beach Boys.... All I would say is to give him one last chance because the consequences of not doing so are awful...."

"Dennis is not a person who you can give a second chance," Mike said. "He's not the kind of person who's trustworthy. What we're considering is sending Dennis home while the rest of us finish the tour. People who like drugs lie, they're not trustworthy. I can dig it because ... I'm an addictive personality but I'm addicted to TM and I meditate my ass off."

Carl interjected, "Michael, I was addicted to cocaine psychologically for many months last year and I know all about that. I was a fucking wreck. I was terrified because I thought Dennis was going through withdrawal."

A few minutes later, Rocky tried to get the production assistant who allegedly sold the heroin to Carl up to the room so he could repeat his story, but David Frost forbade it. "Absolutely not!" he shouted. "That would be a disastrous backwards step."

But Rocky was still not satisfied, and insisted, "People are going to be penalized for their actions around here. We're not going to let Dennis slide."

"We're going to *have* to let everybody slide," Frost said.

Rocky erupted. "You said you were gonna say a few words and now you're telling us what the fuck we're gonna have to do!"

"Don't talk to me like that," Frost said, the proper Englishman. "I haven't talked to you like that and I don't expect you to swear at me."

"Michael, I know all about drug abuse," Carl said. "I abuse drugs, I do not condone them."

"That's a weird statement," Michael mused.

"What I'm saying is absolutely not a threat, it's a scenario," Frost said. "If anyone were to leave, there would obviously be a breach of contract.... But I'm not sitting here saying Paradigm would take action, I'm not saying that.... As one of your greatest fans, it's bizarre and macabre that we're discussing this.... This incident must not be repeated ... it would not be seen as positive if it became public.... Let's plow on to glory."

"Are you going to fire [the procurer of the heroin]?" Frost was asked.

"Yes," Frost said.

The entire room exploded as the group members objected that the production assistant was not at fault.

Still Rocky would not let up, and continued to grill Carl about who had bought the heroin. "I happen to know the fellow's name who paid for it and I won't repeat it," Carl said. "I'll tell David [Frost] or I'll tell Pat [Condon], I'll tell someone else but I won't tell you about it."

"Yeah, they'll come to you, Carl," Rocky snarled.

"Fuck you!" Carl said.

"Fuck me, huh?" Rocky said. He jumped up, leaped across the room, and punched Carl full in the face. Carl fell to the floor unconscious. "Don't ever tell me to get fucked!" he yelled to Carl's motionless figure.

"Jesus Christ! That's about it, guys," Richard Duryea said.

"Fuck you, Duryea!" Rocky said.

"You're the one who should leave town," Frost coolly told Rocky.

When Carl came to, he said, "I won't look good for the photo sessions tomorrow."

Frost couldn't wait to get out of the room. "Sleep well, everybody," Frost said drolly. "Pleasant dreams."

"It's rock-and-roll, David," Michael said.

"Mr. Frost," Stanley called after him as he went out the door. "It was a pleasure meeting you. I enjoyed all your Nixon interviews."

The next night Dennis was ready to perform, completely unaware of what had happened in Stephen's hotel suite. He was shocked and outraged to hear that Rocky had punched Carl. But Dennis was not prepared for a physical confrontation and stayed as far away from Rocky and Stan as he could. Carl showed up for the concert very drunk, and in the middle of the performance he fell down and had to leave the stage. The incident made headlines all over Australia, and Carl had to apologize publicly the next day, telling the press that he had taken a mixture of medications that made him sick.

For the rest of the tour, Carl and Dennis traveled apart from the Love contingent. Their tour funds were collected separately by tour manager Richard Duryea, and they even entered the stage from different sides to keep as much physical distance from the others as possible. Even so, minor tussles occurred, such as a swift knee to the groin and a harsh bump as the group members crowded around the microphones. By now the tactic of cutting each other off in the middle of solo vocals was quite common.

Even with all the sanctions against drugs on this tour and David Frost's caveat that none be made available through his staff, Brian still managed to obtain some pills. On their next-to-last night in Australia, after Stan and Rocky left him alone for the night, Brian went down to the front desk, borrowed $20 in cash against his credit card, and paid a visit to the hotel doctor. Complaining he was pent-up and sleepless from touring, Brian convinced him to prescribe sleeping pills. The next morning Stan and Rocky found Brian lying in bed half conscious, drool pouring out of his mouth. After reviving Brian, Stan and Rocky did a drug search of the room and found several bottles of pills—but evidently not all of them. On the way to the airport, they noticed that Brian's face was contorted and that he was short of breath from an obvious overdose of amphetamines. Carl's personal masseuse was given a letter absolving him of any responsibility, and then gave Brian a massage to relax his muscles. On the plane home, the Beach Boys and their entourage heaved a collective sigh of relief.

The group had broken every concert attendance record in Australia.

On the way back to Los Angeles, they stopped off in Hawaii for one last concert. Brian requested that Debbie Keil be "imported" to see him. There was some discussion about this, as Marilyn was also scheduled to come to Hawaii for a visit and a short vacation. However, since Marilyn was coming primarily to see Rocky, those in authority figured Debbie's arrival would even things out. Even so, they were afraid to put Debbie's name on the Beach Boys hotel roster list lest Marilyn see it, so they asked Debbie to pay her own fare and to check into the hotel with her own credit card, promising to reimburse her. Of course, she was never reimbursed and ended up paying her own bill. But before long, everyone in the Beach Boys organization would have a heavy bill to pay.

5

A renewed surge of bad feeling toward Stephen Love began, and this time he lost one of his most loyal supporters, Al Jardine. Al was highly critical of Stephen Love for not firing Rocky Pamplin after he knocked Carl out in Australia. But Stephen, who did not hide his contempt for Carl and Dennis, seemed to feel Rocky had been justified in punching Carl.

Moreover, everyone in the group was irritated with Stephen for the pressure he was putting on them to meet the January, 1978, deadline on their CBS contract. The group members felt the deadline could easily be extended, because their attorneys, David Braun and John Branca, had a good relationship with CBS. By this time Tom Hulett, one of the top managers and tour agents in the music business, was handling their domestic schedule for a 15 percent fee. It seemed that Stephen Love had become superfluous to the group, and the hard feelings generated by the Australian heroin incident didn't help. It was agreed to fire him a second time, this time for good.

Stephen Love was owed $550,000 on his contract, and a settlement was reached under the guise of a consultancy contract in which the group agreed to pay him half of that, or $75,000 a year for three years, at a rate of $18,750 every three months. Although Stephen Love was reportedly not very happy with the settlement, he was relieved to be finished with the group. He packed his belongings and moved to Hawaii, where he was content, for a time.

I was in such a hole
that I swear to God
every living second
of my life
was just a disastrous calamity.
—BRIAN WILSON

Sixteen

1

Rocky Pamplin and Marilyn Wilson continued their affair, still a well-kept secret from Brian. By now Marilyn was wracked with deep guilt. She loved Brian dearly, and was in the most basic sense a moral, committed wife. But she was also only twenty-nine years old, a lonely, affectionate woman caught in the gothic web of an emotionally disturbed husband and a sexless marriage. Rocky Pamplin, however, was quite clear-headed and calculating. Only a few months into the affair he revealed a long-held desire to have a singing career. According to Rocky, Marilyn supported this wish, as did Brian, who promised to help produce an album for Rocky with Marilyn's group, the Honeys, singing backup. Rocky went into the studio and cut several songs. The results were amateurish, but Brian was fond of Rocky and continued to encourage the project.

Brian had reached a new low after returning from Australia—his emotional stability seemed to disintegrate daily. He still managed to obtain cocaine and barbiturates, no matter how closely his three caretakers watched him. One night, on some untold mixture of drugs, Brian began to vomit in his sleep and would have choked to death if the sound had not awakened Marilyn, who summoned Stanley to help clear the vomit from Brian's windpipe. Stanley and Marilyn spent the rest of the evening dousing Brian under a cold shower to keep him conscious.

The next day Brian disappeared. They searched throughout the house, calling all of his friends, but no one had seen or heard from him. "He was just so drugged out and miserable with himself, he didn't want to be home," Marilyn said. Brian hitchhiked to West Hollywood and ended up in a gay bar. "I know he was playing piano for beers," Marilyn said. He met someone there who drove him down to Mexico. Later Brian hitchhiked up to San Diego and wandered around the city for days, barefoot and unwashed.

"He was on a binge," Stanley said. "A couple of guys felt sorry for him and took him home and let him stay there for a while. He got drugs from somebody in a recording studio who recognized him. They said they'd give him coke if he helped them produce a song. The engineer called Brother Records and immediately got hold of Marilyn, who hired a private detective to go down and find him. The next thing we knew, there was a phone call from a doctor at the Alvarado Hospital who said to Marilyn, 'I'm treating your husband.'"

Brian had passed out in the gutter and had been picked up by an ambulance. "The cops found him in Balboa Park under a tree, with no shoes on," Stanley said, "his white pants filthy, obviously a vagrant with no wallet, no money." Marilyn, Stephen Love, and Stanley went down to San Diego to take Brian home, but decided to follow the doctor's advice instead, allowing him to spend some time detoxifying in the hospital.

Marilyn returned to Los Angeles to take care of the children. While Brian was in the Alvarado Hospital they finally discussed getting a divorce. They were talking on the phone and Marilyn was only half surprised to hear Brian say, "Mare, I think we should separate."

"I wanted it too," Marilyn said, "but still it hurt. The thought of him not wanting me anymore killed me." September 15, 1978, for legal purposes, became the arbitrary date of their separation, although Brian continued to depend on Marilyn for encouragement and stability, and kept in close telephone contact with her.

Brian never moved back into the house on Bellagio Road with Marilyn. By the time he was ready to be discharged from the Alvarado Hospital, the rest of the group was already in Miami, starting work on their long-overdue first album to satisfy their CBS contract. Through their attorney David Braun's intervention, they had received an extension on the due date, but patience at CBS was running low and the boys were under extreme pressure to produce. Said CBS Vice-President Tony Martell, "Obviously there was the feeling that the company was screwed, because we did not know Mike Love was going to take off [to Switzerland] and that all of them would be disjointed.... They were making money because Capitol was putting out repackages up the kazoo. They were making a lot of money on tour and making money from two companies... so they didn't feel under pressure to produce an album."

Since Brian was contractually obligated to produce the CBS albums, he flew by himself directly from San Diego to Los Angeles Airport, where Stanley met him in a limousine and drove him to a private plane. Brian joined the rest of the group at Critereon studios, the lush Miami recording facilities owned by the Bee Gees. Once more, the Beach Boys were together.

The new album was to be called *L.A. (Light Album)*, and its highlight was "Here Comes the Night," a twelve-minute song done in the then-popular "disco" style, the original version of which had appeared on the 1967 *Wild Honey* album. With the disco craze reaching its height, several popular groups had changed their style to accommodate the new music, and the Beach Boys—mistakenly—jumped on the bandwagon. The group was staying at the Doral Country Club Hotel, and it was apparent from the start that Brian was still very ill and wouldn't be much help in producing the album. Eventually, CBS President Walter Yetnikoff flew down to Miami to hear how the album was progressing. Brian had prepared a demo track of some of the songs, hoping to satisfy Yetnikoff that the old Brian Wilson flair was still evident. Yetnikoff and Martell assembled in the control room at Critereon and listened in dismay to the playback. Remembered Tony Martell, "We sat there and listened to the tunes.... At one point, it was a little volatile, because of what we heard. They told us it was one of their finest efforts."

According to a Beach Boys' employee who was present, "Yetnikoff basically said, 'I think I have been fucked.' That was his opening statement. But Yetnikoff was great. His next statement was 'Where do we go from here?' It was a very positive meeting. Yetnikoff has a very subtle sense of humor. He says something to get your attention."

"We refused to put out [what we heard]," said Martell. "It was not up to their capabilities by any stretch of the imagination. I think they were in a hurry.... It bothered them that they still had obligations to us, it really did.... They wanted to fulfill their obligations and by trying to do it fast, the product just wasn't there.... It was typical of them to do something like that. Then they realized what had happened, one by one. They went to Walter and said, 'You're right, this is not what we wanted.'... Walter has a way with artists. He presented a logical explanation of why the company was very upset, and they had a meeting of the minds."

According to Steve Korthof, "Brian was real weird then, real quiet, not saying much. Real depressed. I think he just realized he wasn't going to be able to pick up the slack. Brian eventually suggested that Bruce Johnston be brought back in to help produce the album. I was in the hotel room with him at the Doral Country Club when he picked up the phone and called Bruce Johnston. He said, 'Why don't you come down to Florida? I think we need you.' Brian was right; they needed him, they still do. Bruce jumped in. He flew down the next day." Bruce has been a full-fledged member of the Beach Boys ever since.

When everyone else returned to Los Angeles to continue recording at Western Studios, Brian wanted to stay in Florida by himself. The group agreed that this was out of the question and forced him to return to L.A. Back in Los Angeles, Brian moved in with Marilyn's youngest sister, Barbara, but after one weekend she asked him to leave. He called a real-estate agent and rented a small house on Sunset Boulevard for $2,300 a month. The house was dumpy and dark, with a small pool in the back. The furniture came from a local rental company, and a secondhand car was purchased to chauffeur Brian around.

At first, Brian seemed to fare well alone in the house, but he soon took to drinking heavily. His behavior verged on manic. Stan and Rocky would come by every day to stay with him. Brian would say, "Watch me walk around the pool seven hundred and eighty-five times," because that was a number he liked. Then he would frantically walk in circles around the

pool until he was sweating and exhausted. He had also developed the habit of talking out of the side of his mouth, and
his right leg vibrated constantly.

With Marilyn out of the picture, Debbie Keil now had free
rein with Brian. She would often visit him at his new house,
and once they took a romantic trip to Palm Springs. Unfortunately, Brian discovered Debbie's diet pills in her purse,
devoured them all, and refused to come out of the hotel room
until they returned to L.A. Back at the house, Debbie was often
torn as to how to deal with Brian. When he asked for money,
she knew it was to buy alcohol and would usually refuse to
give it to him, but occasionally she would relent, driving him
wherever he wanted to go lest he get hurt hitchhiking or run
away altogether. Often Brian would disappear, turning up penniless in Watts or East L.A. One morning, after they had spent
the night together, Brian insisted Debbie drive him to his old
house on Bellagio Road. Marilyn had always told him that if
he was lonely he could visit her and the children there.*

Brian let himself into the house and went up to Marilyn's
bedroom. The door was closed and he let himself in without
knocking. Marilyn was asleep, lying on her side. On the other
side of the bed, under a blanket, was Rocky Pamplin.

Brian walked over to where Marilyn lay sleeping, knelt at
her side, kissed her, and said, "I love you." Then he walked
around to Rocky's side of the bed, knelt next to him, kissed
him on the cheek, and said, "I love you." Then he was out the
door.

It took Marilyn and Rocky a few minutes to compose themselves. "I went out to find him and saw him pacing by the
front gate," Rocky said. "I walked up to him, and he turned
to me and said, 'You love Marilyn, don't you?'"

Rocky said, "No, Brian."

Brian said that he needed a pack of cigarettes, and Rocky
offered to drive him to the store. Marilyn came out of the house
and got into the back of her Mercedes while Rocky and Brian
sat in front. All three were silent as they drove to get Brian

*Marilyn Wilson denies that the following incident ever took place, calling it "total
bullshit." Rocky Pamplin, however, in direct, taped interview with the author of this
book, relates the story in detail.

the cigarettes. Suddenly Brian turned to Rocky and said, "It wasn't fair, Rocky."

Rocky said, "Worse than the way you've been treating your kids and wife the last ten years?"

Brian looked down at his lap and said, "No."

When they got back to Bellagio Road, Brian said he wanted to walk back to his rented house alone, and they let him go.

The next day Stan and Rocky arrived at the Sunset Boulevard house to find Brian plastered on muscatel. He was standing on the front porch, "drunker than a skunk," according to Steve Korthof, who had arrived a short time earlier. They took him inside, and he was quiet and morose for a while. Then he said abruptly, "Watch me kick these windows in." Brian was referring to a long row of ceiling-to-floor plate-glass windows that faced the rear of the house. He started hammering away at them with his foot. Korthof grabbed Brian and pulled him away from the glass, but he was obviously out of control. The three men managed to haul him out to the car and throw him in the back, where he was wedged between Rocky and Stan. Korthof drove them directly to the office of a Dr. David Ganz, the medical doctor who had been prescribing various medications for Brian.

They brought him into the doctor's office. Dr. Ganz was sitting behind the desk, smoking a pipe. For a moment, the sight of the man with the pipe in his mouth reminded Brian of Murry. Brian screamed at him, "*You Jew motherfucker!*" and wiped everything off the doctor's desk with one sweep of his arm. While Rocky, Stan, and Steve held Brian down, Dr. Ganz injected him with a sedative. Then they drove Brian directly to the psychiatric ward at Brotman Memorial Hospital, where he would stay for the next several months.

Stanley Love and Rocky Pamplin were fired by Marilyn Wilson's attorney via letter in January 1979 with two weeks' severance pay.* "I stopped seeing Marilyn that day," Rocky

---

*Marilyn Wilson claims she fired Rocky because, during an interview at which she was present, he said Brian would be producing his forthcoming album. "Stan and I got into a big fight," she said. "I looked at them and said, 'You...expect me to go along with you? I'm not going to lie about Brian for your benefit.' I won't have anyone lie about Brian....I fired them the next day."

said. But Rocky would not leave it at that. For months to come Marilyn received obscene messages from Rocky on her answering machine, in which he called her a "kike" and a "Jew." "I told her everything I ever felt about her," he said.

Said Stanley Love, "If Rocky hadn't been sleeping with her, we'd still be there."

2

On April 12, 1978, above the Roxy Theater on Sunset Boulevard, at a private club called On the Rox, Karen caught Dennis flirting with another girl. She punched him out cold. Jack Nicholson, who was sitting nearby, told Karen, "You should leave before he gets up," and she did. That night she wrote in her diary, "I hit him in the mouth and it felt great." But it obviously felt better to be with him—the next day they made up. Two days later, Karen joined Dennis in Houston, where the Beach Boys were performing. She arrived at the hotel to find him "holding court" in the hotel bar.

"He had been drinking and cocaining the whole day," Karen said, "and had picked up some girl. He told me to go back up to the room and wait for him. About two-thirty I called down to the bar, but it was closed. So I called the desk and asked if Dennis was around. They told me he had taken another room." Furious, Karen went to the room and tried to break down the door, until she was stopped by a security guard. The last thing she heard through the door was a girl's voice asking, "Should I put my clothes back on?"

Karen flew back to Los Angeles the next day, only to receive several phone calls from a contrite Dennis. On Monday, April 24, Karen learned that Dennis had been arrested in Tucson, Arizona, for "contributing to the delinquency of a minor." According to Dennis, he was the victim of an angry mother. According to the local papers, "a sixteen-year-old girl was allegedly found alone in Wilson's hotel room following the Beach Boys concert at a local university. The arrest came through a tip by the girl's mother, who called the police at 3:55 A.M. to say her daughter had breached curfew and was at Wilson's hotel room...." Dennis later told Karen it had cost him nearly $100,000 in legal fees to get out of trouble.

Still, Karen found it in her heart to forgive Dennis yet again, and by May they were considering remarrying.* She was hesitant, however, not because of his philandering, but because of his increasing use of heroin. On at least half a dozen occasions in her diary that year she noted that Dennis was either high or nodded out on the drug. However, on the morning of July 28, after she had returned from an appearance in a Michelob beer commercial at Lake Arrowhead, Dennis "begged [Karen] to get married again because he wanted a clean slate."

"I don't know why I did it," Karen said. "I always forgave Dennis, and I really, really, really, really loved Dennis. I loved Dennis more than anything in the world, and nothing meant that much to me." That night they flew to Las Vegas and were married in a small church on the strip.

For a short time Dennis stopped using cocaine and heroin, but less than two months after they were married, he was getting high all the time. Karen encouraged him to seek professional treatment for withdrawal. On September 29 Dennis signed himself in to a hospital in Century City under an assumed name to detoxify himself. When he arrived home chipper and clean, the two hoped to make a new start together.

Dennis had been recording songs for a second solo album at the Village Recorders, the studio owned by George Hormel, Jr. One night in November 1978 he met Christine McVie, keyboardist and singer of the English group Fleetwood Mac, who was there recording background vocals as a favor for musician Danny Duma. McVie was a tall, husky-voiced, blond woman with hard features—a far cry from Karen Lamm's classic American beauty. Born Christine Perfect in Birmingham, England, she joined Fleetwood Mac after a stint as a featured member of the group Chicken Shack. She later married Fleetwood Mac's bass player, John McVie, only to divorce him in February 1978. Still, the two continued to work together in the group, which

---

*Karen is hard-pressed to explain the number of times she forgave Dennis. "If you're worried about fidelity with a rock star, forget it. It's part of the life-style. But if you really love the man, and you need each other, there's justifiable reason to try and work it out. The only absolutely intolerable thing Dennis ever did was to take drugs."

would soon hit megastar proportions, owing to both Christine's exceptional talent as a songwriter and the incomparable voice of group member Stevie Nicks. Christine was a loyal, sensitive woman with strong moral convictions, but she was also lonely and vulnerable, living in a huge four-bedroom house in Coldwater Canyon.

She had been romantically involved with Curry Grant, Fleetwood Mac's lighting director, but the affair had run its course. According to Chris Kable, who was Dennis's secretary and later worked for Christine in the same capacity, "She took one look at Dennis and knew that he was somebody she wanted to be with. The night they met, she went home with him and spent the night with him on the boat. It was very romantic, and they were together ever after that night. She told Curry Grant she had met someone else, and he moved out."

The beginning of this affair contributed to Dennis's slide into a completely dissolute life-style. Just before Christmas 1978, Dennis moved into Christine's house. Like many of the women who fell in love with Dennis, she was generous to a fault, and found herself giving him money almost daily. Yet she was wealthy enough that one of their friends described Dennis's role in her life as an "expensive excuse for her to get up in the morning." At first they spent their time between the *Harmony* and Christine's house, but within a few months, with Christine's blessings, Dennis had set up quarters in a small pool house on Christine's terraced property. He outfitted the place with a brass bed and pump organ, cushions on the floor, and an array of candles for mood lighting.

Karen was by now resigned (and a little relieved) about the impending end of her relationship with Dennis. With Dennis's enthusiastic urging, Karen began to visit him at Christine's house, where she befriended her competitor for Dennis's attention. Karen and Christine had one common bond—the misery Dennis was putting them through. Karen, a magnanimous, and in some ways wise young woman, gave Christine her support. Karen's spirit helped Christine through many dark times to come.

Still, the relationship between the two women was most peculiar. Dennis tried to impart many of Karen's virtues to

Christine. For instance, Dennis didn't like the way Christine dressed, and asked Karen to take her shopping for clothes. (Christine dropped over $50,000 in Charles Galley in Beverly Hills under Karen's guidance.) Karen would sometimes visit Dennis when Christine wasn't home, which led to some odd situations. One day while Karen was there, a messenger arrived with a manila envelope from a lawyer's office and Dennis wasn't home to receive it. Karen was nice enough to sign for it. When Dennis arrived home later, she discovered that Dennis had filed for divorce a second time without telling her and that the envelope she had so helpfully signed for contained her own divorce papers. When she saw what the envelope contained, she asked Dennis sweetly, "What's this, honey?" But Dennis had no answer. The divorce became legal in June 1980. Karen received only $2,000 a month through February 1983 and $1,000 a month thereafter—not as alimony, but merely to pay back the loan Dennis owed her. Attorney Marvin Mitchelson took $19,000 of it in fees. On the bottom of the dissolution decree was a handwritten note that said, "So sorry, Dennis Wilson."

Dennis lived with Christine McVie for over two years, and during this time his drinking and cocaine addiction increased alarmingly. According to reputable sources, Christine McVie loaned or gave Dennis approximately $100,000 during that period, including a $20,000 loan to make repairs on the *Harmony*. Said Bob Levine, who had become Dennis's business manager in 1978, "How can a man with any dignity live in a situation [like that]? Even though she did it without any strings in a very nice manner, [he felt] like he's a gigolo, sponging off her."

Still, Dennis did not have enough money to pay for all the cocaine—at one point he had run up a coke bill of over $10,000 with a hard-nosed dealer. Reportedly, Dennis settled his debt by giving the dealer a 1935 classic Ford automobile—a wedding gift from Karen.

Dennis brought all his personal problems into Christine's life. At one point, on vacation in England, he thought he had stomach cancer. Christine checked him into a hospital for treatment, only to discover he was perfectly healthy. At any time

of day or night half a dozen people might arrive at Christine's
house at Dennis's invitation for shelter and food. Jack Rieley
spent nearly a week with them in the summer of 1979. One
day, Dennis's daughter Jennifer was deposited on Christine's
doorstep with a suitcase and a note, and Christine took her in.
Jennifer's mother, Carol, was besieged with personal problems
at the time. "I had remarried and was getting a divorce. I was
having a very, very big problem," Carol said. "Jennifer loved
living there. She always spoke highly of how nice Christine
was. The problem was that Dennis was a heavy drinker. Jennifer started to experience some of the real things that go on
out in life. She was exposed to drugs and drinking. After a
few months...she didn't want to come back...she was having
a great time."

Dennis's stepson, Scott, also came around the house, and
was soon employed as an assistant to Dennis while he was
there. But relations between stepfather and stepson were less
happy than Dennis's relationship with Jennifer.

With Dennis, any kind of disaster was possible. One night,
because Dennis left candles burning in the pool house, or perhaps because of an electrical short, the pool house burned to
the ground. There were, of course, romantic moments, as only
Dennis could orchestrate them to make up for all the problems.
On a trip to Hawaii with Fleetwood Mac, Dennis bought Christine an unset ruby as an expression of his love. He presented
it to her in Rex's restaurant in Honolulu, where he got down
on his knees in front of the whole band and asked Christine
to marry him. Back in Los Angeles, Dennis was showing the
stone off to her friends and he dropped it on the floor. It was
recovered by Dennis's long-time assistant Chris Kable, who
found it in the vacuum-cleaner bag. One July, for Christine's
birthday, Dennis hired a team of gardeners to construct a heart-
shaped flower bed in the backyard, and even hired a string
quartet to play for her. Unfortunately, the bill for the party was
sent to Christine. That same night, Dennis managed to take
Scott's girl friend to bed, and the entire household was up in
arms over the incident.

"He did crap to Christine," Chris Kable said. "He would be
gone for days, and he would call her every hour while he was

off with somebody else. But for whatever reasons, he didn't intentionally set out to hurt her by his actions."

After an onstage fight with Mike Love at the Universal Amphitheater, where Dennis performed drunk and on Quaaludes, he was officially thrown out of the Beach Boys, learning of the decision by telegram. Now almost broke, Dennis needed Christine more than ever—he became completely dependent upon her, both emotionally and financially.

3

At Brotman Memorial Hospital, Brian was under the care of Dr. Lee Baumel, a psychiatrist he had met socially years before through Tandyn Almer. Brotman had a system of putting patients on "teams." Brian was first on the C team, where the rooms had little furniture and some were padded. The B team was for healthier patients, and the A team was for those who were well enough to be on their own. Brian progressed very quickly from C to B to A. He spent his time playing piano in the lounge, and drinking endless cups of coffee. When the other patients found out who he was, they all wanted to compose with him, and Brian amused himself by writing songs with a female patient.

While Brian was at Brotman, a pathetically small contingent of loyal friends came to see him—writer David Leaf, his wife Eva Easton, Debbie Keil, Fred Vail, and Chris Kable. There was also a list at the front desk of people who were not allowed in to see Brian. Among them were Stan and Rocky. Brian had finally determined that he "hated Stan and Rocky," according to Steve Korthof, who still was permitted to see him. "He told the doctors he didn't want them around and that they scared him."

But Stan and Rocky were perhaps the most loyal to Brian in their own peculiar way—they were determined to get him back and get their own jobs back in the process. "We were only fired in [David Braun and Lee Baumel's] minds," Stanley said. One day they showed up at the hospital and demanded to see Brian. The psychiatric aide at the desk told them it was impossible, and Rocky said, "We work for the guy, so get out of the way."

The aide insisted that they were not permitted to see him. "We went behind the counter," Rocky said, "and said, 'You little fucker, that's my cousin! Don't give me that fucking shit!'" But the aide would not be intimidated and called security guards, who escorted Stan and Rocky out. They later called Steve Korthof, who was permitted to take Brian out of the hospital on passes, and suggested they "hijack Brian." "'You get him out of the hospital on a pass. Don't say anything, and we'll be waiting,'" Korthof claimed Stanley told him. "I got so angry I hung up on him," Korthof said. "I couldn't belive it." Korthof did take Brian out of the hospital to visit his lawyer so he could sign his divorce papers from Marilyn.

Stan and Rocky finally saw Brian at Brotman. A few weeks after they were thrown out, they managed to slip by the desk and visit with Brian in the cafeteria, where they tried to talk him into rehiring them. Brian said to Rocky, "You know, Rocky, you were fucking my wife...."

And Rocky said, "Yeah, and you weren't."

Then Brian accused Stan of having poked him in the chest one day.

"Brian," Stan said, "I poked you in the chest because I love you and you know that."

"Well, I have to think it over about hiring you guys back."

"Brian, now look," Stan said. "We know exactly what you're doing. You're trying to do yourself in. We're trying to save you. We're offering you our love and our help. Now, if you want to play your bedroom game again, and destroy yourself, then go ahead."

Brian got up and left the table.

"So he did it," Stanley said.

Brian was released from Brotman at the end of March, and went almost directly to New York to appear at the Radio City Music Hall date of the L.A. (Light Album) tour. Released on March 16, 1979, the new album provoked outrage among Beach Boys fans. Indeed, the disco song "Here Comes the Night" was roundly booed by the audience at Radio City Music Hall. The criticism of that song was so great that, under pressure from the group, CBS recalled the single. Still, the *L.A. (Light Album)* sold over 400,000 copies worldwide, although it only managed to reach 100 on the album charts.

Back in Los Angeles, Brian stayed at the Westwood Marquis Hotel for a week, and then moved into a house in Santa Monica Canyon on Sycamore, which he rented for $1,300 a month. Before he left Brotman, a round-the-clock psychiatric nursing team of four professional aides had been arranged for him. "There was a full-time staff," Korthof said. "We wrote 'med notes' [reports-on-the-patients' moods] just like in the hospital, which Jim Redman [one of the psychiatric aides] read every morning. It was very professional. It was the only arrangement outside of the hospital setting that made any sense."

Brian's night nurse was a competent psychiatric nurse named Carolyn Williams. A warm, caring black woman with corn rows in her hair, raising three children from a former marriage, she had been one of Brian's favorite nurses while he was at Brotman. In several phone calls to Marilyn from the hospital, Brian had mentioned how fond he had become of Carolyn Williams. But no one suspected that Carolyn would soon become his girl friend. "You know," said Korthof, "a guy is a guy. ...Maybe I would do the same thing....Little by little, I imagine, the nighttimes weren't just professional."

Janet Lent-Coop, who was by then an officer of Brother Records, remembered the first time it dawned on the rest of the group that Brian was involved in a romantic relationship with Carolyn. "We'd have meetings at the Brother Records office," she said, "and sometimes Michael would bring his girl friend. Brian was proud of his girl friend [Carolyn], and he put his arm around her during the meeting. The first time I saw it, I looked at the attorney and said, 'What's going on?' Carolyn looked at me with a totally blank [expression]. Later, when I confronted her about it, she completely denied that anything was really going on. She said, 'Big deal. If it makes him feel good, big deal.'"

When Brian started to go out on the road again, Carolyn accompanied him, much to the mortification of the rest of the group. "Everybody hated it," said Korthof. "Brian arm-in-arm with a black girl backstage. They would say, 'Oh Jesus!' Al would come up to me and say, 'Why does he have to put his arm around her?' But what are you going to do about two people? You can't tell them to live in a little closet. How do you tell a human being not to be with somebody else?"

Aside from the general humiliation the group felt about Brian's attachment to Carolyn Williams, they were also concerned that he would spend too much money on her—although there was no evidence that Carolyn ever took advantage of Brian financially—or even worse, marry her. The couple once went to Las Vegas together for a weekend, and the group held its breath until they came back—unmarried.

Although Carolyn Williams tried her best, life with Brian still left much to be desired. According to visitors, the house they lived in was always a mess. The floor was mottled with thousands of cigarette burns where Brian had tossed his cigarettes instead of using an ashtray. Unable to curtail his drinking, or food intake, Brian was reportedly consuming four or five steaks a day, as well as mountains of ice cream and other fattening foods. There were also rumors within the Beach Boys organization that Brian was using drugs again, in addition to the prescribed medications he was also taking. He managed to find the bottle of chloral hydrate sleeping pills that had been prescribed for him and started taking them during the day. When this was discovered, Dr. Baumel put Brian back in the hospital for a short stay.

Brian's renewed drug use was blamed on Dennis Wilson—indeed, Dennis had been seeing a great deal of Brian in recent months, often bringing him to visit friends in seedy neighborhoods of Venice or to various studios where they produced and wrote songs together. Sometimes Dennis would buy a huge bag of hamburgers at MacDonald's and give one to Brian for every song he worked on. Dennis might also promise Brian a gram of cocaine for every song he wrote. Dennis would lay out the entire gram of cocaine on the piano top and Brian would snort it all in one long, noisy inhalation. Fifteen minutes later he would want another.

In early March of 1982, Brian was pressured to enter St.

John's Hospital in Santa Monica to help him lose weight. When a strapping Beach Boys aide arrived at his house to take him to the hospital, Brian went directly to the phone and called the police to have him thrown out. But the police reportedly refused to interfere, and Brian was taken to St. John's for an involuntary seventy-two-hour stay. Carolyn Williams reportedly complained to a patients' legal-rights group and Brian was released in five days. Now the Beach Boys and their management were furious with her interference.

A few weeks later, on March 24, at the Lee County Airport in Fort Myers, Florida, the Beach Boys were on their way to Tampa to perform. Carolyn Williams was passing through the security check before boarding, when she was asked to open a blue denim carry-on bag as well as a black-and-brown bag. According to the booking report filed that day, security guard Charlotte Maxwell found "a gold cigarette case which contained a razor blade, straw and piece of clear plastic which both contained residue...." There was also a white piece of paper "that contained a white substance that appeared to be a narcotic substance." The report said that Carolyn "grapped [sic] the white paper and deliberately emptied it out the floor." Later, the residue proved "positive to Cobalt Thocyanate Narcotest" as cocaine.

Carolyn insisted she was set up as a means of getting rid of her. (Intimate members of the Beach Boys' circle suspect she was right.) Carolyn spent the day and night in jail before she received an anonymous phone call warning her that she should not try to see Brian again. At one in the morning, after repeated phone calls to the Beach Boys' touring entourage, a $300 bail was paid, reportedly charged to Brian's credit card. A court date was set for April. The next day, Carolyn's arrest was widely reported in the news, and featured on "Entertainment Tonight." Carolyn later entered a plea of "nolo contendere" to possession of a controlled substance. She was fined $5,000 (which Brian reportedly paid himself) and was put on probation for three years.

But Carolyn and Brian could not be kept apart once they returned to Los Angeles. Later that summer Brian asked Carolyn to move her three children and dog into a new house he had purchased at 910 Greentree in the Pacific Palisades, which Janet Lent-Coop had decorated.

By autumn, Brian's weight was 311 pounds and climbing.

4

Christine McVie's personal life was nearly destroyed by the end of 1980. She had tried, unsuccessfully, to end the relationship with Dennis several times. Each time she asked him to leave, he came back like a sheepish dog, and Christine's heart went out to him. Like Karen Lamm before her, she forgave Dennis more times than she should have, and always let him back in. But by Christmas of that year her neighbors were up in arms over the loud arguing and public scenes taking place in the street, and her own lawyers advised Christine to end the relationship. Sadly, Dennis moved out and rented his own house on Wavecrest Avenue in Venice Beach with his friend Steve Goldberg.

Stan Love was in Hawaii at this time visiting his brother Stephen. He claims he got phone calls from both Janet Lent-Coop and Carolyn Williams, telling him that Brian was in desperate straits and needed somebody to protect him from Dennis. "Brian is out of control," Stanley claimed Carolyn told him. Stanley learned that "Dennis had been hanging around and he got Brian to buy maybe fifteen thousand dollars worth of cocaine. Brian would snort up five or six grand in half an hour, and they'd have to put their hands in his mouth to stop him from swallowing his tongue."

Stanley returned from Hawaii to see his old friend Rocky. A few nights later was Superbowl Sunday, and Stan and Rocky were celebrating on the yacht of a friend. "We were partying," said Stanley. "We were on a pump."

Rocky said, "Stanley was going to drive me home because I was too high [to go myself]—I admit it—and [Stanley] said, 'Let's go get Dennis.' And I said, 'Yeah, let's go cruise his pad.'"

"It just happened to fall together," Stanley said.

The two of them drove to Dennis's house and hid in the bushes outside, watching what was going on inside. According to Stan and Rocky, they could clearly see Dennis through the window, snorting coke with seven other people. Later, they followed him on a trip to the liquor store and waited for him outside. When Dennis came out of the store, they said hello and pretended they were there coincidentally, but Dennis was wary of them and went directly home.

"I said, 'Let's go fucking get him....'" Rocky said.

When Dennis went back inside the house, a terrifying assault began. Stanley knocked down the front door with one swift kick, and he and Rocky went barreling inside. Stanley screamed, "Freeze! We're cops!" And before anybody could move, they were on Dennis.

"We broke our hands the first couple of punches," Rocky said. "He doubled up, and we picked him up and dragged him through the house, beating him up for ten minutes. We let him try to run away, and then we grabbed him and threw him through a window."

With Dennis bleeding and badly beaten, Stanley picked up the telephone, and as if he were speaking to other police officers, said, "Okay, we've got everything under control here," and then took the receiver and smashed it into Dennis's head.

"He knocked him twelve feet over a couch into the other room. Then we slammed his head against the bedboard twelve times," Rocky said. "By now the guy is pleading, 'Stanley, please! Stanley, please!'"

"It was one of the most brutal beatings ever," Stanley said.

Dennis pressed charges against Stan and Rocky. They appeared in Santa Monica Supreme Court on March 19, when a restraining order was placed against them. Rocky was fined $250 and Stanley $750 (although he claims that with legal fees and air fare back and forth from Hawaii his actual cost was close to $10,000). Both were put on six months' probation.

According to Rocky, when the judge handed out the fines, Dennis cried out, "Oh no! I got beat up for two hundred and fifty dollars!"

Dennis was now on the last loop of a spiral plunge. He was unable to refuse anyone shelter or money, and the house on Wavecrest was soon filled with a collection of needy wanderers from Venice and the surrounding neighborhoods. One day his daughter Jennifer brought a friend by. She was a short, blond teenage girl named Shawn. Dennis had heard a rumor that she was the very same illegitimate child Mike Love had fathered sixteen years before. When Dennis asked Shawn who her father was, all she would say was "Mike." Later, she admitted that "Mike" was indeed Mike Love. For Dennis, now would come the ultimate revenge.

The whole pathetic thing
was the child, a beautiful child
—BOB LEVINE

Seventeen

1

A disgruntled CBS Records, disappointed with the sales of the previous album, expected another album as soon as possible. From November 1979 to January 1980 the Beach Boys went back to the studio to produce a new LP, *Keepin' the Summer Alive*. The group wanted Brian to return to the studios in an environment that would be comforting to him, so they decided to record the album at Western, where the earliest Beach Boys albums had been produced. According to Carl, "Brian got hot for about three days in the studio. He was singing like a bird. All the protection he usually runs just dropped; he came out of himself. He was right there in the room." But the productive period lasted only three days, and when the album was released, the production credit went to Bruce Johnston. By the time it was finished, over three dozen tracks had been recorded for the album. The single, "Goin' On," with lyrics by Mike Love, was released early in March 1980 and appeared on the charts for only three weeks. The album itself, released two weeks later, fared no better, chalking up six weeks on the *Billboard* hit list at no higher than number 76. Still, according to the terms of their contract, the group was paid $666,000 by CBS.

In 1980 there was no Beach Boys group to speak of—while the band continued to tour, they had concert dates in which Alan and Mike were the only original members present. Dennis had been kicked out of the group. Carl was busy on his own. From September to December 1980 he recorded a solo album,

Carl Wilson, for Caribou Records, produced by James Guercio, and co-written by Jerry Schilling's wife, Myrna Smith. Although the album was distinguished by Carl's beautiful voice, which had given most of the memorable Beach Boys songs their distinctive sound, it was a commercial failure. In April 1981, Carl went on a short solo tour to help promote the album. He told one reporter, "I was hoping my absence would encourage the guys. . . . I felt that by leaving, I was in a rare position to offer them some feedback." According to Steve Korthof, "In 1981, Carl wasn't on the road at all with the Beach Boys. Dennis was there half the time, showing up, leaving the tours, not able to make the show. Sometimes they had only one Wilson family member onstage, and when Dennis didn't show they had nobody. Here we are trying to sell a Beach Boys show and no Wilson. It's kind of stupid. So they said, 'Get Brian out here, I don't care how you do it, we need Brian on the road.'"

The problem was how to do it. By now, Tom Hulett of Concerts West was managing the Beach Boys, while Jerry Schilling handled Carl Wilson's personal management. Under their guidance, an extraordinary event took place. Brian Wilson was fired by the Beach Boys on November 5, 1982, at a meeting held in their lawyers' office. Brian was presented with a letter which read, "This is to advise you that your services as an employee of Brother Records Inc. and otherwise are hereby terminated, effective immediately." The letter added that "this action is taken in your best interest, and is not reversible. We wish you the best of health." It was signed Alan Jardine, Mike Love, Carl and Dennis Wilson.

Just a few weeks before, Brian had been notified that he was "broke" and behind in his taxes by nearly $80,000, according to Rick Nelson and Janet Lent-Coop, who were now his personal business managers. Steve Korthof had also been told Brian was broke and was unable to afford Steve's salary—he was fired on October 28, 1982. Now Brian was left alone, under the total care of Carolyn Williams, who had moved her children into Brian's house.

But in truth, Brian was not broke, and had not really been fired. All of this was merely a ploy to get him away from Carolyn Williams and back to Gene Landy. Suspecting some kind of plot, Brian (or somebody who could type) wrote a letter to the Bank of Beverly Hills, where his accounts were kept, and asked that all his statements, checks, and correspondence be sent to his house at 910 Greentree. The bank automatically got in touch with Rick Nelson about the letter, and Nelson told them to ignore it.

This crisis had taken six months to invent and prepare, with Gene Landy's help behind the scenes. According to Landy, Tom Hulett called him and said, "'We are worried that Brian Wilson is going to follow Elvis. We've got to do something.' He had a year or two left to live and then he would have died.

"No one thought there was hope for Brian," Landy said, "but four people decided to take a shot at saving him anyhow— his brother Carl; Carl's manager, Jerry Schilling; Brian's lawyer, John Branca; and the Beach Boys' manager, Tom Hulett." According to Landy, he told them: "There are certain conditions. I want him in a hospital first; I want to check the man out physically."

When it was first suggested to Brian that he go back to Landy, he refused. Asked if Brian didn't like Landy anymore, Rick Nelson said, "That is putting it mildly. He didn't want to have anything to do with the guy." Instead, Brian suggested that he consult with the mop-headed TV exercise guru, Richard Simmons.

In order for Landy to take Brian back, Brian had to really *want* to be treated by him again, and Brian had to make the phone call himself. Landy's position at the time was that he wasn't available to see any new patients. "That was all part of it," according to Rick Nelson. "Landy masterminded the whole thing." Said Janet Lent-Coop, "The way to get Brian to see Landy was to tell him that he was broke and that he wouldn't be earning any money at all, from touring. He had been getting paid for not touring, and the only way for him to get that money was to see Landy. It took us six months to get ready for that meeting."

Carolyn Williams was not thrilled with the idea of Brian going back to see Landy, and she was not party to the "Brian is broke" ploy. "They were willing to try and work with Carolyn," Janet Lent-Coop said, "but she refused to work it out because she... saw the handwriting on the wall. She tried to make appointments for Brian [herself] but they wouldn't let her call.... Landy had to hear it from Brian directly." Reportedly, Carolyn Williams attended one of the first meetings with Landy's associate, Dr. Arnold Dahlke, who would assist in the new program being designed for Brian. Williams later claimed to reporters that a tape recording was secretly made of the session without her knowledge and that she found the hidden recorder and took the tape with her before she left Dahlke's office. The battle lines were clearly being drawn.

The Beach Boys felt that for Brian's own benefit they had to get him away from Carolyn Williams, so another plan was devised. In January 1983 Brian was told he needed a complete physical examination in order for Landy to treat him. He was brought to Cedars of Sinai Hospital, where, according to Landy, Brian weighed 320 pounds upon arrival and was in a chemical daze. An extensive series of tests was run, including myriad blood analyses, cardiograms, and electroencephalograms. Landy said, "We put Brian through every test imaginable to see what food allergies he had, the levels of medication in his bloodstream. This man was on so much shit! He had forty percent lung capacity and no liver!" Drs. Murray Susser and Sol Samuels put Brian on an intravenous biomedical diet that Landy called "heavy detox."

Two weeks later, after the tests were completed, Brian was whisked away from the hospital on a Sunday—without Carolyn's knowledge—and taken to a rented house in Kona, Hawaii. He was accompanied by Gene Landy, his lady friend Alexandra, his associate Arnold Dahlke, and Dr. Susser, who put Brian on a megavitamin treatment.

The day after Brian's arrival in Hawaii, Landy and his two associates asked him to take a walk. When Brian refused, they drove him to the beach. After a short stroll, Landy asked Brian if he wanted breakfast. Brian, who was always hungry, immediately headed back to the car, but Landy insisted they walk to a restaurant visible in the distance. "How am I gonna get there?" Brian said. "I can't walk that."

"Well, we'll come back for you," Landy said.

"You're gonna *leave* me here?" Brian asked.

"Unless you walk with us," Landy said. And with breakfast as the lure, Brian walked.

Slowly, Landy and his crew began to reintroduce Brian to the basics of normal socialization. From table manners to re-learning how to drive, Brian gradually became independent. "When we started driving with him," Dahlke told a reporter, "back when he was on nine hundred calories a day, we'd give him nine hundred dollars a day in Monopoly money. If he made a mistake driving, we'd pull him over and fine him— twenty dollars for speeding, that sort of thing."

On January 11, before he was taken to Hawaii, Brian signed a notarized letter to Carolyn Williams stating that he was leaving town on a "retreat" and would be unable to speak with her for some time. While he was away, the letter asked, would she remove herself and her possessions from his house? Carolyn Williams was understandably hurt and angry—especially when the electricity and water were turned off in the house. Then a For Sale sign appeared on the front lawn and a moving van arrived to take all of Brian's furniture into storage. Carolyn retaliated by calling a press conference in which she displayed a telegram she claimed had been sent to her from Hawaii by Brian. The telegram read, WHY ARE OUR PHONES DISCONNECTED? PLEASE STAY HOME AND WAIT FOR ME.... THEY FORCED ME TO COME. ... I MISS THE KIDS.... PLEASE HELP ME GET HOME TO YOU. The press jumped on this announcement with great delight, the Los Angeles Herald Examiner running a headline that read, "Brian Wilson, Please Phone Home." Rolling Stone ran a column headlined, "Was Brian Wilson Shanghaied?" In Hawaii, Brian held a press conference at the Kahala Hilton Hotel in which he told reporters, "We are trying to get rid of her, yes, so that we can sell the house. It sure is weird."

Later, Carolyn started a campaign against Gene Landy. She reportedly kept trying to contact Brian throughout the year, once even waiting for him outside of Landy's office. By the late winter of 1984, she would finally report Landy to the Psychology Examination Committee in Sacramento, as well as the California State Psychological Association ethics committee. She accused him of violating moral and legal standards, the welfare of the consumer, and professional relationships.

The results of the Association committee's findings, if any, are confidential.

By March 1983 Brian was back in Los Angeles, some forty pounds thinner. Landy moved him into one of the largest homes in Malibu colony—a seven-thousand-square-foot, six-bedroom, two-story beach house with two kitchens and a Jacuzzi. Several aides moved in with him, including Landy's son Evan, Dahlke's son Greg, two of Greg's classmates at Sonoma State, and Evan's friend Carlos. Brian was cut off from all his old friends, including Debbie Keil; his former wife, Marilyn; and their two children.

That same March, Brian's business manager, Rick Nelson, wrote a cautionary letter to John Branca about Landy's bills. "As of March 17th, Brian had written checks to Eugene Landy totalling $44,000.... Based on Landy's projections expenses will run approximately $57,000 per month, plus any other unpredictable occurrences, such as recording sessions. In addition, Brian has ongoing monthly expenses which total approximately $15,000.... Thus, in the nine months remaining in 1983, we will need about $650,000. This is a good $350,000–400,000 more than Brian's gross projected earnings for 1983 before taxes." But according to Nelson's wife, Janet Lent-Coop, the money no longer mattered. "If Landy could get Brian to produce just one hit album, it would easily be worth it."

2

In January 1980, Brother Records Inc., under Alan Jardine's direction as corporation president, had stopped paying Stephen Love his severance fees. These fees were to have been paid under the terms of a consultancy agreement, but by 1980 relations between Stephen and the group had virtually disintegrated, except for the mimimum dialogue required by Stephen's role in certain real-estate investments. When Stephen learned that his quarterly fees had been halted, he told his brother Stanley that Alan Jardine was a "chickenshit." Then all hell broke loose.

The multitude of lawsuits that followed is a tangled skein of yarn knotted by accusations and recriminations, bringing out the worst in all parties involved. If blood is thicker than water, then nothing is worse than bad blood between family members. Over the years, under Stephen Love's guidance, the Beach Boys had made several group investments in real estate with the help of Paul Gader, a prominent real-estate investment advisor.* One of these was the Spaulding Ranch, a choice piece of raw land, purchased in 1974 at a cost of $500,000 for a down payment of $250,000. The second investment was called Modal, purchased in October 1974. Its asset was a profitable Motel 6, operating in Mesquite, Texas. The purchase price was $762,000 with a down payment of $167,000. An income-producing property, Modal was a self-liquidating deal in which the income from the lease paid for the mortgage with a net cash flow. At the end of twenty years the mortgage would be completely paid off. The third investment, called the South Kona Land Company deal, involved a thirty-acre piece of property on the island of Hawaii. Only a $65,000 investment, the South Kona property was a "symbolic" acquisition allowing the five Beach Boys to own a piece of Hawaiian real estate. The investment was viewed as an introduction to Hawaii, where, it was presumed, the group would retire in later years.

In addition, Mike Love had bought a two-acre site in Santa Barbara at 101 Mesa Lane. There was one acre in front, overlooking the ocean, where Mike lived, and one in the rear, which was undeveloped. Allegedly, Mike made a deal with Stephen to develop the "rear five," as it was called. Paul Gader arranged for mortgage and construction financing and Stephen oversaw the building of five houses on the land. In return he expected 15 percent of the equity. Reportedly, Stephen signed the limited-partnership agreement in December 1976 and Janet Lent-Coop sent it to Mike's attorney in Santa Barbara, but the

*There were sundry other real-estate investments made by the Lefkowitz office, including the Saple property, an industrial site with three buildings, which cost the boys $340,000; the Lisal properties, a ninety-one-thousand-square-foot office building leased to Liberty Savings and Loan, purchased for $2,150,000; and the Anaclara property, which was a North American Aviation plant in Anaheim and a Lockheed plant in Sunnyvale, acquired for a $100,000 down payment against a purchase price of $600,000.

deal was never recorded. These circumstances are hotly disputed by both sides.

The Beach Boys didn't realize that before they had stopped sending Stephen Love his settlement checks, he had already sold the Spaulding Ranch for $1.25 million, a deal in which he was a general as well as limited partner and responsible for the management of the property. The Beach Boys finally learned of this sale in March 1980, a month after Stephen started to sue Brother Records Inc. for breach of contract in Los Angeles Superior Court. Reportedly, Stephen had sold Spaulding without telling them because he became paranoid about the group and felt they might try to avoid paying him his 15 percent of Spaulding. To make matters even more complicated, Stephen had given Stan Love a priority payment of $175,000 from the sale of Spaulding. Marilyn and Brian Wilson joined the other Beach Boys in a suit against Stephen and Stanley.

The crux of Brian and Marilyn's lawsuit was an alleged "oral agreement" between Brian and Stanley. Stanley claimed that Brian had told him that if he was no longer in Brian's employment he could be "cashed out" of his investment in Spaulding. Marilyn and Brian both gave depositions countering this claim, but at Brian's deposition, face-to-face with Stephen and Stanley Love, Brian became so frightened he said "yes, yes" to almost every question he was asked. In a subsequent declaration supporting a request to appoint a court receiver, which Brian's attorney prepared for him, Brian claimed: "At the time of the taking of my deposition in this matter I was emotionally upset.... Further, the presence of Stephen Love and Stanley Love at the deposition was intimidating to me. I find Stanley Love physically intimidating and am physically afraid of him." He went on to say that "I have no recollection of any agreement having been made with either Stephen Love or Stanley Love that if Stanley Love's employment with me was terminated he would be entitled to take his money out of any limited partnership investments...."

Stephen and Stanley Love's depositions went right for the jugular, bringing up a series of allegations not specifically germane to the matters at hand. In Stanley's deposition, taken

November 3, 1981, he claimed that while working for Brian "I had to keep him from giving heroin to his two young daughters." Stephen Love's depositions were potentially so harmful that they were sealed by the court in an unusual move taken for the protection of minors. But it is known that Stephen claimed Marilyn made business decisions based on obtaining sexual favors from other parties. In his declaration he claimed that in 1977 he found out that Marilyn had been having affairs with both Carl and Dennis Wilson.

Marilyn struck back in court papers filed February 11, 1982, saying that Brian was "incapable of caring for himself in any sort of a financial or business sense" and that "it is ridiculous for either Stephen Love or Stanley Love to contend that they have discussed these matters with him and he has agreed to them. He is not capable of responsibly agreeing or disagreeing about such matters." As for Stephen Love's contention that Marilyn's business decisions were made on the basis of sexual favors, she simply said, "This is an absolute lie and a rather transparent attempt to assassinate my personal character." And as for her alleged affairs with Carl and Dennis she called his accusation "a complete fabrication."

When Stanley Love was asked why the depositions and claims became so personal, he said, "Because we thought we would say the heaviest shit possible and they would wake up and say, 'Whoa!, Let's not get into that.' It didn't work."

As of this writing, the lawsuit has not been resolved, but the parties are reportedly working toward a settlement.

The next round of lawsuits started when Mike Love took five second mortgages out on 101 Mesa Lane totaling $600,000, without Stephen's awareness. Mike's contention was that Stephen was not obligated to know about this transaction, because when Stephen tried to point to his partnership agreements as proof that he deserved 15 percent of the mortgages, he learned that the agreement was never recorded. In 1980 Stephen filed suit. Michael in turn sued Stephen over the sale of the Hawaiian property they owned together. Throughout the next four years hundreds of thousands of dollars would be spent on lawyers, which contributed to Mike Love's eventual personal bankruptcy. As of this writing the lawsuits are not settled.

On October 8, 1981, Mike realized a lifelong dream. His solo album, *Looking Back with Love*, was released on the Boardwalk label. Produced by Curt Becher, and recorded on a mobile unit at Mike's Santa Barbara estate, the album was mostly ignored by critics, as well as by fans.

By now Mike was divorcing his fifth wife. In the late seventies he had married Sue Oliver Damon, a pretty Hawaiian woman in her mid-thirties, in a quiet ceremony in a Lake Tahoe chapel. They were divorced two years later. He then had an affair with a pretty Korean girl, Sumako Kelley, whom Mike announced as the fifth Mrs. Love. But instead, he met and fell in love with Cathy Linda Martinez and married her in 1981 at his Santa Barbara home in a ceremony performed by disc jockey Wolfman Jack, who is an ordained minister. Mike and Cathy had a son together, Michael Edward Love II. Cathy was gone in a little over a year. Mike filed in Reno, Nevada, under Nevada's non-community property law. Cathy moved into Mike's vacation home in Incline Village, Nevada.

The lawsuits, divorces, and Mike's extravagant life-style toppled him financially. In 1983 he filed for a Chapter 11 bankruptcy in the Central District Court of California. Among other debts Mike claimed $48,000 in taxes owed to the California State Franchise Tax Board; a $100,000 loan secured against his properties in Santa Barbara and Incline Village; and at least fifteen loans from various banks. Total debt to creditors holding security was $2,854,767. In all there were over a hundred unsecured creditors, including exterminators, his answering service, his dentist (to whom he owed $28), and a telephone bill for $1.16 from Nevada Bell. With the addition of several hundred thousand dollars in legal fees owed for divorces and sundry lawsuits, the grand total came to $2,462,737.80 for unsecured debts to creditors.

In court papers Mike claimed immediate debts payable totaling $163,671.77. In a declaration by Pamela Ann Caughill, his bookkeeper since August 1982, she stated, "Mr. Love has financed his lifestyle by extensive borrowing. All of the properties he owns are fully mortgaged, and as a result, he has substantial monthly obligations....His monthly loan obligations presently total $22,765.59...[and] his total monthly obligations are in excess of $50,000." Pamela Caughill said, "Mr. Love's present financial circumstances are, to say the very least, desperate."

3

On April 5, 1983, the Beach Boys got an unexpected boost from the most unusual quarter. Then Secretary of the Interior James Watt announced that the Beach Boys would not be invited to play the Mall on Independence Day that year because they attracted "the wrong element." He added, "We're not going to encourage drug abuse and alcoholism as was done in years past." A wave of national sentiment and sympathy arose, from such supporters as Beach Boys fans and fellow Californians Nancy and Ronald Reagan. Watt was called to Reagan's office, lectured about the national treasure known as the Beach Boys, and presented with a cast plaster foot with a hole shot in it to symbolize his gaffe. On July 4, the Beach Boys played Atlantic City instead while Las Vegas singer and personality Wayne Newton graced the Washington concert with his presence. On July 17 the Beach Boys were invited to the White House, where they posed for pictures with the president and his wife. Dennis stood in the background, pale and bloated from drugs and alcohol, looking the worst the public had ever seen him.

Dennis's peculiar relationship with Shawn Love had blossomed into a romance. Shawn had moved into Dennis's little house on Wavecrest Avenue, a block from the ocean in Venice. There were so many other people staying in the house (with Dennis paying the bills) that at first it wasn't clear what was happening with Shawn. Hemmed in by the dozens of people crashing at his house, Dennis moved into a tiny broom-storage closet underneath the stairs that led to the second floor—there was hardly enough space for Dennis himself in the room, let alone Shawn.

According to Bob Levine, "Dennis was thinking with his cock. He was an easy mark. When it came to young girls, he was very vulnerable. If there was one thing that acted as a drug on Dennis, it was young sex. Shawn* didn't care about Dennis. She really didn't. She was only trying to get in a situation where she could have close proximity with her father. All she wanted was for Mike Love to look at her and say, 'My daughter.'"

But Mike Love did not say, "My daughter." When Dennis first brought Shawn to a Beach Boys concert, Mike reportedly said, "No daughter of mine takes drugs."

By spring of 1982 Shawn was visibly and unmistakably pregnant, and she and Dennis moved into their own rented house in Trancas Beach, Malibu. On September 3, 1982, Shawn and Dennis had a son, Gage Dennis Wilson. Dennis, on tour in Texas with the group, took a private jet home to be with Shawn. But when he arrived in Los Angeles, he wasn't sure he wanted to see her. Instead, he called Karen Lamm. Once free of Dennis, Karen had completely restructured her life. Her career, which had floundered under the strain and distraction of their relationship, was once again successful. She was exercising daily and neither drank nor did drugs. When Dennis called Karen on the night Gage was born, he asked if he could come see her.

"Absolutely not," Karen told him. "You belong at the hospital with your wife and son."

Once Dennis laid eyes on the boy, his whole world began to revolve around Gage. He talked about him to anyone who would listen and slept with the baby next to him at night. But when the call of the wild sounded, Dennis could easily desert the infant and its mother. On July 28, 1983, he married Shawn for Gage's sake, but marriage only intensified the tension between the couple. Shawn, like all of Dennis's wives before her, could not abide his impossible behavior, and she was not going to be the one to tame him. Dennis complained to his friends that the marriage had been a mistake and almost immediately began to talk about getting a divorce. Less than four months married, he filed for one.

Shortly afterward, he called Karen Lamm again and asked her to come visit him in the Trancas house he was renting.

---

*Shawn Love refused to be interviewed for this book.

Dennis's friend John Hanlon drove Karen out to the beach, and at first she wasn't even sure she recognized the man who answered the door. Dennis had shaved his beard and was bloated and gray. His face was jowly and his eyes lined and tired.

"Look at you!" Karen cried. "What happened to all your muscles?"

"I have muscles," Dennis said, smiling sadly. He pounded himself on the stomach to show her how tough he was. "I run every day."

"Where to? The local bar and back?"

Dennis told Karen he had kicked cocaine and would soon be off the booze, but only a few minutes later he produced a vial of white powder and asked Karen to join him in a few snorts. Karen shook her head no, and disappointed, but resigned, soon left.

Shawn moved into the Santa Monica Bay Inn with Gage. That November, when the lease at Dennis's Trancas beach house was up, he was homeless. Said Bob Levine, "The concept we agreed to was that he go [to a detoxification program], spend a month, six weeks there, and when he came back, we'd find him a place."

But Dennis never actually went to detoxify; every attempt he made was aborted for one reason or another. By autumn of 1983 he was homeless and disconsolate, staying wherever he fell asleep at night—at the homes of friends, at George Hormel's house, or with a new girl, Coleen "Crystal" McGovern. He would go into bars, broke, and ask strangers to buy him drinks. "I'm Dennis Wilson of the Beach Boys!" he would say, and more often than not, some stranger, remembering the music that had orchestrated his childhood, would buy him what he wanted.

All Dennis thought about was Gage, and—oddly enough— Murry. "The last six months of his life Murry was dominant," Bob Levine said. "...and he was totally enraptured by the child." By late November, Dennis had hit rock bottom and on his thirty-ninth birthday, December 4, he discovered Shawn asleep in her room at the Bay Inn with two friends and went berserk. A final attempt to detoxify that began at St. John's Hospital in Santa Monica on December 23, ended a day later when he was told that Shawn and Gage were going to be evicted from the Santa Monica Bay Inn for nonpayment of rent. Late Christmas night, one of Shawn's boyfriends beat Dennis up over a disagreement about whether he could use the telephone in the hotel room.

Three days later, Dennis went diving from his friend Bill Oster's boat to find the lost treasures of better days.

4

Bill Oster stood on the dock waiting for Dennis to reemerge from the cold waters of Marina Del Rey. "Pretty soon I saw him," Oster said. "He came up almost to the surface but he stayed about two feet underneath it and swam to near where my rowboat was tied up. He was up for maybe fifteen seconds and then he slipped straight down from there. I said, 'I wonder where he's going? Is he going to come up the other side of the dock?' I had a few puffs on my cigarette and didn't see him or hear him, and I wondered where he was. I made some noise stomping on the deck, trying to flush him out, but I got no response. All that happened was the girls came up from the boat and said, 'Where's Dennis?' I said, 'I don't know where he is.' At that point we started looking all around. I came around the other side of the boat and started looking under all the docks in the air spaces. After a few minutes of this we started getting panicky."

Oster spotted a Harbor Patrol boat nearby and flagged them in. "We told them the story, and they said, 'Well, are you sure he didn't get off the dock and go up to the bar or to somebody's house or sneak off?'" Oster said he didn't think so, and one of the harbor patrolmen took off his shirt and jumped in the water to look around. Oster and the girls started calling all over the marina, to the local bars and Aggie's Chris Craft. They enlisted the help of anyone they could find to search all the bars of the marina, hoping to find Dennis there.

They found Dennis forty-five minutes later. A four-man dragoon located his body on the muddy floor of the marina, directly underneath the spot where the *Harmony* had been berthed. Oster, his girlfriend Brenda, and Crystal stood on the dock and wept.

One by one the phone calls were made. Carl, Mike Love, Alan Jardine, Audree, the ex-wives, Shawn. But before everyone could be informed personally, the news media descended on Marina Del Rey, and the photographs of Dennis in a body-bag being carried away to the city morgue were flashed all around the nation on the eleven o'clock news.

At Brian's house in Malibu one of Landy's assistants told Brian there was a message for him on his answering machine. It was Jerry Schilling. When Brian called Schilling back, he said, "I'm sorry to have to tell you that Dennis drowned."

"I felt real *strange*," Brian said. "It's a weird feeling when you hear about a death in the family, a weird trip. It's not something you can really talk about or describe. I got tears after about a half-hour. Then I saw it on the news and thought, Oh God, there he is, lying there dead. I was blown out by the whole idea that he *drowned*, although I just let it lay; I didn't fuck with it. I didn't think too much about it. I let it lay.... It pissed me off when he drowned because I felt I wasn't just losing a brother, I was losing a friend, and that compounded it even more."

A meeting was called at Audree's house, attended by Dennis's three former wives—Carol, Barbara, and Karen—and his teenage widow, Shawn, for whom Carl had arranged a limousine. The group had only conversed for a few minutes when it became clear that only one person had any say over what would happen at this point—Shawn. Shawn was legally Dennis's widow, because their divorce had not yet been final at the time of his death, and hers was the ultimate word.

Carl Wilson at first thought Dennis would be buried in a crypt next to Murry, but Shawn had decided that Dennis was to be buried at sea. When Dennis's sons Michael and Carl heard this, they were aghast. "Do you mean Daddy's going to be thrown in the ocean?" they asked their mother. All of Dennis's former wives disagreed with the idea of a burial at sea, but legally there could be no dispute. Carl told Karen Lamm, "It's Shawn's duty now, Karen, and I have to stand behind Shawn."

The family decided on a small, quiet memorial service to

be held at Inglewood Cemetery. Karen asked Shawn's permission to read from I Corinthians 13, and after some consideration Shawn acquiesced. But a half-hour before the service, Karen received a phone call from Shawn saying that she and Dennis's daughter Jennifer would read the Bible segment instead: "Somebody closer to Dennis should read it." Next, the question was raised as to what kind of music should be played. Someone suggested religious music, but Shawn objected, saying that the Police song "Every Breath You Take" was Dennis's favorite song. The rest were dismayed at the idea of playing this current popular favorite at the funeral of a man to whom music meant so much. Karen suggested that "Farewell My Friend" from Dennis's solo album would be more appropriate, and Shawn decided to consider the suggestion. Someone asked that Shawn listen to it right then, and the album was put on the stereo at Audree's house. Up until that moment everyone had remained composed, but when Dennis's voice came over the speakers, they all burst into tears.

That night, unable to sleep, Karen prayed for guidance, seeking to understand why Dennis's life had to end as it had. After she finally fell asleep, she had a dream. She and Dennis were sailing on the *Harmony* out in the open sea, and he turned to her and said, "If I ever die, I want to be buried right here, because when you look out at the ocean I want you to think of me." Karen called Barbara early the next morning and told her. Together, they encouraged Shawn to go ahead with her plan. However, it turned out that there was a federal law prohibiting burial at sea. A personal plea was made to President Reagan for special permission, which was granted. Said Karen Lamm disgustedly, "He was put in a bodybag and dumped in the ocean."

When the coroner's report on Dennis's death was made public, it was disclosed that the alcohol level in Dennis's blood was .26, twice that of legal impairment for driving. His liver was enlarged, there was a narrowing of the coronary artery, and there were traces of Valium and cocaine in his tissues. Deputy Medical Examiner J. Lawrence Cogan reported that the drugs and alcohol "may have...bearing [on his death because] these drugs are associated with impairment of judgment of physical activity." Even Dennis's doctor at St. John's Hospital told a reporter, "I'm not an expert on drowning...but sixty-five percent to seventy-five percent of drownings are drug-related...when you've had a couple of drinks and go in the water, your judgment's altered."

Less than a year before, Bob Levine had obtained a new, $1 million insurance policy for Dennis, which named his four children and Shawn as beneficiaries. Previously, Dennis had a policy for only $250,000, which was in danger of cancellation because of erratic payments. Levine had wisely abandoned that policy and obtained the new one—Dennis passed the examination in Bob Levine's office. But when the results of the coroner's report were made public, the Transamerica Occidental Insurance Company refused to pay for Dennis's life-insurance policy, claiming his death was not an accident but attributable to his misuse of alcohol and drugs.

Barbara and Carol decided to settle with the insurance company for a reported forty cents on the dollar, but Shawn lodged a $20 million suit against the company for refusing to pay her and Gage full benefits. The suit asked for $400,000, which Shawn felt she was owed under the life-insurance policy; $50,000 in general damages; and $20 million in punitive damages. To complicate matters for them, Dennis's last will, written in March 1977 after the dissolution of his first marriage to Karen, stated that while no future wives would share in his estate, "any other child of mine who may hereafter be born" would become a beneficiary. Shawn started a separate suit to share in Dennis's estate. Eventually, Los Angeles Superior Court Judge Billy Mills ruled that two-year-old Gage should be an heir to Dennis's estimated $2 million estate. Attorney Allan Cutrow, representing Dennis's estate, did not object to having Gage added as an heir, but pointed out that Dennis's will specifically excluded future spouses.

In the interim, Shawn was hospitalized in the summer of 1984 for what her lawyer termed "inoperable stomach cancer." After exploratory surgery and extensive radiation therapy she has apparently recovered. She told the press at the time, "My life has been the pits since Dennis died. It's a real tragedy."

5

In November 1982 Mike became engaged to Sharon Lee, a pretty seventeen-year-old Chinese girl. In 1985 his charitable organization, the Love Foundation, donated $5,000 to the committee to have rock lyrics rated for listener acceptability. He recently moved to Beverly Hills. He remains a devout practitioner of Transcendental Meditation, the premiere spokesman and showman of the Beach Boys.

Carl Wilson, divorced from Annie, lives in Colorado with his fiancée, Gina Martin, daughter of singer Dean Martin.

Alan Jardine divorced his wife Lynda and married fellow horse breeder Mary Ann. He lives in Big Sur, California.

Marilyn Wilson and her two daughters live in a large home in Encino, California. Along with her cousin Ginger and sister Diane, they are pursuing singing careers as the Honeys. Carnie and Wendy have recently been allowed to meet with their father in an attempt to reunite them under Gene Landy's auspices.

Stephen Love lives in Hanalei, Hawaii, where he surfs every day.

Stanley Love lives on the Pacific Palisades and is still close friends with Rocky Pamplin.

Karen Lamm lives alone on the Marina peninsula and is pursuing a successful acting career.

Carol Wilson is remarried to movie producer Jeffrey Bloom.

Barbara Wilson is raising Dennis's sons Carl and Michael, and is studying to be a psychologist.

Audree Wilson lives with her grandson, Jonah, Carl's son, in a house in the Hollywood Hills.

Brian Wilson lives in a six-bedroom beach house in the Malibu colony along with a full-time staff working for Gene Landy. He is relatively slim and considerably happier than ever before in life. He jogs five miles a day, cooks some of his own meals, and eschews drugs. Although the *Los Angeles Times* reported he calls Landy "Napoleon," the treatment seems to be working for him. "Dr. Landy taught me things that I didn't know," he said recently. "He taught me that a glass or two of wine every other night is just as good as actually taking drugs. You can carry on a good conversation and appreciate the conversation. And he taught me things like manners. I never realized that I used to rush through my meals. He's taught me to eat slower and enjoy them! God, I could never mention all the things he's taught me." Brian and the entire staff wear telephone beepers around their waists to remain in constant contact with Gene Landy, who lives in a house several miles down the coast.

The Beach Boys' most recent album for CBS was released in summer of 1985. Called simply *The Beach Boys*, it was produced by Culture Club producer Steve Levine. While the album was in production, Gene Landy was interviewed for *California* magazine. When asked if he would consider contributing lyrics to the album, Landy replied, "Listen, all the Beach Boys make some contribution, and I'm practically a member of the band.... Brian's got the talent to make the music.... He's the creator. The other band members are just performers. So I'm the one who's making the album."*

In 1985, the group was dropped by CBS Records when their contract ran out.

The Beach Boys continue as a number-one concert attraction, maintaining a $50,000-a-night guarantee. They are one of the most popular live entertainment acts in the world. For millions of fans, they are, and will always be, the essence of the California dream.

*Gene Landy is credited with contributing the lyrics to three songs on the album.

Index

C

M

S

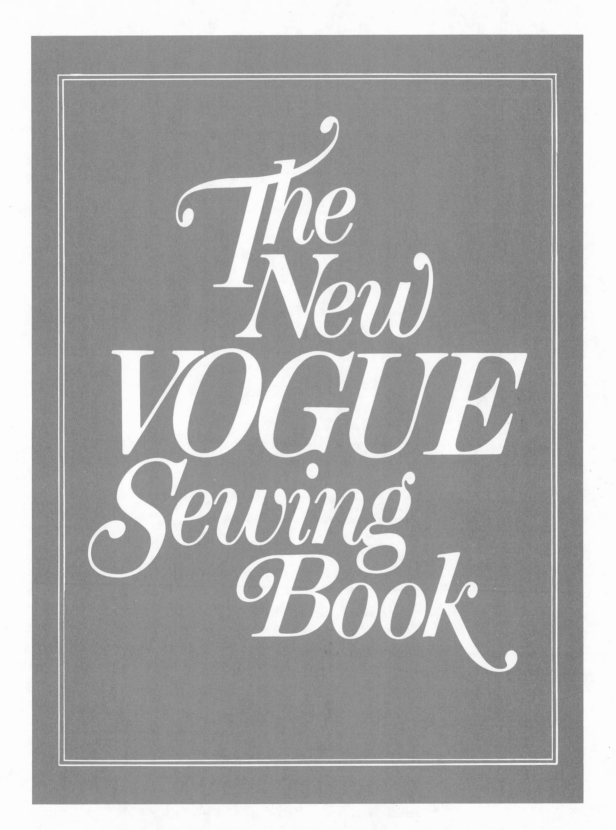

The New VOGUE Sewing Book

BUTTERICK PUBLISHING

Library of Congress Cataloging in Publication Data
Main entry under title:

The New Vogue sewing book.

Previous editions published under title: Vogue
sewing book.
Includes index.
1. Dressmaking. 2. Sewing. I. Title: Vogue
sewing book.
TT515.V63 1980   646.4'04   79-27537
ISBN 0-88421-097-9

Copyright © 1980 by Butterick Publishing   /   708 Third Avenue   /   New York, New York 10017

First Printing, July 1980   Second Printing, December 1980

Manufactured and printed in the United States of America,
published simultaneously in the USA and Canada.

Contents

Acknowledgments

Since 1970 *The Vogue Sewing Book* has been guiding home sewers in the creation of stylish, beautifully constructed clothing. In the years after the first edition appeared, three revisions were made in an effort to keep this valuable reference tool up to date. However, home sewing techniques and materials have changed dramatically in recent years. To ensure that home sewers and students would have the most recent, comprehensive, and accurate information, the editors at Butterick Publishing felt that the time had come for a total overhaul.

To Jeanette Weber, editor of *The New Vogue Sewing Book,* fell the monumental task of updating, reorganizing, and rewriting. Her sure grasp of sewing techniques and fashion is evident on every page. Working closely with the editor was illustrator Phoebe Gaughan, who painstakingly revised existing artwork and created several hundred new fashion and construction illustrations—no small undertaking! Special thanks are due Linnea Leedham and Maryanne Bannon, both of Butterick Publishing; without their perseverance and thorough professionalism, this edition could never have been completed within the time frame allotted. And a vote of heartfelt appreciation to Hugh MacDonald, Director of Operations and Production for Butterick Publishing; the quality of the book's physical appearance is largely the result of his diligent supervision of every stage of its production.

The New Vogue Sewing Book could not have been written without the contributions of the sewing experts at Vogue Patterns. Margaret Lange supplied information on patterns, construction techniques, Very Easy Vogue techniques, and sewing menswear; Timothy Healy assisted with pattern development, fashion vocabulary, and illustrations; Carolyn Galante helped update the sections on Vogue Patterns' designers; Shirley Asper advised on pattern sizes, layouts, adjustments, and alterations, and on construction techniques; and Robin Harding contributed material on garment construction.

Several companies also contributed valuable information. Thanks are extended to E. I. du Pont de Nemours and Company, Inc., Celanese Fibers Marketing Company, The Singer Company, and the American Home Sewing Association for their assistance with technical material, and to the many manufacturers and distributors of sewing notions and materials for their product information.

Although *The New Vogue Sewing Book* has been revised from top to bottom and from front to back, it is still based on *The Vogue Sewing Book.* The first edition of this excellent book involved many talented people from Vogue Patterns. Patricia Perry was the editor, ably assisted by Janet DuBane, Betty Faden, Ellen Kochansky, Jeanne Johnson, Sheila DiBona, Gisela Sachs, Susan Frye, Doreen Williams, Grace Guerrera, Dorothy Martin, Elaine Poprovsky, Lynne Perrella, Joe Molko, and Helen Nemeth.

Subsequent editions required the expertise of Elizabeth J. Musheno, Tony Serino, Barbara Trujillo, Janet Lombardo, Caroline Dill, Marian Bartholomew, Alfred Raphael, Leopoldo A. Hinds, and Paul Milbauer.

Butterick Publishing

1

The Fashion Game

Fashion Sewing as an Art Form

Fashion sewing can be compared, in some ways, to the classic art of sculpture. The sculptor is involved with the medium—manipulating clay or carving stone into a form. Sewing demands the same involvement with a medium—touching, appraising, and working with fabric that will be molded and shaped into a three-dimensional design.

The creative forces necessary to make flat, two-dimensional fabrics take on strong, structural three-dimensional shapes are no less important than those required to chip marble or mold clay. Just as a sculptor expresses dynamic ideas with plaster, bronze, or stone, the seamstress uses fabric to manifest her ideas about fashion.

Inspiration, as both artists know, comes only after attaining a good working knowledge of one's craft, and after a period of deliberation on the specific project. The end result must be firmly in mind before you begin. A sculptor wouldn't tap idly on a piece of marble with a chisel until inspiration came, and it makes no more sense for you to unwrap a length of fabric with your scissors poised until you've considered the relationship between the style and the fabric.

First, the sculptor carefully selects the basic material; it must be just right for the planned creation. No less consideration should be given to the selection of fabric. The silhouette you desire, the mood to be created, the type of body being covered—all are important to the proper fabric selection.

If ten seamstresses were given the same fabric and pattern, probably none of the finished garments would be exactly identical. With an eye to her own pluses and minuses, each would select, adapt, and embellish. The result would be what looks best on her. *A person who sews is a creative artist because she individualizes fashion to her own special preferences and requirements.*

The same principles that make a sculpture visually pleasing apply as well to clothing for the human body. A fashionable woman is aware that she is a three-dimensional form that can be seen from all angles. She must create a pleasing total visual impact by discriminating among colors, textures, and lines to discover the combination that is best suited to her own individual features. She is more than just a seamstress—she is an artisan, too. She draws upon her talents as artist, decorator, and designer to make unique creations which far surpass average ready-to-wear standards. She has, in other words, a good fashion sense.

Like creativity, good fashion sense is not limited only to designers and editors, but is a quality most women have in some degree. If you possess a strong sense of professionalism; if fine workmanship, good lines, and quality impress you; if you find shopping for patterns, fabrics, and trims irresistible; if the world of fashion intrigues and excites you; if you have good personal taste—then you are already on your way to attaining good fashion sense.

One of these qualities, personal taste, is especially important. It is, most broadly, the ability to relate fashion to yourself—your needs, figure, and preferences. Basic to that ability is being able to recognize which clothes and accessories will best accentuate natural good features. Any woman who truly cares about her appearance is very much aware of her figure's limitations, as well as those of her coloring. She analyzes her feelings about clothes—why she never wears pink and loves red; why she feels comfortable in a scoop neckline but not a high one. She forces herself to be open to change, simply for the sake of improving the way she looks and feels.

Just as a sculpture communicates a certain mood or message, a woman's clothes convey much about her. What's your fashion image? Do you picture yourself as a certain type? If not, what image would you like to convey: elegant sophisticate, sweet romantic, perky gamin, tailored classicist, avant garde dazzler? Since there is more than one side to every woman, your wardrobe will undoubtedly reflect the many facets of your personality, with all its feelings and moods. But a woman with strong fashion sense and personal taste relates her various looks to form a unified image, which conveys the confident air of a woman who knows who she is and enjoys being herself. How does one achieve this? Pick up ideas from your pattern catalogues, magazines, advertising, window displays, and other well-dressed women. Even though styles and colors shift seasonally, an awareness of your personal fashion identity will enable you to discriminately choose and select among them to organize your particular look.

The Fundamentals of Your Art

Every artist has had to absorb and apply the basic principles of design to achieve the desired artistic effect. You should do the same; once firmly grounded in them, you may confidently choose to follow them with a strict interpretation or with artistic license to achieve your exact fashion effect.

- ☐ **HARMONY** is achieved when all elements are working together in a pleasing manner. It refers to elements of likeness, but not necessarily sameness; the key here is appropriateness and relativity.
- ☐ **PROPORTION** requires all parts to be related to one another in size, length, and bulk.
- ☐ **BALANCE** is achieved by maintaining equal amounts of interest in either direction from the natural center of interest.
- ☐ **RHYTHM** is created by the eye moving smoothly and easily, connecting points of interest without jerking from point to point.
- ☐ **EMPHASIS** means attracting the eye to one feature and subordinating all others.

Every fashion idea you have should be backed with an understanding not only of these principles, but also of the artistic components of color, print, texture, line, proportion, and balance. Just as the sculptor must understand the qualities of the raw material, whether it be rock, clay, or metal, you must understand the qualities of your fabric—color, print, and texture. Then you transform it into a design with the same components the sculptor uses to transform the material into a sculpture—line, proportion, and balance. Our aim in the next few pages is to provide guidelines in hopes that you'll find inspiration there to create a prettier, newer, and more fashionable you.

Color

What is the first thing noticed about a garment? Invariably the answer is its color. We talk about "the woman in the blue dress" or "my brown suit"; only a designer would refer to "the slim low-waisted dress with inverted pleats and bateau neckline." This fact alone makes color quite worthy of consideration and a power to be placed at your disposal. Thus a fashion-conscious woman must be aware of the language and principles of color, immersing herself in all the thrilling effects that color can produce. Color know-how combined with a comprehension of her own needs and requirements can make the difference between being "sensational" or just "well-dressed."

Elements of Color

This is the technical language commonly used to describe color; learn it well, referring to the diagram and the color wheel in the first section of color photographs.

HUE, a term often used interchangeably with color, is the quality or characteristic by which we distinguish one color from another. The **primary** hues—red, yellow, and blue—are the basic building blocks of color from which all others are blended. The **secondary** hues, produced by mixing two primaries, are orange, green, and violet (purple). The **tertiary** hues (often called intermediates) stem from various combinations of the basic six; they are the "double-name" colors, such as yellow-green and blue-violet.

VALUE is the lightness or darkness of a color. Hues with white added are called **tints** and are higher in value than the original colors. To produce lower values, black is added to hues to create **shades.** Hues differ in their inherent value as well; yellow, for example, is higher in value than blue.

INTENSITY refers to the brightness or dullness of color. Again, certain hues have a higher intensity than others—orange is higher than violet, for example. **Tones** are hues with their complementary color or gray added, which reduces their intensity.

COLOR SCHEMES are many in number, but three of them are most common. A **monochromatic** color scheme uses various values and intensities of one color, or one color with black and white. These are sure and easy schemes to achieve, but the danger of monotony lurks if the variations are too similar. Use both ends of the spectrum to add contrast, such as beige to chocolate brown. An **analogous** color scheme utilizes hues which are closely related on the color wheel, or in other words, that contain similar components, such as blue, blue-green, and green. These are the real "mood makers" and are often the most pleasing and restful combinations. A **complementary** color scheme is one which involves direct opposites on the color wheel, such as red and green or blue and orange. These are exceedingly strong, bold combinations. To truly enhance each other, judgment must be used with variations in value and intensity, as complementaries used in combinations make each other look stronger. Remember that colors should never be seen as isolated entities, but in relation to each other.

Now, armed with an understanding of the basic concepts of color, turn your attention to what color can do for you. As every artist and advertising expert knows, color has profound psychological effects on all of us, as evidenced by such expressions as "seeing red," "green with envy," "black mood," "yellow streak," and "feeling blue." Some colors are cheering, compelling, vivacious, frivolous, active, and just plain fun, while others are restful, serene, relaxed, subtle, and dignified. Some lift the spirits, others subdue them; they can be soft and fresh or brassy and bold. It is not merely by chance, therefore, that we may reach into the closet for our brightest dress on a rainy day, or slip into a pastel dressing gown to relax after a hectic day.

But color can do far more for you than reflect or influence your multitude of moods and images. The skillful use of color can help present you at your loveliest. Too often women are led merely by whim, pure preference, or simple prejudice in their color selection, and not enough by what looks best on them. Always take your personal coloring into consideration. Before you buy any fabric, hold it up to your face and take a long, thoughtful look into the mirror. How does it relate to the color of your hair, eyes, and complexion? Don't mistakenly think that just because that jade green dress looks so good on you, kelly green will be just as becoming; often even a slight variation in value or intensity can make all the difference in the world. Always let your eye—or the helpful eye of a reliable friend—be the final judge.

Play tricks with color by discovering the optical illusions they can create. They can create impressions of size; cool colors of blue, green, and violet make the figure appear smaller, warm colors of red, yellow, and orange increase the apparent size of the figure. The degree of brightness or dullness can also affect size appearance—brighter colors make you look larger, duller colors make you look smaller. Boldly contrasting colors will create an impression of greater size; a more subtle color scheme will appear more compact. Another thing to note is that the eye will be attracted first to the brightest of contrasting colors; use this principle to draw your viewer's eye to or from particular areas.

Accessories can be the answer to many of your color quandaries. Use a gaily colored scarf or belt to add new spark to a dull dress, or dark shoes and bag to bring a boldly colored dress a bit closer to earth. If your figure demands subtle coloring, don't say goodbye to bright colors forever—use them in a scarf, bracelets, or a necklace. Let a bright sash riding on the hipline of your dress distract from bulk above the waist, or use a bright necklace to coax the eye away from excess width through the hipline.

The manipulation of color is not only one of the most artistic elements of fashion sewing but one of the most exciting. Experiment with it—contrast, complement, combine, or go solid. Don't be afraid of new colors or let yourself be boxed into a one-color wardrobe. Go on a creative fling to create a more colorful you.

Dark, cool, or subdued colors recede.
Light, warm, or bright colors advance.

Print

Vivid Print/Subtle Print   Small Plaid/Large Plaid

From plaids to paisleys, stripes to florals, dots to borders, prints are fashion's fun, and often its beauty as well. To create a truly harmonious effect, however, they must be carefully related to all the other design elements of your garment.

Prints are first and foremost combinations of colors, and the same rules apply to them as to solids. Vividly contrasting colors or bright shades will appear larger than subtle combinations or calmer shades. Prints can give you an advantage you may miss with solids; if you love a color that is unflattering on you, you may be able to wear it combined in a print with a more suitable color. Most prints will have a dominant color, and that is the one to consider in relation to your coloring; it will usually be either the brightest shade or the one that occupies the largest area (such as the background). Another thing to keep in mind is that colors used in combination may affect each other's apparent hue—red and blue used together, for example, may appear purple.

Also consider garment lines when selecting a print. While a solid color may require intricate lines for interest, they may be overwhelmed or appear cluttered in a print. Be aware that plaids, stripes, and many other prints have lines of their own, and make sure they are flattering to your build. Also relate the direction and shape of the various lines; a curved bodice seam would only work against an angular print and be lost.

Last and most importantly, relate the print to your own figure. A print that is greatly out of scale with the wearer and the garment will emphasize the contrast, making their size only more obvious. Use the placement of your print to direct attention to or from your pluses and minuses. A border print placed at the hemline will distract from the bodice or hips and draw attention to your legs. A dominant plaid or stripe will attract the eye, so place it only at attractive locations. Placing a dominant large-scale motif at the bust or derrière is definitely to be avoided.

Texture

Nubby Fabric/Smooth Fabric

Stiff Fabric/Soft Fabric

The texture of your fabric is created by the characteristics of its fiber (wool, silk, etc.) and the manner of its construction (knitted, woven, etc.). All too often overlooked or taken for granted, it can be a special asset in the business of illusion-making.

The object is to create fluid eye movements in which the eye stops to rest at attractive, predetermined points of emphasis. Stiff textures hang straight without draping and thus will slide the eye smoothly up and down the lines of a sleek silhouette. One figure problem can be concealed this way, but overall roundness cannot. On the other hand, clingy fabrics rendered in straight or very simple designs do just one thing—reveal. If your figure is less than perfect, use them only in softly draped styles. And, of course, gauzy transparency should never reveal an unattractive body area.

Textural effects also contribute to an impression of size. Rough, thick textures always seem more bulky than they really are. If you adore chunky tweeds but wish to avoid their bulk, use them just at a slender section of your body, perhaps in a vest or skirt. Shiny, lustrous fabrics reflect more light and thus make you appear larger; just the opposite is true of rougher, duller textures. In other words, velvet, which absorbs light, may be a better choice in an evening dress than glittering sequins for a heavier woman.

Line

Line, as it applies to fashion, is often used synonymously with style. Every design is a carefully conceived structure of lines and shapes. The final garment will present three major sets of lines to the viewer's eye: body lines, silhouette lines, and detail lines. The ability to relate them to one another and to you in a pleasing and flattering manner will require, therefore, a basic understanding of the visual element of line. Set out to discover what line can do for you. Realize that lines influence eye movements, establish shape, and form moods, just as color does. Direction and placement of line will be your main concern.

The first thing you should realize about line is that our eyes are conditioned to move naturally in the direction we read—left to right, top to bottom. While there is a certain "pull" between the two directions, if given two equal intersecting lines, the eye will follow the horizontal more readily than the vertical. This leads us to another important concept—lines rarely are equal, as there are several factors that tend to make certain lines dominant. If a line is longer, wider, brighter, or more often repeated than another, it will be more dominant. A final point to keep in mind is that the eye follows a straight line directly and rapidly, making it the most severe and architectural line, while the eye moves more slowly along a curved line, making it a softer, relaxed line often used to lead gracefully from one point to another.

Thus lines often play tricks with our eyes and create illusions, and you want all those illusions to work for and not against you. Your primary target: to be a master of illusion and camouflage by knowing the rules of the fashion game. First, be your own best inspiration by taking a realistic look at yourself. What has nature given you that is worth emphasizing or concealing? Then follow the suggestions below to put line to work to make a more appealing you. After all, beauty is in the eye of the beholder, and the clever use of line can subtly coax the viewer's eye just where you want it.

Never forget the relationship of your design to your raw material. Remember that fabric patterns often have line and direction of their own. For example, horizontal stripes will be dominant even if the dress is vertically seamed, and even a less obviously directional fabric could possibly distract from your intentions. And when buying a plaid, check first to see if the plaid lines are dominant in a particular direction.

These are the basic "rules" for using line, but don't be misled into thinking they are necessarily hard and fast. The relationship of several lines is invariably greater than the direction of one of them. You need not do without unflattering lines entirely; simply do not use them as **dominant** lines. Regardless of your figure or the direction of the line, always be sure that the garment lines do not draw attention to an unattractive portion of the body; a horizontal across too-large hips will not look any better on a tall woman than on a short one.

Vertical Lines

Horizontal Lines

Verticals

Choose the strong classical effect of a vertical line to appear taller and thinner by leading the eye in an up and down direction. Single verticals give the strongest impression of height; when they are repeated at even intervals across the garment, the illusion of length is blunted because our eyes tend to move sideways from line to line as well. A straight or long unbroken silhouette also creates a vertical impression.

Horizontals

It is common knowledge that horizontal lines emphasize width, especially when two are used together. Placing a single horizontal line above or below the median of the body can, however, create an illusion of length throughout the longer area. Since horizontals are the strongest lines, avoid placing them at unflattering locations on the body. You can distract attention from a horizontal by using an opposing vertical, by placing it at other than the center, or by modifying it in the form of a diagonal or curve.

Diagonals

The modifying effect of diagonals depends primarily upon the angle and length of the line. As shown, the shorter diagonal line will lead the eye from side to side, giving an impression of width, while the longer line leads the eye equally downward and sideways for a longer, narrower look. And remember that the line should always move in the same direction as our eyes, from left to right, for the most pleasing effect. Diagonals possess both the discipline of straight lines and the softness of curves.

Curves

Whether they are created by shaped seaming or edges or soft draping, curved lines perform the same function of illusion as straight lines but in a less obvious manner. Curved lines also emphasize the curves of the feminine form by repetition, making them more defined. Many times a line that would be unflattering if straight can be nicely worn if modified by a curve. A curved bodice seam or front closing will be softer visually than a horizontal or vertical seam.

Diagonal Lines

Curved Lines

Proportion and Balance

Have you ever changed the hem on the skirt of a suit, and suddenly the jacket and skirt no longer seemed to go together quite the way they did before? Or seen a woman in a top and skirt that seemed to coordinate in almost every visible way but somehow didn't look quite right together? Perhaps you've stood before a mirror wondering why the style that looked so great on your best friend looks so odd on you. All of these problems may very likely be caused by an error in proportion and balance. The skillful use of the color, print, and texture of your fabric and the lines of your garment will all be for naught unless they are artfully related by these two elements. That beautifully coordinated, "well put together" look that accompanies a truly well-dressed woman is in large part due to an eye well-trained in the subtleties of proportion and balance.

Proportion

Balance

Proportion

This applies to the space relationships within a design, and involves relating such measurements as size and bulk. The most visually pleasing division of an area is one that creates the two aesthetic qualities of unity and variety—in other words, one that creates areas that are similar but not so alike as to be dull. Areas of identical size or exact divisions of space like halves, fourths, or thirds used together, while not displeasing, are often less interesting than divisions that are just far enough away from basic dimensions that the eye does not catch them immediately. Thus the most pleasing relationships, in mathematical terms, are two to three, three to five, five to eight, and so on, rather than two to two, two to four, two to six, etc. *Scale* is a term that also refers to size relationships; similar sizes are in scale with each other, widely disparate sizes are not and are visually jarring.

Balance

A design is balanced when an equal amount of interest is maintained in either direction from the natural center of interest. There are two kinds of balance: formal and informal. Formal balance is achieved when two halves of a design are exactly the same. If two halves are visually balanced but are not identical, it is called informal or asymmetrical balance. This is accomplished by shifting the center of interest with emphasis. *Emphasis* attracts the eye to one feature or area and subordinates the others.

Your Fashion Analysis

On the previous pages we have discussed the basics of artistic theory. As you know, these elements take a very active part in the overall visual impact of clothing. As important as it is to relate the various parts or areas of your garment to one another, several other elements need to be considered in order to establish a total, "put together" look.

Of course, the most important thing is to relate everything to you. Don't forget that you have proportions of your own as well. Thus, a garment that is beautifully balanced and proportioned on the hanger may not be so on you. The next step is to learn how to use art principles in relation to the individual needs of your figure.

Height

To help you learn more about your figure, we, as a pattern company, have done extensive surveys of the possible figure variations that may occur. The results of these studies indicate that *height* is the single most important factor when trying to camouflage a figure problem or trying to emphasize a particularly positive feature.

Automatically, three basic height divisions come to mind: short, average, and tall. But we believe there are really only two true groupings—*Short* and *Tall.* Even though a woman's height in inches may seem to make her average, this designation is misleading. Actually, average is a statistic, not necessarily the ideal. Due to their bone structure, build, and individual features, most women appear to be either short or tall. Described on the following pages are the important principles that the short woman, 5'4" and under, and the tall woman, 5'7" and over, should follow when selecting garments. If you fall somewhere in between, study yourself to determine the category into which your bone structure places you and the impression of height you wish to convey—delightfully small or gracefully tall. You will find that once you have established yourself as either one or the other you will have a fresh approach toward the clothes that are right for you.

Short

Don't consider being short a figure problem. Your attitude toward yourself is crucial; you must consider your height an advantage and boldly proceed with that very important outlook. Of course, there are some practical tips to follow before you can fool the observer into thinking that you are actually more petite or slimmer or perhaps taller than you really are. Above all, dress to your own scale. At this point, if you have not done so already, read Proportion and Balance, on page 16, as small women should be particularly concerned with these principles. For example, a short woman, especially if she is not model-slim, will do well to avoid very large prints; they will be greatly out of scale with her build and the size of her garment, making her seem even shorter and wider.

You should concentrate on an uncluttered appearance with everything in proportion to your height. Begin by avoiding the unnecessary bulk of billowing skirts or very heavy fabrics. Short, fitted jackets, gently flared silhouettes, and delicate detailing are your best choices. The scale of accessories should be appropriate as well. They can help pull an outfit together into a neat, fashionable picture or completely destroy all your devoted efforts. Don't let yourself look overwhelmed by massive jewelry or overpowered by a tremendous handbag.

Line, in both fabric and garment design, will be one of your most valuable tools. If you want to add inches to your height, no matter what your weight, depend upon the illusions vertical lines will provide. One-piece dresses with shoulder-to-hemline seaming will give the strongest, most immediate impression of height. Lengthening details such as long sleeves, V-necklines, pleats, or raised or lowered waistlines will all tend to heighten your appearance. Stay away from anything that may cut your figure by interrupting the up and down movement of the eye, such as wide belts, tight waists, very short skirts, or repeated horizontal construction.

Should you not be as slim as you would like, a little extra thought is required. On the whole, vertical lines are perfect slenderizers, but the appropriate ones for you should be chosen with discretion. Avoid gathers or pleats unless they are stitched down to the hip. Wear simple lines. Use a single vertical line or the repeated vertical seaming of a princess silhouette to whittle away the inches while adding to your height.

Color should be a very influential factor when dressing. In general, one-color outfits or monochromatic costumes will contribute to elongating your appearance. Color-coordinated accessories, such as belts or shoes, can be most helpful to your illusion. Warm colors and bright colors will tend to increase your stature visibly. Subtle colors may seem to diminish your size, but be sure they do so in a beguiling feminine fashion rather than making you blend unnoticed into the background.

If you are slim, your color range is almost unlimited, although you will find that solid colors, neat textures, and small prints are best for your body build. The same is true for the slightly heavy woman, but the use of vivid colors or shiny fabrics should be restricted to well-placed splashes for accent.

Tall

If you are tall, you have an immediate fashion edge. You are the fortunate woman who can carry the exotic prints or dramatic designs that can only be draped over a taller frame. Even though you have this head start, you must be as concerned with proportion and

Proportion

One Color/Contrasting Colors

balance as short women. You will need to make an effort to wear clothes that are right for your size. Very tiny prints on a tall, large woman will emphasize the contrast between their delicacy and the size of the woman wearing them. You should take advantage of your size; select colorful prints, nubby fabrics, and bold stripes. Balance your height with horizontal divisions to present an impression of equality to the observer's eye. Wide belts, medium-long jackets, and crosswise stripes will contribute toward your goal of optical equilibrium.

Accessories should also warrant your concern when trying to maintain proper proportion and balance. Work with your height and lean toward large jewelry and handbags, and do indulge in some of the more daring fashion accents.

Line, in both garment and fabric design, should be consistently utilized to your advantage. Should you have a full figure, lean toward easy fitting, unfussy silhouettes, and curved or diagonal vertical lines. Gently lowered necklines with ties or collars will emphasize a pretty face while balancing a heavier figure. Orderly prints will be better looking than splashy plaids or repeated horizontal stripes. If you are extremely tall and you wish to appear shorter, cut your height dramatically with wide colorful cummerbunds, crosswise yokes, and other horizontal construction lines. Of course, if you are tall and willowy, the world of fashion is open to you. Try using frills to fill out your curves or be dramatic with yards of drapey, clinging fabric in unusual patterns. Appreciate your capacity to follow the whims of fashion or to branch out on your own.

Color can also be cleverly used to your advantage. Remember that cool colors as well as the duller hues make the figure appear smaller. Make your color selections according to your weight and width. As always, to appear more slender, wear medium to dark color values in your solids and soft shades for prints, plaids, and textures. To add bulk and roundness to the slim figure, select bright colors with shiny or chunky textures. Contrasting separates are always recommended for the tall woman. They will cut your height no matter what your girth and successfully balance your appearance. The degree of contrast and the division of the areas will influence the final effect. A note of caution before you get carried away with your use of color: make a conscientious effort to keep your total silhouette in mind and avoid a busy look.

Small Print/Large Print

Vertical Stripes/Horizontal Stripes

Figure

In addition to the basic concepts related to height, your individual physical characteristics also deserve special consideration. Bosom size, width of hips, length of waist, etc., all are prime problem areas for many women, and the solution for these problems is closely related to height. Camouflage can be accomplished with the carefully applied use of color, print, or texture. Well-placed lines in the form of trim or accessories can draw the viewer's attention away from negative features and to figure pluses. If you are large-busted but have small hips, the bodice is already heavier visually than the skirt, and you may need to make the skirt longer, fuller, bolder, or more intricate to balance the impression of weight. Conversely, ruffles or a bold print in the bodice may help distract from the additional width of large hips in a skirt. If you are very long-legged, an Empire style will simply accentuate the lack of natural proportion, in the same way that it will distract from it if you are short-legged. And don't forget to relate the size of a print or fabric pattern to your body proportions as well. Be sure that it is always in scale with both your build and garment dimensions, as a too-large or too-small design will only emphasize your size by contrast.

You can shift emphasis and give an illusion of weight or size by using a print in opposition to a solid, intricacy to simplicity, a bright color to a duller one, a heavily textured fabric to a flat fabric, a shiny finish to a dull one. For example, a print skirt may help to balance a solid blouse for a top-heavy woman, but could overwhelm the blouse for a large-hipped woman. Even a woman with ideal measurements may need intricate seaming, long full sleeves, a shiny fabric, or a bright scarf on the solid blouse if the print skirt is very bright or very full; on the other hand, if the print is quite conservative, she may need a simpler or quieter blouse to balance it properly. In other words, each design element does not work by itself but interacts and relates to the others to create the whole.

But, of course, all the theories and warnings in the world won't do you any good until you train your eye to perceive what is in perfect balance and proportion and what isn't. How can you gain this type of artistic sensitivity? By learning to look honestly and objectively. Analyze the composition of various fashion approaches you see in magazines, illustrations, store windows, and on women you see on the street. But most importantly, **look at yourself**. Learn to "practice" in front of a mirror. Try different combinations, lengths, and accessories, all the time asking yourself questions and answering them objectively. Are your accessories too large or small, delicate or massive, bright or dull? Are your lengths, colors, details, widths, and textures related? Are the design of your fabric and the lines in your garment in proportion to your size and build? Be as honest as possible; if in doubt, ask someone whose judgment you respect. When you have analyzed your present wardrobe, continue to do so with every new outfit you make. It is not an indication of vanity, but just of a desire to always look your very best. After awhile, putting together a well-balanced and proportioned look will seem as second nature as straightening a crooked picture on a wall.

The Vocabulary of Fashion

This list of fashion terminology was collected to give you a firm grasp of the language used by designers and fashionable women everywhere. It includes terms commonly used to describe the silhouettes, styles, and details of clothing design as well as fabric qualities, notions, and construction procedures. We have also included French terms that have become part of our fashion vocabulary. A knowledgeable and conversational use of the words listed here will certainly increase your fashion confidence.

a

A-line Dress or skirt resembling shape of an A.

accessories Articles of apparel that complete a costume, e.g., shoes, jewelry, etc.

allonger (a-lohn-zhay) Fr. To lengthen, to give clothing a longer appearance.

amincir (a-men-seer) Fr. To make thin; to give a slender look.

appliqué (a-plee-kay) Fr. Motif applied to cloth or garment.

ascot Broad neckscarf; tied so that one end falls over the other.

asymmetrical One-sided, not geometrically balanced.

atelier (a-te-lyay) Fr. Dressmaking establishment; work room or studio.

au courant (oh-koo-rahn) Fr. Up to the moment; to know all about it.

avant-garde (a-vahn-gard) Fr. Ahead of fashion or trend.

b

backing Fabric joined to wrong side of garment or garment area, typically for reinforcement or opacity.

balmacaan Loose overcoat.

band Strip used to hold, ornament, or complete any part of garment or accessory.

bateau Neckline following curve of collar bone.

bell sleeve Full sleeve, flaring at lower edge like a bell.

bias Diagonal direction of fabric. *True bias* is at a 45° angle to grainlines.

binding Strip encasing edges as finish or trim.

bishop sleeve Sleeve that is full in the lower part, either loose or held by band at wrist.

blind hem Hem sewn invisibly with hand stitches.

blouson Bloused effect of fullness gathered in at and falling over a seam, typically bodice over skirt.

bodice Portion of garment above the waist.

bodkin Sharp, slender tool used to pull fabrics through narrow enclosed space, such as casing.

bolero Short jacket that ends above waist; Spanish origin.

bolt Unit in which fabric is packaged and sold by manufacturer. Usually contains 12-20 yards.

boning Flexible strips used to stiffen seams or edges.

border Strip of self-fabric or commercial trimming used to finish edge.

boutique A small retail store in which accessories and miscellaneous fashion items are sold. Often part of a couture house.

c

caftan Long, coat-like garment fastened with long sash, having extra long sleeves.

camisole Short, sleeveless underbodice; often joined to skirt and worn under jacket. Also, lingerie-like outer garment worn as a blouse.

cap sleeve Short sleeve just covering the shoulder and not continued under the arm.

cape Sleeveless outer garment hanging loosely from shoulders, covering back and arms.

cardigan Close fitting collarless jacket, sweater, or bodice with center front closing.

cartridge pleat Rounded pleat that extends out rather than lying flat.

chemise Dress or undergarment styled like a loose slip or long undershirt.

COLLARS

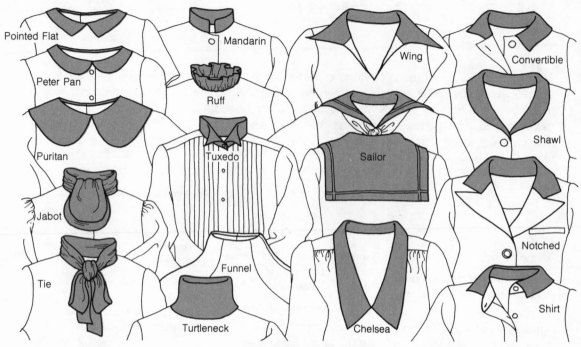

chesterfield Plain coat usually having velvet notched collar.

chevron V-shaped stripes.

chez (shay) Fr. At home, shop of; as chez Dior, Lanvin, etc.

chic (sheek) Fr. Originality and style in dress.

clip Cut in fabric to allow ease on curves or corners.

closure That which opens or closes a garment (buttons, etc.), or area on which they are placed.

coatdress Dress with coat-like lines and front closing.

collection All apparel exhibited at fashion showing. Spring and fall are the two major periods each year when collections are shown to trade and clientèle (customers).

colorfast Refers to fabric that will not fade or run during cleaning or laundering.

contrasting Opposing; showing off differences of color, fabric, shading, etc.

convertible Notched collar that can be worn either buttoned at neck or open with lapels.

couture (koo-tür) Fr. Sewing or needle work. Product of a seamstress; seam.

couturier (koo-tü-ryay) m. or **couturière** (koo-tü-ryare) f. Fr. Dressmaker; designer; head of a dressmaking house.

cowl Soft drape of fabric at neckline.

cravat Necktie folded or tied at front with ends tucked inside garment.

crew Round neckline that hugs the throat.

culotte Trouser-like garment with flaring leg portions to simulate a skirt.

cummerbund Wide sash worn around the waist.

cut-in-one Two or more sections cut in one piece, such as sleeve and bodice.

d

décolleté (day-kawl-ęh-tay) Fr. Cut low at neckline, exposing neck and back or cleavage of bosom as in formal evening dress.

démodé (day-maw-day) Fr. Old-fashioned, out-of-style, unfashionable.

dernier cri (dern-yay-kree) Fr. The latest fashion; the last word.

dickey Detachable shirt front.

dirndl Garment with full gathered skirt.

dolman Sleeve set into a deep armhole so as to resemble a kimono sleeve.

double-breasted Front closing

DRESS SILHOUETTES

Shift

A-Line

Tent

Yoke

Empire

High Waist

Sheath

Low Waist

Tunic

Princess

Blouson

Shirt Waist

Asymmetrical Closing

that overlaps enough to allow two rows of buttons.

dressmaking Art of sewing dresses, skirts, etc., distinguished from tailoring.

drum lining Lining not sewn into garment seams.

e

edgestitch Topstitching placed very close to finished edge.

edwardian Style of 1901–1910 when Edward VII was king of England.

elegance (ay-lay-gahns) Fr. Quality of being elegant; tasteful luxury.

empire Style of French empire period; high waistline, décolleté, loose, straight skirt.

enclosed seams Concealed by two garment layers.

ensemble The entire costume. Usually, dress and coat.

epaulet Shoulder trimming, usually a band secured with a button.

epaulet sleeve Sleeve with square-cut shoulder section extending into neck in form of yoke. Strap sleeve.

eyelet Small, round finished hole in garment or fabric.

f

face To finish an edge by applying a fitted piece of fabric, binding, etc. Also, the right side of the fabric.

fagoting Decorative stitch used to join two fabric sections that are spread apart.

fancy work Hand embroidery and needlework.

favoring Rolling one garment section slightly over another at the edge to conceal the seam.

feathering Removing stains by rubbing lightly in a circular motion from the outside edge of the stain to its center.

finger press Pressing small area by creasing with fingers.

finish Any means of completing raw garment edge.

flap Shaped garment piece attached by only one edge.

flare Portion of garment that spreads out or widens.

fleur de lis (fler-de-lee) Fr. Lily flower; heraldic emblem of former French royalty. Used as design in fabric, embroidery, jewelry, etc.

fly Fabric used as lap to conceal opening in garment.

full-fashioned Garments knitted flat and shaped by dropping stitches, in contrast to circular knits that are shaped by seams.

funnel collar Flaring outward at the top.

g

garni (gar-nee) Fr. Trimmed, garnished.

godet Triangular piece of cloth set into a garment for fullness or decoration.

gore Tapered section of garment; wider at lower edge.

grommet Large metal eyelet.

grosgrain Fabric or, most commonly, ribbon having heavy crosswise ribs.

gusset Fabric piece inserted at underarm to give ease in sleeve area.

h

halter Neckline having band around neck, attached to front of a backless bodice.

harem pants Garment with legs softly draped and gathered to narrow lining or ankle band.

haute couture (oht-koo-tür) Fr. High fashion, creative fashion design. Couturier houses as a group.

i, j

inset Fabric section or trim inserted within garment for fit or decoration.

interlining Layer of fabric between lining and underlining for warmth.

jabot Ruffle worn down front of bodice and fastened at neck.

jerkin Short jacket, coat, or vest; usually sleeveless pullover.

jewel Simple, round neckline at base of neck.

jumper One-piece garment with low cut bodice attached to skirt.

jumpsuit Pants and bodice joined in one garment.

jupe (zhup) Fr. Skirt.

k

keyhole Round neckline with inverted wedge-shaped opening at front.

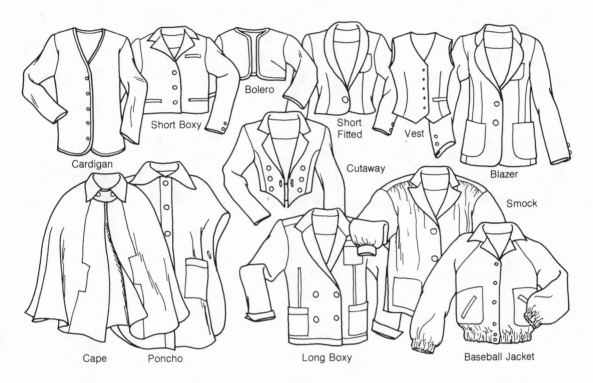

Cardigan

Short Boxy

Bolero

Short Fitted

Vest

Blazer

Cutaway

Smock

Cape

Poncho

Long Boxy

Baseball Jacket

kick pleat Pleat used for ease in a narrow skirt; may be a knife, inverted, or box pleat.

kilt Pleated, plaid skirt with unpleated panel in front.

kimono Loose, wide-sleeved robe, fastened at waist with obi; also used to describe style of sleeve cut in one piece with the bodice.

l

lantern sleeve Bell sleeve with wrist section joining at bottom, creating a shape resembling a lantern.

lap Any edge that extends over another edge, as on a placket.

lapels Part of garment that turns back, especially front part of garment that folds back to form continuation of collar.

layout Cutting chart on instruction sheet showing placement of pattern pieces.

line Style, outline, or effect given by the cut and construction of the garment.

lingerie Women's lightweight underclothing.

longuette Style derived from below-knee hem lengths.

m

macramé Bulky, knotted lace woven in geometrical patterns.

maillot (my-yo) Fr. One piece, tight-fitting bathing suit.

maison de couture (me-zohn-de-koo-tür) Fr. Dressmaking establishment.

mandarin Small standing collar that hugs neck.

mannequin (man-eh-kin) Fr. Dressmaker form, dummy. Person wearing new clothes to present at fashion show or collection.

marking Transfer of construction symbols from paper pattern to fabric.

martingale A half-belt or strap, generally placed on the back of a garment.

matelasser (ma-tla-say) Fr. To pad or cushion.

middy Slip-on blouse with typical sailor collar.

mini Hem length falling at mid-thigh.

miter Diagonal seaming at a corner.

mode (mawd) Fr. Fashion, manner, vogue.

motif Unit of design; used as decoration or pattern.

25

NECKLINES

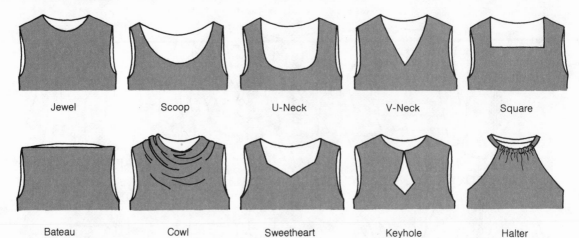

| Jewel | Scoop | U-Neck | V-Neck | Square |

| Bateau | Cowl | Sweetheart | Keyhole | Halter |

mounting Term sometimes used for underlining. Two layers of fabric are based together and sewn as one.

n

nap Soft surface with fibers that lie smoothly in one direction.

negligée Decorative dressing gown, worn indoors by women.

notch *v,* Cutting wedges from seam allowances. *n,* Pattern symbol transferred to fabrics to indicate matching points.

notions Items other than fabric or pattern required to complete garment.

o

obi Broad Japanese sash.

opening Synonymous with closure; also, fashion showing of apparel for season.

overblouse Blouse not tucked in at waistline.

overskirt Decorative skirt worn over another garment.

p

pantsuit Women's suit consisting of jacket with pants instead of skirt.

passementerie (pahs-mahn-tree) Fr. Trimming, particularly heavy embroideries or edgings.

peasant sleeve Full sleeve set into dropped shoulder and usually gathered into wristband.

peignoir Originally, a robe of terrycloth worn instead of a towel; now, a robe that matches a nightgown.

pelt Skin of animal with fur intact.

peplum Small flounce or extension of garment around hips, usually from bodice.

peter pan Flat shaped collar, with round corners.

piece Specified length of goods as rolled from loom.

piece goods Fabric sold in

pieces of fixed length or by the yard.

pin basting Pinning seams before stitching.

pinafore Sleeveless apron-like fashion worn over a dress or other garment.

pinking Cutting raw edge with pinking or scalloping shears to retard raveling.

pivot Stitching around corner by leaving needle in fabric, raising presser foot, and turning fabric in new direction.

placket Garment opening fastened with zipper, snaps, buttons, or hooks and eyes.

plunge Neckline cut so low as to reveal curve of breasts.

prefold Folding and pressing garment section or binding before applying to garment.

preshape Shaping fabric into curves like those of area to which it will be applied; done with steam before stitching to garment.

preshrink Contracting fabric before construction.

prêt à porter (pret-ah-portay)

Fr. Ready to wear; more current than "confection."

princess line Garment fitted with seams instead of darts.

purl Stitch made by bringing needle out across thread so as to hold it; also looped edge of embroidery, lace.

r

raw edge Unfinished edge of fabric.

remnant Unsold end of piece goods, leftover piece of cloth.

répertoire (rep-e-twar) Fr. Collection of works by a designer.

right side Finished side of fabric, outside of garment.

rip Removing stitches improperly placed; also, tearing fabric along straight grain.

roll Desired curve and fold (commonly on a collar); shaping established by pressing, pad stitching, etc.

s

sash Ornamental band or scarf worn around the body.

scalloped Cut into semicircles at edge or border.

scoop Deep neckline cut to shape of U.

seam allowance Width of fabric beyond seamline, not including garment area.

seam binding Ribbon-like tape used to finish edges.

secure Fasten permanently by means of knot, backstitching, etc.

self Of same material as rest of garment.

selvage Lengthwise finished edges on all woven fabrics.

semi-fitted Fitted to conform partly, but not too closely, to shape of figure.

shank Link between button and fabric to allow for thickness of overlapping fabric.

shawl Triangular piece of fabric worn around shoulders.

sheath Close-fitting dress with straight skirt.

sheer Transparent fabric; comes in varying weights.

shift Loose-fitting dress.

shirtwaist Dress with bodice details similar to shirt.

shrinking Contracting fabric with steam or water to eliminate excess in specific area.

silhouette Outline or contour of figure or garment.

PANTS

Straight

Tapered

Bermuda Shorts

Boy Shorts

Short Shorts

Flared

Warm-Up Pants

Jumpsuit

Culottes

Evening Pants

SKIRTS

Straight

Dirndl

A-Line

Gathered

Yoke

Wrap

4-Gore

6-Gore

Knife Pleated

Single Front Pleat

Double Front Pleat

single-breasted Center front closing with enough flap to allow one row of buttons.

slash Cut taken in fabric to facilitate construction.

slit Long, narrow opening; also, to cut lengthwise.

soft suit Dressy suit with a minimum of inner construction, also *dressmaker suit.*

soigné (swa-nyay) Fr. Well-groomed, highly finished, carefully done.

soutache (soo-tash) Fr. Narrow braid trim.

sportswear Garments meant for informal or casual wear.

stay Means of maintaining shape of garment area.

stiletto Pointed instrument for punching holes in fabric; smaller version called *awl.*

stole Long scarf wrapped around shoulders.

surplice Bodice with one side wrapping over the other side.

t

tab Small flap or loop attached at one end.

tack Joining two garment lay-

ers with small, loose hand-stitches or thread loop.

taille (tie-y) Fr. Size, waist.

tailoring Construction technique requiring special hand sewing and pressing to mold fabric into finished garment.

taper Cutting or stitching at slight diagonal, generally to make gradually smaller.

tension Amount of pull on thread or fabric during construction of garment.

thread count Number of threads in one square inch of fabric.

tissu (tee-su) Fr. Textile, fabric; texture.

toile (twahl) Fr. Linen or cotton cloth. Also muslin copy of a design, purchased by firms to copy original. Sometimes made by dressmakers to show customers garments that they are prepared to copy.

topstitching Machine stitching parallel to seam or edge, done from right side of garment.

train Extended part of garment, usually wedding dress, which trails at back.

transfer pattern Commercial pattern having design stamped on paper, usually transferred to fabric by iron.

trim To cut away excess fabric.

trimming Feature added to garment for ornamentation.

tunic Long top, worn over another garment.

turnover A garment section, usually collar or cuff, which folds back upon itself.

turtleneck High turnover collar that hugs throat.

twill tape Firmly woven tape.

u, v

underlining Fabric joined in garment seams to give inner shape or support.

V-neck Neckline shaped in front like the letter V.

vane Web or flat extended part of a feather.

vendeuse (vahn-doos) Fr. Saleswoman. In Paris dressmaking houses, the saleswoman is an important staff member.

vent Faced or lined slash in garment for ease.

vest Short, close-fitting garment without sleeves, similar to man's waistcoat.

volant (vaw-lahn) Fr. Flounce.

w, y

welt Strip of material stitched to seam, border, or edge.

wrap-around Garment or part of a garment wrapped around person, as cape or skirt.

wrong side Side of fabric on inside of garment.

yardage block Guide on back of pattern envelope; includes garment description, measurement, yardage, notions, etc.

yoke Fitted portion of garment, usually at shoulders or hips, designed to support rest of garment hanging from it.

SLEEVES

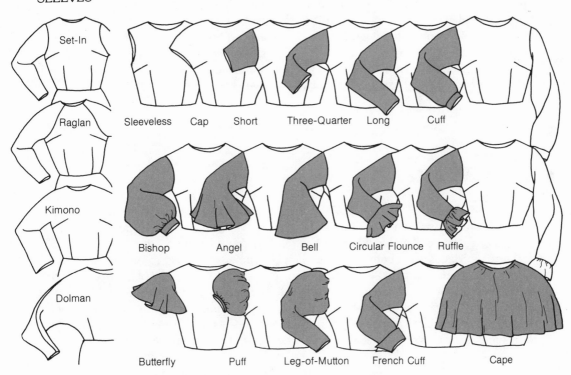

Set-In   Raglan   Kimono   Dolman

Sleeveless   Cap   Short   Three-Quarter   Long   Cuff

Bishop   Angel   Bell   Circular Flounce   Ruffle

Butterfly   Puff   Leg-of-Mutton   French Cuff   Cape

The
Wonderful World
of Fabrics

Fabrics are a delight to the senses. The artist in fashion finds the material she uses a thrill and an inspiration, for she is aware that every aspect of a fabric will influence her finished garment, and she knows how to use it with her own personal flair. Her most valuable asset is that elusive sixth sense that can successfully match style line with fabric texture, color, and character to form a harmonious, pleasing, and flattering whole. While this sense is to some extent instinctive, it can benefit by experience and an understanding of the structure and origin of textiles. They are not made by magic, though some of the procedures they undergo may seem mysterious.

Every aspect of a fabric's history influences its character and hand—the things that have most to do with its success or failure as the medium for your sewing endeavors. Fluid, stiff, crisp, rough, soft, thick, or shaggy, it will lend its personality to the design. From fiber to yarn to cloth, from the loom to the finishing mill to the fabric shop, each detail of its past is a fascinating clue to the way it ultimately looks, acts, and feels. But its characteristics are not limited to tactile and visual ones; among the considerations most important in your busy contemporary world are those of care and performance. New developments in fibers and finishes have placed at your disposal fabrics that lighten your laundry chores and keep you looking your most impeccable self. Ask for the information on fiber content and finishing treatments that will help you choose and care for the fabric on which you will spend so much effort and time. Learn to distinguish quality fabric not by prices, but by a thorough understanding of the components that lend durability and the unmistakable touch of luxury. Fiber content, the tightness of the weave, the amount of twist and the structure of an individual yarn, and the permanence of finishes and color treatment all have a bearing on its quality. These factors determine the amount of wear a fabric can withstand, how it will drape and fold, and whether it is worthy to serve as your fashion signature.

Fibers

Where does fashion begin? The realization of a concept of silhouette, texture, and color depends on the basic stuff of fabric—the fiber of which it is made. Especially since the advent of synthetic fibers, textile classification has developed into a bewildering maze of technical subtleties and chemical terms. Few consumers will need to be familiar with the quirks of the anhydroglucose molecule, but a basic understanding of the general fiber categories is an invaluable aid in the practical business of buying and caring for fabrics. Although its properties may be altered by yarn and fabric structure and by finishing treatments, ultimately a fabric's origin and chemistry are its soul. The primary distinction in fiber types is a very simple one—a fiber is either natural or man-made.

Wool

Silk

Cotton

Flax

Natural Fibers

Fibers exist in nature in many guises. Animal, vegetable, and mineral substances all provide the raw material for cloth. The wool of the sheep, the hair and fur of other creatures, and the fine filament from which the silk worm spins his cocoon are animal fibers composed of **protein.** Dozens of plants produce usable fiber in **cellulose** form. For example, linen is made from the fibrous stalk of the flax plants. The familiar cotton fiber grows as a puff protecting the seeds of the cotton plant, and grasses and leaves provide many other textile fibers. Minerals yield asbestos, which occurs naturally in fiber form and is used for fireproof fabrics, and metals that can be pounded into foils and cut into strips for luxury fabrics.

The unmistakable characteristics of the natural fibers are born in their structure. The familiar warmth of wool, the downy softness of cotton, the rich, dry texture of silk, and the crisp sheen of linen originate in the plant or animal that made them, and from the fact that natural things can never be quite uniform. The irregularities in their formation give them their distinction and explain many of their peculiar properties, such as the ability of wool to lock into felted constructions, the generally high absorbency of natural fibers, and the wide variation in quality among fibers of the same type.

WOOL is among nature's masterpieces. The fuzzy coat of the sheep possesses several remarkable and unique properties that make it especially adaptable to textile use. The wool fiber, which varies in length from 1½″ to 15″, has a natural crimp that facilitates the spinning of yarns and increases elasticity. The fiber itself is covered with minute scales. When wool is subjected to heat and pressure, these scales interlock, holding the fibers together and creating wool's unique felting capacity. The protein molecule of which wool is composed is spiral, or spring-shaped, contributing great resiliency, "loft," and shape-keeping ability. The fabric is highly absorbent and consequently very receptive to dyes but, in contrast, the surface tends to shed water. The hair and fur of other animals contribute fibers that are also classed as wool, and possess these properties in varying degrees.

SILK has a romantic history shrouded in regal legend, and the silk worm's life cycle is itself an exciting drama. A moth lays eggs which, after an incubation period, hatch into tiny, hungry silk worms. In about a month, each worm eats thousands of times its weight in mulberry leaves, growing rapidly and shedding its skin several times. Then it spins its cocoon. If allowed to continue the cycle, the worm transforms itself into a moth, which emerges from the cocoon to mate and lay more eggs. If the cocoon is to be used for silk, however, the worm is baked and dried in its blanket, and the fine protein fiber is unreeled in a continuous filament, which may be from 1500 to 4000 feet long. A stiff natural gum called sericin is boiled away, and silk filaments are combined to form very fine threads. Silk is extremely strong, absorbent, warm, resilient, and highly elastic.

COTTON is a vastly popular, versatile, and relatively inexpensive fiber that produces durable, comfortable fabrics. Magnified cotton has a ribbon-like appearance and is of fairly uniform thickness. The many types of cotton fibers range in length from ½″ to 2½″. It is naturally soft and easily spun into a variety of textures. The cellulose of which cotton is composed is an inert substance, and as a result untreated cotton may have little resiliency and wrinkle easily. However, its normally high strength increases when wet, making it exceptionally easy to launder, and its natural absorbency makes it receptive to a variety of treatments, such as mercerization, color application, and wrinkle-resistant and easy-care finishes, which add to its desirability.

FLAX is the plant from whose stems linen is made. By a process developed at the dawn of civilization, the outer woody portion of the stalk is rotted away, leaving long, soft, strong fibers composed of cellulose. The magnified fiber has a jointed structure similar to that of bamboo, and the thickness may vary widely. Length ranges from 5″ to 20″. Because of their similar composition, linen resembles cotton in many ways, including its ability to withstand high temperatures and its easy launderability and low resistance to wrinkling. In addition, it is extremely durable and, if stored properly, will withstand years of use. However, the flax fiber tends to be stiffer than cotton, and linen fabrics are subject to abrasion and wear along edges and creases.

Man-made Fibers

For thousands of years, natural fibers were the only materials available for the creation of fabric. Then, in the middle of the nineteenth century, scientists began to experiment with the production of "artificial silk" from regenerated cellulose. The resulting fiber, rayon, heralded a new era for the textile industry. Rapid developments have greatly increased the number and refined the properties of man-made fibers, which have become indispensable in the contemporary world.

Each type of man-made fiber has a generic name, such as nylon or polyester. In turn, fiber producers have trademarks or brand names for the various fibers they manufacture. Often a fiber producer has several trademarks for one fiber, indicating one or more variations in its manufacture.

The chemical complexities of man-made fibers are endless, but one of the distinctions among them is the fact that some fibers are derived from **natural** materials such as cellulose or protein, while others are completely **synthesized** or developed from basic chemical sources. In either case, the production involves similar steps. A chemical solution is formed that contains the basic components of the fiber. The solution is forced through the tiny holes of a **spinneret** into a chemical-coagulating bath or air chamber that hardens the substance into filament form. A continuous "rope" of unlimited length is produced, and goes on to be textured and processed. The same solution can produce filaments with varying properties, depending on the size and shape of the holes in the spinneret and the nature of the hardening procedure.

Great advances have been made in the development of man-made fibers since their inception. Today, man-made fibers can be engineered specifically to impart the performance feature required by the end use of the fabric.

Yarns

Yarn is the medium of fabric construction. However the fabric is formed, its character is determined to a great degree by the type of yarn from which it is made.

Before they are formed into yarn, fibers are referred to as either staple or filament. Silk and all the man-made fibers originally exist as long continuous strands, or *filaments*, which simply require a small amount of twist to form yarn. All the natural fibers except silk occur in short lengths, or *staple* form; man-made fibers may also be cut into short staple lengths to imitate them. These require more complex yarn-making techniques. A mat of random fibers is first sorted, cleaned, and blended into a uniform mixture and then subjected to several procedures that align the fibers and impart twist. *Carding* produces a loose strand of more or less parallel fibers about an inch in diameter. Further *combing* eliminates shorter fibers and produces a strand of higher quality. (*Woolen* and *worsted* yarns are, respectively, the wool counterparts of carded and combed yarns in other fibers.) The strand is then further stretched, twisted, and finally spun.

Yarn as it comes from the original spinning frame is called a *single*. Twisting several singles together produces a *ply yarn* and improves uniformity and strength. The character of a yarn is also influenced by the degree of twist. Low-twist yarns, soft and relatively weak, are used for napped fabrics. Tighter twist increases strength and crispness. Very high twist is used for crepe effects, as the tension causes puckering.

COMPLEX OR NOVELTY YARNS include several types, most of which are produced primarily for appearance value since they are seldom strong. They may be single or ply, and often contain components of several colors or fiber types for visual variations. Novelty single yarns, called *slub* yarns, vary along their length in thickness and amount of twist. The typical novelty ply yarn illustrated here is composed of a strong base yarn that forms the support and determines the length, combined with an effect yarn that is held in place by a binder. Examples of this type are *bouclé, ratiné, spiral*, and *knot* yarns.

TEXTURED YARNS are produced from man-made fibers that possess the useful characteristic of thermoplasticity, which means they will melt when subjected to heat. Through the use of this property, filament yarns can be heat-set in interesting textured effects. Several manufacturing methods can change the contour of the filament to a *coiled, crimped,* or *looped* formation from its original rod-like shape. Yarns from such filaments may be lightweight, have great bulk, or have a high degree of stretch.

2-Ply Yarn

3-Ply Novelty Yarn

Coil

Crimp

Loop

Fabric Structure

The thread of textile weaves through history, touching each civilization since the dawn of man and creating a tapestry of variety and excitement. Each culture has made its unique contribution, and the panorama of fabric designs and types provides deep insight into the development of artistic achievement. Despite these subtle cultural distinctions and mechanical developments that have vastly increased the speed at which textiles can be produced, the basic principles involved in textile construction have remained essentially the same for centuries. Weaving, knitting, knotting, felting, and a recent innovation called Malimo are among the techniques by which fabric is formed.

Weaving

A woven fabric is easy to recognize by the fact that it is composed of two sets of yarns at right angles to each other. The loom that produces it, while it may be an extremely complex device, works on a fairly simple principle. A frame holds a series of yarns called the **warp** taut between two rollers, one each at the front and back of the loom. Arranged in a specific order and extending the width of the projected fabric, these yarns are each drawn first through a **heddle**, which has an eye like that of a needle and may be raised to alter the position of its yarn, and then through a space in the **reed**, which is a comb-like device at right angles to the warp yarns, serving to keep each thread straight and in its proper place. The heddles are raised in a specific sequence as the design dictates, and a single crosswise or **filling** yarn or **pick** is drawn between the warp yarns with a **shuttle** and beaten into place against the previous filling threads by the reed. Then the warp yarns are lowered, a different series is raised, and another filling yarn is drawn through and packed in place. This series of crosswise threads forms the **weft** or **woof**. As the fabric is completed, more yarn is released from the back **warp beam** and the fabric is rolled toward the front of the loom and wound on the **cloth beam**.

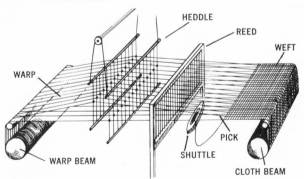

The warp must withstand considerable strain in weaving. It undergoes tension as it is held between the front and back beams and considerable abrasion as the reed slides back and forth through it. Its threads must be strong, tightly twisted, and uniform in structure. Consequently, the lengthwise grain (warp direction) will stretch less, may wear better, and because of its stronger yarn, will drape differently than the crosswise grain (filling direction). The **selvage** is formed along the edges of the warp where the filling thread changes direction. It is likely to be a tighter weave, since the warp edges must support the greatest strain. One indication of durability is in the "balance" of the cloth, or the proportion of warp to filling yarns. Fabric with nearly an equal thread count in both directions often gives longer wear.

BASIC WEAVES

There are several fundamental weaving structures that account for a vast majority of the fabrics we use. All the basic weaves can be produced on a simple loom, requiring no special attachments.

PLAIN WEAVE, true to its name, is the simplest and most common of weaves. Also called *tabby*, it is the prototype of woven structure: each yarn in both the warp and filling directions runs alternately over one and under one of the yarns it crosses. Though basically sturdy, this weave may vary in strength according to the weight of the yarn and the compactness of the weave. Cotton percale, voile, calico, and gingham; linen crash; silk organza and chiffon; synthetic organdy and taffeta; and wool challis are familiar fabrics in plain weave.

The *rib* variation occurs when the yarn in one direction of a plain weave are heavier or closer together than those in the other. Examples of ribbed fabrics, in order of fine to heavy rib, are broadcloth, poplin, faille, grosgrain, bengaline, and ottoman.

When the same alternating construction employs paired or multiple threads, it is called a *basket* weave. Such fabrics tend to be softer and less stable than fabrics of similar weight in single-thread plain weave, and may pose the problem of seam slippage. Examples you may be familiar with are oxford cloth, monk's cloth, and hopsacking.

TWILL WEAVE is often used to produce strong, durable fabrics such as denim and gabardine. A handsome weave characterized by a diagonal ridge usually running from lower left to upper right, its appearance depends to a large extent on the yarn weight and specific twill construction. A frequent variation in the twill weave is the *herringbone*, in which the diagonal ridge switches direction back and forth, creating a zigzag design.

SATIN WEAVE has a characteristic luxurious shine. The surface is composed of *floats*, or warp yarns, which pass over many filling yarns before being caught under one. The surface yarns, usually of filament fibers, intersect cross threads at points randomly spaced so the smooth texture appears unbroken. A variation called *sateen* has similar surface floats, but they run in the filling direction and are usually of a spun staple yarn.

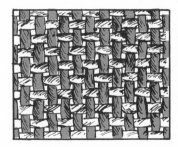

Plain Weave

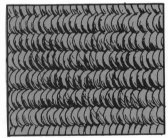

Rib Weave

Basket Weave

Twill Weave

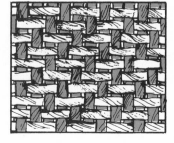

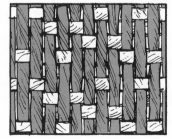

Satin Weave

DECORATIVE WEAVES

There are two basic types of fabric designs—those that are a product of the fabric's woven construction, and those that are applied to the fabric by such processes as printing or embossing. To create woven designs, the basic weaves may be varied and combined, surface floats may form involved designs, and complex mutations of the age-old loom may produce elaborate fabrics whose beauty wins constant attention.

PILE WEAVES provide soft, thick, textured fabrics for many purposes. Several different constructions may be employed to emphasize specific characteristics such as absorbency in terry, density and durability in carpeting, or texture in velvet. Extra warp yarn may be woven over wires, which cut the loops as they are withdrawn. In terry cloth, some of the warp yarns are woven with slack tension and forced up into loops as the filling is beaten back. Corduroy is woven with long filling floats that are cut after weaving to produce wales or cords. Some velvets are woven face to face, sharing warp yarns between two layers which are slashed apart when completed.

Loop Pile   Cut Pile

PATTERN WEAVES are the glory of the weaver's art. Delicate traditional coverlet designs can be created on a simple loom by an intricate order of threading. Other pattern weaves, such as crisp piqués, filmy curtain gauze, and patterns of flowers and scrolls in rich, deep brocades owe their existence to more complex variations of the loom.

Leno weaves are used most effectively in lacy, open fabrics. A special attachment twists the warp yarns around each other in a figure eight as the filling passes through, imparting stability to fabrics with widely spaced yarns. The leno construction is often combined with other weaves in a decorative effect for casement fabrics and may be especially attractive when designed with novelty yarns. Small figured and textured designs such as birdseye piqué are ***dobby weaves,*** produced on a more complicated loom. Usually a geometric pattern in a small repeat, these designs frequently employ heavy "stuffer" yarns in the filling to float on the back of the fabric and add texture to the weave. Further elaborations on the basic weaving process produce ***jacquard weaves,*** some of the most complex and beautiful fabrics available. These include huge repeats, detailed brocades, damasks, and tapestry effects. The jacquard loom controls each warp yarn individually with a series of punched cards like a computer deck. Since one card determines one filling pick, the repeat in the design can include as many threads as there are cards in the deck, permittng an unlimited range of design possibilities.

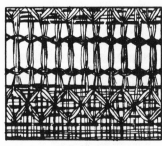
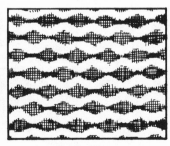
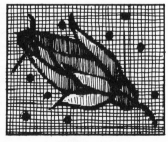

Leno Weave   Dobby Weave   Jacquard Weave

Knitting

A relatively recent development in the history of cloth, knitting has grown through technical advancements from a tedious hand construction to a fast, economical means of producing comfortable, packable, and beautiful fabrics. Knits owe their many advantages to their structure. While the yarn in a woven fabric is in a straight position, the knit construction arranges a continuous yarn into interlocking loops. Since these loops can straighten out under tension without straining the yarn, knit fabrics are inherently stretchy and flexible.

Several terms are used to describe knit goods. The **gauge** of a knit refers to the number of needles in 1″ to 2″ of fabric, depending on the type of knit. **Denier** is a term dating from Roman times, when the weight of a coin by that name was used as a standard for buying and selling silk. It describes the weight of the yarn per unit length. A **wale** or **rib** is a column of loops running parallel to the long measurement of a knit fabric, corresponding to the lengthwise grain of a weave, and a **course** is a crosswise row.

WEFT KNITTING

The first knitting machines were designed to reproduce the type of knitting done by hand. Called weft or filling knit, this construction uses a continuous single thread to form a crosswise row of loops which links into the previous row and is in turn linked into the row that follows it. Two stitches, **knit** and **purl,** are the basis for all knitting constructions. The knit stitch is a loop drawn through the front of the previous one, the purl is drawn through the back. Simple weft knits are uniquely fragile, since all the loops in a vertical row are dependent on each other. A broken loop will release all the others in the row, marring the fabric with a run. Wool knits tend to have greater resistance to runs because of the capacity of the wool fibers to cling together, locking the stitches. Weft knitting produces fabric in both tubular and flat form.

Plain Knit   Rib Knit   Purl Knit

PLAIN KNITS, found in the familiar fabric known as jersey, have a flat surface and a back characterized by short, horizontal loops. The right side exhibits the appearance of the knit stitch, and the loops on the back are the purl stitch. This structure is a common feature of hand knitting, where it is called **stockinette.**

RIB KNITS are made by alternating sets of knit and purl stitches in the same row, forming pronounced vertical ridges. The purl stitch tends to recede while the knit stitch advances, creating a fabric with a wavy cross-section and superior crosswise stretch. Rib knits have good insulation properties, and provide a snug fit.

PURL KNITS also have pronounced ridges, but in a horizontal direction. Entire rows are formed alternately of knit and purl stitches, yielding a fabric which has considerable crosswise stretch. It is completely reversible, since the appearance of the face is identical to that of the back, and similar to the reverse side of the flat knit.

Pattern Knit

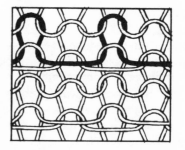

Double Knit

PATTERN KNITS are produced from the two basic weft knit stitches by re-arranging, dropping, adding, alternating, and crossing them. The beautiful "fisherman knits" are prime examples of the vast variety of patterns that owe their depth of texture to the fact that the knit stitch tends to advance and the purl stitch to recede. The machines that produce these fabrics, while they are not very economical to operate, can recreate hand-knitted structures with great fidelity.

DOUBLE KNITS, a versatile form of weft knitting, resist runs and have great stability. Produced by the interlock stitch, a variation of the rib stitch that can only be done by machine, double knitting employs two yarns and two sets of needles that draw loops through from both directions. It yields a heavy, firm, easily handled fabric that has the same rib-like appearance on both sides. Jacquard-type machinery has been adapted to produce highly decorative double knits.

WARP KNITTING

The technique of warp knitting, unlike that of simpler weft knitting, employs many yarns. Wound parallel to each other on a warp beam, the yarns are fed into the knitting machine and form loops in a lengthwise direction. Each yarn is controlled by its own needle and follows a zigzag course, interlocking with its neighbors along the length of the fabric. Warp knitting produces several varieties of durable and relatively run-proof fabrics whose low cost and vast design potential have won them enthusiastic consumer acceptance and a secure place in the future of the textile industry.

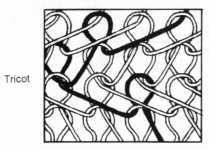

Tricot

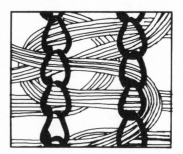

Raschel Knit

TRICOT is used extensively for lingerie because of its good permeability and comfort. Available in a variety of weights, it is suitable for dresses, loungewear, and linings. This strong, drapable fabric can be recognized by a fine crosswise rib that appears on the wrong side, and by the fact that it will stretch much more in the crosswise direction than in length. It is resistant to both running and fraying. The name tricot is taken from the French "tricoter," meaning "to knit."

RASCHEL KNITS are becoming increasingly familiar as they are being produced in a wide variety of fabrics. While tricots and many weft knits are best suited to fine, uniform yarns, raschel knits can take advantage of every conceivable texture and fiber type because of a specially designed latch needle. Raschel knits range from fragile tulles to coarse fur cloths. They may often be identified by a chain of fine yarn, which restrains and stabilizes a heavier textured yarn in a lacy, open construction.

Other Fabric Constructions

Beautiful fabrics are produced by many methods other than weaving and knitting. Some have been developed from old hand processes, while others are strictly a product of modern technology. They may be limited to specific uses by their character or cost.

NETTING is the fabric construction that encompasses both the strong, simple, burly texture of fishnet and the delicate and complicated tracery of lace. Knots may secure sets of threads together where they cross each other, or continuous coils of thread may loop through each other, forming the hexagonal mesh that can create a background for further embroidery. The most elaborate machines in the textile industry can reproduce laces in many styles and weights.

CROCHETING is adapted from a hand process that involves the use of a hook to form a chain of loops from a single continuous yarn.

BRAIDING forms fabric whose yarns lie at acute angles to the edges in a bias-woven structure, usually a narrow strip. All the yarns originate from the same direction.

FELTING is a time-honored method for producing warm, versatile, though not very durable, fabrics of wool or fur fibers by the application of heat, moisture, friction, and pressure. This economical construction doesn't require spun yarn or weaving, but depends on the natural ability of wool fibers to shrink, coil, and lock together to form a mat. As there are no yarns to unravel, edges of felt fabrics require no finishing techniques. Since they do not depend on looped yarns, however, they have little or no elastic recovery. When stretched, they will not return to their original shape. Felt exists in many weights and qualities, from fine garment fabric to heavy industrial padding. Wool may be mixed with a certain proportion of cheaper non-felting fiber and still retain its felting capacity.

FUSING produces a non-woven fabric or a web by using an adhesive or bonding agent to join or fuse together a mat of textile fibers other than wool. The fibers are distributed on a belt and made into fabric by one of two methods. An adhesive may be applied directly to the web of fibers, or the fiber mixture may contain some fibers that melt at a very low temperature, fusing the fabric together when heat is applied. Many different characters of fabric may be produced by this method, depending on the length, concentration, and orientation of the fibers. Non-woven fabrics are generally used for interfacing, and the webs are used as a fusing agent on other fabrics.

BONDING is a term that has come to include those textiles which are technically called *laminated* fabrics. These are composed of two separate layers of knitted or woven cloth that are joined together with a bonding agent to improve stability, opacity, or handling ease. Sometimes a thin sheet of plastic foam is laminated between the face and backing fabrics to add texture and insulation. Plastic film may be given greated durability and made suitable for apparel use by bonding it to a base of woven or knitted fabric. Simulated leather and patent vinyl fabrics are produced this way. Bonding may change the "hand" or draping qualities of the face fabric, and off-grain or impermanent bonding may be unsatisfactory.

MALIMO is a textile process that produces extremely stable fabrics at great speed. Three sets of yarns are used—warp yarns, filling yarns laid across the warp, and a third set of yarns that stitches them together with a chain stitch.

Finishes

Fabrics as they come off the loom bear little resemblance to those that reach your sewing machine. Before they are sold they may have been washed in chemical solutions, brushed, pressed, beaten, and polished. Substances and treatments may alter their texture and appearance and improve their resistance to moths, static electricity, spotting, staining, shrinking, sagging, wrinkling, and burning. All the processes undergone by the fabric after its initial transformation from yarn to cloth are called *finishes.*

Texture Finishes

CALENDERING is a process in which the fabric is passed between heated rollers under pressure. Like a large iron, a calender may simply press the fabric flat. However, there are several variations. Smooth, high-speed metal rollers and a resin application produce a finish called *glazing.* When two layers of a ribbed fabric are calendered slightly off grain, a *moiré* effect results. Thermoplastic fibers, or those which melt in sufficient heat, can be permanently textured by *embossing* with rollers engraved with a raised design. A super-glossy finish, called *ciré,* is obtained by applying a wax or other sheen-producing substance to the fabric before it is rolled.

NAPPING is a common finish by which short fiber ends of spun yarn are raised to the surface of a fabric by a series of revolving wire brushes to create flannel or fleece.

BRUSHING is similar to napping except that long fiber ends are mechanically pulled out of the fabric to produce a mohair-look.

PLISSÉ is a process of printing untreated cotton fabric with a caustic soda solution to shrink the fabric in certain areas creating a puckered effect.

FULLING takes advantage of the natural shrinkage capacity of wool. Subjecting the cloth to moisture, heat, and pressure compacts the yarns, strengthens the weave, and imparts warmth, body, and stability. It is similar to the *felting* of non-woven fibers.

BEETLING, applied to linen or cotton, involves prolonged pounding with wooden blocks to flatten the yarns, fill out the weave, and impart an elegant luster to the cloth.

TENTERING straightens the fabric, setting the width and grain, and dries it in the set position. The conveyor-like frame is lined with pins that hold the fabric's selvages and stretch it into shape. An electronic or hand-operated mechanism controls the two belts of pins, keeping filling yarns at right angles to the warp. Off-grain fabric is a result of improper tentering. If it has been heat-set off grain during tentering, it cannot be straightened.

Temporary Finishes

Several finishes may be added that improve the fabric's hand and appearance, but which are quickly removed by normal wear and care. Some substances may temporarily alter the character of a fabric in such a way that poor quality is disguised.

SIZING, or *dressing,* provides body, weight, and luster. Fabrics are stiffened with glue, clay, or wax, which is not fast to laundering. Starch may restore this finish, but if fabric is of poor basic quality (low thread count) it will wear out quickly.

SOFTENERS give a lighter, fluffier, softer hand to fabrics and can be re-applied during the laundering process.

WEIGHTING is a process applied to silk to restore the weight that is lost when the natural gum is removed. Metallic salts are absorbed, which allows heavier fabrics to be produced but weakens the fiber. Weighted silk water-spots easily.

Performance Finishes

In recent years, manufacturers have been increasingly conscious of the consumer demand for fabrics with improved and specialized characteristics. Finishes can counteract the inherent disadvantages of certain untreated fibers, and give them texture and aesthetic appeal as well as safety, durability, and adaptability to special purposes.

Keep in mind the fact that "permanent," as used in the textile industry, is only a relative term. So-called "permanent" finishes would more accurately be called durable, since they are only designed to withstand normal wear, and must be treated and laundered as the manufacturer recommends. Here is a list of terms that you will find on hangtags, bolt ends, and labels.

ANTI-BACTERIAL Finish that checks growth or effect of bacteria and perspiration.

ANTI-STATIC A finish to help dissipate static electricity and thus reduce clinging.

COLORFAST Color in fabrics so labeled will not fade with normal use if laundered as recommended.

FLAME-RESISTANT Fabrics that have been treated to prevent the spread of flame once its source has been removed.

MERCERIZED A term for cotton and linen fabrics that have been immersed under tension in a solution of caustic soda to swell the fibers for increased strength, luster, and affinity for dyes.

MILDEW-RESISTANT Fabrics that have been treated to resist the growth of mildew and other molds.

MOTHPROOF Fabrics that have been treated to repel moths.

PERMANENT-PRESS or **DURABLE-PRESS** Indicates fabric will wash and dry by machine, shed wrinkles, and retain shape without ironing.

PRESHRUNK Fabrics that have undergone a preliminary shrinking process. *Residual shrinkage*, or the percentage of possible shrinkage remaining in a fabric, must be declared.

SANFORIZED Ensures that fabric will not shrink more than one percent in washing. *Sanfor-Set* means 100% cotton fabric has wash-and-wear properties.

SHRINKAGE CONTROLLED Fabrics that have undergone compressive shrinkage in manufacturing; increases durability by compacting the weave.

SOIL RELEASE Treatment that makes possible the removal of oil stains from permanent-press fabrics.

STAIN- AND SPOT-RESISTANT Fabric finished to repel water- and oil-based stains.

WASH-AND-WEAR Fabrics that can be washed and re-worn with little or no ironing. This property may be produced by heat-setting or resin treatment and varies in permanence. Also termed *easy care* and *minimum care*.

WATERPROOF Fabrics that have been made non-porous so that water will not penetrate them.

WATER-REPELLENT Fabrics that have been treated to reduce their affinity for water yet remain porous.

WRINKLE- OR CREASE-RESISTANT A term applied to fabrics that have been treated to resist and recover from wrinkling caused by normal wear.

Color and Fabric Pattern

We can be sure that when cave men first began painting hunting scenes on walls of caves, the first textile designer was also painting the animal skins he wore. Though the content, construction, and finishing of a fabric provide all of its essential properties, richness of color and pattern have always held the most primary appeal. For centuries, special formulas for color and fabric have been jealously guarded secrets. Vast industries have developed on the basis of changing tastes and new technical developments in color and applied textile design in order to satisfy our unquenchable decorative instinct.

Dyeing

The complex science of dye chemistry has developed in response to demand for fast, vivid color that will withstand wear, sunlight, and the rigors of modern laundering.

Natural fibers, which frequently have distinct colors of their own, often require bleaching before they can be dyed. Many fibers naturally resist color, and among the chief advantages of such innovations as mercerizing is the improvement of a fabric's affinity for dyes. With the advent of synthetic fabrics and the increased importance of the chemical industry in textiles, the number and quality of synthetic dyes has grown by leaps and bounds since their inception in 1856.

Dyes are classified in several ways, including the chemical category and fibers to which they can be applied, the hue produced, and the method of application. The appearance of a fabric is often determined by the stage in manufacturing at which the dye is applied.

STOCK DYEING is used to produce color in a mat of fibers before they are spun into yarn. Colors penetrate the fibers thoroughly, and are likely to be fast. This method is commonly used on wool; hence the expression "dyed in the wool." It permits the spinning of tweed and mottled yarns from several batches of variously colored fibers.

SOLUTION DYEING is a procedure for coloring man-made fibers by introducing pigment into the chemical spinning solution before it is formed into filaments. Since the color is an inherent part of the fiber, it is extremely permanent.

YARN DYEING is one of the oldest methods of coloring textiles. The spun yarn is dyed in a skein, or it may be wound on a cylinder known as a *package*, which is then dyed from the inside out in a machine similar to a pressure-cooker. Typical yarn dyed fabrics are ginghams, plaids, checks, stripes, and those with iridescent effects.

PIECE DYEING is the most common and economical means of coloring fabric. It involves immersing the woven goods in a dye bath. The procedure is practical because it permits manufacturers to store a volume of undyed goods and dye to order as preferences in color change. Piece-dyed fabrics are usually a solid color, but an exception to this rule occurs with *cross dyeing*. Fabrics to be so treated are woven of a combination of fiber types, each with a different affinity for certain dyes. Those dyes which are accepted by one fiber are rejected by others, resulting in fabrics that can resemble either yarn-dyed or fiber-dyed fabrics. Difficulties may be encountered in attempting to dye fiber blends a solid color, and many must be dyed twice to impart the same color to both fibers.

Applied Design

The surface of a fabric provides enticing stimulus to an artist's creative imagination. An infinity of surface patterns can be reproduced in many ways.

TRANSFER PRINTING is the process of applying the print to paper and then transferring it to the fabric by the use of heat and pressure. Fine sharp registry of the design can be achieved by this method as well as the ability to obtain multiple colors and tones. Transfer printing is less expensive than roller printing.

ROLLER PRINTING, or direct printing, is a simple procedure used to produce large quantities of a design that is engraved on a series of rollers, one for each color to be used. These print rollers are arranged around a large drum in exact positions, and color is applied to them. When the fabric feeds between the rollers and the drum, the areas of color coincide to form the complete design. *Discharge printing* uses a bleaching paste to bleach out the design on a solid color fabric. *Resist printing* uses a dye-resistant paste to print the design. The fabric is then dyed and the paste removed, leaving a lighter print. *Burnt-out printing* uses chemicals to dissolve one of the fibers in the fabric, creating a raised motif on a sheer ground. *Flocking* adds textural interest by printing a design on the fabric with an adhesive and then applying short fibers to the surface. The fabric can also be completely flocked to give the appearance of a velvet or velour.

SCREEN PRINTING is a sophisticated version of the stencil process. The design is cut out of a thin sheet of film, which is then adhered to a frame covered with a fine, strong mesh fabric. The fabric to be printed is stretched out on a table, the screen laid on top, and the pigment or dye is forced through the screen in the areas where the non-porous film does not act as a barrier. Adapting photographic processes to cutting the film has allowed screen printing to produce fine gradations of tone and delicate detail. Though it is slower than roller printing, it is often used to produce limited quantities of a print.

TIE DYEING is an ancient craft that produces interesting and varied textile designs. Puffs of fabric are wrapped in waxed thread or sewn and tightly gathered, then dipped in dye, creating intriguing sunburst effects as the dye penetrates the fabric unevenly. The blending of several colors and the combining of techniques contribute to the unique effect. The technique has been copied effectively by a machine process.

BATIK is a process that can be used to create striking and delicate designs. It is a method of resist dyeing in which wax is applied to the cloth in areas that are not to receive color. After dyeing, the wax is boiled off, and the process repeated for each color to be used. It has now been adapted to machine printing.

EMBROIDERY was developed from a tedious hand process into a lucrative industry by the invention of the Schiffli machine. Hundreds of needles embellish the prewoven base fabric with an infinite variety of lace and eyelet designs that are programmed into the machine on punched cards. Holes for eyelet fabrics are punched or cut automatically as the edges are finished by machine stitching. Some varieties of lace are produced by chemically dissolving the base fabric, leaving just the stitched lace design.

Fiber and Fabric Facts
Natural Fibers

	Fabrics	Properties	Care
Cotton	Extremely versatile in weight, texture, and construction. Found in fabric such as organdy, broadcloth, poplin, terry, corduroy, seersucker, denim, tweed. Used widely for summer wear, work clothes, and in heavier weights, for warm transitional garments.	Quite strong, even stronger when wet. Not susceptible to pilling or seam slippage. Comfortable; absorbent; carries heat from body. Free from static electricity. Good affinity for dyes. Will deteriorate from mildew; weakened by sunlight. Tendency to wrinkle. Fabrics may shrink badly unless treated.	Wash 10 minutes in hot water at regular speed with heavy-duty detergent. Can use chlorine bleach on white cottons; however, some finishes react to chlorine bleach and turn yellow (see label). Fabric softener will reduce wrinkling. Tumble dry on regular heat setting but don't over-dry. Press with hot iron while damp until completely dry or use a steam iron with a slightly dampened press cloth.
Linen	Beautiful, durable, and elegant; has a natural luster. Can be made into sheer, medium, or heavyweight fabrics. Used for summer dresses, blouses, and suiting.	Tendency to wrinkle unless treated. Exceptionally strong, but stiff; may show wear at the edges and folds. Comfortable; excellent absorbency; carries heat away from the body. Poor affinity for dyes; bright colors may bleed when laundered. Fabric will shrink unless treated. Will deteriorate from mildew but not from moths. Does not lint.	Usually dry cleaned, but launders well if preshrunk. Wash 5–8 minutes in hot water at regular speed with heavy-duty detergent. Can use chlorine bleach but over-bleaching may weaken the fiber. Tumble dry on regular heat setting, but remove and iron while still very damp. Iron at high setting (unless treated with special finishes; see label). For maximum durability, creases should be finger pressed, not ironed into the garment.
Silk	Beautiful, luxurious to touch; has a deep luster. Available in a variety of weaves and weights from sheer drapable chiffon to stiff rich brocades in brilliant colors and beautiful prints for dresses, suits, blouses, linings, lingerie. Found in fabrics such as crepe, brocade, satin, jersey, tweed.	Good wrinkle resistance. Builds up static electricity and may cling. Exceptionally strong for its fineness. Very absorbent; will hold in body heat. Excellent affinity for dyes, but may bleed. May yellow and fade with age or the use of strong soap or high iron setting. Weakened by sunlight and perspiration; excellent resistance to mildew and moths.	Usually dry cleaned. If marked washable, use mild suds in lukewarm water; can also machine wash for 3 minutes at gentle speed. Avoid using chlorine bleach. Tumble dry at low setting for short time or hang up to dry, but avoid prolonged exposure to light. Iron on wrong side while damp with a low heat setting or use a steam iron; however, silk is easily water spotted, so you may need to protect the fabric with a thin cloth.

| **Wool** | Versatile in weight, texture, weave, color. Unique properties of wool permit constructions not possible in any other fiber. Tailors well because of ability to be molded into shape. Used for coatings, suitings, crepe, tweeds, knits, gabardine, flannel, jersey. | Excellent wrinkle resistance and elasticity. Limited abrasion resistance. Weakens and stretches when wet. Exceptional absorbency; holds a large amount of moisture before it feels damp. Traps air in fibers, providing great natural warmth. Good affinity for dye. Weakened by sunlight. Requires moth proofing; may be attacked by mildew if damp or soiled. Susceptible to shrinking and pilling if not treated. Tailors well. | Should be brushed between cleanings. Usually dry cleaned. For hand washables, use mild suds in cool water; can also machine wash for 2 minutes at gentle speed, interrupting the agitation time for 10 minutes to let the fabric soak, and then completing the cycle. Do not tumble dry; block to shape on a flat surface away from heat. If labeled "machine wash-and-dry," wash 3–8 minutes in warm water at gentle speed with mild suds. Tumble dry at regular heat setting but remove while slightly damp. Do not use chlorine bleach; it will weaken and yellow the fibers. To avoid stretching, press gently at low heat setting on the wrong side using a damp press cloth or steam iron. |

Man-made Fibers

| **Acetate**

☐ AVTEX
△ CELANESE
♦♦ CHROMSPUN
♦♦ ESTRON | Silk-like appearance, luxurious soft feel, deep luster, excellent draping qualities. Found in fabrics such as satin, jersey, taffeta, lace, faille, brocade, tricot, and crepe, and often in blends with other man-made fibers. Used for dresses, foundation garments, lingerie, linings, and blouses. | Tendency to wrinkle. Accumulates static electricity. Takes colors well, but some dyes are subject to atmospheric fading. Relatively low in strength. Resistant to mildew and moths. Weakened by light. Moderately absorbent; holds in body heat. Resistant to stretch and shrinkage. | Usually dry cleaned. If washable, use mild suds in warm or cold water at gentle speed for 3 minutes. Tumble dry at cool setting or hang up to dry. To hand wash, gently squeeze suds through fabric and rinse in lukewarm water. Iron while damp with light pressure on wrong side at lowest temperature; a hot iron may melt the fabric. Place strip of brown paper between garment and seam allowances or darts. Do not use acetone (as in nail polish remover) or other organic solvents. |
| **Acrylic**

●●● ACRILAN
○ CRESLAN
●●● FINA
☐☐ ORLON
●● ZEFRAN | Commonly soft, light, fluffy fabric construction. Available in sheer fabrics, knits, fleece, furlike, and pile fabrics, and blends with natural and man-made fibers. Used for sweaters, dresses, suits, sports, and work clothes. | Good wrinkle resistance. Lightweight. May accumulate static electricity. Low absorbency; quick drying. Good affinity for dyes; colorfast. Quite strong. Excellent resistance to mildew, moths, chemicals and sunlight. Heat sensitive. May pill. Holds shape well, good pleat retention. | Remove oily stains before cleaning. May be dry-cleaned or laundered. Wash for 3–5 minutes. For sturdy fabrics use regular agitation with heavy-duty detergent. For delicate fabrics use gentle agitation with mild suds or hand wash. For bright colors use cool water; otherwise, warm water. Rinse in warm water, using a fabric softener. Chlorine bleach may be used for white fabrics. Dries quickly; may be tumble dried at low heat setting or hung up to dry. (Sweaters, however, must be dried flat.) Seldom requires ironing if removed from dryer as soon as cycle is completed; otherwise use low heat setting, never hot, on wrong side. |

Man-made Fibers

	Fabrics	Properties	Care
Metallic OOO METLON	Fibers glitter in gold, silver, and other colors; used in blended fabrics and trims.	Non-tarnishing if plastic coated. Not affected by salt water, chlorinated water, or climatic conditions.	Can be laundered or dry cleaned if plastic coated. Iron at low setting Mylar polyester covering withstands heat better than acetate covering.
Modacrylic ●●● ELURA ♦♦ VEREL	Available in deep-pile, fleece, and fur-like fabrics; used chiefly in blends and no-iron fabrics for deep-pile coats, trims, and linings.	Good wrinkle resistance. May accumulate static electricity. Non-allergenic. Quick drying. Retains shape well; excellent elasticity. Resistant to moths, mildew, chemicals, and sunlight. Very heat sensitive; softens at low temperatures. Flame resistant.	Fur-like deep-pile garments are most safely cleaned by a furrier; other fabrics may be dry-cleaned or laundered. If washable, follow same directions as for acrylic. If ironing is absolutely necessary, iron at lowest temperature to prevent any stiffening or glazing. Finger press fur-like deep-pile fabrics. Do not use acetone, as in nail polish remover.
Nylon □□ QIANA NYLON 6 ★ CAPROLAN ★ CAPTIVA ● CREPESET ● ENKALURE OO SHAREEN ●● ZEFRAN NYLON 6,6 □□ ANTRON ●●● CADON □□ CANTRECE △ CELANESE ★★ VECANA	Several types of nylon produce a wide variety of fabric textures, from smooth and crisp to soft and bulky. Available in wide range of fabrics both woven and knitted. Nylon 6 and 6,6 often found in blends. Used for dresses, blouses, shirts, skirts, sweaters, lingerie, ties, socks, swimwear, and rainwear.	Very good wrinkle resistance. Exceptional strength. Washes easily. Low absorbency; holds in body heat. Good affinity for dyes; may fade in sunlight. Can be heat-set to hold shape, pleats, and embossed effects. High resistance to moths, mildew. Very elastic. Does not soil easily; may pill. Melts under high heat. Resistant to non-oily stains. Special properties of Qiana: lightweight; colorfast; stable; does *not* hold in body heat; luxurious hand.	Remove oily stains before cleaning. Machine wash for 3–5 minutes with regular agitation for sturdy fabrics and gentle agitation for delicate fabrics, using warm water. For bright colors use cool water. Wash whites separately to avoid graying. Fabrics may yellow; bleach frequently with sodium perborate bleaches. A fabric softener in the rinse water will reduce static electricity. Tumble dry on wash-and-wear setting or drip dry; dries quickly. Wash delicate items by hand in warm water with soap or detergent; rinse well. If removed from dryer immediately, may not require ironing, otherwise use low temperature on the wrong side. Never use a hot iron.
Olefin △△ HERCULON □□□ MARVESS ★★ POLYLOOM ★★ VECTRA	Wool-like hand and slightly waxy feel. Adaptable to textured, bulky yarn types for suit, dress, and coat fabrics. Light weight makes it especially good for deep pile and fake fur constructions.	Excellent elasticity and resiliency. Lightest of textile fibers, will float on water. Virtually non-absorbent; quick drying. Will not shrink unless overheated. Very sensitive to heat; melts easily. Non-allergenic. Resists pilling, staining, and insects. Difficult to dye.	Machine wash in lukewarm water; add a fabric softener to final rinse. Machine dry only on very low setting, and remove immediately after cycle has stopped. Preferably drip dry. Iron on lowest possible temperature setting, or not at all. Stains may often be blotted away with absorbent tissue. Olefins should not be dry-cleaned if perchlorethylene is the solvent used.

Polyester

★ A.C.E.
☐ AVLIN
☐☐ DACRON
● ENCRON
△ FORTREL
♦♦ KODEL
●●● SPECTRAN
★★★ TREVIRA
●●● ULTRON
●● ZEFRAN

Available in many weights, textures, and weaves; often used in blends and minimum care fabrics. Used for durable press (permanent press) and knit fabrics found in suits, shirts, slacks, dresses, blouses, lingerie, and thread.

Excellent wrinkle and abrasion resistance. Accumulates electricity. Wash/wear, quick drying. High strength. Resistant to stretching and shrinking. Low absorbency; may hold in body heat. May yellow, but otherwise colorfast. Retains heat-set pleats and creases. Exceptional resistance to mildew and moths. Occasional seam slippage. May pill and pick up lint.

Remove oily stains before cleaning. Machine wash for 3–5 minutes with regular agitation for sturdy fabrics, and gentle agitation for delicate fabrics, using warm water. For bright colors use cool water. A fabric softener in the rinse water will reduce static electricity; rinse well. Chlorine bleach can be used for whites before the spin cycle; others can be tumble dried at wash-and-wear or low setting. If removed from dryer immediately, may not require ironing; otherwise use a medium warm setting or steam iron.

Rayon

● ABSORBIT
☐ AVRIL
♦ BEAUNIT
○○ COLORAY
● ENKROME
○○ FIBRO
○○ SARILLE
● ZANTREL

Comes in wide range of qualities; can be made to resemble natural fibers; can be lightweight or heavy constructions. May have smooth surfaces or bulky napped textures. Soft hand, drapes well. Used for dresses, suits, blouses, coats, lingerie, slacks, linings, non-woven fabrics, and blends.

Soft and comfortable. Absorbent; holds in body heat. Good affinity for dyes; generally colorfast. Low resistance to mildew. Relatively low in strength; weaker when wet. Wrinkles unless specially finished. May shrink or stretch if not treated. Weakens in prolonged exposure to light.

Usually dry-cleaned; if wet may weaken, ravel, or shrink. If washable, use mild detergent in warm water at gentle speed for 3–5 minutes. When hand washing use mild lukewarm suds, gently squeeze them through fabric, rinse in lukewarm water. Do not wring or twist. Do not soak colored fabrics. Chlorine bleaches or the peroxygen type can be used; some finishes may be sensitive to chlorine bleach. Tumble dry; if hung to dry, avoid direct sunlight. Iron while damp at a moderate setting, on wrong side to prevent shine.

Spandex

☐☐ LYCRA

Found in stretchable, flexible, supple fabrics for foundation garments, swimwear, ski pants, and other sportswear; elastic banding.

Lightweight; great elasticity. High in strength, durability. Non-absorbent so repels body oils. May yellow with exposure to light.

Hand or machine wash in warm water for 3 minutes with gentle agitation. Do not use chlorine bleach, which will cause permanent yellowing. Use oxygen or sodium perborate bleach. Rinse well. Drip dry or tumble dry at cool setting, being careful not to over-dry. Can be ironed at a low temperature.

Triacetate

△ ARNEL

Often found in blends, fabrics such as tricot, sharkskin, flannel, and taffeta. Used for garments that require pleat retention, sportswear.

Good wrinkle and shrink resistance. Antistatic finish can be built in. Low strength. Good affinity for dyes; colorfast. Can be permanently pleated; holds heat-set shape and texture. Easily washed.

Machine wash; tumble dry, except permanently pleated garments which should be hand washed and hung to dry. Usually requires ironing; can withstand higher temperature than acetate. Do not use acetone, as in nail polish remover, or any other organic solvent.

TRADEMARKS

★ Allied Chemical	♦ Beaunit	●● Dow Badische	★★★ Hoechst
○ American Cyanamid	△ Celanese	☐☐ DuPont	○○○ Metlon
● American Enka	★★ Chevron Chemical	♦♦ Eastman Chemical	●●● Monsanto
☐ Avtex	○○ Courtaulds	△△ Hercules	☐☐☐ Phillips

Spot Removal

	Washable	Dry Cleanable
Alcoholic Beverage	Soak in cold water, wash in warm sudsy water, rinse. If stain remains, soak silk, wool, or colored items in 2 tablespoons hydrogen peroxide to 1 gallon water for ½ hour and rinse twice. Soak white linen, rayon, and cotton 15 minutes in 1 tablespoon household bleach to 1 quart water. Rinse twice. Caution: alcohol may remove the dye.	Sponge with water or hydrogen peroxide or dust with an absorbent such as cornstarch.
Ball-Point Pen	Place blotter under fabric. Drip home dry-cleaning solvent through spot. Soak in solution of detergent and warm water. Rinse in cold water. Use mild bleach, but test fabric first.	At dry cleaners, specify stain was made by ball-point pen.
Blood	Soak in lukewarm water and detergent. If yellow stain remains, apply laundry bleach. For stubborn stains, apply a few drops of ammonia.	Treat with cold water to which table salt has been added (1 ounce per quart of water). Salt helps prevent color bleeding. Rinse and blot with towel. Try warm water and hydrogen peroxide to remove final traces.
Chewing Gum	Apply ice and remove gum from surface with dull knife. Soak affected areas in cleaning fluid.	Same as washable fabrics.
Chocolate	Rinse in lukewarm water. If brown stain remains, apply laundry bleach. For sturdy fabrics, pour boiling water through fabric over a bowl.	If colorfast, sponge with lukewarm water.
Coffee or Tea	If safe, pour boiling water through spot from a height of 1–3 feet or soak with a safe bleach.	Follow directions for a non-greasy stain, page 51.
Fruit and Berry	Launder. If stain remains, apply white vinegar. Rinse. If necessary, bleach with hydrogen peroxide.	If safe, apply small amount of detergent locally. Rinse. Or, apply white vinegar; rinse.
Grass, Flowers, Foliage	Work detergent into stain, then rinse. Or, if safe for fabric, sponge stain with alcohol. Dilute alcohol with 2 parts water for use on acetate. If stain remains, use chlorine or peroxygen bleach.	Same as washable, but try alcohol first, to see if it is safe for the dye.
Grease	Place towel under stain. Scrape off as much grease as possible, and pour cleaning fluid through stained area.	Sponge wools with trichloroethane.
Mildew	Pretreat fabric as soon as possible with detergent and launder. Expose to sunlight; if any stain remains, sponge with rubbing alcohol.	Have dry cleaned or try a 4 to 1 solution of water and hydrochloric acid.
Milk and Cream	Immediately soak in cool water and detergent. Rinse and launder.	Sponge with cleaning fluid. If color-safe and stain still remains, sponge with water.
Paint, Varnish	Rub detergent into stain and wash. If stain is only partially removed, sponge with turpentine. For aluminum paints, try trichlorethylene; however, do not use on triacetate or polyester. Soak overnight in detergent.	Sponge with turpentine. If necessary, loosen more of the paint by covering the stain for 30 minutes with a pad of cotton dampened with a solvent. If stain remains, apply one drop liquid detergent and work in with bowl of a spoon.
Perspiration	If garment color has been affected, sponge a fresh stain with ammonia, an old stain with white vinegar. Rinse and launder.	Same as washable fabrics.
Scorch	Alternate applications of detergent, water, and ammonia. Rinse well.	Dampen with hydrogen peroxide until stain is removed. If necessary, mix a few drops of ammonia with 1 tbsp. peroxide and moisten stain. Sandpaper scorch from heavy wools.

Soft
and Delicate

Create an aura of romance with soft
pastels, from barely-there pales to
elegant hues: the pale purples—misty
mauve, soft lilac, heliotrope—
reminiscent of grandmother's parlor . . .
soft blues from periwinkle and robin's
egg to copen and delft blue . . . delicate,
feminine pinks from strawberry to dusty
rose . . . the gorgeous, fruity yellow and
orange tints of apricot, tangerine, peach,
and mango . . . the sophisticated pastels
of pale celery and dusty sage . . . and,
recalling the sea, the cool and limpid
blue-greens.

Quiet
and Calm

Neutrals make subtle fashion statements and form the foundation of your wardrobe. Use them as calm, restful interludes between brights, or let them stand on their own understated character. Black is eternally sophisticated, reserved, serene, and just a little sexy. Whites, from innocent chalk white to elegant ivory, are refreshing alone or as an immaculate accent for any neutral shade. Traditional navy . . . pewter, gray, and charcoal . . . beige, camel, cinnamon, and chocolate brown—play the many neutral variations against each other in harmonious monochromatic color schemes. And look for neutrals in the downbeat tones of any color you like.

Rich
and Dramatic

Rich, glowing colors add drama and elegance to your wardrobe. The wine reds—crimson, burgundy, maroon—are warm and satisfying. Peacock and sapphire blue are vibrant and assertive. Jaunty magenta and violet are both dramatic knockouts. Rich saffron yellow creates a fascinating Eastern glow. Analogous color schemes—closely related color clusters such as blue, blue-green, and green—are effective mood makers.

Bright
and Bold

Make a bright, bold color statement with eye-catching, full-intensity colors. Begin with the primaries—clear red, true blue, sun yellow—the basic building blocks of color. Add the secondaries—grass green, citrus orange, royal purple—to demand attention and drama. Hot pink, vivid chartreuse, and brilliant turquoise are vibrant showstoppers. Complementary color schemes, with opposites attracting, are exceedingly strong, bold combinations that enhance each other and you. To perk up a gray day, or to dazzle at a party, bright, bold colors express a happy, extroverted, high-spirited personality.

COLOR IS…

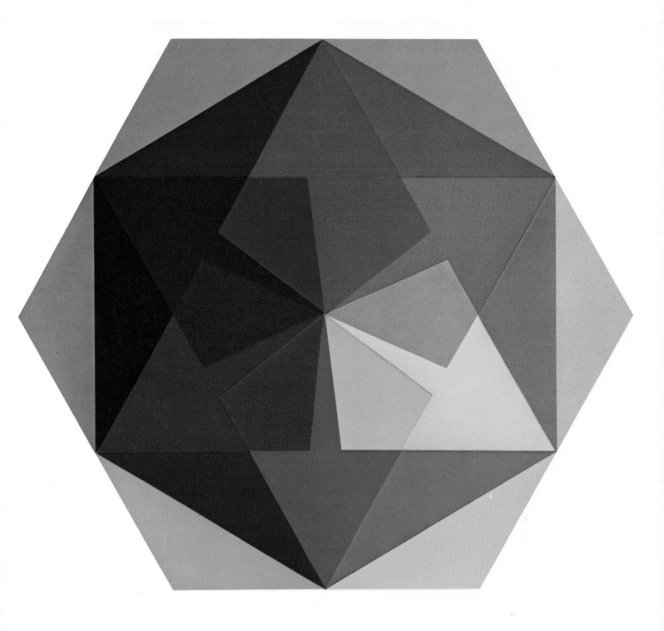

1—PRIMARIES
2—SECONDARIES
3—TERTIARIES
4—TINTS
5—SHADES

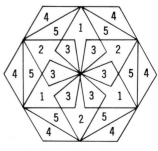

2

Your Pattern Profile

Pattern Design

When you flip through the Vogue catalogue in a store or unfold a Vogue pattern at home, have you ever wondered how pattern designs are created and patterns made? How do the latest couture fashions by your favorite designers become a part of the Vogue pattern collection? The creation of a pattern is a complex process involving many steps in planning, development, and testing before the pattern is finally presented to you. Working six months ahead, Vogue Patterns check and double-check every detail to guarantee that each pattern will serve as an expert guide to sewing.

The Creation of a Pattern

Four times a year, Vogue's design director attends the collections in Europe and America to purchase garments for pattern reproductions. Today Vogue Patterns is one of the largest buyers in the world of couture designs.

Back in New York City, the designer garment along with its flat pattern goes to the pattern maker who drapes a line-for-line copy of the garment, including all interfacings, linings, and details down to the last hook and eye. This muslin copy is compared with the original garment to make sure that all the design lines and details are identical.

For patterns created by Vogue's own designers, the pattern maker first makes a basic silhouette pattern using the designer's sketch or "croquis" along with notes on construction. She then cuts and drapes the muslin.

Next a "master pattern block" is traced from the muslin and marked with all the construction symbols such as darts, seams, and notches. From this master pattern, a dressmaker constructs the garment using a home sewing machine and dressmaking, rather than manufacturing, construction techniques. The pattern is tested for its suitability for striped, plaid, diagonal, and napped fabrics; then a model tries on the garment to check the fit and mobility of the design.

The master pattern block must next be "graded" or scaled up or down for all pattern sizes. The difference between sizes is based on standardized measurements and the style of the garment. The grading is done by a computer that adds a carefully predetermined amount to certain areas to achieve the different pattern sizes.

The pattern pieces are then measured for layout diagrams. Again the computer determines the pattern piece arrangement and the yardage requirements and prints out a picture of the pattern layout. Meanwhile the Sewing Guide instructions are written from the original muslin and construction notes, and the illustrations are drawn to scale using the muslin. Photographs, sketches, yardage requirements, and fabric recommendations are gathered together for the pattern envelope. Everything is checked one last time before being sent to the Vogue Pattern manufacturing centers throughout the world for printing.

All the pattern pieces are printed on a continuous roll of tissue paper. A band saw is used to cut around the individual pattern pieces cutting through 1300 layers of tissue paper at one time! The tissue paper patterns are folded by hand and inserted into the envelope with the Sewing Guide Sheet. From there the completed patterns are distributed to stores around the world for your selection.

They Design For You

Introducing the world's most famous designers of haute couture. Vogue made its first such introduction in 1949, and the enthusiastic reception has grown over the years. And small wonder; as more and more women have begun sewing the most elegant clothes these high-fashion couturiers design, sewing has become, for you and millions like you, a creative art form. Through the pages of your Vogue catalogue you are able to attend the greatest collections Europe and America have to offer, for these exciting designs are not mere copies but actual reproductions of the original toiles.

Vogue Paris Original

Any discussion of haute couture must begin with Paris, which has always been the wellspring of world fashion. Where the genius of the French designers leads, fashion has invariably followed. And so Vogue introduces to you the style-setters, creators of the fashion fireworks that explode twice yearly in Paris to light the world of fashion. These talented designers are the creators of all the exciting clothes offered in Vogue's famous Paris Original patterns. No longer is their genius limited to the elegant apparel of a select few; make it your own with Vogue Patterns.

Givenchy is universally known for his luxurious and dramatic collections. His clientele numbers fashionables from all over the world.

Yves Saint Laurent presents a complete fashion format spiced with originality and imagination. Where St. Laurent leads, fashion follows.

Marc Bohan of the **House of Dior** has a reputation for flouting convention, innovating trends. His youthful silhouettes are dramatic with color.

Pierre Balmain creates clothes based on classicism and simplicity of line, elegant reflections of his early architectural training.

Renata is famous in Paris boutique circles for the gracefulness of her design approach. Her unconstructed clothes are soft, fluid, and lightweight.

Emanuel Ungaro aims his crisp, mobile designs at a youth-oriented but definitely couture market. His look is modern with sporty detailing.

Christian Aujard is known as the "Couturier of Ready to Wear." His soft, feminine clothes can be found in boutiques from Toulouse to Toronto.

Gerard Pipart of the House of Nina Ricci incorporates youth, vitality, and dynamic ideas in his original and energetic designs.

Karl Lagerfeld's designs have flair, finesse, and femininity. He creates his soft, sophisticated clothes for the House of Chloe.

Vogue Designer Original

In recent years, Paris has been joined by the "new couture." Rome, London, Dublin, and Madrid have moved into the fashion world and made it their own, imparting their inimitable personalities and outlook to the fashions they create. Here you will find the Savile Row tailoring and subtle elegance of the British Isles intermingled with the flair and drama of the Latin countries. Their fresh yet chic approach, so obvious in all their designs, has inestimably widened the world fashion scope. Realizing this, Vogue features selections from these great collections in their Designer Original patterns—selections made always with you, the truly fashion-conscious woman, in mind.

Belinda Bellville of London adds a youthful flair to crisp, well-bred daytime wear and thoroughly romantic evening and wedding dresses.

Valentino is the famous Roman couturier whose inimitable design skill and color sense have attracted an overwhelming coterie of the international set's most elegant women.

Jean Muir instills a traditional quality of simplicity into her designs, bespeaking her tranquil Scottish background. Determined to make clothes comfortable, she matches style with fashion sense.

Gianni Versace has the biggest ready-to-wear business in Italy. Art, cinema, and young people's tastes all influence his modernistic fashion approach.

Vogue American Designer Original

American designers no longer have to take a back seat to those in Paris and other international fashion capitals. Brash, young, modern, sparked by originality and excitement, the American collections are as news-making as those anywhere in the world. The casual California way of life and the cosmopolitan atmosphere of New York combine in a fashion melting pot as versatile and changeable as the nation itself. Vogue continues its tradition of seeking out the best fashion creations from the promising American designers. You will find them presented in the Vogue American Designer Original collection, devoted to bringing you the newest and best America has to offer.

Anne Klein's name is identified with creative American sportswear. **Donna Karan** continues that sportive creativity in her distinctive Anne Klein designs.

Bill Blass is the award-winning designer whose fashion message is young, elegant, and cosmopolitan. His clothes are geared to the life of today's active woman.

Geoffrey Beene designs clothes with a beautifully proportioned line that is the hallmark of couture. His great taste and trendsetting approach make him a favorite with fashion pace-setters.

Oscar De La Renta holds a featured position in the roster of American designers. His collections link his natural talent with his firm belief in the importance of tailoring and the mastery of every aspect of design.

Calvin Klein is sportswear's 20th century classicist. His clean lines and naturally easy design approach made him the youngest member of the Fashion Hall of Fame.

Carol Horn brings a fresh, contemporary approach to American fashion. Her interest is the present . . . revivals bore her. Her comfortable, easy-to-wear designs inspire the individualist.

Ralph Lauren creates a look that is always unique, refreshing, and exuberantly Today. His clothes are well-bred, confident, always a bit off-handed in their luxuriousness.

Albert Nipon is a creator of today's classics. His meticulous attention to detail, often expressed in delicate tucking, makes his designs instantly recognizable.

Jerry Silverman and his designer Shannon Rogers express their fashion ideals in their credo "good design, good fabric, good workmanship."

Scott Barrie began his fashion career at Vogue Patterns. Now, as an internationally famed designer, he continues to create young, distinctive, exciting looks.

Edith Head, the legendary costume designer for the Hollywood stars, creates fashions that exemplify her Oscar winning talent.

Kasper, a member of the Fashion Hall of Fame, is noted for his uncanny ability to anticipate trends and for his expertise in combining textures and colors.

Adele Simpson's philosophy has guided her through many successful years in the fashion business: clothes must move easily and never be contrived; they must be comfortable as well as practical.

Don Sayres believes that at the foundation of all good design is a taste level that must remain constant. He designs contemporary classics with a fresh, realistic approach.

Bill Kaiserman, the creative genius behind the **Rafael** label, designs quality apparel. His clothes are tailored to suit the contemporary lifestyle.

John Anthony epitomizes quiet chic. A fashion minimalist, he expresses his philosophy in a few key textures and colors, in masterful draping, and a perfectionist cut.

Diane von Furstenberg's name is synonymous with impeccable taste. Her innate designing talent makes her dresses wonderfully wearable.

Perry Ellis designs clothes to relax in, to feel good in, to be at ease in. He puts everything together with youthful zest, with proportion and shape the key to his philosophy.

The Vogue Catalogue

The Vogue Pattern catalogue offers an abundance of fashion designs to satisfy the desires of women—and men—to be beautifully dressed for every mood and occasion. We literally go to the ends of the earth to bring you the most complete selection of designs—from the great European collections, New York City's Seventh Avenue design centers, to our own design rooms. Great care is taken to feature the finest photography and the most realistic illustrations in order to convey both the fashion concept and the construction details of every design.

The introductory section of the catalogue is a photographic highlight of the very latest fashion trends in styles, fabrics, and colors. The rest of the catalogue is organized into sections to enable you to quickly find whatever style you are seeking. Most of the sections are divided according to the type of garment—dresses, separates, coordinates, sportswear, lingerie and sleepwear, loungewear, and after-five.

The designers show up everywhere in the catalogue—*Vogue Paris Originals, Vogue Designer Originals,* and the *Vogue American Designer Originals*—to offer you the height of the European and American fashion markets. Some designers contribute elegant and dramatic fashions with the intricate detailing of haute couture. Others offer young, sophisticated, contemporary, and easy-to-wear designs. Vogue Patterns' own designers complete the vast selection of garments for every occasion.

In addition to the broad range of fashions included in the catalogue, there are several special categories of patterns. *Very Easy Vogue Patterns* couple fabulous style with simple, easy-to-follow construction and few pattern pieces. *Vogue Bridal Designs* offer an outstandingly beautiful selection of designs for the entire bridal party. *Vogue Maternity Designs* for the mother-in-waiting give her the very latest in fashion trends. *Little Vogue* caters to the carriage set and on up to the school age crowd with marvelous party dresses, sporty separates, and special occasion creations.

Vogue Patterns for Men, created by American and European designers as well as Vogue's own designers, include fashions to suit the most discriminating male. Whether his tastes are classic or innovative, Vogue offers a choice of patterns to reflect his particular needs and preferences. Last but not least, Vogue's *Craft and Accessories* patterns offer a wide range of creative ideas for gift items, fashion accessories, children's toys, and home and holiday decorations.

Although the Vogue catalogue is a wealth of fashion ideas, it also contains some very important information to assist you in your pattern and sewing selections. The caption for each pattern clearly describes all the views and construction details. Information about yardage requirements, fabric suggestions, and notions are also listed. Located on the back, you will find a numerical index for every pattern included in the catalogue, a measurement chart, and instructions for taking body measurements and selecting the correct pattern size.

There is a world of fashion at your fingertips in every Vogue catalogue and a fantastic look in each pattern. Whatever your age, size, life-style, or personal taste, there is something there for you. The choice is yours . . . the Vogue choice.

Choosing the Pattern for You

Choosing the correct pattern size avoids wasting money and effort—not to mention time. Just imagine how many more creations you can turn out if you don't have to spend time needlessly adjusting an incorrect pattern size. To be sure you are buying the correct pattern size, you should consider figure changes that may have taken place. How many women do you know who plunge directly into cutting the same size they've worn for the last five years, only to discover that those few pounds added or subtracted make an irreversible difference in fit once the fabric has been cut? Even if you have maintained the same weight, it is possible that certain body areas may have become fuller while others have become more slender. These small body changes may require a careful re-evaluation of the silhouettes that are most becoming on you rather than necessitating the purchase of a larger or smaller pattern size. Also be aware of how fashion influences the fit of your garments. There are years or seasons when the trend is toward a closer, more revealing fit as opposed to a looser, freer line.

To determine your correct pattern size, follow these three easy steps: measure precisely, select your correct figure type, and gain an understanding of ease. With this knowledge, you can approach your next sewing project with confidence.

Your Body Measurements

Accurate measurements are the starting point in selecting your correct pattern size. When taking your measurements, be sure you are wearing properly fitted undergarments and your usual shoes so that your posture will be normal. Never measure over an outer garment.

Although it is easier if a friend can help you, measurements can be taken unassisted by working in front of a full-length mirror. Make sure the tape measure is held straight and snug, but not tight, against the body. Check in the mirror to be sure the tape is always parallel to the floor for the circumference measurements; do not let it slide down in the front or back (see illustrations). Double-check your measurements for accuracy.

These basic measurements are sufficient for selecting your correct pattern type and size. Additional measurements will be necessary if you have to make any pattern adjustments and alterations (see page 75).

Measure your bust, waist, and hips periodically so you can be aware of any possible changes in your figure. Record your measurements, along with the date, on a convenient chart for easy reference. Even though your weight remains stable, your body contours may shift, and you may find it necessary to change your pattern size or even figure type in the future.

While being measured, look straight ahead and maintain your normal posture. First, tie a string around the thinnest part of your waist to use as a reference point in taking other measurements.

Full Bust: Measure over the fullest part of the bust and then straight across the back (1).

High Bust: Measure across the top of the breasts, under the arms, and across the widest part of the back (2). The high bust measurement is not listed on body measurement charts. However, if the difference between your full bust and high bust is 2" or more, use the high bust measurement for determining your pattern size.

Waist: Measure around the thinnest part of your body over the string (3).

Hips: Measure around the fullest part of your hips (4). Mark the position with pins on your undergarments and measure the distance from the waistline over the top of the bones down to the pins, which is usually 7" to 9" (5).

Back Waist Length: Measure from the prominent back neckbone to your waist (6).

Height: Remove your shoes and stand in your stocking feet against a wall. Stand erect and place a ruler on top of your head, parallel to the floor. Mark its position on the wall and measure the distance to the floor with a tape measure or a yardstick.

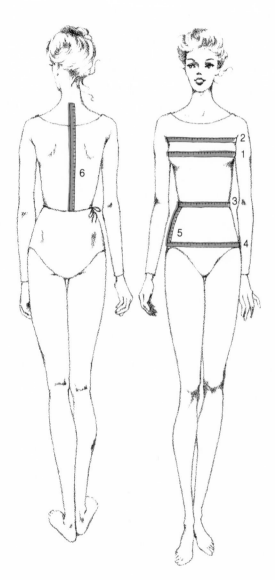

Your Figure Type

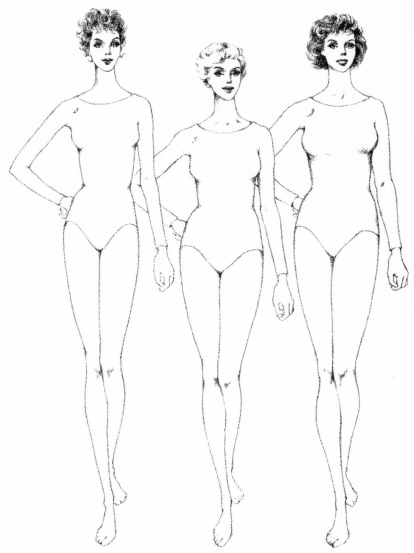

Misses'

A well-proportioned and developed figure that is 5'5" to 5'6" in height; considered the "average" figure.

Half-Size

A fully developed figure with a shorter back waist length and larger waist than Misses'; 5'2" to 5'3" in height.

Women's

A larger, longer and more fully developed figure than Misses'; well-proportioned; 5'5" to 5'6" in height.

The second step in selecting your correct pattern size is determining your figure type. Because women vary greatly in size and shape, average figure types of varying proportions are the basis for the "grading" or sizing of pattern sizes. Standard body measurements have been established by the pattern industry for uniform sizing among all the companies. Thus, patterns offer a choice of proportion—figure type—and measurements in order to most closely approximate the many variations of the feminine figure.

We must stress that figure type is a matter of proportion, not age. Your pattern is your sewing blueprint, from which you will build your exact dimensions for perfect fit. Choosing the correct size and figure type will therefore minimize alterations and further adjustments, and make sewing easier for you.

MISSES': The Misses' size range has been developed to encompass patterns for a well-proportioned and developed figure. You'll find her hip measurement on the chart to be at the 9" level. Without shoes, she stands about 5'5" or 5'6" in height. The Misses' figure is considered the statistically "average" figure.

HALF-SIZE: The woman with a fully developed figure and short back waist length belongs in this size range. Her waist and hips are larger in proportion to her bust than in the other figure types. The fullest part of her hips is 7" down from her waist. She stands approximately 5'2" or 5'3" without her shoes on.

WOMEN'S: The Women's figure is somewhat larger, longer, and more fully developed than the Misses' figure, but is just as well-proportioned. She stands approximately 5'5" or 5'6" tall without her shoes on. According to the chart, the fullest part of her hips has been measured at 9" below the waistline.

To determine your figure type, compare your bust, waist, hip, back waist, and height measurements with those of the figure types on the next page to see which one corresponds with your own body configurations. You will probably find that your measurements do not correspond exactly with those in any specific size. Do not be alarmed; the woman who is lucky enough to have those standard measurements is indeed difficult—if not impossible—to find. The figure type and size you choose should be the one whose measurements correspond most closely to your own.

Height is one indicator of figure type. However, the proportion of your body—the length of your torso, the location of your bust and hips in relation to your waist, and difference between your bust, waist, and hip measurements—is the most important factor in determining your correct figure type.

To evaluate the length of your torso, compare your back waist length measurement with the figure types. Measure the distance of your hips from your waistline to determine the vertical proportions of your figure. The measurements of your bust, waist, and hips will indicate their relative circumference proportions.

If, in comparing your measurements to the size ranges, you find that you fall between figure types, take stock of your body structure. Stand in front of the mirror and ponder awhile. Is your body long and slender or shorter and more closely put together? Then refer to the introductions included with each figure type for a general description of the figures. They will give you a clue to your perfect figure type. Now refer back to the figure types and choose the one best for you.

Measurement Chart

Misses'

SIZE	6	8	10	12	14	16	18	20
BODY MEASUREMENTS *in inches and (centimeters)*								
Bust	30½(78)	31½(80)	32½(83)	34(87)	36(92)	38(97)	40(102)	42(107)
Waist	23(58)	24(61)	25(64)	26½(67)	28(71)	30(76)	32(81)	34(87)
Hip	32½(83)	33½(85)	34½(88)	36(92)	38(97)	40(102)	42(107)	44(112)
Back Waist Length	15½(39.5)	15¾(40)	16(40.5)	16¼(41.5)	16½(42)	16¾(42.5)	17(43)	17¼(44)
PATTERN MEASUREMENTS								
Shoulder Length	4¾(12)	4¾(12)	4⅞(12.5)	5(12.5)	5⅛(13)	5¼(13.5)	5⅜(13.5)	5½(14)
Back Width	13¾(35)	14(35.5)	14¼(36)	14⅝(37)	15(38)	15½(39.5)	16(40.5)	16½(42)
Sleeve Width	11¾(30)	12⅛(31)	12½(32)	13(33)	13⅜(34)	13⅞(35)	14⅜(36.5)	14⅞(38)
Sleeve Length	22⅜(57)	22⅝(57.5)	23(58.5)	23¼(59)	23⅝(60)	23⅞(60.5)	24⅛(61.5)	24⅜(62)
Skirt Length (from back waistline)	22¼(56.5)	22½(57)	22¾(58)	23(58.5)	23¼(59)	23½(59.5)	23¾(60.5)	24(61)

Half-Size

SIZE	10½	12½	14½	16½	18½	20½	22½	24½
BODY MEASUREMENTS *in inches and (centimeters)*								
Bust	33(84)	35(89)	37(94)	39(99)	41(104)	43(109)	45(114)	47(119)
Waist	27(69)	29(74)	31(79)	33(84)	35(89)	37½(96)	40(102)	40½(108)
Hip	35(89)	37(94)	39(99)	41(104)	43(109)	45½(116)	48(122)	50½(128)
Back Waist Length	15(38)	15¼(39)	15½(39.5)	15¾(40)	15⅞(40.5)	16(40.5)	16⅛(41)	16¼(41.5)
PATTERN MEASUREMENTS								
Shoulder Length	4⅝(11.5)	4¾(12)	4⅞(12.5)	5(12.5)	5⅛(13)	5¼(13.5)	5¼(13.5)	5⅜(13.5)
Back Width	14⅛(36)	14½(37)	14⅞(38)	15¼(39)	15¾(40)	16⅛(41)	16⅝(42)	17⅛(43.5)
Sleeve Width	13⅛(33.5)	13⅝(34.5)	14⅛(36)	14⅝(37)	15⅛(38.5)	15⅝(39.5)	16⅛(41)	16⅝(42)
Sleeve Length	22⅛(56)	22⅜(57)	22⅝(57.5)	22⅞(58)	23⅛(58.5)	23⅜(59.5)	23⅝(60)	23⅞(60.5)
Skirt Length (from back waistline	23(58.5)	23¼(59)	23½(59.5)	23¾(60.5)	23⅞(60.5)	24(61)	24⅛(61.5)	24¼(61.5)

Women's

SIZE	38	40	42	44
BODY MEASUREMENTS *in inches and (centimeters)*				
Bust	42(107)	44(112)	46(117)	48(122)
Waist	35(89)	37(94)	39(99)	41½(105)
Hip	44(112)	46(117)	48(122)	50(127)
Back Waist Length	17¼(44)	17⅜(44)	17½(44.5)	17⅝(45)
PATTERN MEASUREMENTS				
Shoulder Length	5½(14)	5⅝(14.5)	5⅝(14.5)	5¾(14.5)
Back Width	16⅝(42)	17⅛(43.5)	17⅝(45)	18⅛(46)
Sleeve Width	15(38)	15½(39.5)	16(40.5)	16½(42)
Sleeve Length	23⅞(60.5)	24⅛(61.5)	24⅜(62)	24⅝(62.5)
Skirt Length (from back waistline)	24⅜(62)	24½(62)	24⅝(62.5)	24¾(63)

Understanding Ease

Each Vogue Pattern takes into consideration your need for comfort and mobility by building in **wearing ease** to allow you freedom of movement without restraint. **Design ease** is an integral part of many styles and will have additional dimensions added to the pattern beyond the wearing ease, as dictated by the garment's design lines.

The pattern caption in the catalogue and on the back of the pattern envelope describes how the garment is intended to fit. Some women prefer loosely fitting clothes while others prefer clothes fitted more closely to the body. Use this information to help you select the type of fit in your garments that is most flattering to your figure.

WEARING EASE Without the built-in "liveability" found in most patterns your garments would not be comfortable—you would not be able to stretch, sit, or walk up or down stairs in comfort.

Wearing ease is additional inches added to the pattern pieces beyond the actual body measurements. Never use this ease to accommodate a larger size or eliminate it when making pattern adjustments and alterations. The approximate wearing ease is 2½″ to 3½″ for bust; 1″ for waist; and 2½″ to 2¾″ for hips. A chart listing the wearing ease for each figure type can be found on page 76.

Some patterns may have little or no wearing ease at all. Halter-neck, extremely cut-away armholes, and strapless bodices must fit very closely to the body. Patterns stating "use only stretchable knits" will have less wearing ease because the fabric's elasticity allows for movement and comfort.

DESIGN EASE The extra fullness added to a garment by the designer to create a wide variety of silhouettes is called the design or fashion ease. The different silhouettes are described in the pattern caption as closely fitted, fitted, semi-fitted, loosely fitted, and very loosely fitted. A **closely fitted** garment would have no design ease and little or no wearing ease. A **fitted** garment would have little or no design ease in addition to wearing ease. A **semi-fitted** dress may have up to 4″ of ease in the bust; a **loosely fitted** dress up to 8″; and a **very loosely fitted** dress over 8″. Coats and jackets have more ease than dresses and blouses to enable them to be worn comfortably over other garments. A chart with the design ease allowances for different types of garments can be found on page 76.

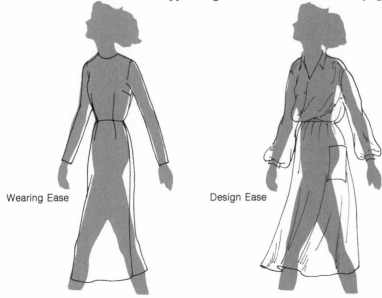

Wearing Ease   Design Ease

Your Correct Pattern Size

After taking accurate measurements, determining your figure type, and gaining an understanding of pattern ease, you are now ready to choose your correct pattern size. Do not select your pattern size on the basis of the size that you take in ready-to-wear clothes. Instead, compare your measurements with the body measurements for your figure type on page 62 and circle those closest to your own. Detailed body measurement charts can also be found on the back reference pages of a pattern catalogue.

When selecting a dress, jacket, blouse, or coat pattern, choose your size by your **bust measurement**. Just as height and back waist measurements were the key measurements in determining your figure type, your bust measurement is the key measurement for choosing your pattern size. If your waist or hip measurements do not correspond to the measurement for this pattern size, it is easier to make adjustments in either or both of these areas than to alter the bodice.

If there is more than a 2″ difference between your full bust measurement and your high bust measurement, you have a fuller bust in relation to your frame. Since patterns are sized for a B cup bust, you will achieve a better fit if you select your pattern size by your high bust measurement. It will be easier to alter only the bust than to make adjustments on the rest of the pattern.

For a skirt, pants, or shorts pattern, select your size by your **waist measurement**. If your hips are much larger in proportion than your waist, select the size closest to your hip measurement and then make adjustments in the waist. When buying coordinate patterns that include blouses, skirts, jackets, and/or pants, select your size by your bust measurement and adjust your waist and hips if necessary. For maternity patterns, choose the same size that you wore before pregnancy.

Remember that the measurements listed in the charts are the actual body sizes; true pattern dimensions have ease built in beyond the actual body sizes for an attractive fit. These dimensions change, adding further fullness when design ease is needed to obtain a certain silhouette, so be sure to always choose your pattern size by the body measurements listed in the charts.

Frequently women fall between two sizes. If this applies to you, consider your bone structure. If you are thin and small boned, choose the smaller of the two sizes. Conversely, a large-boned person will require all the ease of the larger size. Personal preference may also influence your decision depending on whether you prefer a looser or closer fit.

Many women are a combination of two pattern sizes. If you fall into this category, look for **Vogue Doubles** patterns, which combine two sizes in one pattern. The two cutting lines on the pattern enable you to change sizes at the bust, waist, or hip according to your figure. For in-between sizes, simply cut between the cutting lines. **Vogue Doubles** can eliminate pattern alterations, fitting problems, and the need for buying two separate size patterns when one half of you differs from the other.

When a new fashion trend develops, it is often difficult to judge how the style will look on you. Before buying a pattern, try on ready-to-wear garments to check proportions and styling. Above all, when selecting patterns, choose the silhouettes that are most flattering to your figure regardless of current fashion trends. Accent your good figure points and minimize your flaws.

Choosing your correct pattern size will not guarantee an absolutely perfect fit because few women have statistically average measurements. Figure and posture variations affect fit. To assure yourself of a perfect fit, you may have to customize the pattern to your own figure by making some pattern adjustments and alterations.

Pattern Particulars
Envelope Front: Fashion

The pattern envelope presents the total fashion concept originally created by the designer. Through artwork and sometimes photography, the flair of the design as well as the construction details of the garments are shown. The pattern may be shown in different views to give you a wider selection of styles. The fabrics are carefully selected for illustration to show the types of fabric, suitable for different seasons, that are recommended for this particular pattern. Even the accessories are chosen to complement the design and to show the fashion concept.

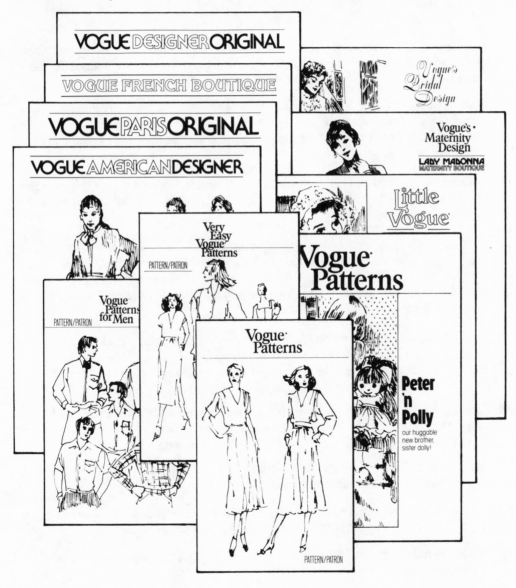

Envelope Back: Information

The envelope front was instrumental in your pattern selection. Now use the envelope back to your advantage. All envelopes contain the complete information you will need to make the proper selection of fabric and notions.

1 **Style Number, Size, and Price:** Buying information is found in the upper corner of the envelope back.

2 **Descriptive Caption:** Sizing category, type of garment, and total number of pattern pieces are stated. The detailed explanation describes the silhouette, pertinent details not visible in the sketch, and any additional instructions included in the pattern.

3 **Body Measurements:** Patterns are computed for these measurements. Included in the pattern tissue are wearing ease and style ease as dictated by the design.

4 **Yardage:** Sizes are across the top. Garment type and/or version letter are just above fabric widths, including interfacing, lining, underlining, and trims needed for each version. Fabric widths have nap indications alongside them.

5 **Width at Lower Edge:** This measurement will tell you the hem circumference of a skirt, dress, shirt, or coat, or the width of the pant leg.
Finished Back Lengths and Side Lengths: These lengths are used as starting points for pattern tissue length adjustments.

6 **Notions:** All required and optional notions with recommended sizes for your garment are listed here. They were chosen in the correct proportion to complement the garment design as featured.

7 **W/WO:** This key indicates whether the yardage shown is for fabrics with or without nap. Fabrics with nap (W) have layouts with all pattern pieces placed in the same direction, as required for directional fabrics. Layouts for fabrics without nap (WO) may have pattern pieces placed in any direction; additional yardage would be required for directional fabrics.

8 **Fabric Design Suitability:** This important information tells if the pattern is not suitable for stripes, plaids, or diagonal fabrics. When these fabrics are suitable you'll find a line stating "No Allowance Made for Matching Stripes and Plaids" because the additional yardage needed varies with the size of the fabric design.

9 **Fabrics:** Suggestions listed in this area are well-known fabric types suitable for the design to give you a wide choice. The most important quality of desirable fabrics, soft or crisp, is given to indicate the silhouette intended by the designer.

10 **Back Views:** These drawings show styling and construction details for all design versions that were not visible in the fashion illustration.

11 **Labels:** This is a reminder to ask at the pattern counter for your Vogue Paris Original, Vogue American Designer Original, or Vogue Designer Original label.

12 **Vogue Pattern Service:** The truly international aspect of Vogue Patterns is reflected by its representative offices in several countries.

1971

SIZE 10

$6.00
$6.60 in Canada

10

1971 MISSES' JACKET, BLOUSE AND PANTS   **22 PIECES**

Loose-fitting, unlined, unconstructed, slightly below-hip length jacket has notched collar, front-buttoned closing, self bias binding around collar and edges, patch pockets and full-length sleeves. Edgestitching. Loose-fitting blouse has V-neckline, front-buttoned closing and full-length sleeves gathered into bias buttoned cuffs (may be worn turned back). Topstitching. Tapered pants with front tucked into front buttoned waistband with belt carriers has mock fly front zipper closing and side front slanted pockets. Edgestitching. Purchased belt.

BODY MEASUREMENTS	Inches					BODY MEASUREMENTS	Metric				
Bust	30½	31½	32½	34	36	Bust	78	80	83	87	92cm
Waist	23	24	25	26½	28	Waist	58	61	64	67	71cm
Hip	32½	33½	34½	36	38	Hip	83	85	88	92	97cm
Back Waist Length	15½	15¾	16	16¼	16½	Back Waist Length	39.5	40	40.5	41.5	42cm
BUST	30½	31½	32½	34	36	BUST	78	80	83	87	92
SIZE	6	8	10	12	14	SIZE	6	8	10	12	14

JACKET						JACKET					
35'' */**	2½	2⅝	2⅝	2⅞	2⅞	90cm */**	2.30	2.40	2.40	2.70	2.70 m
44/45'' */**	1¾	2	2	2	2	115cm */**	1.60	1.90	1.90	1.90	1.90 m
54'' *	1⅝	1⅝	1⅝	1⅝	1¾	140cm *	1.50	1.50	1.50	1.50	1.60 m
60'' *	1⅝	1⅝	1⅝	1⅝	1⅝	150cm *	1.50	1.50	1.50	1.50	1.50 m

PANTS						PANTS					
35'' */**	2⅝	2⅝	2⅝	2⅝	2¾	90cm */**	2.40	2.40	2.40	2.40	2.60 m
44/45'' */**	2⅜	2⅜	2⅜	2½	2¼	115cm */**	2.20	2.20	2.20	2.30	2.40 m
54'' *	1¾	1¾	1¾	1¾	1⅞	140cm *	1.60	1.60	1.60	1.60	1.80 m
60'' *	1½	1½	1½	1⅝	1¾	150cm *	1.40	1.40	1.40	1.50	1.60 m

JACKET AND PANTS						JACKET AND PANTS					
35'' */**	4⅛	4⅝	4⅞	5¼	5⅜	90cm */**	4.20	4.30	4.50	4.80	5.00 m
44/45'' */**	3¾	3¾	3⅞	4⅛	4⅛	115cm */**	3.50	3.50	3.60	3.80	3.80 m
54'' *	2⅞	3⅛	3⅜	3⅜	3¾	140cm *	2.70	2.90	3.10	3.10	3.10 m
60'' *	2⅞	2⅞	2⅞	2⅞	3	150cm *	2.70	2.70	2.70	2.70	2.80 m

JACKET INTERFACING (Optional) (Either Version)						JACKET INTERFACING (Optional) (Either Version)					
36,45''	⅜	⅜	½	½	½	90,115cm	0.40	0.40	0.50	0.50	0.50 m

PANTS INTERFACING (Either Version)						PANTS INTERFACING (Either Version)					
36,45''	⅛	⅛	⅛	⅛	⅛	90,115cm	0.20	0.20	0.20	0.20	0.20 m

PANTS STAY (Either Version) / PANTS STAY (Either Version)

44/45'' Lining	½	½	½	½	½	115cm Lining	0.50	0.50	0.50	0.50	0.50 m

BLOUSE						BLOUSE					
35'' **	2⅛	2⅛	2¼	2⅜	2⅝	90cm **	2.00	2.00	2.10	2.20	2.40 m
44/45'' **	1¾	1¾	1⅞	2	2	115cm **	1.60	1.60	1.80	1.90	1.90 m

INTERFACING FOR FRONT AND BACK FACINGS (Optional) / INTERFACING FOR FRONT AND BACK FACINGS (Optional)

44/45'' Underlining	⅞	⅞	⅞	⅞	⅞	115cm Underlining	0.80	0.80	0.80	0.80	0.80 m

CUFFS INTERFACING / CUFFS INTERFACING

44/45'' Underlining	½	½	½	½	½	115cm Underlining	0.50	0.50	0.50	0.50	0.50 m

Width at lower edge						Width at lower edge					
Jacket	37	38	39	40½	42½	Jacket	94	96.5	99	103	108cm
Pants (each leg)	15	15½	16	16¾	17½	Pants (each leg)	38	39.5	40.5	42.5	44.5cm
Blouse	38½	39½	40½	42	43½	Blouse	98	100	103	106.5	110cm
Finished back length from base of neck						**Finished back length from base of neck**					
Jacket	25¾	26	26¼	26½	26¾	Jacket	65.5	66	66.5	67	68cm
Blouse	24¼	24½	24¾	25	25¼	Blouse	61.5	62	63	63.5	64cm
Finished side length from waist						**Finished side length from waist**					
Pants	41½	41¾	42	42¼	42½	Pants	105	106	106.5	107	108cm

NOTIONS: Jacket: Two ¾'' (line 30) Buttons. Pants: 7'' Skirt Zipper. One ⅝'' (line 24) Button, Hooks and Eyes Size 2, Seam Binding and 1'' Belt. Blouse: Seven ⅜'' (line 18) Buttons and Seam Binding.

NOTIONS: Jacket: Two 20mm Buttons. Pants: 18cm Skirt Zipper, One 15mm Button, Hooks and Eyes, Seam Binding and 25mm Belt. Blouse: Seven 10mm Buttons and Seam Binding.

* with nap, shading, pile or one-way design.
** without nap, shading or pile or with a two-way design.

Obvious diagonal fabrics are not suitable. For one-way design: use nap yardage and nap layout. Allowance for matching plaid and stripes not included in yardages given.

FABRICS: Soft or Crisp fabrics such as Flannel, Medium Weight Pongee, Linen, Lightweight Tweeds and Double Knits for Jacket and Pants. Handkerchief Linen, Crepe de Chine, Crepe and Challis for Blouse.

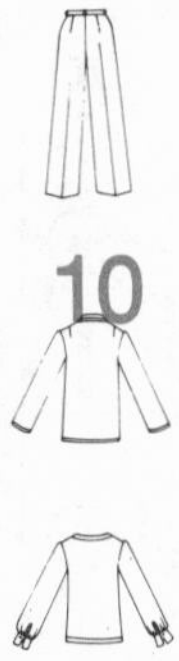

VOGUE PATTERN SERVICE
NEW YORK • LONDON • PARIS • MILAN • TORONTO • SYDNEY
161 SIXTH AVENUE, NEW YORK, NEW YORK 10013

Pattern Pieces: Blueprints

Pattern pieces are like blueprints. The master plans of any dressmaking project, they guide you by including all the construction symbols needed to make your sewing easier and more accurate. Every symbol has been printed on your pattern for a very specific and necessary purpose. Get acquainted with them; learn to recognize the markings on each piece and to understand their uses. Then all you will have to do is follow them faithfully.

1 *Grainline:* This heavy solid line with arrows at either end indicates the direction of the grain. Most often it runs parallel to the fabric selvage, along the lengthwise grain. When the pattern is illustrated in border prints, scallop-edged laces, etc., the tissue will state, "place on lengthwise or crosswise grain."

2 *Cutting Line:* The heavy outer line of the pattern piece is indicated by scissors. It may also be found within the pattern designating a "cut off" line for a style variation.

3 *Seamline:* The long, broken line, ⅝" inside the cutting line (unless otherwise specified) and indicated by a presser foot, is where all seams should be stitched for an ample seam allowance.

4 *Adjustment line:* Double lines are printed to indicate areas where lengthening or shortening must be done before cutting, if necessary.

5 *Center Front or Center Back Lines:* These solid lines indicate where garment is to fall at the center of the body.

6 *Fold Line:* This solid line marks where the garment is to be folded during its construction.
Roll Line: A solid line shows where the pattern piece is to be softly creased to make a soft, rolling fold.

7 *Buttons and Buttonholes:* These symbols give you the length of the buttonhole, size of button, and precise location for each.

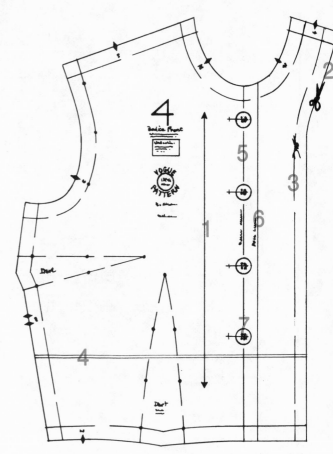

8 *Place-on-Fold Bracket:* Brackets shown on the center front or center back line indicate that a pattern piece is to be placed on the fold of the fabric before cutting.

9 *Notches:* Used for accurate joining of seams, notches are numbered in the order in which seamlines are matched.

10 *Large ●'s and Small •'s:* These symbols are printed on the tissue pattern for accurate joining of garment sections. They are particularly helpful where even distribution of gathers and ease is required, or when you are matching plaids, stripes, etc.

Triangles (▲) and squares (■) are also construction symbols to aid in matching. You must remember to sew to or through the center of all symbols.

11 *Dart:* Corresponding symbols that are to be carefully matched are placed on broken lines that meet at a point to comprise the dart marking.

12 *Zipper Placement:* This symbol indicates the placement of zipper on seamline. Pull tab at top and stop at the bottom indicate the exact length of zipper to be used.

13 *Hemline:* This line indicates the finished edge of the garment. Also included along this line is information concerning the depth of the hem for optimum drape of design and weight of fabric.

14 *Pattern Piece and Version:* Name and letter identifies pattern piece. The numbers relate to you the order in which each garment is to be constructed.

Special Cutting Instructions: Any information on the cutting of interfacing, lining, or underlining pertaining to the pattern piece will be found in this enclosed area to highlight its importance. It also states when a piece is to be cut other than twice.

Vogue Pattern Trademark: Your guarantee of fine styling also includes the pattern style number and size. Each is clearly marked to make identification simple.

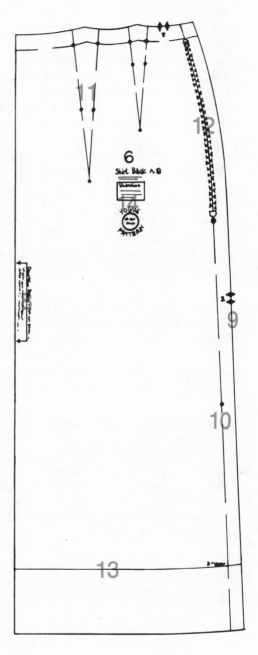

Pattern Cutting Guide

In your Vogue Pattern envelope you will find a Cutting and Sewing Guide along with the actual pattern pieces which, if followed thoroughly and consistently, can answer almost any question you might have about the general planning, pinning, cutting, and construction of your garment.

The information available in the Cutting Guide is everything in capsule form that you will need to know before you begin to actually sew. Spend time studying the correct procedure for preparing your fabric and laying out your pattern. Then no tears will be shed because you've run out of fabric by not placing your pattern pieces correctly or another equally avoidable mistake.

1 **General Instructions:** Helpful hints are given for preparing fabric, arranging fabric for cutting layouts, and for cutting and marking the pattern.

2 **Pattern Markings:** The most important symbols on the pattern tissue are identified and explained. These should be especially reviewed before cutting and marking.

3 **Special Instructions:** These instructions are concerned with the cutting of specific pattern pieces, fabrics, or bias pieces which require additional layout preparation.

4 **Pattern Pieces:** Pattern pieces show center fronts and backs, grainlines, piece numbers, cut-off lines, and notches. Recognition of the actual pattern piece is made simpler by noting this section first.

5 **Layout Piece Requirements:** All pattern pieces needed for each version of the garment and for underlining, interfacing, and lining are listed.

6 **Cutting Guide:** The garment cutting layouts are divided into style versions and then into sizes and fabric widths. Each layout is also marked as to suitability for nap. Underlining, interfacing, and lining layouts are also given in the same manner. Pattern pieces to be placed with the printed side up are shown without shading, while those that are to be placed printed side down are shaded. Carefully follow the illustrations when you fold your fabric. If any pattern pieces extend beyond the fold, they are to be cut on a single thickness after all the other pieces are cut. Circle the layout you are using for easy reference.

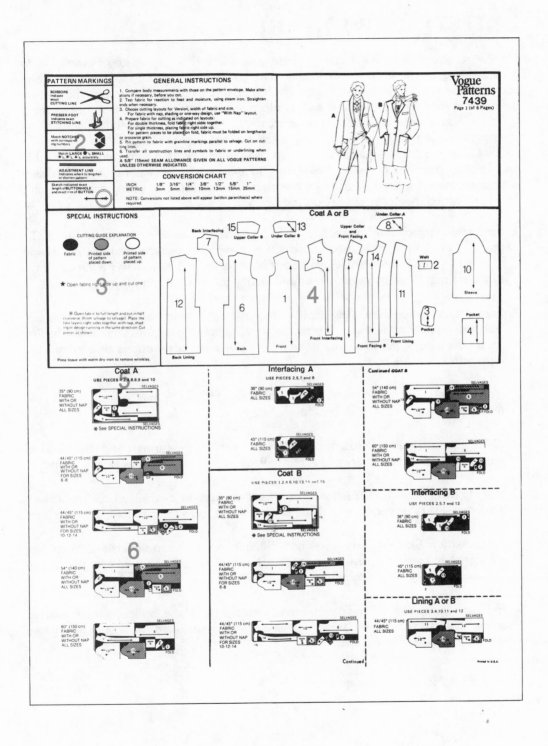

Pattern Sewing Guide

On the reverse side of the Cutting Guide you will find a step-by-step Sewing Guide arranged by garment versions with numbered and outlined instructions for fast reading and comprehension. The large and precise technical sketches that accompany the written instructions are easy to understand and as informative as having a sample of your garment in front of you. Across the top of the sheet are the fabric illustration key and suggestions on stitching, trimming, and pressing, which can serve as excellent reminders.

The Cutting and Sewing guides are indispensable ingredients in achieving the perfect fit and finish to your Vogue pattern. Whether you're a nervous beginner or a highly skilled seamstress, following the instructions diligently to the completion of your garment can only help to make the most professional looking garment possible.

1 **Pattern Identification** The pattern number is given along with the page number. To give you the benefit of couture construction in designer patterns and comprehensive directions for multiversion styles, you may find several instruction sheets in the envelope. Pages are numbered consecutively as well, stating the amount you will find.

2 **Fabric Illustration Key:** This explains the use of shading and texture in technical sketches: underlining is shown by crosshatching, interfacing by dots, lining with shading lines, right side of fabric by tone. **We follow the same distinctions throughout the illustrations in this book.**

3 **Helpful Hints:** Important points to remember on stitching, trimming, and pressing are shown and explained for your benefit.

4 **Titles:** The construction procedures for different parts of the garment and the individual versions are presented separately. A title in large bold type introduces each section.

5 **Sewing Directions:** Construction of each garment section is explained individually as it is needed. Every procedure is outlined and numbered consecutively for quick reference.

6 **Construction Sketches:** Many sewing techniques are easier to understand when they are shown in comprehensive illustrations. They are meant to be used with the written instructions, since some procedures cannot be sketched.

7 **Enlarged View:** You will find that details of important and/or difficult construction areas are enlarged and circled to clarify the sewing procedure involved. Be sure to pay special attention to each enlarged view.

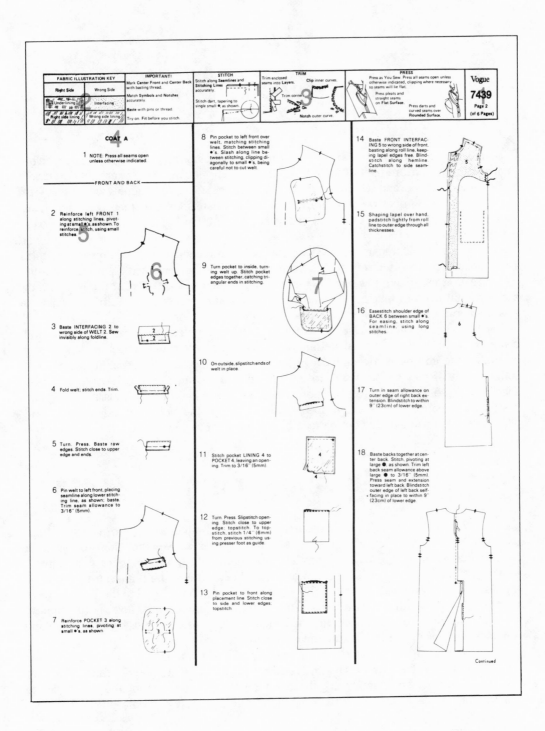

FABRIC ILLUSTRATION KEY

Right Side	Wrong Side
Underlining	Interfacing
Right side lining	Wrong side lining

IMPORTANT!

Mark Center Front and Center Back with basting thread.

Match Symbols and Notches accurately.

Baste with pins or thread.

Try on. Fit before you stitch.

STITCH

Stitch along Seamlines and Stitching Lines accurately.

Stitch dart, tapering to single small ●, as shown.

TRIM

Trim enclosed seams into Layers.

Clip inner curves.

Trim corners

Notch outer curve.

PRESS

Press as You Sew. Press all seams open unless otherwise indicated, clipping where necessary so seams will lie flat.

Press pleats and straight seams on Flat Surface.

Press darts and curved seams over Rounded Surface.

Vogue 7439
Page 2
(of 6 Pages)

COAT A

1 NOTE: Press all seams open unless otherwise indicated.

—————— FRONT AND BACK ——————

2 Reinforce left FRONT 1 along stitching lines, pivoting at small ●, as shown. To reinforce, stitch, using small stitches.

3 Baste INTERFACING 2 to wrong side of WELT 2. Sew invisibly along foldline.

4 Fold welt: stitch ends. Trim.

5 Turn. Press. Baste raw edges. Stitch close to upper edge and ends.

6 Pin welt to left front, placing seamline along lower stitching line, as shown; baste. Trim seam allowance to 3/16" (5mm).

7 Reinforce POCKET 3 along stitching lines, pivoting at small ●'s, as shown.

8 Pin pocket to left front over welt, matching stitching lines. Stitch between small ●'s. Slash along line between stitching, clipping diagonally to small ●'s, being careful not to cut welt.

9 Turn pocket to inside, turning welt up Stitch pocket edges together, catching triangular ends in stitching.

10 On outside, slipstitch ends of welt in place.

11 Stitch pocket LINING 4 to POCKET 4, leaving an opening. Trim to 3/16" (5mm).

12 Turn Press. Slipstitch opening. Stitch close to upper edge; topstitch. To topstitch, stitch 1/4" (6mm) from previous stitching using presser foot as guide.

13 Pin pocket to front along placement line Stitch close to side and lower edges, topstitch

14 Baste FRONT INTERFACING 5 to wrong side of front, basting along roll line, keeping lapel edges free. Blindstitch along hemline. Catchstitch to side seamline.

15 Shaping lapel over hand, padstitch lightly from roll line to outer edge through all thicknesses.

16 Easestitch shoulder edge of BACK 6 between small ●'s. For easing, stitch along seamline, using long stitches.

17 Turn in seam allowance on outer edge of right back extension. Blindstitch to within 9" (23cm) of lower edge.

18 Baste backs together at center back. Stitch, pivoting at large ●, as shown. Trim left back seam allowance above large ● to 3/16" (5mm). Press seam and extension toward left back. Blindstitch outer edge of left back selffacing in place to within 9" (23cm) of lower edge.

Continued

Achieving
a Perfect Fit

Achieving a perfect fit depends on more than just buying the correct pattern size. The standard body measurements compiled by the pattern industry are simply average body measurements of women within a particular size range. Since individuals within that size may vary in any number of ways from the standard measurements, they serve simply as starting points from which you must make adjustments and alterations to fit your own dimensions.

All Vogue patterns, regardless of style, are based on the same standard measurements. Thus, once you have determined how your body differs from the basic pattern figure in your size, you can make the same adjustments or alterations on all your patterns. If, for example, you need to take in ½″ on the shoulder seams of a basic pattern, you will also take in ½″ on the shoulder seams of a blouse, a dress, a suit, or a coat.

The first step for achieving a perfect fit is to take complete body measurements and compare them with the actual pattern measurements. Most differences in length and circumference can be made directly on the pattern, using flat pattern adjustments. For some people, it may be necessary to make additional changes in a pattern to allow for specific body contours. These alterations must first be worked out in a muslin or gingham basic shell because they affect a specific dimension of the body. All adjustments and alterations must be made in your pattern *before* you cut out your fabric.

Accurate Measurements

Custom fit begins with accurate measurements. You shouldn't begin to alter a pattern without knowing your exact contours, so make up a convenient chart of all your measurements. Be sure to wear appropriate undergarments and shoes when measuring.

Whether you take the measurements or a friend takes them—be honest; make sure the tape is held snug and taut (but not tight) against the body and parallel to the floor for most circumference or width measurements. The illustrated figures and the text on the opposite page will guide you in taking accurate, meaningful body measurements. If you are planning to make pants, see page 111 for the measurements to take.

When your chart is completed, keep it ready for adjustment and alteration comparisons at all times. Then you will be able to transfer your adjustments and alterations to most patterns automatically without going through the process of discovering the specific fitting adjustments for each and every pattern. Don't forget to note the date on the chart for future use.

To be sure that small figure changes are not creeping up on you unnoticed, take your bust, waist, and hip measurements often to be aware of any possible changes. Even if your weight remains stable, your measurements may shift. If you are making too many adjustments and alterations, it may be preferable to change sizes and possibly figure types as well.

Take Complete Measurements

Bust: Measure over the fullest part of the bust and then straight across the back (1).

High Bust: Measure around the body, directly under the arms and across the top of the breasts (2).

Waist: Tie a string around the body at thinnest part to establish your waistline and use as a reference point in taking other measurements. Measure circumference at the string (3).

High Hip: Measure 2″ to 4″ below your waist over top of hipbones (4).

Full Hip: Measure at fullest part of hips; mark position with pins on undergarment and measure down from waist over top of hipbones to pins, usually 7″ to 9″ from the waist (5).

Back Neck to Waist: Measure from prominent neck bone down center back to waist mark (6).

Back Width: Measure from prominent neck bone down center back 4″ to 6″ and mark. Then measure at this point from arm crease to arm crease (7).

Front Neck to Waist: Measure from hollow between neck bones to center front waistline (8).

Bust Point: To establish position of bust point, measure from base of neck to bust point, and from bust point to center front at waist. Record both measurements (9).

Shoulder: Measure from base of neck to shoulder bone (hinge) (10).

Arm Length: Measure from shoulder bone to elbow and on to wrist bone with arm slightly bent. Record both lengths (11).

Arm Circumference: Measure around fullest part of arm, generally 1″ below armpit (12), wrist at bone (13).

Neck Circumference: Measure fullest part of neck (14).

Skirt Length: Measure from center back waist to desired point on leg for hem (15), referring to the back of the envelope for a description of lengths. This will help you to estimate any length adjustments necessary on your pattern and any changes from the recommended amount of fabric to purchase.

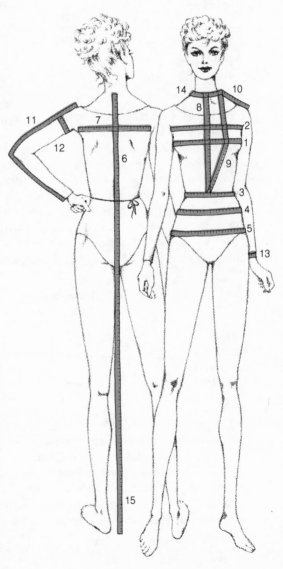

Compare Measurements

You must compare your body measurements with the corresponding pattern measurements to determine if any adjustments have to be made in the pattern before you cut out your fabric. Some body measurements—bust, waist, hip, and back waist length—can be compared to the standard measurements for your size listed on the back of the pattern envelope. For other measurements, it will be necessary to measure the pattern itself.

It is essential when comparing measurements that you always consider the amount of ease necessary in the garment (see page 63). **Wearing ease** is the additional fullness added to a pattern to allow for body movement and comfort. It should not be used to accommodate a larger size. The chart below shows the extra inches of wearing ease added to the pattern pieces beyond the actual body circumference measurements for each figure type.

	Misses'	Half-Size	Women's
Bust	2½″	3½″	3½″
Waist	1″	1″	1″
Hip	2½″	2½″	2¾″

Almost all pattern pieces will measure larger than your actual body measurements. The exceptions are very close-fitting designs such as strapless and halter tops that may have no wearing ease at all. Also, patterns designed especially for stretchable fabrics will have less wearing ease since the fabric will contribute some elasticity for a comfortable fit.

In addition to wearing ease, many patterns have **design ease,** which is fullness added by the designer to create the intended silhouette. The amount of design ease is described in the caption on the back of the pattern envelope and in the catalogue, and states whether the garment is closely fitted, semi-fitted, fitted, loose-fitting, or very loose-fitting.

Below is a chart with the approximate design ease allowances of a pattern over the body measurements for each category of design fullness.

	Inner Wear (*dresses, tops*)	Transitional (*unlined jackets*)	Outerwear (*lined jackets, coats*)
Fitted	0–2½″	0–4″	0–6″
Semi-fitted	2⅝″–4″	4⅛–6″	6⅛″–8″
Loose-fitting	4⅛″–8″	6⅛″–10″	8⅛″–12″
Very loose-fitting	over 8″	over 10″	over 12″

Design ease can be taken into consideration when adjusting a pattern. You may not wish to increase the hip circumference in a very loose-fitting garment if you will not miss the extra fullness intended by the designer.

When measuring pattern pieces, be sure to exclude all seam allowances, darts, overlapping edges, pleat underlays, etc. You can pin the pattern pieces together and measure as a unit, or you can measure each piece from the center or seamline to seamline and add the measurements together.

The bodice is crucial to a good fit. Compare your bust, waist, and back waist length measurements to those listed on the pattern envelope for your size. If the measurements differ, you must make the proper adjustments. The shoulder seam of the pattern and your shoulder length should correspond. Also compare neck circumference. To locate the bust point, measure the pattern from the point where the neck and the shoulder seams intersect, down toward the dart point, and on to the waist at the center front. Compare your personal measurements with the pattern. Bust darts should point directly toward the bust point and end ½″ to 1″ from the point.

For sleeves it is important to determine both the proper sleeve length, including any cuffs, as well as the correct elbow dart placement. It may be necessary to alter the sleeve length either above or below the elbow or in both locations. Sleeve circumference should allow for wearing ease of about 2″, with a greater allowance for heavier arms than for thin ones.

For skirts, both the waist and hip measurements can be compared with the measurements on the envelope. The hipline is established on a pattern at 9″ below the waistline for Misses' and Women's sizes and at 7″ below the waistline for Half-sizes. It is essential for a comfortable and attractive fit that you have the right hip fit in the exact spot. Compare both high hip and full hip measurements, being sure to measure down the exact amount on the pattern that you did when measuring yourself.

Usually the garment's finished length is given on the pattern envelope or you can measure the actual pattern pieces along the center back. Compare it with your personal skirt length measurement.

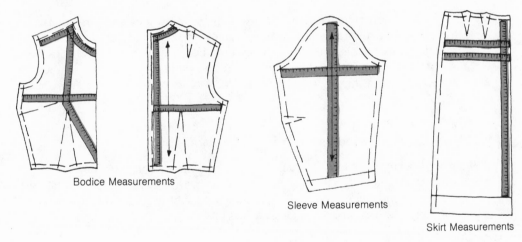

Bodice Measurements

Sleeve Measurements

Skirt Measurements

On the following pages are explained all the specific procedures you will need for personal fitting. The changes you will make are divided into two categories. **Adjustments** are minor changes that are made "in the flat" on your pattern tissue before you cut your muslin. **Alterations** are major changes that are made on the muslin fitting shell to ensure they will relate to your body contours.

All the changes are clearly illustrated for you. **Only the front pattern pieces are shown for adjustments, as equal changes are made for the front and back pattern pieces. Alterations, which are more localized, may not require changes on both front and back pieces, and thus only the affected pieces are shown.** So that you may relate your adjustments and alterations to everything you sew, we will also show you how to make them on other basic shapes (princess lines, raglan sleeves, etc.) when applicable.

Flat Pattern Adjustments

Let us help take the mystery out of pattern adjustments. You need not be reluctant to try an original idea to get a better fit as long as you remember this principle: since all patterns and fabric are flat, any change you make must be done in such a manner that the pattern tissue will also remain flat after it is adjusted.

Flat basic pattern pieces are essential tools of the pattern and clothing industries for maintaining consistency in sizing. Use your adjusted fitting patterns the same way to achieve a personalized and perfect fit.

When making the flat pattern adjustments on the following pages, follow these rules:

☐ Keep grainlines, center front, and center back foldlines straight.

☐ Make adjustments with discretion to carefully preserve style lines of design.

☐ Maintain wearing ease built into pattern.

☐ Use adjustment lines provided for lengthening and shortening. Make sure you have made your length adjustments the same amount along the entire adjustment line. After the changes have been made to your satisfaction, anchor them permanently with transparent tape.

☐ When making circumference adjustments, keep in mind that each major pattern piece represents a quarter of your body. Think of your body as divided in half horizontally by the waistline and in half vertically by the center front and back lines. Since, as a general rule, only the right half of the pattern is given, the amount of adjustment taken on the front bodice piece, for example, is only one quarter of the total adjustment.

☐ Make corresponding changes on all related pieces—bodice front and back, skirt front and back, facing front and back, lining front and back, etc.

☐ When re-drawing printed construction lines that have been interrupted by your adjustments, simply joining the two ends will result in an irregular line. To re-establish a smooth line, you will have to add to one line and subtract from the other equally, thus tapering your new line to the original line.

The cutting line and dart corrections of the pattern pieces on the following pages are indicated by **bold lines**. Correct seamlines accordingly.

Remember that only the front pattern pieces will be shown for all flat pattern adjustments. Be sure to make the comparable adjustments on the back pattern piece.

Length Adjustments

While making pattern length adjustments for your figure, you may find yourself an interesting sizing statistic. You may be long-waisted with a shorter than average hipline, or your arm may be longer from shoulder to elbow and average from elbow to wrist; thus you must adjust the pattern lengths to your personal needs. Shortening or lengthening your pattern pieces is an easy adjustment to make and is crucial to correcting many fitting problems.

SHORTENING PATTERN PIECES: There are areas indicated on every Vogue pattern piece where shortening may be needed to adjust the pattern lengths to your personal needs. Two adjustment lines, placed close together, are shown within the body area, and a note is placed at the lower edges of skirts. The hipline may also need to be raised to the correct position. Remember to make equal changes on front and back pieces.

To **shorten the bodice and sleeves,** crease the pattern between the adjustment lines within the body area and make a fold half the amount needed to be shortened. Secure the change with tape.

To **raise the skirt hipline,** crease just above the hipline of the pattern. Make a fold half the amount needed to bring the hipline into position. Secure the change with tape.

To **further shorten the skirt at the lower edge,** simply cut away excess pattern tissue, following the shape of the pattern.

Correct the seamlines, dart lines, and cutting lines as shown on the pattern pieces.

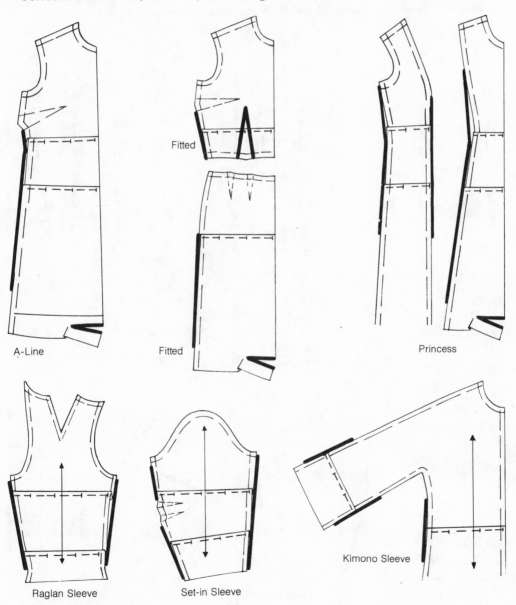

A-Line

Fitted

Fitted

Princess

Raglan Sleeve

Set-in Sleeve

Kimono Sleeve

LENGTHENING PATTERN PIECES: On every Vogue pattern piece there are areas indicated where lengthening may be needed to adjust the pattern to your personal needs. Within the body area are shown two adjustment lines, placed close together, and a note is placed at the lower edge of skirts. The hipline may also need to be lowered to the correct position.

To **lengthen the bodice and sleeves,** cut the pattern along adjustment lines within the body area. Place tissue paper underneath. Spread the cut pattern edges apart the required amount and secure the changes with tape.

To **lower the skirt hipline,** cut the pattern along the hipline. Place tissue paper underneath; lower the hipline into the correct position and secure the change with tape.

To **further lengthen the skirt at the lower edge,** extend the pattern with tissue paper and fasten with tape. Extend the seamlines and cutting lines at the sides, and draw the cutting line across lower edge, retaining the original curve.

Correct all necessary seamlines, dart lines, and cutting lines on the pattern pieces.

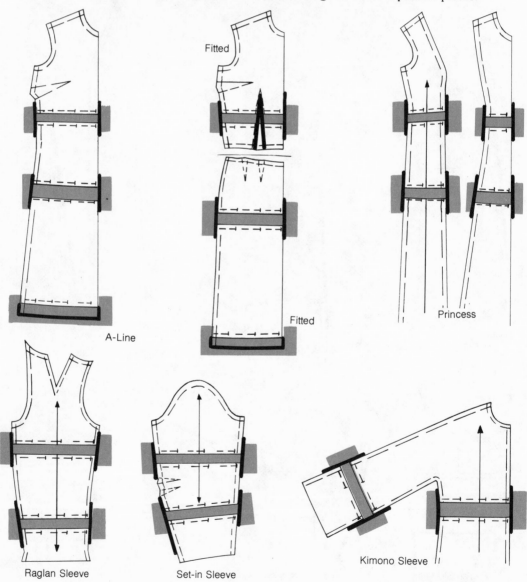

A-Line

Fitted

Fitted

Princess

Raglan Sleeve

Set-in Sleeve

Kimono Sleeve

Circumference Adjustments

Changing the pattern to coincide with your body contours allows you to make the fitting pattern personally yours. You will be amazed how much better your garment will actually flatter your figure when your own curves are really built into the pattern before you ever cut your fabric. Be sure to make equal adjustments on front and back pieces.

REDUCING WAIST AND HIPS: For adjustments *less than 1″*, draw in new seamlines and cutting lines at the sides. First mark ¼ of the amount to be reduced at the waist and hipline and pin the bust dart along the dart lines. Connect markings and draw new seamlines and cutting lines, tapering from waist to bustline. Remove pins and press tissue.

For adjustments *larger than 1″* in the fitted style with a waistline seam, it will be necessary to slash the pattern as indicated and lap the edge ¼ of the amount required. Clip the seam allowance where necessary for the pattern to lie flat.

For a princess style, adjust each seam, dividing the amount by the number of seams.

A-line styles should not be reduced more than 1″ or the style lines may become distorted.

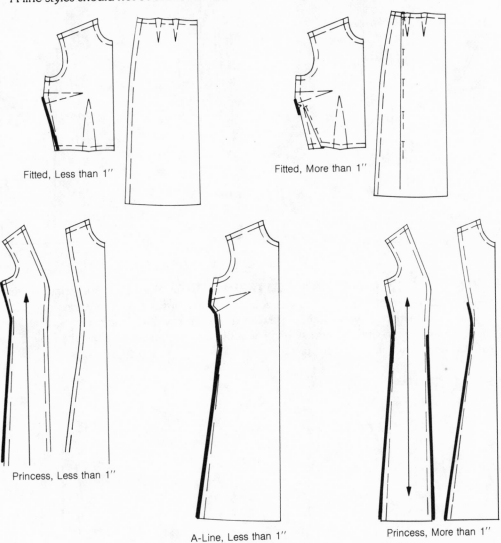

Fitted, Less than 1″

Fitted, More than 1″

Princess, Less than 1″

A-Line, Less than 1″

Princess, More than 1″

ENLARGING WAIST AND HIPS: For adjustments of *less than 1"* (not shown), mark ¼ the amount needed to be enlarged at the waist and hipline and pin bust darts together along the seamline. Connect the markings by drawing new cutting lines and seamlines, tapering above the waist to the bustline.

Correct all necessary seamlines, dart lines, and cutting lines on pattern pieces.

For adjustments *larger than 1"*, slash the pattern as indicated. Place tissue paper underneath. Spread slashed pattern edges ¼ of the amount needed at the waist and hipline. Secure with tape. For a fitted style, make sure you have slashed enough to allow the pattern to lie flat. A small pleat will form in the seam allowance or hem area. For princess styles, divide the amount needed by the number of seams and adjust each seam as indicated.

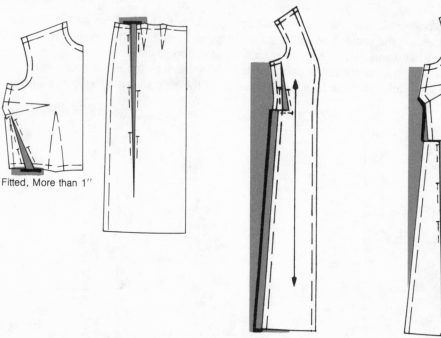

Fitted, More than 1"

Princess, More than 1"

A-Line, More than 1"

REDUCING WAIST WITHOUT ALTERING HIPS: Mark the appropriate pattern pieces ¼ of the amount needed to be reduced at the waist seamline or waist indication. Connect the markings by accurately drawing new seamlines and cutting lines. The lines should taper back to the original seamline near the bust dart and just above the hipline. Be sure to adjust any related pattern pieces.

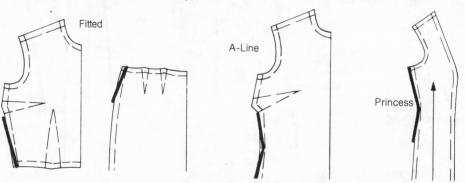

Fitted

A-Line

Princess

ENLARGING HIPS: If the adjustment required is *2″ or less,* place the tissue paper under the side edges. Mark ¼ of the amount needed at the hipline and hemline. Draw new seamlines and cutting lines, connnecting the marks, and taper to the waist.

For adjustments of *more than 2″,* slash the pattern parallel to the grainline or center fold. For skirts, slash from top to bottom. For A-lines, slash to hipline and then cut across hipline to side seam. Over tissue paper, spread each piece ¼ of the amount needed at hipline and secure with tape. Taper seamline and cutting line to bust dart or bust area. For princess styles, be sure to divide the amount needed by the number of seams and adjust each seam as indicated.

Take out excess circumference at the waist by adding darts near the side seam or reducing the pattern along the side edges, retaining hip adjustment.

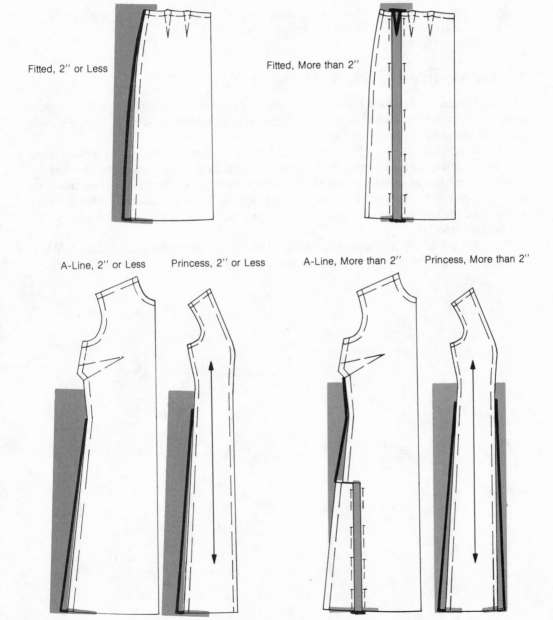

Fitted, 2″ or Less

Fitted, More than 2″

A-Line, 2″ or Less

Princess, 2″ or Less

A-Line, More than 2″

Princess, More than 2″

Vogue's Personal Fit Patterns

Vogue's personal fit patterns allow you to experiment successfully while working toward your ultimate goal—a perfect fit. Fit is what separates an average garment from a truly superior one. Exquisite fabric and couture sewing techniques cannot make up for an ill-fitting garment that sags, pulls, and wrinkles.

Probably every seamstress has had the bitter experience of painstakingly constructing a garment only to find her time and effort wasted because her lovely creation doesn't fit. More often, the pleasure of a garment may be blunted by a minor fitting problem—tight hipline or baggy neckline—which keeps it from being as comfortable and attractive as it should be.

Vogue, understanding this frustration, has developed two patterns to help you better understand all your personal fitting needs.

Measure-Free Body Fitting Guide

Vogue's Measure-Free Body Fitting Guide pattern enables you to understand how your body differs from Vogue's average pattern figure as you fit a basic bodice, sleeves, and skirt shell that you cut from gingham fabric.

The pattern is designed with extra allowances or "outlets" in common problem areas such as shoulders, waist, hip, abdomen, sleeve cap, and hem. This enables you to make the pattern larger as well as smaller; the stitching lines are normal. Each pattern includes five bodice front pattern pieces in bra cup sizes A through DD. Since commercial patterns come sized only for a B cup, this gives you the opportunity to select the bodice front that will fit you perfectly.

The basic pattern is cut out and constructed in ¼″ woven gingham check fabric. When trying on the gingham shell, you can immediately see any problem areas—wherever the

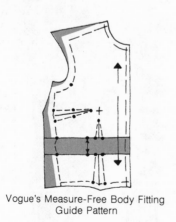

Vogue's Measure-Free Body Fitting
Guide Pattern

Gingham Check Shell

gingham checks are not square on the body. The bodice and skirt can each be fitted separately before attaching the two together.

The pattern includes a comprehensive guide sheet that covers many common fitting problems. Photographs and drawings are used to indicate the fitting problems and their simple solutions. After the gingham has been fitted to your body, you can follow the instructions for transferring the changes made on the gingham back to the pattern pieces.

To achieve a proper fit, it is extremely important to begin with the correct size pattern. To determine what size to purchase, measure your "high bust" and your full bust, and compare measurements. If the difference is 2½" or more, select the size of your Vogue Measure-Free pattern by the "high bust" measurement. If your bust measurement falls between two sizes, select the smaller size pattern.

Once the basic pattern has been customized to fit your figure, you will understand how to fit any pattern to your body. Instructions are given for transferring changes made on the basic fitting shell to the fashion patterns included in the pattern or to any Vogue dress, blouse, skirt, vest, or jacket pattern. Thus, if you have to make a bust alteration on this pattern, you can automatically make the same alterations on all other Vogue patterns, except perhaps for very loose-fitting styles.

The Measure-Free Body Fitting Guide is truly an educational tool for learning how to obtain a perfect fit as well as a permanent personal reference to be used for pattern alterations.

Vogue's Guide to Perfect Fit

Vogue's Guide to Perfect Fit of Fitted Garments is a basic fitting pattern to use for constructing a garment with a waistline seam in muslin and fitting it to your figure. A fully illustrated Cutting and Sewing Guide shows how to make adjustments for any figure problem.

Markings are transferred to the right side of the muslin and are used to check the grainline of the garment sections. Minor adjustments can be made along the seam allowances. Additional alterations, as described in the next section, may be needed to compensate for posture, bone structure, or body contour.

The muslin should be used freely—slash it, mark it, patch it—adding any guidelines that will help in future projects. The altered pattern becomes your personal guide for adjusting Vogue patterns with waistline seams.

Use Your Basic Pattern

With both personal fit patterns, try on the gingham or muslin shell periodically to see if your measurements have changed at all, and adjust accordingly. When constructing a garment with unusually shaped pattern pieces or complex seaming details that cannot be compared with your basic pattern, you may wish to construct that portion of the garment in muslin before cutting out the fashion fabric. Machine baste this muslin together and fit it carefully to your figure, restitching as necessary. When satisfied with the fit, rip the muslin apart and transfer the changes to your pattern.

To preserve your basic pattern, press an iron-on pattern saver or interfacing to the back of the tissue pattern. You will have an easy, handy, and permanent record for achieving perfection each and every time you sew.

Personal Fitting Alterations

The alterations in this section pinpoint areas where you may need further changes to accommodate your body contour or bone structure. Make the necessary alterations as directed, being careful not to over-fit; too precise a fit will tend to accent a figure fault.

Transfer the changes to your pattern pieces, using the same techniques as for flat pattern adjustments. If you find it too difficult to translate any adjustments, take your muslin fitting shell apart to use as a guide. When you have recorded all necessary alterations, they can be transferred to every pattern you use. If ever in doubt about the accuracy of a pattern adjustment, test it by first constructing the section in muslin.

Necklines

The neckline of the muslin fitting shell (called a jewel neckline by our designers) should encircle the body at the base of your neck. All necklines are raised or lowered from this point to give you many variations. For styles other than a jewel neckline, the back pattern piece will have a note stating exactly how much lower or higher it is at the base of neck.

When a neckline pulls, is too large, or does not hug your body in a flattering manner, it will need further alteration. Choose one of the following procedures to help you achieve a perfect fitting neckline.

TIGHT NECKLINE: Neckline pulls uncomfortably around neck. To correct this, draw a line on the garment at the correct neckline location. Stitch along this line. Clip to the new seamline at ½″ intervals until it is comfortable. Adjust the front and back pattern pieces of the bodice and facing in equal amounts by drawing in new seamlines and cutting lines.

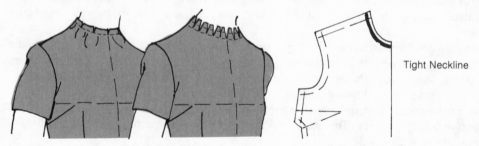

Tight Neckline

LARGE NECKLINE: Neckline is too big and does not reach to the base of neck. To correct, fill in the neckline to the base of the neck with a folded, shaped bias strip of fabric; baste. Adjust the front and back pattern pieces of the bodice and facing in equal amounts by extending the seamlines and cutting lines as indicated by the strip.

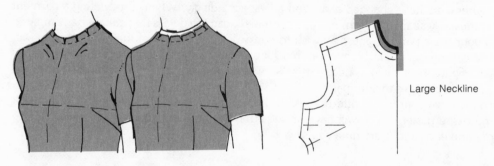

Large Neckline

GAPING NECKLINES: This problem is caused by the wrong bust cup size, too small a pattern, a hollow chest, or a pigeon chest. Even though you bought your pattern by bust measurement, the pattern may not allow enough room across the garment front for your bust cup size or body contour. Therefore, the bodice will not drape smoothly over the body contours, causing gaping and distortion of lower necklines. Cut the bodice in muslin. Try on the bodice to find your problem area. Gaping and pulling can be caused in the same neckline. You may need only one of the alterations listed below or a combination of two. The changes will be the same for square, V-, or U-necklines.

Excess fabric causes the neckline to wrinkle above the bust and to stand away from the body. Pin out the wrinkles, tapering to the armhole seam. Transfer the alteration to the pattern front by lowering the cutting lines and seamlines at the shoulder and neck and by shortening the amount needed at the center front.

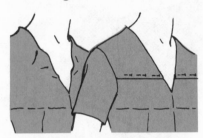

Excess Fabric at Neckline

Pulling at the armhole distorts the neckline above the bust. Slash from the neckline to the armhole seam. Spread as needed. Insert strips of fabric; baste to the cut edges. Transfer the alteration by slashing the pattern front in the same way. Spread as needed and fasten with tape. Correct the shoulder, armhole, and neckline seams and cutting lines.

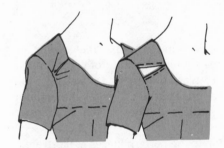

Pulling at the Armhole

DECOLLETE OR LOW NECKLINES: Cut your neck facings in muslin and stitch them together. Stitch along the neck seamline; turn the seam allowance to the inside along the stitching, clipping at ½″ intervals; baste. Try on facing and see where it rests on your body. Fill in a very low neckline to desired depth. Transfer the alteration to facing and front pattern pieces before you cut fabric. Correct cutting lines and seamlines.

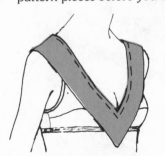

Shoulders

Since your shoulders support the hang of the entire garment, it is essential that they are fitted properly with the fabric smoothly molded over the body. Be sure the shoulder seams rest directly on top of the shoulders and end at the arm hinge and at the base of the neck.

SLOPING SHOULDERS: Wrinkles appear near the bust dart at armhole and across the end of the shoulder in back because the shoulder and armhole seams are not placed at the angle needed for your figure. To correct this, try shoulder pads. If wrinkles remain, remove the sleeves. Pin out the excess fabric at the shoulders, tapering to the neckline. Lower the armhole seamline the same amount. Transfer the alteration to the pattern.

For raglan and kimono sleeves, transfer the alteration to the pattern pieces as illustrated.

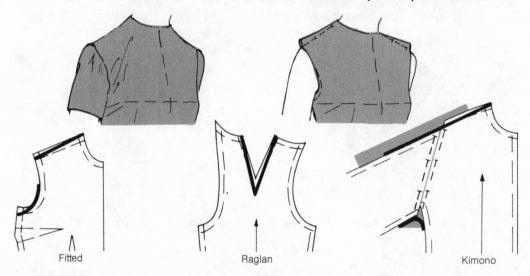

Fitted　　　　　　　Raglan　　　　　　　Kimono

SQUARE SHOULDERS: Pulling around the shoulders and armhole creates wrinkles across the back and front near the neckline because the shoulder area is not wide enough for your bone structure. To correct, remove the sleeve. Slash the front and back near the shoulder seam from the armhole edge to the neckline. Spread the cut edges the amount needed until wrinkles disappear. Insert strips of fabric under cut edges and baste. Transfer the alteration to pattern pieces.

For raglan and kimono sleeves, transfer the alteration to the pattern pieces as illustrated.

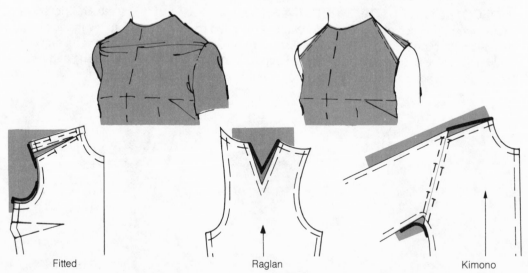

88　　　　Fitted　　　　　　　Raglan　　　　　　　Kimono

NARROW SHOULDERS: The armhole seams fall beyond the end of the shoulder for set-in sleeves. Other sleeve types wrinkle across the upper arm and sometimes pull and restrict movement. To correct the muslin garment, pin the dart in front and back deep enough to pull the armhole seam into place. Adjust the bodice pattern pieces the same amount.

The muslin fitting shell covers only the basic style with a normal shoulder seam and a set-in sleeve. To transfer the alteration to style variations, adjust the pattern pieces as shown below and test in muslin *before* cutting into the fashion fabric.

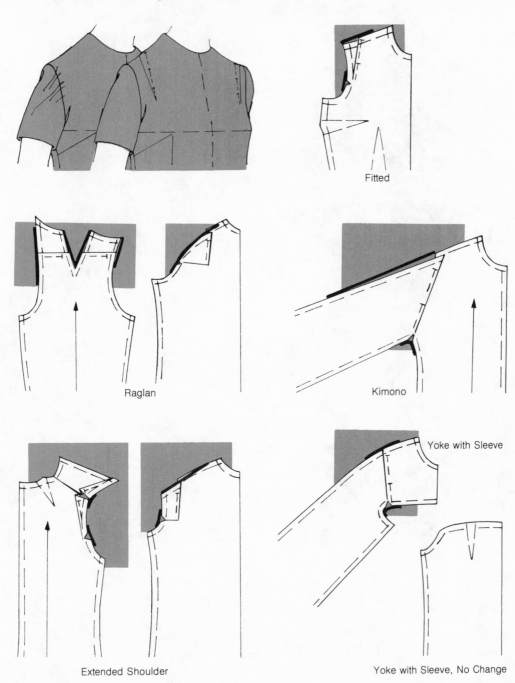

Fitted

Raglan

Kimono

Yoke with Sleeve

Extended Shoulder

Yoke with Sleeve, No Change

BROAD SHOULDERS: The armhole seams draw up over the shoulder, causing wrinkles and pulling in a set-in sleeve. Other sleeve types pull and do not have enough ease in the shoulder area for movement. To correct the muslin garment, slash the front and back from the shoulder seam to the armhole seam. Spread the cut edges the amount needed until wrinkles disappear. Insert strips of fabric under the cut edges; baste. Adjust the bodice pattern pieces the same amount.

The muslin fitting shell covers only the basic style with a normal shoulder seam and a set-in sleeve. To transfer the alteration to other style variations, adjust the pattern pieces as shown below and test in muslin *before* cutting your fashion fabric.

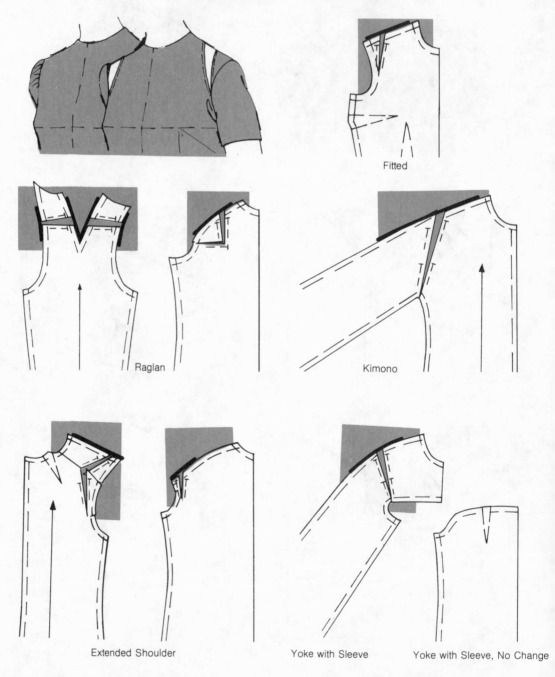

Fitted

Raglan

Kimono

Extended Shoulder

Yoke with Sleeve

Yoke with Sleeve, No Change

Sleeveless Armholes

There is nothing less attractive than an armhole in a sleeveless garment that does not lie correctly on the body. An armhole that is too small will bind and cut. When the armhole is too big it will gap, exposing your undergarments. Stitch along the seamline at the armhole; turn the seam allowance to the inside. Clip at ½″ to ¾″ intervals; baste. Try on the bodice. The underarm portion should be 1″ below the armpit and the garment should fit smoothly around the armhole. It should not bind, pull, or restrict arm movement.

TIGHT ARMHOLE: Draw the correct line at the armhole. Stitch carefully along the line and clip to the new stitching at ½″ intervals until the armhole seam is comfortable. Transfer the alteration to both the bodice and the facing pattern pieces.

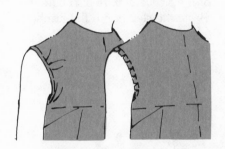 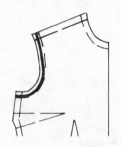

Tight Armhole

LARGE ARMHOLE: To correct a large armhole, insert bias strips of fabric to fill in the amount needed around and under the arm. When placed accurately, baste securely and transfer the alteration to the bodice and facing pattern pieces.

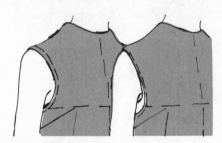 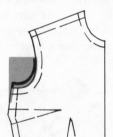

Large Armhole

GAPING ARMHOLE: Pin out excess fabric at the shoulders to bring the armhole into place, tapering to the neck. If the alteration is extensive, you may have to raise the underarm further by inserting a bias strip of fabric; baste. Transfer the alteration to bodice and facing pattern pieces. If gaping still occurs, the pattern is too small at the bust or back and you will need to alter the bodice. Make alteration for bust with a large cup, page 99, rounded back, page 101, or large back, page 103.

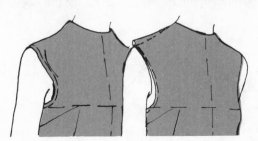 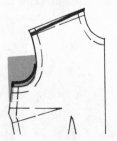

Gaping Armhole

Sleeves

The ease needed in a sleeve cap has traditionally been a stumbling block for many, since the pattern pieces and their markings are designed for the standard figure. Many times the only thing wrong with your sleeve is improper distribution of ease due to your body contour or bone structure. However, these same figure problems can affect the length of the sleeve cap, too.

IMPROPER DISTRIBUTION OF EASE: Diagonal wrinkles will form, starting at the sleeve cap and continuing across the sleeve, distorting the lengthwise grain. When this occurs, remove the sleeve cap from the armhole between the notches. For wrinkles that start at the front of the sleeve cap, re-distribute the ease, moving it forward until the wrinkles disappear. For wrinkles that start at the back of the sleeve cap, re-distribute the ease, moving it backward until the wrinkles disappear. Baste the sleeve into the armhole and check the appearance.

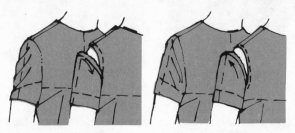

SKIMPY SLEEVE CAP: Sleeve cap pulls and collapses, causing wrinkles. To correct, slash across the top of the sleeve cap. Insert a strip of fabric under the cut edges. Spread the amount needed to increase the ease around the upper armhole seam and baste. Adjust the sleeve cap area of the sleeve pattern the same way.

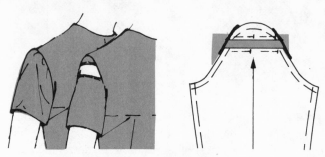

SLEEVE CAP TOO DEEP: The sleeve cap wrinkles across the top of the sleeve just below the seam. Reduce the amount of ease by pinning out excess fabric. Adjust the sleeve cap area of the sleeve pattern the same way.

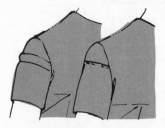
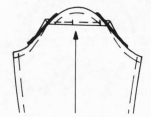

EXCESS EASE IN SLEEVE CAP: The sleeve cap wrinkles around armhole seam. To correct, release the stitching. Smooth the sleeve cap and pin in a shallow vertical dart at the top; baste the sleeve in place. At the shoulder marking, make a slash of 3″ to 4″ into the pattern. Overlap the edges the amount to be decreased (pattern will bubble slightly). Make 1½″ clips at each end of ease so that the seam allowances lie flat. Be sure to maintain the girth across the sleeve cap where the ease ends and to shorten the sleeve cap slightly as indicated.

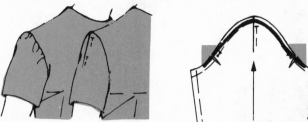

LARGE ARM: The sleeve pulls due to a lack of wearing ease. To correct, slash the sleeve along the lengthwise grain. Insert a strip of fabric under the cut edges and spread the amount needed, tapering to the shoulder seam and sleeve edge. If the sleeve cap still pulls, remove the stitching, add a piece of fabric to extend the cap, and baste. Add ease thread to the strip and insert in the armhole. Adjust the sleeve pattern the same amount, folding the pattern so that it lies flat. Re-draw grainlines.

For raglan and kimono sleeves, transfer the alteration to the pattern pieces as illustrated. Test in muslin *before* cutting the fashion fabric.

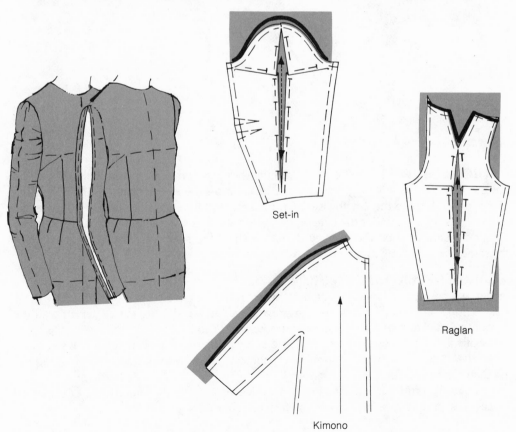

Set-in

Raglan

Kimono

THIN ARM: The sleeve wrinkles and sags. To correct, pin out excess fabric by making a lengthwise fold from the sleeve cap to the lower edge, tapering the fold at the lower edge if necessary to provide room for the hand to slip through. Adjust the sleeve pattern piece in the same way. The sleeve cap will have less ease.

For raglan and kimono sleeves, transfer the alteration to the pattern pieces as illustrated. Test in muslin *before* cutting the fashion fabric.

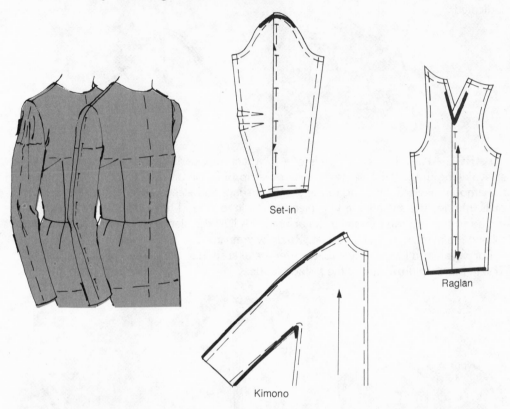

Set-in

Raglan

Kimono

THICK ELBOW: The sleeve pulls from the shoulder and is snug around the elbow. To correct, remove the stitching between the notches on the sleeve seam. Slash the sleeve between the darts to the lengthwise grain marking and then slash to the sleeve cap edge. Insert strips of fabric under the cut edges. Spread the amount needed and baste. Make an additional dart between the existing darts. Re-stitch the seam. Adjust the sleeve pattern the same way. Re-draw the grainlines.

LARGE UPPER ARM: The armhole seam binds and the sleeve is snug above the elbow. To correct, remove the stitching between the notches on the sleeve cap. Make a slash along the lengthwise marking. Insert a fabric strip under the cut edges. Spread the amount needed and baste. Continue ease stitching 1″ to 2″ beyond the markings to make a smooth sleeve cap and re-baste the sleeve in the armhole. If the armhole seam still binds, make the alteration for square shoulders, page 88. Transfer the alteration to the pattern. Re-draw the grainlines.

To make alterations for raglan and kimono sleeves, transfer the alterations to the pattern pieces. Test in muslin *before* cutting the fashion fabric.

THICK ELBOW

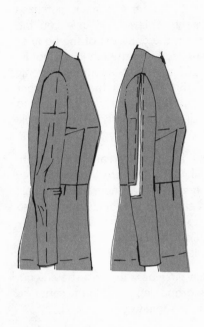

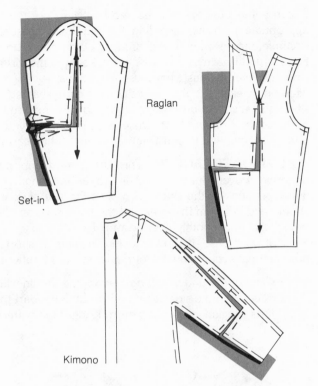

Set-in

Raglan

Kimono

LARGE UPPER ARM

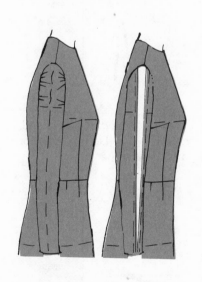

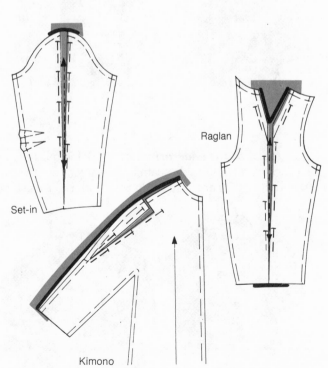

Set-in

Raglan

Kimono

Bust

Because the bust area is the most difficult portion of the pattern to alter, purchase appropriate patterns according to your bust measurement. This should give you the circumference needed in this area. In some cases, however, the contours of the body or bone structure across the **back** can take away the girth needed and the fabric will not lie smoothly over the bust. For these alterations, see pages 101 to 103. Sometimes the only alteration needed is the re-positioning or re-shaping of the darts, but frequently other situations, such as a bust with a large cup or a small cup, can require detailed alterations to fit the contour of your bust. Once you make them, you will see the difference immediately and be on your way to constructing a better fitting garment.

BUST DART LENGTH: This is the most important feature in creating a smooth, flattering fit over your bosom. The proper dart lengths will vary with every woman, as they are dependent on the shape as well as the size of your breasts. The underarm bust dart should end ½″ from the apex and the front darts should end ½″ to 1″ below the apex so fabric will cup smoothly over bosom. Refer to page 75 to determine the location of the apex of your bust. If, however, lengthening or shortening the dart is not sufficient to accommodate your body contour, refer to the alterations listed on the following pages.

To **shorten the underarm dart,** mark the muslin with a pin where the dart should end. To correct, open the side seam and re-stitch the dart the proper length. (Do the same for front darts if included in your pattern.) Adjust the pattern the same way.

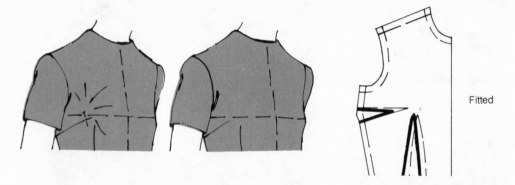

Fitted

To **lengthen the underarm dart,** mark the muslin with a pin where the dart should end. To correct, open the side seam and re-stitch the dart the proper length. (Do the same for front darts if they are included in your pattern.) Adjust the pattern the same way.

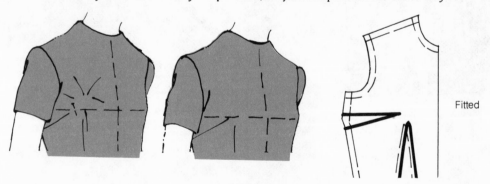

Fitted

HIGH BUST: The bust darts do not fall in line with the fullest part of the bust and need to be raised. Make a line on the muslin where the dart should be. To correct, open the side seam and re-stitch the dart in the proper position. Adjust the position of the dart on the pattern as shown. This alteration is applicable to **all** underarm bust darts, regardless of their angle. Lengthen the front darts as indicated, if necessary.

To alter styles that have bust shaping without the use of darts, place your adjusted fitting pattern underneath the pattern pieces to use as a guide. Above the armhole notch, make a fold ½ the amount needed to be raised and secure with tape. Slash through the pattern below the bust area and spread over the tissue paper, adding the amount the bust was raised to maintain your bodice length. Secure with tape. Make new seamlines and cutting lines for the armhole below the notches.

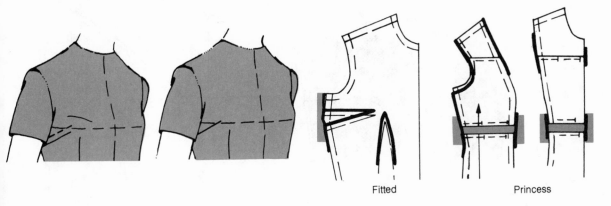

Fitted   Princess

LOW BUST: The bust darts do not fall in line with the fullest part of the bust and need to be lowered. Make a line on the muslin where the dart should be. To correct, open the side seam and re-stitch the dart in the proper position. Adjust the position of the dart on the pattern as shown. This alteration is applicable to **all** underarm darts, regardless of their angle. Shorten the front darts as indicated, if necessary.

To alter styles that have bust shaping without the use of darts, place your adjusted fitting pattern underneath the pattern pieces to use as a guide. Slash through the pattern pieces at the armhole notch. Spread over the tissue paper, lowering the bust shaping area into position. Secure with tape. Make a fold below the bust area ½ the amount the bust was lowered to maintain your bodice length. Secure with tape. Make new seamlines and cutting lines for the armhole below the notches.

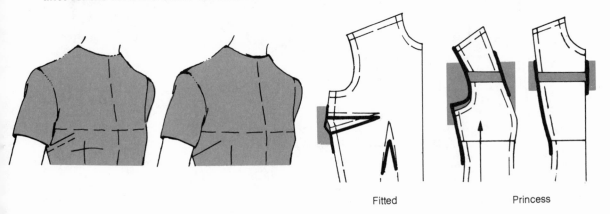

Fitted   Princess

BUST WITH SMALL CUP: The bodice wrinkles over the point of the bust. To correct the muslin garment, pin out excess fabric; taper horizontal folds to the side seams. Taper vertical folds to the waist seam (lower for A-line style garments). Transfer the alterations to the front pattern piece. When the tapering extends into skirt portions, be certain to add the amount taken out to the seams. For A-line styles, slash through the center of the dart to allow these edges to overlap. The darts will become shorter and narrower; adjust their length to your figure. Correct cutting, seam, and dart lines.

To transfer this alteration to garments without darts, place your adjusted fitting pattern underneath the front pieces to use as a guide. Reduce the pattern sections for the bust as indicated. Test in muslin *before* cutting out of the fashion fabric.

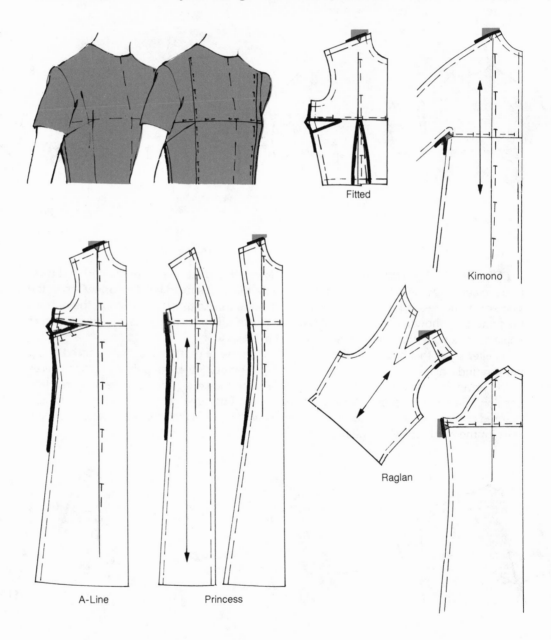

Fitted

Kimono

A-Line

Princess

Raglan

BUST WITH LARGE CUP: The bodice pulls over the bust, flattening the bust at the apex. To correct the muslin garment, slash through the bust darts and across the front. Slash down the front from the shoulder to the waist seam (lower for A-line style garments). Spread the edges the amount needed until the bust is not flattened. Insert strips of fabric under the cut edges and baste. Transfer the alteration to the pattern front. When enlargement extends into the skirt portion, be certain to take out the amount spread at the side seams. Correct cutting, seam, and dart lines. Darts will become deeper; adjust their length to your figure. Trim darts to within ½'' of stitching if necessary to reduce bulk; press cut edges open.

To transfer this alteration to garments without darts, place your adjusted fitting pattern underneath the front pieces to use as a guide. Enlarge the pattern section for the bust as indicated. A dart will be needed in raglan and kimono styles. Test in muslin *before* cutting out of your fashion fabric.

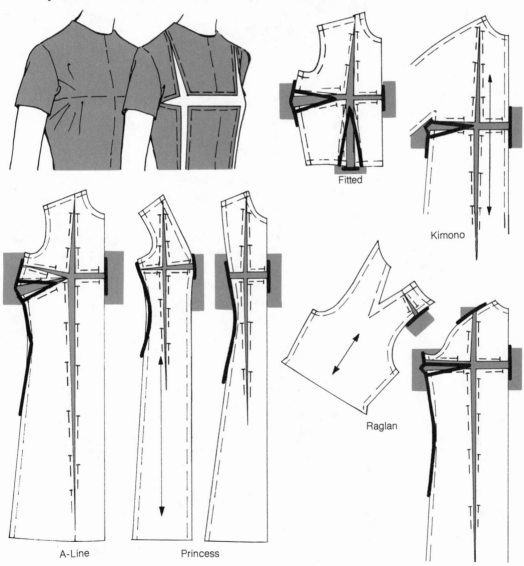

Fitted

Kimono

A-Line   Princess

Raglan

Chest

The upper portion of the chest above the bust would seem to be an area of little concern when fitting a garment. The bone structure of the rib cage and collar bone controls the bodice length along the center front, however, and may create a need for alterations.

HOLLOW CHEST: The bodice wrinkles above the bust and below the neckline. To correct the muslin garment, pin out the wrinkles, tapering to the armhole or shoulder seams. Adjust the front pattern pieces at the neck and shoulder edges the amount needed.

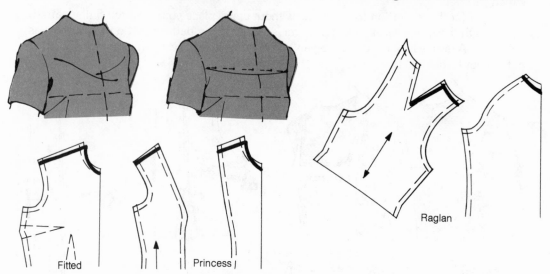

Fitted Princess Raglan

PIGEON CHEST: The collar and breast bones protrude, causing the bodice to pull above the bust and distort the armhole seam. To correct the muslin garment, open the armhole seam. Slash across the front above the bust and up through the center of the shoulder area to the seam. Insert fabric strips under the cut edges. Spread the amount needed to fit the body contour. Baste, keeping the slashed edge flat. Re-stitch the seams. Transfer the alteration to the front pattern pieces as indicated.

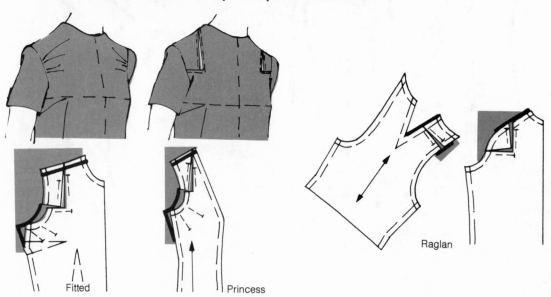

Fitted Princess Raglan

Back

The entire garment back should mold smoothly over your body contour from the neck to the hem edge. There should be no wrinkles or pulling and the hem must be even. Adjusting the pattern to your measurements will give the girth needed, but the fabric may not drape evenly due to bone structure or posture and will require alteration.

VERY ERECT BACK: The bodice back has parallel wrinkles across the back above the shoulder blades. To correct, pin out the wrinkles, tapering to the armhole or shoulder seams. Adjust the bodice pattern the amount needed at neck and shoulder edges.

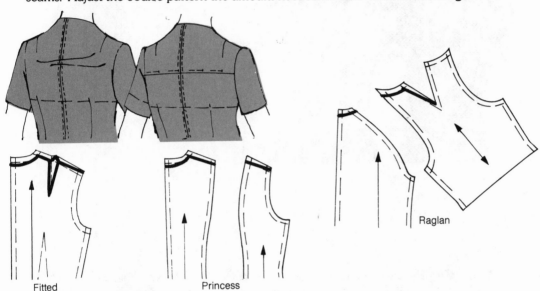

Fitted   Princess   Raglan

HIGH, ROUNDED BACK (DOWAGER'S HUMP): The bodice wrinkles and pulls across the shoulders and near the sleeve tops. To correct the muslin garment, slash across the back between the armhole seams. Remove the stitching from the zipper above the slash. Insert strips of fabric under the cut edges and spread them the amount needed. Baste, keeping the slashed edges flat and allowing for the center back opening. Pin darts in neck edge to fit the contour. Add strips to extend the back edges to the center opening. Adjust bodice back pattern piece same amount, adding a dart at neck edge as indicated.

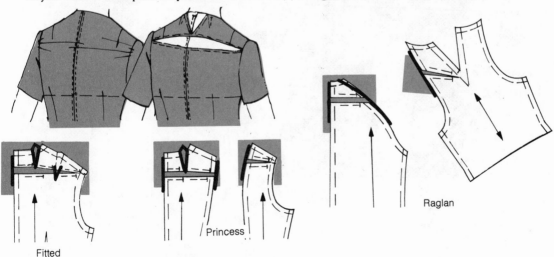

Fitted   Princess   Raglan

NARROW BACK: The bodice is loose through the shoulder area. A garment with a waist seam may have extra fullness above the seam, while an A-line garment may be longer in the back at the hemline. To correct, pin out excess fabric between the shoulder darts and waistline. Transfer the alteration to the pattern back as indicated. For a princess style, simply take a deeper seam.

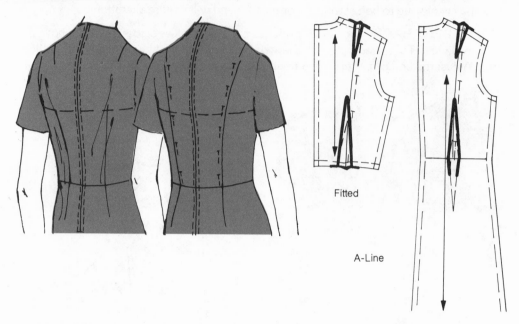

Fitted

A-Line

SWAY BACK: The garment wrinkles across the back below the waistline. To correct the muslin garment, pin out the wrinkles, tapering to the side seam. Transfer the alteration to the pattern back by removing the excess length along the center back seam the necessary amount. The darts will become shorter.

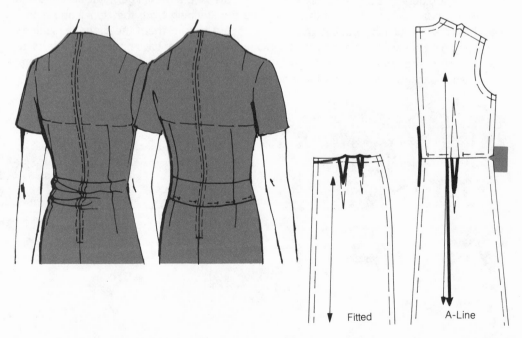

Fitted

A-Line

LARGE BACK OR PROMINENT SHOULDER BLADES: The bodice wrinkles and pulls across the fullest part of the back and is tight when raising the arms. To correct, remove the stitching at the shoulder seams, darts, and side seams. Slash across the back below the armhole and up through the center of the shoulder dart. Spread the edges the amount needed. Insert strips of fabric under the cut edges and baste. Make the existing dart deeper or add a dart to fit the contour and then re-stitch the seam. Transfer the alteration to the pattern back.

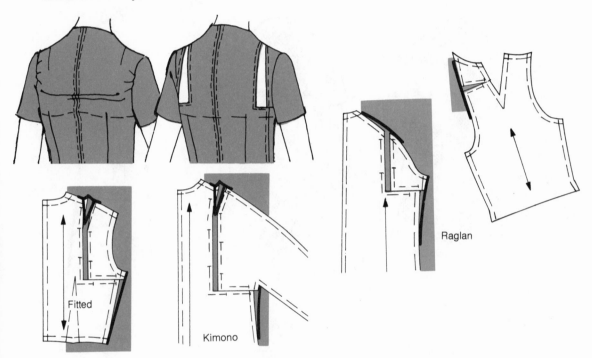

Raglan

Fitted

Kimono

Hips

Since the hip circumference was already taken care of before making the muslin fitting shell, you now must be concerned about the effect your bone structure or posture has on the garment. The fabric should mold smoothly over the buttocks and hip bones without wrinkles or pulling.

PROTRUDING HIP BONES: This is usually noticeable only in fitted garments. The bones protrude, causing pulling across the front. To correct, remove the stitching from the darts and seams. Pin the darts to fit the contour. If this makes the waistline smaller, add to the side seams. Re-stitch darts and seams. Transfer the alteration to the pattern front.

Fitted

FLAT BUTTOCKS: The skirt area wrinkles and sags at the back, causing an uneven hemline. For both styles, release the darts. Pin the darts, making them shorter to fit the body contour and narrower to retain the same waist measurement. To correct an A-line garment, release the zipper below the back bustline. Pin out the excess fabric at the side and center back seams. To correct garments with a waist seam, pin out excess fabric across the hips. Pin out any sag, making the hemline even.

Transfer the alteration to the pattern back as indicated.

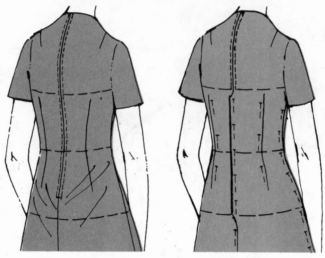

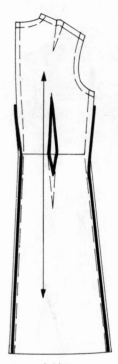

Flat Buttocks, A-Line

A-Line

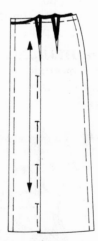

Flat Buttocks, Fitted

Fitted

LARGE BUTTOCKS OR LARGE BACK AT TOP OF HIPS: Wrinkles form between the waist and hipline with pulling that distorts the side seams. The hemline is shorter in the back. To correct an A-line garment, release the darts, seams, and zipper below the back bustline. Place strips of fabric under the center back and side seams. Make equal adjustments at each seam to bring the side seams into position; baste. Pin the darts to fit the contour. To correct a garment with a waist seam, release the darts below the waist and remove the stitching from the waist seam. Pin the darts to fit the contour.

Transfer the alteration to the pattern back as indicated.

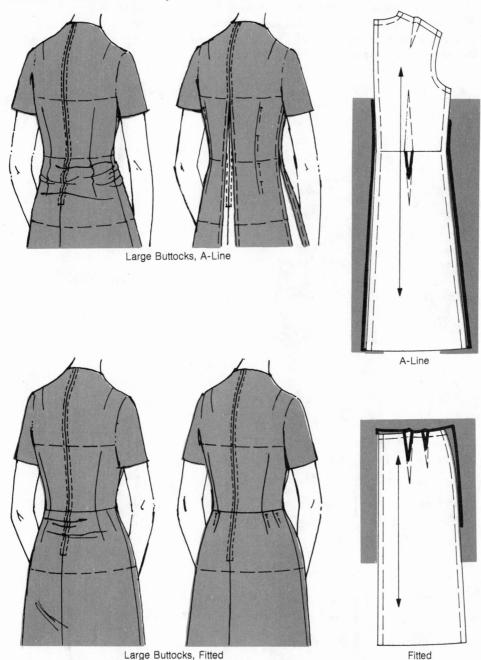

Large Buttocks, A-Line

A-Line

Large Buttocks, Fitted

Fitted

ONE LARGE HIP: The skirt pulls up on one side of the front and back, causing an uneven hemline. It is most obvious in fitted garments, but may also show up in other garments.

To correct a garment with a waist seam, remove the stitching from the side seam, waist seam, and darts on the shorter side. Drop the skirt until the grain and hem are straight. Insert strips of muslin at the sides and top; baste. Pin darts to fit the contour. Re-stitch the seams. For A-line garments, remove the stitching from the side and darts on the shorter side. Spread the edges until the grain and hem are straight. Insert muslin strips at the sides; baste. Pin back the dart to fit the contour. Re-stitch the seam.

Make a paper pattern for the other half of the skirt and transfer the alteration to the side that needs to be enlarged. You will then have a record of both sides of your skirt. (Shown below are the pattern pieces for the altered side only.)

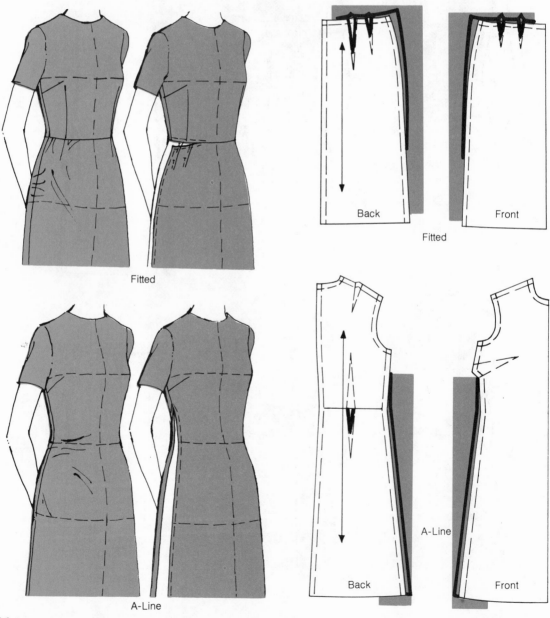

Fitted

Back   Front

Fitted

A-Line

Back   Front

A-Line

Abdomen

The hip circumference measurement allows for the girth of this area, but will not compensate for wrinkles and pulling caused by posture and body contour. As with all figure flaws, fabric molded smoothly over this area will minimize rather than accent it.

LARGE ABDOMEN: The skirt front rides up, pulling the side seams forward and causing the waist and hipline to pull up. To correct a garment with a waist seam, release the front waist seam and darts. Drop the skirt front until it hangs evenly. Baste a fabric strip to the top of the skirt. Pin darts to fit the contour. If this makes the waistline smaller, add to the side seams. Re-stitch the darts and seams. Transfer the alteration to the pattern as indicated.

To correct an A-line garment, slash the front up to the bust area. Spread the edges the amount needed until the side seams, waistline, and hipline fall into position. Place strips of fabric under the slashed edges and baste. Transfer the alteration to the pattern front as indicated, slashing through the bust dart to make the pattern lie flat, and let the edges overlap.

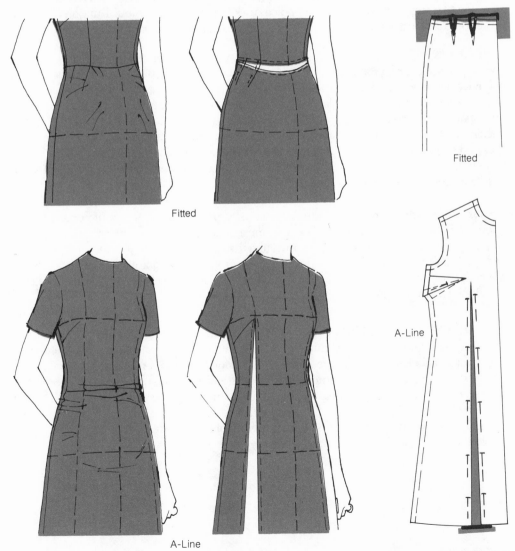

Fitted

Fitted

A-Line

A-Line

Combine Two Patterns

How many times have you wished your pattern had longer sleeves or a different neckline than the one shown? Perhaps you've even passed up a pattern style that you loved because it had a design feature that was not flattering on you. With some initiative and practice, you can avoid such compromises by using parts of different styles to create a garment that is truly custom-designed for your particular taste and figure. This information is intended to allow you to exercise your designer instincts and to provide some guidelines that will help you combine patterns successfully.

Within each size range of a Vogue pattern, the structural body relationships of shoulder to neck, bust to waist, etc., never change—for example, a size 12 bodice from one style number will fit a size 12 skirt from another style number if they both have waistlines and the styles are similar. To achieve the preferred silhouette for your needs, it is possible to combine necklines, collars, and other features from two different style numbers if the structural features of the two are the same.

Most people who understand the alterations required for their particular figure flaws will also know what style lines will minimize them. This knowledge can reduce your style selection at times because either the bodice or skirt is not right for you. But don't let these limitations discourage you. Combining two patterns can expand your fashion horizons.

NECKLINES: The shape of your neckline can either reveal or camouflage your neck and upper body, and you should be aware of which function you wish it to serve. When you have a limited number of flattering necklines to choose from, you must be aware of the bodice style. A bodice with raglan or kimono sleeves requires a different style of draping and shaping to achieve the proper fit than does a bodice wiih a set-in sleeve, so the necklines of the two styles cannot be interchanged. Empire and low-waisted seaming or dropped shoulders are also very stylized and need careful evaluation of the neckline before you cut into your fashion fabric. Do not be afraid to experiment, however, as long as you test your proposed adaptations in muslin.

COLLARS: Do not make a hasty decision when you decide to substitute one collar for another. Even if two collars look alike, you must check the bodice pattern pieces to make sure they match line for line before substituting them. The shape of the neckline must vary with each different collar style in order to get the proper shaping in the collar. Interchange the collars of different styles only when the bodice pieces match closely. Also make sure that the location of the closings is the same.

SLEEVES: While it is obvious that radically different sleeve styles, such as raglan and set-in sleeves, cannot be interchanged, very subtle variations can make a big difference. The bodice style is the deciding factor in interchanging sleeve versions, for it controls the size of the sleeve cap and the amount of necessary ease. The shoulder seams of the two bodices must be at the same angle and end at the same point where the arm joins the body. The lengths of the armhole curvatures must also be alike. If you wish to stray from these general rules, be very sure to test your experiments in muslin before cutting into your fashion fabric to avoid disappointing results.

Combine Two Sizes

Let's face it! Very few of us have perfect figures. Instead, many women are actually two sizes—one on top and one on bottom. Vogue Doubles patterns are ideal for such figures because two sizes are included in one pattern. If your size changes at the bust, waistline, or hip, simply use a combination of the two-size cutting line to accommodate those changes.

If the pattern you select is not available in dual-size patterns, it is often easier to use two pattern sizes rather than alter a bodice or skirt drastically. The secret to combining these two areas is in making the waistline a transitional area.

Note the difference in inches between the waist measurements of the two sizes listed on the back of your pattern envelope. If your waist measurement is the same as one pattern size, adjust the waist of the other pattern to correspond. If the waist needs to be adjusted on both patterns, determine how much to enlarge or reduce the waist of each piece, dividing the amount to be changed by the number of seams involved. Adjust each piece accordingly.

Keep center fronts, center backs, and grainlines straight. For fitted styles with a waist seam, adjust the waist area of the bodice and skirt so the waistlines match when joined. Adjust the position of the darts in the skirt so they will meet the bodice darts at the waist, retaining the distance across the centers of the garment between the darts. For A-line styles, cut both patterns apart and join the sections needed with transparent tape. Shown below, in both styles, are the situations that may require two sizes—the smaller size bodice combined with a larger size skirt and the larger size bodice combined with the smaller size skirt. Mark ¼ the amount needed for the waist at the side seam for both front and back pattern pieces. Draw new side seams from the bust to the hip, simulating original curves as much as possible.

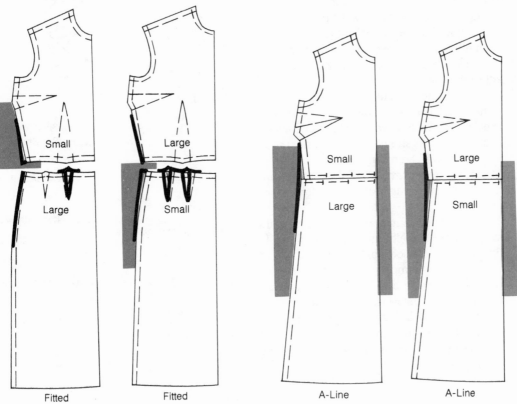

Small	Large	Small	Large
Large	Small	Large	Small
Fitted	Fitted	A-Line	A-Line

Pants, Pants, Pants

A wardrobe including casual, tailored, and luxurious pants will always be an important part of the fashion scene. They can be worn from morning to after dark—on the street, out to dinner and the theater, entertaining at home, or for active sports. Not to be forgotten are shorts: they too can be the basis of a smart ensemble costume.

The length of your pants or shorts is important to your total look. Full-length pants that are too short can have a skimpy, "out-grown" look, and pants that are too long can be clumsy and troublesome. Make sure your shorts do not end at an unattractive point on your leg; sometimes even an adjustment of ½″ in length can make a world of difference in their attractiveness.

At all times you should strive toward a balanced silhouette. A long jacket, tunic, or top can camouflage those few extra pounds or inches or give an illusion of height. You may prefer a shorter top with a shorts costume or if you are short-legged. Consider your accessories; the same ones you wear with dresses may not be appropriate or in correct balance with pants.

Select the pattern for your pants carefully, choosing the type of pants that are best for your figure type. If you have prominent hips, a hip-hugging style with fitted thighs would not only be hard to fit, but would also be unflattering. If you have heavy thighs, pants that are wider and straight-legged from the hips down are a good choice because they will not cling or accent the thighs.

Choose your pants by waist measurement unless your hip measurement is much larger or smaller than that shown with the waist size; if so, select your size by hip measurement and adjust the waistline.

Pants are not difficult to construct, but can be hard to fit because of the endless variations in body shapes. For accurate fit, check several points: the waist should be comfortably snug, the hips should be roomy enough for ease in sitting, the thigh area should not bind, and the crotch area must not be too tight or too loose.

Pants, of all your garments, demand the most perfect fit. Although such accurate fitting can take a good deal of time and effort, you need do the most major alterations only once if you make a fitting muslin. This will require precise measuring, flat pattern adjustments, and detailed fitting; once done with a classic style in muslin, however, you can transfer the alterations to every pair of pants you make in the future.

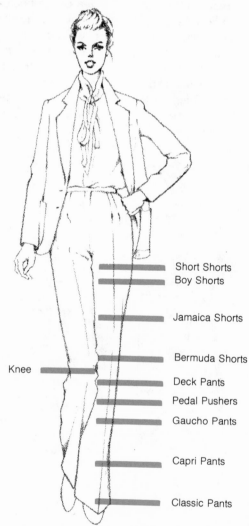

Short Shorts
Boy Shorts

Jamaica Shorts

Bermuda Shorts

Deck Pants

Pedal Pushers

Gaucho Pants

Knee

Capri Pants

Classic Pants

Precise Measurements

MEASURE YOURSELF: Be sure to wear the proper undergarments with your pants. Some can flatten the contour and give a "stuffed sausage" look. Be sure they do not cause unsightly indentations or bulges over the fullest part of your hips or thighs. Wearing the correct undergarments and shoes, take these measurements:

Waist: Tie a string around the body where it settles comfortably at the waistline. Measure your waist at the string (1). (Note: leave the string in place to facilitate measuring from the waist to points at which measurements 2 through 7 are taken.)

High hip: Measure across the top of the hip bones 2" to 4" below the waist (2).

Full hip: Measure the fullest part of your hips. Vogue places this hipline approximately 7" to 9" from the waist, depending on the size range (3).

Circumference of Leg: Measure the fullest part of the thigh (4), knee (5), calf (6), and instep (7).

Length: Measure at the side from the waist to the floor or the desired length (8).

Crotch Depth: Sit on a hard chair and measure at the side from the waist to the chair seat (9).

Crotch Length: Measure from the waist in back to the waist in front. Determine the front and back crotch length at the midpoint between the legs (usually not an even division) (10).

Torso Length: Necessary for jumpsuits. Using two tapemeasures, measure over undergarments from the front waistline over the fullness of your bust to the middle of your shoulder. Continue down to your center back, under the crotch and up to the center front waist (11).

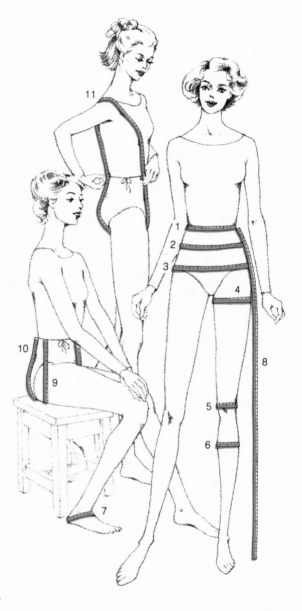

COMPARE MEASUREMENTS: After you have taken your personal measurements, compare them with the actual pattern measurements, taking into account ease (see page 63), to determine if any adjustments have to be made in the pattern. Measure pattern pieces only from seamline to seamline, excluding any darts or tucks. If pants have side front slanted pockets, be sure to include the side front pattern piece.

Mark adjustment and fitting lines on your pattern tissue. Start with the front pattern piece and extend the grainline the full length of the pattern. Draw lines perpendicular to the grainline for high hip, full hip, and thigh, measuring down from the waistline the same amount as when you took your measurements. For slim pants, it may also be necessary to indicate the knee and calf positions.

Lay the back pattern over the front, matching sides. Indicate the end of each line from the front piece along the side seamline. Draw lines perpendicular to the back grainline from these locations.

For waist and hip, first compare your body measurements with the standard body measurements listed on the pattern envelope for your size. If these differ, you will have to make pattern adjustments. Next compare the relationship of your high hip and full hip measurements with the pattern to see if additional hip alterations may be necessary for your figure shape (see pages 118 to 120). Thigh measurement of the pattern should equal your thigh measurement plus at least 1″ for wearing ease.

To compare measurements for both crotch depth and crotch length, you must draw the crotch line on your pattern as illustrated. For crotch depth, measure from the waistline to the crotch line near the side seamline. Crotch depth should exactly equal your crotch depth measurement plus ½″ to ¾″ for sitting ease. For pants that may be attached to a yoke or contour waistband, it is necessary to first pin the yoke or waistband pattern to the pants pattern, matching seamlines. Then measure from the waistline marking or seamline to the crotch line. For pants styles that do not extend up to the natural waistline, compare the pattern pieces with a regular pants patten to determine where the natural waistline is located above the pattern.

For crotch length, use a tape measure or flexible ruler to measure from the waistline along the center front and center back seams to the crotch points, being sure to eliminate the seam allowances. Crotch length should equal your crotch length measurement plus up to 1½″ for ease. Adjustment can be made equally to the front and back pattern pieces or distributed more to one piece than the other, depending on your figure.

For torso length, measure both front and back pattern pieces. Begin at middle of the shoulder seam and measure to waistline marking (do not include blousing allowance) and along the center front and center back seams to the crotch points. Add front and back measurements. If adjustments are needed, they can be made in the back waist length and the crotch length.

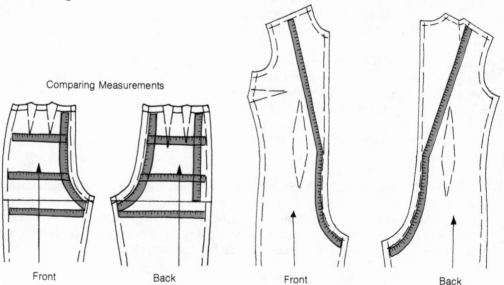

Comparing Measurements

Front   Back   Front   Back

Flat Pattern Adjustments

The most critical step in achieving perfectly fitted pants is to adjust the crotch. Unless the crotch is in the correct position, no amount of adjustment made later can overcome a poor fit. Crotch adjustments should be made first because they can affect other adjustments.

Be sure to keep grainlines straight and connect the seamlines and cutting lines in a smooth, gradual line, tapering to the original lines as indicated on the pattern pieces.

CROTCH DEPTH: The crotch depth should exactly equal your measurement plus ½'' to ¾'' for sitting ease. If not, it must be adjusted by lengthening or shortening the pattern pieces. Be sure to make equal changes on the front and back pattern pieces.

To shorten this area, make a fold ½ the amount needed at the adjustment line on each pattern piece. Fasten with tape. *To lengthen,* cut the pattern along the adjustment line, place tissue paper underneath, and spread the amount needed. Fasten with tape.

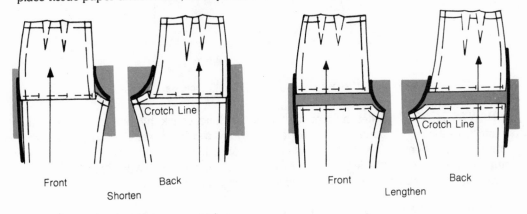

Front   Back   Front   Back

Shorten   Lengthen

CROTCH LENGTH: The crotch length can be adjusted either at the crotch point or along the center front or center back seam. Both types of adjustments affect only the crotch seam and do not change the side seam.

It is important that the adjustment be made according to your figure. Increases or decreases can be made equally to the front and back pattern pieces or distributed more to one piece than to the other. Altering at the crotch point will also affect the upper thigh measurement. Altering along the crotch seam enables fullness to be added or subtracted across the abdomen or the derrière.

To *decrease* crotch length at the crotch point, slim the pattern the required amount. To *increase* crotch length, add to the crotch seam. Remember to retain the crotch curve shaping and gradually taper new lines back to meet the original leg seams.

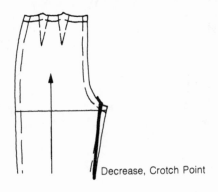 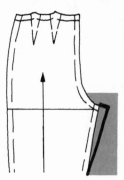

Decrease, Crotch Point   Increase, Crotch Point

To **_decrease_** crotch length along the crotch seam, fold the pattern on the adjustment line ½ the amount needed, tapering the fold out to the side seam. To **_increase_** crotch length, cut the pattern along the adjustment line just to, but not through, the side seam. Place tissue paper underneath and spread the amount needed.

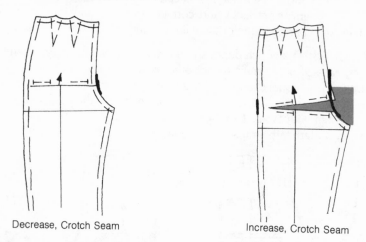

Decrease, Crotch Seam   Increase, Crotch Seam

PANTS LENGTH: After the crotch alteration is done, check the total length (measurement 8) of the pants along side seamline. If they are **_too long_**, make a fold ½ the excess amount above hemline across the leg of pattern front and back; fasten with tape. If they are **_too short_**, slash across the leg above hemline on pattern front and back. Place tissue paper underneath and spread the amount needed. Fasten with tape.

WAIST CIRCUMFERENCE: If your waist (measurement 1) is **_smaller,_** first determine the amount needed to be decreased. Then take away ⅛ of this amount from the pattern front and back at each center and side seam. If your waist is **_larger,_** add ⅛ the necessary amount to the pattern front and back at each center and side seam. Be sure to make corresponding adjustment on the waistband or facing pattern pieces.

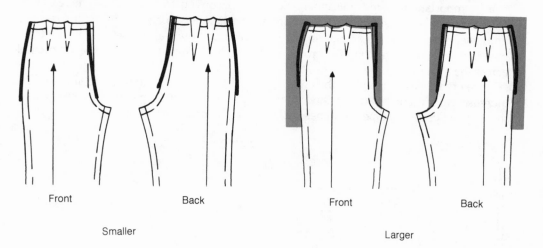

Front   Back   Front   Back

Smaller   Larger

HIP CIRCUMFERENCE: If your hips are much larger or smaller than your waist measurement, be sure to purchase your pattern by your hip measurement. However, adjustments of 2″ or less in hip circumference can be made along the side seam. Mark ¼ of the amount needed to be increased or decreased at the hipline and hemline of the pattern pieces. Draw new seamlines and cutting lines, connecting the marks, and taper to the waist. See skirt adjustments, pages 103 to 106.

LEG CIRCUMFERENCE: If the pattern measurement is close to that of your thigh plus 1″ for wearing ease, no adjustment is necessary. To make the leg *smaller,* slim the pattern ¼ the amount along each leg seam. To make the leg *larger,* add ¼ the amount to each leg seam. Taper the lines gradually from the crotch point or the hipline and extend straight down to the hem edge.

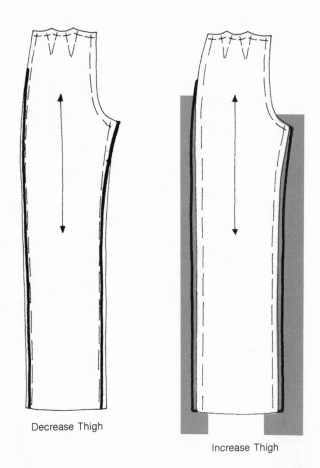

Decrease Thigh

Increase Thigh

If you are making tapered, slim-fitting pants, it would also be wise to check the knee, calf, and instep measurements. If your measurements (plus at least 1″ for wearing ease) are larger or smaller than the pattern measurements, adjust the leg seams accordingly.

Fitting Adjustments

Some minor fitting adjustments can be made in pants after they are constructed. If you are unsure of the fit, cut your seam allowances 1″ wide to allow for any later fitting problems.

If the pants wrinkle at the high hipline, release the darts. Pin to fit body contour, lengthening or shortening the darts as needed. Re-stitch.

If the waist pulls downward at center front or back when you sit or stand, release the waistband. To correct, set waistband higher at the center seam, tapering to the side seams.

Often pants have wrinkles that either point up or down from the crotch line in either the front or the back, indicating that the crotch depth, crotch length, or crotch curve needs adjustment. If the problem is major, alterations can only be done on the pattern before the garment is cut out. Refer to adjustments for crotch depth and length, pages 113 and 114.

Wrinkles Caused by Poor Fit at Crotch

If the problem is minor, adjustments can be made in the crotch seam and at the waistline. If the wrinkles point up toward the waistline, the crotch must be lengthened. Remove the waistband and let out the waistline seam up to ⅜″. Make a deeper curve in the crotch seam by lowering the seam at the bottom of the curve and letting out the center front and center back seams, tapering to the original seamline below the waist.

If the wrinkles point down away from the waistline, the crotch must be shortened. Remove the waistband and take in the waistline seam. To shorten the curve, raise the seam at the bottom of the curve up to ⅜″, and take in the center front and center back seams, tapering to the original seamline below the waist.

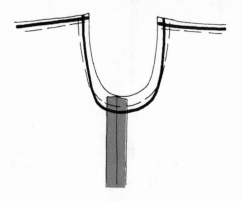 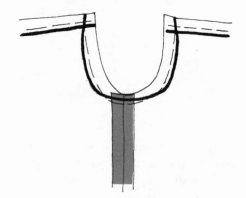

Lengthening Crotch Curve   Shortening Crotch Curve

Vogue's Personal Fit Pants Pattern

The Vogue Measure-Free Pants for Any Body is a specially designed pants pattern with extra fabric allowances in common problem areas such as abdomen, sides, thigh, length, and crotch depth. These "outlets" have been included to enable you to make a pattern larger, in addition to making it smaller. The stitching lines are normal.

The pattern is cut out and sewn in ¼″ woven gingham check fabric. When trying on the pants, you can easily identify any problem areas because the gingham checks will not be square on the body.

The pattern includes a comprehensive guide sheet that covers the most common fitting problems for pants. Photographs and drawings are used to indicate the fitting problems and their simple solutions. After the gingham has been fitted to the body, directions can be followed for transferring the changes made on the gingham back to the pattern.

Once this pants pattern has been customized to fit your figure, you know how your body differs from the average pattern figure. Thus, if you have to make a crotch adjustment on this pattern, you can automatically make the same adjustment on all other Vogue patterns. To compare a new pattern to the basic for a quick analysis of problem areas, simply lay the new pattern on top of the basic pattern, aligning crotch lines. Remember that some pants patterns will include more ease as part of the fashion design and thus will be larger than the basic pattern which fits close to the body. Be careful not to overfit and eliminate the fashion ease.

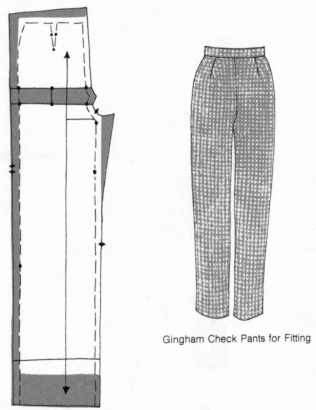

Gingham Check Pants for Fitting

Vogue Measure-Free Pants for Any Body

Pants-Fitting Muslin

A pants-fitting muslin can be made from any basic pants pattern. Alter the pattern, cut out the muslin, and transfer all seamlines and markings with a tracing wheel and dressmaker's carbon. Also trace your hipline (high and full) and your thigh line to the right side of the muslin. Machine baste the pants together. Baste a temporary waistband of grosgrain ribbon to the waist seamline to support the pants while fitting.

Take a critical look in a full-length mirror to spot problems due to bone structure or body contour. The side seams should be perpendicular to the floor. The traced lines should be parallel to the floor. If they are pulled or distorted or if wrinkling occurs, you will need further fitting and pattern adjustments to compensate for your figure flaws. If minor adjustments do not correct the problems to your satisfaction, you may need one of the more specialized alterations on the following pages. For comfort and attractiveness, avoid fitting pants too tightly.

Personal Alterations

These fitting alterations can only be accomplished by fitting your muslin and cannot be made after the fashion fabric has been cut. Since the alterations are quite individualized, the same changes are not always required on both the front and back pattern pieces.

FOR LARGE ABDOMEN: Release the darts. Drop the top of the pants until the side seams fall into position. Baste a strip of fabric to the top and add to the front inner leg seam until the pants hang without wrinkles. Pin darts to fit the contour. Transfer the changes to your pattern.

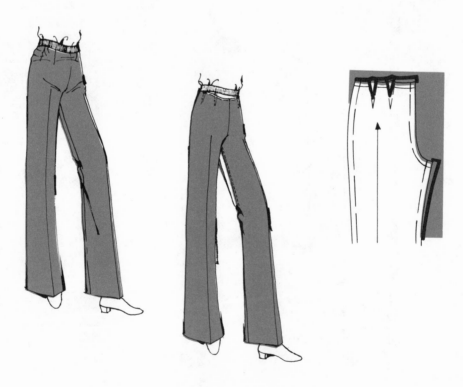

PROTRUDING HIP BONES: Release the darts and pin to fit the contour. This may include widening or shortening the dart. If this makes the waistline smaller, add to the side seams, then transfer the alteration to the pattern.

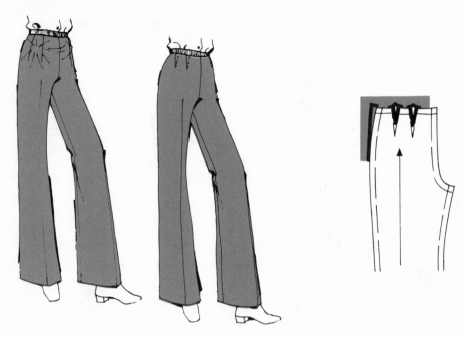

LARGE BUTTOCKS: Buying your pattern by hip measurement will give you girth for a large derrière. However, you may need more length at the center back in order to fit the contour and to let the side seams fall into position. Release the darts. Drop the top of the pants until the side seams fall into position. Baste strips of fabric to the top and add to the back inner leg seam until the pants hang without a wrinkle. Pin darts to fit the contour. If the waistline measurement is not large enough after this alteration, add to the side seams. Transfer the alteration to your pattern piece.

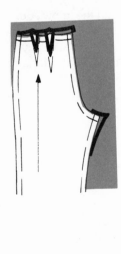

FLAT BUTTOCKS: Eliminate the wrinkles on the muslin by pinning a horizontal fold across the high hipline and a perpendicular fold along each leg to eliminate excess fabric there. Taper folds to nothing at the side seams, waist, and knee. Release the darts and pin to fit the contour, taking out the excess waistline measurement at the side seams. Transfer these adjustments to the back pattern piece, clipping seam allowances to lie flat.

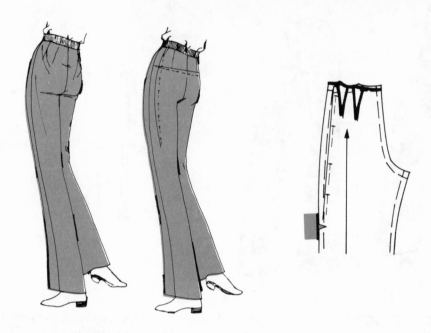

SWAYBACK: If you have a swayback, see treatment for swaybacked skirts on page 102.

FINAL STEPS: When constructing pants, baste and fit to see how your fabric drapes over your body contours, making minor fitting adjustments to compensate for your fabric. Since the crotch area receives considerable strain, use a smaller straight stitch or a very small zigzag stitch when stitching the curve of the crotch seam. Clip the seam at the top of the curve and press open. Add a second row of stitching ¼'' from the first row between the clips. Then trim and overcast this edge. This portion of the seam remains unpressed.

Armed with the knowledge you have gained by making a fitting muslin, make your pants pattern pieces a permanent sewing tool by backing them with an iron-on non-woven. Use them as a guide to alter any style of pants, shorts, culottes, pantskirt, or jumpsuit you plan to make. You will find it is a handy, time-saving device.

Fitting As You Sew

You should always try on your garment after completing each unit of construction to check the fit. But what exactly is good fit? Clothes that fit well are clothes that allow enough ease for comfort and freedom of movement, hang smoothly without wrinkles or bulges, and flatter the figure. If a garment does not conform attractively to your contours, all your efforts at fine construction will have been wasted.

There might seem to be a fine line between fitting and alterations. In reality, however, alterations or adjustments are those **significant** changes that should be made on the pattern tissue before you even reach for the fabric, while fitting involves those **minor** changes necessary to perfect and finalize the garment. Tissue pattern alterations alone may not guarantee a flawless fit, since paper, by its very nature, will behave differently than your fabric.

First Fitting

This fitting should tell you how your fabric will mold into the style you have chosen. It should include only the garment areas that constitute the basic outer layer; omit the collar, cuffs, facings, sleeves, and any other details such as pockets. Baste the darts and press them lightly with the fingers. Pin or baste the major seams at the shoulders, sides, and waistline along the seamlines. Pin shut any openings where the zipper, buttons, or plackets will later be placed. For the best fit, the garment should always be tried on as it will be worn, with the right side out.

Before you attempt to fit any garment, wear the undergarments, shoes, and belt intended for that garment, and work before a full-length mirror in a well-lighted room. Stand naturally and look into the mirror. Make sure the garment provides enough ease for comfort. Sit, bend, walk, and move your arms. The garment should look balanced, with adequate length

from the neck to the waist and from the waist to the hem. Keep in mind that most figures are not perfectly symmetrical. Do not allow yourself to fit so closely that figure flaws such as a high hip or low shoulder become noticeable. Check the placement of closures and fastenings, the number of buttons, and so on to be sure that the closings will not gap. Don't become alarmed by high necklines and armholes; they will be smaller during the first fitting stages because the seam allowances are not turned in the proper direction until these edges are finished.

CONCENTRATE ON THE FABRIC: Learn to use your hands to lightly smooth the wrinkles, easing the fabric into the correct position. Grainlines and remaining wrinkles will tell you how the fabric is reacting to your figure. Check the placement of darts, necklines, armholes, and seams for any indication that the basic structure of the garment does not agree with the basic structure of your body.

SEAMLINES—GRAINLINES—WRINKLES: All lines are very important guides in fitting. Note the positions of your seamlines and grainlines. They should divide the body as intended by the designer. Grainlines should be parallel to the floor if they are crosswise and perpendicular to the floor if vertical (unless a section has been cut on bias grain as part of the design). When you are cutting out and marking your pattern, thread trace the grainlines on the fabric to indicate crosswise and lengthwise grainlines on each of your main garment pieces.

Wrinkles are the telltale signs of a grain distortion or of areas that are too tight or loose. If a vertical seam or grainline is not perpendicular to the floor or does not hang as your pattern envelope illustrates, look at the adjoining horizontal (or approximately horizontal) seams to see whether reducing or increasing their depth will sufficiently correct grainline and seam positions. Changes may have to be distributed between both the horizontal and vertical seams to bring the fabric into position. For these changes, you may open and re-pin seams on your figure, but it is faster to pin or chalk mark new seamlines and then make the change after you remove the garment. Fitting problems should be solved by the least complicated changes possible to avoid unnecessary work and unintentional disruptions of

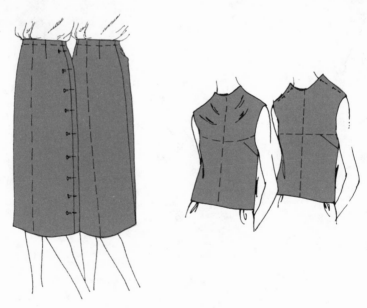

the design. Be aware that moving seamlines will mean that corresponding changes will have to be made in the adjoining garment sections.

Horizontal straining—stress at seams—indicates that a garment is too snug. Even after pattern alterations have been done, heavy or tightly woven fabric may require more wearing ease. Release all your seams slightly in even amounts to produce the needed ease.

DARTS: If the point ends in an unattractive location, remove the basting and adjust length of your dart. Relocate the point end first. You can adjust the depth of the dart to compensate for the thickness of your fabric.

NECKLINES: Necklines often require minor corrections. To remedy tight or high necklines, deepen the neck seamline an even amount around entire neckline to avoid distorting the line. If your neckline is a little large, slightly increase the shoulder seam or the center back seam at the neckline, tapering to the shoulder. Remember, straining at the neckline may be caused by the seam allowance that has not yet been turned under.

TO COMPLETE FITTING: Baste garment sections together along the new seamlines established during the first fitting, stitching any darts or seams that did not require fitting changes, and press. Press basted seams open with fingertips. Try on the garment again, testing the fit before stitching these areas together permanently.

Second Fitting

The second fitting takes place after sewing the darts and major seams, attaching the facings, and basting the sleeves or armhole facings into position. Test a jacket over a blouse, or a coat over a dress or jacket for really precise fit. Turn up the proposed hem. Review the appearance of your garment critically in the mirror. Side, back, and front seams should be straight and perpendicular to the floor by now. Diagonal wrinkles are often the result of fabric slippage as you sew. Smooth fabric perpendicular to the wrinkles to discover where to open and re-stitch the seam. Then check the new seamline. It is important to machine stitch directionally, generally sewing up from the hemline and down from the neckline. If you are letting out seams in fabric that frays easily, extend seam allowances with ribbon seam binding to ensure durability.

CLOSINGS: Pin the closings in position, matching center markings. *Asymmetrical closings* by their very nature need additional care and handling to prevent stretching any bias edges. Center markings should be anchored securely before you proceed with the fitting, or the additional weight of the closing details may distort grainlines and seams.

SLEEVES: The fit of the sleeve affects the entire garment. Raise your arms; freedom of movement is vital. Alterations should be handled during the tissue stage, as in the pattern adjustment section. For set-in sleeves, review pages 274 and 275. Kimono sleeves and gussets can only withstand very minor fitting adjustments.

Make sure that the fabric grainlines on the set-in sleeve cap are at right angles to prevent rippling toward the front or back of the armhole. Minor fitting adjustments can be done at the upper portion of the armhole. Remove the basting between notches. Raise or lower the sleeve cap until it is positioned correctly, taking a deeper or narrower seam allowance on the bodice at the shoulder; do not change the sleeve seam allowance.

The underarm seam below the notches will be trimmed after the sleeve has been permanently set in. About 1″ below the armpit is ample room for movement. Contrary to what may seem logical, the lower the underarm part of the armhole, the more the sleeve or armhole facing may resist movement, causing pulling and straining. Remove the basting across the underarm. Raise or lower the sleeve, taking a deeper or narrower seam allowance on the bodice at the underarm as needed.

Final Fitting

After the garment has been completely sewn and pressed (except for the hem), try it on to determine the length. Review the final pressing to be sure that your seams are flat.

In the second fitting, the hem is pinned up to establish the most flattering length. Experiment with the estimated hem length. Once a length has been chosen, the actual measurement with a pin or chalk hem marker can take place in the final fitting.

Essentially, fashion dictates hem lengths; but the type of garment, the nature of the fabric, and the height of the wearer determine the depth of the hem. Usually the hem allowance is 3″, which adds weight and therefore influences the drape of the garment. Of course, if the hem is for a very full skirt or a sheer fabric, the depth will vary—1″ for a circular skirt and as narrow as ⅛″ or as wide as 6″ for a chiffon overskirt.

It is always more accurate to have someone else mark your hem for you. Make sure you are wearing the same height heels you plan to wear with the finished garment. Stand erect, look straight ahead, and have the person doing the marking move around you. For longer length garments, stand on a stool or a low table. Garments with bias or circular hems should always hang for at least 24 hours to allow the bias to set and prevent the hemline from sagging after it is hemmed.

After the hemline has been marked, pin up the hem and examine it carefully from all angles. Is the length flattering to your figure? Are the proportions of the garment pleasing to the eye? Is the hem parallel to the floor? Sometimes only a small change in length makes the difference between a hemline that is flattering and one that is not. For plaids, checks, and horizontal stripes, it may be necessary to change the curve of the hemline so that it follows the design of the fabric.

Once the best hemline has been accurately established, turn to page 340 for the ideal hem finish to select for your individual fabric and design.

Your honest, objective, critical awareness is vital if you want to improve your sewing with each item you make. We hope that these suggestions have encouraged you to try to solve your individual fitting enigmas undaunted. If the most orthodox solutions don't work for you, don't be afraid to invent others. Be intuitive, flexible, and creative and you'll see how effortlessly you can accomplish a more perfect fit.

3

Planning Your Fashion Approach

(continued on next page)

Choosing the Correct Fabric

Perhaps the most critical phase of any sewing project is that moment in the fabric store when, pattern in hand, you make your fabric decision. Be careful not to make it lightly, for the success of each sewing venture hinges on the quality and the suitability of the fabric you use. Quality is an elusive factor that does not depend on high price. Learn to recognize it by touch, not necessarily by cost, and don't skimp. Sleazy fabric never justifies the time and effort you spend on it. The suitability of the fabric to the pattern design is all-important—a crisp fabric will never create soft, flowing lines just as a soft, fluid fabric cannot be crisply tailored. The best judgment is based on experience, but these guidelines will also help prevent disasters due to a poor fabric choice:

- ☐ Let the back of your pattern envelope be your guide. The fabric suggestions reflect the designer's recommendations. Are crisp or soft fabrics listed? Is the design suitable for plaid, striped, or obvious diagonal fabrics?
- ☐ Look at the photographs or sketches on your pattern envelope to determine the silhouette of the garment. Does it stand away from the body or fall closely against it? Is it crisply tailored or softly gathered? Is the design detailed or does it have only a few seams?
- ☐ Feel the fabric's weight, bulk, and texture. Does it lend itself to your pattern's silhouette and line? Will it drape or gather effectively? Unwrap a length of fabric from the bolt, gather it up in your hand, and see how the fabric hangs.
- ☐ Analyze the design of the fabric. A dramatic print or highly textured fabric is best for a garment with simple lines, while a plain fabric allows the design lines of a garment to be highlighted. Will the fabric require matching? Does it have a nap or pile, shading, or a one-way design?
- ☐ Test the fabric for wearability and performance. Crush it. Is it wrinkle-resistant? Stretch it. Does it give? Does it spring back? Crease it. Is it suitable for pleats? Read the label on the bolt end for fiber content, finishes, and care information.
- ☐ Examine the fabric closely. Hold it up to the light. How strong and close is the weave? Loose weaves ravel easily and require more finishing details. Will it require any special sewing techniques? Is the fabric finished off-grain? Are there any imperfections in the weave or uneven streaks? For a printed fabric, does the design correspond to the grain?
- ☐ How will the fabric look on you? Unfold some and hold it up to your face before a mirror. Do the color and scale suit you? Will the fabric be appropriate for the garment's intended use and care? Carry with you snips or color swatches of other wardrobe items which must coordinate with your new garment. Above all—will you enjoy wearing this fabric?

Special consideration must also be given to the stretchability of knitted fabrics and to the additional yardage requirements of certain fabrics, as explained on the following pages.

Stretchability of Knits

Knitted fabrics have a wide range of stretchability. Some are very stable and can be handled like a woven fabric, while others have considerable stretch in either one or both directions. It is very important to determine the amount of stretch in a knit before you make your pattern and fabric selection.

Many patterns recommend both woven and knitted fabrics as suitable for that particular design. For these patterns, the stretchability of the knit is not as important as the weight and texture of the fabric. Double knits can be tailored for suits, coats, and dresses while single knits are best for softer designs that drape and flow. For loose or bulky knits, patterns that are simple in design are recommended.

However, some patterns have been designed specifically for use with stretchable knits. These patterns have very little wearing ease and rely on the stretchability of the fabric to provide ease for movement and comfort. Thus only stretchable knits can be used for these patterns—regular fabrics or stable knits would result in a garment that fits too tightly. These patterns are marked in the Vogue catalogue and on the pattern envelope with "use only stretchable knits."

Vogue Patterns has developed a Stretch Gauge to assist you in determining the stretchability or "give" of an individual knit. The weight or texture of a knit is not an indicator of its stretchability. Some lightweight knits are very stable, just as some heavyweight knits are very stretchy. The Stretch Gauge appears on the inside back cover of the Vogue catalogue and on the individual pattern envelopes for your convenience.

To use the Stretch Gauge, fold the fabric 2″ from the crosswise edge and place it in a relaxed state on the Stretch Gauge. Firmly hold the left edge of the fabric in place at the end of the gauge and gently stretch the fabric to the right. If the fabric design is distorted or the upper edge curls, the fabric is stretched too much. To be considered a stretchable knit, your fabric should stretch easily to the right end of the gauge, indicating that 4″ of the fabric will stretch to at least 5⅜″.

Now release the fabric end in your right hand to observe its ability to recover. If it springs back immediately, you are assured of a garment whose shape will not change. If the fabric does not recover well, you will have to control the stretch during construction to avoid a misshapen garment.

Some patterns, such as swimwear, require a two-way stretch fabric that must stretch equally in both directions. For these patterns, be sure to check the stretchability in both the crosswise and lengthwise directions to determine if the fabric is a two-way stretchable knit.

KNIT
STRETCH
GAUGE

Fold fabric 2″ (5cm) from crosswise edge and stretch gently
4″ (10cm) of your knit should stretch to | HERE ⟶

Fabrics Requiring Extra Yardage

Some fabrics, due to their construction or pattern design, require additional yardage for the fabric layout. Refer to the back of your pattern envelope for special yardage requirements and information. However, for some other fabrics, you will have to make your own calculations.

If your fabric is directional with a nap or pile, shading, or a one-way design, use the separate "with nap" yardage requirements. Always read the envelope carefully. For some patterns, the yardage for certain fabric widths is the same for both "with nap" and "without nap" fabrics, while for other fabric widths the amount differs. If you are uncertain of either the construction or design of your fabric, purchase the "with nap" yardage amount so that you will be able to follow a nap layout if necessary.

If your fabric is a plaid, stripe, or geometric design, allowance for matching the pattern is usually not included in the yardages given. To calculate the amount of additional yardage required for matching, you must measure the length of one repeat, which is one complete motif of the design. Then multiply this measurement by the amount of yardage required. For example, if the repeat measures 4½″ and 4 yards of fabric are required—you will have to purchase an additional 18″ or ½ yard of fabric for a total of 4½ yards.

A large-scale print may require additional yardage in order to balance the design appropriately on the figure. Use the same calculations as for plaids.

Some fabric designs may fall into more than one category when determining yardage. For example, a large uneven plaid will require a "with nap" layout, matching, and design placement on the figure. Thus, consider all aspects of your fabric to be certain that you will have enough yardage when you start to lay out your pattern pieces. For complete accuracy, some fabric stores will allow you to make a trial layout on the fabric before it is cut for purchase.

Fabric Width Conversion Chart

We have provided this guide to help solve those quandaries that occur when the width of the fabric you've chosen is not included on the pattern envelope. It is strictly an *estimate*, and does not include changes in your fabric requirements caused by pattern alterations, large-scale fabric designs, directional fabrics, and garment designs with unusually shaped or large pieces. In these instances, it's best to exercise your own judgment about how much fabric you'll need.

FABRIC WIDTH	32″	35″-36″	39″	41″	44″-45″	50″	52″-54″	58″-60″
	1⅞	1¾	1½	1½	1⅜	1¼	1⅛	1
	2¼	2	1¾	1¾	1⅝	1½	1⅜	1¼
	2½	2¼	2	2	1¾	1⅝	1½	1⅜
	2¾	2½	2¼	2¼	2⅛	1¾	1¾	1⅝
Yardage	3⅛	2⅞	2½	2½	2¼	2	1⅞	1¾
	3⅜	3⅛	2¾	2¾	2½	2¼	2	1⅞
	3¾	3⅜	3	2⅞	2¾	2⅜	2¼	2
	4	3¾	3¼	3⅛	2⅞	2⅝	2⅜	2¼
	4⅜	4¼	3½	3⅜	3⅛	2¾	2⅝	2⅜
	4⅝	4½	3¾	3⅝	3⅜	3	2¾	2⅝
	5	4¾	4	3⅞	3⅝	3¼	2⅞	2¾
	5¼	5	4¼	4⅛	3⅞	3⅜	3⅛	2⅞

Reprinted courtesy of New Jersey Cooperative Extension Service, Rutgers, The State University

Fabric Terminology

Before preparing and cutting your fabric, it is important to understand the terminology for woven and knitted fabrics.

Grain is the direction in which the threads composing the fabric run. Every woven fabric consists of crosswise threads worked under and over the more sturdy lengthwise threads. The narrow, flat, woven border resulting at both lengthwise sides when the crosswise threads reverse direction is called the *selvage*. The threads composing it are strong and densely woven. This border is a prefinished edge, and may be used to advantage in center back seams, waistbands, etc. The direction of the lengthwise threads running parallel to the selvage is known as *lengthwise grain*, or sometimes "straight-of-fabric." These threads are very strong and stable, since they must withstand great tension during weaving. For this reason, garments are usually cut with the lengthwise grain running vertically for durability. The direction of the crosswise threads, running from selvage to selvage at right angles across the lengthwise threads, is known as the *crosswise grain*. In most fabrics it has a very slight amount of give.

A third term used to describe direction on woven fabric is *bias*. Bias is any diagonal intersecting the lengthwise and crosswise threads. Fabric cut on the bias grain possesses much greater elasticity than that cut on the crosswise grain. Maximum stretchability occurs on the *true bias*, which is obtained by folding your on-grain fabric diagonally so the crosswise threads are parallel to the selvage. Thus, true bias exists at any 45° angle to any straight edge of a fabric whose lengthwise and crosswise threads are perpendicular.

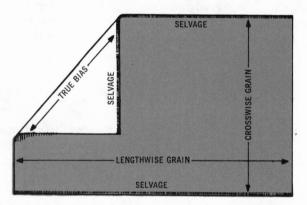

Knitted fabrics are structured of interlocking loops of yarn. *Wales* or *ribs* are columns of loops running parallel to the long measurement of a knitted fabric. They correspond to the lengthwise grain of a woven fabric. *Courses* are the crosswise rows of loops.

Fabric as sold in stores is folded or rolled lengthwise on a cardboard or metal form. In this packaged state it is known as a *bolt*. You will find that on the bolt the selvages may be located at the top and bottom of the retainer, or both selvages may be at one end with a fold at the other. Knitted fabrics come either flat or tubular. Tubular knits can be cut open along one edge.

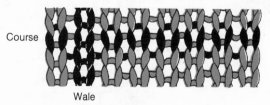

Preparing Your Fabric

You're excited about your new project, and anxious to start sewing immediately. Hang onto your enthusiasm, but don't be so eager to begin cutting that you neglect the all-important preparation. Fabric and pattern may both need attention before you do the final layout, and the success of your finished garment depends on care in these preparatory steps.

First, turn your attention to your fabric. Carefully steam-press it to remove wrinkles and fold lines. If the fabric has been long in the store, this may reveal a soiled mark along the fold, which must be washed out or dry-cleaned before you proceed. In some fabrics, such as knits and permanent-finish fabrics, the crease may not always be removed by pressing. For these fabrics, avoid layouts where pattern pieces are placed on the fold. If no other layouts are included in your pattern, place the pattern pieces so that the crease will not appear in a conspicuous place on your garment.

Straightening Fabric Ends

Straighten the ends of a woven fabric to coincide with the crosswise threads by snipping close to the selvage, pulling a crosswise thread until the fabric puckers, then cutting along that puckered line across the entire width. This is the most time-consuming method, but also the most accurate. If a crosswise thread is readily visible, you may omit pulling threads and cut directly.

Tearing the fabric is the quickest means, but should be used only with extreme caution. The pulling action may throw the first several inches off grain at both fabric ends, or if the tear is not done swiftly and accurately, the cloth may suddenly split along the lengthwise grain.

For a knitted fabric, cut along a course or crosswise line of loops to straighten the fabric ends. If the loops are not easily seen, it may be necessary to first mark the course with chalk or thread tracing. These markings can also be used for determining if the knit is on-grain or not. A tubular knit can then be cut open lengthwise following a rib or lengthwise row of loops.

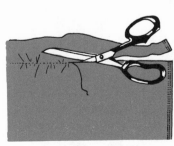

Woven Fabric

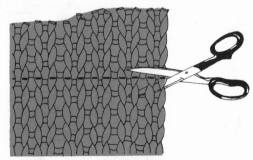

Knitted Fabric

Straightening Grain

We cannot emphasize strongly enough how vital the correct grain is to the final appearance of your garment. Your fabric is on grain when crosswise and lengthwise threads or loops are at perfect right angles to each other.

Check the grain after the ends of your fabric have been evened. Fold the fabric lengthwise, matching selvages and fabric ends. If the edges do not align along all three sides, the fabric is off-grain and must be straightened. If the edges are even, check also to see if the corners form right angles by aligning a corner of the fabric with a corner of your cutting surface. For knitted fabrics, match only the ends of the fabric; unlike the selvages of a woven fabric, the lengthwise edges of a flat knit are not always straight.

If the fabric is only slightly off-grain, it can be straightened by steam-pressing the threads into proper alignment. With the fabric folded lengthwise, right sides together, pin every five inches along the selvages and ends. You may need to pin the fabric to the ironing board to keep it square. Press firmly, stroking from the selvages toward the fold.

 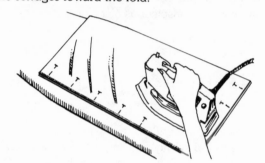

Fabric that is very much off-grain can be straightened by pulling the fabric gently but firmly in the opposite direction from the way the ends slant until a perfect right angle corner is formed. If the fabric is washable, place it in warm water for a few minutes to help relax the finish before pulling the fabric ends. Then pin a selvage to a taut clothesline every few inches or lay on a flat surface, and allow to dry. Repeat if necessary.

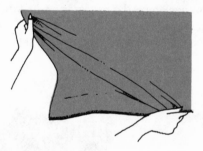

In some cases you may have to try a combination of the above techniques for the best results. Note that permanent-finish fabrics can never be straightened. It is perfectly all right to use them as they are, matching and pinning the selvage only, not the ends. Some printed fabrics may not be off-grain, but the print design does not coincide with the grainline. These fabrics should be avoided. If you should wish to use them, you must allow the print design to dictate the layout, not the grain.

Preshrinking

Many fabrics on today's market are "ready for the needle" and require no preshrinking. Always read the label on the fabric bolt to determine the specifics on shrinkage and whether the fabric is washable or dry cleanable. If the fabric has not been shrunk by the manufacturer or if it will shrink more than one percent according to the label, you must shrink your fabric before cutting it out. If you are unsure, it is always safer to preshrink your fabric rather than discover a shrinkage problem after the garment is completed. Washing or dry-cleaning can also help to remove resins used for finishing some knitted and woven fabrics that can cause skipped stitches.

For washable fabrics, you can launder and dry the fabric following the same methods that you will use with the finished garment. Or fold the fabric evenly and immerse it in hot water for thirty minutes to an hour. Gently squeeze out the water and dry according to the fabric care instructions.

Dry cleanable fabrics such as woolens should be shrunk by a professional dry cleaner if possible. To do it yourself, first straighten fabric ends, snip selvages at intervals, and fold in half lengthwise. Baste across the ends and along the selvages. Place a very damp sheet on a flat surface and lay the fabric on the sheet. Fold carefully, keeping the sheet on the outside. Leave the fabric folded overnight in a tub or basin. Unfold, smooth and stretch the fabric into shape and on grain. Let the fabric dry and press lightly with a steam iron. Then test for grain perfection before cutting, as previously discussed.

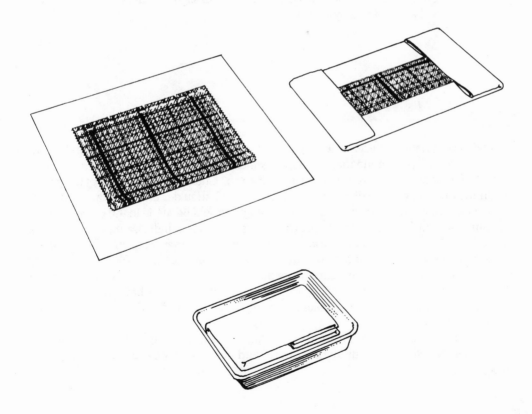

Identifying Right Side of Fabric

Occasionally the right side of the fabric is not readily discernible from the wrong. The way the fabric is displayed on the bolt can be an excellent clue in distinguishing the right and wrong sides, for you will find that certain fabrics are usually wound on the bolt in a consistent manner. For example, cottons and linens are almost always folded in half with their right sides out, then placed on the bolt. Wools can be packaged either prefolded with the right side in and wrapped on a rectangular bolt or rolled unfolded on a tube with the right side toward the inside. Many easily marred, delicate fabrics and imported fabrics are also rolled with their right side on the inside as protection against damage.

If you've purchased the fabric in a state other than its usual packaging, or forgotten which side is which, try the following procedures to differentiate the right side from the wrong side. Look at the center fold, which is parallel to the lengthwise grain or selvages, and refer to the usual packaging procedures mentioned above. Examine the selvages for slubs, nubs, and other irregularities. In general, the selvages will look less finished on the wrong side of the fabric. You can also examine the fabric surface itself to see if the finish used will indicate the right side. The finished side may be shinier, flatter, more brushed, or the weave more pronounced.

For knitted fabrics, the cut edge usually rolls toward the right side when pulled in the direction of the greatest stretch. The right side also may be more decorative or textured.

As a last resort, pick the side you like best! There is no reason why you cannot use either side of many fabrics. Just be very certain to use the same side consistently when laying out your pattern on the fabric. If you neglect to do so, the slightest variation in shading can destroy the good looks of your garment.

Organizing

Sort all of your pattern pieces, selecting those for the view you have chosen, as indicated by your Cutting Guide. Among these, group together the pieces for the main garment, lining, and interfacing and press them with a warm, dry iron. Check the proportion of the garment length to your figure by holding up the pattern to your shoulder or waist, with hems folded up. If a change is indicated, an adjustment in length should be made in the paper pattern at this time. If your basic pattern or your previous experience indicate that alterations are needed, such changes should also be made in the paper pattern. Compare your measurements with those on the body Measurement Chart (see page 62) and allow ample room in the pattern for any measurements that are larger than those given for the pattern size. Remember—when in doubt, leave extra room! Better to have nice, wide seam allowances because you overestimated than to have to skimp because you didn't leave enough fabric.

Take out your equipment for measuring, cutting, and marking and read through your Cutting Guide. Now that your fabric, pattern, and equipment are organized you are ready to begin!

Cutting with Care

Assuming your pattern alterations are double-checked and your fabric is fully prepared, circle the correct layout for your version, size, and approximate fabric width on your Cutting Guide. Be sure to use the "with nap" layout if your fabric is a knit or has a nap or pile, shading, or a one-way design. The pattern layout provides you with a completely reliable guide for laying out your pattern swiftly and economically. If you think you can bend the rules by laying some pieces a little off grain to fit, **don't.** A simple maneuver like this can jeopardize all your future efforts on that garment—one side of the skirt may flare more than the other, the entire bodice section might ripple and pull, and facings cut off-grain will pucker.

Here are some ideas used by professionals—suggestions to follow as you lay out and cut your pattern for perfect results every time.

Layout

- ☐ Pin fabric every three inches or so on indicated foldline and along all ends and selvages. The selvages may have to be clipped every few inches so that the fabric will lie flat. For knitted fabrics, match straightened ends or thread trace along one rib near center of fabric to use as lengthwise foldline or for aligning crosswise fold.
- ☐ Extend a short grainline to pattern ends with pencil, and measure often to be sure that the pattern is placed on the correct grain.
- ☐ Double-check all alterations to see that seam and cutting lines are redrawn and all corresponding pieces are altered, including facings.
- ☐ Lay out all pattern pieces before you begin cutting to be sure you have enough fabric.
- ☐ Place pattern pieces printed side up unless otherwise indicated by the Cutting Guide. Shading of the area on the layout indicates that the piece is placed printed side down.
- ☐ Fold fabric right sides together when double layers are shown on layout. For single thickness, place fabric right side up. If layout shows single and double thicknesses, pin pattern on double layer first, folding fabric as shown in the layout and measuring from the selvage or cut edge to the fold in several places to be sure the fold is exactly on-grain.

Lengthwise Fold—fabric is folded in half on the lengthwise grain, right sides together, matching selvages.

Crosswise Fold—fabric is folded in half with right sides together on the crosswise grain of the fabric, matching selvages along the edges.

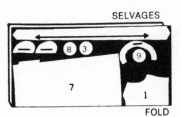

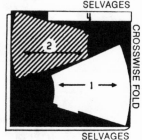

Double Fold—fabric is folded twice along the lengthwise grain, right sides together, with the selvages usually meeting in the center.

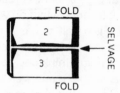

Single Layer—fabric is opened up to single thickness and placed right side up.

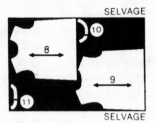

Partial Fold—fabric is folded with right sides together on lengthwise grain, only wide enough to fit the width of the pattern piece or pieces on the fold. Other pattern pieces are placed on the single layer of fabric above the folded portion.

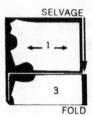

☐ When your layout shows a pattern piece extending beyond the fabric fold, cut the other pieces first, then unfold the fabric, and cut out the remaining pattern piece.

☐ Stars are used to indicate that the pattern piece must be cut right side up on a single layer of fabric.

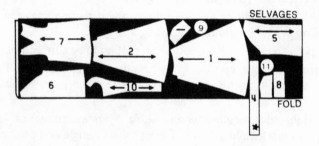

☐ If the layout is marked with a large asterisk and "See Special Instructions," the fabric must be specially folded as for a nap layout (see page 138).

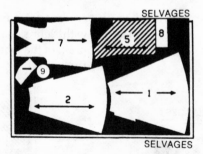

✱ See SPECIAL INSTRUCTIONS

☐ If the fabric design must be matched, always take care to match seamlines, **not** cutting lines. See next section on Special Fabric Layouts.

Cutting

☐ Pin first along lengthwise grainlines and foldlines.

☐ Place pins perpendicular to and ¼" inside the cutting line and diagonally at the corners of the pattern, spacing them about every three or four inches apart, or closer for sheer or slippery fabrics.

☐ Use long, bent-handled shears, and cut with steady, even slashes. Never cut out a pattern with pinking shears. Use them only to finish seams during construction.

☐ To avoid distorting the fabric, cut "directionally" with the grain.

☐ Never lift the fabric from the table. Keep one hand flat on the pattern piece while cutting.

☐ Use the point of the scissors to cut notches outward. Cut groups of notches in continuous blocks for easier matching.

☐ Be sure to use each pattern piece the correct number of times. Such details as pockets, cuffs, welts, and belt carriers are likely to need more than the usual two pieces.

☐ Fold the cut pieces softly and lay them on a flat surface.

☐ Save fabric scraps left from cutting. They are often needed for such things as bound buttonholes, sleeve plackets, and other sections not cut from pattern pieces; or for testing tension, stitch length, and pressing techniques.

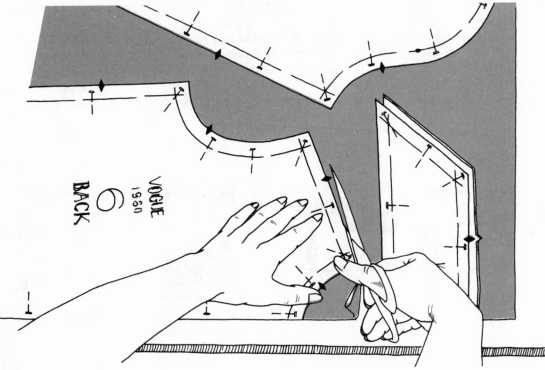

Special Fabric Layouts

If you have been avoiding fabrics that require special layouts, such as napped or pile fabrics, diagonals, plaids, stripes, and border prints, let us dispel your fears by providing a reassuring supplement to your Cutting Guide. You can usually use the same methods for preparing, pinning, and cutting, but do give more than average attention to laying out your pattern pieces and basting the garment together.

If you haven't had any experience with the special demands of an unusual fabric, arm yourself with our suggestions and a spirit of adventure. Choose a fairly simple design until experience bolsters your confidence, and sew ahead.

Directional Fabrics

Fabrics with nap, pile, shading, or one-way designs must be cut with all pattern pieces placed in the same direction. If your pattern suggests these fabrics, your Cutting Guide includes a "with nap" layout, which you must follow.

Napped fabrics, such as fleece, are those which are brushed after weaving to produce a directional, fuzzy surface on one side. Pile fabrics, such as velvet, are actually constructed so some of their component yarns rise at an angle from the woven surface of the fabric. Both give a different impression in color and texture according to the direction of the nap or pile. Cut with nap running down for a lighter, shinier look; with nap running up for a deeper, richer color. The fabric will feel rough when you move your hand against the direction of the nap, and smooth when with the nap. With piles and naps, pin the pattern to the wrong side of the fabric so that the pattern tissue does not shift.

Knits and textured fabrics, such as satins and brocades, also have to be treated as one-way fabrics because of the way light is reflected off their surface, causing a shading effect.

For fabrics with a one-way print, be sure that the print will be right side up when the garment is completed.

Sometimes a special cutting layout is included in your Cutting Guide for directional fabrics. It will be marked with a large asterisk and the words, "See Special Instructions." The fabric must first be folded in half on the crosswise grain with right sides together. Then it is cut along the fold from selvage to selvage. Keeping the right sides together, turn the upper layer around so that the nap, shading, or one-way design runs in the same direction.

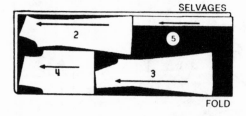

＊ See SPECIAL
INSTRUCTIONS

Diagonals

Diagonal fabrics require special care in pattern selection and pattern layout in order that the direction of the diagonal remains consistent in the garment and does not create any unusual optical illusions. Twill weaves, such as flannel, serge, and gabardine, have a diagonal ridge running from either the lower left corner to the upper right, or from the lower right to the upper left on the fabric. Sometimes the diagonal is hardly noticeable unless the fabric is napped. Other times, it is very distinct because of different colored or heavy yarns used in the fabric. Diagonally striped fabrics are usually printed, not woven, and are treated the same as twills.

Select your pattern carefully, choosing a simple design with set-in sleeves, straight underarm darts, and a slim skirt. If your pattern has the warning "obvious diagonal fabrics are not suitable," it is an indication that diagonal stripes or prints will be difficult or impossible to match. However, many diagonals are less obvious when draped into a garment than lying on a flat surface. Always drape a length of fabric on yourself in front of a mirror to determine how prominent the diagonal will be.

Certain design features are to be avoided with diagonals. Collars cut on the fold and roll-back lapels will have the diagonal pattern running in different directions on the left and right sides. Strange illusions will be created by V-necklines, long bias darts, and any sleeve cut-in-one with the bodice—the diagonal pattern will be parallel to one side of the neckline, dart, or sleeve and will be perpendicular to the other. Garments with bias-cut side seams will have the diagonals meeting each other perpendicularly.

When working with a diagonal fabric, you must plan your layout carefully so that the diagonal is consistent in both front and back. Cut out your fabric single thickness with all the pattern pieces running in the same direction as in a "with nap" layout. If your collar is cut on a fold, change the foldline to a seamline and add a ⅝″ seam allowance. Lay out the collar on the bias with the diagonal running parallel or perpendicular to the original foldline. (For printed fabrics, the diagonal may not be exactly on the true bias.) Or you can lay out the collar on the bias and flip at the foldline to avoid a seam. Now the collar will match on both the left and right sides. For the rest of the garment, match the diagonal at the notches and dots along the seamline.

Features to Avoid
with Diagonals

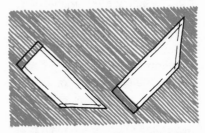

Planning Layout for Diagonal Fabric

If your fabric is identical on both the right and wrong side, the pattern can be laid out so that the diagonal forms a chevron. Cut the fabric into two equal lengths and place one length on top of the other with the right side of one against the wrong side of the other, matching the diagonal. The pattern, which must have a center front and center back seam, can be cut double thickness.

When a diagonal fabric is cut on the bias, the design will run horizontally or vertically. You can use this contrasting effect for pockets, cuffs, and bindings.

Plaids

Plaids present an additional design dimension in any garment. When sewing with plaids, therefore, the idea is to avoid extremely complicated fashions and let the plaid tell the story. Also keep in mind that the size of the plaid should be in scale with both the garment and the person wearing it if it is to flatter rather than overwhelm. For the best results, plaid garments should be made only in designs recommended for plaids by your pattern catalogue or the back of the pattern envelope. If "Not Suitable for Plaids," it is because they cannot be properly matched at the seams.

There are several things to keep in mind when purchasing a plaid fabric. First, always remember to buy extra yardage for matching. The actual amount will be determined by the size of your pattern, the size of the plaid repeat, and the number of lengths of major pattern pattern pieces required by your Cutting Guide. Secondly, never purchase your plaid from a small sample, as it seldom shows the repeat. A strong vertical or horizontal movement in the fabric, which might easily affect your choice of fabric, can only be noted from looking at a large piece of fabric. Thirdly, if you decide on a printed rather than a woven plaid, check carefully to see that the stripes of the plaid are on-grain. If the plaid is printed just slightly off-grain, match the plaid since it is more noticeable than the grain in this particular instance. Do not buy an extremely off-grain printed plaid, since it will not drape or mold satisfactorily when made into a garment.

For the most attractive and professional-looking results, be concerned with the placement of the lines of your plaid, especially the dominant stripe. The lines should always be continuous from front to back and from neck to hem. This also holds true for two-piece dresses and suits; the plaid lines of the jacket or top should match those of the skirt. Horizontally, avoid placing a heavy, dominant stripe at the bustline or waistline. It is generally preferable to place it at the hemline; this means, of course, that you must determine the finished length of your garment and mark it on the pattern tissue before you cut. On an A-line or other curved hem, the horizontal lines will appear to arc slightly downward toward the side seams if the center fold or seam is on the straight grain. In such a case, ignore the traditional rule and place your fabric's least dominant section along the garment's lower edge, thus drawing a minimum amount of attention to the distortion of the plaid design at the hemline. Vertically, place the dominant line of the plaid at center front if possible. Always make all your fitting adjustments on the pattern before you cut out your fabric, or you may destroy all your careful placement and matching efforts.

Since the kind of plaid you buy will determine your layout, you should understand the elements of a plaid design. A plaid is composed of stripes crossing each other at right angles, spaced evenly or unevenly, and repeated in sequence. All manufactured plaids consist of a **repeat** or a four-sided area in which the pattern and color of the design are complete. These units, arranged continuously side by side, form the fabric pattern and determine whether the plaid is even or uneven. In an **even plaid,** the stripe arrangement is the same in both the lengthwise and crosswise directions, creating a perfectly square repeat. When folded in any direction through the center of any repeat, the halves must form a mirror image. In an **uneven plaid,** the design and spacing are different in the lengthwise, crosswise, or both directions.

Plaid test: To test the plaid, first fold the fabric diagonally through the center of any repeat. (Plaid must be perfectly on-grain.) If spaces and colors match, test further by folding the plaid vertically or horizontally through the center of any repeat.

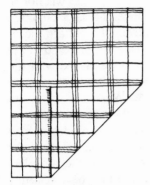

In an even plaid the spaces and colors match in both directions.

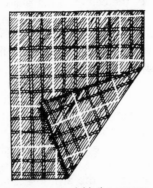

In an uneven plaid, the spaces and colors do not match in both directions.

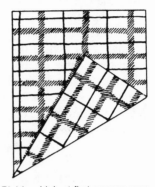

Plaids which at first appear even may, in reality, be uneven.

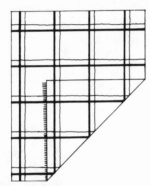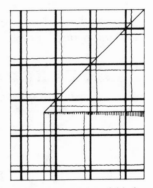

The design in this plaid does form a perfect square when folded diagonally, but does not make a mirror image when folded vertically or horizontally through the center of any repeat.

Slip basting: Slip basting will help to ensure a perfectly matched plaid. To slip baste, work from the right side of the fabric. Crease and turn under the seam allowance along one edge. Lay the folded edge in position on the corresponding piece, matching the plaid at the seamline, and pin. Slip the needle through the upper fold, then through the lower layer using a single long stitch. Continue this stitch for the entire length of the seam. You can now machine-stitch the seam in the normal manner from the wrong side.

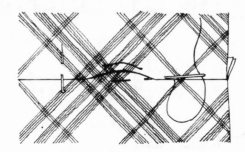

EVEN PLAIDS

Even plaids are relatively easy to match. Prepare your fabric according to the cutting layout. Since the fabric is not always folded correctly on the bolt, make sure the fold is at the center of the dominant line or the center of the plaid design. The selvages will not be even when the fabric has to be refolded. The "without nap" layout can be used, but often the shading or coloring makes the "with nap" layout most effective. The pattern pieces should be placed so the notches and the symbols along the seamline are matched at the side and center of the front and back pieces. Center seams must be placed with the seamline directly in the center of the plaid repeat for a straight seam, while a shaped seam (center or side) should start out in the center of the plaid repeat. When the seams are joined the design will chevron—the angle will depend on the shape of the seam.

Always match the seamlines, not the cutting lines. Start by placing the predetermined hemline along the dominant line of the plaid. Plaids should be matched at the front armhole seamline at the notch, but the curve of the sleeve cap may make the plaid impossible to match around the rest of the armhole seam. You will also have difficulty matching diagonals—darts, shoulder seams, etc. The side seams will not match above the bust dart. With two-piece garments, remember that the plaids should be continuous from the top to the bottom when worn. Always match design details such as cuffs and pockets to the plaid portions they cover on the finished garment. Lapel facings should be cut from the same part of the plaid as the bodice. For interesting fashion details, you may wish to cut pockets, yokes, cuffs, and bound buttonhole strips on the bias.

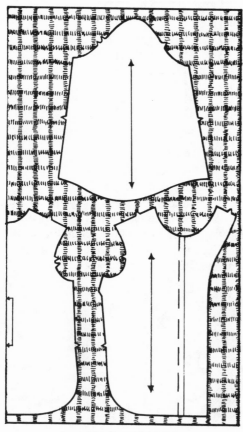

Layout for Even Plaid Fabric

UNEVEN PLAIDS

To be realistic, we must admit that sewing with uneven plaids is not for the novice. But it can be a rewarding experience if you remember to choose a pattern with as few construction lines as possible to reduce the number of matching points.

The matching and placement concepts are the same as for even plaids with the following exceptions. Uneven plaids cannot be matched in both directions. Pick the stripes of the plaid design that you want to be emphasized, both vertically and horizontally, relative to your figure. Choose the desired plaid stripe for the center front. Fold the fabric, matching two desired stripes for front sections. Pin at intervals, matching the plaid lines of both layers. Next, pin the front pattern pieces to the fabric, placing the center front on the desired line. Match the plaid lines for the front sections, either vertically or horizontally as the fabric dictates. When the front pattern pieces are placed satisfactorily, place the back pieces, matching the side seamlines to those of the front. You may need to refold your fabric. Always use a "with nap" layout. Some plaids and fabric widths necessitate planning and cutting the garment on a single thickness, using the same methods as explained above. Be sure to turn the pattern pieces over (printed side down) to cut the left side of garment sections.

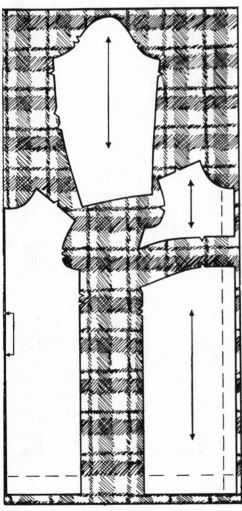

Layout for Uneven Plaid Fabric

CHECKS

In matching checks, let the scale of the pattern be the deciding factor. Checks ½″ square or larger are usually matched, following the same principles as for even plaids. Smaller checks do not require matching unless they would be visually disturbing in the finished garment if left unmatched.

Stripes

Sewing with stripes should definitely influence your pattern selection. Designs illustrated in stripes are especially suitable; if your pattern is marked "Not Suitable for Stripes," it is because they cannot be matched properly or will distract from the design lines. It would also be wise to read Your Fashion Analysis, pages 17 to 20, to help you decide which stripe and direction—balanced or unbalanced, horizontal or vertical—will be best suited to your figure. The amount of extra fabric required for matching horizontal or unbalanced vertical stripes will depend upon the size of the stripe repeat and the number of pattern lengths in the Cutting Guide. The principles for working with stripes also apply to wide wale corduroy and other obviously wide-ribbed fabrics.

While the methods for laying out stripes are basically the same as for plaids, stripes are easier to match because the design runs in only one direction. Stripes should run in the same direction throughout the garment. Other parts of the garment—cuffs, waistbands, and pockets—must be adjusted to match the body of the garment. Stripes on a notched collar should match those on the lapel. Set-in sleeves should match at the notch of the front armhole seamline. Buttonholes should be aligned with the direction of the stripes and, if the stripes are very large, they should match the color of the stripe.

You will have to discover which stripe is dominant in order to plan your layout. Squint at the fabric to see whether the widest stripe, the stripe at the center of the design, or the stripe with the strongest color is dominant. You may even find that a particular group of stripes, acting as a part of the overall design, becomes dominant and is then treated in the layout the same way as a single dominant stripe. Distinguish between balanced and unbalanced stripes by folding the dominant stripe in half along its length. If the stripes match when a corner of the fabric is folded back, the stripe is balanced.

Once you've become familiar with the principles involved in stripe layouts, let the stripes suggest creative visual effects. Don't be afraid to use a bias binding, pocket, or cuff, or perhaps a horizontally striped yoke on a vertically striped dress.

Balanced Stripes

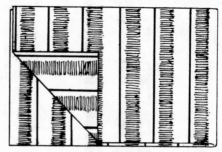

Unbalanced Stripes

BALANCED STRIPES

Horizontal: Matching a balanced stripe horizontally is the easiest of the stripe layouts. The lengthwise grainline arrow should run perpendicular to the stripe. The general rule is to place the dominant stripe at the hem foldline, so you must predetermine the hemline before you cut. There are two exceptions, however; if you have an obviously curved hemline or if thus placing the dominant stripe will also place it at the bustline or hipline, place the hemline at a less dominant location. If you do place the dominant stripe at the hemline, center a portion of it at the hemline in the center front and back of the garment to obtain the proper optical illusion. Match the stripes at center seams and at side seams below the bust dart, and make sure they are continuous from neck to hem, especially with two-piece garments such as suits.

Vertical: With the lengthwise grain arrow of your pattern parallel to the stripes, center the dominant stripe at the center front and back for the best-looking results. For a center fold, simply fold the fabric through the dominant stripe. If the center is on a seam or opening, pin two dominant stripes together and place the center seamline (not cutting line) through the center of the dominant stripe. If the pattern has a straight center front or back seam, you will have to plan carefully to allow for the seam allowances and for matching the stripes. If you are making a two-piece garment, make sure that the dominant stripe is at the centers of both pieces and runs continuously from the top or jacket to the skirt. Place the sleeve so that it matches on the front armhole seamline at the notch.

For an A-line skirt, a chevron will form at the side seams, the angle of which will depend on the fullness of the skirt. Note: Do not use styles for striped fabric that state specifically "not suitable for stripes," as this designation was made because you will not be able to match the stripes at the seams.

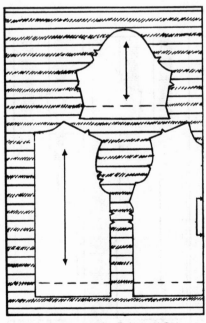

Horizontal Layout for Balanced Stripes

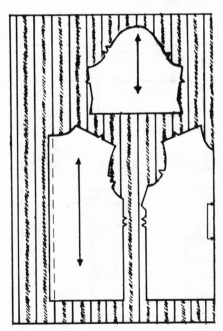

Vertical Layout for Balanced Stripes

UNBALANCED STRIPES

Horizontal: To plan for an unbalanced horizontal stripe, place the dominant stripe in the same manner as for a balanced stripe on the previous page. Be sure the lengthwise grainline arrow is perpendicular to the stripe. Predetermine and mark the hem lengths of all the garment sections before you cut your fabric. Then, using a "with nap" cutting layout, lay all your garment pattern pieces in the same direction. Use the notches and symbols to adjust the layout until the side seams match and the sleeve matches the bodice at the front armhole seamline. Also take care to lay the pieces so that the stripe design will be continuous and running in the same direction from neck to hem, especially with two-piece garments such as suits. For example, the stripe on a jacket hem should be a continuation of the stripe on the skirt.

Vertical: To use an unbalanced stripe vertically, the lengthwise grainline arrow should correspond with the stripe. To have the stripes move in the same direction around the body, use a "with nap" layout. Choose the desired stripe for the center front. Next, fold through the center of the stripe for a center front fold or pin two matching desired stripes together for a center front seam. Pin the pattern to the fabric, placing the center front on the desired stripe. Place the back pieces with the same stripe at the center. Refold the fabric if necessary. Depending on the design repeat, you may be able to plan side seams so stripes are continuous around the garment, but shoulder seams will not match. With shaped seams, sides will not chevron nor is it likely the stripes will match. Some designs may necessitate cutting fabric in a single thickness.

To have both sides of the garment form a mirror image, the center seam must be straight and parallel to the grainline. Place left-side pattern pieces in the opposite lengthwise direction as the right-side pieces. (This treatment cannot be used with fabrics requiring a "with nap" layout.)

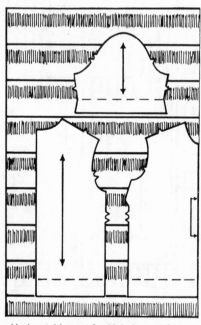

Horizontal Layout for Unbalanced Stripes

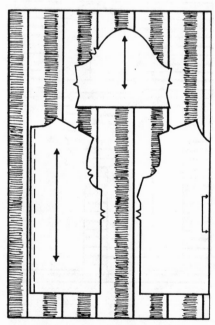

Vertical Layout for Unbalanced Stripes

Bias-cut Plaids and Stripes

Some of the most attractive design effects are brought about by cutting the plaid or stripe on the bias. The final result is a chevron, which is two sets of stripes meeting at identical angles. The specific angle of the chevron will depend upon the angle of the seams in relation to the lengthwise grainline. When selecting your fabric for a bias-cut garment, choose an even plaid or a balanced stripe without a pronounced diagonal weave. (Some plaid and striped fabrics are actually printed or woven on the bias; these are cut on the straight grain and matched as for a bias-cut fabric. See diagonals, page 139.)

Unless your pattern is specifically recommended for bias-cut fabrics, you will need to establish a bias grainline on each of the pattern pieces by drawing a long line at a forty-five-degree angle to the lengthwise grainline. Lay the pattern out on a single thickness of fabric to make sure that the plaid will chevron properly. Cut the right and left sides individually, turning the pattern pieces over (with the printed side down) for the left side. With each pattern piece, be sure that the plaid or stripe design corresponds at the symbols and the notches before cutting the fabric. This will ensure you a perfectly matching design once the seams are joined. To prevent the bias seams from stretching, pin strips of tissue paper to the wrong side of the layer that will remain flat while you are slip basting. Also place the tissue paper under the fabric on the machine bed when stitching the bias seams.

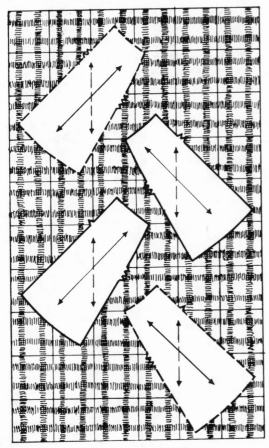

Layout for Bias-Cut Plaid Fabric

Prints

BORDER PRINTS

Special layouts are included with patterns illustrated in border prints; for others, you will need additional yardage. For your initial attempt, choose a fabric with the border running along one lengthwise edge and place it where the hem will fall. When the pattern is laid out along the crosswise grain, the garment can only be as long as the width of the fabric unless you seam it at the waist or bodice. Place the predetermined hemline at the border and the lengthwise arrow along the crosswise grain of the fabric. The pattern hem should be perpendicular to the center front and back and as straight as possible; if the hem is not straight, follow the edge of the border to create the best optical illusion. Avoid obviously A-line patterns. Match the motif at the side seams where feasible; if fabric has a dominant motif, place it at the center front and back.

LARGE-SCALE PRINTS

Carefully place the motifs of a large-scale print. Your goal should be a totally harmonious effect in the finished garment, where nothing stands out as visually disturbing. Large flowers and bold crosswise or lengthwise designs should be placed so that major body curves are avoided. For a pleasing visual balance, it is best to center large-scale designs vertically. You should definitely avoid placing large flowers or circles, etc., directly on the bust or derrière. Some large-scale prints have a definite vertical or horizontal direction, and thus fall into the category of one-way prints. If this is true of your fabric, use the "with nap" layout, letting your own judgment guide you in deciding whether the motif is prominent enough to require matching. It would be wise to analyze critically the scale of the print in relation to the scale of your figure. Very large prints are most effectively presented in styles with few design lines or in long garments, such as evening clothes or loungewear.

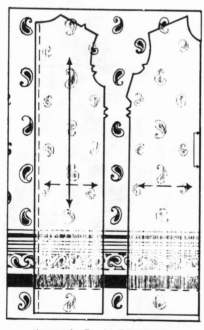

Layout for Border Print Fabric

Layout for Large-Scale Print Fabric

Marking
with Accuracy

Accurate marking of every notation on your fabric makes sewing that much easier. All those symbols and lines are put on the pattern piece for a reason, each having its separate purpose, which ultimately helps to create the shape of your garment. Happily, you will know exactly where to stitch on a curve, where ease should be adjusted, and whether corners will match perfectly.

All markings on pattern pieces should be transferred to the wrong side of the fabric as soon as the garment sections are cut and before pattern tissues are removed. Markings include construction symbols, seamlines, foldlines, darts, center front and center back lines, grainlines, and position marks. Always transfer these markings from your pattern pieces because they serve as continuous reference points for making your garment through all stages—pinning, stitching, fitting, even sewing on buttons. After you've completed marking the wrong side of your fabric, remove your pattern tissue and transfer position marks, foldlines, and any other long lines to the right side of your fabric, temporarily, with thread tracing. At this time, thread trace lengthwise and crosswise grainlines on the right side of each of your main pattern pieces, as special guidelines for fitting. If underlining is being used, you may want to mark it instead of your fashion fabric. Pin it to your fabric with the wrong sides together and then thread trace all necessary markings through both layers of each piece.

The tremendous variety in weights and types of fabric available means that you will need to use more than one method of marking in your sewing projects. Determine the fastest, most accurate, and most appropriate way to mark your particular fabric from among the following methods.

TRACING WHEEL and **DRESSMAKER'S TRACING PAPER** are used with hard-surfaced fabrics and all underlinings. First, test the color that you intend to use on a scrap of fabric. Steam-press the scrap to see if the tracings disappear. You may not have realized it, but white is best for white as well as light colors; red, yellow, or blue are better for dark colors. **Never** use vividly contrasting colors unless you know that they will disappear during pressing or cleaning.

If your garment is not underlined, trace markings on the wrong side of your fabric, one piece at a time. The carbon side of the paper should be next to the wrong side of the fabric when you trace.

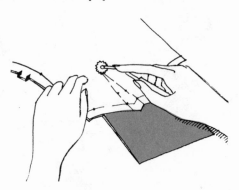

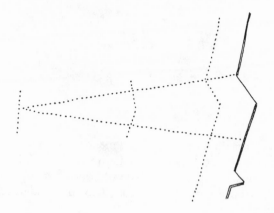

If your garment is underlined, mark only the underlining, not the fabric. Insert double layers of dressmaker's tracing paper around both layers of underlining, with the carbon side next to the underlining. With the fingers of your left hand holding the layers in place, trace over all markings, using just enough pressure on the tracing wheel to make light lines.

Use a ruler to guide tracing of straight lines. Trace through the center of any symbols. Indicate small symbols on seamlines with a short line perpendicular to the seamline. Also indicate the ends of darts, the points of slashes, and other small symbols which do not cross any seamlines with short horizontal lines; mark large symbols with an X; and so on, until you have developed your own shorthand for delineating the differences between the various construction symbols. Refer to the marking equipment section, page 189, if you need information on the types of tracing wheels and tracing paper to buy for your particular fabric.

TAILOR'S TACKS are used on delicate fabrics that might be marred by other methods of marking. They are especially necessary for soft-surfaced fabrics, such as velvet or spongy tweeds with napped or nubby faces. The technique is always the same whether you mark the fabric as a single or double layer. Using a long double strand of thread *without* a knot, take a single small running stitch through the tissue and fabric at a bold symbol. Then, sew another stitch crossing over the first, pulling the thread until a large loop is formed. As you go on to the next symbol, leave a loose thread, as shown. Clip the loops and the long threads connecting each tack. Raise the pattern tissue carefully, roll the upper fabric back gently, and cut the threads between the layers, leaving tufts on either side. When you are marking a single layer at a time, the tufts will appear on the right side, the short stitches on the wrong side. Use the fabric as soon as possible, or fold it carefully to prevent the clipped threads from slipping out of position.

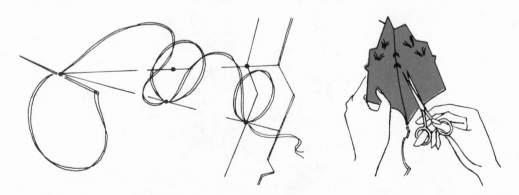

TAILOR'S CHALK or **MARKING PENCIL** are used on soft- or hard-surfaced fabrics. Place pins through the pattern and both layers of fabric at symbols, construction markings, and corners of pattern. Turn the piece over and chalk the wrong side of the fabric at each pin. Turn the piece back to the pattern side. Starting at the edge and working toward the center, hold the pins as you remove the pattern by forcing the pinhead through the tissue, and chalk the fabric. Remove pins as you work. Run thread tracing along the chalk lines if the chalk tends to rub off.

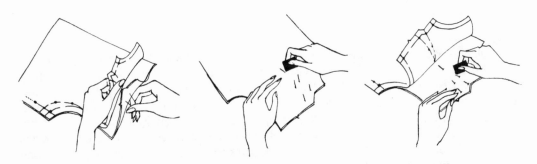

THREAD TRACING is uneven basting for quick marking of grainlines on all garment fabrics and for transferring necessary position marks to the right side of your garment fabric. Using a single thread (do not use knots), begin by taking a small backstitch. The type of uneven basting stitch to use as you thread trace is a matter of personal choice; it should be one that you find works best for you. With very little practice you will be able to develop a rhythm that makes this procedure a simple routine. Use silk thread or a basting thread on napped fabrics, piles, and light colors to avoid leaving an imprint. After all symbols and construction lines are transferred to the wrong side of your fabric or underlining by one of the previous methods, remove the pattern tissue. Pin underlining to fabric where necessary. Thread trace center front and back lines, foldlines, and grainlines on **one** section at a time.

We suggest that you thread trace a lengthwise grainline on sleeves, starting at the shoulder and ending at the elbow, and a crosswise grainline at the bust, hip, and sleeve cap. These lines will save you much guesswork in fittings. With one glance in the mirror, many needed adjustments will become obvious, as distortions in these long, thread tracing lines appear immediately.

Inner Construction:
The
Undercover Story

Designers' styles require fabrics to take many different shapes. They depend on either the fabric's natural ability to flare into a silhouette or hidden inner components that support the fabric in its desired shape. Underlining and interfacing, when chosen and used correctly, will help achieve the designer's intended effect with relative ease. They are the concealed elements that help garments retain their shape and wear longer. In lining a garment, the designer uses only fabrics that will comply with the drape of the style and will be attractive, comfortable, and smooth. The use of these hidden components, correctly executed, is one of the hallmarks of fine couture.

As fashion styles and silhouettes change from year to year, so do the fabric preferences of designers. Some seasons crisp silhouettes executed in firm fabrics predominate; other seasons the fashion pendulum swings to soft, fluid styles with lightweight, flowing fabrics. Therefore the type, weight, and amount of inner construction used in garments varies according to the styles and fabrics highlighted by current fashion.

When choosing underlining, interfacing, and lining, consider the style of your garment, the weight of the fashion fabric, and the type of care required by the fashion fabric. For crisp or tailored garments, an underlining may be necessary to maintain the silhouette, while for soft, woven fabrics and knits, an underlining would inhibit the drapability or stretchability of the fashion fabric. However, interfacing is needed to shape detail areas such as collars, cuffs, and buttonholes in almost all garments regardless of the silhouette or weight of fabric.

To achieve best results when selecting your inner construction fabrics, try draping the fabrics together—placing outer fabric over the underlining, interfacing, and/or lining to see how the fabrics relate to each other. Interfacing fabrics are now available in a wide range of types and weights—from heavy hair canvases for tailoring coats to lightweight interfacings designed with a certain amount of stretch to use with knits. Remember that heavy fashion fabrics do not necessarily require heavy interfacings, nor lightweight fabrics, lightweight interfacings. Also, fusible interfacings may become a little stiffer after fusing.

Inner construction fabrics must be compatible in care with the fashion fabric. A washable outer fabric necessitates washable inner fabrics. A residual shrinkage of less than 1% in the underlining, interfacing, lining, or outer fabric will not require preshrinking. When in doubt, however, preshrink all the fabrics using a suitable method described on page 133.

The durability of the inner fabric should be as great as that of the fashion fabric so that it will last the life of the garment. There is nothing more annoying than having to replace a lining that has weakened and torn from normal use, pulled away from the seams at points of stress, and crumbled at the armholes from moisture and wear; or to have a crisp stand-up collar lose its stiffness after the garment has been laundered.

Inner construction is never seen, except for a beautifully lined coat or jacket, yet its proper selection and application often determine the final appearance of your garment—not only when it is first constructed, but long after it has been worn and cleaned many times. Inner construction should never be overlooked.

Underlining

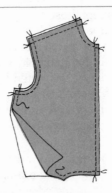

Underlining helps to impart a sculptured look to your garment. It is cut from the same pattern pieces as the garment fabric. Then the underlining and fashion fabric are basted and sewn together to act as one layer throughout construction.

Underlining adds body and durability to your garment by supporting and reinforcing the fabric and seams. It also helps to reduce wrinkling and prevent stretching. Underlining can act as a foundation for the garment so that the interfacings, facings, and hems can be sewn without stitches or ridges appearing on the right side of the garment. With sheer and lightweight fabrics, underlining can be used for opaqueness in certain areas of the garment. When used for crisper shaping, it can give support to the outer fabric to maintain a silhouette that otherwise could not have been achieved.

Underlining helps to facilitate the marking and stitching of your garment. All markings are made on the underlining, which is then pinned to the wrong side of your fashion fabric. Slight changes or adjustments can be recorded on the clearly marked underlining without overhandling the garment.

When selecting underlining, test it with the fashion fabric by draping both together over your hand to make sure they relate well to each other. A tightly woven fabric is best for preventing stretching and preserving the shape of your garment. Test the tightness of the weave by scratching the fabric with your thumbnail. If the threads spread apart or slide, the fabric generally will not wear well.

To achieve different effects in different areas of the same garment, more than one kind of underlining is often necessary. A lightweight wool dress with a soft bodice and A-line skirt will need a soft, lightweight underlining for the bodice and a crisp underlining for the skirt.

Special underlining fabrics are available in a wide selection of colors and fiber blends and may be labeled for softness or crispness. Or you can use other light and mediumweight fabrics such as batiste, China silk, marquisette, organdy, organza, muslin, and taffeta. In general, the underlining should be lighter in weight and as soft or softer than the outer fabric so as not to affect the appearance of the garment, except in cases where subtle shaping is desired. To aid you in your selection, refer to the chart of underlinings and linings, pages 160 to 162.

Method of Underlining

Transfer all markings to underlining fabric only. Center the marked underlining over the unmarked fabric, checking to be sure that the traced grainlines and center fold lines coincide with the grain of your fabric. Pin together along the traced lines and around the raw edges. Your cut edges will not always be exactly even, but that is to be expected since the two layers were cut separately.

To make your underlining and fashion fabric relate to each other the way they will when curving around your body, it may be necessary to make the underlining slightly smaller than the fashion fabric. Remove all pins except those along the center lines, and fold both layers along this pinned center line with your fashion fabric uppermost. Insert a thick newspaper, large magazine, or cardboard between the folded fabric. Smooth the fashion fabric over the underlining, keeping crosswise grain aligned, and pin where it lies along all raw edges and at all construction lines. The underlining will extend slightly beyond the edges of the fashion fabric. The difference between the seam allowances will increase with the thickness of your fashion fabric. After repositioning, trim away the excess underlining. Use a seam gauge to mark the new underlining seamlines so they will align with the fashion fabric seamlines.

From the underlining side, run a line of thread tracing along all markings through both layers of fabric. Baste next to, **not on,** the traced seamlines so the basting threads will be easy to remove later. Or staystitch ½″ from the edge through both layers so that the fabrics can be handled as one throughout construction.

To stitch darts, hand or machine baste along the foldline of each dart through both fabrics, beginning 2″ to 3″ beyond the point of each dart. Fold dart along center, matching markings, and stitch. Remove basting that extends past dart point. Darts can also be stitched separately in the fashion fabric and underlining before basting the two fabrics together; then handle the two fabrics as one.

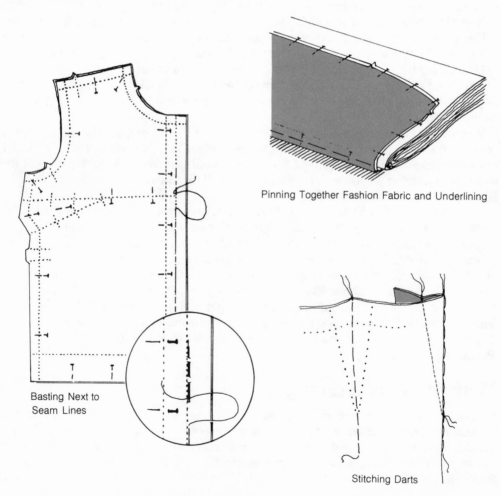

Pinning Together Fashion Fabric and Underlining

Basting Next to
Seam Lines

Stitching Darts

Interfacing

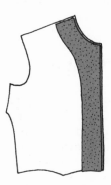

Interfacing is used to shape detail areas in a garment. It can maintain a gentle roll in collars and lapels; add body without bulk to garment edges, cuffs, and pockets; prevent stretching of necklines and buttonholes; and add crispness and stability to waistbands and belts. Almost all garments, regardless of their style or type of fabric, require some interfacing—a tailored jacket may have many areas interfaced while a simple knit dress may have interfacing only in a V-neckline.

Interfacings are available in a wide range of fibers, weights, and degrees of crispness. They are categorized according to their method of application: **sew-in** interfacings are stitched by hand or machine to your garment; **fusible** interfacings have a resin coating on the back that will fuse to fabric when steam, heat, and pressure are applied. Both types can be woven, non-woven, or knitted and are available in white, black, and neutral colors.

Woven interfacings are made of synthetic, cotton, or a blend of fibers; canvases may include wool or goat hair. They are available in different weights and crispness from lightweight polyester to heavyweight hair canvas. Woven interfacings must be cut on straight grain, or they can be cut on the bias for softer shaping in rolled collars and hems. **Non-woven** interfacings are made of synthetic fibers bonded together in weights from sheer to heavy. Pattern pieces can be laid in any direction for stable or "all-bias" non-wovens; however, for those that have crosswise stretch and lengthwise stability, the pattern pieces must be laid out as for woven fabrics. **Knitted** interfacings are made of nylon tricot, which has lengthwise stability and considerable crosswise stretch, providing flexibility for light-weight knits and wovens. Other fabrics such as organza, cotton batiste, and lightweight underlining fabrics can also be used as interfacings.

The selection of the appropriate interfacing depends upon the weight of the fashion fabric, the area in which it will be used, the amount of shaping or stiffness desired, and the type of care the fabric will receive. Sheer or featherweight interfacings are designed for lightweight woven and knitted fabrics; lightweight interfacings for dress weight fabrics; mediumweight interfacings for suitings and medium to heavyweight fabrics; and heavy-weight interfacings are recommended only for accessories and crafts.

In general, your interfacing should not be heavier in weight than your garment fabric, although it can be crisper. Some fabrics may require an interfacing with a certain amount of stretch or flexibility to achieve subtle shaping. With sheer fabrics, a piece of self-fabric can act as interfacing. To determine a compatable weight of interfacing, drape it and your fabric into a shape that resembles how they will be used, such as a cuff or hem edge, and check for the crispness and shaping you desire. Remember that fusible interfacings may be slightly crisper after fusing. Do not hesitate to mix different types and weights of interfacing within your garment in order to produce the desired fashion effect with your fabric.

Finally, be sure to select an interfacing that will have the same care requirements for washing or dry-cleaning as the outer fabric. Interfacing helps to make your clothes look better and last longer. To aid you in your selection, use the Interfacing Chart, pages 163 to 167.

Applying Sew-in Interfacings

Two different methods can be used for stitching interfacing to a garment, depending primarily on the weight of the interfacing fabric. Light and mediumweight interfacings have very little bulk so they can be stitched into the seams. Heavier weight interfacings and all hair canvases are too bulky or rigid to extend past the seamline, so the seam allowances must be trimmed away before the interfacing is attached to the garment.

Interfacing is usually cut from the facing pattern pieces. Separate interfacing pieces are usually provided for tailored jackets and coats that have a large portion of the garment interfaced. Follow your pattern directions for the correct placement of the interfacing on the garment sections. For almost all garment areas, the interfacing is applied to the garment or outer layer of fabric, not to the facing. For most collars, however, it is attached to the undercollar for better shaping.

Interfacing is applied to each separate section of the garment, and then the interfaced sections are stitched together. This method helps to reinforce the seamlines and prevents an outline of the seam allowances from showing on the outside of the garment.

Light and Mediumweight Interfacing

Cut out interfacing, being sure that the pattern pieces are placed correctly if interfacing has grainlines or stretchability. Pin interfacing to wrong side of fabric, matching seamlines and markings. Baste next to the seamline in the seam allowance, or staystitch ½" from the edge. Trim interfacing close to stitching. Stitch seams; trim and grade fabric seam allowances (1).

When interfacing a garment section that has a foldline along one edge, such as a collar, cuff, waistband, or front edge with extended facing, the interfacing should be trimmed at the foldline if the edge will be topstitched or edgestitched. Catch-stitch the interfacing to the garment along the foldline (2). For a softly rounded edge, extend the interfacing approximately ½" beyond the foldline. Secure interfacing to garment along the foldline with long running stitches spaced about ½" apart, with only a tiny invisible stitch catching the garment fabric (3).

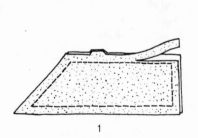

1

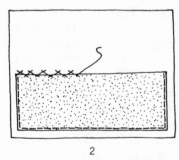

2

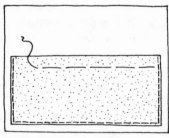

3

Heavier Weight Interfacing

Cut out interfacing, checking on pattern placement as for light and mediumweight interfacings. Stitch any darts or center back collar seam in the interfacing as shown on pages 423 to 426.

Trim away all seam allowances. Pin interfacing to wrong side of fabric, aligning cut edges of interfacing with seamlines of garment; baste in place. Catchstitch interfacing to garment along seamlines. Then pin, baste, and stitch interfaced garment sections together.

To attach interfacing along a foldline, use either catchstitches or long running stitches as shown above.

For additional information on interfacing a jacket or coat, refer to pages 422 to 434 in chapter 8.

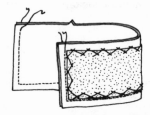

Applying Fusible Interfacings

Fusible interfacings, although very easy to apply, do require the proper combination of steam, heat, and pressure for a specific amount of time in order to achieve a lasting bond. Always follow the manufacturer's instructions precisely, and pretest on a scrap of your fabric before beginning to fuse. Also check the crispness of the fused sample—the fusing process sometimes adds a little body or stiffness to the fabric.

Fusible interfacings are usually applied directly to the garment, not to the facing, just as for sew-in interfacings. However, with lightweight fashion fabrics, you may wish to fuse the interfacing to the facing if the edge of the fused interfacing creates an outline or imprint visible on the right side of the garment. For small detail areas, such as cuffs and pocket flaps, fusible interfacings are always applied to the outer fabric sections.

Cut out fusible interfacing, being sure grainline or stretch direction is positioned as you desire. Trim away ½″ of seam allowances to reduce bulk; for heavier-weight fusible interfacings, you may wish to trim away the entire seam allowance. Make a diagonal clip at any corners to further reduce bulk.

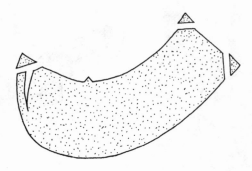

Place interfacing with adhesive side down against wrong side of fabric, aligning seamlines. Hold in position by steam-basting—pressing lightly with the tip of your iron in several places. To fuse, press down firmly using a steam iron and/or damp press cloth for 10 to 15 seconds, depending on manufacturer's directions. Press one area, then lift up iron and press again, overlapping the previous area. Do not slide iron along fabric or you may form wrinkles.

If you make an error, fusible interfacing can be removed by repressing with steam until the two layers of fabric can be gently pulled apart. However, the interfacing cannot be re-fused.

Fusible interfacings can be used to stabilize small areas such as buttonholes, slashes, and plackets. If the edge of the interfacing creates a visible outline on the right side of the fabric, try pinking the edges of the interfacing before fusing.

For additional information on tailoring jackets and coats with fusible interfacings, refer to Menswear, page 501.

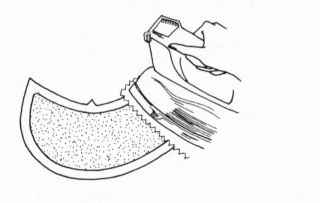

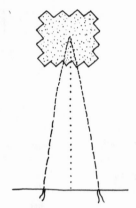

Fusing Agents

A fusing agent is a web of fusible fibers used to hold two layers of fabrics together. Fusible webs are not considered interfacings. Nevertheless, they can be used in detail areas such as hems, cuffs, pocket flaps, and belts to add body simply by fusing the layers of fabric together. Unlike interfacing, fusible webs cannot be used to stabilize an area to prevent stretching.

For information on widths, uses, and method of application, see Notions, page 175.

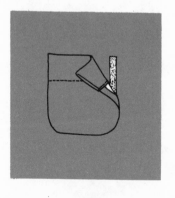

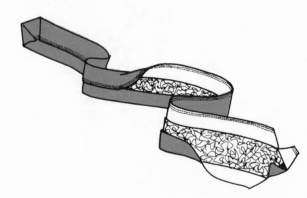

Lining

Lining gives your garment a smooth, luxurious feeling for added comfort as well as a quality finished, custom-made look. It is either cut from the same pattern pieces as the garment or from separate lining pieces, if provided; it is assembled separately, then sewn into your garment by hand or machine. A lining prolongs the life of the garment by covering the inner construction details and protecting the fashion fabric from abrasion during wear. It prevents stretching, helps preserve the shape, reduces wrinkling, and adds body to limp fabrics when desired.

The lining fabric should not affect the fit or characteristics of the outer fabric. Generally it should be softer and lighter in weight than the outer fabric, but not so lightweight as to reveal ridges and bumps from construction details. A lining fabric that is too firm for your fashion fabric may distort the silhouette of your garment.

A lining should be static-free; otherwise it might cling to the wrong side of the garment or to your undergarments. It should also be smooth and slippery to help your garment slide easily over your other apparel, especially in a jacket or coat.

Color is important in choosing a lining fabric, especially in a jacket or coat where the lining may show when the garment is opened. Matching lining and fabric colors are best if the jacket will be worn over different colored blouses and sweaters. Or select a colorful print or snappy stripes to add excitement and verve to a garment that will be worn over a matching dress or top. If the lining fabric is darker in color than the fashion fabric, make sure it does not show through to the outside of the garment.

When selecting a lining fabric, consider how often you plan to wear and clean the garment. Delicate fabrics such as China silk can be used for lining a velvet dress that will be worn occasionally for elegant evenings, but will not last in a garment worn or dry-cleaned often. Lining fabrics, like interfacings and underlinings, must be able to receive the same care as your outer fabric. For example, for a garment made of a permanent-press fabric, be sure to choose a lining that is washable and requires no ironing. When shopping for a lining, note the special characteristics of the fabric listed on the bolt in addition to its fiber content. The majority of trade-name linings are colorfast, perspiration-proof, wrinkle-resistant, and have non-cling finishes, as well as other desirable atttributes. To insert a lining by hand, refer to pages 438 to 441.

Interlining

Interlining is a separate layer of wool, fuzzy cotton, or non-woven polyester fleece placed between the lining and underlining or fashion fabric for additional warmth, especially in coats. For application, see page 442. Some linings designed for coats and jackets are backed with wool, a metallic reflective finish, a napped finish, or a foam-type insulation. Since the wool or foam types add more bulk than a plain lining, you must make an allowance for this added thickness when cutting the pattern.

Guide to Underlinings And Linings

	Fabric Name	Fiber Content	Weight	Color	Use
★	**Armo-Press**	100% polyester	light, with soft or firm finish	white	soft underlining for lightweight fabrics; crisp underlining for mediumweight fabrics
★	**Armo Wool**	90% wool, 10% other fibers	medium	natural	thermal interlining for coats and jackets
	batiste	cotton or blends of cotton and man-made fibers	light	range of colors	fine, soft underlining for all fabric weights
	brocade	silk or man-made fibers	medium to heavy	range of colors	elegant lining for fur coats and evening coats
△	**Butterfly**	100% polyester	light	range of colors	"silky" underlining and lining for all fabric weights
	China silk	silk	light	range of colors	soft, supple underlining and lining for all fabric weights
★	**Ciao**	100% polyester	light	range of colors	soft crepe underlining and lining for all fabric weights
●	**Cintilla**	100% acetate	medium	range of colors	"creped" satin lining for coats, jackets, and mediumweight dresses
○	**Coupe de Ville**	100% polyester	light	range of colors	fine, "silky" lining for all fabric weights
	crepe	acetate, rayon, polyester, or silk	light to heavy	range of colors	light and mediumweight—soft underlining or lining for most fabric weights; heavyweight—lining for coats, jackets, and suits
	crepe-back satin	rayon, acetate, or other man-made fibers	medium	range of colors	lining for coats, jackets, and suits
●	**Designer's Touch**	100% acetate	medium	range of colors	jacquard-woven lining for coats, jackets, and suits
●	**Devonshire**	100% acetate	medium	range of colors	striped lining for coats, jackets, and suits
●	**Earl-Glo Acetate Satin**	100% acetate	medium	range of colors	lining for coats, jackets, and suits

Guide to Underlinings and Linings *(continued)*

	Fabric Name	Fiber Content	Weight	Color	Use
		100% acetate with Milium	medium	range of colors	Milium insulated lining for coats and jackets
		100% acetate with polyurethane batting and rayon back	heavy	range of colors	quilted lining for coats and jackets
●	**Earl-Glo Acetate Twill**	100% acetate	medium	range of colors	lining for coats, jackets, and suits
△	**Easy Knit**	100% nylon	light	neutral colors	fusible knit underlining for knit and woven fabrics
	fake fur	man-made fibers	heavy	range of colors	pile lining for coats and jackets
○	**Keynote Plus**	80% polyester, 20% combed cotton	light	range of colors	underlining or lining, especially for permanent-press fabrics
	lawn	cotton or blends of cotton and man-made fibers	light	range of colors	underlining or lining for lightweight fabrics
□	**Loomgold Satin**	100% acetate with Milium	medium	limited range of colors	Milium insulated lining for coats and jackets
	marquisette	silk or man-made fibers	sheer	range of colors	sheer net underlining for chiffon and other sheer fabrics
●	**Marvelaire**	100% polyester	light	range of colors	underlining and lining for all fabric weights
		100% polyester with polyester batting and acetate back	heavy	range of colors	quilted lining for coats and jackets
★★	**Miracle Lining**	100% polyester	light	range of colors	lining for all fabric weights
	muslin	cotton; occasionally a blend of cotton and man-made fibers	medium	natural and white	underlining for tailored coats and suits
★★	**Nite Lite**	87% acetate, 13% nylon	medium	range of colors	crepe back satin lining for coats, jackets, and suits
	organdy and organza	cotton, silk, or man-made fibers	sheer	range of colors	fine, crisp underlining for sheer and lightweight fabrics
	percale	cotton or blend of cotton and man-made fibers	light to medium	range of colors	lining, especially for cotton fabrics

Guide to Underlinings and Linings *(continued)*

	Fabric Name	Fiber Content	Weight	Color	Use
●	**Poli-air**	100% polyester	light	range of colors	underlining and lining for all fabric weights
★	**Poly-Sibonne Plus**	100% polyester	light	range of colors	soft underlining and lining for all fabric weights
♦	**Sew Easy Tricot**	100% nylon	sheer to light	range of colors	soft knitted underlining or lining, especially for knit fabrics
	silk broadcloth or surah	silk	light to medium	range of colors	lining for suits and mediumweight dresses
□	**Sunbak Satin**	59% rayon, 41% acetate	heavy	limited range of colors	lining with napped back for extra warmth in coats and jackets
	taffeta	rayon, acetate, or silk	medium	range of colors	crisp lining for medium to heavyweight coats, suits, and dresses
○	**Ultra Vino**	75% polyester, 25% combed cotton	light	range of colors	underlining and lining, especially for permanent-press fabrics
△	**Veriform Durable Press**	50% polyester, 50% rayon	light	white and black	underlining, especially for permanent-press and polyester fabrics
	voile	cotton or blends	sheer	range of colors	crisp underlining and lining for sheer and light-weight fabrics
□	**Warmline**	60% acetate, 40% rayon	heavy	limited range of colors	lining with napped back for extra warmth in coats and jackets
†	**Wistful**	65% polyester, 35% combed cotton	light	range of colors	soft underlining for all fabric weights

★ The Armo Company
○ Burlington/Klopman Fabrics
● N. Erlanger, Blumgart, and Company
♦ Sew Easy Lingerie, Inc.
□ Skinner Company

† Springmaid Company
△ Stacy Fabrics Corporation
★★ Pago Fabrics Corporation

PHONESIA (fo ne' zhuh) n. The affliction of dialing a phone number and forgetting whom you were calling just as they answer.

pressing   437 X 3144

431, 433, 451
341, 351,   menu

SNIGLETS (snig' lit): any word that doesn't appear in the dictionary, but should

Guide to Interfacings
Sew-in Interfacings

Fabric Name	Type	Weight	Fiber Content	Color	Use
★ Acro	woven hair canvas	medium	51% polyester, 43% rayon, 6% goat hair	natural	multipurpose washable hair canvas for medium to heavyweight fabrics
△ Add-Shape	non-woven	feather and medium-light	70% nylon, 20% polyester, 10% rayon	white and charcoal	crosswise stretch and lengthwise stability for light and mediumweight knit and woven fabrics
★ Armoflexxx	woven waistbanding	heavy	62% nylon, 38% polyester	white	stabilizing waistbands and belts
★ Armo P-26	woven hair canvas	medium	62% cotton, 30% rayon, 8% goat hair	natural	economical hair canvas for tailoring medium to heavyweight fabrics
★ Armo-Press	woven	light, with soft or firm finish	100% polyester	white	soft or crisp shaping for light and mediumweight woven fabrics, especially permanent-press
★ Armo-Wool	woven interlining	medium	90% wool, 10% other fibers	cream	shaping and padding sleeves, shoulders, collars, hems
△ Bravo Canvas	woven canvas	medium	45% polyester, 45% rayon, 10% wool	natural	luxury canvas used for tailoring medium to heavyweight fabrics
★ Fino II	woven hair canvas	medium	35% wool, 30% cotton, 19% rayon, 16% goat hair	natural	quality hair canvas for tailoring medium to heavyweight fabrics
△ Hair Canvas #77	woven hair canvas	heavy	59% cotton, 32% rayon, 9% goat hair	natural	hair canvas for tailoring medium to heavyweight fabrics
△ Interlon	non-woven	light, regular, heavy	75% rayon, 25% nylon	white and black	firm, stable shaping; heavyweight for accessories and crafts
△ Interlon Bias	non-woven	feather-weight light	100% polyester	white and black	bias "give" in all directions for light and mediumweight fabrics

Sew-in Interfacings *(continued)*

	Fabric Name	Type	Weight	Fiber Content	Color	Use
△	**Interlon Durable Press**	non-woven	light	100% polyester	white and black	interfacing used for permanent - press fabrics
● ●	**Pellon Fleece**	non-woven fleece	heavy	100% polyester	white	fluffy fleece for padding, quilting, trapunto, interlining
□ □	**Poly-Fluff**	non-woven fleece	heavy	100% polyester	white	fluffy fleece for padding, quilting, interlining
●	**Reemay**	non-woven	light	100% polyester	white	stable shaping for light and medium-weight fabrics
● ●	**Sew-in Pellon**	non-woven	sheer	100% polyester	white and beige	crosswise stretch and lengthwise stability for sheer to lightweight fabrics
			light	100% polyester	white and grey	bias "give" in all directions for feather-weight to medium-weight fabrics
			medium	100% polyester	white	bias "give" in all directions for mid-weight to heavy-weight fabrics
● ●	**Shapewell**	woven	light	100% cotton	white	soft shaping for light and mediumweight fabrics
□ □	**Shaping Aid**	non-woven	feather light medium heavy	100% polyester	white white, black white, black white	interfacing all fabric weights; heavy-weight for accessories and crafts
□ □	**Shirt Maker**	non-woven	light and medium	100% polyester	white	crisp shaping for collars, cuffs, front openings
△	**Sta-Shape #50**	woven canvas	light	100% polyester	white and grey	lightweight washable canvas for tailoring medium-weight fabrics
△	**Sta-Shape Durable Press**	woven	light	50% polyester, 50% rayon	white and black	interfacing used for permanent - press fabrics
□ □	**Stretch & Bounce**	non-woven	light	50% polyester, 50% rayon	white and charcoal	crosswise stretch and lengthwise stability for woven and knit fabrics

Sew-in Interfacings *(continued)*

	Fabric Name	Type	Weight	Fiber Content	Color	Use
★	Stylus Featherweight Bias	non-woven	light	100% polyester	white	soft, bias "give" for lightweight knit and woven fabrics
△	Thermolam	non-woven fleece	heavy	100% polyester	white	fluffy fleece for padding, quilting, interlining
★	Ti-Rite	woven	medium	60% polyester, 40% rayon	cream	interfacing for ties, rolled collars, cuffs; interlining
△	Tri-Shape	woven	medium	90% polyester, 10% rayon	eggshell	interfacing for ties and tailored garments; interlining
△	Veriform Durable Press	woven	light	50% polyester, 50% rayon	white and black	interfacing used for permanent - press fabrics

Fusible Interfacings

	Fabric Name	Type	Weight	Fiber Content	Color	Use
★	Armo-Weft	weft insertion	light	100% polyester warp; 50% acrylic, 50% rayon weft	white, beige, grey, and black	crosswise stretch and lengthwise stability for medium to heavyweight knit and woven fabrics
△	Easy-Knit	knit	light	100% nylon	white, beige, grey, and black	soft, drapable tricot with crosswise stretch and lengthwise stability used with knit and woven fabrics
△	Easy-Shaper	non-woven	light suit weight	70% nylon, 20% polyester, 10% rayon	white and charcoal	crosswise stretch and lengthwise stability for both gentle shaping and soft tailoring
●●	fuse'n fold	precut non-woven strips	light to medium	100% polyester	white	precut widths for interfacing plackets, cuffs, straight facings, waistbands, belts
★	Fusible Acro	woven hair canvas	medium	51% polyester, 43% rayon, 6% goat hair	natural	multipurpose washable hair canvas for medium to heavyweight fabrics

Fusible Interfacings *(continued)*

	Fabric Name	Type	Weight	Fiber Content	Color	Use
★	Fusible P-91	woven	light	100% cotton	white	for interfacing small areas on medium-weight woven fabrics
●●	Fusible Pellon	non-woven	sheer	100% polyester	white and beige	crosswise stretch and lengthwise stability for sheer to lightweight fabrics
			light	100% polyester	white and grey	bias "give" in all directions for feather-weight to medium-weight fabrics
			medium	50% polyester, 50% nylon	white	crosswise stretch and lengthwise stability for medium-weight to heavy-weight fabrics
□□	Jiffy Flex	non-woven	super light	100% polyester	white	soft, flexible shaping for lightest weight fabrics
			light	50% polyester, 50% rayon	white and charcoal	supple shaping for lightweight fabrics
			suit weight	50% polyester, 50% nylon	white and charcoal	flexible shaping for mediumweight fabrics
●●	Pel-Aire Pellon	non-woven	suit weight outerwear	100% nylon	natural	luxury fusible for tailoring suits and coats
□□	Poly-O	non-woven	sheer	100% polyester	white, beige, grey, and charcoal	crosswise stretch and lengthwise stability for sheer and lightweight fabrics
△	Shape-Flex All Purpose	woven	light	100% cotton	white and black	supple shaping for light and medium-weight fabrics
△	Shape-Flex Non-Woven	non-woven	light	65% polyester, 35% rayon	white and black	for interfacing and stabilizing detail areas
□□	ShapeUp	non-woven	light	100% polyester	white	soft shaping for all fabric weights
●●	Shapewell	woven	light	100% cotton	white	soft shaping for light and medium-weight fabrics
□□	Shirt Maker	non-woven	light	100% polyester	white	crisp shaping for collars, cuffs, front openings

Fusible Interfacings (continued)

	Fabric Name	Type	Weight	Fiber Content	Color	Use
△	Shirt-Fuse	non-woven	medium	100% polyester	white beige charcoal	crisp shaping for light to medium-weight shirt fabrics
●●	Sof-Shape Pellon	non-woven	sheer	100% nylon	white	ultra-soft, bias shaping for light to heavyweight fabrics
★	Stylus Detail Fusible	non-woven	light	75% polyester, 25% rayon	white	stabilize and reinforce detail areas
★	Stylus Fashion Former	non-woven	light to medium	75% polyester, 25% rayon	white	stable shaping for light or medium-weight woven and knit fabrics
★	Stylus Uni-Stretch	non-woven	light suit weight	75% polyester, 15% nylon, 10% rayon	white	crosswise stretch and lengthwise stability for light or mediumweight knit
△	Suit-Shape	weft insertion	light	84% polyester, 16% nylon	white natural	tailoring medium-weight to heavy-weight woven and knit fabrics
△	Sure-Fuse	non-woven	light	65% polyester, 35% rayon	white beige	soft shaping for lightweight fabrics
△	Waist*Shaper	precut non-woven strip	medium	80% polyester, 20% cellulose	white	precut widths for interfacing waist-bands and belts

Fusing Agents

	Fabric Name	Fiber Content	Weight	Width
★	Fusible Web	100% polyamide	sheer	18″ wide
□□	Jiffy Fuse	100% polyamide	sheer	20″ wide, 1″ strips
○○	Magic Polyweb	100% nylon	sheer	9″ wide, ¾″ and 2″ strips
♦♦	Press'n Fuse	100% polyamide	2 weights— regular and super	14½″ wide
●●	Sav-a-Stitch	100% polyamide	sheer	15″ wide, ¾″ strips
△	Stitch Witchery	100% polyamide	sheer	18″ wide

★ The Armo Company
○○ Coats and Clark
△ Stacy Fabrics Corporation
□□ Staple Sewing Aids

♦♦ Dritz/Scovill
● N. Erlanger, Blumgart and Company
●● Pellon Corporation

Notions:
Your Sewing Accessories

Having chosen your fabric, you must now remember to stop at the notions counter and pick up those little necessities that might otherwise cause another trip back to the store. Generally, it is a good idea to keep on hand a supply of the more standard notions, such as pins, needles, snaps, and hooks and eyes, to save yourself the frustration of having to continually interrupt your sewing to purchase some small item you have forgotten. There are some notions, however, that you will have to buy each time you purchase fabric to ensure that they will match and be appropriate to your particular fabric and style; buttons, thread, zippers, and bindings or tapes are perfect examples. Still other notions are so specialized that you will need to purchase them only as they are called for by a specific garment, such as horsehair braid for the hem of an evening gown. Special shaping notions, such as shoulder pads, boning, and weights, are described in The Shapekeepers, pages 446 and 447.

Couture finishing requires the proper sizes and types of notions. Since the notions counter contains a seemingly endless array of gadgets, use the back of your pattern envelope and the following descriptions to guide your selection.

Pins

Pins vary in size and type. Pin size is stated in sixteenths of an inch according to length: a size 16 is $^{16}/_{16}''$ or 1″ long, a size 8 is ½″ long. For general sewing, #17 (1 $^1/_{16}''$) dressmaker pins are most commonly used. These are slender pins of medium diameter. For fine sewing and delicate fabrics, #17 silk pins—very slender with very fine points—or #16 pleating pins are recommended. Larger, coarser pins are advisable only on heavy, coarse, or very loosely woven fabrics. Ball point pins should be used on knitted fabrics as their rounded tips slip between the yarns to avoid snags. T-pins are good for deep pile, loosely woven, and bulky, knitted fabrics because the large heads are easy to locate and will not slip through the fabric.

All pins must be rustproof; brass, nickel-plated steel, or stainless steel pins are all good. Plastic or glass-headed pins, available in various sizes, are easy to see because they contrast with the fabric.

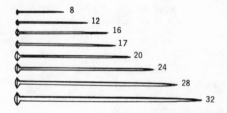

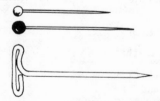

Needles

Hand sewing needles are classified by type and size, each designed for a specific use. Choose the type of needle according to the job it will be doing, and the size of needle according to the thread it will be pulling through the fabric. The finer or sheerer the fabric, the sharper and more slender the needle should be.

Two size scales are generally used for needles—1 through 10, and 14 through 22. For each needle type, the smaller the size number, the longer and thicker the needle. Sizes 7 through 10 are best for most dressmaking, while the other sizes are for heavier or specialized sewing.

Dressmaking Needles

SHARPS are all-purpose medium-length needles with small, rounded eyes used for general sewing.

BETWEENS are shorter needles with small, rounded eyes used for detailed handwork requiring short, fine stitches.

MILLINER'S needles are long with small, rounded eyes used for long basting stitches, gathering, and millinery work.

EMBROIDERY needles are medium length with long oval eyes; generally used for embroidery and crewel work, they can also be substituted for sharps.

Needles are also available with *ball-point* tips for use with knitted fabrics. The slightly rounded tip slips between the yarns to help prevent snagging the fabric. *Calyx eye* needles have an eye with a slit on the side for easy threading.

Sharp

Between

Milliner's

Embroidery

Specialty Needles

BEADING needles are extremely long and fine with a small round eye; generally used for beading due to their flexibility, they can also be used to sew fine, lightweight fabrics.

CHENILLES are short, thick needles with long, oval eyes and sharp points for embroidery use.

TAPESTRY needles are short and thick with large eyes and blunt points for use with tapestry or needlepoint.

COTTON DARNERS are long needles with long eyes which can be used for darning or basting.

YARN DARNERS are very long, coarse needles with large eyes used for darning with heavy or multiple yarns.

Beading

Chenille

Tapestry

Cotton Darner

Yarn Darner

GLOVER'S needles are medium length with a wedge-shaped point, designed to penetrate leather and plastic without splitting or tearing.

SAILMAKER'S needles are long, coarse needles with a wedge-shaped shank and sharply tapered point designed for use on heavy coating, canvas, and heavy leather.

CURVED needles are semicircular with a large oval eye and sharply tapered point, ranging from 1½″ to 3″ in length; used for upholstery, lampshades, mattresses, braided rugs, and wherever a straight needle is impracticable.

Sewing machine needles are selected according to the type and weight of fabric to be sewn. They are available with different points: sharp for woven fabrics, ball point for knitted fabrics, and wedge point for leathers and plastics. Sizes range from fine (size 9) for lightweight fabrics to heavy (size 18) for very heavy and firm fabrics. Sizes 11 and 14 are used most often for regular sewing. Refer to The Sewing Machine, pages 182–183.

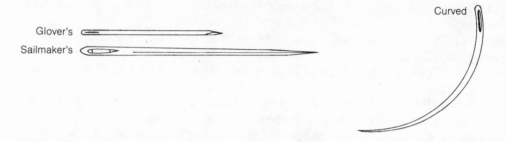

Thread

A quality thread is strong, smooth, and consistent in thickness, and it resists tangling. Select the proper thread according to fabric weight, purpose, and color. Thread should be the same color or slightly darker than the fabric. For multicolored prints and plaids, select thread colors according to the predominant hue in the fabric.

POLYESTER THREAD, either 100% polyester or cotton covered, provides strength and elasticity for sewing on fabrics made of synthetic, natural, or blended fibers. It is especially desirable for knit, stretch, and permanent-press fabrics because of its stretch and recovery, and its non-shrinkage. 100% polyester thread can be made from strands of long staple polyester multifilaments or spun short staple multifilaments, which are then twisted tightly together. Cotton-covered polyester cord thread is formed by twisting together two or more strands of polyester multifilaments wrapped with mercerized cotton. The cotton sheath provides resistance to heat, while the polyester cord gives strength and elasticity. Polyester thread is available in different weights for specific uses: extra fine for lightweight fabrics and machine embroidery; extra strong for heavyweight fabrics; topstitching and buttonhole twist for decorative stitching and hand-worked buttonholes; button and carpet thread for hand sewing buttons and very heavy fabrics; basting thread; and hand quilting thread.

MERCERIZED COTTON THREAD is strong and lustrous, without any stretch or give, for use on woven natural fiber fabrics. It is formed by twisting together three strands of spun staple cotton fibers that have been mercerized for added strength, luster, affinity for dye, and color fastness. Size 50, a medium diameter thread, is suitable for hand and machine sewing on light and mediumweight fabrics. Size 40, a heavy-duty thread, is used for heavier fabrics, slipcovers, and draperies. Black and white mercerized cotton is available in the widest size range—from fine (60) to heavy (40, 30, 20, 8). Some threads have six strands or "cords" twisted together for added strength. Other types of cotton thread are: button and carpet thread for hand sewing buttons and heavy fabrics; soft basting thread, which breaks easily under tension; and quilting thread for hand and machine quilting.

SILK THREAD is durable, pliable, and lustrous for sewing silk and woolen fabrics. It is formed by tightly twisting two or more strands of silk fibers together. It is excellent for tailoring and basting because it can mold permanently with the fabric and leaves no imprint or lint when pressed. Size of silk thread is designated by letters: size A is a fine thread used for general sewing and basting: size D is a thick, loosely twisted thread used for decorative topstitching, hand-worked buttonholes, buttons, thread loops, and gathering.

NYLON THREAD is a very strong thread with twice the tensile strength of the same size cotton thread. It is made from one continuous filament or several filaments bonded or twisted together. It is available in colors for sewing nylon tricot and in a clear or dark transparent shade for sewing heavy fabrics such as canvas and for crafts.

Thread can also be waxed or glazed, which creates a smoother surface, adds strength, helps to eliminate tangling when hand-stitching, and prevents fraying and twisting of the thread when machine-stitching. The following chart is a guide for selecting the proper thread, needle, and stitch length for your particular fabric.

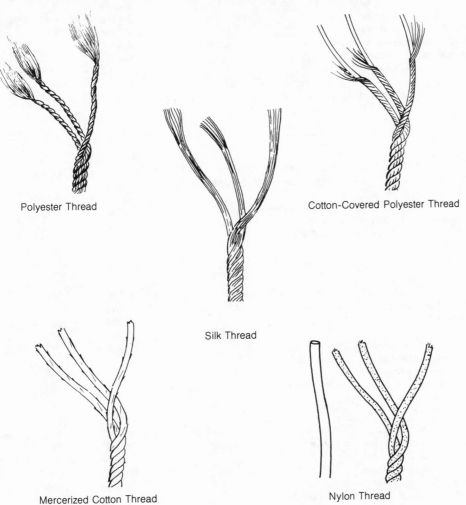

Polyester Thread

Cotton-Covered Polyester Thread

Silk Thread

Mercerized Cotton Thread

Nylon Thread

Needle and Thread Chart

Uses	Threads		Needles	
FABRIC WEIGHT AND TYPE	**FOR ALL FABRICS**	**FOR NATURAL FIBER FABRICS**	**HAND**	**MACHINE**
VERY LIGHT: chiffon, georgette, marquisette, ninon, fine lace, organdy, organza, net, tulle, lingerie fabrics	Cotton-covered polyester—extra fine △ Cotton-covered polyester ○△■ 100% long staple polyester ★□△♦●■▲ 100% polyester □	Mercerized cotton—size 50, 60 □△■ Silk—size A □	9, 10, 11, 12 Sharps Betweens Milliner's Beading	Finest: 9 Stiches per inch: 16–20
LIGHT: bastiste, voile, lawn, dimity, dotted Swiss, pure silk, crepe de chine, sheer crepe, silk jersey, paper taffeta, chambray, handkerchief linen, synthetic sheers, ciré, single knits	Cotton-covered polyester—extra fine △ Cotton covered polyester ○△■ 100% long staple polyester ★□△♦●■▲ 100% polyester □	Mercerized cotton—size 50, 60 □△■ Silk—size A □	9, 10 Sharps Betweens Milliner's Embroidery Beading	Fine: 9, 11 Stitches per inch: 12–16
MEDIUM LIGHT: gingham, challis, percale, sheer wool crepe, peau de soie, taffeta, satin, pongee, silk surah, wool jersey, cotton knits	Cotton-covered polyester ○△■ 100% long staple polyester ★□△♦●■▲ 100% polyester □	Mercerized cotton—size 50, 60 □△■ Silk—size A □	8, 9 Sharps Betweens Milliner's Embroidery	Fine: 11 Stitches per inch: 12–14
MEDIUM: flannel, corduroy, broadcloth, poplin, linen, chintz, muslin, pique, shantung, faille, ottoman, moiré, satin, sharkskin, serge, bouclé, lamé, lace, velvet, velveteen, satin-backed crepe, double knits, jacquard knits, velour, leather, synthetic suede	Cotton-covered polyester ○△■ 100% long staple polyester ★□△♦●■▲ 100% polyester □	Mercerized cotton—size 50 □△■ Silk—size A □	6, 7, 8 Sharps Betweens Milliner's Embroidery	Medium: 11, 14 Stitches per inch: 12
MEDIUM HEAVY: denim, tweed, gabardine, twill, brocade, bengaline, felt, terry, burlap, textured linen, fleece, sweater knits, quilted fabrics, leather, vinyl coated fabrics, fake fur	Cotton-covered polyester ○△■ 100% long staple polyester ★□△♦●■▲ 100% polyester □	Mercerized cotton—size 40, 50 □△■ Silk—size A □	5, 6 Sharps Betweens Milliner's Embroidery	Medium Coarse: 14, 16 Stitches per inch: 10–12

Needle and Thread Chart (continued)

Uses	Threads		Needles	
FABRIC WEIGHT AND TYPE	**FOR ALL FABRICS**	**FOR NATURAL FIBER FABRICS**	**HAND**	**MACHINE**
HEAVY: sailcloth, ticking, double-faced wool, heavy coating, fur, fake fur, drapery fabrics, upholstery vinyls	Cotton-covered polyester ○△■ Cotton-covered polyester—extra strong ○ 100% long staple polyester ★△♦●■▲ 100% polyester—heavy duty □	Mercerized cotton—heavy duty size 40 □△■ Silk—size A □	4,5 Sharps Betweens Milliner's Embroidery Darners Glover's Sailmaker's	Coarse: 16,18 Stitches per inch: 8–10
VERY HEAVY: canvas, duck, work denim, upholstery fabrics	Cotton-covered polyester—extra strong ○ 100% polyester—heavy duty □ Cotton-covered polyester Button and Carpet (hand sewing only) ○△ Nylon □△■	Mercerized cotton—heavy duty size 8, 20, 30, 40 □△■ Cotton Button and Carpet (hand sewing only) □△■	1, 2, 3 Sharps Betweens Milliner's Embroidery Darners Glover's Sailmaker's	Coarse: 18 Stitches per inch: 6–8

Special Uses

Uses	Threads	Needles
Basting	Cotton Basting △ Silk—size A □	Milliner's Cotton Darners Sharps
Buttonholes, hand-worked	Silk Twist—Size D □△ 100% long staple polyester Buttonhole Twist □△♦■▲ Cotton-covered polyester Topstitching and Buttonhole Twist △	Embroidery 6, 7
Buttons and Fasteners on heavier fabrics	Silk Twist—size D □△ 100% long staple polyester Buttonhole Twist □△♦■▲ Cotton-covered polyester Topstitching and Buttonhole Twist △	Embroidery 6, 7

Uses	Threads	Needles
Buttons and Fasteners on heavier fabrics *(continued)*	Cotton Button and Carpet □△■ Cotton-covered polyester Button and Carpet ○△	
Embroidery and Other Decorative Stitching	Cotton-covered polyester—extra fine for machine embroidery △ Cotton-covered polyester Topstitching and Buttonhole Twist △ 100% long staple polyester Buttonhole Twist □△♦■▲ Silk Twist—size D □△ Metallic ■ Embroidery Floss Yarn	Sharps, Embroidery 9, 10 Embroidery 6, 7 Yarn Darners
Hand Quilting	Cotton Quilting ○□■ Cotton-covered polyester Quilting △	Betweens 7
Topstitching (light)	Cotton-covered polyester ○△■ 100% long staple polyester ★□△♦●■▲ 100% polyester □ Mercerized cotton □△■ Silk—size A □	Sharps, Betweens, Milliner's, Embroidery appropriate to fabric weight
(heavy)	100% long staple polyester Buttonhole Twist □△♦■▲ Cotton-covered polyester Topstitching and Buttonhole Twist △ Silk Twist—size D □△	Embroidery 6, 7

★	Amann Thread Company—Seralon	♦	Mölnlycke Inc.—Mölnlycke
○	American Thread Company—American	●	Swiss-Metrosene Inc.—Metrosene
□	Belding Lily Company—Corticelli, Super Spun	■	Talon/Donahue Sales—Gutermann, Talon
△	Coats & Clark Inc.—Drima, Dual Duty Plus, Supersheen, Best Cord	▲	Wm. E. Wright Company—Couturier

Fusing Agents

Fusing agents are web-like bonding materials used to hold two layers of fabric together without stitching. The web is placed between the two layers of fabric and dissolves into the yarns when heat, steam, and pressure are applied. When properly fused, it is both washable and dry cleanable. Always follow the manufacturer's directions precisely, and pretest on a scrap of fabric before fusing your garment.

Fusibles can be used for hems, facings, belts, trims, and appliqués. For most detail areas, the web is cut the same size as the area to be fused. For hems, a crisp edge can be obtained by fusing the entire depth of the hem. For a softly rolled hem, fuse only the upper portion of the hem. A fused area can be separated by re-pressing with steam until the fabric can be gently pulled apart. To re-fuse, insert a new strip of fusible web.

Fusibles are available in precut strips of ¾'', 1½'', and 2'' widths and in wider widths sold prepackaged and by the yard.

Strip of Fusible Web

Buttons

Make your buttons work as an accent to your garment. Buy them to enhance your creation, not merely to finish it. Although buttons are available in a wide range of shapes and contours, there are basically only two types. A **sew-through button** has two to four holes for attaching the button to the garment. A **shank button** has a metal, plastic, or fabric shank behind the button through which the button is attached. The shank allows room for the overlapping fabric so that the button rests on top of the buttonhole. You can cover your own buttons using a two-piece button form or mold. See pages 325 to 327 for a detailed discussion of buttons and how they may be used.

To determine button size, use the button gauge below. Technically, buttons are sized in "lines"—40 lines equal one inch. When the size is known in inches, refer to the chart to convert the size into lines.

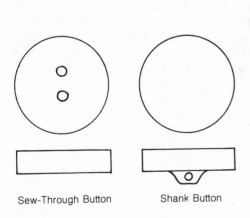

Sew-Through Button   Shank Button

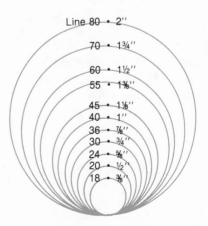

Line 80 • 2''
70 • 1¾''
60 • 1½''
55 • 1⅜''
45 • 1⅛''
40 • 1''
36 • ⅞''
30 • ¾''
24 • ⅝''
20 • ½''
18 • ⅜''

Zippers

Zippers are now available in a variety of colors, sizes, and weights for almost any conceivable fastening task. Choose a zipper according to the style needed for your garment opening and a weight that is compatible with your fabric. The conventional or regular zipper, the oldest and most common type, can be used for most standard zipper applications on most garments. Specialty zippers designed for specific openings or garments are also available.

The weight of a zipper is determined by its construction and the type of tape used. A coil-constructed zipper is made from a continuous strand of nylon or polyester twisted into a spiral and attached to a woven or knitted synthetic tape. It is lightweight and flexible, yet very strong, and is ideal for light and mediumweight fabrics and all types of knits. A coil zipper can be easily repaired if fabric catches in the zipper. Just bend the zipper in half, pinch the fold tightly, and twist to open. Pull the slider down past the opening and then up again to close.

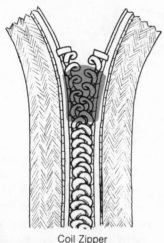

Coil Zipper

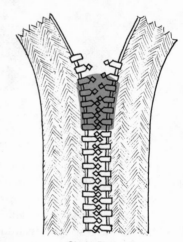

Chain Zipper

A chain-constructed zipper has metal or plastic teeth attached to a cotton or cotton-blend tape. It is a little heavier and more rigid than the coils; some metal styles are excellent for heavy-duty use.

Your pattern will specify the proper zipper length for your garment. If you make any length adjustments in the zipper area of your pattern, you may need to either purchase a longer or shorter zipper or shorten the one you have as directed on page 329. Zippers can be inserted by hand or by machine, using a special zipper foot, for any type of zipper application. Protect the zipper from excessive strain by closing it before laundering or dry-cleaning. If the zipper seems stiff and sticky to operate after laundering or cleaning, run a piece of beeswax or soap over the teeth or coils or use a zipper lubricant.

The **CONVENTIONAL ZIPPER** is designed so that one end opens at the edge of a garment and the other end has a bottom stop to prevent the slider from running into the seam. It can have synthetic coils or metal teeth and is available in 7″ to 22″ lengths. Shorter lengths (4″ and 6″) and extra long lengths are usually available only in limited colors.

The **SEPARATING ZIPPER** opens at both ends for use on coats, jackets, parkas, vests, and detachable hoods and linings. Lightweight types with metal or nylon teeth range in length from 10″ to 22″. Heavyweight types have heavy brass or molded teeth in 14″ to 24″ lengths. The separating zipper is also available in a reversible version that has a pull tab on both sides of the slider and comes 16″ to 22″ long.

The **TWO-WAY ZIPPER** has two identical sliders on both the top and bottom of the zipper, enabling the garment to be opened from either end. Two-way separating zippers are ideal for parkas, ski pants, and snowsuits. Two-way zippers closed at the bottom can be used for jumpsuits and coveralls. Lengths range from 20″ to 34″.

The **TROUSER ZIPPER** is a heavy-duty variation of a conventional zipper with metal teeth, special bar supports on the slider to withstand frequent laundering, and extra wide tapes for double reinforcement stitching. It is available in 9″ and 11″ lengths.

The **BLUE JEAN ZIPPER** is a variation of the trouser zipper with a brass finish for use on jeans, skirts, and work pants. It is available in 7″ length.

The **DECORATIVE** or **INDUSTRIAL ZIPPER** has large metal or plastic teeth, matching or contrasting tape, and a big ring pull. It is available in both conventional and separating types in limited lengths. It is usually applied with the zipper teeth exposed for added emphasis.

The **INVISIBLE ZIPPER** is designed so that the teeth or coil is totally concealed behind the tape when the zipper is closed, and the completed application looks just like a seam. The zipper must be applied before the seam is stitched, using a special invisible zipper foot. It is available in lengths of 7″ to 22″.

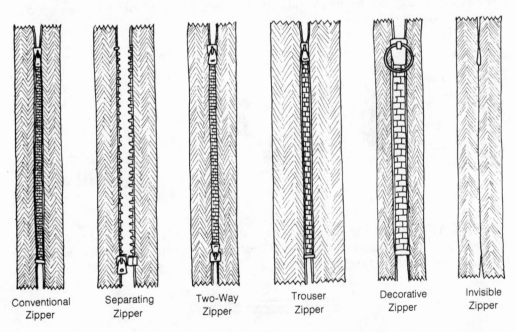

| Conventional Zipper | Separating Zipper | Two-Way Zipper | Trouser Zipper | Decorative Zipper | Invisible Zipper |

Fastenings

SNAPS, used for closing and anchoring garments, are available in many sizes and types. Snaps come in nickel or black enamel-coated metal with the smaller sizes, 4/0 to 1, the most popular. The larger sizes, 2 to 4, are suitable for heavy-duty use. Large silk-covered snaps, ideal for suits and coats, are available in neutral colors. You may cover your own for special color combinations (see page 449) or purchase see-through nylon snaps to blend with the color of your garment. For casual clothes and children's wear, snaps prespaced on cotton tape and no-sew snap fasterners applied with special pliers or attaching tool can be used. Fur snaps are perfect for attaching fur collars and other accessories to your garment.

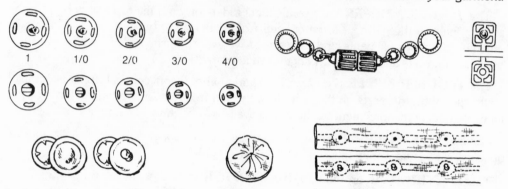

HOOKS AND EYES come in a variety of designs for special holding purposes. The standard type is made with brass, nickel, or black enamel finish, and comes in sizes 00 to 2 for lightweight fabrics and sizes 3 to 5 for bulky and heavyweight fabrics. The eye can be curved or straight.

Large hooks and eyes, either plain or silk-covered, make sturdy fastenings for coats or other items, especially fur. Specially shaped hook and bar closures, both sew-on and prong, make practical fasteners for waistbands on skirts and pants. Hooks and eyes are also available prespaced on cotton tape.

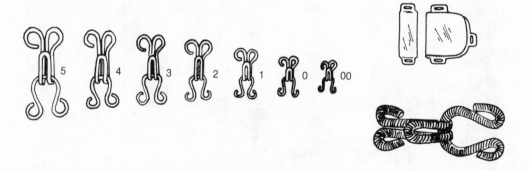

HOOK AND LOOP TAPE consists of two strips, one with tiny hooks and one with a looped pile, that intermesh when pressed together and open when peeled apart. It is available in precut shapes and by the yard.

BUCKLES are available in a wide variety of shapes and sizes, with or without prongs. They come in all types of materials such as metal, wood, plastic, and leather; or they may be covered with fabric for a custom finish. They can be purchased singly or in kits with belting. Eyelets are available with a nickel, gilt, or colored enamel finish and are applied with special pliers or attaching tool. They can be used for belts, lacing, and decorative ties.

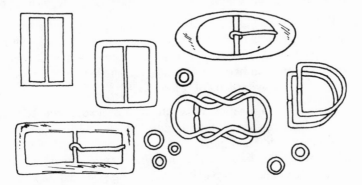

Elastics

Elastics are available in many different types and widths to be used in casings or applied directly to the garment. Elastics are made from a rubber or stretchable synthetic core that is wrapped with cotton, synthetic fiber, or a blend of fibers. Elastic thread is a very thin, covered core that is used for shirring. Elastic cord is a round or oval covered cord in varying diameters that can be sewn directly to the garment or used for loop closings.

Elastic braid, ribbon, and ribbed elastic are made of several covered cores woven, knitted, or braided together. They range in width from ¼″ to 3″ and are available in soft and hard stretch. Woven and knitted elastics retain their original width when stretched and thus can be sewn directly to the garment or inserted into a casing. Because braided elastics become narrower when stretched, they are recommended only for casings.

Special purpose elastics are available for pajamas, lingerie, intimate apparel, and swimwear. They are usually constructed of a softer strip or band, sometimes with a decorative edge, so that they are more comfortable when worn next to the skin. Do not use rayon elastic for swimwear because it stretches when wet. Special elastics are also designed for stretchable waistbands on both men's and women's wear.

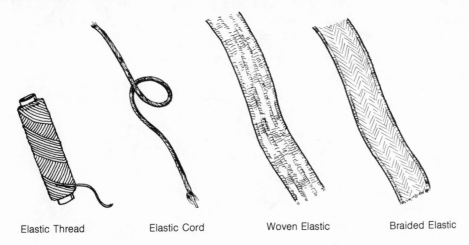

Elastic Thread   Elastic Cord   Woven Elastic   Braided Elastic

Tapes and Trims

Completing the inside of your garment in an aesthetic manner will result in a finished garment that is a delight to wear. Tapes, laces, and bindings in matching colors will give the inside of your garment a custom-made look—not to mention perfectly finished edges!

SEAM BINDING, a truly indispensable sewing notion, is used for finishing hem edges and straight facing edges. Ribbon seam binding is a woven tape approximately ½″ wide, which can also be used to reinforce or extend seams. Lace seam binding can be used for a decorative finish on seams and hems; stretch lace is suitable for use on knitted fabrics. It is available prepackaged, in a wide range of colors.

BIAS TAPE is available in a variety of widths with prefolded edges to use for binding curved or straight edges, casings, ties, and trims. Single-fold bias tape is ½″ wide with edges folded to the wrong side and meeting at the center. Double-fold is ¼″ wide and has been folded again just slightly off-center; also available is an extrawide ½″ width. Wide bias tape is ⅞″ to 1″ wide with edges folded ¼″ to the wrong side. Bias tape is prepackaged in a wide range of colors and prints. Stretchable lace binding, prefolded to ½″ width, can be used as bias tape for binding edges, seams, facings, and hems.

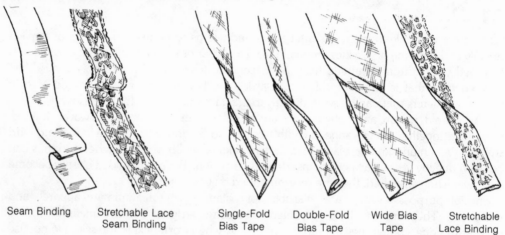

| Seam Binding | Stretchable Lace Seam Binding | Single-Fold Bias Tape | Double-Fold Bias Tape | Wide Bias Tape | Stretchable Lace Binding |

HEM FACING is a 2″ wide bias tape or lace strip used for facing hems and binding edges. Bias hem facing has both edges folded to the inside and is available in both a polyester and cotton fabric and a taffeta. Stretchable lace hem facing has a decorative lace design. Both are prepackaged in many colors.

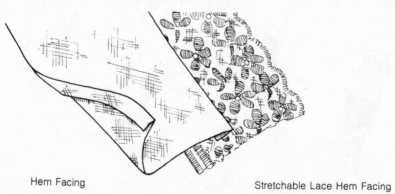

Hem Facing

Stretchable Lace Hem Facing

TWILL TAPE is a very firmly woven tape used in tailoring and for reinforcing seams. It comes only in black and white in ¼″, ½″, ¾″, and 1″ widths.

GROSGRAIN RIBBON is a firmly woven, ribbed ribbon used for staying waistlines, facing waistbands and belts, and for decorative trims. It is available in a wide range of widths, colors, geometric patterns, and prints.

PIPING is a narrow, corded, bias strip with a ¼″ seam allowance, which is inserted into a seam for a decorative accent. It comes in several colors in prepackaged lengths.

CABLE CORD is used as a filler for piping, cording, tubing, and trapunto and for making corded buttonholes and tucks. It is sold by the yard in ⅛″ to 1″ diameters.

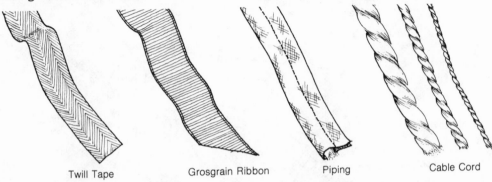

Twill Tape   Grosgrain Ribbon   Piping   Cable Cord

FOLD-OVER BRAID is a knitted braid with finished edges that is folded in half, sometimes with one edge slightly wider than the other. It is used for binding and trimming an edge without a hem or facing. It is available in different colors and designs, both prepackaged and by the yard.

RIBBING is a knitted band with a variety of types, weights, and widths that is used to finish the neckline, armhole, sleeve, pants leg, or waistline of a garment. The stretchability of ribbings varies, depending upon the knit—some are quite stable while others are very stretchy. Ribbing is available prepackaged or by the yard.

HORSEHAIR BRAID is used to stiffen hem edges, especially on evening and bridal wear, so they will softly flare. A stiff, bias braid woven of transparent synthetic yarns, it may have a heavy thread along one edge for easing. It is available in different widths.

BELTING is a very stiff band used to reinforce self-covered belts and waistbands. Available in both regular and iron-on types, it is sold in prepackaged lengths or by the yard in ½″ to 3″ widths. Specially designed waistband strips, used to finish the inside of a waistband, are also available.

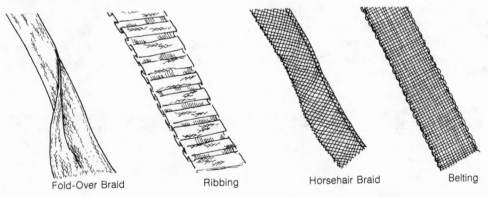

Fold-Over Braid   Ribbing   Horsehair Braid   Belting

The Sewing Machine

Sewing machine manufacturers, keeping pace with new fabrics and the upsurge of fashion sewing, offer a wide range of makes and models. When buying a sewing machine, you must decide how many special features your projects require.

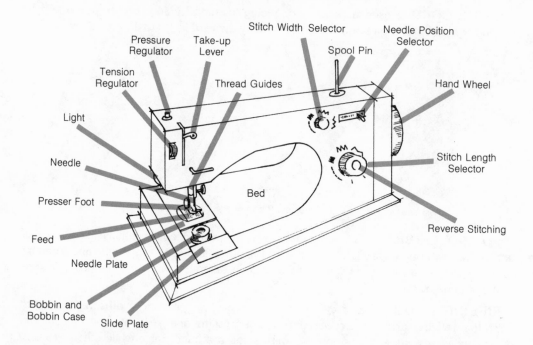

Zigzag stitching, in addition to straight stitching, is offered on all but the most basic machines. Automatic stitch machines have pattern discs that mechanically control stretch and decorative stitches. With solid-state memory machines, a wide variety of stitches can be selected instantly by simply touching a picture of the desired stitch on the control panel.

All sewing machines share one feature—***the thread tension.*** The strength of your seams depends upon using the correct thread tension. Before stitching any garment, you should test the tension and determine the correct stitch size on a fabric scrap. Stitch about 3″ on the bias of both lengthwise and crosswise grains.

The upper tension controls the thread that goes through the needle. If it is too loose, the thread on the underside of your stitching will appear to lie flat on the surface of the fabric (1). Should the thread appear to lie flat on the upperside of your fabric, the upper tension is too tight (2). In the ideal stitch, the thread tensions are in balance and both threads are drawn equally into the fabric (3).

| 1 | 2 | 3 |

To test further, hold the fabric at both ends of the stitching line and pull sharply until one of the threads breaks, indicating which tension is too tight. If both threads break evenly, the tension is balanced. No matter which tension is wrong, the correction should always be made by adjusting the upper thread tension. **Do not** adjust the bobbin tension until you have exhausted all other methods possible.

Machine Equipment

Needles should be selected according to the weight and type of fabric used. Needle sizes range from 9 (for delicate fabrics) to 18 (for heavyweight fabrics). Refer to the needle chart, pages 172 to 174, for the specific needle size recommended for your weight of fabric.

Needles are available in three different needle points, depending upon the type of fabric. A sharp point is recommended for stitching woven fabrics. A ball point, which has a slightly rounded point to slip between the fabric yarns, should be used for stitching knits. A wedge-shaped point is designed for sewing leathers and vinyls. Some needles are color coded for easy identification.

Double and triple needles mounted on a single base are used for decorative stitching. Needles should be changed frequently, often with each new sewing project. Many stitching problems are due to the needle being blunt or damaged, improperly inserted, or the wrong size.

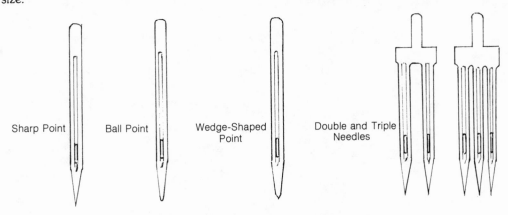

Sharp Point Ball Point Wedge-Shaped Point Double and Triple Needles

A **straight stitch foot and straight stitch needle plate** may come with your machine. Use them for straight stitching and whenever extra fabric control is needed, such as for edge stitching. Use them also for stitching delicate and spongy fabrics as the small hole in the needle plate helps to prevent the fabric from being pulled down into the machine and puckering during stitching.

A **general purpose foot and general purpose needle plate** are essential for zigzag stitching as they have a wider hole and opening to accommodate the sideways motion of the needle. They can also be used for straight stitching on firm fabrics.

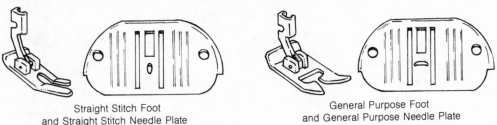

Straight Stitch Foot
and Straight Stitch Needle Plate

General Purpose Foot
and General Purpose Needle Plate

Bobbins are made of either metal or plastic. Keep several wound with the basic colors you use most frequently. Have extra bobbins on hand to avoid winding one color thread over another. There are several types of bobbins, so consult your sewing machine's manual before purchasing them. Replace any damaged bobbins as cracks or knicks in the bobbin can cause stitching problems.

Tools to keep your machine in the best possible condition are vital. An assortment usually comes with your machine. The most important ones are a brush for removal of lint from the working parts, a small screwdriver to open areas for easier cleaning, and sewing machine oil to keep the parts moving freely without friction and wear.

Special Feet

The ***zipper foot*** is designed to stitch very close to a raised edge during straight stitching and can be adjusted to the right or left side of the needle. Used most often for zipper insertion, it can also be used for covering and applying cording in seams.

The ***hemming foot*** turns a narrow hem and stitches it in one operation with either straight or decorative stitches. It may be used to attach ruffles and lace and works best on lightweight fabrics.

The ***gathering foot*** locks fullness into every stitch. It is used for both shirring and gathering.

Zipper Foot

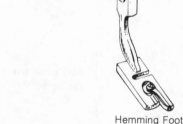

Hemming Foot

Gathering Foot

The ***roller foot*** is used to feed hard-to-handle fabrics such as nylon, polyester, or vinyl between the throat plate and the needle. The grid on the foot's round, rolling-pin type construction prevents fabric from slipping while stitching.

The ***even feed foot*** is used for sewing hard-to-feed pile and stretch fabrics, as the foot feeds both layers of fabric evenly under the needle. It is also excellent for stitching plaids, stripes, and topstitching.

The ***overedge foot*** is used with an overedge stretch stitch for seams in stretch fabrics.

Roller Foot

Even Feed Foot

Overedge Foot

The **button foot** will hold any two-hole or four-hole button securely for zigzag or automatic stitching. It should have a groove to hold a needle over which a thread shank can be formed.

The **darning and embroidery foot** is used for all types of free-motion stitching. The foot holds the fabric firmly as the needle enters and rises out of the fabric.

The **special purpose foot,** usually of clear plastic, is used for all kinds of decorative stitching.

Button Foot

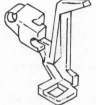
Darning and Embroidery Foot

Special Purpose Foot

Special Purpose Attachments

A **seam guide** attaches to the machine bed for accurate stitching of straight, curved, and topstitched seams. Some machines have markings on the throat plate for the same purpose.

A **ruffler** can make uniform gathered or pleated ruffles on light- to mediumweight fabrics. Some make and attach them in one operation.

Seam Guide

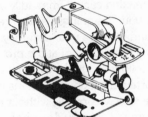
Ruffler

The **buttonholer** makes durable, strong, attractive buttonholes quickly and easily on all fabrics. All models come with templates to make different sizes ($\frac{5}{16}$" to $1\frac{1}{2}$") and types of buttonholes.

The **binder foot** applies packaged bias binding or self-fabric bias to an unfinished edge. It ensures a uniform binding without pinning and basting. Use it with either a straight or zigzag stitch.

The **quilting foot** consists of a short open foot and an adjustable space guide for accurately following curved lines and keeping stitching rows evenly parallel. Especially adaptable for lightly padded fabrics, it guides the placement of straight stitching on block, floral, or scroll designs.

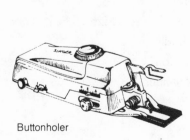
Buttonholer

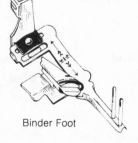
Binder Foot

Quilting Foot

Tools
for
Every Sewing Need

A vast assortment of tools and gadgets have been manufactured to serve the woman who sews. Each one has been carefully designed to save time and simplify construction. You should begin by acquiring tools according to your immediate needs (shears, steam iron, etc.) and then start to purchase those extra, handy time-savers that are constantly appearing on the market. The more basic items will be your only expenditure in the very beginning, while the more complicated tools will become necessary as your skill and interest increase. Thus, your purchases will be spread out as you go along.

Because your equipment is essential to your sewing success, it must be of good quality and always kept in the peak of working order. Experiment with various types of equipment and see which one is best for you. If possible, it is wise to test the tool before you purchase it to be sure the parts are working smoothly. Most importantly, give each tool the same scrupulous attention you would give any other household appliance and there will be no need to buy replacements.

To save yourself time and confusion, have your equipment stored systematically in categories, making each item readily accessible at all times. Keep together all your marking equipment, your fastenings, your thread, and so on. Having them handy will accelerate your work and increase your accuracy. If you follow this advice, it will be easy to get into the habit of using the right tool at the proper time.

Use the following guide as a reference when purchasing your equipment. We have carefully sorted through the extensive variety of tools sold, creating a list of those you should have to sew correctly without needing to improvise. Turn to the following pages to find each item individually described in detail. The illustration on each page is designed to present a fairly complete cross section of all the equipment available.

Bent-handle shears	Needles
Scissors	Thimble
Tape measure	Dressmaker's Silk Pins
Ruler	Pincushion
Yardstick	Steam Iron
Tracing Wheel	Ironing Board
Dressmaker's Tracing Paper	Press Cloths
Tailor's Chalk	Tailor's Ham or Press Mitt
Seam Gauge	Full-length Mirror
Assortment of Thread	Extension Cord
Sewing Machine	Waste Container

Measuring

Measuring tools are among the most important items in your sewing box. Good quality equipment and correct usage will assure you a better-fitting garment. Be sure you have a variety available to avoid the temptation to guess or the need to substitute. The key to success is to measure often and accurately.

Tape measures are indispensable. They should be 60″ long with metal tips and made of a material that will not stretch, preferably fiberglass. It will be most helpful if the numbers, in inches or centimeters, are clearly printed on both sides (1).

Rulers are necessary for all your sewing projects. You must have at least one 12″ to 18″ long and one 5″ to 6″ long. They can be found in a variety of materials. If you select wood, keep in mind that it may warp. It should have a metal edge for accuracy. The plastic see-through type easily retains its straight edges, is well suited for buttonholes, pleats, etc., and can readily serve all your needs. The numbers should be clearly indicated.

Yardsticks are invaluable for general marking purposes. They should be made of shellacked hard wood or metal. Those made of metal are the sturdiest.

A **sewing gauge** is a small 6″ metal or plastic ruler with a sliding indicator. It is ideal for quick, accurate measurement of hems, buttonholes, and pleats (2).

A **dressmaker's gauge** is another small, handy marking tool. One side is straight for marking tucks and pleats, the other scalloped for marking scallops, etc. (3).

A **hem gauge** is generally made of lightweight metal with one gradually curved edge designed to accommodate the shape of your hems. The different hem depths are clearly indicated on its surface. The straight edges are also marked in inches to provide yet another measuring tool (4).

A **French curve** is a marking tool that is sharply curved along one side. Use it to re-draw curved areas such as armholes, necklines, and princess seams when altering patterns (5).

T-squares can be made of either clear plastic or metal. Use the T-square for straightening grain, locating opposite grains, altering your pattern tissue, or for other marking tasks (6).

A **skirt marker** is the quickest, easiest, and most accurate way to mark hems. There are several types: pin, chalk, and a combination of both. The pin marker is more precise but does require the assistance of another person, which is not necessary for the chalk variety with a blower on a tube. A skirt marker that combines pin and chalk allows you to have the best qualities of both. Be sure the base is heavy and steady and that the marker extends high enough to be suitable for all your fashion lengths (7).

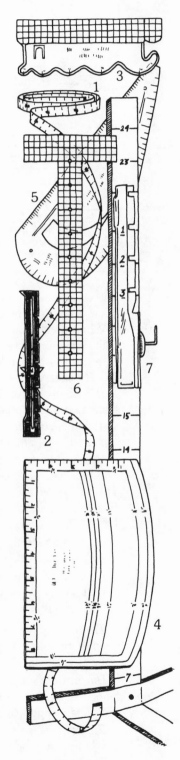

Cutting

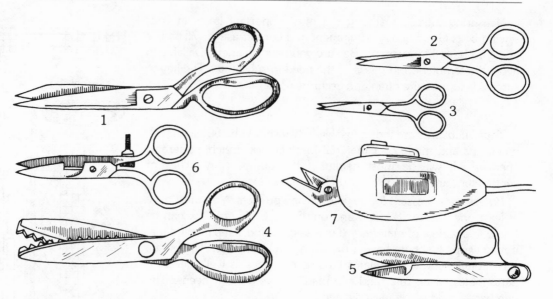

It is vital to be accurate when cutting out the individual pieces of your garment. An even edge, an obvious notch, and a true curve will make sewing much simpler.

When purchasing shears or scissors, look for steel or molybdenum that has been coated with nickel for protection and chrome plated to prevent rusting. Test the mechanism to be sure the scissors work smoothly and cut sharply from the back of the blades to the point. Quality shears are put together with an adjustable screw to allow the user to adjust the "run" of the shears to her particular feel. Shears and scissors should be periodically lubricated and sharpened. Oil the screw portion with sewing machine oil and wipe with a soft cloth. You may sharpen them at home or send them back to the manufacturer for repairs. Keep in mind that cutting paper heavier than tissue will dull the blades.

Dressmaker's shears are bent-handle shears with 7″ or 8″ blades hinged with a screw. The two differently shaped handles accommodate more fingers and yield better control. The bent handles are preferred because the fabric can rest flat on the table when being cut. Some have a serrated edge on the blade that helps control the cutting of lightweight fabrics. Left-handed shears are also available (1).

Sewing scissors have small round handles and range from 4″ to 6″ in length. Used for more delicate cutting and trimming (2).

Embroidery scissors, 3″ to 4″ long, are used for buttonholes and detail work (3).

Pinking or scalloping shears are used to finish raw edges of fabrics that do not ravel easily. Select 7½″ to 9″ blades with a ball-bearing pivot (4).

Thread clips are a scissor variation with short blades and an inner spring mechanism to keep them apart. They fit neatly into your hand and are used with a clipping motion to cut stray threads quickly and easily (5).

Buttonhole scissors are constructed to allow you to begin cutting within the body of the fabric. A screw and nut arrangement makes it possible to set the blades to cut only a prescribed length (6).

Electric scissors are available with or without a cord for fast cutting. Be sure they are small enough to hold comfortably (7).

The ***cutting area*** should be large and flat, preferably about 38″ high, at least 36″ wide, and 6′ to 8′ long. Ideally the area should be accessible from all four sides.

Marking

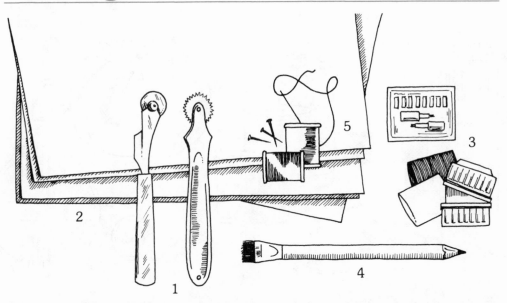

Marking plays an important role in the construction process. Haphazard stitching of seams and darts or arbitrary placement of collars, pockets, etc., caused by incorrect markings will unquestionably yield unfavorable results. The pattern tissue has specific construction lines and symbols printed on its surface for you to transfer to your garment pieces. If you have been accurate in marking these guidelines, construction will be greatly simplified and errors kept to a minimum.

Since you will be working with many varieties of fabric, from lush woolens to transparent voiles, you should have on hand the accompanying types of marking equipment.

Tracing wheels come in two types. A dull serrated edge is best for most fabrics. Delicate or smooth fabrics require a plain, unserrated edge and may be marked by impression without using tracing paper (1).

Dressmaker's tracing paper is a form of carbon paper. It is used in conjunction with a tracing wheel to transfer construction markings. Don't use contrasting colors on light fabrics. Choose a color close to that of your fabric, yet still discernible. Always use white on white fabric. Test the color you selected before marking to be sure it is removable, and always mark on the wrong side of your fabric. The double-faced variety is a time-saver when marking two layers of fabric (2).

Tailor's chalk, found in several color squares, is ideal for many marking tasks. The type with a refillable holder and built-in sharpener is most convenient. Since it may be made of either chalk or wax, test first to see which type is easiest to remove. Do not use wax on synthetic fabrics because it will be difficult to remove by any method (3).

A *dressmaker's marking pencil* is chalk in pencil form and is practical for most hard-surfaced fabrics. Do have at least one with a brush for erasing the marking (4).

Thread is used for thread tracing, general basting, and tailor's tacks. Special basting thread can be used for marking because it breaks easily and thus is easy to remove. Silk thread is recommended for fine fabrics and when basting stitches are not to be removed before pressing. Choose thread in a slightly contrasting color for easier removal (5).

Stitching

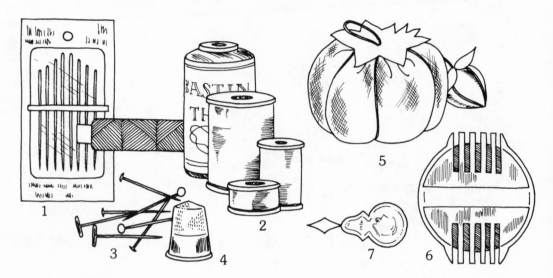

1 2 3 4 5 6 7

Needles and thread are the essence of your sewing equipment. Although considered basics, both are available in a wide variety of types and sizes for many different uses.

Needles most commonly used for hand sewing range in size from #1 for coarse work to #10 for fine sewing. Sharps are a commonly used medium length, all-purpose needle. For very fine hand sewing on heavyweight fabrics, use the short, round-eye betweens. Ball-point needles have a rounded point for use with knits. Milliner's needles are best for basting and millinery. Buy embroidery or crewel needles for embroidery or other sewing requiring a long eye for easy threading. Self-threading needles come in an assortment of sizes (1).

Thread should be selected in a matching shade or one shade darker than your fabric. An assortment of sizes and colors is a must for any sewing kit. Color and size numbers are printed on the spool. Greater numbers denote finer thread, using #50 as a midpoint. Polyester or cotton-covered polyester thread is recommended for most sewing tasks; silk thread is used for fine fabrics and basting; buttonhole twist for topstitching and hand-worked buttonholes; mercerized cotton for sewing on natural fiber fabrics; and heavy-duty thread for use with heavier fabrics. Special threads are available for basting, quilting, sewing on coat buttons, and carpets (2). Also see the needle and thread chart, pages 172 and 174.

Pins should be rustproof stainless steel or brass dressmaker's silk pins. For easily marred, special, or delicate fabrics use a slightly finer size 17 pin. Ball-point pins have a rounded tip to slip between the yarns of knitted fabrics. Pins with round, colorful plastic heads are especially easy to see and remove. The T-pin, with a larger T-shaped head, is convenient for heavy pile or bulky knitted fabrics (3).

A **thimble** should fit snugly on your middle finger. They are available in a range of sizes 6 to 11 for both small and large hands (4).

Pincushions are convenient tools. We suggest having two: the large type for the bulk of your pins with an attached emery bag for sharpening and removing rust from pins and needles; and the wrist variety for quick service while sewing and fitting (5).

Beeswax should be kept handy in a holder to coat your hand sewing threads. It strengthens the thread and reduces tangling, knotting, and breaking (6).

A **needle threader** is a little device to help you through those frustrating days when you can't thread your needle (7).

Sewing Aids

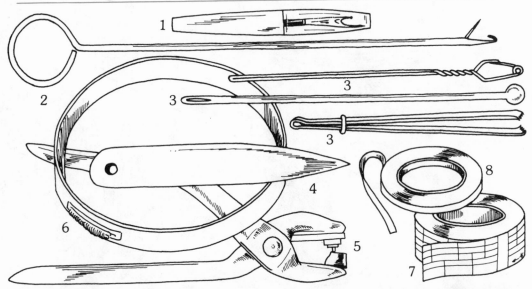

These additional sewing aids help contribute to fine workmanship. Although not essential, they enable you to perform your hand tasks more quickly and easily.

A *seam ripper* is a simple and safe pen-like device that allows careful ripping of adjustments and mistakes. Never, never use a razor blade as a substitute (1).

A *loop turner* is a specially designed tool with a latch-hook device at one end. It is used to turn tubing or bias cording to the right side (2).

A *bodkin* is used to draw elastic, belting, and cording through casings. Gripper teeth or a safety pin closing hold the elastic or cording. Another type has an eye for threading and can be used for turning bias tubing (3).

A *pointer and creaser* is a flat wooden tool approximately 4″ long. One end is pointed, the other is rounded. The pointed end is for pushing out small corners; the rounded end is used in conjunction with an iron to flatten seamlines or to assist finger pressing (4).

Fastener pliers are used to apply snap fasteners, eyelets, and grommets and are available in several sizes (5).

An *embroidery hoop* is a two-part frame. One hoop fits snugly over another to hold a section of fabric taut for embroidery or beading. It can be purchased in both metal or wood and in a variety of sizes and shapes. The wood hoops are intended for crewel work. Select a hoop with a spring mechanism that permits adjustment for various weights of fabric. A cork-lined outer hoop will hold the fabric more securely (6).

Sewing tape is measured on one side to use as a stitching guide, especially when topstitching. One type can be separated into various widths (7).

Basting tape is very narrow and has adhesive on both sides. Use it to hold a zipper in place or two layers of fabric together for stitching. Do not stitch over tape and be sure to remove it after sewing seam (8).

Tissue paper should always be on hand. Use it when stitching those fabrics that may need special treatment to go through the feed dog and presser foot of your machine. The tissue is also used when lengthening your pattern tissue, making alterations, or transferring monograms and designs.

Pressing

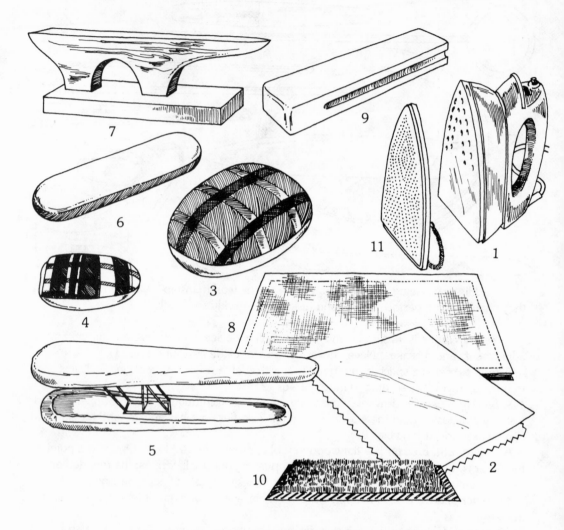

The real secret of success in sewing is to press as you sew. Careful, thorough treatment during each stage of construction will result in a good-looking garment that requires only a light touch-up when completed. You will find that it is quicker and easier to press in units as you sew. For example, stitch and press all darts or all pocket flaps, and so on.

The **iron** should combine the characteristics of both a steam iron and a dry iron. The steam vents should be located at the end of the soleplate to provide concentrated steam when it is needed. Be sure the iron has a wide temperature range for the best care of all your fashion fabrics. A controlled spray mechanism can also be helpful (1).

The **ironing board** should be sturdy, level, and adjustable to different heights. Pad the board with cotton batting or purchased padding already cut to fit. Place a silicone-treated cover over the surface to prevent scorching or sticking. Keep the cover smooth and soil-free.

Press cloths should be selected in relation to the weight of your fabric. They should be similar in weight for best results. Have at least two on hand: a transparent variety for seeing details, and a two-part wool and cotton type for most general pressing needs. For pressing on the right side, use a scrap of the garment fabric as a press cloth. Keep cheesecloth available for ready use as a press cloth (2).

A *tailor's ham* is an oblong, firmly stuffed cushion with subtly rounded curves. It is designed for pressing the curved areas of your garment such as darts, sleeve caps, princess seams, or any place that requires a rounded, curved shape pressed in. There are no substitutes for this item as it simulates actual body curves. Hams come in different sizes and should be covered in half cotton and half wool. One version has a concave as well as a convex section (3).

A *press mitt* is similar to a tailor's ham, but small enough to fit over your hand. It has pockets on either side to protect your hand. The mitt is good for small hard-to-reach areas or it may be slipped over the end of a sleeve board for sleeve caps. It also may be covered on one side with wool and on the other with cotton (4).

A *sleeve board* is actually two small ironing boards attached one on top of the other. They are designed for pressing small or slim areas, such as sleeves or necklines, that do not fit over your regular board. It should have a silicone cover and padding (5).

A *seam roll* is a long, firmly stuffed, tubular cushion that is rounded at each end. It is used to press small, curved areas and long seams in hard-to-reach areas such as sleeves. Because the roll is rounded, you press only the seam and not the surrounding fabric. This prevents ridges from forming on the right side. Again, one side should be covered with wool and the other side with cotton. To make a seam roll, cover a tightly rolled magazine with scraps of fabric (6).

A *point presser* or *pressing board* is made of wood and provides many differently shaped surfaces for pressing points, curves, and straight edges. The different sizes of curves and narrow straight edges allow you to press seams flat and open without wrinkling the surrounding area. The board can be used as it is for firm fabrics and sharp edges, or covered with a contoured pad for softer edges (7).

A *pressing pad* is three or four thicknesses of soft fabric stitched together to make a padded surface for pressing monograms, buttonholes, sequined fabric, and other raised surfaces. Place the raised surface face down on the pad and press on the wrong side. The pad prevents puckers and flattening of the decoration. A heavy turkish towel may be substituted (8).

A *pounding block* or *clapper* is a block of wood used with steam to flatten seam edges. It was originally designed to be used on hard-finished woolens and linens, but it may be used to form soft rolled hems. It is a must for tailoring. First make as much steam as possible with a steam iron and a damp press cloth. Remove the iron and cloth and pound firmly, regulating your pressure and slapping motions to suit the desired edge (9).

A *needleboard* is a bed of needles mounted on a flat surface that is placed between your fabric and the ironing board to prevent flattening pile fabrics. When the fabric is placed face down on the board, the pile falls in between the needles. It is essential for pressing velvet and other high-piled fabrics and very useful when pressing easily marred woolens. Also available with a stiff, high-pile fabric surface instead of needles (10).

An *iron cover* is placed over the soleplate of your iron and is used instead of a press cloth to prevent shine and scorching. One type is made of pre-formed heat-resistant fabric stretched over a metal frame and attaches to the iron with a spring; another is made of wool or canvas and has a drawstring for adjustment (11).

Brown paper is essential. Strips should be placed under the folds of darts or the edges of pleats, etc., to avoid unsightly ridges from appearing on the right side.

Dress Form

Have you ever had to compromise on fit because you could not reach that puckered seam or extra back fullness? Such compromises could lead to disappointing results; as every fine seamstress knows, an accurate fit is as vital as good workmanship to the lovely look of a finished garment. The perfect solution to these and other tricky fitting problems is a dress form, which duplicates your figure and allows you to fit and alter from all angles.

Whichever type you choose, it should have a heavy, sturdy base and be adjustable for figure changes, different heights, and convenient storage. Compressible shoulders are also a definite plus, as they allow you to slip your garment on and off the form easily.

A *foam form* is covered with a fabric shell that can be individually fitted to your contours. It can be adjusted by altering the fabric shell, and will not be harmed by pinning fabric to its surface. It is also available in pants forms (1).

A *molded, sectional form* can be adjusted both horizontally and vertically in several places to correspond to your own measurements, but it cannot duplicate your figure variations (2).

A *wire mesh form* can be slipped on and shaped to your own body and posture. It is then unsnapped and attached to a stand. Although easily adjustable, it does not have a smooth contour. It is also available in pants forms (3).

A *fabric-covered cotton batting form* is smoothly shaped, takes pins, and is good for working with very heavy fabrics or garments. However, it can be adjusted only by adding padding to the outside of the form (4).

Remember to check your measurements occasionally to make sure your dress form is still accurate, and adjust accordingly if necessary.

Once you begin using a dress form as part of your sewing equipment, you will be happily surprised at the many uses and the convenience it provides. Fitting, of course, will be quicker, easier, and more accurate. You will also be able to see and understand more completely the reasoning behind darts, structured seams, and built-in ease. It will help you check such details as the fall of a hem or the roll of a collar before it is too late to easily make any necessary adjustments. You can steam press directly on the dress form to perfectly set design lines. Most importantly, you can stand away from your garment and see it as others will, giving you greater objectivity and a three-dimensional view you can't get in a mirror.

Construction Basics

Your Complete Sewing Handbook

Now you're about to begin your adventure into the actual creation of fashion. Let's suppose that you have already made your fabric selection and chosen your pattern. Thread, bindings, trims, interfacings, all the things you need to shape fabric into fashion are at hand, and you are ready to make your first move. This is the time for you to consult your sewing handbook.

Since your pattern instructions cannot possibly elaborate on every variation of your particular garment, we've designed chapters 4 and 5 to be used along with your pattern instruction sheet. They provide step-by-step guidance that will help you to understand **why** certain procedures should be followed, and **how** to put these procedures to use. These chapters will help you to sew creatively with a minimum of effort and a maximum of fun. Turn to them often, and the results you achieve will be worth every minute you invest.

Here you will find a multitude of different sewing techniques that represent the most practical approach to good dressmaking.

Since making your sewing quicker and easier is our job, let us point out a time-saving plan that should serve as a guide for every project you sew:

☐ Do all preparatory steps first—cutting, marking, and basting the underlining to your fabric—as these operations definitely require a large, flat, clean surface that may be difficult to find once you've begun sewing.

☐ Complete sewing of small details, such as pocket flaps and buttonholes, on each garment section **before** it is joined to the other sections, as the weight of the entire garment can be extremely cumbersome when you are trying to be so precise.

☐ Make all buttonholes at one work session to assure consistent results.

☐ Organize yourself by attempting to finish a complete stage of construction at each sitting.

☐ Spend your extra moments on those often envied finishing details such as overcasting seams, attaching lingerie straps, etc.

☐ And, as a final word of professional advice, be sure to press seams as you finish each section.

Hand Stitches

With the advent of the sewing machine, the drudgery of making clothes was eliminated and fine hand sewing was elevated to the position it so rightly deserves. Hand sewing plays such an important part in the construction of clothes that no properly made dress can be completed without it. It is the attention paid to the hand-sewn details that determines the quality of your finished garment. As hand sewing becomes less of a necessity, it becomes an increasingly desirable luxury. Whether you love hand sewing or regard it as a necessary evil, there are ways you can do it quickly yet precisely enough to pass the closest scrutiny.

Choose a needle size in accordance with your fabric and thread, consulting the thread and needle chart on pages 172 to 174. Use a single 18″ to 20″ length of thread, coated with beeswax for added strength and slipperiness. It may seem elementary, but learn to wear a thimble on the second finger of your sewing hand. You'll be able to sew hard-surfaced fabrics more quickly and easily and with greater assurance.

THREADING THE NEEDLE: Cut thread at an angle; never break, bite, or tear the end; pass cut end through the needle eye, then knot the same end you put through the eye like this: using the left hand, hold the thread between the thumb and first finger (1). With your right hand, bring the thread over and around the fingertip, crossing it over the thread end, as shown (2). With your thumb over the crossed threads, and the longer thread taut, gently push the thumb toward the fingertip, causing the thread end to roll around the loop (3). Slide the loop off the fingertip and, lightly pinching the rolled end between the thumb and second finger, pull the longer thread in the right hand taut to set the knot (4).

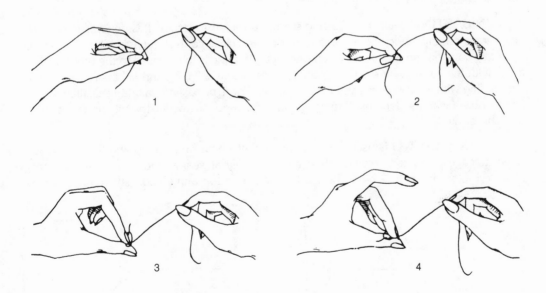

FINISHING STITCHING: To end your hand stitching, you have two choices—several backstitches or a knot. Begin the knot by taking a tiny stitch on the wrong side of your fabric, directly over your last stitch. Pull the thread until a small loop remains. Run your needle through the loop, pulling the thread a second time, until another small loop is formed. It is through this second loop that you insert your needle for the last time. Pull the thread taut, forming an inconspicuous knot at the base of your stitches.

Basting

Basting is a **temporary** stitch used in the preparatory phase of your sewing. Whether matching plaids, indicating markings, attaching interfacing, or holding fabric pieces together for stitching, the trick is to use the right stitch in the right place and to follow these common-sense principles. Always work on a flat, smooth surface. Pin your garment pieces together before basting, and use contrasting colored thread. Begin with a knot or a backstitch, and always remove basting **before** pressing permanent stitching. Silk thread is recommended for fine fabrics or when basting stitches are not to be removed before pressing, as in the case of pleats or hems. Always baste alongside the seamline within the seam allowance for easy removal of your basting threads.

EVEN BASTING is used for basting seams subjected to strain. It is generally used for long seams on any fabric and for areas that demand close control, such as set-in sleeves. It is usually done flat on a table, or when one layer of fabric is to be eased to the other, in the hand, with the eased layer on top. Space stitches evenly, ¼″ long and ¼″ apart, beginning and ending with backstitches rather than a knot. For firm basting, take a backstitch every few inches. Gear the length of stitching and the type of needle to suit the fabric and probable strain (1).

UNEVEN BASTING is used for marking, for attaching underlining and interfacing to fabric at edges, and for holding fabric together only at seams and edges that are not subjected to strain, as in a hem. Take a long stitch on top and a short stitch through the fabric (2).

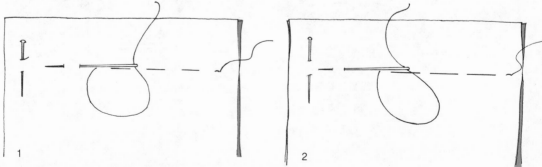

DIAGONAL BASTING or **TAILOR BASTING** is used for holding facings, interfacings, and linings in place during fitting. Take short stitches through the fabric at a right angle to the edge, spacing them evenly. This results in diagonal stitches on the upper side and short horizontal stitches on the underside.

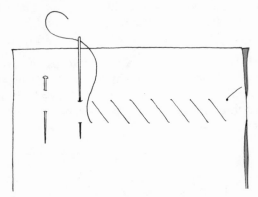

SLIP BASTING is used for matching stripes, plaids, and prints; intricate curved sections; and for fitting adjustments made from the right side. Crease and turn under the seam allowance on the edge. Right sides up, lay the folded edge in position on the corresponding piece, matching the fabric design at the seamline; pin. Slip the needle through the upper fold, then through the lower garment section, using a stitch ¼″ in length. The result is a plain seam with basting on the wrong side.

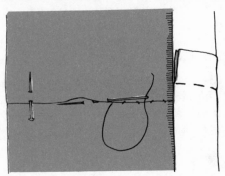

MACHINE BASTING is used for firm fabrics that won't slip or show needle marks. Set your machine for the longest stitch and loosen the upper tension slightly so thread is easily removable. To remove, clip the top thread at intervals and pull out the bottom thread.

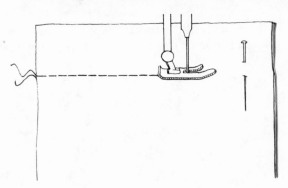

Hand Sewing

Hand sewing means to stitch **permanently** in place by hand. Keep stitches fairly loose to avoid a puckered, strained look. Work from right to left unless otherwise stated, reversing direction if you are left-handed. To secure the thread in the fabric, start with a few small backstitches or make a knot at the end and conceal it in the wrong side of your fabric.

The **RUNNING STITCH** is the most basic of stitches. It has many uses—easing, gathering, tucking, mending, and sewing seams that are not subjected to much strain. Take several small forward stitches, evenly weaving the needle in and out of the fabric before pulling the thread through; pick up as many stitches as your fabric and needle will allow. For permanent seams, use stitches ⅟₁₆″ to ⅛″ long; for easing and gathering, ⅟₁₆″ to ¼″ long.

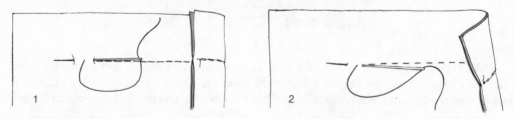

The **BACKSTITCH** is one of the strongest hand stitches. It is especially useful for repairing hard-to-reach seams that have ripped. It has the appearance of a machine stitch on the right side, but the stitches overlap on the wrong side. With right sides together, following the seamline, bring the needle through the fabric to the upper side. Take a stitch back about ⅟₁₆″ to ⅛″, bringing the needle out again ⅟₁₆″ to ⅛″ forward on the seamline. Keep inserting the needle in the end of the last stitch and bringing it out one stitch ahead. The stitches on the underside will be twice as long as those on the upper side (1).

The **HALF-BACKSTITCH** is suitable for any seam. It is also used to understitch finished facings to prevent the edge from rolling toward the outside of the garment. Follow the same method as the backstitch, but carry the needle back only half the length of the last stitch while continuing to bring it out one stitch ahead (2).

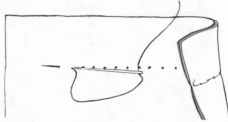

The **PRICKSTITCH,** a variation of the backstitch, is often used for inserting zippers. The needle is carried back only one or two threads, forming a tiny surface stitch with a reinforced understitch.

The **HAND PICKSTITCH** is used as a decorative finish and has the same appearance as the prickstitch. The only difference is that the bottom layer of fabric is not caught when backstitching. The thread should not be taut, and should lie beadlike on the fabric surface.

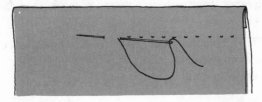

The **HEMMING STITCH,** used for all types of hemming, is most often used for hems finished with seam binding, especially when the garment is not underlined. Take a tiny inconspicuous stitch in the garment, then bring the needle diagonally up through the edge of the seam binding or hem edge. Continue in this manner, spacing stitches about ¼'' apart (3).

The **SLIPSTITCH** is used to hem, attach linings, and hold pockets and trims in place, and it provides an almost invisible finish. Slide the needle through the folded edge and at the same point pick up a thread of the under fabric. Continue in this manner, taking stitches ⅛'' to ¼'' apart; space the stitches evenly (4).

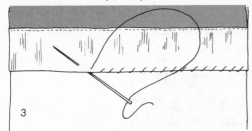

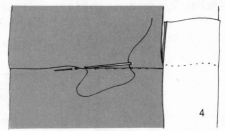

The **CATCHSTITCH** is used for holding two layers of fabric together in place while still maintaining a degree of flexibility. Its most common uses include attaching raw edges of facings and interfacings to the wrong side of garment sections, sewing pleats or tucks in linings, and securing hems in stretchy fabrics such as knits. Working from *left* to *right*, make a small horizontal stitch in the upper layer of fabric a short distance from the edge. Then, barely outside the edge of the upper layer, make another stitch in the lower layer of fabric diagonally across from the first stitch. Alternate stitching along the edge in a zigzag fashion, keeping threads loose (5).

The **BLIND CATCHSTITCH** is good for hemming heavy fabrics. Finish the raw edge of the hem and roll the hem back about ¼''. Make catchstitches between the two layers of fabric, keeping stitches loose (6).

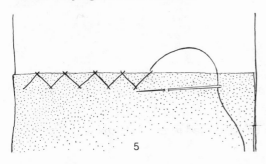

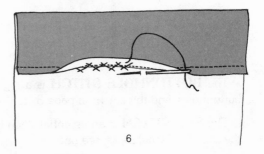

The **BLINDSTITCH,** used for hemming and holding facings in place, is inconspicuous on both sides of the garment. First, finish the raw edge of the hem or facing. Roll this edge back on the garment about ¼''; take a small horizontal stitch through one thread of the garment or underlining fabric, then pick up a thread of the hem or facing diagonally above. Do not pull the stitches tight (7).

The **OVERCAST STITCH** is the classic stitch used to finish raw edges to prevent them from raveling. Working from either direction, take diagonal stitches over the edge, spacing them evenly apart at a uniform depth (8).

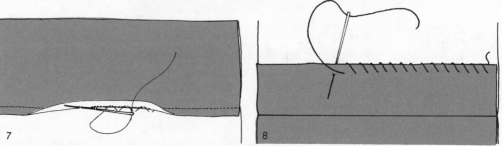

The **OVERHAND STITCH** holds two finished edges together with tiny, straight, even stitches. It is primarily used to join lace edging or to attach ribbon to a garment. Insert the needle at a diagonal angle from the back edge through to the front edge, picking up only one or two threads each time.

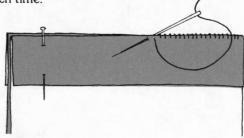

The **WHIPSTITCH** is a variation of the overhand stitch. It may serve the same purpose, differing in that the needle is inserted at a right angle to the edge, resulting in slanted stitches.

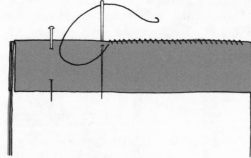

The **BUTTONHOLE STITCH** is a highly specialized stitch for making hand-worked buttonholes; find this stitch on page 321.

The **PAD STITCH** is an essential stitch in tailoring used to precisely shape and control the collar and lapel areas; see page 428.

The **BLANKET STITCH** is used for a wide variety of hand-finished details. Always work from *left* to *right* with the edge of the fabric toward you. Anchor your first stitch at the edge. For the next stitch and each succeeding one, point the needle toward you and insert it through the right side of your fabric, approximately ¼″ above the edge and ¼″ over from the preceding stitch. Keep the thread below your work and under the needle, as shown. A variation of the blanket stitch is generally used to form inconspicuous thread eyes, loops, and belt carriers (9).

The **BAR TACK** is used to reinforce points of strain, such as pocket corners or the end of a slit. It is formed by working a blanket stitch over two or three long stitches (10).

The **FRENCH TACK** is used to hold two parts of a garment together, such as the hems of a lined garment, and is constructed the same way as a bar tack (11).

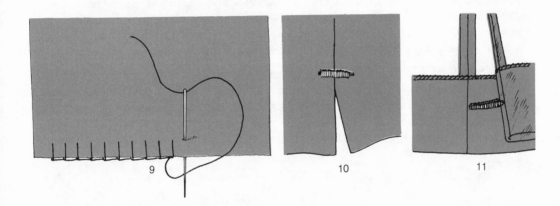

The **CHAINSTITCH** is a substitute for the blanket stitch when making thread loops and fastenings; see page 324.

The **CROSS-STITCH TACK** is used to hold two layers of fabric together. A single tack can be used to hold a facing edge in place at a seamline and is usually stitched several times (12). A series of cross-stitches is used to hold folds of a jacket lining in place at the center back or at the shoulder (13).

The **FAGOTING STITCH** is a decorative stitch used to join two fabric sections across an open seam; see Decorative Seams, page 214. Stitch through folded edge and diagonally across opening, entering material from underneath. Place needle under the thread, creating a twist, and stitch diagonally across opening again, spacing stitches evenly (14).

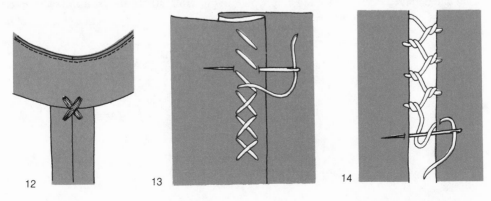

Seams and Seam Finishes

Be it plain or fancy, the mark of professional sewing is a perfect seam—a seam that is never puckered, never stretched, never wobbling, and is finished without a tangle of ravelings or crooked edges.

To stitch a perfect seam, always adjust the machine tension, pressure, and stitch regulator to suit the fabric texture and weight. See chapter 6 for additional hints on handling of special fabrics and pages 172 to 174 for thread and needle sizes before you begin. The usual seam allowance set by the pattern industry is ⅝'' unless otherwise specified. If your machine doesn't have a seam guide attachment or stitching lines marked on the needle plate, place a small piece of colored tape ⅝'' from the needle as a guide.

A smooth, sleek appearance is the result of careful seam handling. If you are not satisfied with the way your seam looks, it is easy to remedy. Simply rip the seam out by using a pin, a seam ripper, or small scissors—but never a dangerous razor blade. Correct any unhappy results at an early stage, and you will be rewarded by a professionally finished garment.

STAYSTITCHING: Prior to pinning, basting, and permanent stitching, curved areas that require extra handling should be staystitched. This will act as a guideline for clipping and joining the curved edge to the other edges, as well as prevent stretching. Staystitch in the direction of the grain ⅛'' away from the seamline in the seam allowance, using the regular machine-stitch length suited to your fabric. For zipper openings, stitch ¼'' from the cut edge.

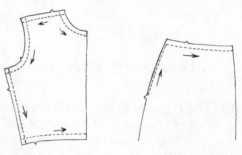

DIRECTIONAL STITCHING: To prevent stretching seam areas of your garment you should stitch seams in the direction of the grain just as you do when staystitching. If it is hard to tell from the cut piece which is the direction of the grain, run your finger along the edge. The threads with the grain should lie smoothly; those against will come loose and the edge will begin to fray. Without testing, you can generally stitch from the widest part to the narrowest part of each pattern piece.

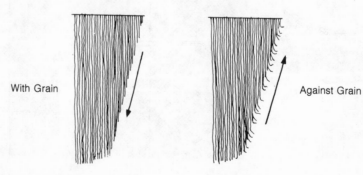

With Grain   Against Grain

Constructing a Seam

The main purpose of all seams is to hold your garment sections together.

JOINING SEAMLINES: When pinning the edges of your fabric together, place the pins at right angles to the seamline with the heads toward the seam allowance. Your seams will be held in place accurately, and in this position pins can be stitched over by most sewing machines. You may wish to baste next to the seamline in the seam allowance.

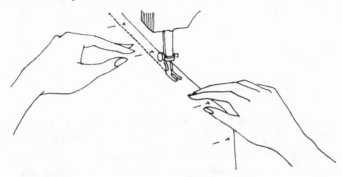

STITCHING: Begin to stitch ½'' from the end, backstitch to the end, and then stitch forward. Keep stitching along the seamline, following seam guidelines on the needle plate of your machine. Keep the cut edges of the fabric even. Secure by backstitching at other end of seam.

The seam may also be stitched from end to end without backstitching and the ends secured by tying a knot. Hold the thread in your left hand. Form a loop (1). With your right hand, bring the thread ends around and through the loop from the back (2). Holding the loop in your left hand, work the intertwined thread down to the base and hold in place with your left thumb (3). With your right hand, begin pulling the thread taut until the loop disappears and forms a knot (4).

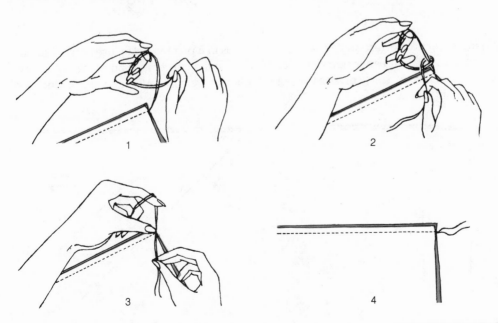

If you must end your stitching before reaching the edge, pull one of the thread ends through to the other side (5). Then tie both thread ends together (6). For best results, learn to tie all your knots by these two methods and to automatically clip the threads to ½″ after you finish each knot.

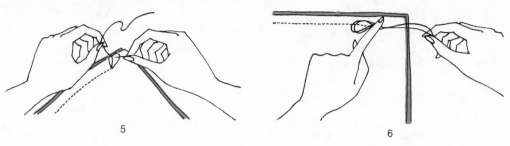

5   6

REINFORCING A CORNER SEAM: Whenever you stitch a seam with a corner, use *reinforcement* stitches (15 to 20 per inch depending on your fabric) to strengthen the point. If it is a corner that will need to be clipped for easy sewing, reinforce it before joining in a seam. Just inside the seamline, stitch for about an inch on either side of the point (1). Clip to the point. Pin both sections right sides together with clipped section up and stitch, pivoting at the point (2).

1   2

When joining two corresponding pieces of fabric, as in a pointed collar, use reinforcement stitches for an inch on either side of the corner (3). If the corner is at an acute angle, you should take one small stitch **across** the point for lighter-weight fabrics, and two stitches for heavier-weight fabrics (4).

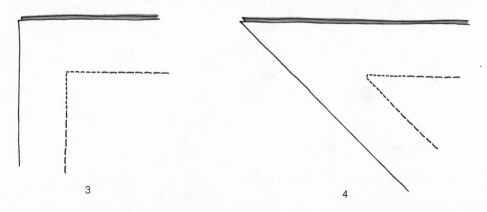

3   4

TRIMMING: Seam allowances should be trimmed only where less bulk is desired. In general, enclosed seams call for ¼″ seam allowances, but if the fabric is very light you may want to trim less. Cut diagonal corners from the ends of the seams, especially if they will later cross other seams (1).

For corners of an enclosed seam, trim across the point close to the seam. Then trim diagonally along either side of the point to eliminate any bulk when the corner is turned (2).

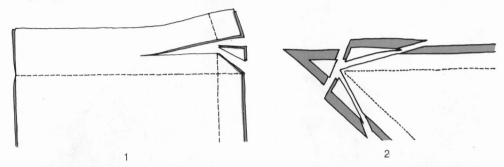

GRADING: When seam allowances are turned together in one direction, they must be graded to avoid making a ridge and to make seams lie flat without bulk. Grading is especially important when the fabric is heavy or if there are more than two layers of fabric. Each layer should be trimmed to a different width. Enclosed seams may be trimmed a little narrower than exposed seams. Generally the garment seam allowance is left widest (1).

NOTCHING and **CLIPPING:** Curves must be graded first and then trimmed in a special way in order to lie flat. On an outward curve, cut small wedges or notches from the seam allowance at even intervals; on an inward curve, clip into the seam allowance at even intervals. These intervals should be about ½″ to 1″, depending on the sharpness of the curve. Be very careful not to clip past the seamline (2).

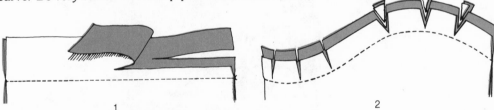

PRESSING: Pressing any seam is a two-step operation. First press the stitching line flat to blend the stitches into the fabric; then press the seam open (1). For enclosed seams in collars, cuffs, and pocket flaps, press the seam open with a point presser so that the seamed edges will be sharp (2).

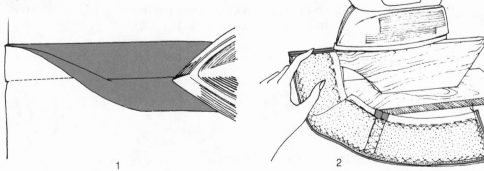

UNDERSTITCHING: When a seamline is pressed to form an edge that encloses the seam allowances, the underside should be understitched. This technique is often used for facings to prevent them from rolling to the outside of the garment. Grade both seam allowances and press toward the facing. Be sure to clip or notch curved edges when necessary. From the right side of the facing, work the half-backstitch (1) or machine-stitch (2) close to the seamline and through all the seam allowances. Turn the facing in and press the seamed edge.

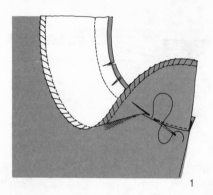

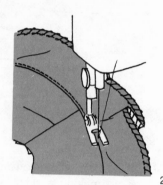

1

2

Special Seam Situations

INTERSECTING or **CROSSED SEAMS:** Stitch one seam and press open. Stitch the second seam in the same manner. Pin the two seams with right sides together, using a pin point to match the crossed seams exactly at the seamline. Then pin on either side of the seams and stitch. Trim corners diagonally as shown.

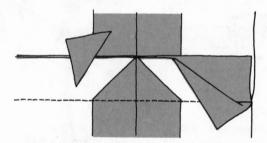

SEAM WITH EASE: To ease, stitch close to the seamline with long machine stitches extending the stitching slightly beyond markings. Pin the two layers right sides together with the eased side facing up. Pull up the ease thread between the markings and distribute the fullness evenly. Baste carefully to control the extra fabric and stitch.

SEAM WITH GATHERS: See page 227 for techniques to use on gathers.

TAPING A SEAM: A seam may be stayed or taped to strengthen and prevent stretching in the finished garment by using twill tape or woven seam binding. This technique is often used at waistline and shoulder seams. The tape should be placed over the seamline of one garment section, with the edge extending ⅛″ into the seam allowance. Baste next to the seamline and sew the tape on permanently as the seam is machine-stitched (1).

TISSUE PAPER UNDER SEAMS: You may have discovered that some lightweight fabrics are inclined to stretch or shift during sewing, creating uneven seams. To prevent mishaps, try placing tissue paper on the machine bed under the seams. Stitch through both the fabric and the paper; then tear the paper away (2).

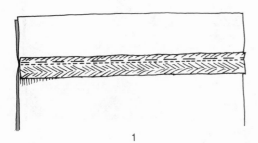

1

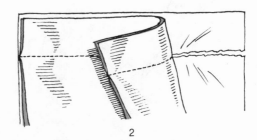

2

BIAS-CUT SEAMS: If you are joining a bias edge to a straight edge, pin and baste the bias edge to the straight edge. When stitching, be sure to always keep the bias side up in order to control the stretch of the bias and to avoid puckers (3).

If you are joining two bias edges, stretch the fabric slightly as you stitch over tissue paper so that the finished edge will hang correctly. Otherwise the seam may pucker and the threads will break when the garment is worn.

If it is a lengthwise seam, baste the fabric together, and let the garment hang for 24 hours to allow the bias to stretch before stitching the seam.

PRINCESS SEAM: Staystitch both curved edges ⅛″ from the seamline within the seam allowance. Clip the inward curved seam allowance on the center panel of the garment to the staystitching. Pin the seamline, spreading the clipped edge so that it will lie smoothly. Make any additional clips if necessary. With clipped side up, stitch the two edges together, being careful to keep the underside smooth. Press seam open over a tailor's ham, notching the seam allowance on the side panel until it lies flat. Wherever possible, stagger the position of the clips and notches (4).

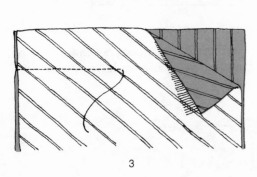

3

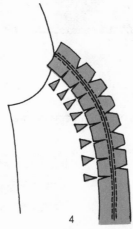

4

SCALLOPS: Stitch the curved scallop seam with small reinforcement stitches (15–20 per inch). Take one stitch across each point to make turning easier later. Now clip into each point, being careful not to cut through the stitching. Grade the seams and notch all the curves (5).

JOINING NAPPED FABRIC TO NAPLESS FABRIC: First pin, then baste closely using small stitches along the seamline. Always stitch in the direction of the nap with the napless fabric uppermost. This procedure will help to reduce any slippage caused by the nap (6).

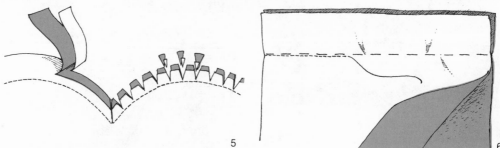

5   6

Seam Finishes

Since the inside story is as important to fine couture as the outside, all seams should be finished by the most suitable method if they are not covered by a lining. A seam finish helps the seam allowances to support the garment shape, ensures durability, prevents raveling, and contributes to the overall neatness of the garment.

HAND OVERCAST: This finish is suitable for most fabrics. For a seam pressed open, stitch ¼″ from each raw edge, then trim to ⅛″. (For firm fabrics, stitching and trimming may be omitted.) Overcast the edge by hand, using machine stitching as a guide (1).

MACHINE ZIGZAG: For fabrics which tend to ravel easily, use a zigzag stitch to reinforce each raw edge. Use a smaller stitch for lightweight fabrics and a larger stitch for heavy, bulky fabrics, pretesting for the best results (2).

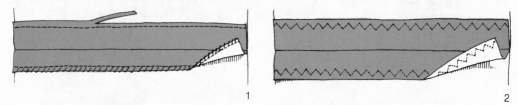

1   2

PINKED: If you are working with a firmly woven fabric which does not ravel, pink the edges with pinking or scalloping shears. For an even more secure finish, you may wish to stitch ¼″ from each edge before you begin to pink.

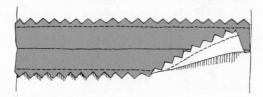

TURNED UNDER: Use this method for lightweight fabrics and plain-weave synthetics. It is not suitable for fabrics with bulk. Turn under the raw edges of the seam allowances, press if necessary, and stitch close to the edge (3).

BOUND EDGE: For heavy, bulky, easily frayed fabrics, especially in unlined jackets or coats, encase each raw edge in purchased double-fold bias tape. Place the slightly narrower edge of the tape on top and edgestitch (4).

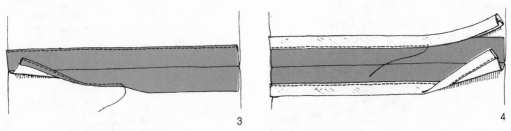

3   4

HONG KONG FINISH: For a couture touch, see page 450.

Self-Finished Seams

Some seaming techniques enclose the seam allowances as the seam is stitched. This gives a very neat appearance to seams that are visible such as in sheer fabrics and in unlined jackets.

FRENCH SEAM: This seam is well suited to sheer fabrics. It looks like a plain seam on the right side and a small, neat tuck on the wrong side. It is used on straight seams. Pin *wrong* sides together and stitch ⅜" from the seamline in the seam allowance. Trim to within ⅛" to ¼" of stitching. *Right* sides together, crease along the stitched seam; press. Stitch along the seamline, encasing the raw edges (1).

SIMULATED FRENCH SEAM: This seam can be made after first making a plain seam. Do not press it open. Instead, turn both of the seam allowances toward each other ¼" and press. Now edgestitch the folded edges together (2).

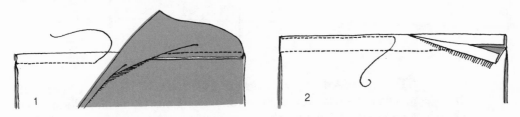

1   2

FRENCH WHIPPED SEAM or **DOUBLE-STITCHED SEAM:** For lace and embroidered fabrics or curved seams on sheer fabrics, stitch a plain seam, then stitch again ⅛" away in the seam allowance. Trim to ⅛" from this stitching and carefully overcast the raw edges by hand or with a fine zigzag stitch.

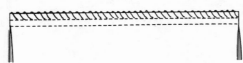

FLAT-FELL SEAM or **FELLED SEAM:** This seam is very sturdy and is often used on sportswear and menswear. Place **_wrong_** sides together (right sides together for an inside fell), stitch a plain seam, and press it toward one side. Trim the lower seam allowance to ⅛″. Turn under the edge of the other seam allowance ¼″ and place over the narrow seam allowance. For non-bulky fabrics, machine-stitch close to the folded edge; for bulky reversible fabrics, slip-stitch the fold in place (3).

SELF-BOUND SEAM: Trim one seam allowance of a plain seam to ⅛″ or ¼″, depending on your fabric. Turn the edge of the other seam allowance under and slipstitch or machine-stitch over the seam, encasing the trimmed seam allowance (4).

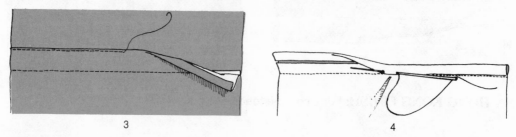

3   4

HAIRLINE SEAM: Use on sheer fabrics for collars, cuffs, and facings where there is no strain. Place a narrow row of zigzag stitching along the seamline, then trim away the seam allowances as close to the stitching as possible (5).

DOUBLE-STITCHED SEAM: This seam can be used on soft knits which have a tendency to curl at the edges. Stitch a plain seam, then stitch again ⅛″ away within the seam allowance using either a straight stitch or a zigzag stitch. Trim seam allowances close to stitching (6).

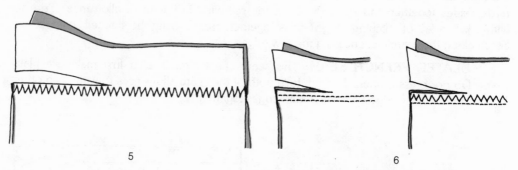

5   6

OVEREDGE-STITCH SEAM: If your machine has an overedge stitch, you can join and finish a seam on knit or stretch fabrics in just one operation. Trim seam allowances to ¼″. Stitch so that the straight stitches go along the seamline and the zigzag stitches enclose the raw edges.

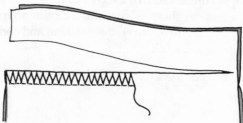

Decorative Seams

You can be creative in your sewing by letting your seams show. Topstitching on the right side of the fabric adds a special decorative touch. Choose one as a design feature in your garment and be inventive—your finished product will be an original!

TOPSTITCHED SEAM: Press a plain seam to one side as indicated on the pattern. Topstitch the desired distance from the seam on the right side of the fabric through all thicknesses (1). See Stitchery, page 463, for further instructions.

DOUBLE TOPSTITCHED SEAM: First press a plain seam open. Topstitch the desired distance from each side of the seam on the right side of the fabric. Be sure your stitches go through both thicknesses of the fabric (2).

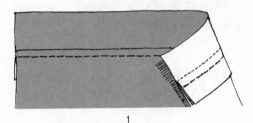

1

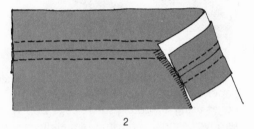

2

WELT SEAM: Stitch a plain seam and press it toward one side. Trim the lower seam allowance to ¼″. Then stitch through only the upper seam allowance and garment close to the trimmed edge, encasing the lower seam allowance (3).

DOUBLE WELT SEAM: When completed, this seam gives much the same appearance as a flat-fell seam. First construct a welt seam as directed above. Then topstitch close to the seam on the right side of the fabric, as shown (4).

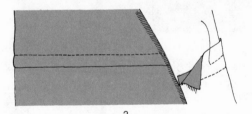

3

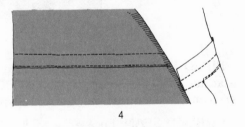

4

SLOT SEAM: Machine or hand-baste a plain seam; press open. Cut a strip of fabric as long as the seam and slightly wider than both seam allowances. From the right side, topstitch the same distance on each side of the seam. Remove basting threads.

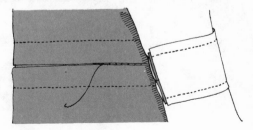

LAPPED SEAM: Turn in the edges of the overlapping section along the seamline and press. Working from the right side, pin the folded edge over the remaining section with the fold along the seamline. Stitch close to the fold through all thicknesses (5).

TUCKED SEAM: Follow the directions for a lapped seam and slip baste the fold in place. To form the tuck, stitch the desired depth from the fold through all thicknesses, stitching no closer than ¼″ from the raw edges. Remove the basting (6).

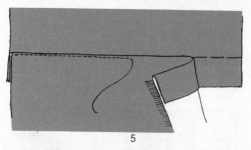

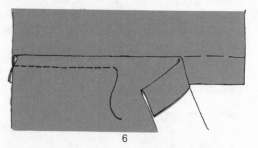

5

6

FAGOTED SEAM: Turn seam allowances under and press. Pin edges to strips of heavy paper, spacing edges ⅜″ apart and baste through all thicknesses. Stitch between the two edges using a fagoting stitch, page 203, or other embroidery stitch. After finishing stitching, remove basting, and trim seam allowance to ⅛″.

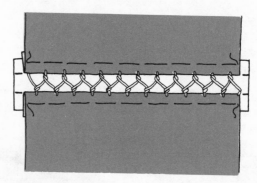

PIPED SEAM: Baste piping to the right side of one of the fabric sections along the seamline. Place the second section over the piping right sides together and baste; then stitch on the seamline through all thicknesses (7).

CORDED SEAM: Encase the cording in a bias strip, using a cording or a zipper foot. Attach the cording and baste the fabric sections together, like the piped seam. Stitch along the seamline through all thicknesses, using a cording or zipper foot (8).

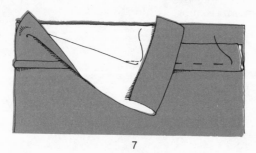

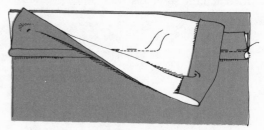

7

8

Darts

Darts create the difference between the flatness of fabrics and the curving third dimension of the feminine form. They rank highly among the basic sewing concepts that must be understood before you can construct a garment with any degree of fit. Their function is to provide carefully shaped fullness. Although the fitting of darts is dealt with on pages 96 to 99, it is always wise to keep a few working axioms in mind. A low bustline will detract from what otherwise could be a youthful appearance. For this reason, if you have an inkling that a low bustline is the cause of your fitting problems, adjust the straps of your foundation garments before you adjust your patterns or fit your garment. Then make certain that the dart position provides fullness that conforms with the lengthwise and crosswise contours of your figure. The dart should point to the fullest part of the body—to the point of the bust, to the curve over the pelvic bone, and so on. Since the length of the dart has been designed for a person of average height, you may have to adjust the dart length to agree with your own proportions—for a short figure, slightly shorter darts; for a tall figure, slightly longer darts. If the vertical bodice darts require relocating, the skirt darts should be realigned to match.

Constructing a Dart

MARKING: Transfer the dart markings to your fabric, using the most suitable method. You may not notice until the dart is folded that the subtle styling of many designs requires concave or convex curves as opposed to straight darts. Use your tracing wheel or tailor's chalk to make short horizontal lines indicating the bold symbols for matching sides, as well as the end of the dart. Always have the darts on the left and right sides of the garment mirror each other in length and placement.

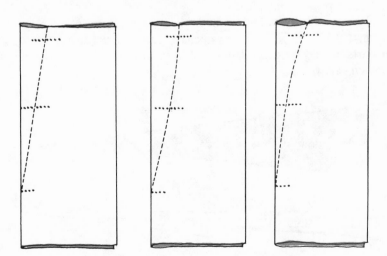

STITCHING: Begin sewing all darts at the wide base and taper to nothing at the pointed end. In fact, your last two or three stitches (12–15 stitches per inch) should be directly on the fold. Sew these stitches very slowly to be sure that they are only catching a few threads of the fabric. The thread ends of all darts, particularly at the point, should be secured with a knot rather than by backstitching. Tie the knot, as shown, working it to the end of the dart using the point of a pin. Backstitching often results in an unsightly bubble or pucker because the previous line of stitching was not duplicated exactly (1).

PRESSING: Always press darts before the major seams are stitched or before they are intersected by seams. The dart fold and stitching line should be pressed flat first to blend the stitches together. Be careful not to crease the fabric beyond the end point. Next, spread open the garment and press each dart over the curved surface of a tailor's ham or press mitt to maintain the built-in shape. Once you've steamed the dart into its proper position the area around the dart may become slightly wrinkled. Touch up this area while the dart is still on the tailor's ham with a dry iron (2).

Vertical darts should be pressed toward center front or center back, depending on their location. Horizontal darts are pressed downward unless otherwise specified. Deep darts, however, are pressed open with the point pressed flat. Place brown paper between the dart and garment to prevent ridges if your fabric mars.

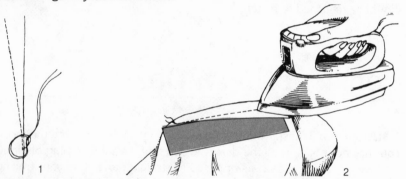

TRIMMING: Generally, darts require little additional handling other than pressing, but there are some situations that require special techniques.

Deep darts or darts in medium to heavy fabrics should be slashed to within ½″ to 1″ from the point and pressed open (3).

Sheers look best when the dart is trimmed. Make a second row of stitching approximately ⅛″ from the first; then trim ⅛″ from this stitching. Overcast the raw edges (4).

Contour darts should be clipped several times on the fold along the curve to relieve strain, as shown below.

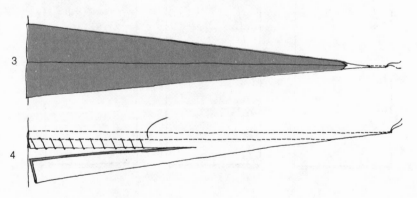

French Dart and Contour Dart

French darts and contour darts are both long darts that help to shape the waistline area of a garment without a waistline seam.

The French dart begins at the side seam and extends diagonally from the hip to the bust. Staystitch ⅛″ away from stitching line, ending about 1″ from point. Slash through center of dart up to end of staystitching. (Some patterns trim away center of dart when the pattern is cut out.) Pin stitching lines together, matching lines carefully. Stitch dart from end to point; knot thread ends securely. Clip seam allowances to allow dart to curve smoothly.

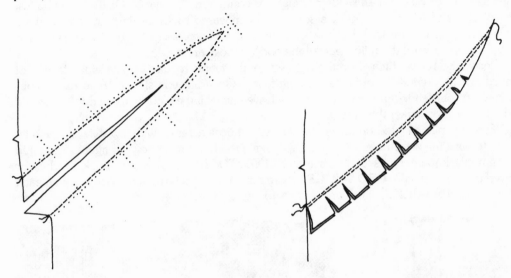

The contour dart tapers upward toward the bust or back and downward toward the hip. Fold dart along center line and pin stitching lines together. Stitch from the waist out toward each point, overlapping the stitching at the waist and knotting the thread ends at the points. Clip dart at waistline and at several places along the fold, if necessary, to relieve strain.

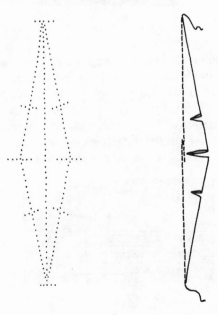

Tucks

The tuck is a versatile element in the designer's repertoire and fulfills a multitude of structural and ornamental needs. Each tuck is a slender fold of fabric that can be stitched along all or part of its length. Tucks are usually folded on straight grain, and, if chosen for decoration, the fold is generally formed on the outside of the fabric.

When tucks are used to control fullness and shape the contour of the design, the fold is formed on the inside, stitched to a designated point, and then released. They may be stitched on- or off-grain and either straight or contoured, like darts. Or they may be just small pleats of fabric secured by a seam. These released tucks, or dart tucks as they are sometimes called, are found at the shoulder line and waistline of a bodice or skirt, and should point toward the fullest part of the body in those areas.

Decorative tucks, stitched on the right side of the fabric, require very careful selection of needles and thread to coordinate with the fabric. Generally you should try to match your thread to your fabric. However, you may achieve interesting effects by using thread just one shade lighter or darker than the fabric.

If you are planning to add tucks to a garment, choose a design with few style lines and be sure to have the placement, width, and spacing of the tucks relate to your figure. The three commonly known types of tucks are: **BLIND TUCKS**, where each tuck touches or overlaps the next, **SPACED TUCKS**, where there is a predetermined space between each tuck, and **PIN TUCKS**, which are very narrow spaced tucks.

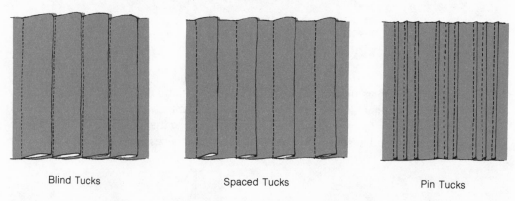

Blind Tucks   Spaced Tucks   Pin Tucks

ADDING TUCKS: If you would like decorative tucks on a garment, and the pattern does not call for them, tuck the fabric before cutting the pattern piece. To determine the amount of additional fabric width needed, multiply the width of a tuck by two to allow for both thicknesses. Then multiply this figure by the number of tucks you plan. Because the extra width required may interfere with the pattern layout, you may need additional fabric to lay out your pattern. A rule of thumb: purchase the amount of fabric required on the back of the envelope *plus* the length of one main pattern piece.

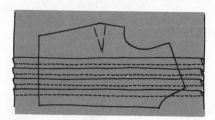

Making Uniform Tucks

Tucks are usually made on the straight grain. Do be sure to make the fold of the tucks parallel to the threads in the fabric.

MARKING and **BASTING:** Mark stitching lines of each tuck on either the outside or inside of your fabric. Remove pattern, fold tucks either to inside or outside of garment, matching stitching lines. Baste in place.

Or eliminate marking your tucks by making a cardboard measurement gauge, cutting a notch for the depth of the tuck and a second notch to indicate the space from fold to fold. Place the top of the gauge along the fold of the first tuck. Using the first notch as a guide, make a row of basting stitches parallel to the fold, sliding the gauge as you stitch. For the next tuck, move the gauge so that the second notch is now even with the first fold, and make your next fold at the top of the gauge. Continue this procedure for each consecutive tuck.

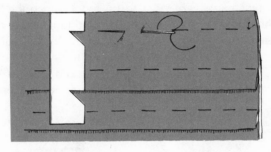

STITCHING: To control the finished look and the evenness of the stitching, be sure to stitch from the side of the tuck that will be seen. For narrow tucks, from ¼″ to ¾″, you can use the needle plate on your machine as a guide for stitching. Tucking may be pieced, if necessary, by carefully lapping, then stitching the tucks.

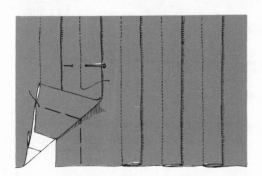
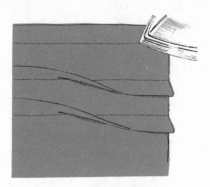

PRESSING: Press tucks as you stitch each one, or directly after stitching the series. First press the crease in the tuck from the right side of your fabric but on the underneath side of the fold. This step makes the final pressing much easier. Press the entire tucked area from the wrong side. Use very little steam to prevent puckering or the tuck fold from making unwanted indentions in the fabric. To prevent the latter problem in some fabrics, you may have to use strips of brown paper under the fold of each tuck as you press. Touch up the right side of the tucks as necessary.

Special Tucks

CROSS TUCKS are done before the fabric is cut into pattern sections. Measure, baste, and stitch the base rows first. Press carefully before dealing with the crossing tucks. Again measure, baste, and sew with these new tucks at right angles to the earlier set. The earlier rows of tucks should lie with the folds facing downward as you stitch. Press all the tucks in the proper direction. Cut out the garment and staystitch around the seam allowances of the tucked area to keep the tucks in place and lying in the right direction (1).

CORDED TUCKS have a piece of cording enclosed in each fold. Place the wrong side of the fabric over the cord; pin and baste each tuck. Using a zipper foot, stitch close to the cord. This type of tuck is best used as a hem edge, as it tends to be stiffer and heavier than most tucks (2).

SHELL or **SCALLOPED TUCKS** are generally ¼" wide. Baste each tuck. To form the scallop by hand, lightly mark every ½" with small dots along the length of the tucks. Sew tiny running stitches between dots and, at the same time, sew over each tuck at the designated intervals using two overhand stitches. Draw the thread taut before making the next set of running stitches. If you prefer a quicker and more sturdy method, stitch along the tucks by machine. Then hand-sew two tight overhand stitches at the marked ½" intervals, running the needle and thread inside the tuck between scallops (3).

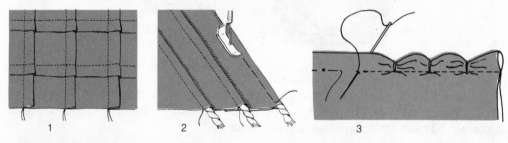

1   2   3

RELEASED TUCKS or **DART TUCKS** may have fullness released at one or both ends of the tuck. Construction techniques will vary greatly according to where the tuck is located on the garment. Regardless of construction, the most significant factor to remember about all released tucks is that the released fullness below the stitched fold should **never** be pressed flat. The stitching line at the point of releasing fullness can be backstitched, or the thread ends tied securely. When the tucks are pressed to one side, stitch across to the fold and backstitch or knot the thread ends.

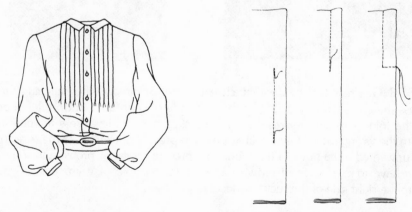

Pleats

Pleats are always in style, adding a special swing to your fashions whether they're crisp, sharp pleats in a tailored skirt or supple, rolled pleats in a soft dress. Pleats are, quite simply, folds of fabric which provide controlled fullness where you want it. The time and patience required to make them perfect will seem well worthwhile as soon as you see yourself in your new pleated creation.

Although there are many variations, basically pleats are of just two types: folds in the fabric made by doubling the fabric over on itself, and folds with an underlay or separate piece stitched to the pleat extensions on the underside of the garment. There are four well known variations, used either singly or in series: **KNIFE** or **SIDE PLEATS** with all folds turned to one side; **BOX PLEATS** with two folds turned away from each other and underfolds meeting at the center; **INVERTED PLEATS**, box pleats in reverse, with folds turned toward each other and meeting; and **ACCORDION PLEATS**, always pressed along the entire length with folds resembling the bellows of an accordion.

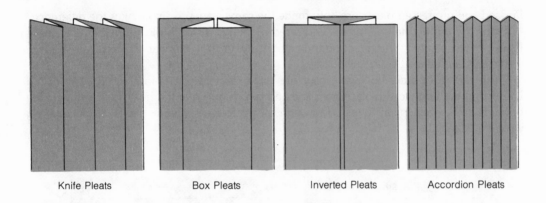

| Knife Pleats | Box Pleats | Inverted Pleats | Accordion Pleats |

Whether the pleats are pressed or hang freely, they look best when executed in fabrics that have good resiliency and drape, such as wool, wool blends, cotton blends, silk, and most synthetics. Some of these can be more crisply pleated than others. If you want a sharp edge on permanent-press fabrics or other fabrics that have been treated with a crease-resistant finish, try edgestitching both the front and back edges of the pleats.

Fabrics and completed garments can be professionally pleated with knife pleats or accordion pleats. To find a firm that does commercial pleating, refer to your yellow pages, check fashion magazines, or inquire at the notions counter of a department store.

The proper pattern size for a pleated skirt should be determined by your hip measurement, because the waistline is easier to adjust. All pleats should be shaped with precision. Complete mastery depends on transferring the pleat markings accurately, basting pleats to keep them in place during preparation, fitting with care, and pressing correctly.

Before you begin, it is important to be aware of and understand the three "line" indications in pleat patterns. The *roll line* used in unpressed pleats is meant to alert you to the fact that the pleats will form soft rolling folds, not creases, while the *foldline* used for pressed pleats indicates a sharply creased fold that can be edgestitched. The *placement line* indicates that the rolled edges or folded edges are brought to this line.

Straight Pleats

It's best to do pleating on a surface large enough to hold the entire pleated garment. For multiple pleats, the hem should be completed before making the pleat folds. Your length can then be adjusted from the waistline after the pleats are formed. For treatment of hems in pleats, see page 342.

Marking

Your pleats can be made either from the right or wrong side, depending upon the designer's intended appearance of the garment and the method that works best for you. Whichever method you choose, be sure to transfer your markings to the right side of the fabric when forming pleats on the right side, or to the wrong side when pleating on the wrong side of the fabric.

Use different colors of thread to key the various "line" indications.

Pleating

Pressed and unpressed pleats are both made the same way; pressing makes the difference.

From the wrong side: Bring the indicated markings for each pleat together and baste. Press or turn pleats in the direction indicated for your type of pleat. Baste pleats in place along waistline edge (1).

From the right side: Following your markings, turn the fabric in along foldline or roll line. Bring the edge to the placement line and pin. Starting at the hem edge and working upward, baste each pleat in place through all thicknesses. Baste pleats in place along waistline edge (2).

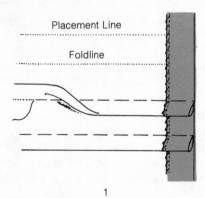

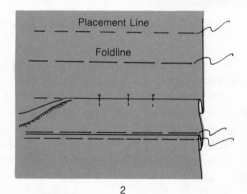

1

2

Fitting

After basting the pleats in place, and before trying on your garment, baste a temporary belt of grosgrain ribbon at the waistline on the inside to ensure that the pleats will be supported and hang properly as you fit your garment.

When fitting you may find that the waistline is too large or too small if you have adjusted your pattern to accommodate your hip measurement. Distributing the change evenly between the pleats, make a hairline adjustment on the placement line of each pleat at the waistline. The tiny dotted lines on each side of the placement line indicate the small change needed to make the difference in fit. On straight pleats it is very important to maintain the straight grainline on the outside fold of each pleat by carefully controlled tapering of the placement line. If you adjust the waistline area, be sure to retain ½″ to 1″ extra for ease.

After pleats and hems are completed, retain the basting only at the upper edge. Baste grosgrain ribbon to the skirt again. Try it on before attaching to the garment or waistband. If your pleats do not fall straight to the hem but tend to open up, raise the skirt at the waist until the hem is even, using a larger waistline seam allowance. However, if the pleats overlap, drop the waist until the hem is even, using a smaller waistline seam allowance.

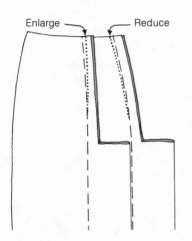
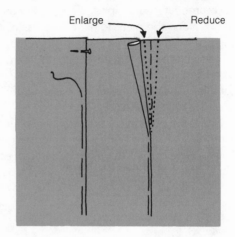

Pressing

For pressed pleats, make certain the pleats are accurately measured, marked, and basted. Pin them to the ironing board at their edge and steam them on both sides just enough to set them. Use a press cloth on the right side to avoid shine. Support overhanging fabric by a chair or table to prevent the weight of the fabric from pulling the pleats out of shape.

If you discover that light pressing creates an unattractive ridge or line on your fabric, insert strips of brown paper under the fold of the pleat before you press. To assure yourself of a sharp, lasting press, iron on both sides of the pleats. Unpressed pleats may require a very slight steaming just to set the shape and fall of the pleat as the designer intended. This can be done most effectively as the garment hangs on your dress form.

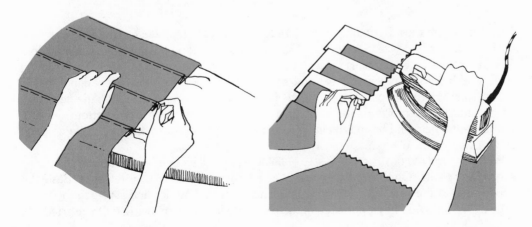

Zipper Applications

A zipper is the easiest and most secure way to close a pleated garment.

For box or inverted pleats, the zipper is usually placed at the left side or center back seam, where the folds of the pleats meet. Use the centered zipper application on page 330.

For a knife-pleated skirt, the placket opening is usually located at the center back or the left side and is the last seam to be stitched. Stitch this last seam, leaving an opening for the placket. (Your last pleat is made *after* this seam is stitched.) Be sure to have the seam at an inside fold so that it will not show and that the underfold of the pleat will be deep enough to accommodate your zipper. To make your last pleat, turn the overlapping section to the inside along the pleat foldline and baste. Clip the seam allowance of the undersection at the placket marking, as shown. Turn the seam allowance of the undersection to the inside ⅝″ and baste (1). Place the edge of the undersection over the zipper tape with the bottom stop even with end of the opening. Have the edge close to the teeth with just enough room for the pull tab to slide easily. Baste carefully, then stitch the undersection to the zipper tape near the zipper teeth (2).

Place the remaining side of the zipper face down on the underlay of the overlapping section. The zipper teeth will extend beyond the seamline. Baste the zipper to the underlay, keeping the rest of the skirt free. Then stitch ⅛″ away from the zipper teeth, continuing across the end of the zipper below the stop; backstitch (3).

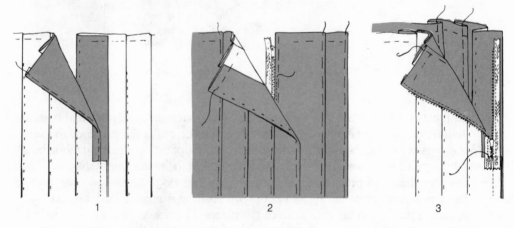

Shaped and Stitched Pleats

These pleats are most frequently used to reduce bulk in the hip area by trimming away the upper portion of the pleat, leaving a ⅝″ seam allowance along the stitched seamline. Join all skirt sections together. Start pleats 6″ to 8″ from the lower edge (to allow for hemming later), and bring the indicated pleat and/or seamlines together following markings; baste. Before stitching, try the garment on to see if adjustments are needed. When the necessary adjustments are completed, stitch along the indicated seamlines from bottom upward. Complete the hem and baste remainder of pleats into place before pressing. Refer to page 342 for ways to handle hems in pleats (1).

With this type of construction, a stay of lining fabric will be needed to support the upper edge of the pleats. On the straight grain, shape a stay to fit into the desired area. Baste the upper edge to the pleated area at the waistline; then turn under and slipstitch the lower edge of the stay over the upper edge of the pleats along the seamlines (2). On inverted box

Seams

Seams are the structural basis of
fashion, the designer's tool for creating a
three-dimensional sculpture from a flat
piece of fabric. Seams can shape a
garment to the figure in a variety of
ways, curving softly for subtle emphasis
or angling abruptly for silhouette
definition. When joining contrasting
fabrics, seams can become the focal
point, creating a linear pattern of their
own. Artful seaming is the claim to fame
of many a successful couturier.

Vertical seams give a strong impression of height, horizontal seams emphasize width. Curved seams create an illusion of softness, repeating the shape of the feminine form. Diagonals—slanting across a bodice or dramatically dividing the entire body—possess both the exactness of straight lines and the softness of curves.

Seams can dramatize any area of a
garment: a shaped waistline or bodice, a
sculptured sleeve or hem. Seams are
the essential ingredient in any design.

Tucks

Tucks create an ornamental design as they control and shape fullness in a garment. Each slender fold of fabric can be stitched inside to a designated point, resulting in a graceful flow of fabric fullness; or tucks can be formed on the outside of the fabric and spaced close together or far apart to create visual emphasis. Tucks are an important component of any designer's repertoire.

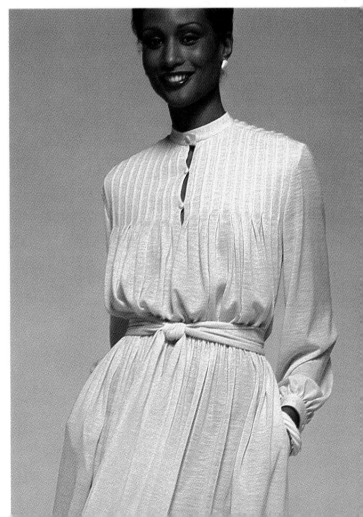

For detail and subtle shaping, tucks
march down the front . . . across the
shoulders . . . around the waist . . .
along a hem. Horizontal, vertical, or
diagonal, the soft touch of tucks is a
perfect accent.

Pleats

Pleats add a special swing to fashion, whether marching around a skirt or centralized in a single box pleat. There's nothing like the snappy swing of pleats to put a lilt in your walk. Rippling gracefully as you dance, they can reflect an upbeat tempo. Whether you choose inverted or box pleats, knife or accordion pleats, they set your fashion stride toward style and comfort.

Crisp and sharp, or soft and rounded—released from a waistline, or accenting a hemline—pleats are versatile and timely, and well worth the effort.

Gathers

Gathers create a touch of softness, rippling around a neckline or curving into a nipped waist. They are the substance of many silhouettes and, if deftly used, terrific camouflage. Gathers love soft knits and fluid crepes; they create enthralling folds, alternately shy and clingy, reflecting the texture of the fabric. Graceful gathers bring suppleness to fashion.

Gathers create softness around a
neckline . . . across the shoulders . . .
above a cuff . . . below a handsome
hipline yoke. The soft swirls of a
gathered skirt or the classic folds of a
draped gown reflect the beauty and
spirit of gathers.

Ruffles

Ruffles lend a touch of romance and elegance, reminiscent of days gone by. Cascading down the front of a blouse, rippling around a neckline or cuff, encircling the hem of a gown— ruffles are graceful, flowing, and expressive. Try them in surprising textures. Use their softness in contrast with the strictness of tailoring, and give them character with a crisp, strong-willed taffeta or a soft, sensuous crepe.

Ruffles always lend a graceful note—framing your face, encircling a wrist, or peeking out from a more hidden spot. However you use ruffles, let your fabric and your mood inspire this romantic look.

pleats, a self-stay can be formed by trimming away only half of the top of the pleat, leaving a seam allowance of ⅝″. The remaining pleat fabric can then be basted across the upper edge for support (3).

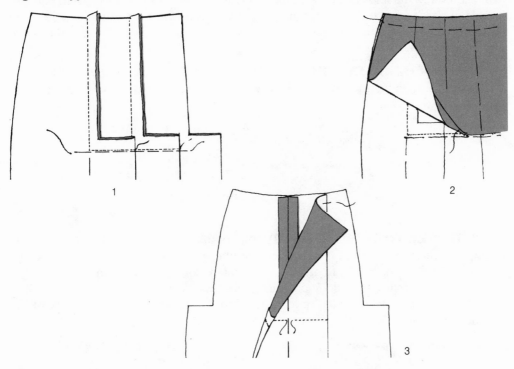

Pleats with a Separate Underlay

These pleats are made from the inside and are often used singly. Bring the coordinating markings together and baste. Open out the pleat extensions. Stitch the pleat underlay to the pleat extensions and baste in place across the upper edge.

Press the seam allowances flat, not open. Check the fit for necessary adjustments. Then join all seams and prepare your hem. For ways to handle hems on pleats, see page 342.

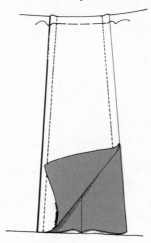

Edgestitching and Topstitching

When you are certain that your pleats fit and hang properly, are well pressed, and are hemmed evenly, the folds can be edgestitched to keep creases sharp. The pleats can also be held in place by topstitching through all thicknesses from the hip area to the waist. Both edgestitching and topstitching should be done before the skirt is permanently attached to the garment or waistband.

EDGESTITCHING STRAIGHT PLEATS: Stitch close to the outside creased edge of each pleat from the hem up toward the waistline. You may also want to stitch the inside folds on the wrong side.

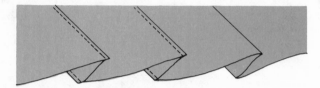

TOPSTITCHING STRAIGHT PLEATS: Always stitch on the right side of the garment, through all thicknesses, from the hip area to the waist. Mark each pleat where the topstitching will begin. For knife or side pleats, stitch along the fold to the waist (1). For inverted pleats, topstitching is done on both sides of the pleat. Make 2 or 3 stitches across the pleat, pivot, and stitch along the fold to the waist. Repeat on other side of pleat (2). Pull thread ends to inside and tie.

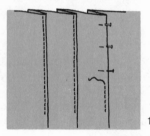

1

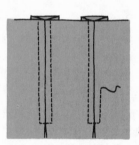

2

EDGESTITCHING AND TOPSTITCHING SHAPED PLEATS: Release the stitching for about 1″ at the hipline of each pleat. Edgestitch the creased edge of each pleat on the outside from the hem to the hipline. Connecting stitches, topstitch along the seam through all thicknesses from the hipline to the waistline. Then pull the thread ends to the inside and tie.

Gathering and Shirring

Softness and suppleness will always be associated with the graceful fullness produced by gathering and shirring. Gathers are small, soft folds made by drawing fabric up on a line of hand- or machine-stitching. Shirring is formed by numerous rows of gathers and is both decorative and functional. It can be used to achieve varied surface effects such as smocking and may be used at waistline, yokes, and sleeves.

Use an extrastrength thread in the bobbin to make it easier to pull up gathers without breaking the threads. (The bobbin thread can be pulled more easily by loosening the upper tension.) In order to have small, even folds when stitching for gathering and shirring, do not use a longer stitch than necessary. First, try approximately 8 stitches per inch. If the fabric still does not gather easily, lengthen the stitch accordingly. Normally, thick and closely woven fabrics need longer stitches than lightweight and sheer fabrics.

Gathering

With the right side of the fabric up, stitch along the seamline and again ¼″ away in the seam allowance. To form the gathers, pin the edge to be gathered to the corresponding edge at notches, centers, and all remaining markings. Draw up the bobbin threads at one end until almost half of the gathered edge fits the adjoining straight edge. Fasten gathers by winding threads around a pin in a figure-eight fashion. Draw up the remaining half and again fasten the threads. Adjust gathers evenly between pins; then stitch on the seamline with the gathered side up. Press the seam, taking care not to flatten the gathers, and then lightly press in the desired direction.

When you are using a gathering stitch on heavy, bulky fabrics, try to avoid stitching across your seam allowances. When applying your gathering stitch, stitch up to the seamline and stop; then begin on the other side of the seamline (1).

If you have a zigzag machine, you may gather by using a large zigzag stitch over fine strong cording (see page 395). Gathering by hand is done with small, even running stitches, the same length on both sides of the fabric. Sew at least two rows. For hand-gathering it is best to work on an individual fabric piece *before* the pieces are joined to each other.

STAYING GATHERS: Seam binding or twill tape can be used as a stay to reinforce and finish off a gathered seam. Place seam binding or tape with one edge right next to the seam line. Stitch along lower edge through all thicknesses.

Trim seam allowances even with top edge of stay. If fabric has a tendency to fray, zigzag along top edge of stay and seam allowances (2).

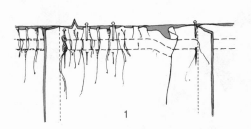

1

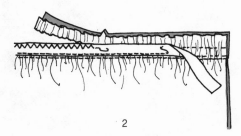

2

Shirring

Shirring is formed by several rows of gathering, requiring **absolute accuracy** for best results. Make as many rows as you desire, using only soft or very lightweight fabric that has been steam-pressed to eliminate any stiffness of fabric and to soften the finish. Gather on the bias or crosswise grain for the most satisfying effect. Never press directly on the shirred area, but work the point of the iron into the area below the shirring. When using more than two rows of shirring, secure each row separately with a knot and stitch over knots. If rows of stitching are not further secured by a seam, fold fabric on the wrong side and stitch narrow pin tucks over knotted ends to hold them securely.

Stay shirring by placing a strip of self-fabric over the wrong side of the shirred area; turn in the raw edges of the strip and slipstitch it in place.

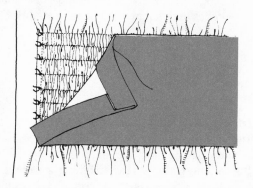

ELASTICIZED SHIRRING is used to snug fabric into place comfortably and prettily. It consists of multiple rows of flexible gathering stitches. Wind elastic thread on the bobbin by hand, stretching it slightly and winding it firmly until the bobbin is almost full. Then set your machine for a long stitch (about 7 stitches per inch) and use a scrap of your garment fabric to test the tension, which might have to be loosened. Mark the location of the shirring with thread tracing or tailor's chalk clearly visible on the right side of your fabric. Now stitch from the right side, holding the fabric taut as you stitch. Continue to stretch the elasticized fabric in each of the preceding rows as you sew so that the shirring will be evenly distributed. You may use the previously stitched row as a guide along with your markings to keep the lines straight. Be sure to knot all the thread ends and, in addition, stitch over the knots in a seam or encase them in a narrow pin tuck, as explained above.

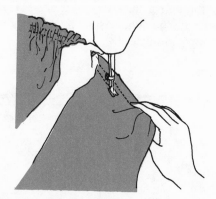

Ruffles

Whether they are of eyelet, organdy, or self-fabric, gathered or circular, ruffles always lend a graceful touch. Let them frame your face, border your hem, or become the perfect ending to a graceful sleeve. The effect can be soft or pert; the mood, sophisticated elegance or spring-like freshness. However you choose to use the ruffle, let your fabric and your mood inspire this softer, more romantic look in fashion.

If you do not have a pattern piece for your ruffle or if you want to estimate its fullness, remember that you will need a fabric strip three times the length of the edge to which it will be joined for a very full ruffle; a fabric strip twice the finished edge length for minimum fullness. Wide ruffles should have more fullness than narrow ones to keep them from looking skimpy. The sheerer your fabric is, the fuller the ruffle should be. You should realize that inward corners will require less fullness and outward corners more fullness than the rest of the ruffle. Always keep in mind the proportions of the ruffle and the garment so that neither overwhelms the other. There are two types of ruffles: the **straight ruffle,** whose fullness is created by gathering a rectangular strip of fabric; and the **circular ruffle,** whose fullness is created when the inner curve of the circle is straightened.

Straight Ruffle

A straight ruffle is gathered and constructed from a continuous strip of material. It can be cut either on the straight grain or on the bias. If the ruffle must be seamed, the seam should be made on the straight grain. Bias ruffles applied to a small area, such as a sleeve, are the exception—in this case, make the seam of the ruffle on the bias to match the seam of the garment.

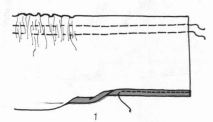
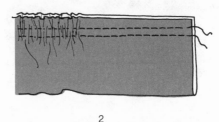

1   2

A straight ruffle may be constructed of a single layer of fabric with a narrow hem at the lower edge (1). Or the ruffle may be self-faced by folding the fabric in half lengthwise with wrong sides together (2). For gathering a ruffle, always stitch two rows of long machine stitches—one on the seamline and the other ¼" away in the seam allowance. The two rows will help to distribute the fullness evenly and will protect each other, should one break during the ruffling process. Use an extrastrength thread in the bobbin to reduce the chance of the thread breaking under tension.

Draw the gathers to the proper length. When adjusting gathers over a short distance, secure both threads at one end and gather from the opposite end. For longer distances, begin gathering from one end, secure the threads, and then gather from the other end. For very long ruffles, gather it in quarters. After you have attached the ruffle, remove any gathering stitches that might show.

Pin the ruffle to the garment edge, matching seamlines. Adjust the gathers until they are evenly distributed and baste in place (3). To make machine stitching and turning easier, press the basted seam allowances flat, holding the tip of your iron parallel to the seam, not on the ruffles (4). With ruffle up, stitch along seamline. Finish the application with a bias facing as directed on page 232.

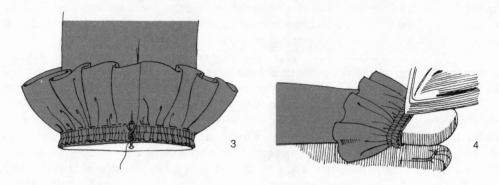

3   4

To sew a ruffle into a seam or along a faced edge, pin the ruffle to the right side of garment. Check to see if the gathers are distributed evenly and the ruffle will be facing the desired direction after the seam is completed. With ruffle side up, stitch a scant ⅛'' within seam allowance. When rounding a corner, be sure to provide extra fabric at the corner (5). Pin to second garment section so that the ruffle is between the right sides of the fabric. Stitch just beside the first row of stitching so that no stitches will show on the right side of the garment or ruffle (6).

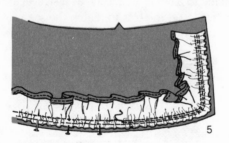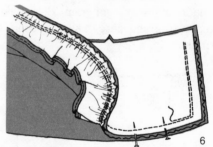

5   6

Double Ruffle: A variation of the straight ruffle, the double ruffle has two free edges and is gathered in the center or off-center for a more asymmetrical look. When gathered off-center it is also known as a ruffle with a heading. Both types can be easily applied by simply stitching them on to the garment rather than having to sew them in during construction.

Make a narrow hem along the two free edges. Or the fabric can be doubled for a self-facing, having the raw edges meet directly under the gathering line. If the ends will be left hanging free, finish with a narrow hem. Or seam and trim ends that are to be joined.

Stitch two lines of long machine stitches ¼'' apart, one on either side of the gathering line.

To apply the ruffle to a finished edge, pin it wrong side down on the right side of the garment. Baste, adjusting the gathers. Topstitch twice, stitching close to both rows of gathering stitches, as shown on next page (7).

To apply the ruffle to a raw edge, trim garment seam allowances to ¼″. Pin wrong sides together with the ruffle side up. The bottom row of gathering stitches should be even with the seamline of the garment. Baste, adjusting the gathers and stitch close to the bottom of gathers.

Press the garment away from the ruffle. Baste the ruffle to the right side of the garment, enclosing the raw edge; stitch close to the top row of gathers. Remove basting (8).

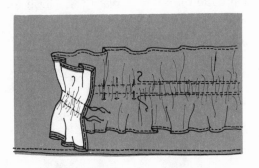

7

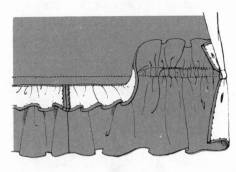

8

Circular Ruffle

A circular ruffle can be added to any edge—cuffs, V-neckline, rounded neckline—wherever you wish. It is cut from several circles that are first slashed and then joined along the straight grain. This method produces a maximum amount of fullness. Exert great caution when laying out, pinning, and cutting the ruffle sections. You will find that exact location and maintenance of the grainline is most important if the circular ruffle is to drape correctly.

You may staystitch each ruffle section ⅛″ from the inner seamline in the seam allowance before joining (1).

The edge of a circular ruffle may be faced with self-fabric or it may have a narrow hemmed edge. Should a narrow hem be required, join the circles and complete the hem before basting the ruffle to its proper edge. If your ruffle has a facing of corresponding circles, stitch the seamed facing and ruffle sections together along the outer edges. Trim seam allowance to ¼″ (2). Turn the ruffle and press. Baste the raw edges of the ruffle and facing together for handling ease.

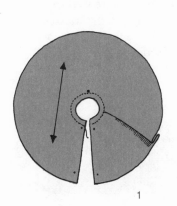

1

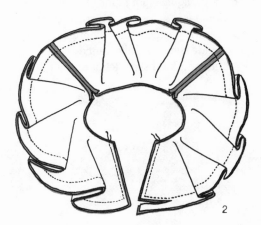

2

If you are applying ruffles to a neckline or any other curved edge, first stay the seamline so that its shape will not be distorted by the weight of the ruffle. Whether the ruffle is cut single or is faced, the inner circle should be staystitched and then clipped where necessary as you pin the ruffle to the garment in order to fit smoothly on the seamline. As a rule, deep curves require a clip at almost every ½″ up to the line of staystitching; shallow curves will, of course, require fewer clips. If the ruffle does not lie flat, do not cut through the staystitching; merely clip more frequently. Then baste the ruffle in place (3). Finish the ruffle application with a shaped facing, as directed below (4).

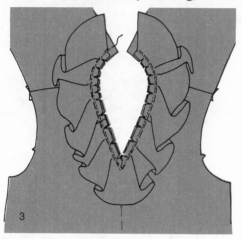

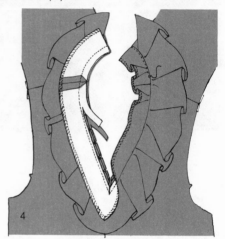

Finishing Ruffles

SHAPED FACING: For ruffles contained by a facing, pin the facing to the garment edge over your ruffle. The ruffle is now sandwiched between the two layers, right sides together. Stitch along the seamline. Trim, grade, and clip the seam allowance so that the facing will lie flat when turned. Turn the facing to expose the finished ruffle. Press, being careful not to press over the ruffle. Understitch the facing by hand through all thicknesses to prevent it from rolling to the outside. If you are using a zipper, insert your zipper and slipstitch the facing along the zipper tape. Blindstitch the facing to the garment or underlining.

BIAS FACING: For a fine finish on ruffles at the hemline, cut a bias strip of your fashion fabric, or a firm, lightweight fabric, 1¼″ wide and ½″ longer than the length of the seam to be faced. Stitch a ¼″ seam at the short ends of the strip. With the raw edges even, pin the bias strip over the basted ruffle. Then stitch a ⅝″ seam through all thicknesses, trim, and if necessary, grade the seam allowances (1). Turn the bias to the inside and press. Turn the raw edge under ¼″ and slipstitch it to the garment or underlining (2).

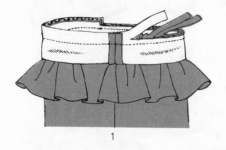

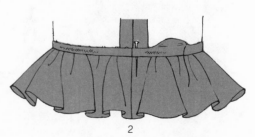

Mitering

Like the use of wine in cooking, mitering is a subtle art. When successful, it merely enhances the total effect; it is noticeable only when incorrect. Mitering is a neat and easy means of eliminating bulk at corners. Since your goal is to achieve a flat, neat-looking miter, you must concentrate on trimming at just the right moment in your mitering plan. Also remember that most miters involve folds, either at right angles or 45° angles to the seam or strip being mitered. The method you use to miter depends on many factors—whether you are working with garment areas, binding, or continuous strips of trim, and whether the miter is made as you attach the trim or before application.

Continuous Strips

If your band or trim has seam allowances, press them to the inside before you begin mitering. To miter the band before it is applied, pin the band to the garment for an accurate measurement of where the miter should be made. Measure to the outermost point where the corner will be formed, and mark with a pin.

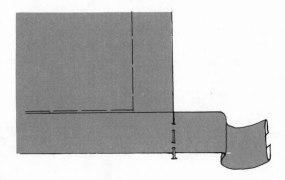

Remove band and fold it with right sides together at marked point (1). Turn the fold diagonally to meet the turned-back edges of band, as shown, and press (2). Open the diagonal fold and stitch along the pressed crease. Since it is important that the knots do not show once the miter is finished, pull the thread ends to one side of the band and knot. Trim to ⅛" and press the seam open (3). Then attach the strip (4).

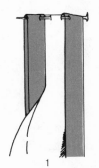

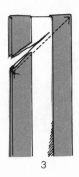

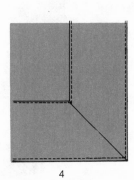

1　　　　2　　　　3　　　　4

To miter while you are attaching the trim, use trim with a finished edge such as ribbon or braid. Pin the trim in position, then edgestitch or hand-sew the inner edge (5). Fold the band back on itself, then diagonally to the side, making a right angle; press.

Again fold the band back on itself and stitch on the diagonal crease—through the band and garment. Since it is important that the knots be invisible once the miter is finished, pull the thread ends to one side of the band, as shown, and knot (6). If trim is bulky, you may trim the small corner close to the stitching. Press flat from the right side, miter remaining corners, and edgestitch or hand-sew outer edge in a continuous motion (7).

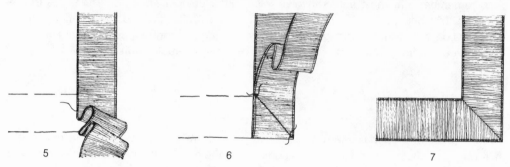

5   6   7

Square Corners

Pockets, appliqués, or any other applied areas requiring square corners, need to be mitered so the excess fullness can be easily trimmed away. Pressing is the key feature. Turn all seam allowances to inside and press (1). At the corners, open the seam allowances and turn them to the inside diagonally across the point, as shown, and press. Trim corner to $\frac{3}{8}''$ from the pressed diagonal crease (2). Slipstitch to fasten miter (3).

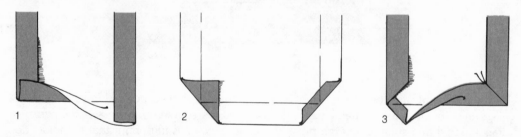

1   2   3

For a quick sturdier method, make a diagonal fold in the turned-back seam allowances at the corners and press. Stitch along the pressed diagonal crease (4). Trim the seam to $\frac{3}{8}''$ or less for bulkier fabrics, as shown. Press diagonal seam open (5), then turn the corners to the inside (6). Press.

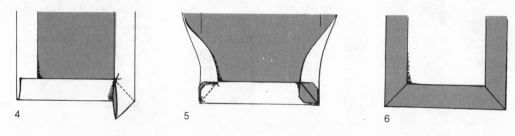

4   5   6

5

Construction Techniques

(continued on next page)

Facings
and Other
Edge Finishes

The edge of a garment can be finished in a variety of ways—either inconspicuously with a facing that is concealed on the inside, or accented with cording, piping, binding, banding, or a casing. Whatever finish you choose, apply it carefully and smoothly to achieve that custom-made look. Never take shortcuts or you may sacrifice the appearance of the entire garment, no matter how much loving attention you have given to other details.

Facings

A well-applied facing does much for the look and comfort of your new garment. The purpose of a facing is to neatly finish and conceal a raw edge by turning it to the wrong side of your garment. Your facing will always perform this task beautifully if you consistently strive for a smooth, flat appearance.

Although the shape and actual construction of facings vary stylistically, they fall into three basic categories—a **shaped facing,** an **extended facing**, or a **bias facing**. Let your fabric and the edge to be faced determine the most suitable method.

There are some construction procedures that can be used on all types of facings to produce the best results, as well as to simplify the work at hand. The garment edge is usually stabilized or reinforced in some manner, either by small stitches, interfacing, or ribbon seam binding. Except for the bias facing, one edge of most facings must be finished since it will be exposed on the inside of the garment. A sturdy way of finishing many facings is to stitch ¼″ from the unnotched edge, trim to ⅛″ and overcast; or zigzag.

For a more attractively finished appearance with added fashion interest, you may try enclosing the edges with bias binding, stretch lace, or other lightweight, flexible trims. When the facing is attached, press the seam or foldlines carefully before you turn and tack the facings to the inside of the garment. To prevent any shaped facing or variation of it, such as the combination facing, from rolling to the outside, open out the facing and understitch it to the seam allowances. If the facing edge is at a visible area, you can *favor* the garment slightly along the seamline so that the facing does not show. You should, however, use caution or you may destroy the clean line of the edge.

Always tack the facing to the inside of the garment to keep it in place. Blindstitch the facing to the underlining only, or if the garment is not underlined, sew it to the inner seam allowances. Tack loosely; many short, tight stitches will give your garment a strained or puckered appearance. When making adjustments and alterations on your garment, don't forget the facings! They must be changed to conform to the new lines of the garment.

Shaped Facing

A shaped or fitted facing is the most commonly selected method used to finish necklines and sleeveless armholes. It is a separate piece provided with your pattern and cut to match the shape of the area to which it will be applied.

Prepare the facing by stitching, trimming, and pressing the seams. The outer edge of the facing must be finished since it will be exposed on the inside of the garment. Stitch ¼" from the unnotched edge, trim to ⅛", and overcast (1); or zigzag stitch the raw edges.

Pin and baste the facing to the garment, matching the seams and markings. Then, with the facing side up, stitch the facing to the garment. Trim, grade, and clip the seam allowances. Press the seam allowances toward the facing (2).

To keep the facing from rolling to the outside, open out the facing and understitch it to the seam allowances, pulling it taut as you stitch. Understitch by hand on custom clothes, using small backstitches close to the seam through the seam allowances and facing. On casual clothes this can be accomplished by machine stitching. Turn the facing to the inside and press. Tack the facing to the inner seams, or blindstitch the free edge to the under-lining (3).

For a neckline facing with a zipper opening, insert the zipper first. Turn the facing ends under to clear the zipper teeth and slipstitch the ends in place. Tack the facing at the shoulder seams or blindstitch facing edge to underlining. Fasten with a hook and eye at top of placket (4).

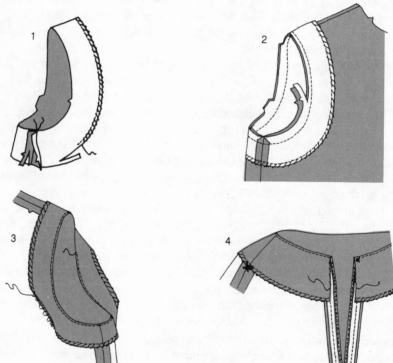

When working with soft or loosely woven fabrics that tend to stretch, stabilize the garment edge with interfacing or ribbon seam binding. Attach either reinforcement to the wrong side of the garment, not to the facing which must be able to mold to the garment edge. Necklines that are cut on the bias must also be reinforced to prevent stretching of the curved or bias edge.

SEAM BINDING: Center the ribbon seam binding over the seamline on the inside of your garment, fold out any fullness at points or corners and baste in place (1).

Pin and baste the facing to the garment edge. Stitch, pivoting at any points or corners. For sharp corners such as those on a V-neckline or a square armhole, reinforce with small stitches (15–20 stitches per inch) on the seamline for an inch on either side of the point. Grade and clip the seam allowances. Press the seam toward the facing and understitch (2). Turn the facing to the inside and press.

1

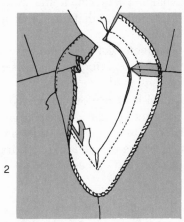

2

INTERFACING: If your pattern doesn't include an interfacing tissue, cut the interfacing the same as the facing and trim ⅜″ from the inner edges. Pin the corresponding interfacing sections to the front and back garment pieces and stitch them in place (1). Stitch the garment sections together and press open.

For a slashed neckline, pin and baste the facing to the garment along the stitching lines of the opening and neck edge. Stitch the opening to within 2″ of the point. Then change to smaller stitches (15–20 per inch) for 2″ on either side of the point and take one stitch across the point. Stitch remainder of opening and neck edge, pivoting at corners. Slash opening to machine stitching, being careful not to cut through it. Trim opening edges if necessary for firmly woven or heavy fabrics. Trim, grade, and clip the neck seam so that the garment seam allowance is left widest (2). Complete facing as above.

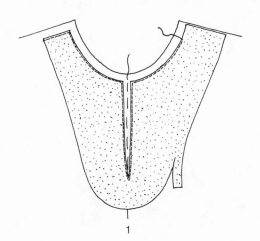

1

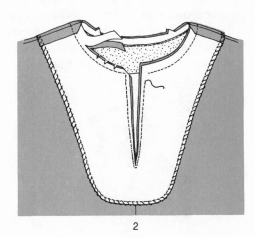

2

Combination Facings

This is a variation of the shaped facing in which the neckline and armhole facings are cut and applied as one piece. It is often used on garments with narrow shoulder seams, as a dress with cutaway armholes. You will find it quite simple to apply if you remember one rule; do not sew the shoulder seams of either the garment or the facing until after the facing is stitched to the garment.

Prior to pinning the facing to the garment, pin a minute tuck in both garment shoulders, as shown. This ensures that the seams and facing will not show on the right side once the facing is turned (1).

Join the garment sections at the side seams, leaving the shoulder seams open, and press. Join the facing sections together in the same manner and press. Then, finish the unnotched facing edge as desired.

You may wish to reinforce a curved neckline with ribbon seam binding, or a square neckline with small stitches at the corners.

Pin the facing to the garment, right sides together. Since the raw edges will not be even, follow the seamline of the facing. Stitch to within ⅝″ from shoulder edges and backstitch. Grade; clip seam allowances (2).

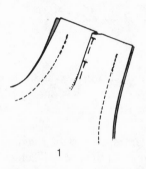

1

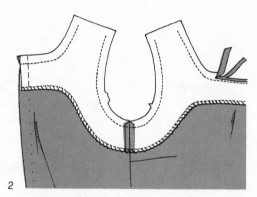

2

Release the tuck in the garment shoulders. Turn the facing to the inside and press. To prevent the facing from rolling to the outside, understitch it to the seam allowances close to the seam. Fold the facing seam allowances back and stitch the garment shoulder seams, carefully keeping the facing free (3).

Do not tie threads at the seam edge. Bring both threads to one side and tie so the knots will not show when the facing is completed.

Trim and press open the garment seams. Turn in the facing edges and slipstitch them together over the garment seam (4). On bulky fabric you may wish to trim the facing seam allowance to ¼″ before turning them in.

3

4

Extended Facing

An extended facing is cut in one piece with the garment, and folded to the inside. It is used for finishing edges cut on straight grain which can simply be extended to create a fold at the edge rather than a seam.

Because extended facing edges are usually overlapped, be sure to transfer position lines with thread tracing. Interface for reinforcement, especially if a buttonhole closing is intended. Your pattern will usually include a tissue for the interfacing.

If your pattern doesn't include an interfacing piece, cut the interfacing from the facing portion of the garment pattern, plus a ⅝" extension at the foldline for a softly rolled edge. Trim ⅜" from the edge opposite the foldline. Attach the interfacing to the garment, using long running stitches to hold the interfacing along the foldline (1). For a garment that will be topstitched, trim the interfacing at the foldline and catchstitch the edge in place.

If additional facing sections are to be joined to the extended facing, such as the back neck facing, attach these sections before stitching the facing to the garment.

Turn facing to the right side along the foldline of the garment. Pin and baste the facing to the garment along the neck seamline. Stitch the seam; trim, grade, and clip the seam allowances (2). Turn the facing to the inside and press. Understitch close to the neckline seam through the facing and the seam allowances just as you would a shaped facing. Finish the raw edge and tack the facing in place at the shoulder seam (3).

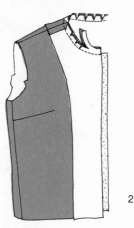

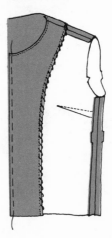

Bias Facing

Ease of handling and versatility make a bias facing a suitable replacement for your regular shaped facing. It is particularly useful when you do not want to use your garment fabric (if it is scratchy or bulky) or where a wide facing may be objectionable (as in sheers).

Cut a bias strip from your lining or underlining fabric four times the desired width plus ¼″ to ⅜″ to allow for shaping (or use double-fold bias tape with folds pressed open) and the length of the garment edge plus 2″ to allow for finishing the ends.

Fold the strip in half lengthwise. Press the strip lightly, steaming and stretching it into curves corresponding to those of the garment edge. As the bias takes shape, its width will become distorted. Equalize the width of the bias facing by measuring from the folded edge the desired facing width plus a ¼″ seam allowance, marking the strip as you work. Trim away excess fabric along markings.

Your closure should be completed before you apply your bias facing. If you have a zipper, trim the zipper tape away below the seamline. Trim the garment seam allowance to ¼″. With raw edges even, place the folded strip on the right side of the garment with 1″ extending beyond the closing edges. Pin, baste, and stitch directionally with grain continuing to the ends of the bias strip (1).

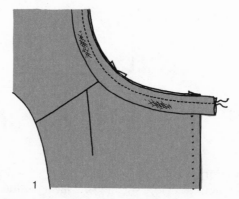

Clip the seam allowances, and trim the two extending bias ends to ¼″. Turn the bias strip to the inside, *favoring* the garment edge slightly so that the binding is inconspicuous. Turn the bias ends in (2). Pin the bias strip in position and slipstitch the folded edge to the underlining (3). Finally, fasten the closing edges with a hook and eye.

If the facing ends meet, as on an armhole, fold in the ends ¼″. Trim the excess length and slipstitch free ends together to finish.

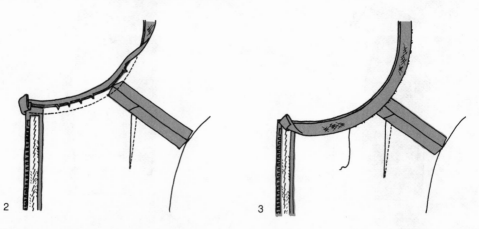

Cording and Piping

This finish can be added to any edge—a neckline, armhole, or hemline—before the facing is applied. The distinction between piping and cording refers to the size of the filler used: piping is thin; cording is thick. First cut a bias strip the size of the filler plus ¼'' to ⅜'' and two ⅝'' seam allowances. Allow at least ⅝'' for finishing the ends. Bring the bias strip around the filler, matching the raw edges. With your zipper foot and using 8–10 stitches per inch, stitch close to, but not on, the filler.

Baste the corded or piped strip to the right side of the garment, matching seamlines.

To finish ends at a closing, pull the bias back, removing stitches for 1½'', exposing the filler. Cut the filler off just inside the end of the opening, leaving the empty bias strip. Fold in the bias ends (1). Slipstitch the ends and restitch the bias, enclosing the filler. Using a zipper foot, apply a shaped facing (2). For thick cording, apply snaps to the ends (3). Narrow cording or piping requires a regular hook and eye closure on the garment.

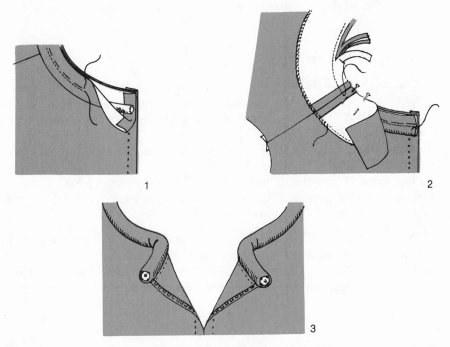

On an edge without a closing, place the joining at an inconspicuous location. For narrow piping, pull the bias back, removing a few stitches from the bias so you can cut the filler off where the ends cross. Overlap the two empty bias ends, easing the ends of the bias slightly toward the seam (4). For thick cording, do not enclose the filler with bias until you have stitched one edge of the bias to the garment and pieced it. Then, using the proper length of filler for the edge, enclose it in the bias, using a zipper foot (5). Apply a facing over all piping or cording with a zipper foot.

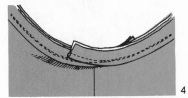 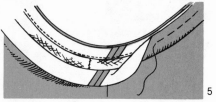

Bindings

The versatile bias binding was designed to enclose raw edges, thus providing a finish that both conceals and strengthens them. A binding can be beautiful as decorative trim around closure edges—whether you use self-fabric or a contrasting fabric. It can be helpful around a neckline or armhole when used in place of facings. One of the great satisfactions of sewing is a bias binding that turns smoothly and evenly over an edge with nary a twist, a pull, or a ripple to mar its flat surface. To achieve a perfect binding, cut strips of fabric evenly on the true bias, join them on the grain, and press and shape them before application.

You can also purchase bias strips ready-made in a variety of colors and a choice of several widths. Whether single- or double-fold, the edges are usually pressed under for your convenience. Depending upon your needs, the folds can be pressed open and the full width of the bias made available. The techniques used for applying or piecing the commercial bias strips are the same as those suggested for bias-cut strips you have made yourself.

Cutting Bias Strips

The ideal bias strip is cut from one piece of fabric long enough to fit the desired area. However, this is not always the most economical usage of the fabric, so piecing becomes a necessity. This can be done in one of two ways—by continuous pieced strips or by individual pieced strips.

For either method, take a rectangular piece of fabric cut on the straight grain. Fold it diagonally at one end, as shown, to find the true bias. Using the bias fold as a guide, mark fabric with parallel lines the desired width of the bias strips, marking as many strips as needed, allowing for ¼″ seams. Cut away the triangular ends. Mark a ¼″ seamline on the lengthwise grain along each edge as shown (1).

CONTINUOUS PIECED STRIPS: Continuous pieced strips are easy to make. On the marked piece of fabric, join the shorter ends, right sides together, with one strip width extending beyond the edge at each side. Stitch in a ¼″ seam and press it open (2). Begin cutting on the marked line at one end and continue in circular fashion (3).

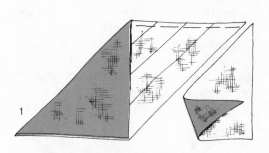

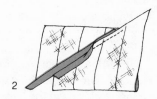

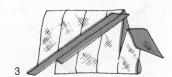

INDIVIDUAL PIECED STRIPS: Individually pieced strips are more time consuming. Cut along the markings for the bias strips. The short ends, previously cut on the grain, will appear diagonal. Mark a seamline ¼″ from each end. With right sides of the strip together, match the seamlines (not the cut edges), pin, and stitch. Press the seam open.

Preshaping the Binding

To preshape the strip and to take out the extra slack, the bias should first be pressed, steaming and stretching it gently (1). You will then have a slightly narrower, taut strip to work with, eliminating the problem of a wobbling seamline. Fold the strip in half lengthwise, wrong sides together, and press again lightly (2). For single binding: open, fold cut edges toward the center, and press lightly (3). Lastly, shape the tape into curves that correspond to those on the garment by positioning it on your pattern piece and steam pressing (4). Since one folded edge of the finished binding will be even with the seamline of the garment, you must always trim the seam allowance from the edge to be bound. When applying the bias strips to the garment, try to place the piecing seamlines at inconspicuous locations wherever possible. Also, leave 2″ extra on the bias strip free at the beginning of any application for finishing. (Note: Commercial binding can be shaped, but the slack has already been removed by the manufacturer.)

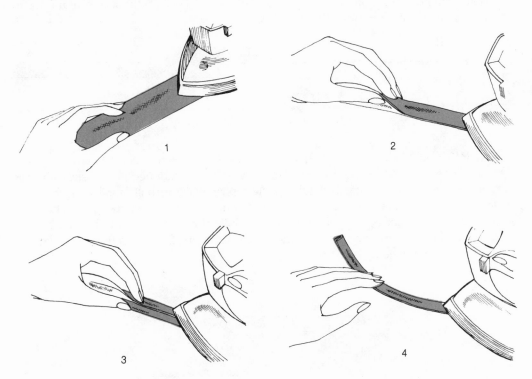

Applying the Binding

SINGLE BINDING: Trim the seam allowance from the garment edges to be bound. Cut bias strips four times the desired finished width plus ¼'' to ⅜'', depending on your fabric. This will give you ample width for stretching and turning. Preshape your bias strip with a steam iron, as shown earlier, to match the curves of the garment edge. Open out the bias strip and, with right sides together and the raw edge of the strip even with the raw edge of the garment, pin it to the garment. Baste the strip at a distance from the edge slightly less than the width of the finished binding. Stitch next to but not on the basting, so that the basting threads can be easily removed (1). Turn the bias over the seam allowance. Pin and slipstitch over the seamline (2).

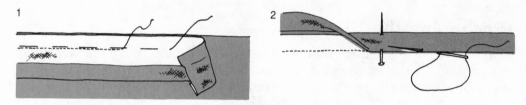

DOUBLE BINDING or **FRENCH BINDING:** This method makes an attractive finish for sheers. Trim the garment seam allowances. Cut bias strips six times the desired finished width plus ¼'' to ⅜'' to allow for stretching and turning. Fold the strip in half lengthwise with wrong sides together, and press lightly. Preshape the bias to match the garment edge. Trim raw edges so entire strip can be folded equally. Divide it into equal thirds and press again. Open out the folded edge of the strip. With raw edges of strip and garment even, pin the strip to the right side. Baste the strip at a distance from the edge slightly less than the width of the finished binding; stitch next to the basting (1). Turn the strip over the seam allowances and slipstitch in place (2).

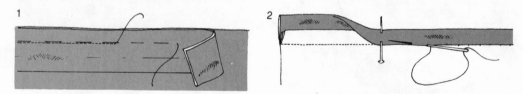

MACHINE-APPLIED BINDING: This is a speedy, one-step method in which success depends upon careful pressing. Preshape the bias strip as mentioned previously, with one very notable exception. Instead of folding the tape equally in half lengthwise, fold the bottom half slightly wider than the top half, as shown. This overlap on the bottom half will ensure its being caught by the machine stitching. With the wider edge on the wrong side, encase the trimmed garment edge with the folded bias strip. Edgestitch through all layers, as shown, and your binding is completed.

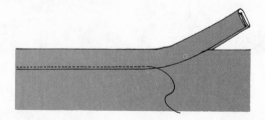

Special Techniques

When bias bindings are used as trim, they will often have to be applied around corners, joined together, or ended at a seam or opening.

OUTWARD CORNERS: Open out one prefolded edge of your bias strip; then pin or baste it in place as for single or double binding. Stitch from one end to the corner and backstitch for reinforcement (1). Fold the strip diagonally, as shown, to bring it around the corner. Pin or baste, then stitch the adjoining edge through the corner from one end to the other end (2). Fold to form a miter at the corner on the right side and turn the bias over the seam (3). To finish the wrong side, form a miter (with the fold of the miter in the opposite direction from the one formed on the right side, so that the bulk of the miter will be evenly distributed). Turn, pin, and slipstitch the binding over the seamline, fastening the miter at the corner, if desired (4).

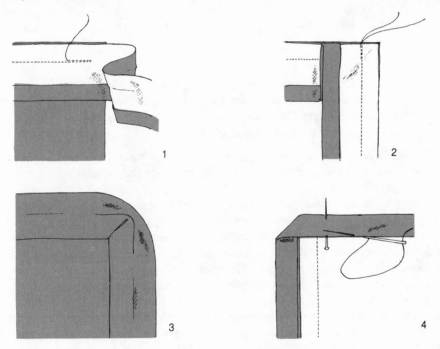

INWARD CORNERS: Reinforce the corner along your planned seamline, as instructed on page 206 (1). Open out one prefolded edge of your bias strip; then pin and baste it to the garment, pulling the corners so the binding remains straight. Stitch from the wrong side of the garment, keeping the binding straight (2).

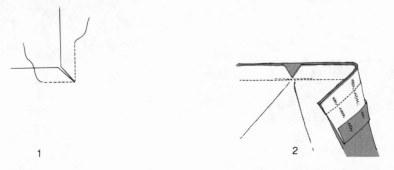

Form a miter on the right side (3). Pull the fold of the miter to the wrong side through the clip, and form a miter on the wrong side in the reverse direction from the one on the right side (4). Turn, pin, and slipstitch the binding over the seamline, fastening the fold of the miter at the corner, if desired (5).

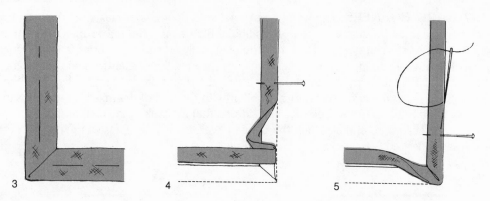

When making machine-applied binding for an outward or inward corner, pin and baste the bias strip to the edge as for single or double binding. Form a miter at the corner, as above. For machine-stitching, follow the directions for machine-applied binding, page 246, remembering to pivot at the corner. If desired, fasten the fold of the miter with slipstitches.

JOININGS: When the binding is applied to a long or continuous edge, such as a front closure or hem, a joining is often required. Try to locate the joining at an inconspicuous place.

A binding applied as described in single or double binding is joined by stopping your stitching slightly before reaching the area of the joining. Open out the strip and fold the garment so the strip ends are at right angles as they are for piecing, page 245. Stitch the ends close to the garment, but without catching the garment in the stitching. Trim the seam allowances to ¼″ (1) and press open. Complete stitching the strip to the garment across the joining. Now you may finish by slipstitching the binding over the seam.

To lap a machine-applied binding, edgestitch to within 2″ of the starting point, leaving extra binding on both ends. Fold one end to the inside on straight grain and trim to ¼″. Trim the other end as shown, also on the straight grain. Pin or baste and continue stitching across the joining. Slipstitch the joining if desired (2).

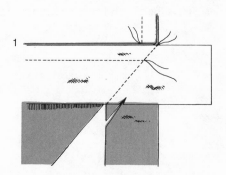

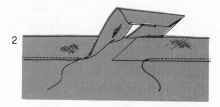

ENDINGS: Binding an edge which ends at a seam or opening requires a special finishing technique. In any of the following cases, the facings should be completed and the seam allowances turned under or the zipper inserted before the binding is applied.

To finish a single or double binding, pin, baste, and stitch the binding to the garment through all layers and to the ends of the bias, which extend about 1″ past the garment opening edge on both ends (1). Trim the bias ends to ¼″ beyond the garment edge. Then trim the garment seam allowance on a diagonal at the corner and fold the extending bias ends back. Turn the strip over the seam allowance, matching the folded edge with the line of machine stitching. Slipstitch the open ends; then pin and slipstitch the folded edge to the garment (2).

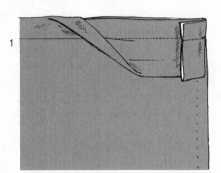

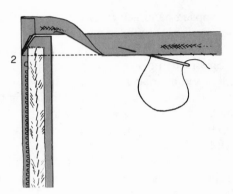

A machine-applied binding, since it is applied and stitched in one step, requires care in trimming and stitching the ends to achieve a tidy finish. Fold in about ½″ at one end on the bias grain and trim, as shown. To encase the raw edge of the garment with binding, make sure the under edge is deeper than the top edge and that the ends are even (3). Starting at one end, edgestitch in place through all layers to about 3″ from the other end. Measure and cut off the binding ½″ past the garment fold. Trim; fold in the binding end. Complete stitching; finish the open ends with slipstitching (4).

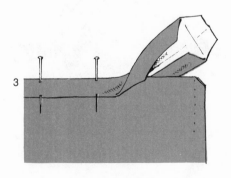

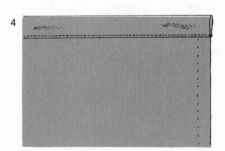

Bandings

Fabric bands can be an important design feature of a garment as well as finish the edge of a neckline, armhole, sleeve, center front opening, or hem. They can take many shapes, such as square, round, keyhole, V-neck, or straight. Sometimes the band will extend only part way down the garment front to form a placket. Knit bands can be used for neckline or sleeve finishes on knitted garments. Subtle in self-fabric or bold in contrasting colors, fabric bands can accent any edge.

Applied Band

An applied band is usually cut from a shaped pattern piece. The two layers are stitched together and then the band is applied to the garment edge. For a hemline, the band may be cut on the bias with an extended facing, which is turned up along the fold line.

Staystitch the edge of the garment directionally and insert the zipper, if necessary. Stitch the interfacing to one band section and trim close to the stitching. (If the band sections have seams, stitch them before you join the band to its facing.) Then pin and baste the band sections together, leaving the notched edge open. Stitch; then trim, grade, and clip the seam allowances, leaving the interfaced band seam allowance widest (1). Turn the band and press it flat.

Pin and baste the edge of the interfaced band section to the garment, matching markings at shoulder seams and clipping the garment seam allowance. Stitch from the band side for the best control, then trim and grade the seam, leaving the garment seam allowance the widest (2).

Notch the band seam allowances to eliminate extra fullness so that all seam allowances can be pressed toward the band. Turn the band, rolling the seam just slightly to the inside to prevent it from being seen on the finished garment; pin.

Turn the remaining free edge under where it falls over the stitching and baste close to the edge. Trim away any excess seam allowance close to the basting. Slipstitch the band over the seamline (3). Fasten the band with hooks and thread eyes.

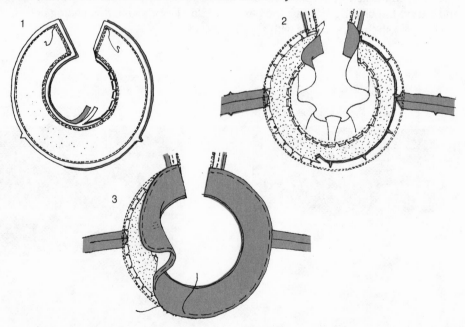

When a flat finish is desired for the band, finish the free edge with a stitch-and-overcast or zigzag treatment. Do not turn the edge under, however. Just blindstitch the free edge where it falls, covering the band seam completely (4).

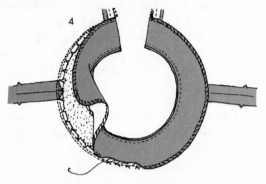

Topstitched Band

If a band will be topstitched, it is often constructed in a slightly different method—the inner band or facing is stitched to the garment and then the outer band is folded over and topstitched in place.

Interface the band as previously described and stitch any seams in the band sections.

Turn in the seam allowance on the notched edge of the interfaced band and baste close to the fold. Trim seam allowance to ¼″ and press.

Pin the two band sections together; stitch. Trim and clip the seam allowances. Turn the band and press (1).

Pin the right side of the band without interfacing to the wrong side of the garment, matching markings, and baste. Stitch seam, trim, and press seam toward band (2).

On the outside, pin the basted edge of the band over the seamline and baste. Topstitch close to the inner and outer edges of the band (3).

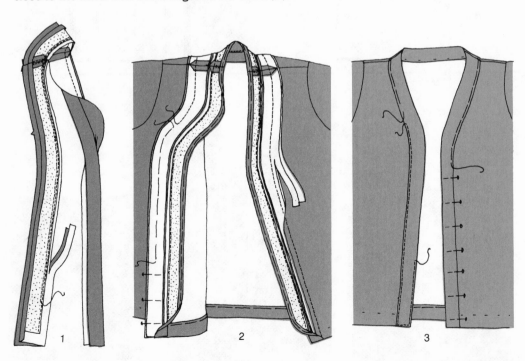

One-Piece Placket Band

A placket band is a variation of the applied band and is used for an opening extending only part way down a garment. Baste the interfacing sections to the wrong side of the band. Turn in the seam allowances on the sides and lower end of the front band, as shown, folding in the fullness at the corners; baste close to the folds. Trim the basted seam allowances to ¼" and press (1). Pin the right side of the band to the wrong side of the garment front, matching all markings. Stitch along the stitching lines, pivoting at the corners, and reinforcing the corners with small stitches (15–20 stitches per inch) along the seamline. Clip diagonally to the corners and trim the seam allowances (2).

Turn the placket to the right side of the garment. Press long seams toward the band and the triangular end down. Fold the shorter side of the placket along the foldline, placing the basted edge over the seamline, and baste in place. Stitch close to the basted edge, ending at the marking. Baste upper edges together at the neckline (3).

Fold the other side of the placket along the foldline, and baste in place as above. Stitch close to the basted edge ending at the marking, being sure to keep the other side of the placket free. Baste upper edges together (4).

Place lower end of the placket band along the placement line and topstitch in place (5).

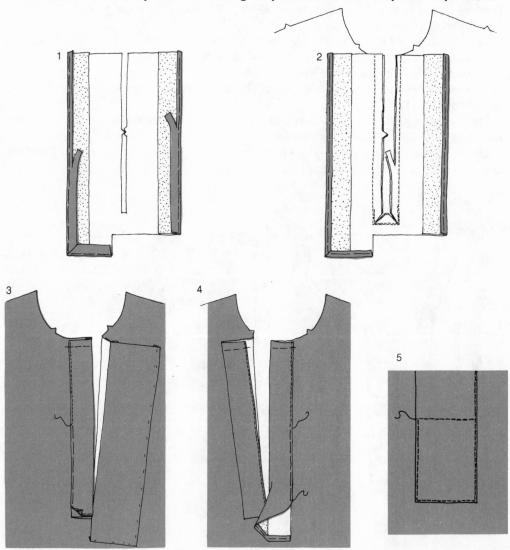

Two-Piece Placket Band

The two-piece placket band must be used at curved areas when the neck and placket bands are combined. Reinforce the front opening corners on the garment with small stitches on the seamline, pivoting at corners. Clip to corners. Stitch shoulder seams, then staystitch the neck and front edges of garment (1). Insert your zipper, if necessary. Interface and construct each band as for the applied band, page 250, stitching along the curved unnotched edges and center back. Leave the lower ends free. Trim and grade the seam allowances, clipping and notching where necessary to allow the bands to lie flat (2). Turn the bands and press them flat.

Leaving the lower end free, baste the interfaced edge of the left neckband to the left half of the garment, clipping where necessary. Stitch with the neckband up. Trim, grade, notch, and press the curved seam allowances toward the band. Turn the free edge of the band under, and baste close to the fold, clipping as necessary for the band to lie flat; slipstitch (3). (Or, for bulky fabrics, use the flat finish for applied bands, page 251.) Do not turn the band under at the lower edge. Just stitch across the end through garment and band (4). Press the lower end toward the garment.

Apply the right neckband to the right half of the garment as above, ending stitching at the right front corner (5). Finish the lower end by turning in and grading the seam allowances and slipstitching them together (6).

Lap the right band over the left band, matching centers. You may wish to slipstitch the lower edge in place along the seamline.

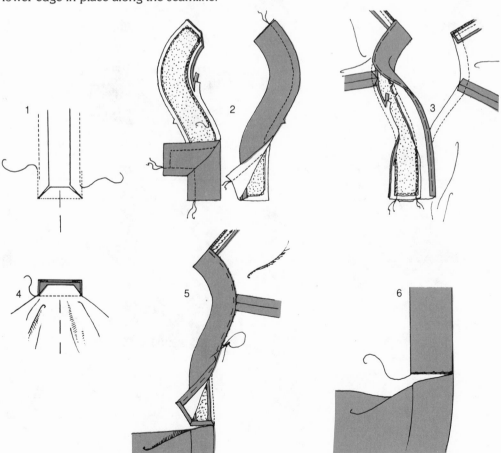

Knit Bands

Knit bands give a professional look to the edges of a knitted garment and allow you to take advantage of the stretchability of the fabric. The band can be cut from self-fabric or you can use purchased ribbing, which is sold by the yard or prepackaged.

A knit band is always cut a little shorter than the edge to which it is applied. Then the band is stretched slightly as it is stitched to the garment, resulting in a smooth, unpuckered seam.

With right sides together, seam the band to form a tube, if necessary. Double stitch the seam and trim close to the second row of stitching. Fold the band in half lengthwise, wrong sides together (1). (Some purchased ribbings have only one layer of fabric.)

Pin the band to the right side of the garment, stretching the band to fit the garment edge. With band side up, stitch the band to the garment, being careful not to stretch the garment edge. Stitch again ⅛″ away from the first row of stitching with either a straight or zigzag stitch, or use an overedge stitch if your machine has one. (See Seams, page 212.) Trim seam allowances close to the second row of stitching (2).

Holding the iron above the seam, steam the band gently to allow it to return to its unstretched state. Press seam allowances toward the garment (3).

For a self-fabric band, your pattern may include instructions for stitching a narrow piece of elastic between the two rows of stitching or for stitching a seam binding stay to the seam, depending on the amount of stretch in your fabric and the shape of the band.

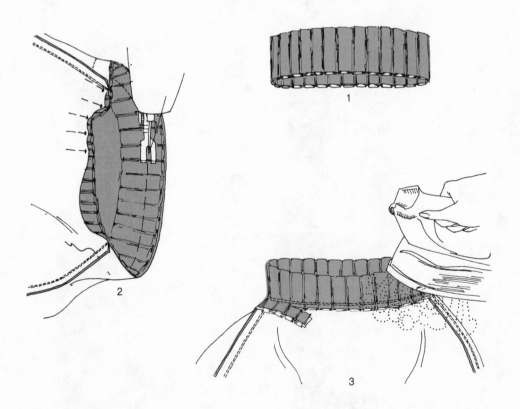

Casings

Casings, which often go unnoticed, are significant in that they enable fabric to be snugged into place with elastic or pulled into graceful folds with a drawstring. Most important, they provide comfort while adapting to the body shape. One essential principle to be remembered is that a casing must always be wide enough to allow the elastic or drawstring to be pulled comfortably. It should be equal in width to the elastic or drawstring, plus ⅛" to ¼" for their thicknesses, plus another ½" for seam allowances. It should be equal in length to the area to which it is to be applied, plus ½".

Applied and Self-Casings

A self-casing is formed by an extension of the garment that has been folded to the inside (forming a hem) and edgestitched. An applied casing is a separate strip of fabric cut on the straight or bias grain or like a shaped facing. You may use prepackaged bias tape for a quick applied casing. Trim garment seam allowances to ¼" wherever casing is to be applied. For the self-casing, allow an extra ¼" seam allowance on the long edge. Allow ¼" seam allowances on all edges for an applied casing. Either type can be used on a finished edge, such as the lower edge of a sleeve; at the waistline, to create a blouson effect; or with a heading, which extends beyond the casing to form a ruffle.

AT FINISHED EDGE: For a self-casing, mark and then turn in the fabric along the foldline; baste. Turn in raw edge ¼" and edgestitch to the garment, leaving the desired opening (1). Self-casings used on a slightly curved edge must be extremely narrow. The stitched fold may need to be stretched or gently eased while stitching. For an applied casing, cut the casing as indicated above. Right sides together, pin one edge of the strip to the garment, turning ends to inside. Stitch in ¼" seam, turn to inside, and press. Finish as self-casing (2).

WITH A HEADING: The extension for a heading requires extra fabric. For a self-casing, extend the garment edge, twice the desired width of the heading, plus the casing and a ¼" seam allowance. Mark heading foldline. Turn fabric to inside and baste close to fold. Mark casing seamlines. Stitch, leaving desired opening (3). For an applied casing, extend the garment edge twice the width of the heading plus a ¼" seam allowance. Mark heading foldline. Turn fabric to inside; baste along foldline. Cut casing as instructed in introduction. Turn all edges under ¼" and press. From the wrong side, baste casing in place, matching raw edge of casing with raw edge of heading. Edgestitch bottom and top edges of casing to garment, leaving desired opening (4).

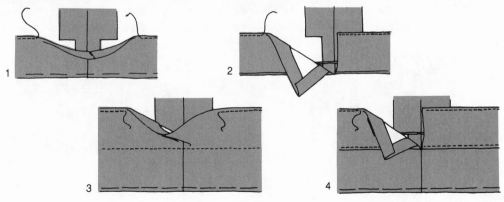

Elastic

Using elastic in a casing will ensure regularity in fit. Unlike the drawstring tie, an elastic pull is not adjustable. It will breathe and move with you, but will not change from the specific measurement you give it. Elastic is used most commonly in sleeves and waistlines. The opening for its insertion is inside the garment. The length of elastic depends upon its stretchability and should be slightly less than the measurement of the body at the casing position, plus ½" for lapping. Usually, the narrower the elastic, the shorter it will have to be. Pull elastic through casing with a bodkin or a safety pin, being careful not to twist it. Lap the ends ½" and stitch securely (1).

Close the opening at the edge of the casing, stretching the elastic as you stitch (2). For an opening across the casing, slipstitch the opening edges together securely (3).

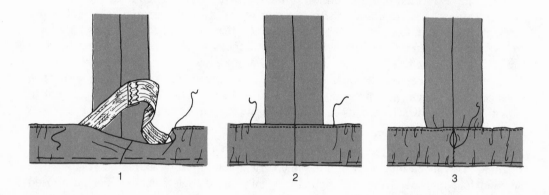

Drawstring

Cord or tubing knotted at the ends, braid, leather strips, ribbon—anything that captures your fancy can be used as a drawstring. Its length should be equal to the measurement of your body at the casing position plus an extra amount to allow for tying a knot or bow. Often quite decorative, the openings for the drawstrings are usually made on the right side of the garment before you make the casing.

There are two types of casing openings for drawstrings. The first, the eyelet or buttonhole type, is made in the outer fabric between the casing placement lines before the casing is applied. From the wrong side, stitch casing in place. When the casing is completed, pull drawstring through the casing with a bodkin or safety pin (1). The second type of opening is in a seam. Stitch seam, leaving an opening the width of the drawstring; reinforce each end (2).

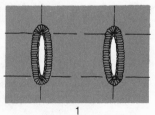 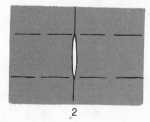

Collars

A visible mark of quality workmanship on a garment is its collar. Regardless of style, the collar is a detail that requires careful handling in every stage of construction in order to retain its quality appearance. When you're browsing through a fashion magazine or pattern catalogue, you'll find the variation in collars can be quite staggering. But however exotic the collar shape may seem, three basic shapes—*flat, standing,* and *rolled*—are the starting point for all variations.

The deeper the curve on the collar neck edge, the flatter your collar will lie, especially as the curve corresponds more closely to that of your garment neck edge. A flat collar is almost identical to the garment in the shape of its neck edge; while the opposite extreme, the standing collar, will have a straight or very slightly curved neck edge. The neck edge of a rolled collar can vary in shape from straight to a curve opposite that of the garment. This collar gently rises from the neck seam and turns down to create a rolled edge around the neck. The line along which the collar is turned is called the *roll line* or *roll.*

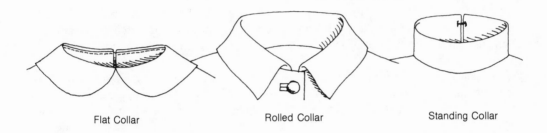

Flat Collar   Rolled Collar   Standing Collar

Here are some guidelines for determining whether or not a collar is well made. All collars with corners and center front or back openings should be symmetrical—with identically shaped curves or points, and the inside edge should smoothly encircle the neck without straining or rippling. The underside, or **undercollar,** should never show, nor should seams at the finished edge. Your collar should hug the garment closely without the corners flipping up or the neck seams showing unintentionally at the back or front of the garment.

To achieve these results, always stitch the collar sections together directionally; then trim and grade the seam allowances. Corners should be reinforced with tiny stitches (15–20 stitches per inch), trimmed diagonally, and turned gently. Careful pressing will shape the collar as well as prevent the undercollar or outer seam from showing. For detailed information, refer to page 272.

The necessary body and shape of the collar are maintained by interfacing, which is usually cut from your collar pattern. Lightweight interfacing can be stitched into the collar seams and then trimmed close to the stitching. For heavier-weight interfacings, the seam allowances are first trimmed away. Then the interfacing is catchstitched to the collar along the seamlines. For fusible interfacings, the seam allowances and corners are trimmed away before fusing to the undercollar. A collar meant to be softly rolled, made of a soft or sheer fabric, or part of a very soft style (as in many blouses), may not require interfacing. For more information about interfacing selection, see pages 163 to 167.

Flat Collar

The flat collar with curved edges and angular or curved corners is unquestionably the easiest collar to make. Often called a Peter Pan collar, it has very little roll because it is cut on straight grain with a neck edge curved like the garment neck edge. Both the upper and undercollar sections are cut from the same pattern piece. The collar itself may be one- or two-piece, with or without a front or back opening.

Attach the interfacing to the section that will be your undercollar. Stitch the collar sections together, leaving the neck edge open. Trim, grade, and notch the seams (1). Then turn and press the collar, favoring the outer edge seam of the section that is to be your upper collar.

Even collars with very little roll need some help from you if they are to be set correctly on the garment. With the upper collar on top, work your collar into the shape shown on the pattern envelope: roll the neck edge, as shown; then pin along the roll and just above the neck seam (2). To make attaching the collar easier, baste the neck edges as they fall together along the seamline of the undercollar. If your collar is made in two sections, baste the sections together at the center front neckline.

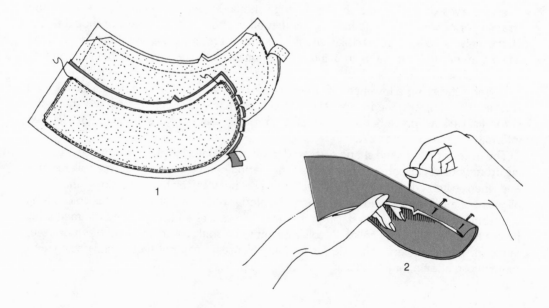

1

2

For either a front or back opening, prepare a buttonhole closure by checking the buttonhole placement, then attaching your interfacing to the garment and making the necessary buttonholes. If using a zipper, you may insert it now or after attaching your collar.

With the interfaced section of the collar next to the garment, pin the collar in place, matching markings, and baste (3). The upper collar will bubble slightly, but that is as it should be, since you've shaped the collar over your hand.

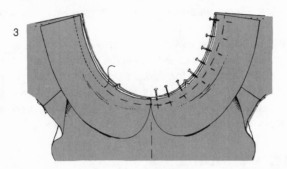

If you are finishing the collar seam with a shaped facing, prepare the facing and finish the unnotched edge. Pin or baste the facing to the neck edge over the collar; again match markings, and stitch. Trim, grade, and clip the seams. Turn the facing to the inside and press. Understitch the facing to the neckline seam allowance (4).

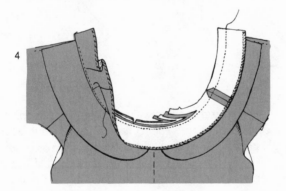

For a zipper closing, turn under the ends of the facing to clear the zipper after it has been turned to the inside. Anchor the facing and fasten the closing with a hook and eye. For a buttonhole closing, turn the facing to the inside, anchor the facing, and complete the back of the buttonholes.

There are other means of finishing the collar and garment seam. You can also use a standard bias facing application (found on page 242) when you wish to reduce bulk in a heavy fabric. Or, for one-piece collars, you may stitch the undercollar to the garment neck edge, keeping the upper collar free to be turned in and slipstitched over the seam.

Rolled Collar

Any molded collar with a pronounced roll around the neck is considered a rolled collar. It is usually cut with a one-piece upper collar and a two-piece bias undercollar that is slightly smaller. The center back seam brings the collar close to the neck, giving excellent control and fit. The standaway version of the rolled collar is cut in one piece on bias grain and folded at the outer edge. The rolled collar can be applied with or without a back neck facing.

The method of construction for a rolled collar depends upon the weight of the garment fabric. For light and mediumweight fabrics, the collar can be stitched to the garment and then the facing attached, as illustrated for Version I. For heavier weight or bulky fabrics, the undercollar should be stitched to the garment and the upper collar to the facing, so as to divide the bulk at the neckline between the two seams. For this method, see Version II, page 262, or the tailoring section, pages 430 to 431.

Rolled Collar, Version I

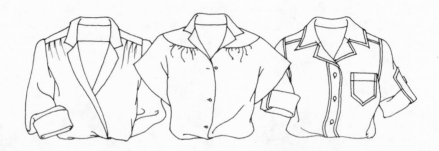

This version is suitable for light and mediumweight fabrics as the collar is attached to the neckline before the facing is applied. The collar is usually cut with a two-piece bias undercollar and a slightly larger one-piece upper collar cut on crosswise grain. For the one-piece version, the collar is cut on bias grain for a smoother roll. Both types of collars are applied in the same manner. Careful molding and handling of the roll helps to shape the collar.

Attach interfacing to wrong side of each undercollar section. Stitch center back seam, press open, and trim. For one-piece collars folded at the outer edge, use long running stitches to sew interfacing to collar at the foldline.

Stitch collar sections together, stretching the undercollar to fit and using small stitches at the points. Trim corners carefully so the points will be sharp when turned (1). Turn and press the collar, favoring the upper collar at its outer edges so that the seam is on the undercollar side.

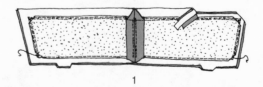

1

Now establish the **roll line.** Shape your collar until it looks like the pattern illustration, continuing to favor the outer edge of the upper collar. Baste raw edges together from the undercollar side as they fall, and thread trace the roll line (2).

Lap collar over garment, matching neck seamlines; baste (3).

Try the garment on or put it on a dress form to check the collar set and roll. The roll should be smooth, even, and unbroken from front to back. Be sure that the points lie symmetrically against the garment when closed (4). The finished edge of the collar should cover the back neck seam. Adjust the collar at the neck seamline until all of these features are correct. When satisfied with the appearance of your collar, transfer any adjustment lines and remove the collar. Attach garment interfacing and front facing, if necessary.

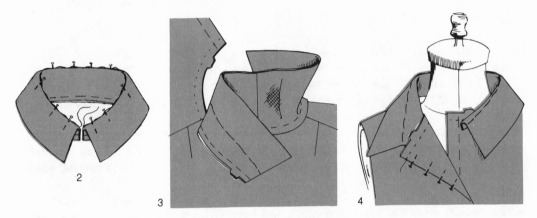

Staystitch the neck edge of the garment and the facing. Baste the collar to the garment, clipping the garment neck edge only where necessary, and stretching or easing the collar to fit as indicated on your pattern. The upper collar will bubble along the roll when opened out (5). Staystitch the neck edge of the back facing and join to the front facing. Baste the completed facing over the collar, matching markings. Clip the facing edge only where necessary. Stitch from the garment side. Then trim, grade, and continue clipping the seam through all thicknesses. Turn the facing to the inside, baste close to the folded edges, and press. Understitch the facing to the seam allowance close to the neckline seam and to within one inch of the opening edges (6). Or you can use a bias facing to finish the collar seam.

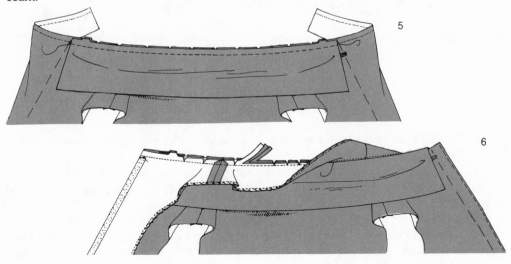

Rolled Collar, Version II

A rolled collar made of heavier weight or bulkier fabric should be constructed so as to eliminate as much bulk as possible in the neckline seams. When a rolled collar has lapels added, the notch area between the collar and lapels can be tricky. This construction version reduces the difficulties. For the best results, this collar should be constructed following the shaping techniques in the tailoring section, page 422.

Although your upper collar is generally larger than the undercollar, heavy fabrics may require an additional ⅛″ to ¼″ added to the upper collar to allow for the roll. Add this additional amount to the unnotched edges of your collar. Taper back to original seam allowances at neck edge.

First stitch and press the undercollar's center back seam. To reduce bulk, overlap the center back seam of the interfacing, stitch and trim. Or trim away the center back seam allowances, and place ribbon seam binding over the abutted edges and stitch. Attach interfacing to the undercollar (1).

Stitch collar sections together, stretching the undercollar to fit. Use small stitches at the points and trim corners carefully. Turn and press the collar, favoring the upper collar at its outer edges so that the seam is on the undercollar side (2).

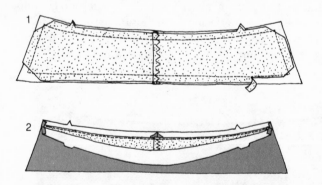

Shape your collar to establish the roll line as for Version I, page 260. Baste the collar neck edges together.

Staystitch garment neck edge directionally and interface lapel area. Lap and baste collar to garment neck edge. (Turn any extended facing back at foldline and baste along neck edge before basting collar.)

Begin rolling the lapel at the top buttonhole marking. Check the fit of your collar and garment, as for Version I. Make any necessary adjustments at the neckline seam until the collar sits close to the back of the neck, rolls smoothly, covers the back neck seam, and falls symmetrically. When you are satisfied with the collar, mark the roll line and transfer adjustment lines before removing it from the garment (3). If you are making bound buttonholes, do them next. (See page 315.)

Baste the undercollar to the garment, clipping the garment neck edge; stitch between the markings (4).

Prepare the facing and staystitch the neck edge. Baste the upper collar to the facing, clipping the facing. Stitch together between markings. Stitching from the garment side to eliminate bubbles that sometimes occur when the collar meets the lapel, join the facing to the garment. Start where it meets the collar, reinforce the corner, and continue around the facing. Trim, grade, and clip the seams (5).

Press collar and garment neck seams open. Turn the facing inside and press. Try on the garment to check the roll of the lapels. Favoring the outer edge of the upper collar and the garment edge below the top buttonhole, pin along the roll and again above the neck seam. Loosely blindstitch both neck seams together as they fall (6). Complete the facing side of buttonholes and anchor facings.

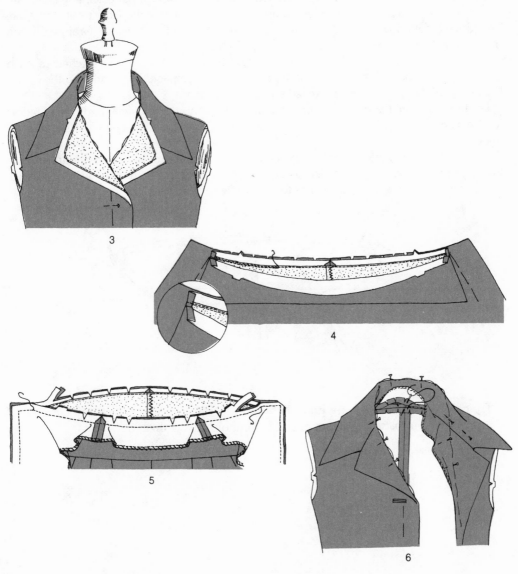

Shawl Collar

A shawl collar is a special version of the rolled collar in which the upper collar and lapels are cut as one piece. It can vary greatly in shape, having a curved, scalloped, or notched edge. Traditionally found on wrap coats and robes, the shawl collar is usually wrapped in the front and held with a sash, but it can also be buttoned.

For light and mediumweight garment fabrics, the interfacing can be stitched to each undercollar section as for Version I of the rolled collar (see page 260); and then the center back seam of the undercollar is stitched and pressed open.

For heavier weight and bulky fabrics, the interfacing should be overlapped or abutted as for Version II of the rolled collar (see page 262) and then attached to the seamed undercollar.

Then attach the interfacing to the garment front and neck edges. Stitch the undercollar to the garment, stretching the collar to fit and clipping the garment neck edge as necessary. Notch the undercollar seam allowance to make it lie flat and press the seam open (1).

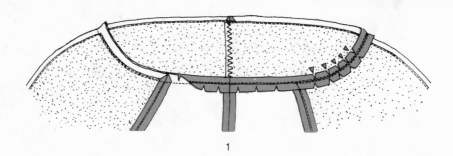

1

Try on the garment or put it on a dress form to check the fit. Check any buttonhole placement. If your pattern includes bound buttonholes, make them now.

Before joining the collar/facing section to the garment, reinforce the inner corner with small stitches along the seamline, pivoting at the marking. Clip to the corner (2).

Stitch the center back seam of the collar/facing and press it open. Then pin it to the back facing along the neck and shoulder edges, clipping the back neck facing where necessary. Stitch, pivoting at corners. Press the seam open. Trim excess fullness at corners and catch-stitch. Finish the unnotched edge of the facing. Stitch the collar/facing unit to the garment and undercollar, stretching the undercollar to fit. Trim and grade seams, leaving the garment seam allowance widest; notch curves (3).

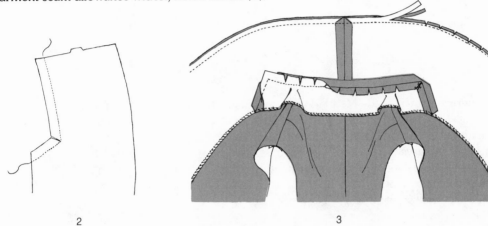

2   3

Turn the collar/facing to the right side and press. Favor the outer edge of the collar so that the seam is on the undercollar side. Below the place where the collar begins to roll, favor the front edge of the garment so that the seam is on the facing side.

Try the garment on again or put it on a dress form to set the roll of the collar. The roll should be smooth and unbroken and the collar should lie close to the back of the neck. When you have achieved the desired effect with the collar/facing in its proper position, pin the facing in place. Continue to favor the collar and garment edges as mentioned previously. Blindstitch the facing seam allowances, as they fall, to the garment seam allowances at the neck edge. Also blindstitch the facing edges in place (4). Complete the underside of any buttonholes.

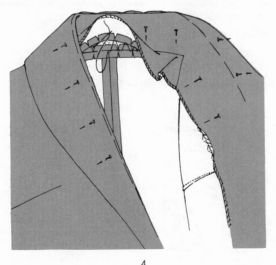

4

Standing Collar

Generally known as the Mandarin or band collar, this basically uncomplicated collar is able to take on many exciting forms. It can be a stiff and close military collar or a soft loose band, and it can be cut in one or two sections depending on whether the finished edge is straight or curved. The depth of the collar and how closely it is fitted to the neck greatly affect the overall design of your garment. This collar will always work and look better if you cut your interfacing on the bias. It will curve around your neck smoothly—without stiff cracks or breaks that mar a fine appearance.

Cut a bias strip of interfacing and attach it to the collar. If collar is cut in one section, use long running stitches to hold interfacing along foldline. Fold the collar and stitch the ends to within ⅝'' of the neckline edge. Trim and grade the seam allowances (1). Turn and press the ends only, **not** the foldline, or you may have an undesirable crease in the finished collar.

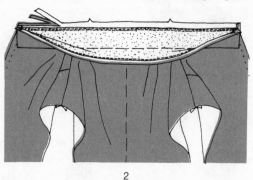

1

For either a front or back opening, insert your zipper or facings.

Baste and stitch the interfaced side of the collar to the garment neck edge, matching all markings and clipping the garment where necessary. Trim and grade the seams, leaving the garment seam allowance widest (2). Press the seam toward the collar. Trim and turn in the remaining edge of the collar and slipstitch over the seam. For hard-to-handle fabrics, you may want to baste close to the fold of the turned-under edge before slipstitching the edge in place (3). Fasten the collar ends with hooks and thread eyes. Complete the buttonholes and anchor the facing in place as required.

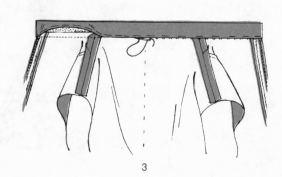

2

3

Foldover Bias Collar

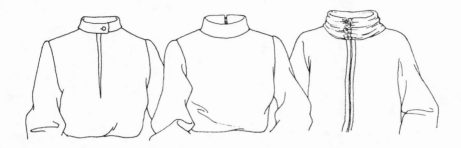

A foldover bias collar, which is commonly known as a turtleneck collar and sometimes misnamed a rolled collar, is really a one-piece standing collar cut on the bias and rolled or folded over to cover the neck seam.

Cut interfacing on the bias to extend ⅝″ beyond the foldline of the collar; stitch to collar and sew along the foldline with long running stitches (1). Fold the collar and stitch the ends to within ⅝″ of the neck edge. Trim and grade the seams. Turn and then press the ends only; do not press the foldline. Staystitch the bodice neck edge and insert zipper or apply facings where needed.

Baste the interfaced collar edge to the garment, clipping the garment neck edge where necessary, and stretching or easing the collar to fit. Stitch, trim, and grade all seams, leaving the garment seam allowance widest (2).

Press the stitched seam allowances toward the collar. Lap the remaining raw edge in place at the seamline and baste loosely. To establish the roll on the garment, turn the finished edge of the collar down to just cover the neck seam, stretching gently until it fits the contour. Thread trace the roll line through all layers. Remove basting, trim, and turn in remaining edge as it falls over seam; slipstitch (3). (For bulky fabrics, overcast edge and blindstitch in place.) Fasten the ends with hooks and eyes.

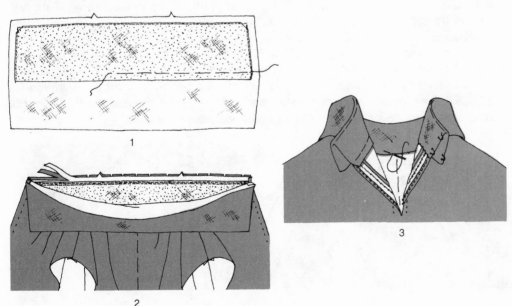

Tie Collar

This collar, basically a foldover or standing collar ending in a tie, adds a delightfully graceful touch to any garment. The difference between the two collar styles is only a matter of dimension; the tie will generally be wider on the foldover collar.

Attach the interfacing to the collar and sew along the foldline with long running stitches. Do not interface ties: added bulk would cause difficulty when tying. Reinforce the seamline at the point where collar and tie meet; clip to the seamline. Fold the collar; stitch the tie along the ends and to its termination points. (For a back opening, you have two collar sections. Stitch the back opening ends; then, stitch the tie ends to their termination points.) Trim and grade seams and corners (1). Turn the collar and tie ends; press the seams lightly.

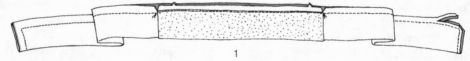

1

Staystitch garment neck edge. Stitch facing to the garment, stopping where the collar begins. Clip to the end of the stitching. Trim and grade the seam allowances. Turn and press. Baste facing and garment neck edges together and anchor the facing at the shoulders.

Baste one edge of collar to garment, clipping the garment neck edge where necessary. A space has been allowed between the termination point of the collar and center marking in order to knot the tie. Stitch, trim, grade, and clip the seam (2). Press the seam toward the collar. Turn in the remaining edge and slipstitch over the seam (3). Complete buttonholes. For a back closing, fasten the collar with hooks and eyes.

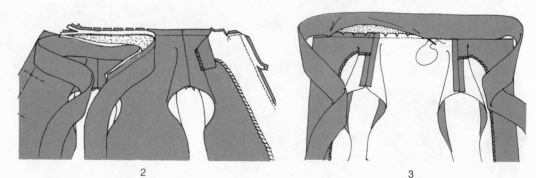

2   3

Collar with Stand

Many man-tailored shirts and jackets have collars with stands. Such a collar has practically no roll; it turns down at the top of the stand and nearly always has a front closure.

Prepare the collar the same as you would for a flat collar, page 256. Apply the interfacing to the wrong side of one collar stand section. (Sometimes the stand is an extension of the collar, and then the interfacing is applied to both the undercollar and stand in one piece.)

Pin the interfaced stand to the undercollar and the remaining stand to the upper collar, right sides together, and baste. Stitch the ends and upper edge to within ⅝" of the neck edges. Trim, grade, clip, and notch the seam allowances (1). Then turn the stand and press. The collar is now encased in the stand.

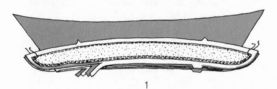

1

Complete the garment front opening. Staystitch the garment neck edge. Pin or baste the interfaced stand to the garment neck edge, clipping the garment as necessary. Stitch; trim, and grade the seams, leaving the garment seam allowance widest (2). Press the seam toward the stand. On the remaining free edge of the stand, trim and turn the seam allowance under and baste close to the fold. Slipstitch the folded edge over the seam (3). Topstitch if desired. Make machine-worked buttonholes.

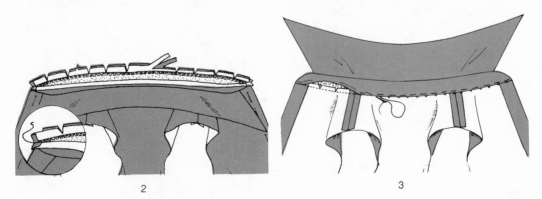

2   3

Cowls

Cowls can drape softly around the face or plunge dramatically down the back of a garment. A cowl collar is simply a very wide foldover bias collar crushed down around the neckline. A cowl neckline usually consists of a yoke cut on the bias for draping ability and a stay cut on straight grain for reinforcement so that the cowl will drape as the designer intended.

Join the yoke sections at the shoulders. Press seams open and clip. Baste ribbon seam binding over the back seamlines of the yoke between the markings.

Prepare a narrow, shaped facing, finishing the inner unnotched edge as desired. Pin, baste, and stitch the facing to the yoke; trim and grade the seam, press it open and clip where necessary. *Roll* the facing to the inside.

Stitch the back and front stay at the shoulders. Press seams open. Finish the stay neckline with bias tape or a 2″ wide bias strip of fabric, applied as a bias facing. Place the right side of the stay on the wrong side of the yoke. Baste the raw edges together, stretching the lower yoke edge to fit (1).

Baste and stitch the yoke to the garment. Insert your zipper and blindstitch the facing in place. If your fabric needs a weight in order to drape properly, cover a flat weight (page 447) and attach it to the cowl with a French tack (2). Experiment with the placement of the weight to determine its most functional position.

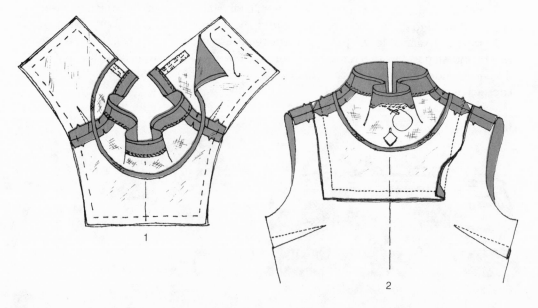

Detachable Collar

This category includes two types of collars—the first lies on top of an existing collar; the second fits inside a collarless neckline. You can use this collar to provide a removable, washable trim on a garment that requires dry cleaning.

The most familiar type of detachable collar forms a decorative overlay to your garment's original collar. It must be longer and wider in order to cover the existing collar. Unless your pattern is designed for a detachable collar, you will probably have to adjust its dimensions so that the decorative collar has the same shape and size as the garment collar when it is worn. Determine how much to add to the pattern by comparing the weight and depth of your garment fabric with the fabric for your detachable collar.

Construct the desired collar and stitch its neck edges together ⅛″ from the seamline in the seam allowance. Clip the seam allowances to the stitching every ½″ so the detachable collar neckline can spread to fit the garment neckline smoothly (1).

Extend the collar neck edge with bias binding to allow for fastening it to the garment. For a ½″ finished binding, cut a bias strip 1¾″ wide and the length of the neckline plus 1″. Then apply the bias as a single binding to the collar neck edge, shaping the binding and clipped edge of the collar as you work so it will fit the garment neck edge (2). Grade seam allowances if necessary. Pin the collar to the neck edge of the garment, matching seamlines, and slip baste the binding to the neck facing (3).

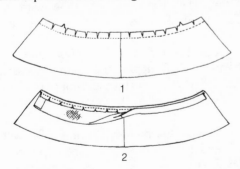

If you don't have a pattern for the second type of detachable collar, it is possible to use a collar from another pattern with the same neckline. Construct the collar and finish the edges with bias binding in the same manner as described above. Then attach it to your garment with snaps or slip basting. If the closure on your collar does not correspond to that of the garment, fasten the collar in place with snaps rather than slip basting.

If you wish to add matching detachable cuffs to complement your detachable collar, refer to Cuffs, page 293, for detailed instructions.

For a More Perfect Collar

Here are some professional techniques that contribute so much to the finished appearance of every collar.

Always stitch the collar sections together directionally, stitching with the collar grain. Start stitching at the center first, then stitch toward one end. Repeat for the other half, overlapping stitches ½''. At corners use 15 to 20 stitches per inch and one stitch across the point when the point is very sharp.

Any rolled collar should be characterized by a smooth roll with the neck seam completely covered. The pattern piece for the upper collar is usually larger than that for the undercollar. This ease allows the collar to roll and accommodates the depth of your fabric. However, only an average roll depth can be allowed on most pattern pieces, so you may have to add as much as ¼'' to ⅜'' to the upper collar to allow for very bulky or heavy fabric. Then be sure to ease or stretch the collar sections to each other when you stitch them together.

The importance of trimming to reduce bulk cannot be stressed enough as it can be the single contributing factor to an unattractive collar. Trim the seams, grading the ones to be enclosed so that the seam allowance of the upper collar is left the widest. Trim the corners diagonally as closely as possible without cutting into your stitching to ensure that the corner seams will miter once the collar is turned. You should not trim ravelly fabrics closer than ¼'' from the seamline. Notch or clip curves so that the seam allowances will lie flat without pulls or bumps when the collar is turned.

There is a professional way to turn and press a collar swiftly and accurately. Prepress the collar *before* you turn it to the right side and you will not only obtain a more finished appearance, but eliminate problems with "shine" and handling of the fabric on the right side as well. Press the collar seam allowances open over a point presser or a tailor board. Then press the seam allowances toward the undercollar side. Holding the seam allowances together at one corner, turn the collar corner by pulling the upper collar over your hand. Repeat for the other corner. If necessary, use a needle or pin from the right side to pull the corners to a point. *Never* use the point of a scissors to poke corners out because you can easily poke a hole in your fabric.

Press the outer edge, using a press cloth. Carefully *favor* the upper collar edge by rolling the outer seam just slightly to the underside of the collar. This ensures that the seam will not be visible at the edge of the completed collar. For thick or resilient fabrics, flatten and smooth the outer edge with a pounding block.

The best way to ensure that your collar will look right is to fit it before you permanently attach it to the garment. Baste the collar to the neck edge, *lapping* the seams for easier fitting, rather than matching them right sides together. Then try on the garment or put it on a dress form and check the features mentioned above, as well as those mentioned in the preceding pages.

When you attach the collar, take special care to align the markings of the collar with those on the garment at the shoulders, front, and back. To help ensure a perfectly symmetrical collar, stitch the neck edge directionally also.

Sleeves, Sleeve Finishes, and Cuffs

A sleeve should be a thing of beauty and comfort. It should look handsome, conforming to the shape of your arm without signs of pulling or straining. Since the arm is probably the most active part of the body, the sleeve should perform well in motion without causing discomfort or distorting the fit.

The comfort of a sleeve is determined mostly by the fit and ease of the two points of action—the upper arm and elbow. The sleeve cap must be neither too tight nor too loose, and in any long or three-quarter sleeve there must be room for the elbow to bend. When the arm is at ease, the sleeve should hang evenly and gracefully in a curve that corresponds to the natural curve of your arm.

Sleeve Types

A profusion of sleeves is at your disposal, in lengths and shapes to suit every whim. Most of them fall into three basic types. The first type is the **SET-IN SLEEVE,** which joins the garment in a seam that encircles the arm over the shoulder. The area of the sleeve at the end of the shoulder or upper arm, called the *sleeve cap*, must be shaped and eased to curve smoothly into the armhole.

The second type, the **RAGLAN SLEEVE,** joins the bodice in a diagonal seam extending to the neckline area, providing a smooth, round silhouette and a great degree of comfort. It tends to be a good choice for hard-to-fit shoulders, since the diagonal seam can be readily adjusted to accommodate differences in the individual figure. Shoulder shaping is achieved by a curved seam or a shaped dart.

The third type, the **KIMONO SLEEVE,** is cut in one with the garment or a part of it, such as a yoke. If it is loose-fitting or short, it may simply be reinforced in the underarm seam, but tighter versions frequently call for gussets or further refinements designed to combine greater comfort with a finer degree of fit.

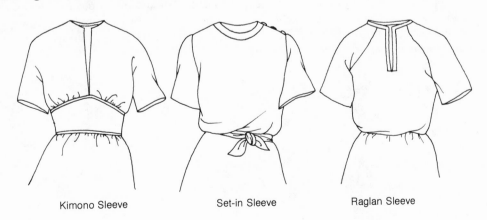

Kimono Sleeve   Set-in Sleeve   Raglan Sleeve

Set-in Sleeve

The one-piece set-in sleeve is the most classic and most popular of these sleeves, and allows for many variations in style. Slightly more refined in fit, the two-piece set-in sleeve is inserted in exactly the same manner, but often calls for the fairly sophisticated sleeve finishes explained in the tailoring section, page 433. If you are using heavy or bulky fabrics, or fabrics such as permanent press or velveteen, which cannot be eased, see page 92 as a guide to adjusting the pattern tissue.

To begin your sleeve, run a line of thread tracing, as shown, along the crosswise grain of the sleeve cap. Easestitch on the right side of the sleeve cap (about 8–10 stitches per inch) just inside the seamline in the seam allowance between markings, as shown. An additional row of easestitching ¼″ from the first row in the seam allowance will give you more control over the fullness and simplify the process of easing (1).

If the sleeve is long or three-quarter length and snug, elbow shaping is needed for comfortable movement, either by easing or using darts. To ease, stitch with large stitches along the seamline on the back edge of the sleeve between markings. Pin the sleeve seam, matching notches and markings; adjust ease (2). Where darts are indicated, stitch and press downward. Match markings; pin and stitch the sleeve seam (3).

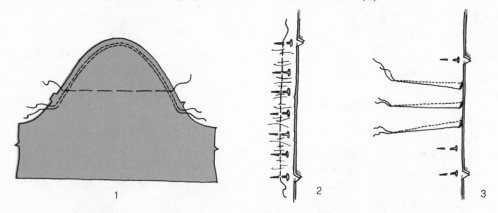

1   2   3

With the garment wrong side out, place sleeve in the armhole, right sides together. Pin together at the notches, markings, and underarm seam, being sure to use the stitching line at the underarm for the sleeve when indicated on your pattern (4). Pull the easing threads up until the sleeve fits the armhole; secure thread ends around a pin in a figure-eight fashion (5). Adjust the fullness and pin about every ½″. If not indicated by markings, be sure to leave one inch of flat area at the shoulder seam where the grain will not permit easing. Baste firmly along the seamline (6).

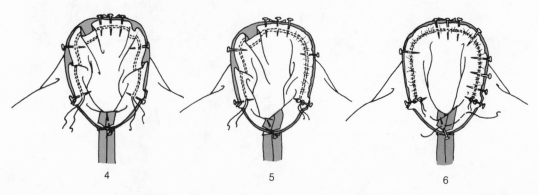

4   5   6

Now try on the garment. First check the line of thread tracing. If it is not perfectly parallel to the floor, you have an obvious indication that a slight adjustment is in order. If the grainline slants or ripples, you will find a quick referral to Sleeves, page 92, extremely helpful. Then check the length, allowing for the anticipated finish (hem, cuff, etc.) and any blousing in a full sleeve. Finally, be sure that the ease is located where it is needed, adjusting it for your particular upper arm shape and shoulder curve.

After fitting, tie the ease thread ends securely and remove the sleeve from the armhole. Holding the curve of the sleeve cap over a press mitt, shrink the fullness by using a steam iron. Begin by steaming the seam allowance to shape the sleeve cap, being careful not to press beyond the stitches (7).

Hold the sleeve in your hands, and turn in the seam allowance along the ease thread. You should have a smooth rolling sleeve cap without puckers or pulling. If dimples remain on the roll near the seamline, slide fullness along the threads until your problem has been eliminated and steam again. Do not be overly alarmed if your unattached sleeve still retains some puckering, as some fabrics do not respond well to shrinking and may need additional handling when the sleeve is being placed into the armhole for permanent stitching (8).

Before you permanently set in the sleeve, complete the sleeve finish. The separate piece will be easier to maneuver than the entire garment. Replace the sleeve in the armhole, pinning and basting it in place. Try it on, checking the shoulder and arm shaping and the sleeve finish.

For a problem sleeve, place the garment on a dress form. Turn in the sleeve seam allowance along ease thread and, from the right side, pin into armhole. Pin and slip-baste in place, working with the sleeve cap until you have a smooth rolling shape (9).

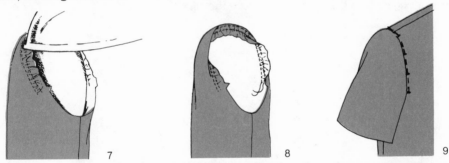

When the sleeve is set in to your satisfaction, start at the underarm and stitch the armhole seam with the sleeve side up, controlling the fullness as you work (10).

Stitch again in the seam allowance ¼″ from the first row of stitching. To reduce bulk, trim close to this second row. If the garment is unlined, overcast or zigzag the seam allowances to prevent ravelling (11). Never press sleeve cap seam after the sleeve is set in. Simply turn the seam allowances toward the sleeve to give a smooth line to the seam and support to the sleeve cap.

There are a few extreme instances when the sleeve cap seam is still not perfectly smooth and rounded—such as lightweight or limp fabrics, fabrics which do not ease, certain designs, and certain figure irregularities. These situations can prove difficult and may call for lambswool padding. We must stress that it is not a remedy for a poorly set-in sleeve. For detailed instructions on how to insert sleeve padding, put lining in a sleeve, or set in a two-piece sleeve, refer to the tailoring section, page 432.

Raglan Sleeve

This sleeve is well liked for its comfortable fit and relatively easy construction. Its diagonal seamline can lead into another seam or form part of a neckline. It can be cut on the straight or bias grain, with a one- or two-piece construction. The shoulder curve is part of the sleeve shape, and is created by a dart, a seam, or gathers.

First stitch the dart or shoulder seam and the sleeve seam. Press the seams open (1). Pin and baste the sleeve into the armhole, matching notches, symbols, and underarm seams (2). Try on the garment.

The curve of the dart or seam should conform to your own shoulder and upper arm shape, with the sharpest part of the curve neither above nor below the point of your shoulder. Test it, standing in a normal position with your arms down. Then swing your arms, making sure there is enough room for comfortable movement. Adjust if necessary, referring to the hints in the adjustment section, pages 93 to 95.

Stitch, then stitch again ¼″ away in the underarm seam allowance between the notches. Clip at ends of the second row of stitching, trim close to this stitching, and overcast or zigzag the edge. Press the seam open above the clips (3).

1

2

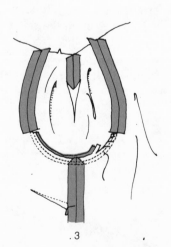

.3

Kimono Sleeve

The classic kimono sleeve is a gem of simplicity. The T-shaped garment that every child has made for a favorite doll is a perfect example. However, arms are seldom at right angles to the body; when they are in a relaxed position, the T-shape creates folds. This draped effect can be a graceful design feature in a kimono sleeve with a large opening; however, as the arm opening becomes smaller and shaping adjustments are made to eliminate folds, further sewing refinements are necessary for comfort and strength.

INVISIBLE REINFORCEMENTS: If the sleeve is cut as an extension of the bodice, the main thing to remember is that the underarm area must be adequately reinforced, since it undergoes considerable strain with arm movements. Pin the back to the front at shoulders and sides. Center a piece of stretched bias tape over the seamline at the underarm. Baste both seams, then clip the curve, being careful not to cut the tape. Fit your garment, then stitch the seam, using a smaller stitch (15–20 per inch according to your fabric) on the curves. Press the seam open (1).

An alternative method is to stitch the underarm seam, using smaller stitches on the curve. Clip the curve; press the seam open. Center a piece of stretched bias tape over the open seam and baste through the seamline. Stitch on both sides of the seamline as you spread the clips, catching only the tape and seam allowances (2).

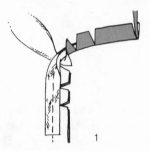

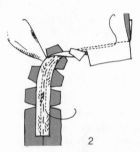

KIMONO SLEEVE CUT WITH YOKE: When the kimono sleeve is cut in one with a yoke, you will get a closer fit without the additional construction of a gusset. The seaming detail allows for easier shaping and fitting adjustments. Reinforce the inner corners at the point where the yoke ends and the sleeve begins; clip to markings. Stitch the yoke/sleeve front and yoke/sleeve back sections together along the shoulder and sleeve seams. Press the seams open (1).

With the yoke/sleeve section dropped into the dress section, place right sides together. Pin and baste the yoke/sleeve section to the dress along the bottom of the yoke and underarm, matching markings. Stitch from the yoke/sleeve side, pivoting at corners. At the underarm, stitch again ¼'' away. Trim close to the second row of stitching and overcast. Press the garment seam toward the yoke. The underarm seam remains unpressed (2).

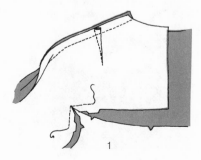

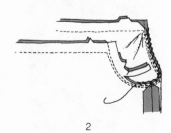

Gussets

Just the mere mention of the word "gussets" can cause panic if you aren't accustomed to sewing them. But don't despair—you can attain foolproof results with even the trickiest of gussets by using appropriate reinforcement and *very careful* stitching.

A gusset is a triangular or diamond-shaped piece of fabric set into a garment at a slash. Most commonly it will be found at the underarm curve of a kimono sleeve, set in a slash that cuts across the garment from front to back. It makes possible a longer, slimmer kimono sleeve with an armhole closer to the body—in general, a more sophisticated fit than the kimono sleeve without a gusset. Another by-product of the gusset is added comfort through increased flexibility of the sleeve. Because the area under the arm receives a maximum amount of strain and needs ease for movement, the gusset should always be cut on the bias.

The gusset can be of one- or two-piece construction—with a seam joining the two sections. Occasionally the gusset is combined with a portion of the garment, such as the underarm section of the sleeve or a side panel of the bodice.

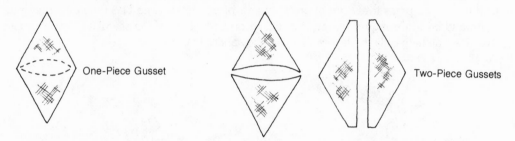

One-Piece Gusset   Two-Piece Gussets

There is very little difference between the insertion of one- and two-piece diamond gussets. The gusset can be shaped by either a contour dart or a seam to eliminate bulk under the arm. The other variation, a triangular gusset, is quite simple to construct because the gusset and the garment side seams are continuous.

REINFORCING: Before you slash the garment, it must be very carefully reinforced. Cut 2″ bias squares of underlining or 4″ long pieces of ribbon seam binding for each slash point. Center them over the slash points and stitching lines on the right side of both front and back sections. Or, for fabrics that ravel easily, use a *very lightweight* fusible interfacing on the wrong side of your fabric at the slash point *before* you underline. For all reinforcements, stitch along the stitching lines, using short stitches (15–20 per inch) and taking one stitch across the slash point (1).

Cut between stitching lines right up to the point. Turn reinforcement squares or seam binding to wrong side of garment so they can be treated as a seam allowance while you are pinning and stitching (2).

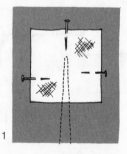

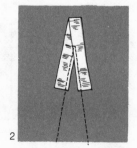

DIAMOND GUSSETS: Stitch all bodice seams, ending stitching at markings as shown on your pattern and leaving gusset area open. Press all seams open. Prepare gusset by stitching any dart or shaped seam, if necessary. Pin or baste gusset to garment, right sides together, placing stitching line of garment along seamlines of gusset.

From the garment side, stitch gusset to garment. Use small stitches and stitch on the garment alongside the previous stitching, beginning at the seams or markings and pivoting carefully at the point, treating the reinforcement patch or seam binding as seam allowances. End stitching at seams or markings so that the side seam allowances of the garment are not caught in the stitching. Press all gusset seams toward the garment.

TRIANGULAR GUSSETS: Stitch shoulder seam only and press open. Right sides together, pin or baste the gusset pieces into their corresponding garment slashes, placing stitching lines of garment along seamlines of gusset. Stitch gussets in place the same as for the diamond gusset, being very careful at the slash points. Press gusset seams toward garment. Matching gusset seamlines of the garment front and back, stitch underarm seam of bodice and sleeve in a continuous seam. Press the side seam open, clipping where needed.

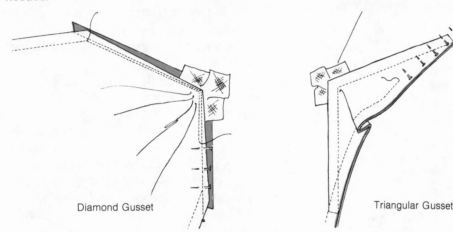

Diamond Gusset   Triangular Gusset

FINISHING: Pull all thread ends to wrong side of gusset and knot. If you use squares of underlining for reinforcement, trim the square of fabric to ⅜″. Press the gusset seam toward the garment (1). To further strengthen the gusset on sporty or casual clothes, topstitch close to the gusset seam on the outside, as shown (2).

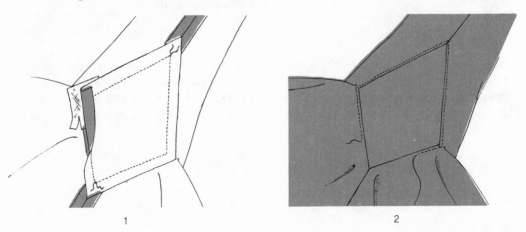

1   2

Sleeve Finishes

Let every gesture of the arm display a perfectly polished sleeve finish—tastefully suited to the overall design, neatly pressed, and flawlessly completed. Feel free to adapt the finish in accordance with the pattern design and your fabric.

The style description on your pattern envelope includes mention of the sleeve length preferred by the designer. Check the length of your sleeve when it is pinned into the armhole, referring to the diagram below for an explanation of the designer's length. If a cuff is a part of the design, be sure to take its depth into account in the total sleeve length. Also allow for blousing in a full sleeve.

Here are the suggested lengths that should be used for reference when you are adjusting your pattern or fitting your garment.

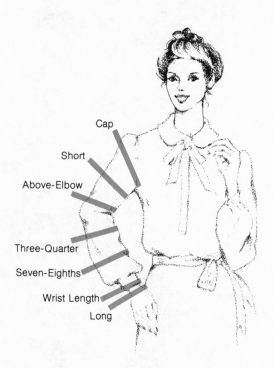

Cap: This is a very, very short sleeve, actually an extension of the shoulder and not usually continued under the arm.

Short: The typical short sleeve lies with its lower edge relatively straight across the upper arm.

Above-Elbow: As the name suggests, the arm above the elbow is completely covered by the sleeve.

Three-Quarter: This sleeve is three-fourths the length of the arm. It ends halfway between the elbow and the wrist bone.

Seven-Eighths: A sleeve which terminates approximately 2″ above the wrist bone or halfway between the three-quarter and the long sleeve.

Wrist Length: This sleeve grazes the wrist just at the prominent wrist bone.

Long or *Full Length:* Falls 1″ below the wrist bone at a comfortable length before reaching the hand.

Keep in mind that the "correct" sleeve length for you is one that is in proportion to your figure. Sleeves influence the total silhouette of your garment. Their shape, length, and finish can exaggerate a figure flaw or lead the eyes away from it. Select a length and type that becomes you and choose your finish from those on the following pages.

Finish a Sleeve with Finesse

A well-made finish enhances the sleeve and handsomely sets off the completed garment. Be precise—avoid sloppy plackets, uneven hems, and mismatched closures with half-sewn snaps. Consider the mood of your garment when choosing a sleeve finish, because varying the finish can give your sleeve an entirely different appearance. A shirt-sleeve placket is perfect for casual clothes, while a fragile thread loop and button closing would be more suitable for dressy or couture garments.

Try on the sleeve. For any of the lapped closures, check to see that the lap will open properly when finished. It should be in back of the sleeve (above the little finger) and open toward the body. Be doubly sure that the right and left sleeves open in opposite directions so that your careful work won't result in two left openings. Establish the location of any buttons or fastenings. Remember that a long sleeve without a closing needs to have an opening big enough for the hand to pass through, while the sleeve with a closing can have a smaller opening circumference. Allow ½'' to 1'' for ease between the circumference of the arm and the opening when the sleeve is fastened.

Fit the sleeve, then remove it from the garment for easier handling when you apply your sleeve finish. Use interfacing for a precise, well-shaped look that lasts through the rigors of wearing and cleaning. Careful matching, stitching, and trimming are natural steps toward achieving a sleeve finish with savoir-faire.

Straight Hem

Although it is the most basic and easiest of all sleeve finishes, the straight hem can be quite elegant as it gracefully circles the arm in a smooth curve. Careful construction and an appropriate interfacing are necessary for a hem that is to hold its curved line without "breaking." The interfacing you use should be determined by your fabric for the desired effect—whether it be a creased edge or a rolled edge. Cut the interfacing in bias strips equal in length to the circumference of the finished sleeve plus ½'' and equal in width to the depth of the hem.

Stitch the underarm seam of the sleeve. Place the lower edge of interfacing ⅝'' below the hemline; overlap ends ½'' and sew, as shown. Sew the interfacing to the garment or underlining along the hemline with long running stitches and along the upper edge of the interfacing with long catchstitches. For a sleeve edge that will be topstitched or edgestitched, trim interfacing along foldline and catchstitch in place. Turn up the hem to cover the interfacing. Baste close to the fold. Check to see that the hem is an even depth all around, and trim if necessary. Finish the raw edge of your hem with a stitch and overcast, or zigzag finish. Blindstitch the edge to the underlining of your garment fabric.

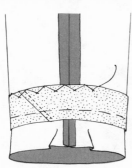
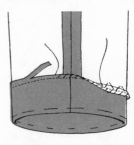

Facings

SHAPED FACING: Overcast the unnotched edge of the sleeve facing with hand or machine stitching. Stitch the facing ends together. Trim the seam allowances to ¼'' and press open (1). Stitch the facing to the sleeve; then trim and grade the seam (2). Turn the facing to the inside, favoring the outside of the sleeve, and press. Blindstitch the free edge to the garment or underlining (3).

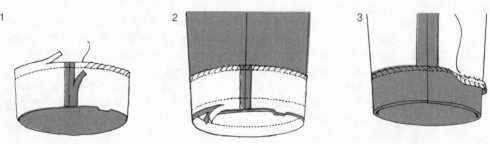

SELF-FACING WITH SLIT: This finish continues partway up the vertical seam and usually includes mitered corners. Interface the opening and hem before you stitch the sleeve seam. If you do not have an interfacing pattern piece, use your sleeve pattern as a guide, and cut the interfacing on the bias equal in width to the depth of the hem and equal in length to the circumference of the sleeve plus 1¼''. Position the interfacing so that it extends ⅝'' past the hemline and slit foldlines, as shown. Sew the interfacing to the sleeve or underlining with long running stitches along the hemline and slit foldlines and with catch-stitches along the upper edges (1).

Miter the corners of your sleeve by turning the edges to the outside along the hemline and foldlines; then stitch to the corners (2). Trim and press the seams open (3). Stitch the long sleeve seam to the appropriate marking. Turn the corners and the facing to the inside along the foldlines and hemline; press. Baste close to the fold. Overcast the raw edges, by hand or machine. Blindstitch the free edges to the sleeve or underlining. Reinforce the end of the slit with a bar tack on the inside sleeve (4).

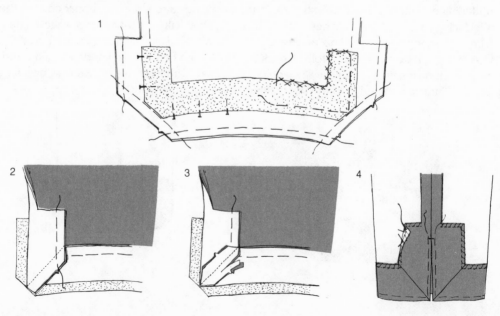

BIAS FACING: Cut a 1½'' wide bias strip in a length equal to the circumference of the sleeve plus 2''. With raw edges even, pin the bias strip to the sleeve, right sides together. Pin ends together on straight grain. Remove bias strip from sleeve and stitch ends in a diagonal seam; trim to ¼'' and press open (1). Then stitch the bias to the sleeve; trim and grade the seam allowances (2). Turn the bias inside, favoring the right side of the sleeve, and press. Turn the raw edge under ¼'' and slipstitch to the sleeve or underlining (3).

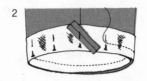

LAPPED CLOSING WITH ROLLED HEM: Generally used with a buttoned cuff, this closing allows for a cuff opening without the necessity of making a sleeve placket. Reinforce the area to be hemmed, using small stitches along the seamline through the markings; clip to the markings. Trim the seam allowance between the clips to ⅜''; trim any underlining up to the stitching (1). Turn raw edge along stitching to form a rolled hem and slipstitch (2). Whipstitch the ends. Stitch underarm seam, add gathers, and apply cuff (3).

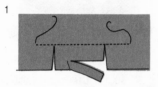
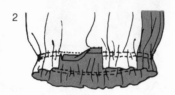

Casings

For a casing at the edge of a sleeve, turn up the fabric along the foldline and baste. Turn in raw edge ¼'' and edgestitch to sleeve, leaving the desired opening (1). Or an applied casing can be formed from a separate strip of fabric or bias tape and applied like a shaped facing. Insert elastic into casing, overlap ends ½'', and stitch securely. Complete edgestitching (2).

For a casing with a heading, which forms a ruffle at the edge of the sleeve, extra fabric is required for the extension. Turn fabric to inside along heading foldline and baste close to fold. Mark casing seamlines and stitch, leaving desired opening (3). An applied casing can also be used with a heading. Insert elastic and stitch securely. Stitch opening closed.
Refer to section on casings, page 255.

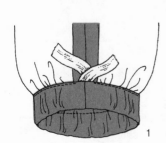

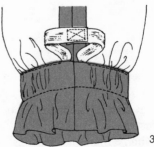

Placket Opening for Cuffs

For cuffs which fit snugly around the wrist, a placket must be inserted into the sleeve before the cuff is applied.

FACED PLACKET: For the placket facing, cut a 2½" wide strip of self-fabric the length of the opening plus 1". Finish the raw edge on the sides and one end of the facing with hand overcasting or zigzag stitching. Right sides together, center it over the slash markings with the raw edge at the bottom. Stitch along the stitching lines with small stitches, taking one stitch across the point. Slash carefully to the point, without cutting through the stitching (1). Turn the facing inside and press (2). Complete sleeve with a binding, cuff, or hem; then blindstitch the facing to the underlining or the garment (3).

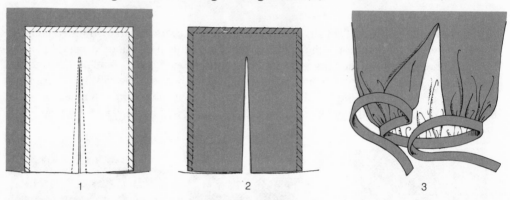

CONTINUOUS BOUND PLACKET: Inserted in a slash or a seam, the continuous bound placket can be an extremely durable and simple opening for sleeves. Since the edges of the placket overlap, it can be used with any lapped cuff.

TO INSERT IN A SLASH, reinforce the area to be slashed with small stitches along the stitching line, taking a stitch across the point. Slash to the point (1). Cut a straight strip of self-fabric 1½" wide and twice the length of the slash. Spread slash open and, right sides together, place its stitching line ¼" from one long edge of strip. Stitch with small stiches on garment beside previous stitching (2). From the right side, press lap away from garment. Turn the free edge in ¼" and slipstitch over the seam (3). To keep the lap from turning to the outside, stitch a diagonal line at the top of the fold (4).

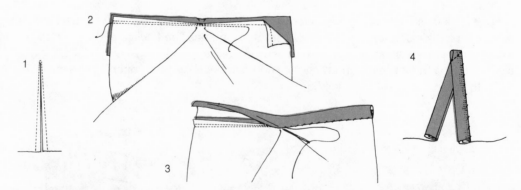

Bulk may be decreased by cutting 1¼" wide strip on a selvage. Use the raw edge for the first seam; then slipstitch the selvage over the seam allowance without turning it under. When a more durable finish is desired, substitute topstitching for slipstitching.

TO INSERT IN A SEAM, stitch the seam, leaving an opening for the placket. Backstitch at the end of the seam for reinforcement. Press the seam open, leaving the placket seam allowances unpressed. Clip the seam allowances at end of opening and trim the opening edges to ¼" (1). Cut a straight strip of self-fabric 1½" wide and twice the length of the opening. Spread the seam open and, right sides together, stitch the strip to the opening edge with small stitches in a ¼" seam. Grade the seam (2). Turn the free edge in ¼" and slipstitch over the seam (3). Stitch diagonally at top of fold (illustration 4, page 284).

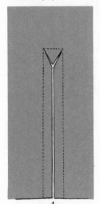
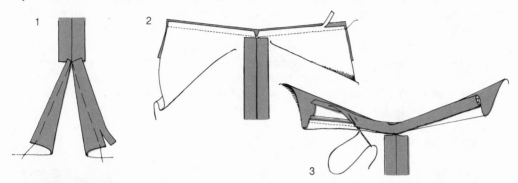

SHIRT-SLEEVE PLACKET: This sporty finish designed for a man-tailored shirt requires precision and care in its making for a fine professional look. First reinforce the sleeve opening by stitching along the seamlines, using small stitches. Slash between the stitches and carefully clip to the corners (1).

Stitch the right side of the underlap piece to the wrong side of the back edge of the sleeve (the edge nearer the underarm seam). Trim and press the seam allowances toward the underlap. Then turn under the remaining long edge of the underlap ¼" and press. Place the pressed edge over the seam allowances and edgestitch through all thicknesses (2).

Stitch the right side of the overlap piece to the wrong side of the remaining slashed edge. Trim the seam and press it toward the overlap. Stitch the base of the triangular end of the slash to the end of the overlap. Press the stitched end of the overlap up. Turn in the overlap at the seam allowances and along the foldlines; press and baste. Pin the overlap in place along the folded edges (3).

Keeping the underlap free, stitch the outside fold of the overlap to the top of the opening. Tie thread ends securely on the wrong side. Stitching through all layers, stitch across the placket, securing both the point of the slash and the top of the underlap in the stitches; pivot and stitch along the remaining edges of the overlap. Tie ends securely on the wrong side (4).

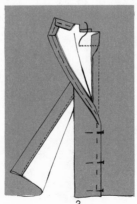
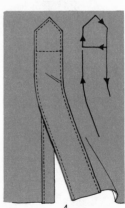

Special Sleeve Closings

Long, narrow sleeves tapering to the wrist are extremely elegant and graceful. They can be closed with snaps, thread loops and buttons, fabric loops and buttons, or a zipper.

SNAP CLOSING: Stitch the sleeve above the marking. Clip the back seam allowance ½'' above the opening. Press the seam open above the clip, and the front edge to the inside along seamline. Turn up the lower edge of the sleeve along the seamline or hemline and baste close to the fold. Finish the raw edge with ribbon seam binding, easing if necessary. Sew the hem in place. To finish opening edges, place ribbon seam binding ⅛'' over the raw edges, turning under the top ends as shown and leaving ½'' extending past the hem fold. Stitch close to the edge of the seam binding (1). Turn in the seam binding ends. Turn the front edge inside along the seamline; turn the back edge inside along the seam binding edge, as shown. Press. Slipstitch the lower ends and long edges of the seam binding in place. On the inside, lap the back seam allowance over the front below the clip, matching seamlines. Slipstitch the upper edge in place, taking care not to sew through to the right side (2). Fasten with snaps (3).

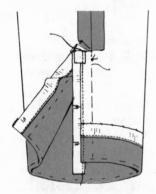

1

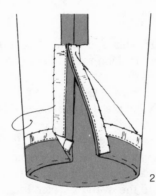

2

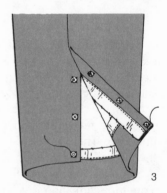

3

THREAD LOOP AND BUTTON CLOSING: This finish is perfect for the row of tiny buttons that is such an elegant touch on a sleeve. It eliminates the bulk of fabric loops, enabling you to use many small buttons spaced closely together. Finish the lower and opening edges of the sleeve with ribbon seam binding, as described above for the snap closing. Lap the opening and align the buttons on the undersection with the edge of the overlap. Space the loop markings evenly. Make the loops as instructed in Thread Loops, page 324. The loops should be uniform in size and shape and just large enough for the buttons to pass through. Secure the ends of the loops on the wrong side.

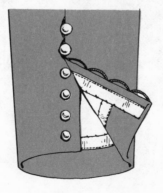

FABRIC LOOP AND BUTTON CLOSING: On the back edge only, clip the seam allowance ½″ above the opening. Turn up the lower edge of the sleeve along the hemline and baste close to the fold. Finish the raw edge with ribbon seam binding, easing if necessary. Sew the hem in place. Make fabric loops according to the instructions in Fabric Loops, page 322. Machine baste them along the seamline of the overlap, as shown, and check to see that they are just large enough for the buttons to pass through (1).

Press seam open above clip. Place ribbon seam binding along the seamline over the loop ends and ⅛″ over the back raw edge, leaving extra seam binding at both ends. Stitch close to seam binding edge. Turn front edge to the inside along the seamline and back edge to the inside along the seam binding, turning under seam binding ends (2). Slipstitch upper and lower ends in place and blindstitch long edges to underlining or garment (3).

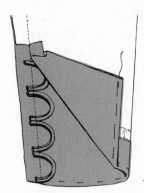

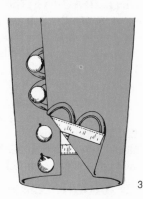

ZIPPER CLOSING: Stitch and press open the sleeve seam above the marking. Finish the hem edge. Baste and press open the remainder of the seam, clipping at the hemline (1). To shorten zipper, whipstitch several times over zipper teeth ¼″ below desired new length and cut off excess. On the inside, center the closed zipper face down over the basted seam with the zipper tab just above the hemline; baste. Trim the zipper tape away below the hemline to eliminate bulk (2). On the outside, prickstitch the zipper in place along the sides and across the upper end.

Turn and pin the hem and baste close to the fold, turning in the ends to clear the zipper teeth. Slipstitch the ends to the zipper tape. Blindstitch sleeve hem to underlining or garment (3).

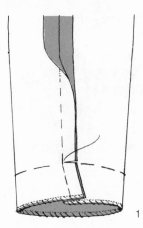
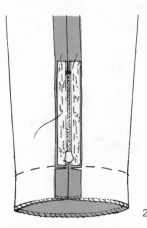
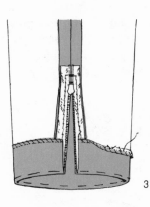

Cuffs

The cuff is one design detail that constantly changes, but never goes out of style. Of the two main categories, the primary function of the **EXTENDED CUFF** is to add length to the sleeve, whereas the **TURNBACK CUFF** rolls back to cover the base of the sleeve and often serves solely as a decorative feature. Both may control fullness. They can be straight bands folded in half, or may be shaped from separate fabric pieces. If a sleeve opening is used, a cuff should fasten closely around the wrist; but without an opening, a cuff must be big enough for the hand to pass through. Remember that trimming and grading of all seams is essential to a well-made cuff. For pressing tips, refer to page 344.

INTERFACING: The outer layer of the cuff should be interfaced. For a cuff cut in sections, use the cuff pattern piece and cut the interfacing on the bias for softer shaping. For a cuff made from one piece, cut the interfacing to extend ⅝″ past the foldline to help maintain a smoothly rolled edge. Sew interfacing along the foldline with long running stitches. However, if this cuff is to be topstitched or edgestitched, trim the interfacing along the foldline.

Lightweight interfacing can be stitched into the seamlines. Pin interfacing to the wrong side of the outer cuff section and stitch ½″ from the edge. Trim interfacing close to stitching. For heavier-weight interfacing, trim away the seam allowances and catchstitch the interfacing along the seamlines of the cuff. For fusible interfacings, the seam allowances and corners are trimmed away before fusing.

BUTTONHOLES: Transfer the placement markings to the right side of the cuff with thread tracing before applying interfacing. Make bound buttonholes before stitching the cuff sections together. Machine- or hand-worked buttonholes are made after the cuff is completed.

Extended Cuffs

BAND CUFF: This cuff is the simplest of all cuffs to make. Stitch the cuff ends together and press open. Stitch the gathered sleeve to the interfaced half of the cuff, right sides together. Trim and grade the seam (1). Press the seam allowances toward the cuff. Turn the cuff inside along the foldline, wrong sides together, and baste close to the fold. Trim and turn in the raw edge along the seamline; slipstitch it in place over the seam (2). You may find it easier to attach a thickly gathered sleeve to a band cuff *before* you close the sleeve or cuff seams. Stitch the gathered edge of the sleeve to the open cuff, matching markings. Trim and press the seam allowances toward the cuff. Then stitch the long underarm sleeve seam and cuff seam at the same time.

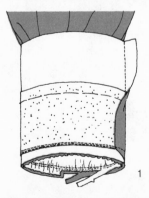

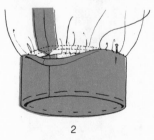

1

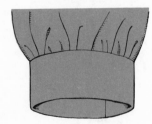

2

Facings

A perfectly applied facing finishes a raw edge and lies neatly concealed, hidden from view. A facing serves its purpose invisibly, finishing a neckline in a variety of shapes—simple jewel or plunging V, square or round, bateau or scooped. A facing can also be found finishing an armhole or at the edge of a sleeve . . . down the front of a jacket, dress, or blouse . . . along the hem of a top or skirt. The one exception to invisibility: A facing always comes into full view on a smoothly rolled lapel.

Piping, Binding, and Banding

An elegant edge, accented with fabric or trim, adds a custom touch of snap and style. Contrasting piping can outline an edge and define a seam for sculptured detail and refinement. Finely molded binding in smooth bias curves is always smart finishing—a subtle accent of flattery in self-fabric, or a decorative highlight in contrasting fabric. Banding, in many widths and fabrics, can enhance a neckline or define a hem. Smoothly and evenly applied without a ripple or twist, these flattering edge finishes are handsome fashion accents.

Casings

Casings enable fabric to be gathered into graceful folds with a drawstring or snugged into place with elastic. Forming a ruffle around a neckline or bodice top, casings add softness and interest to the fabric edge. They provide seductive, off-the-shoulder glamour . . . flowing fullness in gathered sleeves . . . easy comfort in an adjustable waistline. Casings subtly adapt to the body shape and often go unnoticed.

Collars

Collars vary the fashion landscape, offering flattering silhouettes for every mood and figure. The innocent round-shaped collars can grace your face with charming symmetry. The classic lines of a notched lapel reward sewing patience with handsome distinction. Collars on stands subtly lend a hint of swagger. Buttoned up to the neck or opened wide, collars are the face framers of fashion.

Long, unbroken curves make the shawl collar a perfect figure lengthener. The perky stand-up collar expresses flair and form. The bias rolled collar adds grace and softness, while a tie collar in a voluptuous pussy-cat bow is a real mood lifter. The soft cowl, while not a true collar, is still a flattering face framer.

Sleeves

Short and snappy or long and
skinny, trim and efficient or flowing
generously from a gathered wrist,
sleeves offer a wealth of design
potential. Perfect shoulders
distinguish a well-set sleeve and
form the focus of a smoothly curving
raglan or kimono sleeve. Ranging
from trimly tailored to soft and
sheer, sleeves should be both
beautiful and comfortable. Cuffs may
be unassuming finishing details or
eye-catching design features.
Matching or contrasting, turned back
or extending from sleeves of any
length and shape, cuffs often sport
the extra emphasis of beautiful
buttons or cuff links.

Pockets

Pockets—from practical carryalls to decorative accents—are as varied as they are versatile. From shy pockets hiding in seams to brazen contrasting flaps, pockets present many fashion fronts and many personalities. Patch pockets can blend unobtrusively or be accented with a buttoned flap. Tailored single or double welts provide a crisp and precise design detail. High or low, horizontal or diagonal, pockets can serve both the hand and the eye.

Waistbands and Belts

Waistlines may be high, low, or natural as fashions vary, but wherever they span the silhouette, a handsome belt defines them in style. A tailored belt, topstitched for emphasis . . . a skinny, bias-covered cord, knotted or bowed . . . a soft fabric tie, nestled in gathers . . . a wide wrapped sash, accenting the midriff—each makes a different style statement. Even an unadorned waistband is a design detail of proportion and line.

Closures

There is a multitude of methods for closing a garment. Whether buttons are a focus or a convenience, let them show off faultless buttonholes. Your buttonholes may be bound in any of several ways: looped, corded, or placed in a seam, or made of stitches by hand or machine. Marching down the front of a dress, or gracing a smoothly fitting cuff, buttons and buttonholes are a winning combination. Zippers, concealed discreetly or boldly displayed . . . hooks and snaps hidden away . . . perky bows and graceful ties—are all practical components for fashion fastening.

Hems

Narrow or full and flowing, straight or deeply curved—hems are the final finish in the art of sewing. There's a wide selection for every fabric and style of garment: narrow rolled hems for delicate sheers . . . invisible hems for tailored perfection . . . topstitched hems for added detailing. Though hemlines fluctuate up and down as fashion dictates, a well-made hem is the perfect ending of any design.

LAPPED CUFF WITH AN OPENING: A buttoned cuff is most often used on full-length, gathered or pleated sleeves with a continuous bound placket (see page 284). Make your bound buttonholes. Fold the cuff lengthwise, and stitch the ends from the fold to within ⅝″ of the long edge. Trim, grading seams (1). Turn and press. Fold under the front lap of the sleeve placket so that the folded edge is even with the cuff edge. Place the back lap of the sleeve on the cuff at the marking. Stitch the gathered sleeve to the interfaced half of the cuff (2). Press, trim, and turn the cuff in the same manner as for a band cuff. Baste close to the fold. Trim and turn in the raw edge along the seamline and slipstitch it over the seam and extension end (3). Complete your button and buttonhole closure (4).

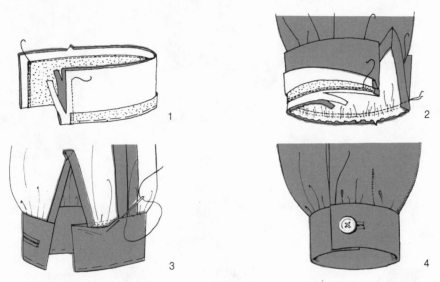

LAPPED CUFF WITHOUT OPENING: You will probably want to put a button trim on this cuff. Fold the cuff lengthwise. To form a finished extension, start stitching at the fold, pivot at the corner, and stitch as far as the marking. On the other end, stitch from the fold to within ⅝″ of long edge. Clip the seam allowance to marking on the long notched edge. Trim and grade the seam. Turn to the right side and press (1). Stitch the gathered sleeve to interfaced half of the cuff. The end of the cuff section will meet the extension marking at the clip, as shown. Clip the sleeve seam allowance at the marking (2). Press, trim, and turn the cuff in the same manner as for a band cuff. Baste close to the fold. Trim and turn in the raw edge along the seamline; slipstitch (3). Fasten extension in place on the right side, as desired (4).

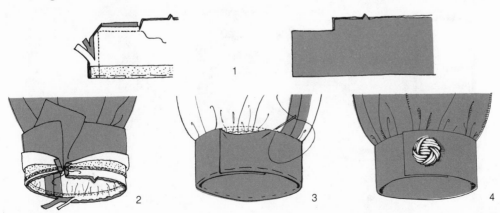

SHIRT-SLEEVE CUFF: A shirt-sleeve cuff is used with a shirt-sleeve placket and is usually topstitched. Stitch the cuff sections together, ending ⅝" from the long notched edge. Trim, turn, and press (1). Stitch the *wrong side* of the gathered sleeve to the *non-interfaced* section of the cuff, placing the placket edges even with the cuff edges. Trim and grade the seam (2). Press the seam toward the cuff. On the outside, turn in the remaining edge where it falls over the seam and baste in place. Topstitch close to all edges of the cuff and again ¼" away from the first line of stitching. Fasten with a machine-made or hand-worked buttonhole and button (3).

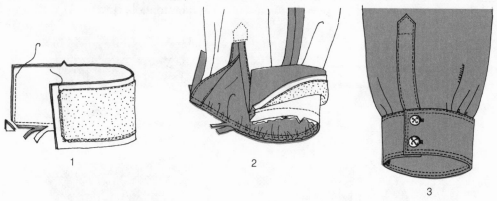

FRENCH CUFF or **BUTTON-LINK CUFF:** These cuffs are worn with the ends extending rather than lapping. The French cuff is folded back on itself and fastened by cuff links passing through four buttonholes. Bound buttonholes should be made on the outermost cuff only, after inserting the interfacing. The two buttonholes that do not show are machine-worked to prevent bulk. The button link cuff is constructed the same way, but is not folded back and has only two buttonholes for the link buttons.

For a French cuff, the inside layer of the cuff will be on the outside when turned back; therefore, apply the interfacing to the inside cuff section and sew it along the foldline with long running stitches. Stitch the cuff sections together, ending ⅝" from the long notched edge; trim, grade, turn, and press (1). Matching markings, stitch the gathered sleeve to the non-interfaced side of the cuff. Trim and grade the seam (2). Press the seam toward the cuff. Turn the raw edge under on the inside and slipstitch over the seam. Slipstitch the extended ends when applicable. Make any remaining buttonholes by hand or machine. Turn the lower edge to the outside along the roll line so that the buttonholes meet; press lightly. Fasten with link buttons or cuff links (3).

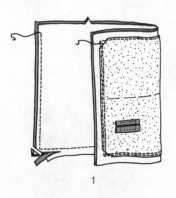
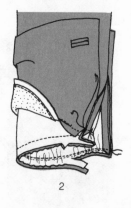

Turnback Cuffs

We have illustrated here only the most classic examples of straight and shaped cuffs. Their variations are unlimited, including scalloped, slashed, and sculptured design edges that may circle the sleeve in a continuous seam or stop at multishaped finished ends. They can be attached to the sleeve in many ways as well, and often serve a dual role as extended cuffs by simply not folding them back.

STRAIGHT TURNBACK CUFF WITH SELF-HEM: These cuffs should taper out slightly to be somewhat larger than the sleeve at the finished edge; this will ensure that the sleeve will not pucker when the cuff is turned back.

After you have determined the finished length of your sleeve, add twice the desired width of the cuff plus 1″ for a hem to the finished length of the sleeve; be sure to taper the cuff out from the hemline to the cuff foldline. Interface the cuff area before stitching the seams. Cut the interfacing the same width as the cuff plus 1¼″ and extend the interfacing ⅝″ beyond the foldline and roll line for a softer edge. Sew to the cuff at foldlines and roll lines with running stitches. Stitch the sleeve seam and press it open (1).

To form the rolled cuff, finish the raw edge and turn the cuff inside along the foldline. Baste close to the fold (2). Roll the folded edge to the outside, forming the cuff. Baste through all thicknesses to hold the roll in place (3). On the inside, blindstitch the hem edge to the sleeve (4).

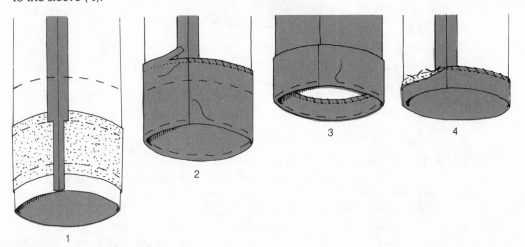

VARIATION WITH A SLIT: Prepare your cuff as in step 1, above. Finish the raw edge, then turn the interfaced side to the outside along the foldline. Mark the position of the slit and stitch along the markings, taking a stitch across the point. Clip the slit close to the stitching, and, using a sleeve board, press just the slit area. Turn the cuff to the inside and finish, as above

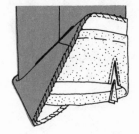

STRAIGHT TURNBACK CUFF: Usually a single rectangle cut on the bias or straight grain, a straight cuff can also be two fabric sections. This cuff should be slightly larger in circumference at its foldline than the sleeve to which it is attached so that it can turn back easily. Apply interfacing to one half of the cuff, extending ⅝" beyond foldline and roll line for a softer edge. Stitch the ends of the cuff together. Trim the seam allowances to the foldline as shown and press them open. Stitch the non-interfaced side of the cuff to the sleeve, right sides together; trim (1). Press the seam open. Finish raw edge with stitching, lace, or seam binding. Then turn the cuff inside along the foldline, wrong sides together; baste close to the folded edge. Blindstitch the hem to the sleeve or underlining (2). Roll the cuff to the outside over the sleeve (3).

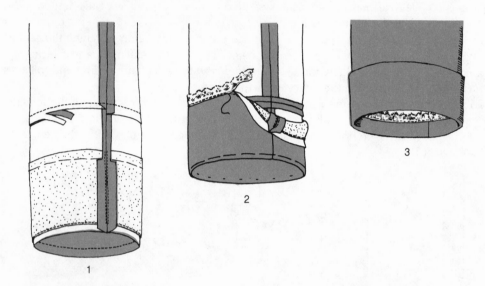

SHAPED TURNBACK CUFF: Made from two fabric pieces, this cuff has many variations. Apply interfacing to one fabric piece. Stitch the cuff sections together, leaving the notched edge open; then trim and grade the seam allowances (1). Turn and press the cuff. Then baste and stitch the cuff to the right side of the sleeve through all thicknesses (2). Finish the notched edges with a bias or shaped facing (page 282), stitching through all the layers. Roll the cuff to the outside along the seam, favoring the cuff so the seam is on the inside (3).

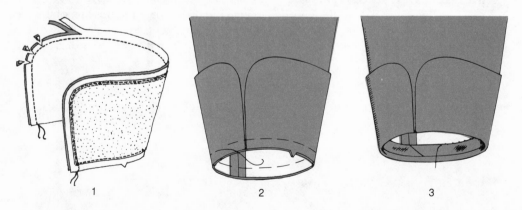

Detachable Cuffs

There are few fashion accents more elegant than the crisp, trim appearance of detachable cuffs. They can be straight or shaped. You can make them in a continuous band, open, or partially open with a slit or a slash. They may be designed to turn back over a sleeve or an existing cuff, or they can simulate a shirt cuff by extending below the hem of a jacket sleeve. They are often used to provide a removable, washable trim on a garment that requires dry-cleaning.

Detachable cuffs that are designed to turn back must taper so that the finished edge, which fits over the sleeve will be somewhat wider than the inside edge, which slips inside the sleeve. Cuffs that are meant to extend below the sleeve will have to be made to fit just the inside measurement of the sleeve to which they will be applied.

BAND CUFF: This is usually made by stitching the ends of the cuff together and pressing the seam open. Fold along the foldline with wrong sides together. Turn in the remaining raw edges along the seamline and slipstitch (1). From the right side, lap the sleeve over the cuff the desired depth and pin. Turn to the wrong side and slipstitch or snap the cuff in place (2).

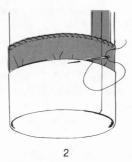

1   2

CUFF WITH A SLIT: Fold cuff, right sides together, and stitch each end. Grade seams, turn, and press. Join cuff by slipstitching ends together, leaving a slit. Baste raw edges together. Then encase them in a bias strip (self-fabric or commercial binding) cut to fit the inner circumference of the sleeve. Simply edgestitch the binding to the raw edges, overlapping the ends (1). From the right side, lap the sleeve over the cuff the desired depth and pin. Turn to the wrong side and slipstitch or snap the cuff in place (2). Roll the folded edge to the outside, forming the cuff, and anchor the corners with a bar tack if desired (3).

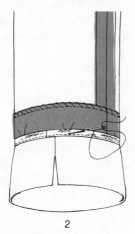

1   2   3

Pockets

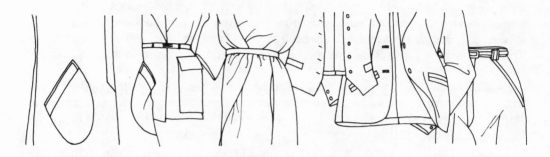

If you are a novice at the art of sewing, or even if you've acquired a great amount of skill, you probably will be confused at the seemingly endless variations in pocket types and names. To help clear your mind, just remember that pockets branch out from two basic constructions—pockets of self-fabric applied to the garment, and pockets of lining pushed to the inside through a seam or slash, and sometimes covered by a flap or a welt.

Pockets can beautifully accent a professional seam or they can expose a poor construction job. A few simple but vital rules will bring about successful results: thread trace all pocket markings to the right side of all pocket and garment parts; pull pockets through openings very gently; keep all corners true; use interfacing for body; strive for even, balanced welts or flaps; and anchor the side edges of flaps and welts **invisibly** to the garment.

One excellent rule for positioning pockets below the waist is that they should be located at a level where your hands can slip into them naturally and comfortably. If placed too near the hem, they will look and feel awkward. However, there are instances when the rules are meant to be flexed a little. Pockets above the waist, and patch pockets anywhere, are so often meant to be strictly decorative that you should concentrate on whether their position is flattering, regardless of how accessible the pocket may be. When adjusting your pattern, the pockets may require relocating if you shorten or lengthen your garment.

All types of pockets made in lightweight or loosely woven fabrics need to be interfaced. Interfacing provides added strength, reinforces the opening, and preserves the pocket line. Welts and flaps should be interfaced if their shape and resiliency are to be preserved. The interfacing is generally cut on bias grain to extend ⅝″ past the foldline unless the welt or flap is going to be topstitched. Patch pockets usually need no interfacing, but are often lined for a custom finish. In-seam pockets will not require interfacing, but may need the reinforcement of a stay to keep the pocket edge from stretching.

As a decoration or means of emphasizing a design line, topstitching is superb. As a method of applying your pocket, however, topstitching is not generally recommended. The patch pocket in particular will have a neater appearance if the topstitching is done before the pocket and garment are joined. It will then be easier to topstitch a straighter, more even line than when you are trying to concentrate on connecting the pocket and the garment. The topstitched pocket is then sewn to the garment by hand. It is possible to topstitch your pocket in place on lightweight, closely woven fabrics, but stitching over many thicknesses of bulky fabric or napped fabric can become a problem.

Patch Pockets

Patch pockets are made from self-fabric and applied to the outside of the garment. They can be lined or be left unlined. When constructing a pair of patch pockets, check carefully to be sure both pockets are the same size and shape and are attached to the garment evenly.

UNLINED: Turn under the top edge ¼" and stitch. Then turn the upper edge of the pocket to the outside along the foldline. Stitch ends and trim, as shown. If yours is a rounded pocket, easestitch the rounded area ¼" away from the seamline on the seam allowance to ensure a flat finish (1). Turn both the hem and the seam allowance to the inside. On a rounded pocket, pull in the easestitches to shape the pocket curve. If the pocket is square or rectangular, miter all corners (if you need mitering instructions, refer to page 233). Baste around the edges, notching away the excess fullness. Slipstitch the hem to the pocket (2).

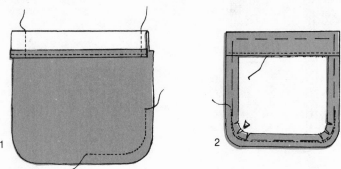

When topstitching is desired, do it before you attach the pocket. Then, from the right side, pin and baste the pocket in place. If the pocket is to be applied to a curved area of your garment, such as the front hip, place the garment over a curved surface such as a tailor's ham in order to pin the pocket in place. From the wrong side, work a small backstitch through garment and pocket. Be sure the stitches do not show on the right side. Or you can slipstitch the pocket to the garment from the right side, taking care not to pull the stitches too tight, or the pocket will pucker.

SELF-LINED: Cut the desired pocket shape twice the length of the pocket plus seam allowances on all sides. Simply fold your pocket right sides together and stitch both sides and a portion of the bottom. Leave an opening for turning. Trim and grade the seam allowances (1). Turn the pocket, press it, and slipstitch the opening shut (2).

Attach to the garment in the same manner as for the unlined pocket.

LINED: There are two methods for constructing a lined patch pocket. In the first method, the lining is slipstitched by hand to the inside edge of the pocket; in the second method, the lining is stitched by machine.

With right sides together, stitch the pocket lining to the pocket self-facing. Press the seam toward the lining. For rounded pockets, easestitch the rounded areas on both the pocket and the lining ¼'' away from the seamline on the seam allowance. Turn in the edges of the pocket along the seamlines, drawing up the ease thread where necessary. Starting at the foldline, taper the seam allowances of the lining ⅛'' so that the finished lining edge will fall ⅛'' inside the finished pocket edge. Baste close to the edge (1). Turn the lining and self-facing to the inside along the pocket foldline. Slipstitch the lining in place around the inside pocket edge (2).

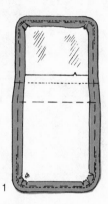

1   2

For the machine method, pin the pocket lining to the pocket self-facing, with right sides together. Stitch seam, leaving a small opening in the center for turning the pocket. Press the seam toward the lining. To ensure that no lining will show at the edges of the completed pocket, trim ⅛'' from around the lining edge. Fold pocket along pocket foldline with right sides of fabric together. Align bottom and side edges; stitch along pocket seamline. Trim and grade the seam allowances.

For a square pocket, trim diagonally across the seam allowances at the corners; for a rounded pocket, notch out the excess fabric in the curved areas (3).

Turn pocket to the right side by pulling it gently through the opening. Press pocket, rolling outer seam slightly to the lining side. Slipstitch opening closed (4).

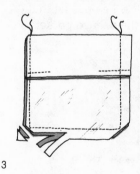
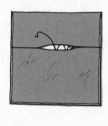

3   4

Pocket Flaps and Welts

Just about any type of pocket can be covered or set off by a flap or welt. Both may also appear by themselves as decorative fakes. The major distinction between a flap and a welt is that a flap hangs downward freely while a welt generally points upward and is securely attached along its sides.

The example shown is a decorative flap, but the same construction principles apply to any flap or wide welt. Interface the outer half of the flap so that the interfacing extends ⅝" past the foldline. Sew along the foldline with long running stitches. For flaps that will be topstitched, trim interfacing away at the foldline and catchstitch the edge in place (1). With right sides together, fold and stitch the flap ends to ⅝" from the flap base. Trim and grade the seam; clipping or notching will be necessary for a shaped flap (2). Turn and press.

When the direction of the seam allowance coincides with the direction of the finished flap or welt, you must establish the roll of the flap at the seamline so that it will lie flat. Turn the seam allowances of the flap down over your hand to establish the roll line, adjusting the flap or welt if more upper fabric is required (3). Pin and baste along the new seamline of the upper portion through both layers. Remember this treatment will be necessary only when the flap or welt turns over its own seam allowance.

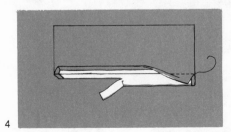

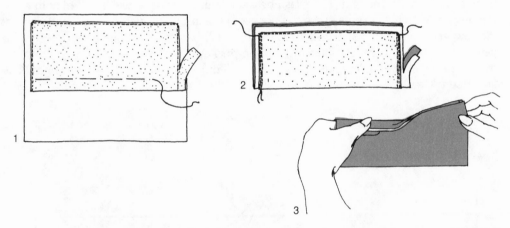

To attach the flap, place the new seamline along the placement lines on your garment and stitch through all thicknesses. Turn back the upper seam allowance and trim the lower one close to the stitching. Turn in ¼" on the long edge of the upper seam allowance, folding the ends in diagonally, and turn it down over the trimmed edge (4). Then edgestitch. Fold the flap down and press, being careful not to overpress or unsightly ridges from the flap edges will appear on the garment. To secure upper sides of corners, slipstitch to the garment from right side, or backstitch heavy fabrics from the wrong side (5).

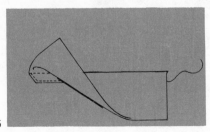

Welt Pockets

A welt pocket gives a very crisp, neat, and precise look to create an essentially tailored appearance. The construction of a welt pocket is similar to a bound buttonhole. It can be made with a single welt, a double welt, or covered with a pocket flap.

To make construction easier, mark precisely and stitch accurately. Use short stitches and begin and end your stitching exactly at the markings. Cut carefully when you are slashing the pocket open. Finally, take time to press after each step and you will be rewarded with a professional-looking welt pocket.

Single Welt Pocket

For this pocket the welt is pressed upward over the opening of a lining pocket. If your fabric needs more body, interface the welt in the usual way. Construct and press the welt. It will be easier to work with if you baste the raw edges together on the seamline and trim them to ¼" from the seamline. Always do any required topstitching before you attach the welt. Then pin the welt to the garment, placing the seamline of the welt over the lower stitching line on the right side of the garment; baste. Now pin and baste the lining pocket over the welt with the deeper portion above the welt. Stitch along the stitching lines, backstitching or using small knots at the ends (1). Slash between your stitching to within ½" of both ends; clip diagonally to the corners. Turn the pocket to the inside, turning the welt up. Overcast the raw edges of both narrow seam allowances (2). Press. Positioning the pocket and garment as shown, carefully stitch around the pocket edges, being very sure to catch the base of the small triangular ends in your sewing. Trim and overcast the pocket edges. The final step takes place on the outside; just slipstitch the ends of the welt in place (3).

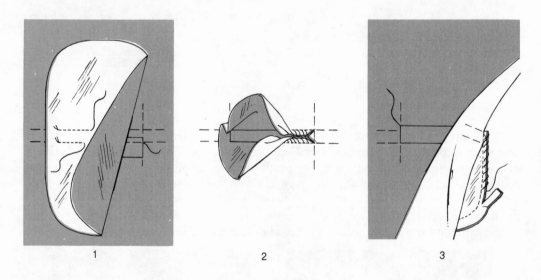

1   2   3

Double-Welt Pocket

This pocket opening looks like a large bound buttonhole. It has two very narrow welts that face each other and is the exception to the rule that welts point upward. Fold both long edges of the welt, wrong sides together, to meet at the center; press. With cut edges up, center folded welt over the pocket markings; baste. Slash through center of welt; do not cut the garment (1). Baste garment fabric section of pocket in place along upper stitching line over welt, matching markings. Baste lining section in place along lower stitching line in same manner. Stitch through all thicknesses along the indicated lines; backstitch or knot the ends (2). From the wrong side, slash through the center for pocket opening. Clip diagonally to ends of stitching, making triangular ends ½" deep. Pull pocket parts to inside through slash (3).

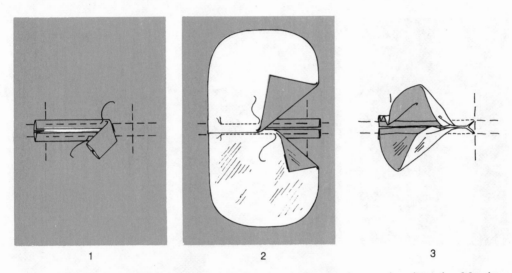

1   2   3

Press welts to meet in center of opening and whipstitch together loosely. Matching pocket edges and starting at the top, stitch side and lower edges together, catching base of the small triangular ends in stitches (4). Trim and overcast edges. To support weight of pocket, catchstitch upper edge to underlining (5).

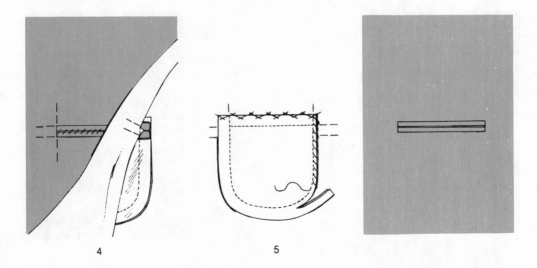

4   5

Welt Pocket with Flap

In this instance, the flap and a narrow welt are combined for a very tailored, precise appearance. Make flap according to directions on page 297, steps 1 and 2. Baste raw edges along seamline. To make welt, fold wrong sides together and baste along seamline on long raw edge. Trim basted seams of both flap and welt to ¼''. On the outside of the garment, baste the flap to the upper stitching line and the welt to the lower stitching line; the long raw edges will meet (1). Matching markings, baste larger pocket section over flap and smaller section over welt. Stitch through all thicknesses along the indicated lines; backstitch or knot ends (2). From the wrong side, slash through the center to within ½'' of end of stitching for pocket opening. Then clip diagonally to the ends of the stitching without cutting the flap or welt. Pull all pocket parts to inside (3).

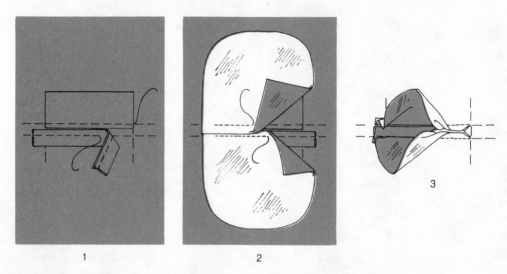

1

2

3

Press welt upward (over opening) and flap downward. Matching pocket edges and starting at the top, stitch side and lower edges together, catching the base of the triangular ends in your stitches (4). Trim and overcast these raw pocket edges. To support the weight of the pocket, catchstitch the upper edge to the underlining (5).

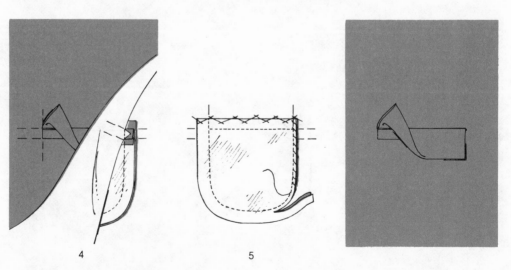

4

5

Side-Front Slanted Pockets

Side-front slanted pockets are constructed from two different size pattern pieces—a pocket section and a side front section. The pocket section can be of self-fabric or lining fabric, but the side front section must be of self-fabric because it becomes a part of the main garment at the side seams and the waistline. If any hip or waist alterations must be made in the garment pattern pieces, be sure to include the pocket pattern pieces as well.

Because the pocket opening is in a slanted or bias seam, the garment front should be reinforced with a stay to prevent the pocket edge from stretching. Cut a piece of ribbon seam binding 2″ longer than the pocket opening and center over the seamline on the wrong side of the garment front; baste (1). For pockets that have a curved, rather than a slanted seam, the pocket opening should be interfaced for reinforcement. Cut a strip of interfacing 2″ wide and same shape as the curved seam; baste to wrong side of garment front along seamline.

Pin and stitch pocket section to slanted edge of garment front and trim seam to $\frac{3}{16}$″, being careful not to cut the seam binding (2). Turn pocket to inside of garment and press. Understitch close to the seamline through pocket and seam allowances to prevent the pocket from rolling to the right side of the garment (3). Or you can topstitch along the finished edge.

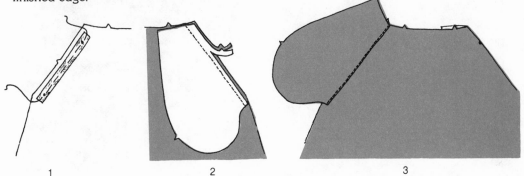

1   2   3

Pin side front section to pocket section, right sides together, and stitch around the seamline to the side of the garment, keeping the front free. Press and finish raw edges with overcasting or machine stitching (4).

Turn pockets down and baste pockets to the garment front along the upper and side edges (5). Pin and stitch front and back sections of garment together at the sides, catching in the pocket and side front seams; press. Treat the upper edge of the pocket as one with the garment when stitching the waistline seam.

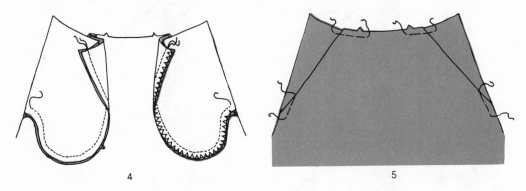

4   5

In-Seam Pockets

This inconspicuous type of pocket is concealed in side or front seams. The pocket top may be controlled from the inside by a waistline seam. An in-seam pocket is generally made of lining fabric and can be stitched to an extension of the pocket opening or directly to the seamline, depending upon your pattern.

With many fabrics, the seamline on the garment front should be reinforced with a stay to prevent the pocket edge from stretching. Cut a piece of ribbon seam binding 2'' longer than the pocket opening and baste in place as shown below.

IN-SEAM POCKET WITH EXTENSION: Place stay on wrong side of garment front with one edge next to the seamline, as shown. Baste, then stitch by hand or machine ⅛'' from edge of stay nearest seamline (1). Stitch one pocket piece to each front and back extension, with right sides of fabric together. Press seams open (2).

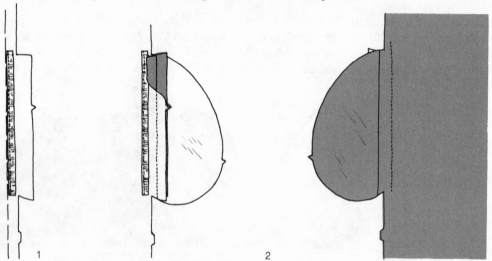

Baste the garment sections together at the seam and across the pocket openings; also baste the pocket edges together. Start stitching from the lower edge and continue around the pocket, pivoting at the corners. Use reinforcement stitches at all pivot points (3). Turn the pocket toward the front along the foldline or roll line. Clip the back seam allowance above and below the facing extension so you can press the seam above and below the pocket. Press lightly for a fold or steam for a soft roll (4).

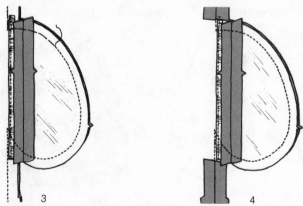

IN-SEAM POCKET WITHOUT EXTENSION: Center stay over seamline on wrong side of garment front; baste (1). Join pocket pieces to front and back garment sections, right sides of fabric together, matching pocket markings. Stitch a ¼" seam, and press seam toward pocket (2).

Baste the garment sections together at the seam and across the pocket openings. Then baste the pocket edges together. Start stitching from the lower edge and continue around the pocket, pivoting at the corners (3).

Turn the pocket toward the front and clip the back seam allowance above and below the facing extension. Press (4).

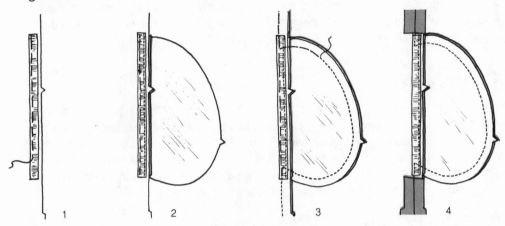

1   2   3   4

How to Add an In-Seam Pocket

You can add this type of pocket in lining fabric or self-fabric to your garment. The dimensions are given in scale. Seam allowances of ⅝" should be added to all edges. Cut two for each pocket. The pocket with a straight upper edge is the style suitable for waistline seams.

Just align the pocket opening edge with the seamline on your garment, being sure that the pocket is at the correct level for your hands. Then construct and press the pocket as described above. If desired, pocket and garment can be cut in one piece, eliminating the seam at the pocket opening (refer to *Very Easy Vogue* section, page 389).

Each Square Equals 1"

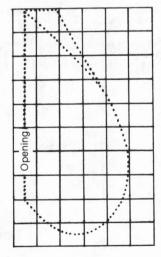

Opening

Waistlines, Waistbands, and Belts

Fashion dictates the location of the waistline, which may or may not be at the natural waistline, and whether it is fitted closely or loosely or not at all. A waistline can be defined in many ways—with a seam, a casing, a waistband, or a belt.

Waistlines

Although in many garments the waistline falls at the natural waistline, other styles are highlighted by a waistline either above or below the natural waistline. The range is wide— from the Empire style with the seamline just below the bust, to the lowered waistline with the seam located at the hipline. A waistline seam is used to join the top and bottom sections of a garment together and may be straight, curved, or sharply angled.

Waistline Seams

Usually the skirt section is larger, if only slightly, than the top and must be eased onto the bodice section. Slip the bodice inside the skirt with right sides together. Carefully match all seamlines, notches, and markings. For a fitted skirt, distribute any fullness evenly around the waistline. With bodice side up, stitch along the seamline (1).

For a gathered skirt, pull up the gathering until the skirt is the same width as the bodice. Adjust gathers evenly. (See page 227 for gathering techniques.) With skirt side up, stitch waistline seam taking care that unwanted tucks or pleats do not form in the gathers (2).

Trim ends of darts and seam allowances diagonally. Press seam toward bodice and overcast or zigzag raw edges, if necessary.

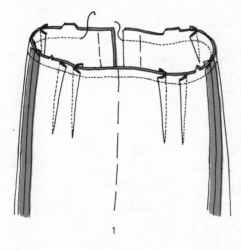

1

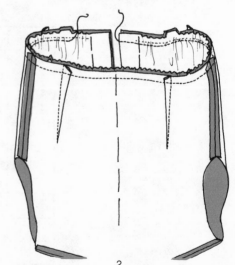

2

Waistline Stays

For some fabrics, it may be necessary to apply a waistline stay to prevent the seamline from stretching. Use ribbon seam binding, twill tape, or grosgrain ribbon ½″ to 1″ wide.

Cut the stay the exact measurement of the waistline from placket seamline to placket seamline. Pin and baste to the seam allowances on the skirt side with one edge along the waist seamline and the ends at the placket seamlines. Machine-stitch through both seam allowance layers just above the stitched seam. Trim seam allowances to the same width as the stay; do not trim the stay.

For bulkier fabrics, the skirt seam allowance can be trimmed narrower than that of the bodice. For fabrics that ravel, stitch upper edge of stay and seam allowances together.

A second type of waistline stay can be applied inside a garment after the zipper is inserted to help relieve stress in the zipper area and to hold the waistline area in place. It is recommended for sheath or princess style dresses, delicate or stretchy fabrics, or when the skirt fabric is heavier than the bodice fabric. Refer to the couture section, page 446.

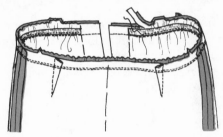

Waistline Casings

A casing enables fabric to be easily gathered at the waistline with elastic or drawstring. Casings are simple to construct and can be easily adjusted to your waistline measurement. For a waistline casing along the edge of a garment such as a casing at the top of a skirt or pants, or a casing at the bottom of a blouse or jacket, refer to edge finishes, page 255.

A waistline casing on a one-piece garment takes the place of a waistline seam. Use self-fabric (if lightweight), lining fabric, or single-fold bias tape. The width of finished casing must be ¼″ wider than elastic or drawstring to allow either one to be pulled smoothly through the casing.

Cut the casing; turn in both edges ¼″ and press gently. Mark the garment waistline and prepare an opening if drawstring is to be used. (See drawstring section, page 256.) From wrong side, place the bottom edge of casing along waistline markings. Stitch along both edges. Insert elastic or drawstring and finish as required (1). If a zipper is used with a waistline casing, end casing at zipper seamline. Insert elastic or drawstring and sew raw ends securely to casing at each end, keeping garment free (2). Insertion of zipper will secure ends of casing and elastic or drawstring. After zipper is applied, whipstitch seam allowances securely to casing and elastic or drawstring (3).

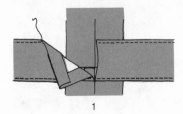

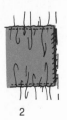

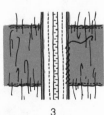

1   2   3

Dress Placket

This type of placket is usually placed in a side seam and centered at the waistline. It is an effective closing for lightweight, sheer, or lace fabrics, where a zipper tape would be unsightly.

Stitch the seam and press it open, leaving an opening between markings for the placket. Use two straight strips of self-fabric or lining fabric 2″ longer than the opening for the placket. Cut front strip 1¼″ wide and back strip 1¾″ wide. Finish one edge of each strip as you plan to finish your garment seams. With raw edges matching and right sides together, center front strip between markings and stitch to opening edges along seamline. Trim and grade seam allowances, leaving garment seam allowances widest. Fold strip to inside along the seam; press (1).

Clip the garment back seam allowance ½″ beyond each end of the opening. Right sides together, center and stitch the back strip to the opening seam allowance ¼″ from the edge. Press small seam open. Lap back strip over front so that folded and finished edges cover garment seam allowances (2).

Stitch both strips to the front seam allowance at the upper and lower ends of the placket opening, keeping the garment free. Blindstitch long free edges in place on front and back placket. Catchstitch raw edges to garment seam allowances (3).

Fasten opening with snaps; place a hook and eye at waistline. When pressing, do not let the iron rest on the placket (4).

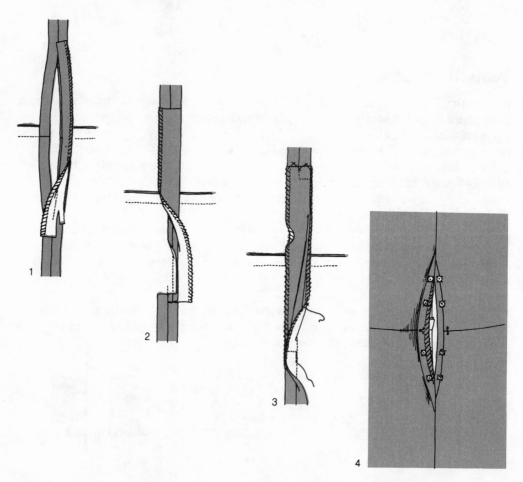

Waistbands

A properly sewn and fitted waistband is a joy to wear. It never stretches, wrinkles, or folds over as some waistbands have a way of doing, nor does it bind you or slip down on your hips. To attain this ideal combination of fit, good looks, and comfort, you must know a few general facts about waistbands.

Your preference and garment style determine waistband width. Most waistbands need the reinforcement and body of interfacing or ribbon seam binding to prevent stretching—particularly loosely woven fabrics and wide or contour waistbands. With knits, use elastic in the waistband to ensure the proper stretch and fit. Unless the garment is gathered, the skirt is usually eased to the waistband to accommodate the curve of your body directly below the waistband. For this reason, your skirt should be ½" to 1" bigger at the waistline than the finished waistline measurement of the garment. If the ends of the waistband overlap, the overlapping edge faces toward the left or the back. Side closings are on the left side. The underneath section usually extends at least 1¼" for the underlap. Put in the zipper before you apply the waistband, unless directed otherwise by the pattern instructions.

Straight Waistband

This waistband is cut on the lengthwise grain for the least amount of stretch, and can be constructed in many ways. Base your construction on the type of fabric, the style of the garment, and the wear that it will receive. If using a zipper, position the zipper stop ⅛" below the waist seamline.

Cut interfacing for the full width of waistband and baste to wrong side of fabric ½" from edge. Trim interfacing close to stitching. To hold interfacing to waistband along foldline, stitch through both layers on the facing side of the waistband ½" below foldline. Turn waistband, right sides together, along foldline. Stitch ends to within ⅝" of the edge. Grade seams and trim corners (1). Turn and press.

Pin and baste the waistband to the garment, matching markings. Ease the garment to fit the waistband; stitch. Trim and grade seams, leaving garment seam allowance widest. Press seam toward waistband. Turn in the remaining raw edge and slipstitch over the seam, continuing across the underlap (2). Fasten with hooks and eyes (3).

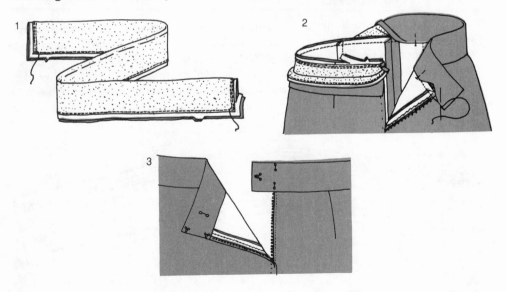

Variations on a Straight Waistband

If your fabric is fairly heavy or bulky, you may wish to use one of the following methods to eliminate bulk and make a flat, smooth waistband.

First, to reduce the ridge caused when all seam allowances at the waistline are turned in the same direction, lay the waistband pattern piece with **seamline** of the unnotched edge even with selvage. The selvage acts as a finished edge and is not turned under (1).

The second variation produces a thinner, less bulky appearance. Cut the waistband from your fabric equal to its finished width plus two seam allowances. Lap grosgrain ribbon (purchased in the same width as the finished waistband) over the upper seam allowance, even with the seamline; stitch ribbon close to edge (2).

Finish both waistbands by folding them right sides together along the upper seamline or foldline. Stitch across both ends. Trim corners and grade seam allowances. Turn and press. Attach them to the garment as usual. Slipstitch the selvage of the fabric or the edge of the grosgrain ribbon over the seam, continuing across the underlap. Be sure that the ribbon does not show on the outside.

The last variation is a quick, sturdy way to finish a waistband on a casual or sporty garment. Stitch the right side of the waistband to the **wrong** side of the garment. Press seam toward the waistband. Turn in the remaining edge and baste it over the seam on the right side of the garment. From the right side, topstitch close to basted edge through all thicknesses (3).

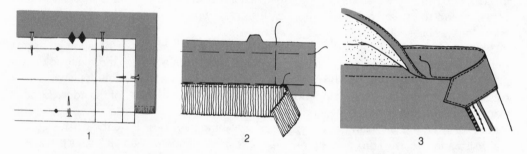

1   2   3

Contour Waistband

A wide contour waistband should be interfaced with two layers of interfacing for stiffness and reinforced with pad stitching and twill tape. Baste two layers of interfacing to wrong side of waistband facing and machine padstitch through all layers. Stay the upper and lower seamlines by basting ¼'' twill tape over seamlines. Pin waistband sections together along the upper edge and ends. Baste, then stitch the upper edges and both ends to within ⅝'' of the edge. Trim corners and grade the seam allowance. Turn and press.

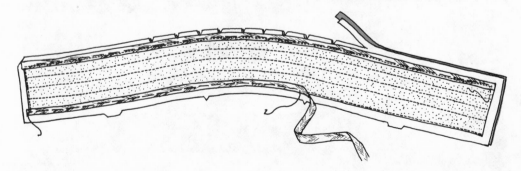

Pin the waistband to the garment with the right sides together, matching all markings. Adjust the ease; baste and stitch. Trim and grade seam; press toward the waistband. Turn in the remaining edge and slipstitch over the seam, continuing across the underlap. Fasten the end of the waistband with hooks and eyes. Be sure to keep hooks aligned with the edge of the waistband and eyes directly above the zipper opening.

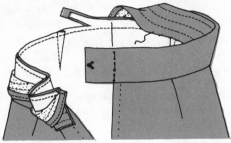

Faced Waistline

Skirts or pants without visible waistbands are usually finished with a facing made from lining, lightweight fabric, or ribbon to reduce bulk.

FABRIC: Cut and prepare facing. Stay the facing waist seamline with ribbon seam binding or twill tape, placing one edge ⅛″ inside seam allowance; baste. Pin the facing to the garment, easing garment to fit. Stitch, trim, and grade seams. Understitch facing to keep it from rolling to the outside (1). Turn and press. Turn in ends; sew to zipper tape. Tack facing to garment at seams and darts. Add a hook and eye at top of closing (2).

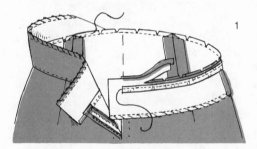

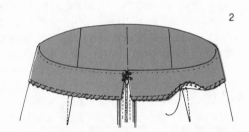

RIBBON: Shape a ¾″–1″ wide strip of grosgrain ribbon by steaming it into curves corresponding to those of the waistline edge. Shape by stretching the edge that is to be left free; if you shrink the edge to be joined to the garment, it will stretch during wear. Fit ribbon to your body, allowing 1″ for ends. Trim garment seam allowance to ¼″. Place grosgrain over raw edge of garment with unstretched edge along seamline and ends extending ½″. Because you are joining two opposing curves, pin or baste carefully, easing the garment to fit. Stitch close to edge of ribbon and complete as for a fabric facing above.

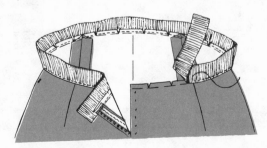

Belts and Carriers

Since ancient Grecian times, belts and belt carriers have been moving up and down fashion's silhouette in an amazing variety of shapes and widths. Modern belt-making techniques can best be exemplified by the basic types shown below.

If you are adding a belt and your pattern doesn't include one, you must plan the belt carefully. To find the proper length, encircle your body where the belt will be worn with belting or interfacing in the desired width; add 7'' to this measurement for finishing your belt. Wider belts extending above your waistline require additional length.

TIE BELT or **SASH:** Your personal preference will determine the type—narrow or wide, bias or straight grain. Cut fabric twice the finished width and the desired length (long enough to tie) plus seam allowances. Piece where necessary, then fold the sash in half lengthwise. Stitch the ends and the long edge, leaving an opening, as shown. Trim corners and grade seams. Turn and press the sash. Slipstitch the opening.

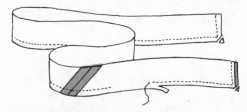

STRAIGHT BELT WITH INTERFACING: On the lengthwise grain, cut two strips of fabric the required length and width of the finished belt, adding ⅝'' seam allowances on all edges. Shape one end as desired. If your fabric is stretchy or loosely woven, staystitch the long edges ⅜'' from the raw edge (1). Cut two interfacing strips the finished width and length. Stitch the interfacing sections together in rows at ¼'' intervals, or substitute one strip of grosgrain belting for the interfacing (2).

Center the interfacing over the wrong side of the belt and pin. Turn the belt seam allowances over the interfacing. Notch pointed end where necessary to make the fabric lie flat. With long running stitches, sew the seam allowances to the interfacing only (3). Staystitch the belt facing ½'' from the raw edge. Turn in the edges of the facing ¾'' and baste, notching pointed end as necessary; trim to ⅜'' (4). Center and pin the facing over the belt, then slipstitch in place (5).

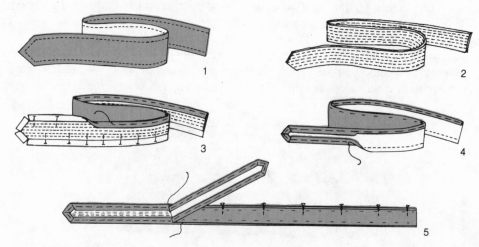

STRAIGHT BELT WITH COMMERCIAL BELTING: Follow manufacturer's directions, or cut one fabric strip on the lengthwise grain the required length and twice the width of the belting plus seam allowances. Shape one end of the belting as desired. Fold belt strip right sides together over the belting, and stitch with a zipper foot close to the belting. Do not catch belting in stitches. Trim seam allowances to ¼'' (1). Slide the seam around to the center of belting, and press seam open with the point of your iron. Stitch the shaped end and trim (2). Remove belting and turn; do not press. Slip the belting into the belt, shaped end first, cupping slightly for easier insertion (3).

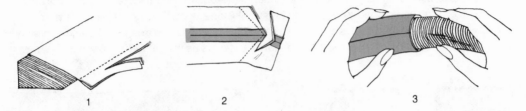

CONTOUR BELT: Follow the instructions for cutting the straight belt. Easestitch the shaped ends and outer curved edges. The interfacing will require some special handling. Pin two layers of interfacing together and trace an outline of your contour belt on them. Stitch the layers together within the outline at ¼'' intervals along the lengthwise grain. Cut out belt along traced outline. For a stay, baste a strip of stretched bias tape to the inner curved edge of the interfacing and stitch in place directionally. Then construct the belt as you would a straight belt, adjusting the ease threads as necessary.

CUMMERBUND: Cut a bias rectangle the measurement of your rib cage plus ½'' and at least 9'' wide. Stitch ¼'' from the long edges and overcast. Turn in long edges 1''; press lightly. Make a row of gathering stitches ¼'' from each end for a back opening and two rows ¼'' apart for gathers at sides of belt. Pull gathers to the desired depth and fasten threads on the inside. Check fit, respacing gathers if necessary to make it snug.

Cut four pieces of feather boning ¼'' to ½'' shorter than the depth of the belt; remove casing. For sides, cover boning with seam binding as shown (1). Center over gathers, and sew in place. For back opening edges, stitch ½'' wide grosgrain ribbon along gathering stitches, extending ends ½''. Catchstitch boning over gathers. Turn in ends, folding ribbon to wrong side; favor cummerbund. Sew ribbon securely to underside of gathers (2). Fasten with hooks and eyes so ends meet. Make and attach grosgrain or self-fabric underlap.

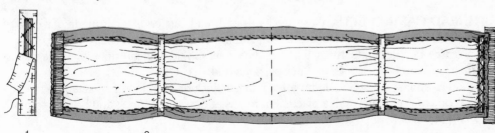

There are several ways to fasten a belt—with a prong and eyelet buckle, a clasp buckle, hooks and eyes, or snaps. Try on your finished belt. Mark the center front position on both ends for all fastenings but the clasp buckle. Trim the unfinished straight end to measure 2″ from the center front line. Stitch ¼″ from the trimmed end and overcast.

PRONG AND EYELETS: Pierce a hole for the buckle prong at the center front marking nearest the overcast end. Overcast the raw edges of the hole (1). Slip the buckle prong through the hole; turn back the end and sew securely in place (2). For a half buckle, make a fabric belt loop; slide it over belt close to the buckle and secure. Then secure the belt end (3). On the finished end of your belt, make one eyelet at the center front marking and one or more on both sides for adjustments. You may use commercial eyelets, which come in a variety of colors, or make hand-worked eyelets as instructed on page 321.

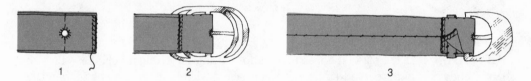

1   2   3

CLASP BUCKLE: Slip the ends of the belt through the buckle and bar fastener, folding the ends back along the bars, and try it on. Trim excess at ends to 1″. Stitch ¼″ from each end and overcast. Slip the ends through the bars; turn back and attach securely.

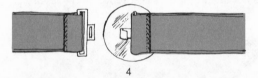

4

FABRIC CARRIERS or **BELT LOOPS:** The loops should be long enough to accommodate the belt width plus ¼″ (possibly a little extra if your fabric is very thick). Cut a straight strip from a selvage edge three times the desired width, and make two folds with the selvage edge on top. Slipstitch the selvage in place (1). Bring ends together and whipstitch. Place the carrier over the markings and sew to the garment at both ends (2). For other methods of making loops, see page 322.

1   2

THREAD CARRIERS: There are two kinds of thread carriers. One is made of a core of long threads reinforced with blanket stitches, and the other is a thread chain. Fabric carriers or loops are often design features, but thread carriers should be nearly invisible. Use thread that matches your belt. See Thread Loops, page 324.

If you are adding a belt and your pattern doesn't include markings, first establish the belt position on your garment. Make placement marks at desired intervals, and be sure to mark the width of the belt for your carriers.

Closures

Although closures are primarily functional, their precision and workmanship can add a special dimension to your garments. From tailored, bound buttonholes to delicate thread loops—from decorative buttons to inconspicuous snaps—there is a wide variety of closures from which to choose.

Buttonholes

Let the design and the fabric determine your choice of buttonhole. Couturiers use bound buttonholes for a tailored, professional look on all garments, hand-worked buttonholes for soft or delicate fabrics, and machine-worked buttonholes for man-tailored and casual garments. Your pattern markings include exact placement and size of buttons and buttonholes as recommended by the designer.

Any changes from the designer's intended placement or size should be carefully planned. If you have adjusted the length of the pattern tissue, adjust the buttonholes by evenly spacing them between the top and bottom buttonholes. If you are adding buttonholes, the most important consideration in the placement is the size of your button. Remember that large buttons are placed farther apart than small ones. If your button is larger than recommended, do not move the buttonhole away from the edge, as this will change your center line; rather, extend the closing edge to accommodate the button. (Make this adjustment on the pattern *before* you cut your fabric so the underlap on the left side will be as wide as the overlap on the right side.)

Always test the buttonhole on a scrap of your fabric with the appropriate underlining and interfacing to discover any problems you might encounter. Refer to Pressing, page 348, for tips on pressing your buttonholes.

BUTTONHOLE SIZE: The size of the buttonhole should always be determined by the button. Minimum buttonhole length is equal to the diameter plus the thickness of the button. Add ⅛″ to allow for the shank and slight size reduction due to fabric thickness(1).

To find the buttonhole length needed for a thick or ball button, wrap a ¼″ wide strip of paper around the button and mark with a pin where the ends meet. Then fold the paper strip flat and measure between the pin and the fold to determine the correct buttonhole size. Add the ⅛″ mentioned above(2).

In general, attractive buttonholes are slim, about ¼″ wide with each lip ⅛″ wide. They may be slightly narrower for lightweight fabrics and a little wider for bulky fabrics, but total width should not exceed ⅜″.

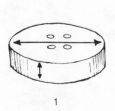

1

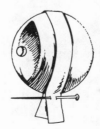

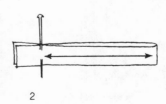

2

PLACEMENT MARKING: Make your buttonhole markings on the right side to make certain that the finished buttonhole will follow the fabric grainlines. First mark the position and length of your buttonhole with pins or chalk, then thread trace for precise markings.

Begin all *horizontal buttonholes* ⅛'' to the side of the buttons nearest the closing edge to allow for the natural tendency of the garment to "pull" away from the closing. This "pull" is downward for *vertical buttonholes;* begin them ⅛'' above the actual button placement and directly on the lengthwise placement line.

The reference point in placing your buttonholes is the garment center line; center lines must meet when your closing is fastened. Thus it should always be the first line marked. Next mark the short horizontal lines for the position of the buttonholes and, lastly, the long continuous vertical lines to indicate their length.

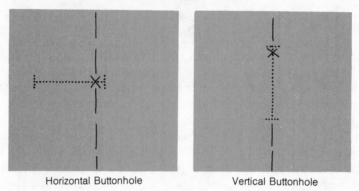

Horizontal Buttonhole   Vertical Buttonhole

For a center closing, the buttons are positioned on the underlap center line, the buttonholes in corresponding positions on the overlap center line (1).

The top buttonhole is generally placed below the neckline edge at least half the width of the button plus ¼''. The last buttonhole should be 3'' to 4'' from the bottom, *never through the hem.* Buttonholes are not usually placed closer than ⅝'' from a closing edge; for a large button, the extension should be no less than half the button's width plus ¼''

For a double-breasted closing with functional buttonholes, place each row of buttons an equal distance on each side from the underlap center line, and buttonholes in corresponding positions from the overlap center line. Remember the *buttons* are placed equal distances from the center line, not the buttonholes, and make certain both rows of buttonholes extend in the same direction from the buttons (2). For an asymmetrical closing, first make sure center lines match. Mark the short placement markings perpendicular to the edge and the long length lines parallel to the edge (3).

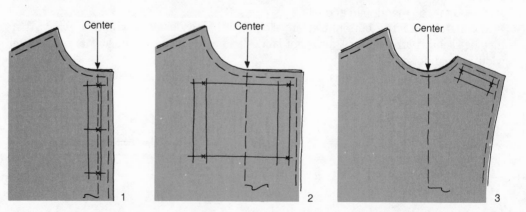

Center   Center   Center

1   2   3

Bound Buttonholes

Make bound buttonholes before attaching the facing. They are formed from strips of fabric cut on either straight or bias grain. Those cut on the bias can add an interesting design feature in plaid or striped fabrics.

There are several methods for making a bound buttonhole—choose the one that you prefer. There are, however, some techniques that are basic to all the methods.

STITCHING: Carefully stitch, using small stitches (15–20 stitches per inch) and follow the buttonhole markings exactly for precise corners and even buttonhole lips.

SLASHING OPENING: After stitching, there are two methods of slashing your bound buttonhole. After securing your thread ends, cut through garment at the center of the buttonhole, cutting between stitching lines from the wrong side with small sharp scissors. Slash along the center of the stitching, stopping ¼" from each end, and clip diagonally to the ends of the stitching or into the corners, being careful not to cut the stitching. Or, you may cut diagonally through the center of the buttonhole, slashing directly to the ends of the stitching or corners.

SECURING CORNERS: You must carefully secure the ends of your buttonholes if they are not to pull out or ravel when worn. With the garment placed right side up, fold garment back at each end of the buttonhole to reveal the strip ends with the fabric triangle on top. Then stitch back and forth across the base of each triangle several times with small stitches to square the corners and strengthen the ends. Trim ends to ¼" and catchstitch them to the underlining.

INTERFACING: If you are using lightweight interfacing, make the buttonholes through it so they will be reinforced and supported (1).

To reinforce the buttonhole area in fabrics or garment areas that may not need interfacing, cut a rectangle of interfacing 1" wider and longer than the buttonhole. Center it over the buttonhole markings and baste it in place before making the buttonhole.

Heavier-weight interfacing and all hair canvases are too stiff or bulky to be sewn with the buttonhole. Instead make the buttonholes through just the fabric and underlining and then attach the interfacing. Cut openings in the interfacing slightly larger than the buttonhole openings. Pull buttonholes through, and catchstitch the edges of the buttonhole to the interfacing (2).

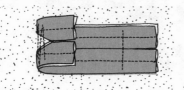
1

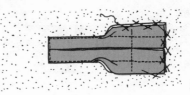
2

TO COMPLETE BOUND BUTTONHOLES: For a quick and easy finish, pin or baste facing to garment through all thicknesses. Hold buttonhole lips together with diagonal basting for hard-to-handle fabrics. Stick a pin from the outside through each end of the buttonhole opening. Be sure that the pins are in line with the grain of the facing. Slash the facing between the pins and turn in the raw edges. Hem around the buttonhole, as shown, taking a few stitches at each end for reinforcement (1).

To make a better-looking finish on garments to be worn open, establish the length of open buttonhole on the facing with pins. Then cut to within ¼″ of each end and clip diagonally into the corners. An additional finish for a thoroughly professional look, or for extremely difficult fabrics, is presented in the couture section, page 448 (2).

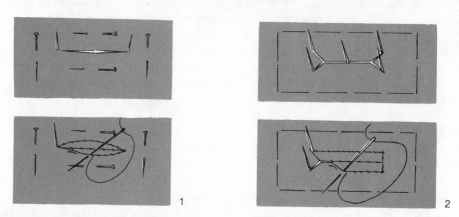

1 2

FIVE-LINE PATCH METHOD: This is a very easy method that enables you to measure the five rows of stitching for accuracy before you slash the buttonhole.

Cut a patch of garment fabric 3″ wide and 2″ longer than the finished buttonhole. With right sides together, center the patch over the buttonhole markings and pin. Machine- or hand-baste through the center of the patch exactly on top of the buttonhole positon line. Baste again exactly ¼″ on either side of the center line to form three parallel rows of basting (1).

Fold the top edge of the buttonhole patch down along the basting line and press. Using a short stitch, sew exactly ⅛ from the fold, beginning and ending exactly at the marking lines which indicate the length of the buttonhole (2).

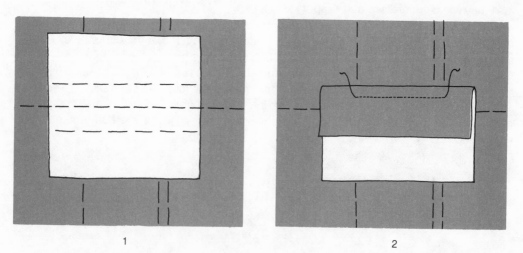

1 2

Fold the other edge of the patch up along the basting line to form the second lip of the buttonhole; press and stitch as above (3). On wrong side of garment, measure to see that the five rows of stitching are exactly ⅛'' apart along their entire length. Restitch if necessary. Pull thread ends to wrong side of fabric and tie securely (4).

Remove three rows of basting. Cut through the center of the patch, being careful not to cut into the garment (5). On wrong side of garment, slash along the center line and diagonally into the corners, being careful not to cut the stitching (6). Turn patch through slash to the wrong side of the garment and press. Baste the buttonhole lips together (7). To cord your buttonhole, see page 320. Secure corners as on page 315. Trim fabric patch to within ¼'' of stitching lines, rounding corners, and press.

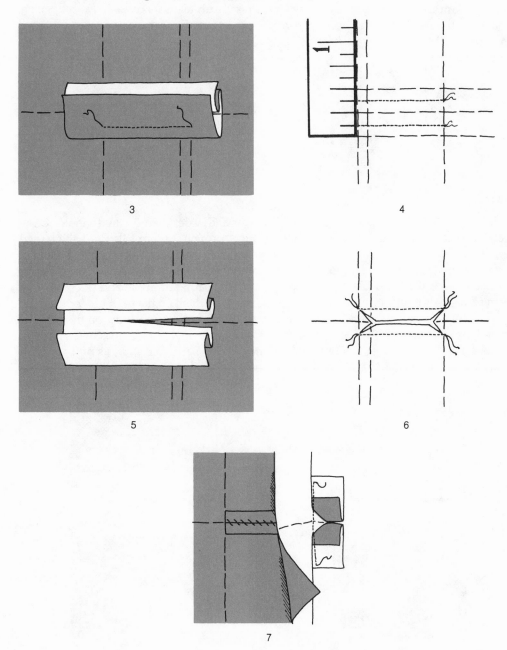

3

4

5

6

7

ORGANZA PATCH METHOD: This method is almost foolproof, and is especially suitable for fabrics that ravel easily or are bulky. Eliminate another problem with these fabrics by applying the interfacing *after* making buttonholes, rather than making them through all layers. Turn to page 315 for directions.

For your patch, always use a crisp, sheer fabric with the same qualities as organza. Cut patch 1″ bigger than the buttonhole. Center the patch over the buttonhole marking on the right side of the garment; pin. If you find the markings difficult to see, emphasize them with tailor's chalk. Stitch ⅛″ from each side of marking, using small stitches. Start at middle of the marking, pivot at corners, and carefully count the stitches at ends for accuracy. Overlap stitches where you began. Slash, being careful not to cut stitching (1). Turn patch through slash to the wrong side of garment. Press seam allowances away from opening. You now have a neatly finished hole in your garment the exact size of your finished buttonhole (2).

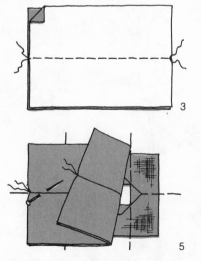
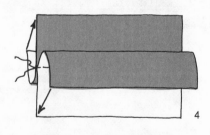

Cut two strips of your fashion fabric 1½″ longer and wider than the buttonhole. Baste the two strips right sides together along the center, forming a seam (3). Press the basted seam open (4). Then accurately place the strips on the wrong side of the opening with the basted seam at the center. This forms the two even lips for your buttonhole. Pin the strips in place close to each end (5). Turn the garment to the wrong side. Pin and stitch the long seam allowances to the strips to hold the lips in place, stitching on the garment (outside the buttonhole) alongside the previous stitching so the organza does not show on the outside. Extend the stitching lines ½″ on both ends of the seam through the organza and strips (6). To cord your buttonhole at this time, refer to page 320. Secure corners, as on page 315. Apply interfacing. Trim excess fabric from patch and strip, rounding out corners, and press.

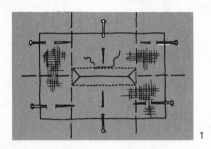
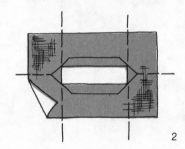
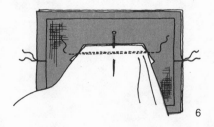

ONE-PIECE FOLDED METHOD: This method requires only one fabric strip per buttonhole and is suitable for light and mediumweight fabrics. Cut a strip of self-fabric 1″ wide and 1″ longer than the buttonhole. Mark a center line along the length of the strip. With wrong sides together, fold edges so they meet at the markings; press (1). With the cut edges up, baste the center of the strip over the buttonhole markings. Stitch with small stitches ⅛″ from each side of the center, starting at the middle of the side and going across the ends. Carefully count the stitches on the end for accuracy. Overlap stitches where you began (2). Slash, being careful not to cut through the stitching. Turn strip to the inside and press (3). If you wish to cord your buttonhole, refer to page 320. Fold back the garment and secure the corners as on page 315.

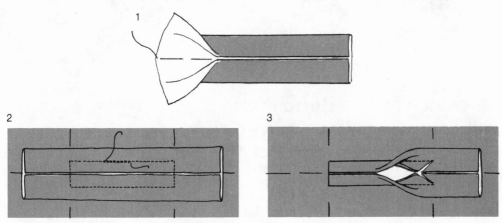

TWO-PIECE METHOD: This method is fast and easy for firm fabrics and textured knits. Cut a strip of self-fabric 1″ wide and long enough for all the buttonholes. For the length of this strip, multiply the length of each buttonhole plus 1″ by twice the number of buttonholes. Wrong sides together, fold strip in half lengthwise and press lightly.

Machine baste ⅛″ from folded edge. Strip can be easily corded as you baste; see page 320. Cut the strip into sections the length of the buttonhole plus 1″ and trim the cut edge to a scant ⅛″ from the stitching (1).

Baste one strip to the right side, placing the cut edge along the thread-traced position line. Using small stitches, stitch the length of the buttonhole through all thicknesses directly over the stitching on the strip. Leave the thread ends long enough to tie. Repeat for the second strip on the opposite side of the thread-traced line so that the cut edges meet (2). Pull the thread ends through to the wrong side and tie. Slash, being careful not to cut through the strips. Turn the strips to the inside and press (3). Finish the corners as on page 315.

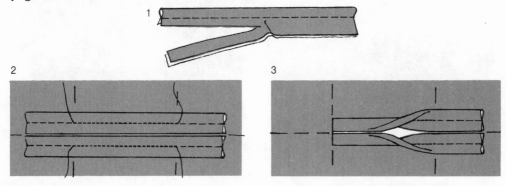

TO CORD BOUND BUTTONHOLES: Cording buttonholes reduces their elasticity, but adds body, strength, and durability. Their raised appearance also provides a finer finish. There are two methods for cording bound buttonholes. For the five-line patch, organza patch, and one-piece folded methods, draw a strand or two of string or yarn through lips just before stitching triangular ends (1). For the two-piece method, fold strip, wrong sides together, around cable cord or twine before you begin to construct the buttonhole. Machine baste close to the cord using a zipper foot (2).

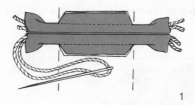

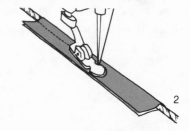

Machine-Worked Buttonholes

These buttonholes are particularly suited to casual and man-tailored clothes or clothes that require frequent laundering. Attach facing before making buttonholes. Thread trace buttonhole markings through all layers. Make buttonholes with a buttonhole attachment or zigzag machine. For a stronger buttonhole, stitch over buttonhole a second time (1).

Some machines have a special built-in mechanism that automatically stitches buttonholes—usually one half of the buttonhole is stitched forward and the other half backward. Refer to your sewing machine manual for complete instructions.

Machine-worked buttonholes are not cut open until after the stitching is completed. To cord the buttonholes, use a special buttonhole foot through which a fine cord can be drawn as you stitch. Or guide the cord by hand as you stitch over it.

Seam Buttonholes

These buttonholes are actually small openings in a seam. Mark buttonhole placement; pin and baste seam. Cut two strips of ribbon seam binding for each buttonhole 1" longer than opening. On one seam allowance, place strip next to seamline along markings and stitch close to each edge. Repeat on other seam allowance (2). Then stitch garment seam, ending stitching at markings; backstitch. Press seam open. Remove basting from opening. Add bar tacks at ends on wrong side (3).

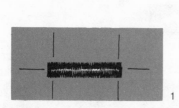

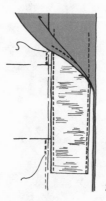

Hand-worked Buttonholes

These buttonholes are sewn through all layers after the facing is applied. Machine-stitch a scant ⅛″ on either side and across both ends of the buttonhole marking. Carefully slash along the length marking.

Take an 18″ length of buttonhole twist and insert the needle at one end, anchoring the thread with backstitches on the wrong side. Work the buttonhole stitch by inserting the needle through the slash from the right side and bringing it out just outside the stitching line. Keep thread under eye and point of needle as shown (1). Draw up the needle so a purl (knot) is formed at the buttonhole edge (2). Repeat, keeping stitches even and each purl exactly on the edge of the slash. Fan stitches at the end closest to the finished edge as shown (3). Place a bar tack at the remaining end.

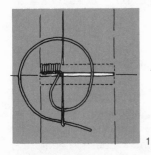
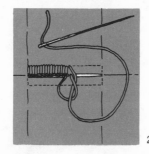
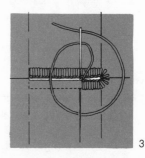

BAR TACK: Finish both ends of the buttonhole with a bar tack. First take 3 or 4 long stitches across the width at each end of the buttonhole. Then work the blanket stitch over the core threads, catching the fabric underneath (4).

KEYHOLE: If you prefer a keyhole buttonhole on man-tailored clothes, follow instructions for hand-worked buttonholes, with one exception: make a hole with an awl at end nearest opening edge to form keyhole. Then work buttonhole stitches around hole and slash; finish remaining end with a bar tack (5).

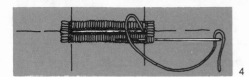
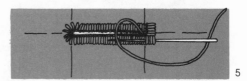

CORDED: Hand-worked buttonholes can be corded by working the buttonhole stitch over buttonhole twist secured at one end with a pin. Add bar tack to end; clip cord (6).

EYELETS: This type of buttonhole is used with studs, cuff links, drawstrings, and belts. Sew around placement marking with small running stitches. Cut an opening the desired size or punch a hole with an awl. Bring needle up through fabric from the wrong side a scant ⅛″ from edge of hole. Leave 1" of thread on the wrong side and work around the hole with buttonhole stitches. Fasten threads securely on the wrong side (7).

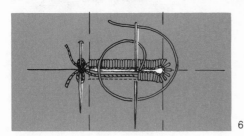
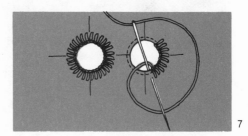

Fabric and Thread Loops

Some details, no matter how time-consuming, are those little touches that add greatly to the pleasure of wearing a garment you have made. Fabric and thread loops are perfect examples. With careful planning and accurate marking they can be easier to make than they look.

Fabric Loops

Fabric loops can add an impressive touch to a simple style whether used with purchased buttons or formed into frogs and Chinese ball buttons. They can be made of self-filled or corded bias tubing, in contrasting or self-fabric; purchased braid; or other tubular material that complements your garment fabric.

SELF-FILLED TUBING: Cut a bias strip the desired length and the finished width plus enough seam allowance to fill the tubing. The additional seam allowance depends upon your fabric—the bulkier the fabric, the narrower the seam allowances. Experiment to determine the correct width for your particular fabric. Remember also that the strip will become somewhat narrower as it is stretched during stitching. Right sides together, fold bias in half lengthwise and stitch, stretching bias as you sew. At end, slant the stitching diagonally, making the tube wider. To turn, pass a heavy thread and a tapestry needle, eye first, through the bias or use a loop turner or bodkin. For a narrow tubing, turn in the raw edges, roll bias between your finger, and sew edges together, eliminating turning process.

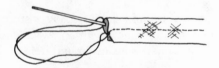
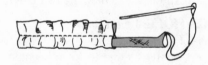

CORDED TUBING: Cut a bias strip of fabric the desired length and wide enough to fit around the cord plus ½″ for seam allowances and stretching. If necessary, piece the bias as directed on page 245. Cut a piece of cable cord **twice** the length of the bias; the extra cord will facilitate stitching and turning. Fold the bias over the cord with right sides together and edges even. Place one end of the bias ¼″ beyond the center of the cording. Using a zipper foot, stitch across the end at the center of the cording. Then stretch the bias slightly while stitching the long edge close to the cording. Trim the seam allowance (1). To turn right side out, slowly draw the enclosed cord out of the tubing; the free cord will be pulled into the tubing automatically (2). Cut off the stitched end and the excess cording.

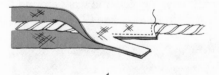
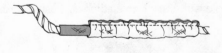

1

2

ATTACHING LOOPS: Fabric loops can be applied singly or in a continuous row, depending on the fabric weight and spacing desired. Mark the seamline the length of the closure area on a strip of lightweight paper. Make a line for the distance that the loops are to extend (approximately half the diameter of the button, plus the thickness of the cording). Make spread of each loop equal to button diameter plus twice the cord thickness (1).

Single loops: Cut each loop the correct length to fit within the markings plus two seam allowances. Form each loop with the seamed side up and the loop pointing away from the edge, keeping the edges of the paper guide and the loops even. Use narrow masking tape to hold them in place. Using large stitches, stitch on the paper close to the seamline within the seam allowance. Then remove the masking tape. Pin paper guide to the appropriate garment edge on the right side of the fabric, matching seamlines. Stitch close to seamline near first stitching (2). Tear away paper and apply facing.

Continuous loops: With a long strip of bias tubing, form a continuous row of loops on the paper guide within the markings, extending them ½″ into the seam allowance. Tape and stitch them to the paper and then apply them to the garment in the same manner as single loops (3). The short looped ends in the seam allowance may be trimmed to ¼″ to reduce any unnecessary bulk before applying facing.

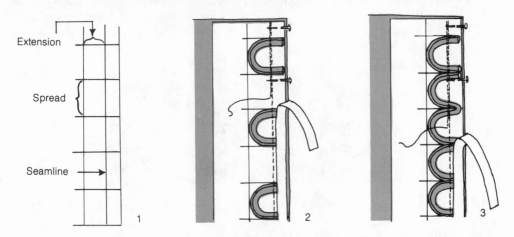

FROGS: Follow the diagram, using soutache braid, round braid, or self-filled or corded tubing. Keep tubing seamline on top while forming the frogs. Use small hand stitches to tack each successive loop as it is formed and tiny invisible stitches to attach the finished frog. You can vary the shape by changing the size of the loops, but remember to keep one loop large enough to extend beyond the garment edge and pass over the button. For intricate shapes, form the frog on paper with masking tape and basting, before stitching.

Thread Loops

Thread loops can be used for a variety of purposes in different locations, as indicated by their names. A thread loop is usually placed at the corner of a neck opening and fastens to a small button. It is also often used in place of a metal eye on delicate fabrics or in conspicuous locations. Its length should be equal to the diameter plus the thickness of the button. A longer loop is used to form a **belt carrier**. Usually placed at the side seams, it should be just large enough to let the belt slip through. A **thread eye** is often used with a metal hook in place of a metal eye, especially on delicate fabrics or in conspicuous locations. Relatively taut, it is the same length as the metal eye it replaces.

A **French tack** or **swing tack** holds two parts of a garment together, such as the two hems of a lined garment, and is usually placed at seams on the wrong side. All types can be formed by either a blanket stitch or a thread chain.

BLANKET STITCH: The blanket stitch is the classic stitch used for most thread loops. Use matching double thread or single buttonhole twist. Take 2 or 3 foundation stitches the desired length and depth of your loop, securing the ends with small backstitches. These stitches form the core of your loop, and it is essential that they be the correct size; if you are using a belt, button, or hook with your loop, make sure the loop size accommodates them and allows for ease. Then, with the same thread, work blanket stitches closely over the entire length of the foundation threads.

THREAD CHAIN: If you prefer, a thread loop can be made with the chainstitch. Use a double thread or single strand of buttonhole twist securely fastened to the garment with one or two small overlapping stitches (1). Form a loop on the right side by taking another short stitch. Slip the thumb and first two fingers of your left hand through the loop while holding the needle and thread end in your right hand (2). Using the second finger of your left hand, pick up a new loop and pull it through the first loop, tightening as you proceed (3). Continue to work the chain to the desired length. Place the needle through the last loop to form a knot and end the chain (4). Secure the free end with several small stitches.

 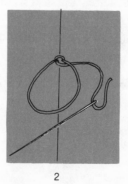  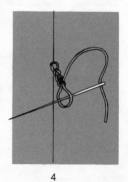

| 1 | 2 | 3 | 4 |

Buttons

Buttons are an important finishing touch not only in their more practical sense as fasteners, but also as adornments and essential parts of the garment design. Gone are the days when buttons simply closed the front or back openings and cuffs of a garment. Today you will see them perching on shoulders, outlining seams, closing skirts and pants, fastening waistbands, attaching belts, ending sleeve vents. They can match, contrast, or complement; give a tailored, casual, or dressy look.

Think of the many different ways you can use them to close a garment—with buttonholes, loops, frogs, or a short chain between two buttons. You might care to group your buttons in clusters, space them irregularly, or use a row of small ones instead of a few larger ones.

However you use buttons, remember that they must relate to the fabric, the design of the garment, and especially to the wearer. Spacing and proportion are the keys to expert selection and placement. For example, a petite figure calls for many small buttons, or a few larger ones. It is best to remain with the button size recommended by the designer. If you prefer to experiment, the best way to find the correct size for your button is to pin on different sizes and see how they look *before* stitching your buttonholes. Refer to the button chart on page 175 to determine correct button sizes.

If you've lengthened or shortened your garment, you may need to adjust the number of buttons and the buttonhole placement accordingly. Be sure that there are buttons located at all points of stress. Place a button at the waist of a fitted jacket or coat to prevent gapping unless you have a belt. If you are using a belt or sash, place your buttons sufficiently above and below the belt so they won't interfere. It is also wise to have a button at the fullest part of the bustline for a large-bosomed figure. If your garment still gaps between buttons, close these spaces with covered snaps.

BUTTON PLACEMENT: The time it takes to see that your buttons are placed correctly is well spent, for it ensures that your garment will close in a straight line and lie flat. Pin the garment closed, matching center basting lines. For a horizontal buttonhole, push a pin through the end of the buttonhole near the finished edge of the garment. The center of the button should be sewn at this point and directly on the center front or center back line. Vertical buttonholes have the buttons placed ⅛″ below the top of the buttonhole and on the center front or center back line. Place each button directly in line with the button above.

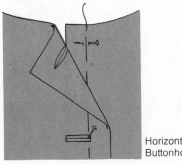

Horizontal
Buttonholes

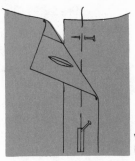

Vertical
Buttonholes

THREAD: To sew on the button, use a double strand of polyester or cotton thread, heavy duty thread, or buttonhole twist. For buttons on heavier weight coats and jackets, button and carpet thread may be used. Drawing your thread through beeswax will prevent knots from forming in the thread while you sew. For easy handling, your thread should not be much longer than 18". Secure your thread with a couple of small backstitches on the right side under the button, rather than with a knot, for a neater application.

SEW-THROUGH BUTTONS: These should have a thread shank to allow the buttoned fabric to lie smoothly and not pull around the buttons. The length of the shank should equal the thickness of the garment at the buttonhole plus ⅛" for movement. Always begin sewing on the right side. Place a pin, matchstick, toothpick, or other object over the button and sew over the object when sewing on the button. Remove the object, raise the button to the top of the stitches, and wind the thread tightly under the button to form the thread shank. Backstitch several times into the shank for a secure finish. Buttons used for trim will not need a shank (1).

REINFORCED BUTTONS: For coats and suits, reinforced buttons are advisable. Place a small flat button on the back of the garment under the larger button. Sew directly through from one to the other for added stability. Use a small folded square of ribbon seam binding in place of the reinforcement button for delicate fabrics. Place it inside the garment directly beneath the holes where it cannot be seen when worn (2).

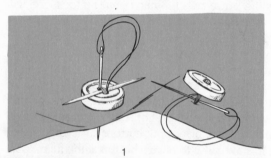

1

2

SHANK BUTTONS: Attach the button with small stitches sewn through the shank. If your garment fabric is very thick and bulky, a thread shank must be made as with the sew-through button. Remember that the direction of the shank should always be aligned with that of the buttonhole (3). To make your shank buttons detachable, insert them through eyelets and secure with toggles (4). Stud buttons are simply inserted through eyelets.

LINK BUTTONS: Link buttons are most commonly used with cuffs, but may also be used to close vests or capes. You may use either purchased or covered buttons. Run heavy thread through two buttons, leaving the thread long enough to form the link and to pass through the joined garment edges. Work over the thread with a blanket stitch (see page 324). Fasten thread securely (5). Buttons can also be sewn to the ends of a narrow turned fabric strip (6).

3

4

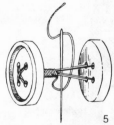
5

6

CHINESE BALL BUTTONS: These can be made of purchased braid or either self-filled or corded tubing. (See page 322.) Cut a piece of tubing 16″ long and follow the diagram for the loop formations. Keep tubing seamline on top and loops open while shaping the button. Then draw the ends to pull the loops closer together, easing and shaping the loops to form your button. Clip off any excess tubing and fasten the ends securely to the button.

COVERED BUTTONS: If you want your buttons to be inconspicuous or if your fabric is hard to match, buttons covered with self-fabric may be your answer. Use a commercially prepared kit available in many sizes and shapes or make your own with bone rings.

For a covered ring button, select a bone ring the size of the button you need. Cut a circle of fabric slightly less than twice the diameter of the ring. Gather the edge of the fabric with a small running stitch. Insert the ring, pull up the gathering thread, and secure. Add a special touch by sewing a small running stitch just inside the ring through all layers with buttonhole twist. Back can be covered with a smaller fabric circle, gathered around edge, and slipstitched in place. (See Finest Fastenings, page 449.) Attach with a shank.

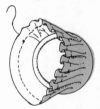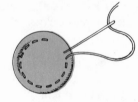

JEWELED BUTTONS: To use jeweled or rough-edged buttons on fabrics that might snag or pull, sew your button directly to the buttonhole, and use covered snaps underneath to secure the opening. This technique will give you the look of a buttonhole closing without the possible mishaps.

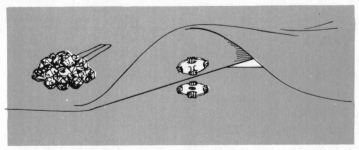

Zippers

Zippers are those mechanical wonders used to close an amazing variety of fashion features. They provide a fast, readily accessible means of getting in and out of your clothes, an asset so valuable in our busy, time-conscious days. Since their invention, zippers have grown lighter, less obvious, and more supple.

Zippers can be made of metal or synthetic teeth or coils and are available in a variety of sizes and wide range of colors to coordinate with your fabric. Specialty zippers, such as separating, invisible, and heavy-duty versions, can also be purchased; refer to the notions section in chapter 3, pages 176 and 177, for additional information.

Know Your Zipper

For your own information and to unravel any difficulties you may have in use or application, you should be able to identify and understand the function of the various parts of your zipper.

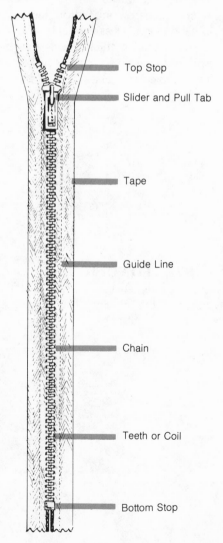

The **TOP STOP** is the small metal bracket or thread bar tack at the top of the zipper that prevents the slider from running off the tape and the teeth from pulling apart.

The **SLIDER AND PULL TAB** is the mechanism that enables you to work the zipper. It locks the teeth together to hold the zipper closed, and unlocks the teeth to open the zipper.

The **TAPE** is the fabric strip on which the teeth or coil are fastened and is the part that is sewn to the garment. It can be woven or knitted, and sometimes covers the back of the coil.

The **GUIDE LINE** is a raised line woven into some zipper tapes to act as a stitching guide.

The **CHAIN** is formed by the interlocking teeth when the zipper is closed.

The **TEETH** or **COIL** is the locking part of the zipper upon which the slider runs. It may be made of metal, nylon, or polyester.

The **BOTTOM STOP** is the metal bracket or bonded part of the coil at the bottom of the zipper and garment opening. The slider rests here when the zipper is unzipped. For separating zippers, the bottom stop separates into two parts to allow for complete opening of the zipper.

Basic Application Procedures

The length of the zipper and the specific type required, if any, will be indicated on the back of your pattern envelope. When you make your zipper selection, consider the weight of the zipper in relation to the weight of your fabric. For example, a synthetic zipper that is lighter in weight and more flexible than a metal zipper is preferable for lighter-weight fabrics.

Complete instructions for all of the major methods of zipper insertion are offered here. You will find that zippers won't be the least bit tricky if you follow the directions carefully and rely on these basic application tips:

- ☐ Close the zipper and press out creases before application. When pressing on the right side of the garment, use a press cloth to prevent any unsightly shine, puckers, or impressions.
- ☐ Always close the zipper before laundering or dry cleaning.
- ☐ Staystitch the zipper opening edges directionally in the seam allowance.
- ☐ Bias seams or stretchy fabric may require a stay before inserting the zipper. Cut two strips of seam binding the length of the opening, and baste to the wrong side along the seamline in the seam allowance.
- ☐ Extend seam allowances of the zipper opening with ribbon seam binding if they are less than ⅝'' wide.
- ☐ For zippers with cotton tape, preshrink the zipper if it will be applied in a washable garment.
- ☐ Always pin the zipper from the top downward.
- ☐ Remember that plaids or stripes should match at the zipper closing as well as at other seams; baste the closing shut, matching the pattern of the fabric.
- ☐ A zipper foot is essential for machine-stitching and, if it is adjustable, permits stitching on either side of the zipper without turning the fabric.
- ☐ Always sew both sides of your zipper in the same direction.
- ☐ For an easier and a truly custom-tailored way to apply a zipper, use the prickstitch.

SHORTENING A ZIPPER: If the required length zipper is not available, you can purchase a longer zipper and shorten it. Measure the desired length and whipstitch tightly across the teeth or coil 8 to 10 times to form a new bottom stop. Cut away excess zipper ½'' below the stitching. Apply zipper, stitching slowly across the teeth or coil at the bottom of the zipper.

Separating zippers should be shortened only from the top. Open zipper and whipstitch over the teeth or coil on each side of the zipper. Trim away excess zipper ¾'' above stitching.

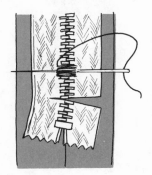

STITCHING A ZIPPER: For an attractive appearance, the final stitching that shows on the outside of the garment must be straight and an even distance from the zipper opening. For best results, topstitch from the right side of the garment using thread basting or sewing tape as a guide. Always begin your stitching at the bottom of the zipper placket and stitch to the top. To stitch past the slider, pull the tab up and turn the slider on its side, or leave the needle in the fabric, raise the zipper foot, and move the slider down before completing your stitching.

One of the easiest methods of achieving straight, even stitching is to use a tiny prick-stitch and complete the final stitching by hand. This method is a custom technique and is especially desirable on delicate and pile fabrics. See the couture section, page 448, for complete instructions.

Centered Application

This application is the one most frequently used for center front and center back openings. Attach the facing before installing the zipper. Trim and grade the seam; understitch the facing to the seam allowances. Then turn and press the facing. Waistbands are applied after zipper is inserted.

Open out facings. Machine-baste opening edges together along seamlines, and press seam open. Face down, place closed zipper on opened seam allowances with zipper teeth centered over the seamline and baste (1). Locate the pull tab ¼" below neck or waist seamline.

On outside, stitch by machine or hand across lower end and continue along one side, ¼" from basted seam (2). Begin again at lower end and stitch other side in same manner.

Completing the facing is both quick and easy. Simply turn the facings to the inside, folding in the ends to clear the zipper teeth. Slipstitch the ends in place. Anchor the remaining facing edge. Fasten the neck edge with a hook and eye on the inside of your garment (3).

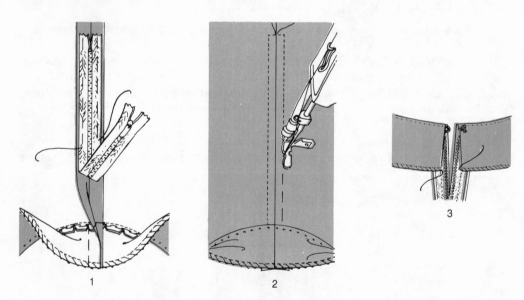

For another method of inserting a centered zipper before the facings are applied, refer to the Very Easy Vogue section, page 410.

Lapped Application

This method neatly conceals your zipper, making it particularly suited for zippers that do not match perfectly with the color of your fabric. It is also used for openings in the side seams of garments. When the garment edge is faced, the facing should be attached before the zipper is inserted. Because the facing may have a tendency to catch in the teeth of the closure and provide excess bulk over the zipper pull tab, we recommend a technique calling for special manipulation of the facing *before* it is stitched to the garment.

FACING: As you are pinning the facing in place, turn back 1″ on the end of the overlapping side and trim to ⅝″. Then stitch the facing to the garment, continuing to the very end of the opening. Trim, grade, and clip all seam allowances, stopping just short of the unfaced portion of the seam allowance (1). Understitch the facing to the neckline seam allowances, then turn and press (2). Insert zipper as directed below. Turn the facing and zipper tape to the inside. The overlapping facing end will automatically clear the zipper teeth. Turn in the other end to clear the zipper. Slipstitch the facing ends in place and the upper neckline edges together. Anchor the remaining facing edge (3). Complete with a hook sewn on the inside and an eye sewn to the outside of your garment (4).

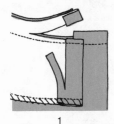
1

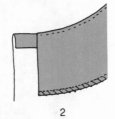
2

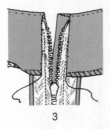
3

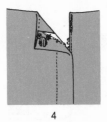
4

APPLICATION: Complete steps 1 and 2 if you are applying your zipper to a faced garment edge. Then mark the seamline on the underlapped opening edge with thread tracing. Turn in the edge ⅛″ from the traced seamline in the seam allowance; baste and press. A tiny fold will appear in the seam allowance at the lower edge. Then turn in the full seam allowance on the other opening edge; baste and press (5).

Place the underlapped edge over the zipper tape with the bottom stop of the zipper even with the end of the garment opening. Baste close to the zipper teeth, leaving enough room for the tab to slide easily. Stitch close to the edge by hand or machine (6). Position the overlapping edge to just cover the stitching on the opposite side of the opening. Baste the remaining zipper tape in place to be sure it does not shift during stitching. Stitch by machine or hand across the lower end, pivoting at the corner and continuing along the side ⅜″ from the edge (7).

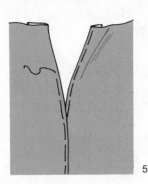
5

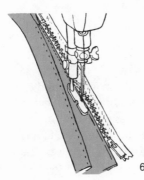
6

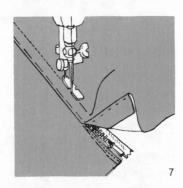
7

Separating Zipper

FACING: Begin by treating both sides of the facing as shown for the overlapping side of the facing in the lapped application. Follow steps 1 and 2 on the previous page.

APPLICATION: Machine-baste the opening edges together along their seamlines, keeping the facing and hem free; press open. Face down, center the closed zipper on the opened seam allowances with the zipper stop at the bottom of the opening. Turn down the tape ends at the top on each side of the pull tab; tack securely. Baste the zipper in place (1).

On the outside, stitch ¼″ from each side of the center front by hand or by machine as you would a centered application, still keeping the facing and hem free. On the inside, turn the facing and hem ends in to clear the zipper teeth; slipstitch. Catchstitch the remaining facing and hem edges in place. Turn in any lining seam allowances, making sure the long edges clear the zipper teeth; baste close to the edge. Slipstitch in place (2).

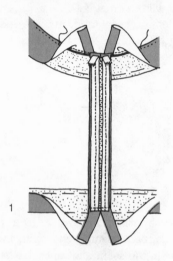 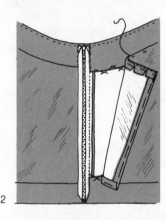

REVERSIBLE GARMENTS: Separating zippers with two pull tabs for reversible garments are available. The zipper area inside the reversible garment is finished so that it is identical in appearance to the outside. Baste zipper in place as above, keeping the long edges of the opening free on the inside. From the inside, turn under the seam allowances so the edges meet over the center of the zipper; baste. From the right side, stitch ¼″ from each side of the center front through all thicknesses.

QUILTED OUTDOOR GARMENTS: To eliminate bulk in the zipper area, baste ¾″ seam and trim away fiberfill in the seam allowances. Stitch ⅛″ from each side of the center front through the fabric and the seam allowances to flatten the zipper area. Insert zipper as above, but stitch ⅜″ from center.

Fly-Front Placket

Traditionally used for men's trousers, the fly-front zipper is often found on women's pants and skirts and may be used occasionally on jackets and coats. You can use a regular zipper or purchase a specially designed trouser zipper. We recommend that you use the fly placket only when your pattern is specifically designed for it.

This version is the simplified method usually found in women's patterns. For the traditional fly front with a fly shield, refer to Menswear Sewing, page 492. Remember that the placket in women's garments always laps right over left, just the opposite of men's.

Turn in both front extensions along the foldlines and baste close to the folds. Pin or baste the closed zipper under the left front, with the teeth close to the basted edge and the pull tab ⅛" below the waist seamline. Stitch close to the edge (1). Lap the right front over the zipper, even with the center front marking on the left front, and baste close to the fold through all thicknesses (2). On the inside, baste remaining zipper tape to the right front, through all thicknesses (3). On the outside, stitch on the right front along the stitching line, ending at the seamline marking. Pull threads to the inside and tie (4).

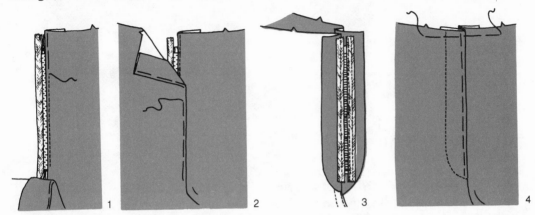

Special Applications

EXPOSED ZIPPER: The exposed zipper application can be used where there is no seam. A fabric patch is first stitched to the placket area to stabilize the opening, prevent raveling, and to eliminate bulk when sewing sweater knits. Use organdy, a lightweight interfacing, or a lining fabric for the fabric stay. Cut fabric stay 2½" wide and 2" longer than the zipper. Place center of stay strip over the center of the garment opening. With right sides of fabric together, pin or baste in place. Stitch ⅛" on each side of the center line and across the bottom at the end of the zipper marking. Slash along the center line between the rows of stitching and diagonally into the corners (1).

Turn fabric stay to the inside of the garment and press. Center the zipper under the opening with the bottom stop of the zipper at the end of the opening; pin in place. Slip baste the edge of the fabric to the zipper tape, exposing only the zipper teeth or coil. Using a zipper foot, stitch across the base of the triangle through the garment fabric, the stay, and the zipper tape as shown (2). Turn back one side of the garment opening and stitch the garment to the zipper tape along the reinforcement stitching line, beginning at the bottom (3). Repeat for the other side of the opening (4).

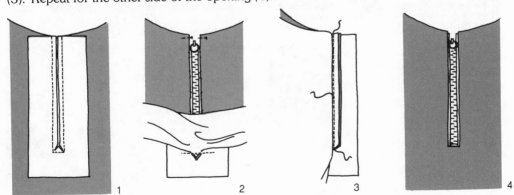

DRESS SIDE PLACKET: For a placket located on the side of a dress, the zipper is inserted in a seam that is closed at both ends. To make a top stop for the zipper, simply whipstitch the upper edges of the zipper tape together. Before inserting zipper, be sure the opening length is equal to the zipper length, with the bottom stop barely concealed. If the zipper is too long, shorten it as on page 329. Insert your zipper, using the lapped or centered application, ignoring facing instructions. As you complete the zipper, stitch across the bottom end, along the long edge, and across the top end by machine or by hand.

INVISIBLE ZIPPER: The invisible zipper, which has no rows of stitching on the outside of the garment, must be stitched with a special invisible zipper foot. Unlike other zippers, the invisible zipper is applied to the opening edges **before** the remainder of the seam is stitched. The facings are usually applied after the zipper is installed.

Open the zipper and place it face down on the right side of the fabric. Have the teeth lying on the seamline and the tape in the seam allowance. Lower the right-hand groove of the foot over the teeth, and stitch from upper edge to pull tab (1). Keep stitches as close to the teeth as possible. Close the zipper to position the other side on the opposite seam allowance. Pin or baste as desired. Open the zipper and stitch with the left hand groove of the foot over the teeth (2). Close the zipper. To finish the seam below the zipper, slide the zipper foot to the left. Lower the needle and begin stitching just slightly above and to the left of the last stitch. Stitch seam closed (3). To complete the application, stitch each end of the zipper tape to the seam allowances (4).

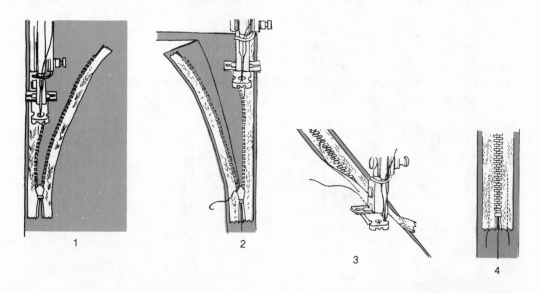

Fasteners

There are many commercial fasteners available. The key is to select the one best suited to your individual needs. These fasteners, to be truly functional, should be chosen in a size appropriate to the fabric weight, the amount of strain the closure will receive, and the type of cleaning and care the garment will require. For types and sizes of fasteners, refer to page 178. Choose a fastener that will also be inconspicuous while the garment is being worn. To simplify matters, we have divided the commercial fasteners into three basic categories—*snaps, hooks and eyes,* and *hook and loop tape fasteners.*

Snaps

These fasteners are used on overlapping edges that receive a minimum of strain. The ball half of the snap is sewn on the underside of the overlap. The socket is sewn on the upper side of the garment section closest to your body. Sew the ball on first. Take several small stitches close together through each hole, picking up a thread of the garment with each stitch. Carry the thread under the snap from hole to hole. To mark the location for the socket, rub tailor's chalk onto the ball and position the garment as when fastened, or use a pin through the ball section.

For a couture finish, use fabric-covered snaps that are ready-made, or you can cover your own. To use a snap on garment edges that just meet, choose either an extended snap or a hanging snap application; refer to the couture section, page 449.

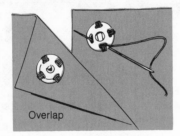

Overlap

Hooks and Eyes

Hooks and eyes are most frequently found at neck edges or waistbands. To attach the hook, work stitches around the circular holes, picking up a garment thread with each stitch. Secure the thread, but do not clip. Slip the needle through the fabric, surfacing to sew the hook end to the garment to hold it flat. To fasten straight or curved metal eyes, work stitches around the circular holes as for the hook. For curved metal eyes, continue to sew a few stitches on either side of the eye to hold it flat. For a thread loop, see page 324.

If the edges overlap, sew the hook even with the overlapping edge on the inside. Then sew a straight metal or thread eye on the outside of your garment on the underlap.

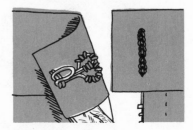

If the closing edges just meet, such as a neckline, sew a hook and a curved metal eye on the wrong side of the garment. Place and sew the hook $\frac{1}{16}''$ from one edge. The curved eye should be placed with the loop extending slightly beyond the other edge (1). Or make a thread eye, the same length as the metal eye it replaces (2).

Large or heavy-duty hooks and eyes are used on areas that receive excessive strain, such as waistbands. Position them as you would regular hooks and eyes and sew them on through the holes (3). In addition to the slide type shown here, large covered hooks and eyes are available for closures on heavyweight garments, such as furs and coats.

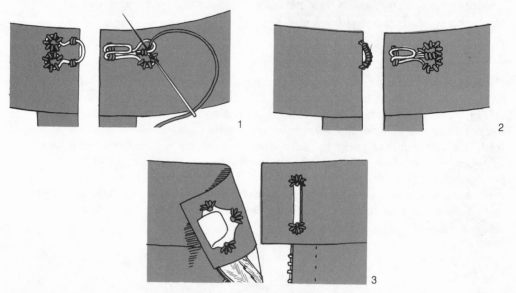

Hook and Loop Tape Fasteners

This fastener operates on the same principle as hooks and eyes. One strip is faced with tiny hooks, the other with a pile fabric serving as minute eyes. When pressed together, the two strips fuse until pulled apart. They are excellent on loose-fitting garments such as jacket fronts, belt overlaps, etc., but are not suitable on tight-fitting garments, on very lightweight fabrics, or whenever extra bulk is not desirable.

There are several effective methods of application. You may machine-stitch the lower strip in place through all layers and the upper strip through just one layer where it cannot be seen. This application must be done during the construction process. Another method is to apply the upper strip by hand, using a sturdy slipstitch through just one layer of fabric, and the lower strip by machine through all layers. Topstitching both strips through all garment layers is also popular as a design detail on casual clothes.

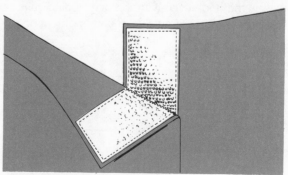

Hems

O ne of the most important fashion aspects of any garment is its hemline. Although the real purpose of the hem is to help your garment hang well by adding weight to the edge, variations in hem lengths will also change the silhouette and proportion of your garment. To be really complete, your wardrobe should include several different hemlines and the accompanying illustration will show you the principal lengths.

We wish to emphasize the fact that there is no standard hem length that is correct for every woman. Always let the lengths most becoming to **you** influence your choice of hem levels.

Although fashion and proportion dictate hem lengths, the type of garment, the nature of the fabric, and the height of the wearer determine the depth of the hem. Usually the hem allowance is 3″, which adds weight and therefore influences the drape of the garment. This is suitable for straight garments and for medium and lightweight fabrics. Flared skirts, stretchy fabrics such as knits, and heavier-weight fabrics should have a narrower hem of 1½″ to 2″. Very full or circular skirts need only a 1″ hem. Narrow-rolled hems only ⅛″ wide or very deep hems up to 6″ wide are suitable for sheer fabrics.

A well-made hem is always the least noticeable hem. Always take the time to eliminate bulk, reduce extra fullness, and press carefully to prevent ridges. Above all, never pull the stitches tightly as you sew.

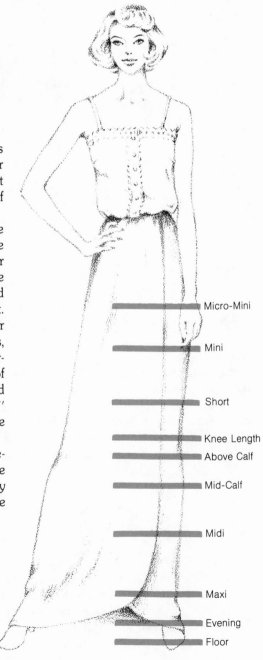

Micro-Mini

Mini

Short

Knee Length

Above Calf

Mid-Calf

Midi

Maxi

Evening

Floor

MARKING HEMLINE: When preparing a hem, there are several fundamental steps to follow. As with any other phase of fitting, the proper undergarments and shoes must be worn when measuring the hem. If you plan to add accessories such as a belt, sash, or jacket, wear it while you are measuring. It will be a factor in determining the hem length in proportion to the total garment design and will affect the garment length considerably when worn.

For absolute accuracy, always have someone mark your hem for you. To avoid discrepancies, stand stationary and have the person doing the marking move around you. Pins should be placed every 3″ for a straight skirt and every 2″ for a flared skirt. If your garment has a bias or circular hem, let it hang for 24 hours before measuring, allowing the bias to set and preventing hemline sag.

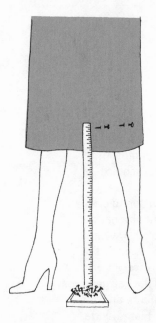

After the hemline has been marked, pin up the hem to see if it looks good. Insert the pins at right angles to the hemline, letting it fall in a natural manner. Regardless of length, the hem should look right. It should be parallel to the floor, but occasionally a perfectly straight hem will appear uneven, especially in garments with pleats, plaids, or that are bias-cut. If such a situation occurs, the hem must be changed to adapt to the optical illusion. Make the correction, using a carefully controlled, gradual change in the hem depth; then try the garment on again to see if the hemline appears to be even.

Types of Hems

PLAIN HEM: This hem, the simplest and most basic of all the hems, has little or no fullness. The procedures used to complete it are the preliminary steps for most hems.

After determining the length, trim any seam allowances below the hemline to ¼″, eliminating bulk that could cause ridges when the hem is pressed. Then baste close to the fold of the hem, measure the hem depth, and trim evenly. Press the hem with brown paper between the hem and the garment, steaming out any fullness. Finish the raw edge in the

manner best suited to the style and fabric. Sew the hem in place with a slipstitch or
hemming stitch for turned-under or steam binding finishes and a blindstitch for pinked or
overcast finishes. Then use the pressing techniques applicable to the hem edge desired, as
described on page 350.

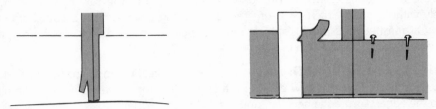

EASED HEM: When your hem has excess fullness that must be adjusted, an eased hem
should be used. To ease, stitch ¼″ from the raw edge, using long stitches. Pull up the ease
thread every few inches, then shrink out the fullness with a steam iron. Refer to Pressing,
page 350, for detailed information on how to shrink hems. Finish the raw edge and sew as
suggested for the plain hem.

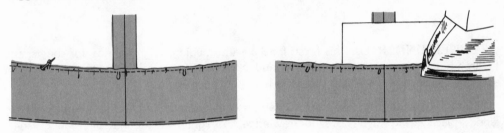

CIRCULAR HEM: This hem should be about 1″ in depth to eliminate bulk and excess
fullness. Let the garment hang for 24 hours before marking. Then mark and complete
hem, following the steps for the eased hem above (1).

NARROW HEM: For blouses, lingerie, and accessories, use a narrow hem. Trim hem
allowance to ½″. Turn under raw edges ¼″ and press. Turn up edge again and press.
Stitch by machine through all thicknesses for casual clothes, or slipstitch to complete the
hem (2). Silks and sheers require the couture touch of a hand-rolled hem; refer to
page 451.

1
2

MACHINE-STITCHED HEM: A topstitched hem is suitable for garments in which
topstitching has been used elsewhere. Fold hemline to desired width. For woven fabrics,
turn under hem edge ⅜″ and press. From right side of fabric, topstitch close to upper edge.
If desired, a second row of topstitching can be placed ¼″ below the first row (3).

For other machine-stitched hems, turn to the Very Easy Vogue section, page 413.

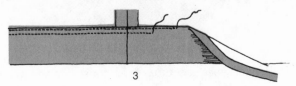

3

Hem Finishes

STITCHED AND OVERCAST: This method creates a very fine finish. The completed hem is inconspicuous from the outside after pressing, and the raw edges are finished securely without bulk. Stitch ¼'' from raw edge, using a large stitch if your hem will be eased. Overcast edge, using this stitching as a guide. To ensure an invisible hem, turn the edge back ¼'' and blindstitch (1).

STITCHED AND PINKED: Here is a quick and effective finish for fabrics that ravel slightly. Stitch ¼'' from the raw edge; use a large stitch for an eased hem. Then pink or scallop the edge. Turn edge back ¼'' and blindstitch to garment (2).

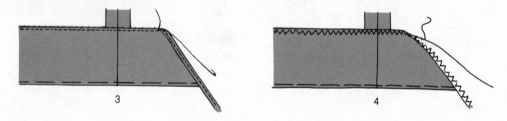

1   2

TURNED-UNDER: Use this finish for light and mediumweight fabrics, for sheers, and for limp hems. Turn in the raw edge ¼'' and stitch close to the fold. (Omit this stitching for sheers.) Use hemming stitch to complete hem (3).

ZIGZAGGED: A fast, easy finish for fabrics of all weights. For heavier-weight or firmer fabrics, place zigzag stitches over the raw edge. For lighter-weight and softer fabrics, stitch about ⅛'' away from the raw edge. Attach hem to garment with a catchstitch; use a blind-stitch for heavier fabrics (4).

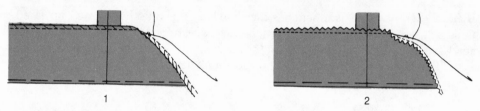

3   4

SEAM BINDING or **BIAS TAPE:** This finish is best for loosely woven fabrics that tend to ravel. Use ribbon seam binding for straight hems and bias tape or flexible lace for eased and circular hems. Stitch tape or seam binding ¼'' from the raw edge of the fabric. For bias tape, easestitch the hem, adjust fullness, and machine-stitch the tape to the raw edge. Then complete the hem using hemming stitch. For bulky fabrics, fold back tape and blindstitch fabric edge to garment.

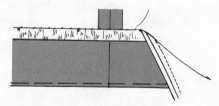

HONG KONG FINISH: A special couture finish for seams and hems; see page 450.

Special Hems

BIAS-FACED HEM: A facing constructed of a lightweight fabric will provide a smooth finish for garments with inadequate hem allowances, very full skirts, or very bulky fabrics. You may use either commercial bias facing or your own bias strip cut from a lightweight material the desired width plus ½'' for seam allowances.

Mark your hemline, leaving at least ½'' additional fabric at the bottom edge. For a very curved hemline, shape the bias to the garment. Match raw edges and stitch in a ¼'' seam, joining the ends of the facing as on page 248. Press seam open. Turn in raw edge ¼'', turn facing up, and slipstitch (1).

DOUBLE-STITCHED HEM: This hem is ideal for unlined heavy fabrics and knits. Stitch and overcast the raw edge. Mark the hemline with thread tracing; shrink and adjust any ease. Baste along the center of the hem. Fold back the hem along the basting and blind catchstitch the hem. Do not pull the stitches too tightly; this line of stitching is for support only. Turn up the top edge of the hem and sew it with a second line of loose catch-stitching (2).

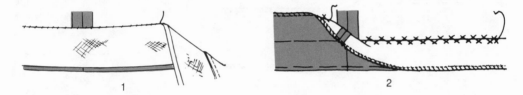

1   2

INTERFACED HEM: Your garment style or fabric may require the control of an interfaced hem to create a smooth, unbroken line. Mark the hemline with thread tracing. Finish raw edge of hem.

For lined garments, the interfacing extends above the hem to prevent any impression of the hem on the right side of the garment. Cut interfacing 1⅝'' wider than hem. For unlined garments, cut interfacing the same width as hem. Use regular interfacing fabrics for body or lamb's wool for a very softly rolled effect. Cut a bias strip long enough to lap the ends ½''. Piece if necessary. For curved hemlines, preshape the interfacing to correspond with the curve. Place interfacing over hemline with one edge extending ⅝'' below the thread tracing. For hems which will be topstitched or edgestitched, cut off interfacing at hemline.

Sew interfacing to garment with invisible catchstitches along both edges. Turn up hem and baste close to fold. For lined garments, catchstitch hem to interfacing only. For unlined garments, blindstitch hem, easing fullness if necessary. To press, steam the hem, never resting your iron on the fabric. Refer to Pressing, page 350, for additional information.

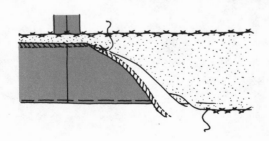

HEMS WITH PLEATS: Press open the seam within the hem area where it crosses the hem at the edge of a pleat fold. Finish the raw edge of the hem, then measure up from the hemline the width of the hem and clip the seam. Both seam allowances above the hem will face in one direction, helping to keep the pleat fold flat (1).

An effective way to ensure that any pleated hem stays creased is to edgestitch the fold of the pleat. Stitch through all thicknesses of the hem on the inside (2).

To handle fullness effectively in a pleated hem, restitch the seam below the hemline at a slant opposite that of the garment seam above the hemline. Remove previous stitching and trim the seam below the hemline to ¼″ (3). Complete the hem.

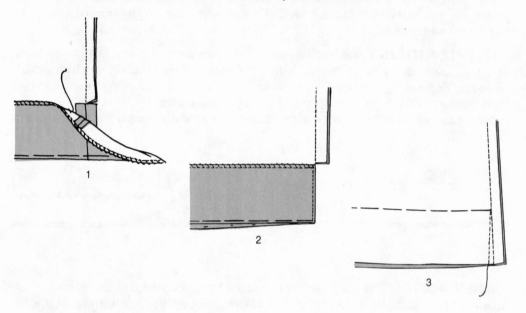

HEMS WITH GODETS: A godet can be used to give extra width to a hem. It can be inserted into a seam, dart, cut-out, or slash. A pie-shaped godet (the most common shape) is usually cut with the straight grain down the center of the fabric, leaving bias edges on the sides.

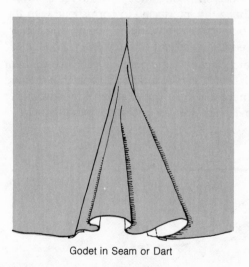

Godet in Seam or Dart

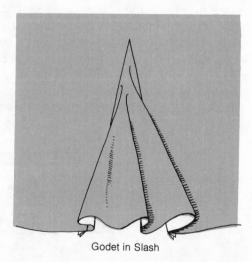

Godet in Slash

For insertion into a seam or dart, pin godet to garment, matching seamlines and markings. For heavy or stretchy fabrics, center ribbon seam binding over seamlines for support. Baste and stitch on either side from point to hem (1). Clip seam allowances 1″ below the point. Press seam allowances open below the clip, toward the garment above the clip, and open again above the point (2).

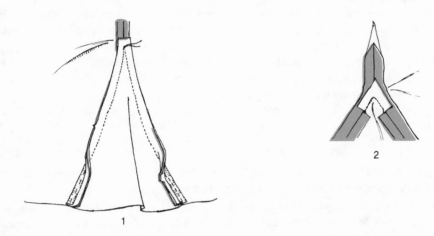

For insertion into a slash, reinforce the slash by sewing just inside the seamlines in the seam allowance, using small stitches (15–20 per inch) on both sides of the point and pivoting at the point. If fabric is especially fragile, reinforce point with a patch of underlining. At point, clip exactly to stitching (3). Pin godet to slash, turning patch inside and matching the godet marking to the clipped point first. Baste and stitch, slashed side up, from point to hem (4). Press seam allowances toward garment (5).

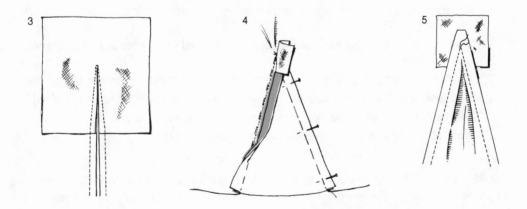

With heavy or loosely woven fabrics, stitch the godet to the garment for only a few inches on either side of the point and let the remainder of the godet hang free for 24 hours to allow the bias to set. Before hemming, allow all garments to hang 24 hours.

For other couture hem finishes—soft hems, extremely curved hems, and horsehair braid finish—see pages 451 and 452. To achieve a smooth corner when a facing folds back at the hemline, see the tailoring section, page 436. For an explanation of pressing techniques and equipment to use on hems, see page 350.

Pressing

That finely finished look every woman strives for is as much a product of good pressing as it is of careful construction. Do not ignore pressing directions in your haste and zeal. If you postpone your pressing until the garment is completed, it will be too late to accomplish well-defined edges and sculptured contours. Set up your pressing equipment near your sewing machine and use it faithfully.

The most important idea to remember is that pressing is *not* ironing. Pressing is the process of lifting the iron and setting it down in the proper position. You can use pressing to accomplish feats not possible with a needle and thread.

Specifically, pressing techniques depend on the particular fabric and garment construction, but there are some basic rules which should always be followed:

- [ ] Have an assortment of equipment available so that you can place the fabric in the most practical position for the area being pressed.
- [ ] Always test an odd scrap or an inconspicuous area to determine the best technique for your fabric. Test a piece large enough to allow a comparison between the pressed portion and the unpressed portion.
- [ ] Check your fabric's reaction to **steam** and **moisture**. Both should be used sparingly, or water marks, puckering, and dulling may result.
- [ ] Press with the grain of your fabric whenever possible; be very careful not to stretch edges or curves by pulling the fabric.
- [ ] Whenever possible, press on the wrong side of your fabric. If you must press on the right side, use a press cloth.
- [ ] Use brown paper strips to prevent impressions of seam allowances, darts, or pleats from appearing on the right side of your fabric. Cut strips at least 2″ wider than the area to be pressed.
- [ ] Always press seams and darts before they are crossed with other seams to eliminate any extra bulk.
- [ ] Never press any sharp creases until the fit of your garment has been double-checked.
- [ ] Try to use only the tip of your iron and work in the same direction as you stitched.
- [ ] To avoid marring fabric, do not press over basting threads or pins.
- [ ] Above all, know your fabric, and *do not over-press.*

PRESS CLOTH: To prevent shine and protect your fabric from the heat of the iron and its impression, use an appropriate press cloth between the fabric and the iron. Press cloths are made of a variety of fabrics. The one you use depends upon the nature of your garment fabric. Select one of a weight similar to the weight of your fabric and use a size approximately 12″ by 18″. An extra scrap of your fabric makes an excellent press cloth. In general, a wool press cloth is best for preserving the spongy texture of woolens, while firm cotton is ideal for most flat-surfaced cottons and mediumweight blends. Cheesecloth, used singly or folded several times, will readily adapt to most of your needs because it is supple and you can see through it for pressing details.

You may use a dry press cloth with either a dry or steam iron. A uniformly damp press cloth may be necessary. If so, moisten it with a sponge, or immerse, wring, and press it until the proper dampness is achieved. To avoid shrinkage, **never** place a really wet cloth on your fabric and don't have the iron so hot that the cloth dries immediately. Keep in mind that there are several very suitable commercial press cloths in addition to making your own.

STEAM: The moisture of steam provides the slight amount of dampness needed to get truly flat seams or edges. Curved or softly draped sections of your garment may be "set" to hang correctly by steaming them into position. Steam is of special value for collars and lapels. They will always roll correctly if carefully steamed in position on a dress form or a rolled towel during construction.

Use a press cloth if you apply the iron directly. If the iron is held about 3″ from the fabric, no cloth is needed. Let the steam do most of the work. Steam, then mold the fabric with your fingers while it is still damp. Allow the steam to dissipate and the fabric to dry before you resume working.

Seams

Initially, all seams are treated alike. Press along the stitching line in the same direction as the seam was sewn to merge stitches with fabric. Open the seam flat with the tip of your iron. Then let the shape of the seam dictate further handling.

FLAT SEAMS often leave ridges in the right side of your garment. Steam press with the garment over a seam roll or with brown paper under the seam allowances. To get some seams truly flat, you may have to steam the surface and use short quick movements with a pounding block on the seamline only (1).

CURVED or **ROUNDED SEAMS** pose different problems. The seamline should be pressed flat, but the seam area should maintain its built-in roundness. Employ the techniques used for a flat seam, but vary the equipment. Use a tailor's ham, press mitt, or dressmaker's cushion, alone or with a sleeve board, as your pressing surface (2).

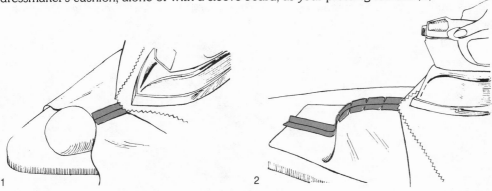

1

2

SEAMS AT FINISHED EDGES with allowances completely enclosed within parts of your garment (such as facings, cuffs, pocket flaps, and collars) should be pressed before turning. Due to the confined area, narrow seam allowances, and the necessity of precise pressing, you will find it easier to work without a press cloth. After stitching, place the seam over the edge of a point presser or tailor's board and open it with the tip of your iron to facilitate turning and ensure a flat seam that will not roll (1). Then lay the section flat on the ironing board with the underside up. Turn pressed seam allowances toward the section until the stitching line shows and press very lightly to make turning and favoring the outer edge easier (2). Turn right side out and press with a cloth from the underside; keep the seam on the underside (3).

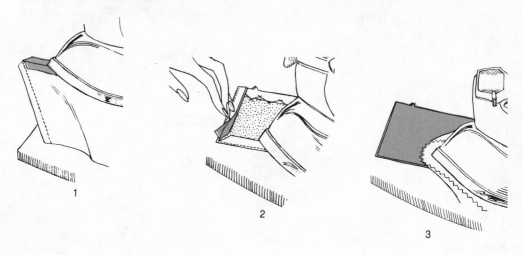

Darts

Darts require a subtly rounded pressing surface such as a tailor's ham, dressmaker's cushion, or press mitt. First press the dart flat, as it was stitched, being careful not to let your iron stray past the pointed end. Then open the garment and press the dart in the proper direction, working from the wider end toward the point. Do not give the dart a sharp crease until the garment has been fitted. In general, vertical darts are pressed toward center back or front and horizontal darts are pressed downward. Press contour or double-pointed darts like single-pointed darts, one half of the dart at a time, working from the middle to the pointed ends. Slash darts in heavy fabrics along the fold to within ½″ to 1″ of the point. Over a rounded surface, open the dart edges with the tip of your iron. Using a press cloth, press darts completely open. After pressing the dart, press the surrounding garment area.

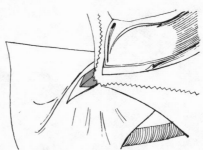

Tucks

First press tucks from underneath side of fold. To retain the soft fold of a released tuck, never press past stitching line. Be cautious with steam; too much may cause puckering. Press the fold of released tucks toward center front or back from wrong side. Tucks made on right side are pressed from stitching line toward folds; put brown paper under folds of wide tucks. Use a press cloth when pressing from right side (1).

Gathering and Shirring

Press from the wrong side wherever possible. Hold the gathering along the stitching as you work. Move your iron from the flat, ungathered area toward the rows of stitching. Use the tip of your iron to get between the folds of fabric. Repeat the procedure until no sharp creases remain. Press gathered seam allowances flat before stitching (2).

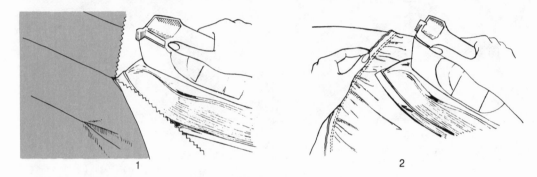

Pleats

When you are sure of fit, baste the length of each pleat; then press on both sides of the pleat, using a press cloth and very little steam. Press just enough to *set* the pleat. If the pleats fall correctly, press again to within 8″ of the lower edge, setting the creases permanently; use strips of brown paper under the folds. Hem and set remainder of pleat creases. (Press the full length if the hem is already completed.) To prevent overhanging fabric from distorting the pleats, support with a chair or table.

Soft or unpressed pleats should be steamed gently into folds rather than sharp creases. Place the garment on a dress form so the folds fall naturally and steam thoroughly with your iron. If a dress form is not available, pin the pleats in place on your ironing board cover and steam them, holding the iron 2″ to 3″ from the fabric. Let the fabric dry completely before removing the garment from the board.

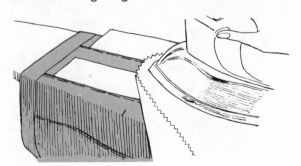
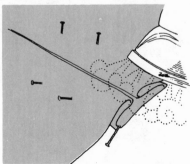

Plackets and Zippers

Because these features can be found in curved or flat areas, let the shape of the garment area determine the appropriate equipment to use. Position your placket right side down on a press pad, thick woolen scrap, or a heavy towel placed on your ironing board, or a tailor's ham. The padding will prevent unwanted ridges from appearing as you press. Work from the wrong side; use a press cloth and limited moisture since excess dampness may create puckers. Do not press directly on zipper teeth, hooks and eyes, or snaps to avoid marring them or the sole plate of your iron. Should you need to touch up the right side of your fabric, place brown paper between the placket lap and the fabric underneath and press, protecting the fabric with a press cloth. Again be especially sparing in your use of steam and moisture.

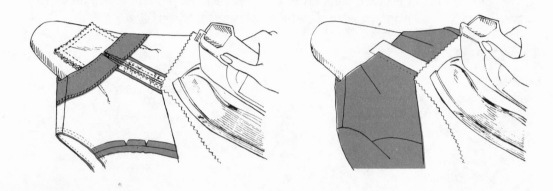

Buttonholes

Since buttonholes call for detailed construction techniques, you'll find that careful pressing applied at the appropriate times will greatly simplify the entire procedure. After stitching the buttonhole to the garment, use a press cloth and brown paper under the strip edges to press the buttonhole from the right side, merging fabric and threads. Then use a sleeve board, placing the wrong side of the buttonhole area on the larger side of the board to prevent the surrounding garment area from becoming wrinkled. Lift up the strips and touch up portions of the garment between the buttonholes, if necessary. Then lay garment flat on ironing board and press the surrounding garment area.

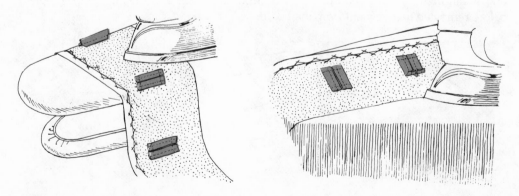

Pockets

The procedure for pressing pockets is quite similar to that of buttonholes. After stitching the pocket to the garment, press from the right side, using a press cloth. For welt or flap pockets, first put brown paper between the garment and the welt or flap. Then turn to the wrong side and press along seamlines, using a press pad. Then lift up the pocket and touch up the garment area underneath the pocket, using the moisture appropriate to your fabric.

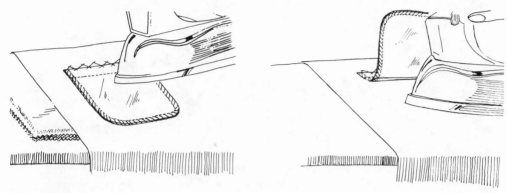

Sleeves

Start by pressing the sleeve seam open over a sleeve board. After easing and fitting the sleeve cap, remove the sleeve from the garment and place it on a press mitt slipped over your hand or the narrow end of a sleeve board. Then use the tip and side of your iron to shrink the fullness from the seam allowance only. Be very careful not to press beyond the stitching line or flatten the sleeve cap. Some fabrics, such as permanent press and velvet, do not respond well to shrinking. If your fabric and sleeve cap need additional handling, see Set-in Sleeves, page 274. After the sleeve has been stitched into the garment, press along the seam over a tailor's ham to blend the stitches into your fabric. Avoid extending the iron into the sleeve cap and use steam sparingly.

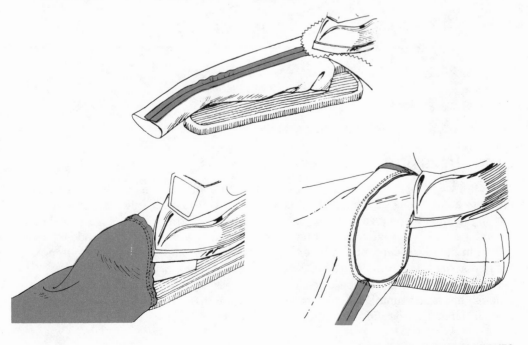

Hems

After marking, baste hems near the fold. Place brown paper between hem and garment and steam out any excess fullness. Avoid pressing over basting threads. For a great amount of fullness, easestitch along upper edge as directed on page 339. Then, holding iron above hem, steam it, shrinking as much fullness as possible. Once hem has been sewn in place, remove basting. Steam again. Use a pounding block if a crisp edge is desired.

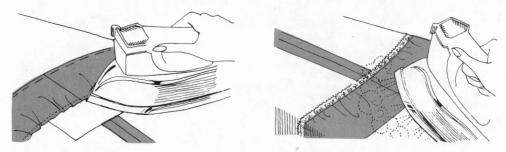

SOFT HEMS with a gently rolled edge may be preferred in place of a sharp crease. To achieve this finish, simply hold the iron 2″ to 3″ from interfaced hem, steaming the fabric thoroughly. Never rest the iron directly on the fabric. Pat *lightly* with a pounding block or ruler to mold the hem. Let the garment dry thoroughly before wearing (1).

PLEATED HEMS with seams at the fold must be pressed carefully before hemming. First clip the pleat seam at the top of the turned up hem before the raw edge is finished. Press seam allowances open below clip. Grade the seam allowances of bulky fabric. Finish the raw edge and complete the hem. Press a sharp crease in the underfold with the edge of your iron. If the folds still do not lie flat, stitch close to the edge of the fold. For more on pleated hems, see page 342 (2).

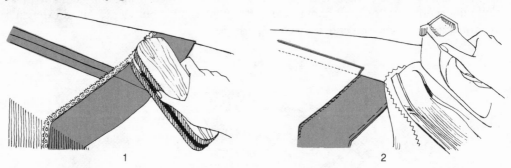

1   2

Final Pressing

The last pressing operation should be a mere touch-up job, never a cure-all for haphazard pressing during construction. Soft pleats, godets, collars, and other areas that need "setting" should be pressed with the garment on a dress form or hanger. Just steam and pat into position without touching iron to fabric. You may use tissue paper padding under collars, inside sleeve caps, and in other areas to hold them in place while fabric dries. Do not remove garment from dress form until fabric is completely dry.

Certain fabrics (satin, crepe, metallics, velvet, silk, synthetics) and trims (paillettes, sequins, beads, trapunto) will require special pressing techniques and equipment; see Special Handling, page 352, and Trims, page 453.

6

Fabrics Requiring Special Handling

Fabrics with Give

Comfort and good fit, two important criteria for clothing, are characteristic of fabrics with give. Whether knitted or woven, these fabrics offer a wide range of stretchability—from maximum stretch needed for active sportswear to minimum stretch used for shape retention of the fabric. New developments in fiber and fabric technology are creating interesting new fabrics for evening dresses, sportswear, lingerie, and swimwear. With the proper techniques, sewing with these fabrics can be easy and rewarding.

Knit Fabrics

The versatility of knits is almost unlimited since they are available in every weight, texture, color, and fiber. From soft jerseys and lacy raschels to firm double knits and bulky pattern knits, these fabrics are inherently flexible—resulting in comfortable, wrinkle-resistant, easy-care clothes.

Knits vary in stretchability; some are very stable and can be handled like a woven fabric, while others have considerable stretch in the crosswise direction or in both the crosswise and lengthwise directions. It is very important to determine the amount of stretch in a knit before you select your pattern, as the applicability of the design and the construction techniques to be used depend upon this fact. Use the Stretch Gauge printed on the inside back cover of the Vogue Catalogue or on the envelope of a pattern designed for stretchable knits; see page 128.

STABLE KNITS have a limited degree of stretch and retain their original shape well. Although they move with the body to a somewhat greater extent than woven fabrics, use the same construction techniques as you would for a woven fabric of similar weight.

STRETCHABLE KNITS have pronounced stretch and recovery characteristics and are perfect for the Vogue Patterns designed specifically for stretchable knits, as well as for regular patterns with soft styling. Construction techniques either maintain or limit the stretchability of the fabric depending upon the specific area of the garment—a hemline should be flexible; a V-neckline may need to be stabilized.

TWO-WAY STRETCHABLE KNITS must be used for swimwear and tight-fitting garments that require maximum stretch and recovery in both directions. Because spandex has been blended into the fabric, these knits have greater elasticity than regular knits. Special sewing techniques are necessary to retain maximum stretchability in the seams.

BEFORE CONSTRUCTION

As with woven fabric, knits may have to be straightened and preshrunk; see page 131. If tubular, split the fabric on one fold and press out the crease on the other. Occasionally, the crease will not press out. In that case you will have to refold your fabric so that the pattern layout avoids the crease. Make any necessary pattern alterations; do not use the stretchability of the fabric to compensate for minor figure variations. Fit is even more important for knits than wovens because of the tendency of the fabric to cling to the body.

Because many knits have a directional shading that is visible from certain angles, use a "with nap" layout. Mark the lengthwise grain with pins or thread tracing if the vertical ribs are not clearly discernable. Allow two-way stretchable knits to relax for at least 24 hours after being unrolled from the bolt before you begin cutting.

Lay out your fabric on a large flat surface, being sure that none hangs off the edge to distort or stretch the knit. Pattern pieces that are to be cut on the bias can also be cut on the crosswise grain for maximum stretch. To prevent lightweight knits from curling, place pattern pieces on the wrong side of the fabric. For two-way stretch fabrics, place pattern so greatest stretch goes around the body. Always use ball-point pins or fine dressmaker's pins, and cut with very sharp shears to avoid snagging the fabric. Slippery or bulky knits should be cut one layer at a time. For stretchable knits, you may wish to cut 1″ seam allowances on vertical seams to allow for any slight fitting changes in your garment.

Mark with tailor's tacks or chalk on stretchable knits and knits with a textured surface. A tracing wheel and dressmaker's carbon paper can be used for smooth, stable knits.

CONSTRUCTION POINTERS

Use a ball-point needle in a size appropriate to your fabric—ball-point needles are designed to separate rather than pierce the yarn loops. Dull or rough needle tips may cause snags or skipped stitches; insert a new needle if you experience stitching problems.

When sewing knits, use a thread that has some give—polyester or polyester-wrapped thread is recommended. Test the tension, stitch length, and pressure on a folded scrap of your fabric before actually stitching your garment; see page 182. A slightly shorter stitch length (12–15 stitches per inch) has less tendency to break when the fabric is stretched than a longer stitch. Often the tension must be loosened. Light pressure may help the fabric to feed evenly.

A plain seam can be used for most knits. Stretch the fabric very gently as it passes under the presser foot to add a little more stretch to the seams and to prevent puckering. Be careful not to pull the fabric or the seam will have a wavy appearance. A narrow zigzag stitch or special stretch stitches can also be used for seams. Seam finishes are seldom needed; only very loosely constructed knits have a tendency to unravel. For knits that have a tendency to curl, it may be necessary to staystitch ¼″ from the fabric edge before stitching the seams. For knits with a loopy surface, such as stretch terry, you may have to wrap a piece of tape around the ends of the presser foot to prevent the small toes from catching in the loops.

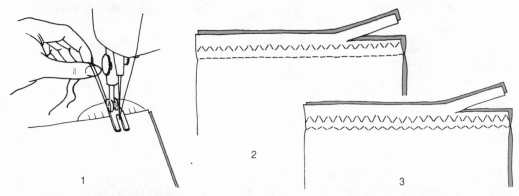

To prevent lightweight knits from being drawn down into the needle hole, use the straight stitch presser foot and needle plate, and hold both thread ends taut behind the presser foot when you begin to stitch. Lower the needle by hand for the first stitch (1).

To prevent seam allowances from curling or to eliminate bulk, you can double-stitch the seams with a row of straight or zigzag stitching. Trim away seam allowances close to stitching; press to one side (2). For two-way stretchable knits in swimwear or tight-fitting garments, combine a narrow zigzag seam with a wide zigzag stitch within the seam allowance, stretching the fabric slightly, to obtain maximum elasticity. Trim away seam allowances (3).

Although stretch may be desired in some seams, it may need to be controlled in others—such as shoulder or waist seams—by using the taping technique discussed on page 209. Interfacing should be used in garment areas where stretch is not desired, such as a V-neckline and buttonholes. Many interfacings, both regular and fusible, have been designed especially for use with knits to give soft shaping without added bulk. Refer to the Guide to Interfacings, page 163. If a lining is desired, select a lightweight, flexible fabric with the same care requirements. A lightweight tricot is often suggested.

Use regular **PRESSING** techniques for knits, but be wary of the tendency to overpress, as this causes irreparable stretching and distortion. Always test press your fabric; some knits are composed of fiber types that may be damaged by heat. For lightweight knits, first press the seams closed and then open to obtain a smooth, flat seam. Place strips of brown paper under the seam allowances to prevent leaving an imprint on the right side.

CLOSURES must be handled according to the stretchability of the knit. Bound, hand- or machine-worked buttonholes can be worked in almost any knit, but should have interfacing for support. If your garment is not interfaced, use lightweight interfacing cut into ovals and catchstitched or fused in place behind each buttonhole area (1). To avoid fabric distortion from too-heavy buttons, choose your buttons to suit the weight of the material. If your garment is not interfaced, reinforce button stitches with a small square of ribbon seam binding or fusible interfacing placed between the garment and the facing (2).

Choose a lightweight synthetic zipper for use with knits. Staystitch ½″ from the fabric edge to stabilize the zipper area. For very stretchy knits, you may have to stitch ribbon seam binding over the seamline before inserting the zipper.

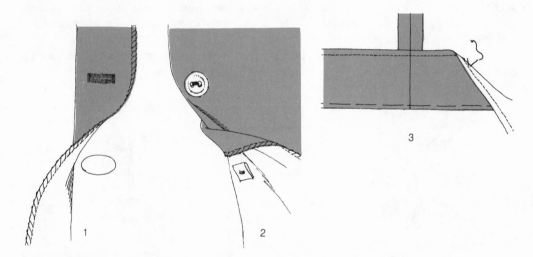

TRADITIONAL FINISHES on knits can be applied in a variety of ways at neck, sleeve, edges, and hems. Facings or bindings, in self-fabric or contrasting fabric, can be applied. Strip bands cut from a stretchable knit or purchased ribbing can also be used; see page 254.

Allow knit garments to hang for 24 hours before marking the hem. To hem most knits, simply turn up the hem allowance and stitch or fuse in place; no hem finishes are necessary.

To ensure an invisible, hand-stitched hem, staystitch ¼″ from the raw edge (3). Turn the edge back along the staystitching and blindstitch in place. Be sure to keep your stitches loose to prevent them from popping when the fabric stretches. Heavier weight knits may require a double-stitched hem (page 341). For lightweight stretchable knits, a narrow topstitched hem (page 339) or a hand-rolled hem (page 451) give the best results.

Lingerie Fabrics

Elegant lingerie trimmed with lace is a wonderful addition to any wardrobe! Nightgowns, robes, slips, camisoles, and panties can be made of lightweight knits, crepe, satin, batiste, China silk, and crepe de chine. Tricot, a single knit available in several weights, is often used for lingerie because of its stretchability and run-resistant qualities.

BEFORE CONSTRUCTION

Woven fabrics may be cut on the bias for undergarments so that they will give and mold more closely to the body. Because tricot stretches most in the crosswise direction, place pattern pieces so the fabric will stretch horizontally on the garment. As for all knits, use ball-point pins and work on a large surface, being sure no fabric hangs over the edge. Because tricot is very strong despite its light weight, use very sharp shears or special lingerie shears to cut smoothly. It may be necessary to pin the fabric to your cutting board to prevent slipping. Mark with tailor's chalk.

CONSTRUCTION POINTERS

Refer to the section on Knit Fabrics, page 352, for complete information on sewing lightweight knits. Use a ball-point needle (size 9 or 11), polyester thread, shorter stitch length (12 to 15 per inch), and a loose, balanced tension; take care to prevent tricot from being drawn down into the needle hole. Incorporate "give" into the seam by gently stretching the fabric as you stitch, or use a narrow zigzag stitch or special stretch stitches. Never stitch over pins, as that may pull the fabric up and cause the seam to be uneven. Seams in tricot should be double-stitched, preferably with a row of zigzag stitching. Side seams can be finished with a very narrow French seam, if desired. Elasticized edges are often used as a substitute for casings to finish waist and leg edges; use lingerie elastic which is softer and more resilient.

To cut elastic, follow the pattern's cutting guide, or cut ½" to ¾" wide elastic 3" to 4" shorter than body circumference; cut ¼" to ⅜" wide elastic 2" shorter than leg circumference. Then join elastic in a ½" seam, reinforcing as shown (1).

To position, place elastic so seam allowances are away from the body. Then divide both elastic (2) and garment edge (3) into quarters; mark. Reduce the spaces between the marks on the fabric if it is greater than 6", dividing the elastic accordingly. Then pin to garment as suggested below.

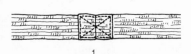  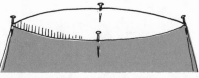

1   2   3

EXPOSED ELASTIC FINISH: Place elastic on outside of garment with one edge along the seamline; match markings; pin. Stretch elastic and fabric as you stitch inner edge of elastic; use a zigzag or straight stitch. Do not stitch over pins (1). Trim seam allowance to ¼". Turn elastic to inside favoring garment edge, encasing raw edge of fabric. Stitch both edges of elastic to garment, stretching elastic and removing pins as you sew (2).

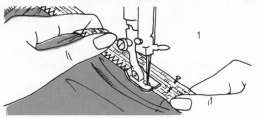 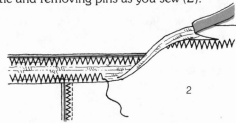

ENCLOSED ELASTIC FINISH: Place elastic on inside of garment with bottom edge along seamline or foldline; match markings and pin. Stretch elastic and fabric as you stitch inner edge of elastic, using a zigzag or straight stitch. Do not stitch over pins (1). Turn garment edge to inside enclosing the elastic, favoring garment edge. Stitch raw edge in place, catching remaining elastic edge and outer garment layer in the stitches (2). Note: Illustrations show a ⅝'' seam allowance and ½'' elastic. Cut wider seam allowances when using wider elastic.

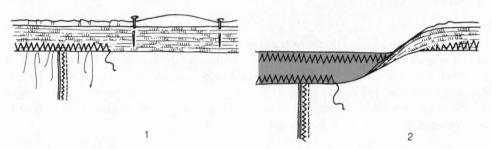

1   2

Lace adds an elegant finish to lingerie. It can be stitched to a hemmed edge, inserted with the fabric underneath trimmed away, or appliquéd. Refer to Lace and Ruffles, pages 458 and 459. Shell or scalloped tucks can also be used to finish an edge; see page 220.

Stretch Woven Fabrics

Gabardine, satin, denim, corduroy—these are just some of the many woven fabrics that have been developed with a certain amount of give. These fabrics have the appearance of traditional wovens, not "stretch" fabrics. However, their stretchability gives them the advantage of better shape retention and wearing comfort. Sewing techniques for stretch wovens include some of the same methods used for knits to maintain the stretchability of the fabric—yet they can be easily tailored like a regular woven fabric.

BEFORE CONSTRUCTION

Allow the fabric to "relax" on a flat surface before cutting, being sure that none hangs off the edge. Lay out pattern pieces so that the fabric will stretch in the direction desired. Use very sharp shears and avoid stretching the fabric as you cut, as this can distort the garment sections.

CONSTRUCTION POINTERS

Use a sharp regular needle or a ball-point needle in a size appropriate to your fabric. To provide stretchability in the seams, just as for knits, use a polyester thread, 12 to 15 stitches per inch, and a slightly looser tension. Always test the stitching on both the lengthwise and crosswise grain before you begin your garment. A tiny zigzag stitch or special stretch stitches can also be used.

Finish seams with overcasting or a double-stitched seam (page 212). Use interfacing to stabilize garment areas where stretch is not desired, such as buttonholes and V-necklines. Many of the lightweight interfacings designed for knits can also be used to softly tailor stretch wovens.

A flexible hem finish must be used to allow the fabric to remain stretchable. Use overcasting, zigzag stitching, or stretchable lace seam tape, and be sure to keep your hemming stitches loose.

Fabrics that Flow and Float

Supple, drapable fabrics that glide and glow on your body—sheers, crepe, and laces—deserve special attention. They may be cotton, wool, synthetic, even metallic; they can be firm or loosely constructed, soft or crisp, knits or wovens. Sheers can also have embroidered or flocked surface interests.

Complete your usual pattern adjustments and alterations. Sheer and lace fabrics should not be fitted tightly, as the tenuous nature of the fabric may not endure stress.

Sheer Fabrics

Crisp sheers—such as voile, organdy, and dimity—are quite durable and easy to manage. Softer sheers—chiffon, georgette, organza, or batiste—are airy and drapable, requiring greater care when cutting and stitching. Think sheer as you select the pattern; remember that sheers reveal all. If you're in great shape, why not show it? If you have some extra pounds, choose a style that will look well with sheer sleeves and underline the rest of the garment.

Sewing sheer fabrics requires extra care. Underfabrics may be necessary for certain parts of your garment, to provide support and to shield the see-through quality. The underfabrics should match sheer in both fiber type and care. Eliminate interfacing if possible. Self-fabric or underlining fabric is an appropriate substitute if interfacing cannot be entirely avoided. Use a lining only if the garment is entirely underlined. An underdress, underskirt, or camisole made from lining or other suitable fabric is an apt partner to any sheer garment.

BEFORE CONSTRUCTION

If your sheer has a nap, or sheen, use a "with nap" pattern layout. Net does not have a grain and can be cut in any direction. However, the edges should be bound, as it is scratchy. Delicate sheers should be pinned to your cutting board or to a sheet that is fastened to your cutting surface. Use silk or ball-point pins and extrasharp scissors to prevent the fabric from becoming caught in the blades. Mark carefully using pins, chalk, or tailor's tacks; tracing wheel and/or dressmaker's carbon may permanently damage fabric. Handle gently to prevent stretching cut edges. Underlined garments should be marked on the underlining fabric only.

CONSTRUCTION POINTERS

The nature of the soft sheers makes seams hard to stitch. The threads tend to shift, so the crosswise fibers do not always remain perpendicular to the lengthwise fibers. To avoid mangled fabric, stitch seams with tissue paper under seam between fabric and feed. Use straight stitch plate or cover the ends of zigzag stitch plate to help prevent fabric from being drawn down into the needle hole.

Use a fine needle (size 9 or 11) and a shorter stitch length—seams should be narrow and inconspicuous.

The most appropriate seam finishes for translucent sheers are French seam, French whipped seam with overcast or zigzag finish, mock French seam, or self-bound seam; see pages 211 and 212.

To finish sheers for a translucent look, omit facings at neck, sleeve, and opening edges, and substitute self- or contrasting single or double binding, following procedures on pages 244 to 249. If you retain facings, trim seam allowances to about ⅛″ wide. This holds true of collar seams, etc., without interfacing. Or use a hairline seam (page 212) for collars, cuffs, and facings.

PRESS with care using scraps of your sheer to test the heat, pressure, and steam of the iron. Enclosed seams should be pressed over a press pad or thick towel so no lumps or ridges will come through to the right side. Use a press cloth and press lightly, smoothing the seam flat with your fingers.

CLOSURES: Underlined sheers will usually support buttonholes, loops, or buttons. Translucent sheers must be able to support the button weight, with only hand- or machine-worked buttonholes. Zippers are usually too heavy for translucent sheers. Substitute a continuous bound placket (page 284) for loosely fitted sheers (1), using snaps, hooks, and thread eyes. For more fitted sheers, use dress placket (page 306).

For a zipper in a garment with an underlined bodice and an underskirt with a sheer overshirt, turn in the edges of the overskirt along seamline and narrow hem, matching finished edges to the seamline of the underskirt. Insert the zipper in the bodice section by hand or machine. Finish stitching the zipper to the underskirt only, keeping the hemmed edges of the overskirt free (2).

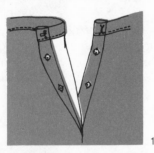
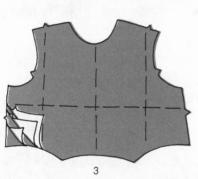

In a **layered sheer** garment, use four or more layers of one color for a "watered" look or each a different color for a moiré look. Place the layers of fabric on your cutting surface, right sides up; pin together. With very lightweight thread and a sharp needle, "quilt" the layers together with long running stitches 6″ to 12″ apart. Proceed with cutting (3). Treat the bodice layers as one in construction; make and gather skirt layers separately; baste each skirt layer to the bodice in graduated levels. Stagger hems, making the outer layer the correct length and each following layer ¼″ to ½″ shorter (4).

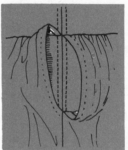
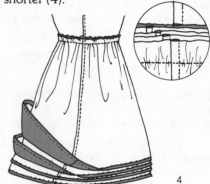

HEMS in translucent sheers that stand alone can be very narrow or very wide. Soft sheers are best hemmed with a hand-rolled narrow hem (page 451). Crisp sheers with a straight hem edge can have a very deep—up to 6″—turned-up hem.

Lace Fabrics

Lace fabrics are unique because of their intricate nature. Once the product solely of hours of hand work, lace is now made mostly by special machinery.

Lace can be used for an entire garment or just a portion such as a bodice, sleeves, or inset, and it works equally well with velvet, sheers, crepe, taffeta, or even gingham. Choose a pattern with simple design lines as there is much beauty and elegance in a lace garment. A camisole and underskirt or slip of crepe, satin, or taffeta provide modesty and comfort for sheer or openwork lace. Opaque lace needs no underlining, but it can be added if you desire. Should you wish underlining, however, lightweight satin or taffeta, organdy, batiste, crepe, polished cotton, nude marquisette, tricot, or jersey are recommended. Sheer, fragile laces should virtually never be interfaced, but the more substantial opaque, underlined laces may need it. Use interfacing that will suit the weight of your lace.

Check washability when purchasing lace—most laces made from synthetic fibers can be machine washed. Linen and silk laces, however, require either hand washing or dry cleaning.

BEFORE CONSTRUCTION

Most laces are designed with a net background, so no grain straightening is necessary. The main concern is the pattern of the lace and its direction, as lace can usually be cut either crosswise or lengthwise. Look at the lines of your pattern to determine if any lace motif can be used as a decorative edge, without facing or hem.

To use the lace design as a finished edge, cut out around the motif to create your own decorative edge (1). For straight edges, such as those found on a V-neckline or at the hem of a sleeve or skirt, position the seamline or hemline at the outer edge of the motif as shown (2).

A *curved edge* as is found in an A-line skirt or bell sleeves requires several steps to achieve a completed garment edge. For an A-line skirt, fold fabric matching the scallops. Position the pattern hemline along the outer edge of the scallop. To raise the edge of the lace fabric to conform to the hemline curve, cut along a motif to form a lace strip as indicated. Raise strips, overlapping edges until pattern hemline curve is accommodated, making tiny clips between motifs if necessary so strip will lie flat. Baste strip in position and cut out skirt section. Appliqué strip to skirt by hand or machine. The results—a couture finish (3).

1

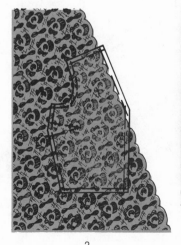

2

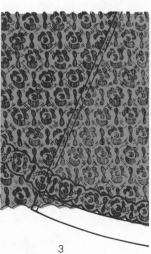

3

CONSTRUCTION POINTERS

Since lace is both sheer and delicate, apply the suggestions made for sheer construction or translucent and underlined garments. Translucent lace seams may require a self-finish such as a French seam, mock French seam, or double-stitched seam.

You may want to appliqué the seams and darts for an elegant finish. The edges are overlapped, matching motifs, and sewn together by hand or machine. Before **cutting out** the garment sections, match the motifs along the seamlines. Cut one edge with a ⅝'' seam allowance for the underlap (or wider for a larger design) and the other edge along the motif design for the overlapping layer. Match seamlines and design with overlap uppermost; pin, then baste, keeping overlap smooth. On the outside, appliqué the motif edges to underlap with tiny whipstitches or machine zigzag stitches (1). On the inside, trim away underlap close to the stitching (2). Finish darts in same manner, determining their depth before overlapping.

To retain the beauty of sheer or open-work lace, substitute a single or double binding instead of neck facings and hems for sleeve, skirt, or pant edges. Cut the bindings from satin, taffeta, crepe, or any other suitable fabric. Binding made from scraps of a companion slip-dress would be ideal. To make a successful binding, follow the directions on pages 244 to 249, or use self-trim instead of a facing to accent a scooped neckline or finish a hem edge. Cut along a line of motifs to form a lace strip. Place strip over garment with one edge along seamline or hemline; baste. Appliqué inner edge to garment same as for the seam above (3). For exceptionally curved edges you may find it necessary to make small clips between the motifs so the strip will lie flat. Overlap the motif edges and sew securely.

When the facings are retained, trim the seam allowances to about ⅛'' in width. Do the same for other enclosed seams such as collars to preserve the sheerness.

When **PRESSING** lace fabrics, take care not to snag the lace pattern.

HEMS are the final touch in a lace garment. Use scalloped or decorative edge as hemline by cutting around the motif, or use self-trim for a decorative finish. For lightweight laces, use the same hemming techniques suggested for sheers. To face a hem in lace, use a doubled net strip in place of the bias facing suggested on page 341, or use horsehair braid for long gowns as described on page 452 (1).

To retain the beauty of a scalloped edge and still underline the lace garment, attach underlining in either of two ways: Cut the under fabric with a straight edge level to the inner points of the design. Turn up the underfabric and whipstitch in place (2). Or trim the underfabric to match the shape of the scallops and staystitch ⅛″ from the trimmed edge. Whipstitch shaped edge of underfabric to the lace (3).

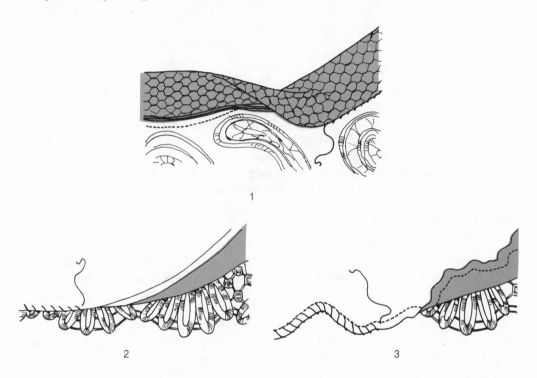

Crepe Fabrics

Choose your crepe according to the pattern style—light and mediumweight for draped, flowing designs and heavier, sturdier weaves for more tailored or fitted garments. Underlinings, if you use them, should be compatible with crepe, such as soft, uncumbersome batiste or organza. If you underline the crepe, omit interfacing, or substitute it with another layer of underlining. Do not use fusible interfacing.

Use the same cutting and marking techniques as for sheers. Since crepe can stretch and slip, use tissue paper between fabric and feed. It may be necessary to lengthen stitch and loosen tension slightly to avoid puckering. Very soft crepes may need the seams taped at stress points such as neckline and shoulder seams.

When **PRESSING**, test effect of heat and steam on fabric scraps. Some crepes may shrink or pucker from steam. Use a press cloth, and press on the wrong side to avoid shine. Crepes can usually support a zipper. Buttons and buttonholes are applicable too. See the closures section in sheers (page 358) for more sewing tips.

Allow your crepe garment to hang at least overnight before completing the hem.

Fabrics with Luster

Satin, taffeta, brocade, metallic, beaded, and sequined fabrics add dimensions of opulence to your wardrobe. Sewing these fabrics requires a knowledge of their nature, rather than special techniques.

For some garments you may want a soft, elegant look that can only be achieved with underlining. Choose an underlining fabric that will support your fashion fabric, as it will be used as a "hanger" for hems and facings so that no seam will leave an impression on the outside of the garment.

Make your normal adjustments and alterations. If your fabric is fragile and if fitting changes could leave permanent marks in the fabric, you may wish to make a test muslin. Follow the preliminaries before cutting, as explained on pages 131 to 134.

Satin and Taffeta

There was an era when satin was worn only for formal occasions—now it can go anywhere at any time of the day. Satin may be single-faced or double-faced, with a crepe or twill weave back so it can be used on either side. It varies from soft and drapable to a firm and crisp weight that will hold sculptured design lines. Some weights do not need interfacing, but use it if you are not underlining your garment.

Crisp, fresh-looking taffeta garments are a long-time fashion choice for day, evening, and lingerie wear. Taffeta is found in many weights and fibers.

BEFORE CONSTRUCTION

The sheen of satin comes from its weave—the lengthwise threads are caught by the crosswise threads after a longer space than usual, which creates "floats" on the right sides of the fabric. These "floats" reflect light and produce a shiny surface, which requires that satin garments be cut according to a "with nap" layout. Some taffetas, such as iridescent and moiré, must also be cut using a "with nap" layout.

Use silk or ball-point pins and pin within the seam allowance only, because pin holes will show on the completed garment (1). Use very sharp shears to avoid snags; mark with tailor's tacks and silk thread within the seam or dart allowance.

CONSTRUCTION POINTERS

Handling the fabric is most important—use polyester or silk thread to avoid puckering. Set your machine for a medium stitch, 12 to 15 per inch, and hold the fabric taut during stitching to prevent sliding and bubbling. Stitch carefully as any removed stitches will leave holes in the fabric. Satin and taffeta ravel easily so the seams must be finished with machine or hand overcasting.

TO PRESS, test your fabric for heat and possible discoloration from steam; use a low temperature setting. For fabrics that water spot, use a dry iron. Press lightly with a press cloth, using brown paper or a seam roll to protect the fabric; folded edges should not be pressed flat.

For **CLOSURES**, zippers are suitable for most satins and taffetas with the exception of the very fragile—for better control, insert by hand with a prickstitch, page 448. Any type of button and buttonhole may be used, though buttons with rough edges may mar your fabric.

The final touch is an invisible **HEM** from the outside of the garment. Choose any of the standard finishes or one of the specialty hems described in the Couture section, pages 450 to 452.

Brocade Fabrics

At one time these luxurious fabrics were worn for only the most auspicious occasion, but with the advent of synthetics, beautiful brocades can now be worn anytime. These fabrics have a flat or raised woven-in design and are reversible; therefore, you have a choice. Use one side to make the entire garment, or make a portion of an ensemble from the reverse side—make pants and jacket from one side with a color-coordinated, contrasting vest from the other. Some may have metallic threads that require the same techniques as metallic fabrics in addition to those required for the surface interest.

Brocades are handled almost identically to satin and taffeta with the exception of pressing. Be sure to pad your ironing board with a towel so the design won't be flattened, and test heat endurance on scraps. Cover loose design threads with a press cloth to avoid accidentally pulling them.

Metallic Fabrics

Metallic fabrics is the name given to any fabrics that contain some metallic threads. They range from knits to wovens, soft to crisp, shiny lamé to rich brocades.

Underlining is optional, but may be necessary to prevent the metallic threads from breaking at the seams. Lining may be mandatory to prevent the fabric from irritating the skin—use a soft but tightly woven fabric. Line garment to the edge, or cut facings from lining fabric to protect skin.

BEFORE CONSTRUCTION

Follow a "with nap" layout because the shiny threads cause a directional glow. Pin within the seam allowances and cut with old shears, since the metallic threads will dull the blades. Mark with tailor's tacks.

CONSTRUCTION POINTERS

Use polyester thread and a fine machine needle, which may have to be changed several times, lest it become too dull. If your fabric is sheer, use tissue paper when stitching seams. Test before stitching. Or, if the fabric is heavy, tape the shoulder, neck, and armhole seams to preserve the lines. Seam finishes may be necessary to avoid skin irritation.

PRESSING requires caution since steam may tarnish and discolor metallic threads, just as an iron that is too hot may melt some synthetic metallics or make them brittle. Press lightly—too much pressure may break the metallic threads. Or, finger-press seams open or edges in place, covering your finger with a thimble.

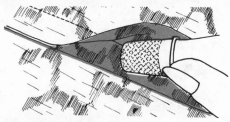

Most standard **CLOSURES** are acceptable for metallics. If you use a zipper, make sure the threads will not break when creased. Buttons and buttonholes are also appropriate, but do not make bound buttonholes on fabric that ravels.

The **HEMMING** methods are the same as for satin and taffeta if the fabric is non-irritating. However, if the fabric irritates, use the bias-faced hem, page 341.

Beaded and Sequined Fabrics

Found in many forms, beaded and sequined fabrics may have some hidden characteristics—they can be attached with a continuous thread, secured with prongs, or sewn individually to a base of knitted or woven fabric. Beads or sequins may form an all-over design, may be sprinkled in random motifs, or used individually, adding glitter to brocades, lace, and other special fabrics.

Choose a pattern that will complement your fabric—simple lines without gathers, pleats, or buttonholes, and avoid set-in sleeves if possible. Consider a beaded or sequined bodice, sleeves, midriff section, or collar and cuffs to add sparkle to another fabric.

BEFORE CONSTRUCTION

Make your usual adjustments and alterations and do make a test muslin if expenditure is great and the silhouette unknown to you. Use an expendable pair of shears for cutting—beads are unavoidable and can easily dull the blades. Cut around the beads where it is impossible to cut through, cutting one layer at a time (1). Staystitch seam allowance edges immediately after cutting to prevent losing beads when attached continuously. Tailor's tacks usually work best for marking. Be sure to line the garment to protect your skin from the roughness of the fabric. Cut all facings from lining fabric (2).

CONSTRUCTION POINTERS

Use stitch length, tension, and needle size required by the base fabric. Remove beads from seam allowances and dart area, then sew with a zipper foot. Rest foot in seam allowance only, since beads would break under pressure. For beads or sequins attached by a continuous thread, fasten by hand or catch them in the seam (2).

Never use steam for pressing—it may cause the backing to curl and erase the sheen from the beads and sequins. Use a low heat setting as the beads could melt, then press along the seam or edges with the tip of the iron. When the garment is nearly finished, go over it and replace any missing or broken beads near seams or edges. Remove beads from hem allowance to prevent snagged hosiery or use a faced hem. Some garments may need an interfaced hem or a double-stitched hem. (See page 341.)

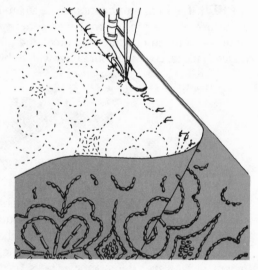

1

2

Fabrics with Surface Style

Intriguing surface interests make fabric selection even more diversified—from deep-textured velvets and fake furs to smooth, shiny cirés and vinyls. Woven or knitted, these fabrics can be made from a wide range of fibers. Some are very luxurious such as cashmere, camel's hair, and vicuña.

The most important feature to consider when using these fabrics is how they will look on you—will they complement your figure? The surface depth, the design (crosswise, lengthwise, floral, or geometric), and its brightness may work against you—creating an optical illusion making you appear shorter or taller or thinner or heavier. Be realistic: Select the fabric and the pattern that is just right for you.

Pile Fabrics

Plushy, luxurious pile fabrics come with many different faces—velvet, velveteen, corduroy (ribbed or uncut), plush, velour, terry cloth, bouclé, melton, and fleece. All have many common characteristics. The most important is **nap**—stroke the surface with your hand—the smoother feel is the "run" or the direction of the pile or nap; the rough feel is caused when you brush the pile or nap in the opposite direction (1). This affects the color and texture of your garments; when the nap or pile runs up, the color is deeper, richer, and the textured surface is more visible.

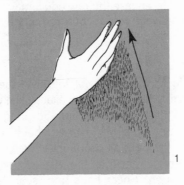

BEFORE CONSTRUCTION

Decide in which direction you want to place the nap or pile; use a "with nap" layout (see page 138), placing pattern pieces as they will be worn. Depending on the fabric weight and the pile depth, cut the pattern from either a single or double thickness of fabric. To avoid crushing the pile on velvets and velveteens, pin pattern to fabric within the seam allowance.

Mark with tailor's tacks and baste denser pile such as velvet with silk thread to prevent slippage. To reduce bulk, make facings from lining or other lightweight fabric. For knitted pile fabrics, apply appropriate cutting and marking methods; see page 352.

CONSTRUCTION POINTERS

Use 10 to 12 stitches per inch, matching needle size and thread to fabric weight. Stitch in direction of nap wherever possible. For velvet, use a fine needle and stitch carefully as removed stitches may leave holes in the fabric. It may be necessary to decrease pressure on presser foot and to hold fabric taut while stitching. To reduce bulk, slash darts and press them open.

PRESSING: All pile fabrics must be pressed carefully to avoid flattening the pile. If the pile is crushed on velvet, it can never be restored. Test-press a fabric scrap before you start. Place fabric, pile down, on a needle board; press carefully on the wrong side of the fabric. You can substitute a piece of self-fabric or a fluffy towel for a needle-board. Use low temperature setting for velvet.

When pile is exposed on both sides, use a self-fabric press cloth on the inside of the garment (1). Or, cover your iron with a damp cloth, then hold fabric lightly. Run the inside of the garment across covered iron to press seams open and steam out wrinkles (2).

CLOSURES should not present a problem. Select appropriate buttonhole, loop, or zipper application according to the weight of your fabric.

HEMS should be finished according to the weight and depth of the pile. Most pile fabrics can be hemmed like any mediumweight fabic. Because velvet can mar easily, a softly rolled hem is often used. Either interface the hem or add additional padding. The Hong Kong finish, using a strip of nylon net to encase the raw edge, may be used on velvet to finish the hem edge. For these techniques, refer to the couture section, pages 450 and 451.

Fake Fur Fabrics

The long-haired fake furs add a dimension not found in the usual pile fabrics, although there are many fur-like fabrics that can be handled exactly like velvet. Follow the techniques suggested for pile fabrics, plus these additional tips. For long hairs, lay out fabric with nap running down. Cut one layer at a time, using a razor blade, and cutting only the backing. Baste seams firmly, pushing hairs back as you work. Stitch seams in the direction of the pile, using a size 14, 16, or 18 regular needle. Use a needle to work out hairs caught in the seam (1). Slash darts; press open. Shear hairs from seam allowance and exposed dart edges to reduce bulk using a sharp scissors or a razor blade (2).

Never press the face of a fur—some are easily melted or the hairs may mat from the steam. Use a dry iron on the inside of the garment. Substitute snaps, hooks, and decorative closures for buttons and buttonholes. If unavoidable, some fabrics adapt to machine or bound buttonholes (substitute leather or other fabrics for the lips). For an attractive hem, use a double-stitched hem or a bias-faced hem; see page 341.

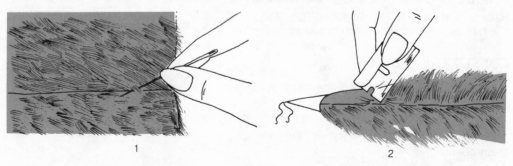

Ciré and Vinyl Fabrics

Ciré and vinyl fabrics require some special handling techniques. Ciré is a very shiny finish applied to woven or knit fabics by a calendering process. Vinyls are plastic and can be single-ply or backed with a woven or knit fabric. The surface can be smooth and shiny or textured to simulate other materials. These fabrics are often semi water-repellent and somewhat windproof—ideal for sportswear and outerwear garments.

BEFORE CONSTRUCTION

Since pins leave permanent marks in cirés and vinyls, pin only within the seam allowances or use tape to hold the pattern pieces in place when cutting.

Because coated fabrics are difficult to ease, you may need to reduce the fullness at the cap of a set-in sleeve. Make a tiny horizontal fold at the top of the sleeve pattern above the notches, taking out a total of ¼" (1). Be sure to make any other needed alterations in the pattern before cutting out the fabric.

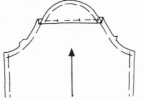

Mark the fabric on the wrong side with tailor's chalk.

CONSTRUCTION POINTERS

For lighter weight fabrics, use a size 11 or 14 needle and a longer stitch length (8 to 12 per inch) to avoid puckering. For heavier weight fabrics, use a size 14 or 16 needle and 6 to 10 stitches per inch. A wedge-point needle is specifically designed for use on vinyls to help prevent splitting the fabric. However, a sharp-point needle can be used on vinyls backed with fabric. Hold the fabric slightly taut in front and behind the needle to help eliminate any seam puckering; do not pull the fabric through the needle. Sew carefully to avoid any later ripping, as needle marks show on the fabric.

Whenever possible, stitch with the right sides of the fabric together as the coated side has a tendency to stick to the machine foot. If you must stitch on the shiny side, use tissue paper or a roller foot to avoid sticking.

PRESS carefully with a warm, dry iron on the wrong side of the fabric. Be sure to test on a fabric scrap first.

HEMS are best topstitched although some vinyls can be glued; refer to Leather, page 374. Buttonholes can be marked with tape to avoid marring the right side of the garment. Regular bound buttonholes or machine-worked buttonholes with a slightly wider stitch setting can be made on most cirés and vinyls. For other closure techniques, refer to the Leather section.

Ribbed Fabrics

Ribbed fabrics can be knitted or woven, soft or crisp, and the ribs can be lengthwise, as in corduroys, piqué, and Bedford cloth, or crosswise, as in bengaline, broadcloth, ottoman, and faille. Knits produce body-clinging, ribbed fabrics in crosswise velours or lengthwise sweater ribs. Treat your ribbed fabric according to its weight, stretchiness, drapability, and surface depth, choosing the special handling techniques from any of the preceding pages. For a couture touch, match the ribs if they are ¼" wide or wider.

Quilted Fabrics

Quilted fabrics—whether prequilted or do-it-yourself—require no special sewing techniques except for eliminating bulk wherever possible.

BEFORE CONSTRUCTION

Always quilt your fabric before cutting out your pattern pieces as quilting draws up the fabric. Refer to the section on Quilting, page 469.

CONSTRUCTION POINTERS

Use a sharp needle (size 11–14) and a slightly longer stitch length (8 to 12 per inch), depending on the thickness of your fabric. It may be necessary to loosen the tension slightly.

To eliminate bulk, trim away batting from the seam allowances and darts. Or slash the darts and press open. To eliminate bulky hems or edges on a quilted garment, you can use a bias facing or follow this special method. Trim the seam or hem allowance to ⅜"; then stitch 1" from edge of fabric. Remove quilting stitches from outside the stitching line, pull thread ends to inside and knot. Trim batting close to stitching (1). Turn in edge of outside fabric and backing fabric along hemline and baste. Stitch close to the edge through all layers (2). **PRESS** quilted fabrics very lightly to avoid flattening the quilting.

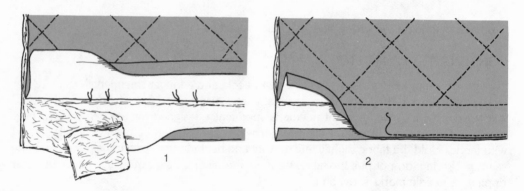

1 2

Double-Faced Fabrics

These fabrics combine two fabric layers that are held together with fine threads or bonding. There is no wrong side so, with the proper finishes, the garment can be reversible.

Choose a pattern with simple lines as the seams must be clean-finished so no raw edges are exposed. This fabric is usually too bulky for gathered styles and too firm for soft ones—classic or tailored garments with few details are best.

BEFORE CONSTRUCTION

Allow wider seam allowances for flat-fell seams and only 1" hems for sleeves and lower edges. Omit facing—interfacings are not used either. All markings must be made with tailor's tacks and thread tracings.

CONSTRUCTION POINTERS

Separate the layers by clipping the threads or pulling them apart. There are three ways to finish the seams: For a flat, plain finish, separate layers to a depth of 1½". Stitch the one

Fabrics with Give

Knits move with the body for comfort and good fit and can be found in a multitude of fibers, weights, textures, and colors. From soft, silky jerseys to bulky sweater knits . . . from lacy raschels to stable double knits . . . from body-hugging swimwear to intricate jacquards—knits have a wide range of stretchability. And knits boast the added pluses of wrinkle resistance and easy care, making them desirable for evening gowns as well as active sportswear.

Lightweight, silky knits drape and gather softly, flowing with the body movement. Knits with moderate stretchability have tremendous versatility and can be used for all types of garments. Two-way stretchable knits are ideal for swimsuits, leotards, and lingerie.

Fabrics That Flow and Float

Soft, fluid sheers, from ruffled voile to gracefully floating chiffon, reveal the body in an alluring way. Long, flowing sleeves gathered at the wrists and floating skirts that swirl around the legs lend a feminine, romantic aura. Lace fabrics with their intricate designs can be bold and dramatic or soft and delicate. Often the lace design can be used as a scalloped finished edge for added elegance and beauty.

Lightweight crepe drapes and glides around your body for sensational figure flattery. Crepe can also be softly tailored for fluid styling—and touched with the shimmer of satin for added elegance.

Fabrics with Luster

Brocaded, metallic, beaded, and sequined fabrics opulently glitter and shimmer in the light. Creating an elaborate pattern or an overall design, these fabrics radiate a feeling of luxury and elegance. However, brocades and metallics need not be limited to special occasions but can be worn almost anywhere—and beads and sequins can trim even casual clothes.

Fabrics with Surface Style

Intriguing surface interest adds excitement and variety to the fabric story. Feel free to use the plush, luxurious piles—velvet, velveteen, corduroy, velour, terrycloth, and fleece; the smooth, shiny surfaces of ciré and vinyl; and the three-dimensional, long-haired fake furs and puffy quilted fabrics. These textures offer endless fabric flair.

Leather and Suede

Leather and suede—and their marvelous look-alikes—have a luxurious appearance and hand. Simple designs highlight leather and suede and enhance their natural, understated beauty.

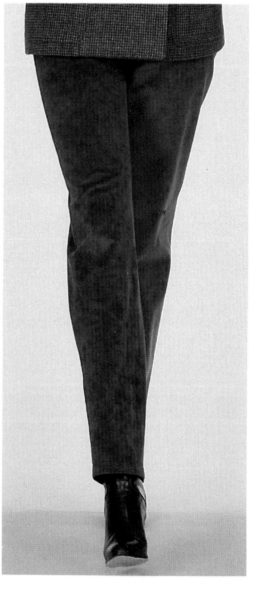

layer in the usual ⅝" seam; press open. Trim remaining layer ¼", then turn in edges over the first seam, slipstitching folded edges together (1).

For a flat-fell seam, stitch the sections together along seamline. Separate the seam allowance layers, then trim and grade all but the uppermost layer. Turn in the edge and edgestitch in place (2).

For a strap seam, stitch the sections together along the seamline; press open. Separate the layers, then trim and grade. Cover the entire seam with a trim or a bias strip of the fabric. Separate the two layers so you have a single thickness. Make a bias strip as long as the seam and about 1⅞" wide. Turn in the edges ¼"; press. Position over the seam and edgestitch through all layers (3).

Edges for the hem, neck, and collar edges can be bound or the layers can be turned in and slipstitched together. Separate layers to a depth of 1½", turn in along seamline or hemline, and press lightly. Trim one edge ¼" and slipstitch or edgestitch together (4).

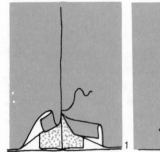 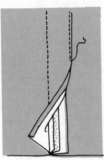 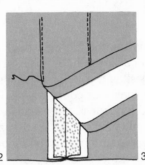 

A *curved seam* is accomplished quite easily if all seam allowances fall in the same direction—the collar joining the garment is the most common example. Separate the inner curved edge to a depth of 1½"; staystitch each layer. Clip curves to staystitching as you turn in these edges; baste. Press carefully, keeping the curve smooth. On the outer curve section, make clips about ¼" deep (5). Place the outer curved section between the turned-in seam allowances of the other section; match seamlines and symbols as you pin and baste. Slipstitch each side separately, or edgestitch close to fold through all layers (6).

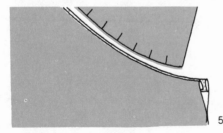 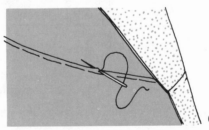

CLOSURES do not present a problem—use machine buttonhole and buttons or any decorative closure. Make one set of buttonholes, but sew on two sets of buttons for reversible garments—one in the normal position and the second set on the reverse side of the first. When the garment is reversed, the closure will be in the opposite direction.

Zippers can be inserted quite effectively. Separate the layers to a depth of 1½". For a slot zipper in a skirt, turn in the edges of each layer along the seamline; press lightly. Sandwich zipper between folded edges and stitch as usual. For an exposed separating zipper, turn in the edges beyond the seamline enough to clear the zipper teeth and allow the pull tab to move freely. Sandwich zipper tape between folded edges and edgestitch through all layers, catching the zipper tape in the stitching.

Leather and Suede

Leather and suede, with their luxurious beauty, are available in many weights, styles, and colors. Real leather is any animal skin that has been treated or tanned such as kidskin, chamois, reptile, calfskin, and buckskin. Suede is a type of leather that has been buffed to create a napped surface. The look of suede can also be obtained with synthetic suede, a very elegant fabric that was first featured by leading fashion designers. It has the look and feel of suede but can be handled like fabric.

For best results, select a pattern design with simple lines that will highlight the leather or suede. Avoid styles that require extensive easing because leathers and suedes—real or synthetic—do not ease well.

Leather

Leather, unlike cloth, is sold by the individual skin rather than by the yard. Think of the pattern shapes as you calculate the number of skins needed. It may be necessary to add horizontal seams suggesting a yoke or vertical seams suggesting gores or princess lines—this adds to the individuality of your project. Use the chart on this page to convert the fabric yardage specified for your size into leather square footage. Be aware that this formula does not give measurements of quantity that are as precise as the yardage given: Since there are 13 square feet in one yard of 54″ fabric, you must multiply the number of yards specified for this width in your size by 13. Allow additional footage for piecing and irregularities in the leather: 0.15 for a large skin or 0.20 for a small skin.

Specified yardage		4
Conversion figure	×	13
Converted yardage (square feet)		52
Piecing percentage (for large skin)	×	0.15
		260
		52
Piercing allowance (square feet)		7.80
Converted yardage (square feet)	+	52
Total square feet needed		59.80

BEFORE CONSTRUCTION

Leathers crease easily—roll them in a tube until ready for use. Because stitching marks leave permanent holes in leather, letting out darts or seams can be disastrous. Make a test muslin if you are unsure of how the pattern fits, since alterations are generally impossible. Felt is a perfect substitute for muslin as it handles like leather and the seams can have the same treatment.

Check leathers for irregularities and holes. For suede, use a "with nap" layout. Smooth leathers and heavy buckskin types have no nap or bias to consider so a "without nap" layout can be used. However, lay out major pattern pieces in the lengthwise direction of the skin for greater stability (although leather has no grain, it does have greater crosswise stretch). Smaller pieces can be laid in any direction. Cut a single layer at a time, holding pattern pieces in place with tape or weights. Use very sharp fabric shears, single-edged razor blade, or another suitable cutting tool. Or, if you prefer, trace around the cutting line of the pattern pieces on the wrong side of the skin with tailor's chalk; remove the pattern and cut. Mark the wrong side with chalk or a smooth-edged tracing wheel and dressmaker's carbon paper.

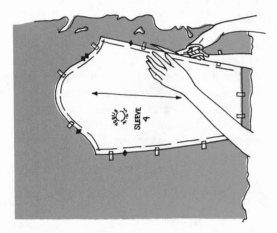

CONSTRUCTION POINTERS

Since seams are a focal point, especially on leather, your sewing machine must be clean and set up correctly. For best results, use a wedge-point needle in the size appropriate for the weight of the skin. Use 8 to 10 stitches per inch and test the pressure on the presser foot; it may have to be reduced since leather is thicker and spongier than cloth. Stitch slowly, taking care not to pull or stretch the leather. Do not backstitch as it might tear the skin; knot thread ends securely. Hold regular seams together with tape (1) or paper clips (2). Overlapped seams can be held together with rubber cement before stitching (3).

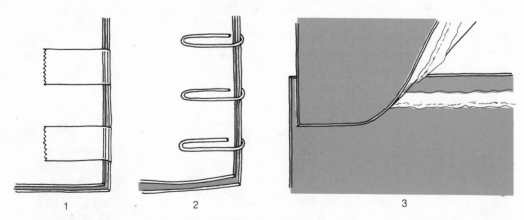

Some seams may need to be reinforced with seam binding or twill tape to prevent stretching.

To reduce bulk in seams, grade the seam allowances. Bevel the edge of thicker leathers with a single-edged razor blade (4).

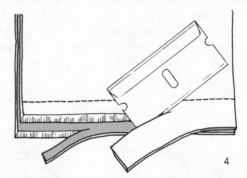

PRESS seams or flatten edges using a warm dry iron, with brown paper serving as a press cloth. Or, use a mallet or a hammer padded with cloth for pressing. Topstitch seams or apply rubber cement under each seam allowance to flatten (1). Pound cemented edges in place; when dry, lift seam allowances and peel away the rubber cement (2). Seams will stay open and flat, without leaving an impression on the outside of the garment. Darts are slashed open and flattened the same way as seams.

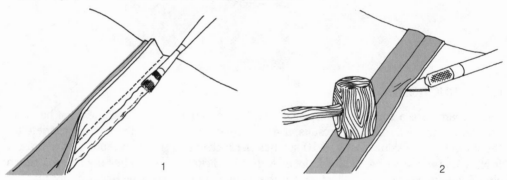

SEAM FINISHES can be modified for leathers. For a flat-fell seam, trim away one seam allowance; lap sections, matching seamlines. Hold in place with a thin line of rubber cement. Topstitch ⅛″ from trimmed edge and again ¼″ away (1). For a lapped seam, topstitch ⅛″ from trimmed edge (2). For a slot seam, eliminate both seam allowances of sections to be joined, cut strips the length of the seam and twice the desired stitching width from the seam, plus ½″. Center trimmed edges over the strip, cement in place. Topstitch each side of the trimmed edges, catching strip in stitching (3). Note: Rubber cement may be hard to remove, so do not cement beyond seamline.

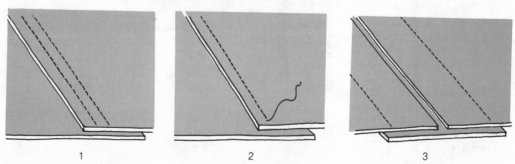

For details like collar, pocket, and facings, eliminate seam allowances from both layers. With wrong sides together, match cut edges; glue. Topstitch ⅛″ from edge to match lapped seams (4) and again ¼″ away to match flat-fell seams (5).

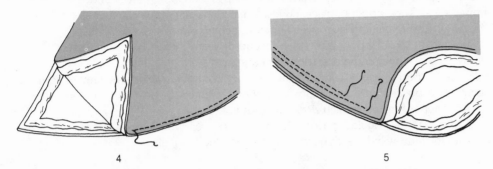

4   5

CLOSURES: The *buttonhole* method shown here is excellent for leathers.

Cut a rectangular opening the length of the buttonhole marking and ⅜″ in width. For each buttonhole cut two strips ½″ longer than the rectangle and 1½″ wide. Fold strip lengthwise, grade edges, and flatten. Center strips over buttonhole opening, with folded edges meeting. Hold in place with a thin line of rubber cement. Then cement the facing in place smoothly over the buttonhole (1). On the outside, edgestitch the rectangle through all thicknesses to anchor the buttonhole lips and hold all layers in place (2). To complete the buttonhole, trim away facing just inside the stitching (3).

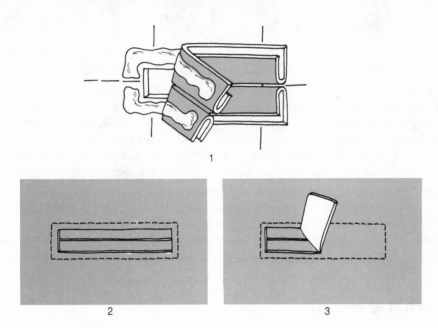

1

2   3

Zippers are inserted in the supple leathers in the same manner as for fabric. Heavier leathers can use another approach when a flat-fell seam is used. Before stitching seam, make a ½" clip through zipper symbol on the underlapping layer and trim away ½" to upper edge. Tape zipper in place; edgestitch in place across the clip and along the trimmed edge (1). Lap remaining layer over zipper, matching seamlines; tape. Stitch ¼" to ½" from edge; start at top of zipper and stitch to end of seam through all thicknesses. Then stitch across end of zipper and along trimmed edge, completing flat-fell seam (2).

For an exposed zipper, trim away just enough of both layers of the leather so the zipper teeth are exposed and the pull tab works easily. Center zipper under trimmed edges; tape. Using a zipper foot, edgestitch zipper to garment (3).

Don't overlook toggles, clasps, etc., that work well with leather. Remember, too, that grommets and rawhide laces go with the rugged look of leather.

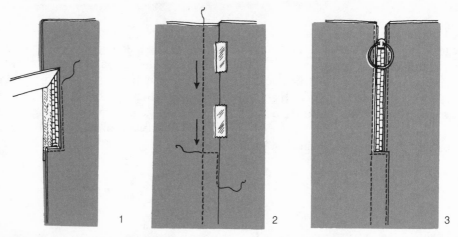

HEMS are simple for leathers and suedes—a 1" to 2" deep hem is adequate for most. Mark hemline with chalk. Apply rubber cement, fold up hem allowance, and flatten as required for the seams. Notch curved hems so they will lie flat. A topstitched hem is also a good finish for leather. Hold the hem in place with paper clips and use long stitches (6–8 per inch). One or two rows of stitching can be used. Press the hem with a warm dry iron and a press cloth. Heavier, firmer leathers can simply be trimmed at the hemline.

The final touch . . . Some leathers and suedes spot easily, so avoid getting them wet. If any do get wet, allow to dry away from direct heat. Wipe smooth leathers first with a soft cloth. Suedes can be brushed when dry to restore the nap. When your leather needs to be cleaned, send it to a professional dry cleaner who specializes in leather cleaning. Store your leather garments in a cool spot and cover with cloth, never plastic, to prevent the leather from drying out.

Synthetic Suede

Synthetic suede has the fashion look of suede without the disadvantages. It is lightweight, wrinkle-resistant, colorfast, and machine washable. The fabric can be constructed with conventional seams or with lapped seams—or a combination of the two methods.

Interfacing is needed for most synthetic suede garments. Because the fabric can be pressed with steam, fusible interfacings are recommended. Use a fusible web to baste two layers of fabric together before stitching or to fuse one layer to another permanently. Refer to the section on fusibles, page 157. Jackets and coats should be lined to make them easier to slip on and off.

BEFORE CONSTRUCTION

Synthetic suede has a nap that gives a richer, darker appearance when the nap is running up on a garment. Because this luxurious fabric is very expensive, you may wish to pre-measure your pattern layout in order to determine the exact fabric that you will need. Be sure to make any alterations in your pattern, and if you are using the lapped seam construction method for any seams, to first trim away hem allowances before measuring your layout. If you are unsure of the pattern fit, you may wish to first construct the garment in felt or nonwoven interfacing that hangs like synthetic suede.

Use the "with nap" layout, although bias collars and cuffs can be cut on the crosswise grain. Facings and pieces that do not show can be tilted off-grain to save fabric (1). Pin marks will disappear when the fabric is steamed; however, it is best to place pins vertically within the seam allowances or to use tape to hold your pattern pieces in place. Use sharp scissors to achieve a clean-cut edge. Mark with tailor's chalk or a smooth-edged tracing wheel and dressmaker's carbon paper. Identify the wrong side of the fabric with pieces of tape.

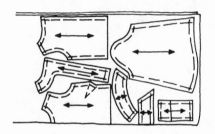

CONSTRUCTION POINTERS

Use 10 to 12 stitches per inch and a fine needle (size 9 or 11). For topstitching with silk or polyester topstitching and buttonhole twist thread, use a size 16 or 18 needle. When hand sewing, use a fine needle and a thimble as the fabric is strong and resilient. Use tape or paper clips to hold the fabric together as you stitch; see Leather, page 371. Or use basting tape placed ⅛″ away from the seamline within the seam allowance. Be sure to remove the tape after stitching the seam.

To prevent puckering in seams, hold the fabric taut in front and behind the presser foot, feeding the fabric evenly through the machine. Do not stretch the fabric. Press on wrong side of fabric using a synthetic setting, lots of steam, and a press cloth. If it is ever necessary to press on the right side, use a piece of self-fabric as a press cloth.

To avoid puckers at the end of a dart, stitch to a very finely tapered point with the last four stitches just on the fold of the fabric. Slash the dart open to within 1″ of the point. Slip strips of brown paper under the dart edges to prevent imprints on the right side. The edges can be topstitched or fused in place if you desire.

Seams can be constructed in either the conventional or lapped method.

For **_conventional seams_**, stitch seam and press open over a seam roll. Use a wooden clapper to help flatten the seam allowances. Or fuse them in place with a ¼'' strip of fusible web under each seam allowance (1). The seams can also be topstitched (2) or double-topstitched (3).

For best results, conventional seams should always be used for a set-in sleeve seam, neckline seam of a rolled collar with lapel, sleeve underarm seam, pants crotch seam, and pants inseam.

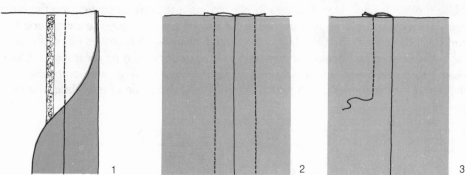

For **_lapped seams_**, you must carefully plan your garment and then trim or fold the overlapping allowance away: Side seams and shoulder seams lap front over back; yoke seams lap over both front and back bodice sections. This method results in lots of topstitching, which gives a sportier appearance to your garment. It also requires less fabric when the seam allowances are trimmed before cutting out the pattern pieces.

Trim ⅝'' seam allowance away from the overlapping layer of fabric (4). Mark seamline with chalk on the right side of the under fabric. Place ¼'' strip of fusible web between the two layers of fabric and press for 2 to 3 seconds just to "baste" in place. Or use basting tape along the outer edge of the bottom layer, being sure that it will not get caught into the stitching. Topstitch ¼'' from the seamline and again close to the overlapping edge (5).

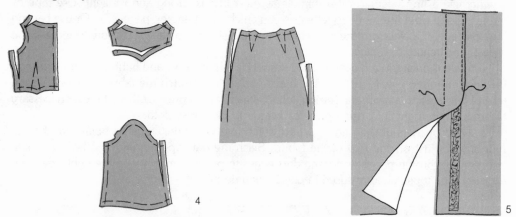

Collars and facing edges—such as lapels, front closings, collarless necklines, and cuffs—can be constructed with enclosed seams as for regular fabrics. For the best appearance, use the conventional method for a rolled collar with lapels; follow your pattern instructions. However, collars and facing edges can also be constructed using a flat method of trimming away all outer seam allowances and then topstitching around the edge, wrong sides of fabric together. The following illustrations and text describe this second method.

For a collar with stand, trim away all seam allowances except for the neck seam. Trim interfacing ¼″ smaller than the collar and fuse to upper collar. Stitch collar sections, wrong sides together. Staystitch neck edge ½″ from edge and clip. Trim away all seam allowances from collar stands and interface both stands. Lap stands over neck edge of collar, encasing the collar in the stand, and topstitch along upper edges of stand (6).

Staystitch neck edge of garment and clip. Encase garment between collar stands and complete topstitching (7).

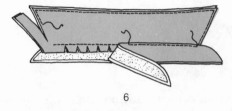

6

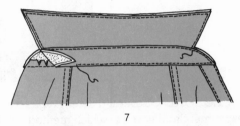

7

For a sleeve placket, cut placket facing and fuse to sleeve, wrong sides together. Slash through center of placket to point and stitch close to edge (8).

For a cuff, trim away all seam allowances and cut the cuff in half along foldline. Trim interfacing ¼″ smaller than cuff and fuse to wrong side of upper cuff. Before attaching cuff, line sleeve if desired. Lap both cuff sections over seam allowance of sleeve and hold in place with tape or fusible web. Topstitch around entire cuff as desired (9). Cuffs can also be stitched following the conventional method.

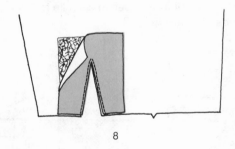

8

9

For patch pockets, trim away ⅝″ seam allowances. For an unlined pocket, cut along foldline to separate self-facing; topstitch facing to pocket wrong sides together; topstitch to garment (10). For a lined pocket, trim ¾″ from lining edge and stitch to pocket self-facing. Fold wrong sides together along foldline and topstitch across top of pocket. Topstitch pocket to garment (11).

For pocket flaps, cut two layers and trim away all seam allowances. Fuse wrong sides together. Topstitch sides and bottom edge; then topstitch top edge to garment (12).

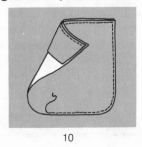

10

11

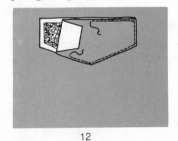

12

For waistband, trim away all seam allowances. Fuse interfacing to wrong side of outer waistband section, with top edge along foldline and other edge ¼″ from edge of waistband. Lap waistband over waist seam allowance of garment and topstitch in place close to edge. Fold band to wrong side and topstitch ¼″ from edge on outside of waistband through all layers. Continue topstitching around waistband, if desired.

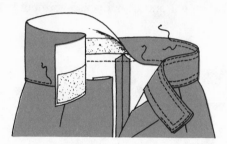

CLOSURES: Several different types of buttonholes can be made on synthetic suede—experiment to determine which method you like best.

For bound buttonholes, you can use the method shown for leather on page 373, except use fusible web instead of rubber cement to hold the buttonhole strips and the facing in place. Also insert a strip of web inside the buttonhole strips to hold the lips flat.

A regular bound buttonhole can be made conventionally using a patch method that does not require machine-basted markings.

Center a rectangle of self-fabric over the button area, right sides together. Stitch two rows of stitching the exact length of the buttonhole and slash diagonally to corners (1). Turn patch to wrong side of garment. To form buttonhole lips, fold patch over the opening so that the folds meet exactly in the center. Place strips of fusible web in each lip to hold lips flat (2). Fold back garment and stitch across ends of buttonhole (3).

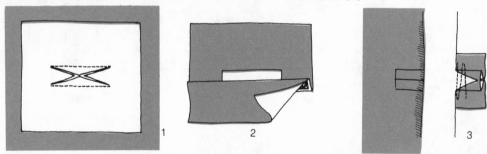

Machine-worked buttonholes can be made through all thicknesses after the garment is completed.

Zippers can be inserted with a centered application, or use the lapped application illustrated for leather; see page 374.

HEMS can also be finished on synthetic suede with different methods, depending upon your preference. For a conventional hem, turn up 1″ to 1½″, and fuse in place (1). For a more casual look, simply trim along the hemline and topstitch close to the edge to prevent stretching (2). Or face the hemline with a strip of ½″ wide fabric cut the same shape as the hem. Topstitch to hem edge, wrong sides together (3).

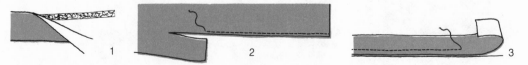

The Elegance of Fur

From time to time, the experienced sewer needs a project that challenges her capability. Making a fur garment not only tests your skill, but also furnishes its own reward. Whether you choose to purchase new fur or remodel an old favorite, you can't go wrong if you follow the directions below closely.

You will need the following equipment for sewing with fur: single-edged razor blades, chalk pencil, safety pins, thumbtacks, or pushpins, heavy-duty needles (size 7 glover's needles are perfect), large board for blocking fur, button and carpet or heavy-duty waxed thread, ½" twill tape, interfacing, and heavyweight muslin for a test pattern.

BEFORE CONSTRUCTION

Choose your pattern carefully. A style with simple lines is best. Consider one with few pattern pieces, seams, or darts, and front opening edges that can be converted to extended facings. Make a test garment in muslin and try on as it will be worn; try on coats over another garment. Make any changes in muslin, then transfer changes to pattern. Since fur is sewn edge to edge, trim pattern away along seamlines and dart lines.

When working with old fur, pinch the skin side to test for suppleness and pliability. Wet a sample on the skin side and stretch it to test the skin's strength. Bend the fur hairs to be sure they are not too dry or brittle. To revive the fur side, dampen slightly, then gently brush it with the grain. Fluff against the grain and allow it to dry overnight before working with it.

Find the best parts of the pelts by placing your pattern pieces on the fur side first. To ensure similarity throughout the garment, place pattern pieces with respect to shading, spotting, and color of adjoining pelts. Outline pattern pieces with a sufficient number of safety pins so you will know where to place them on skin side of pelt. You may need to join pelts to get a fur area large enough to cut out a pattern piece.

Use a razor blade to cut fur. Cut from the skin side and raise the pelt to avoid cutting the hairs. Cut over a board. Place the pelts edge to edge, skin side up, or cut area needed to complete a section (1).

To piece pelts, use strong waxed thread and sew through skin only using an overhand stitch. Work out any hair from the seam with the point of a needle. Reinforce by sewing twill tape over the seam with running stitches along the taped edges (2).

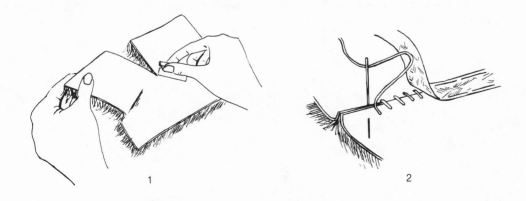

1

2

If there are worn spots in any of the pelts, mark them on the fur side with safety pins; place the pins in a triangle with one point toward the top of the garment (1). From the skin side, mark the triangle with tailor's chalk, drawing lines from pin to pin (2). Cut out the triangle and use it as a pattern for a replacement piece cut from leftover fur. Match texture, color, and grain of the fur carefully **before** you cut out the triangular replacement piece (3).

Use a small overhand stitch to sew the replacement piece (4).

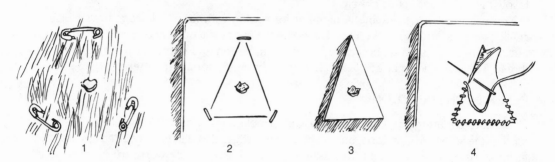

With your pelts atop the work board, place pattern pieces on the skin side and tack in place with thumbtacks or pushpins. For jackets and coats with collars, eliminate neck facings to reduce bulk. Chalk mark the pattern outlines and darts. Cut out pieces with razor blade without cutting fur. **Do not** cut out darts at this time.

Mark the outline of all the pattern pieces on the board. Using a brush, wet the skin side of each pelt, and place it fur side down over the pattern outline. Carefully matching the outline, tack each pelt in place and allow to dry thoroughly (at least 24 hours). This makes the skin easier to work with.

Remove the tacks when the pelts are dry. Pin the pattern pieces to the skins, check for stretching, and redraw the outline with a fine chalk pencil if necessary. Cut along the corrected outline and cut out the darts. Mark the notches but do not cut them. Also mark center fronts, foldlines, and hemlines.

CONSTRUCTION POINTERS

SEAMS: Sew twill tape to edges to be sewn in seams or darts with a hand zigzag stitch, keeping edge of tape flush with edge of skin. Join seams and darts with a close overhand stitch. Work with one skin side toward you and fur sides together (1). Keep edges even and push hairs away. Since tape is necessary for reinforcement, be sure to catch it in the seam. Smooth seams with warm, dry iron, being sure point of iron touches only taped edges, not the skin.

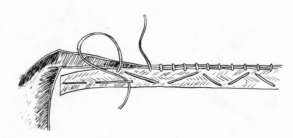

FINISHING EDGES: Hems or other edges that will become a finished edge of your garment must be finished with tape. The tape is then used to anchor linings. These edges are prepared after the seams and darts are sewn. Place the tape on the fur side and sew with small overhand stitches, mitering any corners (1). Finish all edges, then turn the tape to the skin side and sew it in place with long running stitches (2).

INTERFACING: Extended facings are interfaced to give the finished edge a soft rolled effect. Cut a strip of interfacing the length of the facing and twice its width. Place it ¼'' from the facing edge on the skin side and sew along both long edges with running stitches. Attach hook for closure at this time (see Hooks and Eyes on next page). Turn facing to inside along foldline; sew the two layers of interfacing together halfway between the raw edges of the interfacing and the foldline (1). Then sew the same layers together close to the edge (2). For garments lined to the edge, slide one edge of interfacing under taped edge, and sew both long edges in place.

COLLARS: For a detachable collar, back the skin with flannel and lightweight interfacing. Sew both layers to the skin ¼'' from edge with long running stitches. Prepare collar edges as you would finished edges (1). Make lining to fit; slipstitch to collar. Sew to garment (2).

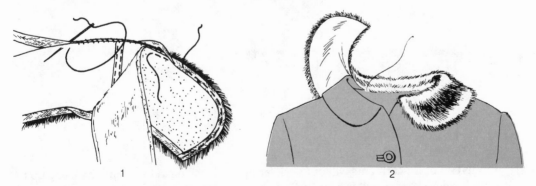

To make your fur collar easily removable as a separate accessory, simply sew a hook and eye to the ends before attaching the lining so they will meet at the neckline.

For a fur garment with a collar, finish edge of upper collar and undercollar as for seams. Sew them together. Then sew undercollar to garment. Shape the roll of the collar, then tack it loosely to the neck seam. This edge will later be finished with the garment lining.

BUTTONS and **BUTTONHOLES:** Using button and carpet thread, sew the button through the fur and interfacing, reinforcing the underside with a flat 1″ button. Be sure to make the thread shank long enough to accommodate the thickness of the fur.

From skin side, make a slit the buttonhole size in facing and garment with razor blade. Finish edges with tape on skin side as instructed for seams. On fur side, place additional tape as described for finished edges (1). Turn tape on fur side through to skin side and sew together with running stitches (2). Join facing to garment, working overhand stitches around buttonhole openings.

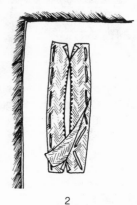

1

2

POCKETS: The two types of pockets usually made in fur are in-seam pockets (page 302) and buttonhole pockets. For the latter type, follow the buttonhole instructions above, cutting the slit long enough for a pocket. Make pocket sections out of lining fabric and stitch together. Sew securely to twill tape on inside of garment.

HOOKS AND EYES: Use large hooks and eyes especially made for fur. For an opening edge with an extended facing, mark placement of hooks and eyes on skin side with chalk. Make a tiny hole through the interfacing and skin at the foldline to allow the bill of the hooks to extend from the fur side. Sew the remainder of the hook to the interfacing and skin (1). Work bill to fur side (2). On opposite side of opening, sew the ring eye (3). For other closures, sew the hooks and eyes to twill tape before attaching the lining.

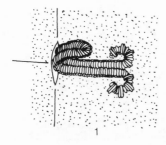

1

2

3

LINING: For fur garments without neck facings, you will need to extend the lining up to the neck edge. Add neck facings to the lining pattern piece, overlapping seams and allowing for a back pleat before cutting. Cut and sew the lining with seam allowances according to pattern instructions. Slipstitch to the fur, covering taped edges.

7

Very Easy Vogue

The Very Easy Vogue Concept

Very Easy Vogue patterns are created for the contemporary woman with "too much taste and too little time." These specially designed patterns combine high fashion styling with easy construction techniques—a concept that appeals both to the skilled sewer who desires to create a fashionable garment in a minimum amount of time, as well as to the beginner sewer who wants to make a fashionable garment while still perfecting her sewing skills.

However, the Very Easy Vogue concept goes beyond pattern design to include all phases of sewing—fabric selection, planning, cutting, marking, stitching, pressing, and finishing. It offers you alternative methods of sewing that are quick, easy, and fun to do. Which methods you choose depends upon the style of your garment, your fabric, the amount of time you have, and your own sewing experience and ability.

The following pages are filled with simplified sewing methods or "shortcuts" that reflect this concept of sewing. These ideas have come from dressmakers and sewing experts, who have learned through years of experience how to achieve professional results using time-saving techniques. The development of new fabrics, interfacings, notions, and equipment has made sewing easier and more pleasurable. Many traditional construction methods can be simplified or even eliminated. Machine stitching or fusing can replace hand sewing, even in tailoring.

Sewing is a very creative experience. Every project offers you a choice of styles and fabrics from which to choose. Now you also have a choice of sewing methods—simplified, traditional, or a combination of the two—that should be a part of your sewing repertoire. As with all creative arts, the final choice is up to you!

Very Easy PATTERNS

Easy-to-sew, fashionable clothes begin with your pattern selection. Choose a pattern that has a minimum number of seams, design details, and pattern pieces. The descriptive caption on the back of the pattern envelope and in the pattern catalogue will list the number of pattern pieces and describe the design and construction features of the garment. For example, a banded effect around the edge of a jacket can either be created simply with topstitching or constructed with a separately applied band and facing.

To eliminate minor fitting adjustments, choose styles that are more loosely fitted. Flared or gathered skirts are easier to fit than straight skirts; blouson or body-skimming styles are easier than fitted bodices with darts or seams; raglan and kimono sleeves are easier than set-in sleeves. If your figure is two different sizes, such as a size 10 bodice and a size 12 skirt, try Vogue's Doubles patterns, which include two sizes in one pattern. You can easily follow the cutting lines for whichever size you need without spending time altering various parts of the pattern. This is a great time-saver! If you are between sizes, simply cut between the two cutting lines.

For more major alterations, always keep a record of the fitting corrections made on your basic pattern so that you can easily make the same alterations in any pattern that you are cutting out. This is much easier than having to fit and adjust as you sew.

Very Easy Vogue patterns are specially designed for easy construction. Each has only a limited number of main pattern pieces such as front, back, sleeves, and collar. Details that require additional handling and sewing, such as cuffs, yokes, bands, pleats, tucks, and gathers, are kept to a minimum. Difficult-to-construct details such as complicated collars, welt pockets, bound buttonholes, mitered corners, gussets, and scallops are eliminated. Topstitching is done only on flat areas, and edgestitching is recommended only when it will make construction easier. If a lining is recommended, the garment is lined to the edge. Hand-stitching is kept to a minimum, and tailoring is not required.

The Sewing Guide for Very Easy Vogue patterns is clearly designed to show the garment, the diagram of all the pattern pieces, and the layout in one compact unit. Illustrations and descriptions of special construction terms such as layering, clipping, and interfacing are included in the Guide Sheet. Sewing instructions are concise and easy to follow, featuring flat construction where ever possible and many shortcut methods. Large, uncomplicated sketches and the use of color help to make the construction of Very Easy Vogue patterns as easy as possible.

Very Easy FABRICS

Easy-to-handle fabrics that require no preparation and no lining or underlining are the best selection for easy construction. Choose a fabric that is firmly woven or knitted with body and resiliency. Learn to recognize quality—fabrics that are sleazy, finished or printed off-grain, or contain flaws will cause sewing problems. Fabrics without a nap, a one-way design, or a matching pattern are easier to lay out; fabrics that do not ravel will need no seam finishes.

Always check your pattern envelope for fabric recommendations. Some Very Easy Vogue patterns may include a separate fabric listing stating: "The following fabrics are also suitable but may be more difficult to handle." This alerts you to fabrics such as crepe, chiffon, and matte jersey, which require special handling techniques.

Your pattern envelope will also state whether plaids, stripes or diagonal fabrics are suitable for this particular design. All of these fabrics require special handling to match the fabric design. However, if you do choose a plaid or stripe, you can avoid matching detail areas such as collars and pockets by cutting those pattern pieces on the bias.

You may need to purchase a little extra fabric if you plan to use certain simplified construction techniques, such as a self-lined pocket or a waistline casing, which require an extension of the pattern pieces. Also, if you are like many women who sew, you may often purchase fabric before you purchase a pattern, planning to make a garment "someday." To avoid later disappointment, be sure to purchase ½ yard more fabric than the "average" pattern requires. Thus, you are usually assured of having enough fabric for whatever pattern you finally select.

Very Easy PLANNING

One of the secrets to easy, successful sewing is planning your project before you begin. Preplanning includes your fabric selection and preparation, cutting, and marking as well as organizing your materials, equipment, and sewing area.

When selecting a pattern and fabric, you may be unable to decide if the style, fabric, or color will be flattering to your figure and personality. This feeling is shared by many sewers, including professionals. For a very easy solution, turn to ready-to-wear! There you are certain to find a similar design in the same type of fabric that you can try on and analyze in front of a three-way mirror.

If you purchase your fabric before your pattern, make up a little notebook containing fabric swatches and yardages to carry with you when you make your pattern selection. Use the swatches for choosing color-matched notions, such as thread, zipper, and buttons, so you can avoid a second shopping trip. To be superorganized, use your notebook whenever you shop to help you coordinate your entire wardrobe.

If your fabric requires preshrinking, this step can not be eliminated without disastrous results. However, most washable fabrics can be tossed right into your washing machine, along with any trimmings and lining, and laundered just as the finished garment will be. Follow the washing and drying directions, which are available on the fabric bolt or hang tag, recommended for your fabric. Washing also helps to remove finishes that sometimes cause stitching problems, especially on lightweight woven and knitted fabrics.

Organize

Next, organize your sewing area. Gather together all your supplies and keep them in a fabric-lined basket or fabric-covered box. Many basic notions such as a variety of pins, needles, snaps, and hooks and eyes should always be kept on hand. Other notions that are color-coordinated with the fabric will have to be purchased for each specific garment.

Although only a needle and thread are needed to sew a garment, a wide variety of sewing tools and equipment can make sewing much easier and faster. Refer to chapter 3 for information on such items as: special sewing machine feet and attachments for performing special tasks; differently sized scissors for cutting, trimming, and clipping; tailor's ham for pressing curved areas; bodkin for threading elastic through casings; and basting and sewing tapes to simplify stitching. Many of these sewing aids are truly timesavers.

Keep your equipment in good condition. Scissors, pins, and needles need to be sharp and smooth without any nicks or burrs for easy cutting and stitching. Professionals replace their needles and pins frequently to avoid snags and skipped stitches. Many follow this rule: a new machine needle for every new project. By keeping your equipment together and in good condition, you will always be ready to begin sewing without any fuss.

Tape a pin cushion or piece of flannel to the top of your sewing machine to hold your pins so they don't scatter all over your working surface and end up on the floor. Tie a ribbon to your scissors to hang around your neck or chair back, so they are always accessible. Tape a small bag to the base of your machine or sewing table so you can sweep all threads and fabric trimmings into it as you sew and avoid a messy clean-up job afterwards.

If possible, set up your ironing board right next to your sewing machine to save extra steps, and to ensure that you always press as you sew. If this is not practical, then set up a small travel board or sleeve board which you can use to press all but the largest areas.

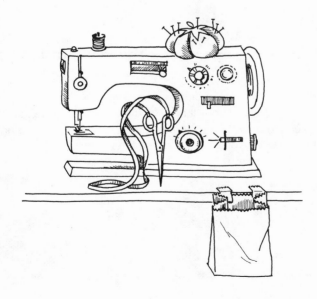

Layout and Cutting

Although there are many shortcuts to follow when laying out and cutting your pattern, always handle your fabric carefully. Accuracy in cutting and marking is truly your best guide and a "time-saver" when you begin sewing. An error of only ⅛″ in cutting along the edge of a seam allowance can be multiplied into a 1″ error for all four seams. Be sure your scissors are sharp. Dull scissors will only chew your fabric, causing inaccuracy, frustration, and a very tired hand! Use sewing scissors only for cutting fabric, never for other household tasks.

Press your pattern pieces with a warm iron. Circle the correct layout on your cutting guide before you begin. Always lay out **all** your pattern pieces on your fabric before you begin to cut even one pattern piece. If you are a couple of inches short at the end, you can always move your pattern pieces closer together **before** you begin cutting.

Try using weights to hold your pattern in place the pinless way (1). Or you can use sewing tape or cellophane tape on some fabrics, testing the tape first for easy removal. If you do use pins, keep them in a pin cushion to prevent the frustration of spilling an entire box of pins. To prevent snagging your fabric, discard any pins that become dull or rough. With knits, use ball-point pins instead of sharps.

A prescaled cutting board can be an aid in straightening and aligning your fabric as well as for measuring. For easy and accurate placement of your pattern, be sure to use a long tape measure, not a short ruler. Never disregard the grainline on a pattern piece in order to save fabric—it will only result in later problems as you stitch, press, and fit your garment.

If you have to make minor fitting adjustments in your garment, plan ahead and cut 1″ seam allowances on all side seams. Then if any seams have to be let out, you will have sufficient fabric to make the adjustment (2).

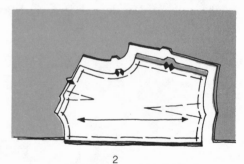

1

2

Certain construction techniques can only be used if you preplan and make the necessary changes when you are cutting out your fabric. Some garments with the center back seam on straight grain can be placed with the cutting line on the selvage for instant seam finishes (3). Clip the selvage at intervals to avoid puckering after washing (4).

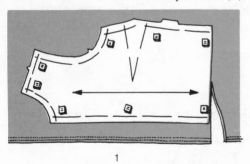

3

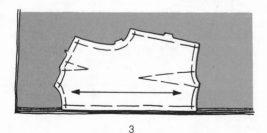

4

Waistbands, belts, ties, and straps can also be cut on the selvage to eliminate the added bulk of a seam allowance. Place pattern piece so that the **stitching** line is even with the edge of the fabric (5).

Pockets can also be simplified by eliminating extra seams. In-seam pockets can be cut as part of the garment by overlapping the pattern pieces, matching stitching lines, and pinning or taping the pieces together (6). Pockets with a facing and separate lining can be easily converted to a self-lined pocket. Flip the pattern piece over along the foldline at the top of the pocket to create a "double" pocket (7).

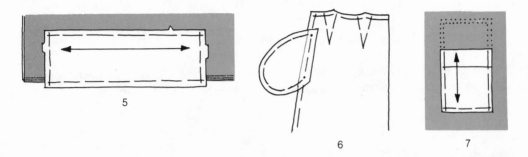

5 6 7

Plaids and stripes create special problems when laying out your pattern pieces. To help you match the fabric design at the **seamline**, not the cutting line, circle the match point in red on each pattern piece. If your pattern pieces do not have dots indicating match points, draw a line intersecting the seamline and the point of the notch to use as your match point for layout (8).

To make matching as easy as possible, lay out your pattern pieces side by side, or one above the other, exactly as they will be worn. Center front will always match horizontally if both sides are cut at one time from carefully folded fabric. The back should match the front horizontally along the side seams, below the bustline dart; and vertically at the shoulder seams. Sleeves should match vertically at the shoulder seam and horizontally at the front armhole notch; the back notches usually will not match. For collars, match at center back; for detail areas, match to corresponding garment area (9).

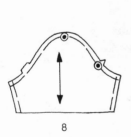

8

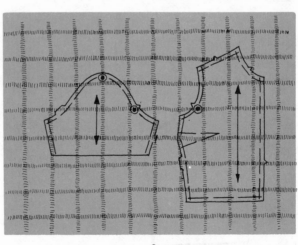

9

For the easiest method of handling plaids and stripes, cut all detail areas such as collar, cuffs, and pockets on the bias for "unmatched" construction. To change the grainline of a pattern piece from straight to bias, fold the pattern in half crosswise near the center of the grainline arrow (1). Bring the folded edge up to the arrow (2). Open out pattern and draw along one diagonal crease for bias grain of the pattern (3).

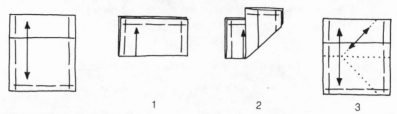

1   2   3

A special tip: When making calculations for changes or alterations in garments, you may find it easier to convert all measurements into eighths—⅛, ²⁄₈ (¼), ³⁄₈, ⁴⁄₈ (½), ⁵⁄₈, ⁶⁄₈ (¾), ⅞.

Marking

Accurate markings on all your fabric sections will help you construct your garment more easily and quickly. Mark all your pattern pieces at one time, being careful not to overlook any important markings. It is very time-consuming to have to repin a pattern piece to your fabric to check a marking when you are sewing!

The marking method you choose depends upon your fabric and how soon you plan to construct your garment. Clips are clearly visible on firmly woven or knitted fabrics, but are lost in loosely constructed fabrics. Pins are simple to use but may fall out if the fabric will be handled several times before stitching. Try one or more of the following methods for quick and easy marking:

PINS: Many garments can be marked with pins if you plan to construct the garment immediately. Place pins through the pattern at all symbols and dots and carefully remove the pattern, leaving the pins in place (1). On the other side, insert additional pins at each marking. Then carefully separate the two fabric layers and secure the pins in each layer of fabric (2).

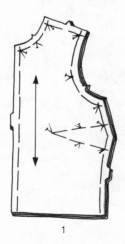

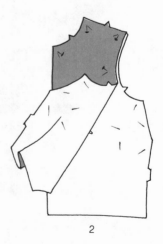

1   2

CLIPS: Tiny clips can be made in seams that you are certain will not be let out during fitting. Make ¼″ snips in the seam allowances to mark notches; ends of darts, tucks, pleats, and foldlines; and the location of the zipper stop and top of sleeve (1).

PRESSING: Foldlines, tucks, and pleats can be marked by pressing the fabric with the pattern still attached. Pin along both sides of the foldline through the pattern and fabric (2). Fold the pattern and fabric together and press along the fold with a dry iron. (3).

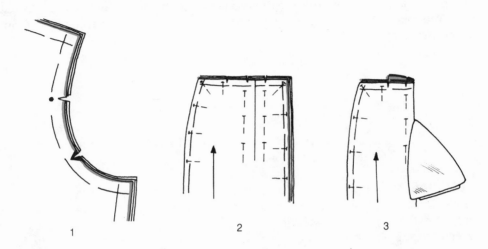

1

2

3

MACHINE-BASTING: The pivot point on a V-neckline or yoke can be marked with machine-basting, stitching two intersecting lines right on the seamline. Use the basting as a stitching guide when joining the two sections together to achieve a perfect point. Machine basting can also be used on many fabrics to mark buttonhole and button placements (4).

CARDBOARD GAUGE: Instead of marking certain areas of a garment, you can make a cardboard gauge to use as your sewing or pressing guide. Simply notch a piece of lightweight cardboard the desired width of the garment area and use it for measuring pivot points, tucks and pleats, hemlines, and topstitching (5)

4

5

DRESSMAKER'S CARBON PAPER AND TRACING WHEEL: Both layers of fabric can be easily marked at the same time by folding the carbon paper in half and placing it under the pattern, making sure the carbon faces the wrong side of both layers of fabric. Use a ruler to help you make straight lines with the tracing wheel.

Some dressmaker's carbons on the market are water soluble. If your fabric is washable, you can mark details such as pocket or buttonhole placement on the right side of your fabric, and the markings will wash out.

A combination marking pen and remover also allows you to mark on the right side of the fabric. Use the "ink" tip of the pen to make your markings; use the "remover" tip to eliminate the ink marks after the garment has been completed. Be sure to test the ink and remover on a scrap of the fabric before marking.

Very Easy SEWING

Many basic sewing techniques, traditionally done by hand, can now be done entirely by machine stitching or fusing. Become familiar with your sewing machine, its attachments, and its variety of stitches so you can use it effectively. Experiment with fusibles—both fusible interfacings and fusible webs have created an entirely new approach to sewing. From preliminary basting to final hemming, new methods of construction have simplified many sewing tasks.

Basting

Traditional pattern construction methods always recommend basting fabric sections together before stitching. However, hand-basting can be very tedious and time-consuming. Instead, use pins, tape, machine-basting, or no basting at all for Very Easy Vogue construction.

PIN BASTING: If you have a hinged presser foot, you can sew directly over pins placed perpendicular to the seamline. Insert pins about 1″ to 4″ apart with the heads far enough away from the seam so they will not be hit by the presser foot. For best control, reduce your sewing speed as you stitch over each pin.

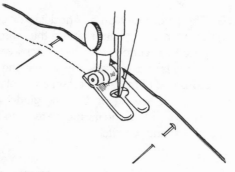

MACHINE-BASTING: Some sewing machines can do speed basting or chain stitching, which are very easy to remove after fitting or permanent stitching has been completed. However, your longest stitch length (6 to 8 stitches per inch) can also be used for basting. Clip the stitches about every inch so they will be easy to pull out later (1). Or use a contrasting color thread, especially in the bobbin, to identify the basting more easily.

For fabrics that must be carefully matched, such as plaids, use machine-basting to keep the fabric perfectly aligned as the seam is stitched. Place fabric right sides together, then fold back one seam allowance so you can match the fabric design. Machine-baste using a blind hemming stitch; press seam allowances together, and then stitch the seam (2).

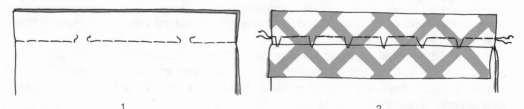

1   2

BASTING TAPE: For hard-to-handle fabrics or for fabrics that must be carefully matched, use basting tape or double-faced tape to hold the two fabric layers together. Place tape ¼″ away from the seamline so it will not be caught in the stitching (1). Be sure to remove it after completing the seam.

NO BASTING: Seamstresses for garment manufacturers are able to sew seams quickly and evenly without any pinning or basting. Although this takes practice, the technique can be used for many fabrics. Match the top edges of your fabric and align the notches or markings. As you begin stitching, guide the fabric with your right hand in front of the needle and with your left hand in back of the presser foot. Keep the two layers of fabric even and anticipate any easing. You may have to stop occasionally to adjust the layers until you can eventually stitch a seam in one continuous operation (2).

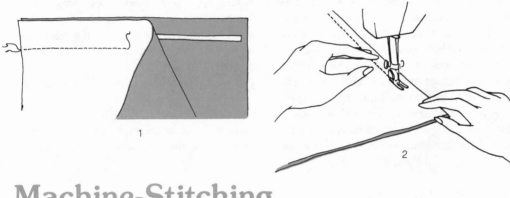

Machine-Stitching

The goal here, as with all steps of construction, is accurate stitching so that no time is spent ripping out stitches. A regular straight stitch can be used for most of the simplified techniques shown below; a zigzag stitch is needed for the others. However, if your machine has additional stitches, use them! Stretch stitches can "give" with knitted and stretch fabrics; overedge stitches can sew a seam and finish the edge at the same time; patterned stitches can be used for topstitching and a multitude of decorative trims.

Refer to chapter 3 for information on needle and thread selection for all types of fabrics. If you have a stitching problem, first check your needle. A bent, blunt, nicked, or improperly inserted needle is usually the cause, so change your needle frequently.

CONTINUOUS STITCHING: Take a tip from assembly lines and stitch as many pieces together as possible without cutting threads until you are finished. Darts, facings, shoulder seams, collars, cuffs, sleeves, and pockets—sew from one piece right into the next. If a seam must be secured at the end, do it with your stitching instead of tying knots (page 394).

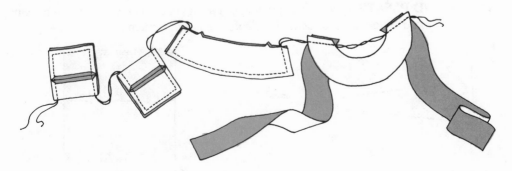

SEAMS: There are several different ways to secure the end of a seam without tying a knot. Either backstitch several stitches (1), use a lockstitch at the end of the seam (2), or complete the seam using very small stitches (3).

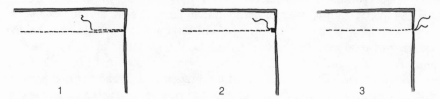

1   2   3

When stitching lightweight fabrics, you may have trouble with the fabric puckering or being pulled down into the needle hole as you stitch. Try placing tissue paper between the fabric and the feed; it can be easily torn away after the seam is completed. Use the straight stitch needle plate or place tape over the hole of the general purpose needle plate, and always hold both thread ends securely behind the presser foot as you begin stitching (4).

Curved edges should always be staystitched to prevent stretching and misalignment when stitching facings or seams. Use the staystitching as a clipping guide, so that the clips do not extend into or past the seamline (5).

Always reinforce corners such as collar points, V-necklines, and sleeve plackets to prevent the frustrating experience of having fabric threads pull out as you are turning the seam. Use tiny stitches on either side of the corner, or reinforce the area with a piece of fusible interfacing before you stitch (6).

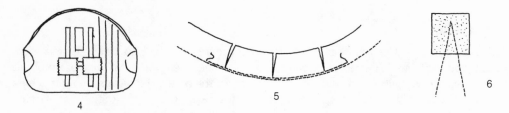

4   5   6

SEAM FINISHES: For most light and mediumweight fabrics, you can simply stitch and pink to prevent raveling. For heavier weight fabrics, zigzag stitching is a quick and easy seam finish. If your fabric does not ravel, no seam finishes are necessary. However, lightweight knits can be double-stitched and trimmed for a narrow seam finish to prevent rolling. If the seam allowances will show, such as on roll-up sleeves, clean-finish the edge by turning under ¼″ and stitching.

DARTS: To achieve a smooth point at the end of a dart is to gradually decrease the length of your stitches as you near the point. This secures the threads without having to tie a knot or backstitch, which can cause a bubble at the end of the dart (1).

TUCKS AND PLEATS: Rather than pinning or basting each tuck or pleat, use a seam guide or cardboard gauge to keep tucks and pleats even as you stitch (2).

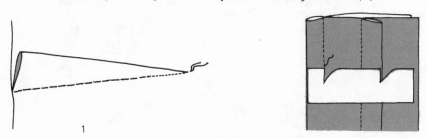

1   2

EASING: For areas that have only a moderate amount of ease, use your fingers to ease in the fullness as you stitch on a single layer of fabric. Press your index finger against the back of the presser foot, causing the fabric to pile up against your finger. This forces the fabric to ease in a little fullness under the needle. After stitching several inches, release the fabric, then repeat until the entire area is eased (1). Pin the two layers of fabric together, and stitch the seam from the eased side.

For areas that have a lot of ease, such as a set-in sleeve, always use the longest stitch possible and loosen the tension so the bobbin thread can be pulled up easily without breaking. After distributing the fullness evenly, press the seam allowances flat to help prevent tucks from getting caught in the stitching as you sew the seam (2).

GATHERING: To help prevent the thread from breaking when you pull up gathering, use heavy-duty thread or buttonhole twist in the bobbin. Or try this method for easy, break-proof gathering: Place a narrow string or cord, or a piece of button and carpet thread just above the seamline, between ½″ and ⅝″ from the edge of the fabric. Using a wide zigzag stitch, stitch over the cord, being careful not to catch the cord into the stitching. Pull up gathers. Using your zipper foot attachment, stitch along the seamline just below the cord. Pull out the cord after the seam is completed (3).

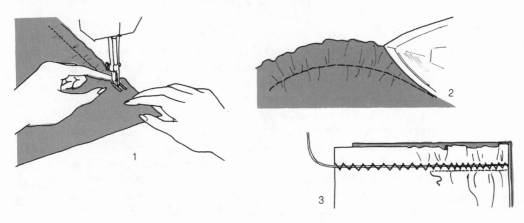

"STITCH IN THE DITCH": A clever name for a clever technique—"stitch in the ditch" can be used to hold layers of fabric together and to eliminate handwork. Stitch on the right side of your garment directly in the ridge or "ditch" of another seam, using 10 to 12 stitches per inch. Be sure that the under layer of fabric is smooth and properly positioned before you begin stitching. Use this technique to finish facings, bindings, collars, cuffs, and waistbands; to hold cuffs in place on pants or roll-up sleeves; and to prevent elastic from twisting in a casing. For complete instructions, see the section on Very Easy Construction Techniques, page 400.

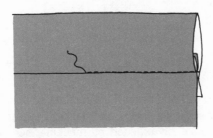

KEEPING STITCHING STRAIGHT: When stitching seams or topstitching sections of a garment, it is important to keep the stitching straight for appearance and accuracy. Here are several techniques to help you accomplish this.

Use the seam markings on the needle plate of your machine as your guide (1). If your plate is not marked, place a piece of white or colored tape exactly ⅝'' away from the center of the needle hole. To aid you in turning a corner, place another piece of tape ⅝'' in front of the hole. When the corner of the fabric is aligned with the intersecting tapes, it's time to pivot or turn your fabric (2). Or use a seam guide, which is placed on the base of the machine and can be adjusted both for distance from the needle hole and for curves (3).

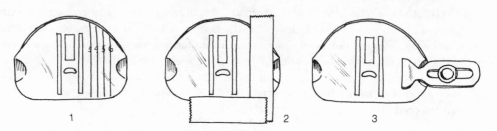

TOPSTITCHING: Both decorative and functional, topstitching can be used to secure facings and hems without any need for hand sewing. For easiest results, topstitch your garment while it is still flat. When topstitching along the edge of a garment, you can use the width of your presser foot for narrow edgestitching, or the markings or tape on the needle plate for wider stitching. When topstitching seams within a garment, you can use your presser foot, a quilting foot (1), or adhesive sewing tape as a guide (2). Stitch slowly but smoothly for straight, even topstitching. For two perfectly parallel rows of topstitching, use a double needle. Very Easy Vogue patterns recommend regular thread for topstitching. For added emphasis, silk or polyester topstitching and buttonhole twist thread can be used. However, some machines have difficulty stitching with a heavy thread; instead try using two strands of regular thread. If your machine does not have two spindles, wind thread on an extra bobbin and place on the same spindle under the spool of thread (3).

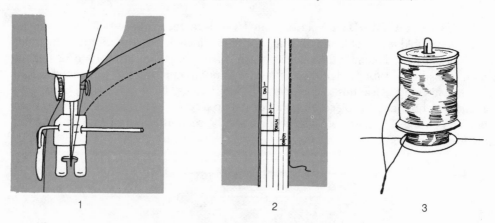

Machine stitching can also be used to finish many details which traditionally have always been done by hand. Hems, thread loops, bar tacks, buttonholes, buttons, and other fasteners can all be constructed or attached by machine; see pages 409 to 414. Your sewing machine can be a great time-saver for so many Very Easy Vogue techniques.

Pressing

"Always press as you sew"—this is one sewing adage that should not be bypassed. Careful pressing is vital to the final appearance of your garment. It is easy to press seams while your garment is still flat, but very difficult and sometimes impossible to press certain areas after the garment has been completed. However, the following techniques can help to simplify your pressing procedure.

Save time by not running back and forth between your sewing machine and ironing board. Organize your sewing construction so that you stitch as many darts or seams in different units as possible, and then press them all at the same time.

To be able to see what you are pressing, use a see-through press cloth or a special iron cover that is placed over the soleplate of your iron to prevent shine and scorching (1). To avoid making imprints of seam allowances on the right side of your fabric, use envelopes instead of brown paper strips. They don't have to be cut and are easy to slide along (2). To obtain a sharp seam edge on collars, cuffs, and lined pockets without using a point presser, preset the seam edge. Press the facing seam allowance back toward the facing before turning the fabric right side out (3). The seam edge will be smooth and even without having to tug or pull at the fabric.

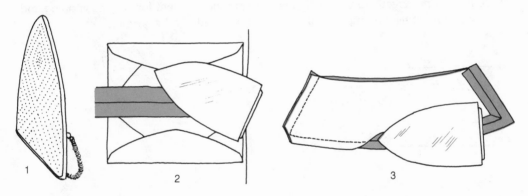

When pressing detail areas such as collars, lapels, facings, cuffs, and pockets, always "favor" the top layer of fabric. Press the outer seam so that it rolls slightly to the underside of the garment. This helps to prevent the facing side from curling or rolling up and becoming visible along the seamline (4).

Hems can be measured and pressed in one easy step by using a hem gauge or cardboard gauge. Place the gauge between the fabric and the hem allowance to prevent an imprint of the hemline from showing on the right side of the fabric (5).

To avoid crushing the pile on velvet, velveteen, corduroy, fake fur, and other pile fabrics, use a thick towel or a piece of self-fabric as a substitute for a needle board.

Occasionally use an iron cleaner to remove built-up fabric finishes, starch, detergent, and fusing agents from the soleplate of your iron. Your iron will glide more easily and smoothly.

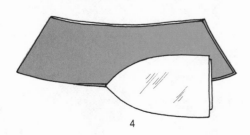

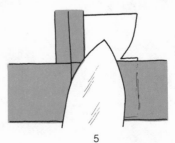

Fusing

Fusing has revolutionized many sewing procedures. Heat-sensitive fusibles—both interfacing and webs—can eliminate hand sewing, achieving professional results in just a fraction of the time. Your iron can also replace your sewing machine for basting, interfacing, and hemming applications.

Although fusing is quick and easy to do, **always** follow manufacturer's directions carefully to achieve the proper results. See page 157 for complete information on where and how to use fusibles. Always take time to pretest on your fabric before you begin fusing, checking the appearance and crispness of the fused fabrics. Although fusibles can be removed if you make a mistake, they cannot be reused and extra steps must be taken to remove any fusing agents remaining on the fabric.

For additional time-savers when working with fusibles, try these suggestions:

FUSIBLE INTERFACINGS: When cutting out sheer or lightweight fusible interfacings, place the interfacing over the pattern piece and trace along the seamline. Cut just inside the traced line and clip corners diagonally to eliminate the time-consuming task of trimming seam allowances separately (1).

Fuse interfacing directly to the facing instead of to the garment for easy positioning and to assure that no outline or imprint will show on the outside of the garment (2).

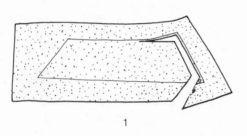

1

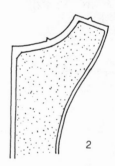

2

If you decide you need extra shaping or body in an interfaced area, fuse another layer of interfacing on top of the first. This method can be used for small areas such as the point of a lapel or the stand of a collar, as well as for an entire waistband or belt (3).

Detail areas such as individual buttonholes, plackets, and V-shaped slashes can be easily reinforced and stabilized by fusing a small piece of interfacing to the fabric before it is stitched or slashed. Pink the edge to help prevent an outline from showing on the right side of the fabric (4).

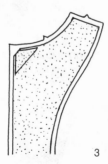

3

4

The use of a damp press cloth when fusing guarantees that enough steam is provided, even if you use a steam iron. The press cloth also prevents any fusing resins from touching the soleplate of your iron.

Fusible interfacings can be used to preserve a favorite pattern or a basic fitting pattern to use time and time again. Just press the interfacing to the back of each pattern piece. Some fusibles are specially designed for just this purpose.

FUSING AGENTS: Use a narrow strip of fusible web to "baste" two layers of fabric together. Pockets, straps, tabs, trims, and appliqués can all be positioned and held in place without shifting as you stitch.

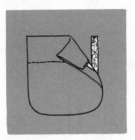

When folding narrow strips of fabric together for buttonhole lips, belt carriers, and fabric loops, insert a narrow strip of fusible web between the fabric layers. When pressing the fabric, the web will fuse the layers together for a smoother appearance, added body, and sharper edge.

When fusing a hemline, place the fusible web ¼″ below the edge of the hem allowance to prevent any web from accidentally touching the soleplate of your iron and to make the outline of the hem less conspicuous on the outside of the garment.

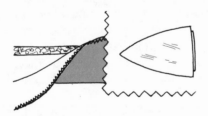

When cutting narrow strips of fusible web from a wide width, fold the fusing agent as many times as you can so that you only have to make one short cut.

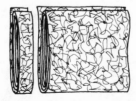

To mend a rip or burn in a garment, just fuse a piece of self-fabric behind the area for a no-stitch, invisible repair job!

Very Easy
CONSTRUCTION TECHNIQUES

Before you begin the construction of any garment, always read the Guide Sheet completely. When you understand how a pattern is to be constructed, the procedure is always easier. Also, you can decide what shortcut methods will be applicable to your particular garment, as some methods necessitate a slightly different order of construction procedures. From collars and cuffs to buttonholes and belts, these simple construction techniques will ease your sewing efforts.

Flat Construction

Very Easy Vogue patterns feature flat construction techniques wherever possible. Flat construction means that you complete each section of a garment before you stitch the major seams together. Sleeves, zippers, pockets, facings, and bands can all be stitched much more easily when a garment is still "flat." Topstitching each area as it is constructed is easier than waiting until the entire garment is completed.

For ***set-in sleeves,*** stitch garment shoulder seams. Finish lower edge of sleeve unless it is going to be cuffed. Easestitch sleeve cap between notches, pin sleeve to armhole edge, and adjust gathers. With sleeve side up, stitch along seamline and again ¼'' away (1). Trim close to stitching and press seam toward sleeve. Stitch back to front at side seams and sleeve edges in one continuous seam (2). Clip, if necessary, and press open.

For ***raglan sleeves,*** stitch neckline dart in sleeve and finish lower sleeve edge unless it is going to be cuffed. Pin sleeve to garment front and back, matching symbols, and stitch. Clip seams along underarm curve and press open. Stitch side of garment and sleeve in one continuous seam; press open (3).

For ***armhole facing,*** finish outer edge of facing and pin to armhole edge. Stitch, trim and understitch. Turn armhole facing to inside of garment and press. Open out facing and stitch side seams, including facing, as shown (4).

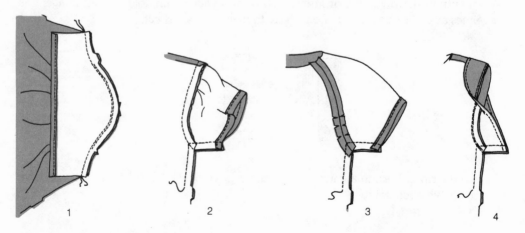

1   2   3   4

Insert a zipper before the facing or waistband is attached, using a centered application whenever possible. Stitch the center back or center front seam below the zipper opening. Insert zipper, following directions on page 410 before the shoulder or side seams are stitched. For a neckline facing, stitch the shoulder seams and then apply the facing before the side seams are sewn. For a skirt or pants facing, stitch the facing sections separately to the garment front and back. Then stitch the side seams of the garment and facing in one continuous seam (5).

When applying a bias binding, banding, or decorative trim to a garment edge, leave one seam open for easier construction. Stitch the binding, band, or trim to the garment, then enclose the ends in the final seam (6).

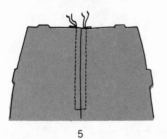

5

6

Facings and Other Edge Finishes

A smooth, even finish at the edge of a garment—whether it is a facing, banding, or bias binding—can often be difficult to achieve. Here are some easy methods to simplify your facing task, as well as alternative ways of finishing an edge.

FACINGS: Use the flat construction method when applying a neckline, armhole, or front edge facing. Not only is it easier to stitch the facing to the garment edge before the side seams are completed, but the tasks of trimming, pressing, and understitching are also simplified.

For a smooth, flat appearance, the seam allowances must be trimmed to eliminate any bulk. With light and mediumweight fabrics, you can grade both seam allowances at the same time by holding your scissors at an angle and cutting the facing seam allowance narrower than the garment seam allowance (1). Always press a facing seam, "favoring" the outside of the garment. Roll the seam slightly toward the facing side to help prevent the facing from showing along the garment edge (2). Then hold the facing securely inside your garment by using machine stitching instead of hand tacking (3). Either understitch through just the facing and the seam allowances, topstitch through all layers, or stitch in the ditch along another seam. You may also use a small piece of fusible web to hold the facings in place.

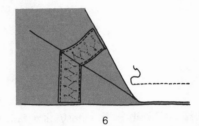

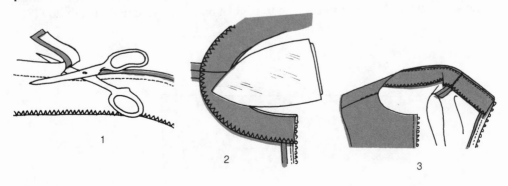

1

2

3

BINDINGS AND BANDINGS: Use the stitch-in-the-ditch method to eliminate any hand finishing when applying bias bindings, and fabric or knitted bands. Stitch binding or band to garment, right sides together; wrap over raw edges, and pin in place on inside of garment. On right side of garment, stitch in the ditch to hold the binding or band in place. If your fabric ravels, finish the inside edge before you begin.

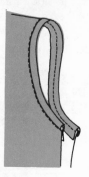

OTHER OPTIONS: For easy alternatives, try these methods for finishing edges. For armholes and necklines on casual knitted garments, such as T-shirts, just turn and topstitch the edge. Fold the fabric along the seamline; turn in raw edge ¼″; and stitch close to the edge, as shown (1). For curved areas, first staystitch just inside the seamline to help the fabric fold smoothly to the inside of the garment.

For a casual appearance on sportswear, try trimming away the seam allowances and stitching along the edge with an overedge or overlock stitch (2). Or for fabrics that do not ravel, simply trim or pink along the seamline and stitch ¼″ from the edge to prevent stretching.

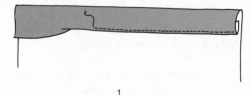

1

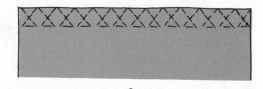

2

Fold-over braid is another option for edges. Be sure to trim away the seam allowances and preshape braid with a steam iron to match curved areas. As a guide for encasing curved edges, staystitch along fabric edge with the distance just slightly narrower than the width of the braid. Place braid over raw edge with widest side underneath and top edge covering staystitching. Machine-stitch close to edge of braid, catching underneath side (3).

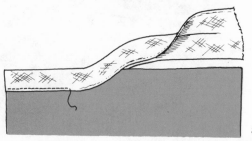

3

Collars

Because a collar frames your face it should always look well made. Symmetrical points, smooth edges, and a perfect roll can be easily achieved with these sewing tips.

For sharp points, always trim the interfacing away at the tip of the point before it is stitched or fused to the collar. When stitching your collar, use short reinforcement stitches for about 1″ on both sides of the point to help prevent any fabric threads from pulling out when the collar is turned. To eliminate extra bulk at the point, make one or two diagonal stitches across the tip and trim close to the stitching, being very careful not to cut into the stitches (1). When turning the collar, you can use a pin to gently coax out the point on the right side; never use scissors to poke it out. "Favor" the upper collar when you press the outer edges to help keep the undercollar always hidden. For bulky fabrics that are not going to be topstitched, try understitching the collar just as you understitch a facing. From the right side, stitch through the undercollar and seam allowances from center back to as close to each point as possible. This helps to keep the undercollar out of sight (2).

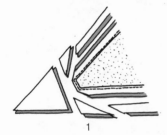

1

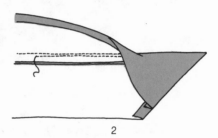

2

When attaching a collar, you have several shortcut options depending upon your fabric and style of garment. Many collars can be simply "sandwiched" around the neckline of the garment. Trim seam allowance of upper collar to ¼″ along the neck edge, and press to wrong side of collar at seamline. Stitch upper and undercollars together, trim, and turn right side out (3). Stitch undercollar to garment, right sides together, catching only the seam allowances of upper collar (4). Fold free edge of upper collar over seam allowances and topstitch in place (5).

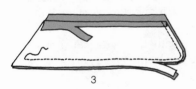

3

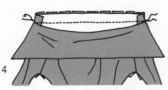

4

5

This method can also be used for a collar on a garment that has a front extended facing. Before the collar can be attached, complete the neck edge between the collar and the front foldline, and press the facing in place as shown (6). Sandwich the collar over the garment and facing seam allowances and stitch as described above, eliminating the back facing (7).

6

7

Or you can use the stitch-in-the-ditch method to eliminate a back facing. Before you begin, clip the upper collar at the shoulder markings almost to the seamline, and finish the neck edge between the clips with a ¼″ hem. Pin collar to garment and front facings, keeping finished back neck edge free; stitch, trim, and clip neck seamline (8). Pin free edge of upper collar along neckline, making sure that the collar rolls properly. Then stitch in the ditch along the neckline seam from shoulder to shoulder to secure the collar without any hand stitching (9).

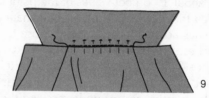

To easily make a stand-up or roll collar on a knitted garment, just pin both collar layers to the garment and stitch in place using an overedge stitch or a straight and zigzag stitch. Trim close to stitching, and press seam allowances toward garment (10).

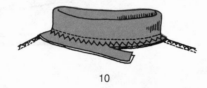

10

Sleeves and Cuffs

For easiest construction of set-in and raglan sleeves, use the flat construction method described on page 400. Many of the same techniques for collars can also be used for cuffs, making construction smoother and easier.

SLEEVES: If a set-in sleeve has a lot of ease, always use two rows of gathering stitches to help distribute the ease evenly and to act as security in case one thread breaks. If the sleeve cap has only moderate ease, try easing in the extra fullness with your finger as you stitch; see page 395. If you still need more ease because the sleeve cap is too large, use a pin to pull up several stitches. If the sleeve cap is too small, just clip the stitches every 2″ or so.

Certain fabrics, such as heavy velvet, vinyl, leather, and synthetic suede can not be smoothly eased. Instead, take out a little fullness in the sleeve cap by pinning a narrow tuck in the pattern above the notches before you cut out the fabric.

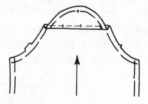

To help avoid any tucks in the sleeve cap when you stitch, be certain that the cut edge of the sleeve does not extend beyond the armhole. Then distribute any gathers evenly, and stitch accurately on the ⅝″ seamline.

PLACKETS: Sleeve openings for cuffs need not be time-consuming. Many traditional plackets can be entirely machine-stitched instead of finished by hand. Or try these very easy openings, using a dart, seam, or facing.

For a dart opening, stitch a small dart beginning about 2" above the edge of the sleeve. Slash fabric to form opening, ending at stitching. Roll raw edges of opening to wrong side of garment and stitch (1).

For a seam opening, just end your stitching at the marking or about 3" above the sleeve edge, keeping the lower seam open. Machine-stitch or fuse seam allowance in place (2).

For an easy faced opening, reinforce the point or corners with small stitches; trim, clip, and turn. Fuse the facing in place, or turn under the raw edges and machine-stitch (3).

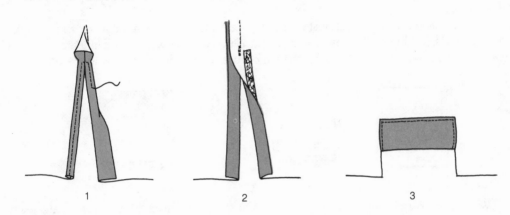

CUFFS: To complete a straight cuff with machine stitching, try this reverse seaming technique. Trim seam allowance of upper cuff to ¼", turn under and press. Stitch right side of cuff to wrong side of garment; trim. Fold cuff right sides together, complete ends, and turn cuff right side out. Pin upper cuff over seamline and topstitch in place (1).

Or use the stitch-in-the-ditch method to eliminate both bulk and hand sewing on the inside of the cuff. Finish raw edge of under cuff with ¼" hem or pinking. Stitch outer cuff to sleeve, trim seam allowance, and pin finished edge along seamline. Stitch in the ditch along the seam from right side of garment (2).

For simple band cuffs and knitted cuffs, attach cuff to sleeve before underarm seam is stitched. Stitch cuff to sleeve edge using overedge seam or two rows of stitching. Trim close to stitching. Complete underarm seam, including cuff. To prevent the seam allowance from showing, fold corners under and machine-tack to the seam allowance (3).

Or eliminate cuffs entirely and finish sleeve with elastic casing! A special tip: To hold roll-up sleeves in place, just stitch in the ditch through all layers.

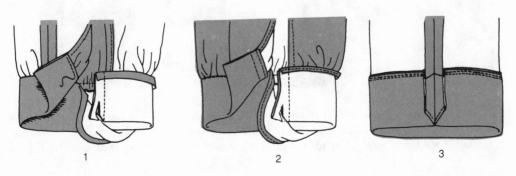

Pockets

Pockets can be easy to sew—whether decorative or functional, prominent or hidden in a seam. Choose patch or in-seam pockets and avoid difficult welt pockets. Some techniques depend upon special pattern layouts; others are done by machine stitching or fusing.

Patch pockets can be lined, topstitched, or stitched invisibly to your garment all by machine. For the easiest lined pocket, cut a self-lined or double pocket, page 389. Stitch pocket and lining, right sides together. Trim, clip and grade seam allowances (1). Preset edge of pocket by pressing seam allowance toward lining. Make a slit in the lining near the bottom of the pocket, and gently pull pocket right side out. Cover slit with a small piece of fusible interfacing (2).

For an unlined pocket, stitch just inside the seamline in the seam allowance to help the fabric fold smoothly to the inside. Trim and clip seam allowance to eliminate any bulk before the pocket is stitched. Machine-stitch or fuse upper edge of pocket in place (3).

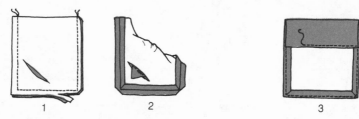

Whenever possible, topstitch patch pockets to garment before the side seams are sewn. Use fusible web to hold pocket in place and eliminate any problem of topstitching over pins. Place ¼" strip of web under edge of pocket and fuse. Or you can use pieces of sewing tape or masking tape to position pocket. Use the inner or outer edge of your presser foot, depending upon desired width, as a guide for straight stitching (4). Machine bar tacks can be used to reinforce corners of pockets that will receive a lot of strain such as those of sportswear and children's clothes (5).

Large, curved patch pockets can be applied invisibly to a garment using this clever method. Machine-stitch or fuse pocket hem in place. Stitch around pocket on seamline, and press seam allowances under, rolling stitch slightly to the inside. Notch out fullness and pin pocket to garment (6). Machine-baste around pocket, barely catching pocket edge with long, narrow, zigzag stitches. On inside of pocket, stitch on top of first row of stitching, ending at the middle and beginning again from the other side until the stitching is completed (7). Remove zigzag basting.

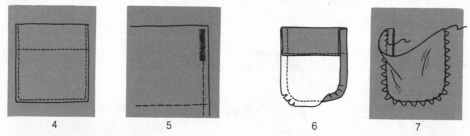

If you have enough fabric, cut pocket and garment in one to eliminate the seam at the pocket opening; see page 389. In-seam pockets can be easily added to a garment. Just use a pocket piece from another pattern, and make sure that the opening is at hand level.

Waistlines, Waistbands, and Belts

Waistlines can be finished with a casing or a waistband, and further emphasized by many types of belts. All three details can be constructed easily and quickly by letting your sewing machine do all the work for you.

CASINGS: Whether along the edge or in the middle of the garment, a casing is one of the easiest ways to control fullness. To convert a pattern from a waistband to a self-facing, you must extend the pattern above the waistline seam twice the width of the casing plus a ¼'' seam allowance. For a casing without a zipper, omit darts and redraw the side seams straight up from the hipline, as shown.

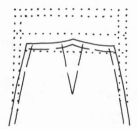

Mark foldline of casing with a clip at each seamline. Machine-baste (1) or fuse (2) seam allowances to garment in casing area to make it easier to thread the elastic or ties through the casing. Turn under the ¼'' seam allowance and press. Stitch the casing in place along the top and bottom edges to help prevent rolling. With firmly woven fabrics and knits, you can eliminate some bulk by finishing the raw edge with zigzag stitching instead of turning the edge under.

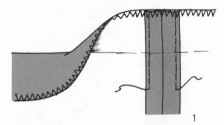
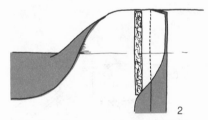

1

2

For easy insertion of elastic, be sure it is narrower than the casing, and try using a bodkin instead of a safety pin. To keep fullness adjusted evenly and to prevent elastic from twisting, stitch in the ditch at each seam through all thicknesses (3).

Or try stitching the casing with the elastic already inside. Measure elastic, including seam allowances, and mark into quarters. Leave one seam open and secure elastic ends in open seam allowance. Pin elastic along casing foldline, matching markings, with pins on outside of garment. Fold casing over elastic and stitch, stretching elastic so fabric lies flat. Complete final seam, catching in elastic ends (4).

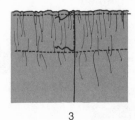
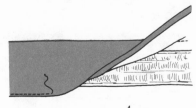

3

4

For an interior casing in a garment, use single fold bias tape. Fold in ends and stitch close to both long edges. Thread elastic or ties through casing (5). For an easier method, eliminate the casing and stitch the elastic directly to the garment. Measure elastic, mark into quarters, and pin to inside of garment between placement lines. Use one or two rows of stitching, depending upon width of elastic, stretching elastic as you sew (6).

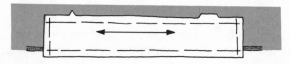

5

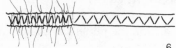

6

WAISTBANDS: Try these alternative methods of constructing a waistband whenever you sew. Interfacing should be used to prevent rolling—for best results choose a special waistband interfacing or use a crisp fusible interfacing. For a simplified version of the straight waistband application, cut waistband with unnotched seamline along edge of selvage to reduce bulk. Stitch waistband to garment; then stitch ends. Trim and press. Turn waistband to inside and pin or fuse selvage edge along seamline. From right side of waistband, topstitch close to seamline, catching in selvage.

Or try the reverse seaming technique, the same one used for cuffs. Reverse the pattern piece when cutting waistband. Trim seam allowance on unnotched edge to ¼", turn under and press. Pin right side of notched waistband edge to wrong side of garment. Stitch, trim, and press seam toward waistband (1). Complete ends; then pin folded edge along seamline and topstitch in place (2).

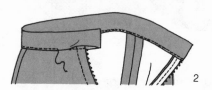

1

2

The stitch-in-the-ditch method is especially good for bulky fabrics because it gives a flatter appearance to the waistband seam. Cut waistband with unnotched edge along selvage so that the seam allowance is only ⅜" wide (3). Or trim the edge to ⅜" and finish with zigzag stitching. With right sides together, stitch waistband to garment, trim and press seam toward waistband. Stitch ends, trim, and clip seam allowances at center back underlap. Turn waistband right side out and pin finished edge along seamline, tucking in corners at ends. Stitch in the ditch along the seamline from right side of garment (4).

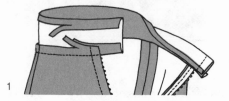

3

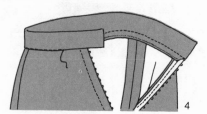

4

For knitted fabrics, you can attach the waistband using an overedge seam. If fabric is stretchy, you may wish to stay the seam by basting a piece of twill tape or seam binding along the seamline. With right sides together, stitch ends and underlap section of waistband; trim, turn, and press. Pin both edges of waistband to right side of garment. Stitch using an overedge or straight and zigzag stitch; trim close to stitching. Press seam toward garment.

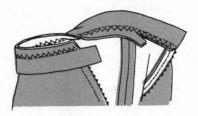

BELTS: Self-tie belts at least ⅜'' wide are the easiest belts to make. For firmer fabrics or fabrics that are too bulky to turn, press under raw edges, fold belt in half and topstitch in place (1). Soft or lightweight fabrics are best stitched right edges together and turned.

For a belt with buckle, use fusible web instead of stitching to hold the layers together. Cut belt with one edge along selvage. Form point at one end and fold in edges of fabric so that selvage slightly overlaps other edge. Fuse layers together with strips of fusible web (2). If extra stiffness is desired, insert a piece of interfacing or belting between the layers of fabric before fusing. Attach a no-prong buckle. Or leave both ends unfinished and attach an interlocking buckle.

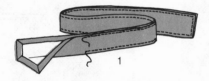
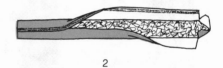

1

2

BELT CARRIERS: Both fabric and thread carriers can be easily made without any hand finishing. For fabric carriers, prepare one long strip using the selvage edge to reduce bulk. Stitch or fuse; then cut into the desired number of pieces when completed. If you plan to topstitch, cut fabric three times the desired finished width, fold strip lengthwise into thirds with selvage on outside, and press. Topstitch along both edges. If you plan to fuse the layers together, cut fabric twice the desired width plus ⅛''. Center a strip of fusible web on wrong side of fabric. Fold in edges, overlapping ⅛'' with selvage on top; fuse. To attach carriers, turn ends under and topstitch in place or enclose ends in seam.

Thread carriers can be made by machine much faster than crocheting by hand. Twist several strands of thread together and hold taut as you stitch over them with a zigzag satin stitch (3). Pin carriers in place before you sew side seams of garment.

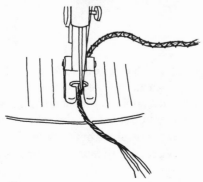

Fasteners

There are many different types of fasteners that can be used to secure garments—some of them can be easily adapted to shortcut methods.

ZIPPERS: Very Easy Vogue patterns recommend a centered zipper application whenever possible. For easiest construction, insert zipper before facings or waistband are attached and before side seams of garment are stitched.

Stitch seam below zipper, reinforcing end of stitching. Machine-baste zipper opening closed; clip basting stitches for easy removal; and press seam open.

Use basting tape or pieces of cellophane tape to hold zipper in place. Position top stop of zipper 1'' below fabric edge. However, if you want to eliminate the need for a hook and eye above the zipper, place zipper stop ¾'' below edge (1). Stitch on right side of garment, using sewing tape or cellophane tape placed ¼'' from zipper seam as a guide for straight stitching (2). Always stitch from bottom to top along each side of zipper to prevent any distortion of zipper placket. Remove bastings.

To secure facing to zipper tape without hand sewing, try this easy method. Turn under ⅝'' seam allowance of facing and pin in place from right side of garment. Use a zipper foot and stitch on the right side directly on top of the zipper stitching line for the width of the facing (3).

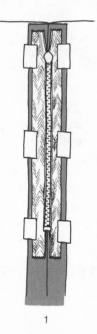

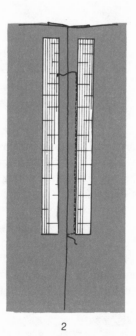

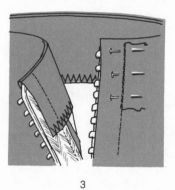

3

1

2

BUTTONHOLES: Very Easy Vogue patterns include only a limited number of buttonholes, which can always be machine-stitched for easiest sewing.

If your machine does not stitch buttonholes automatically, it is sometimes difficult to get the zigzag stitches perfectly parallel and the proper distance apart. An easy solution is to use pieces of tape to mark the dimensions of the buttonhole. Cut tape to exact buttonhole length and place about ⁵⁄₁₆'' apart on outside of fabric to form a stitching guide (1). Always test removing tape from a scrap of your fabric to be sure it is not too sticky; otherwise use machine basting as a guide.

When cutting buttonholes, place a straight pin at each end of the buttonhole so you will not cut through the stitches (2).

When interfacing dark colored fabrics, select dark interfacing so that you will not have to spend time trimming away white threads that may be visible when the buttonhole is cut open. If garment is not interfaced, use fusible interfacing to stabilize each buttonhole area. Cut out a small rectangle of interfacing and fuse to wrong side of fabric before marking buttonhole. If outline shows on right side of fabric, try pinking edges. Or stabilize the buttonhole with cording, guiding the cord as you stitch over it (3).

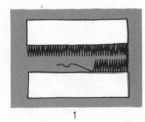
1

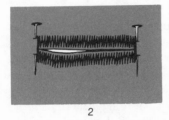
2

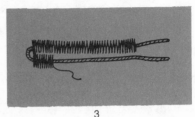
3

Although bound buttonholes are feared by many sewers, try these tips to help make their construction less difficult. Use fusible interfacing behind each buttonhole to stabilize the area and to prevent raveling when the fabric is slashed open. Place pieces of tape across the ends of each buttonhole to mark where stitching must stop (4).

For uniform results, always stitch all of your buttonholes at the same time. Use the production line method and complete each step for all buttonholes, before going on to the next step. This is faster than completing every buttonhole separately. If using fabric strips to form the buttonhole lips, make one long strip and cut into individual pieces. With bulky or very firm fabrics, try inserting a tiny strip of fusible web inside the buttonhole lips before they are stitched so they will lay flat after pressing.

Finishing off the back of a bound buttonhole can sometimes be tricky when you slash the facing and turn the edges under around the buttonhole. Stabilize the area with a piece of lightweight fusible interfacing pressed to the wrong side of the fabric. Or try the stitch-in-the-ditch method with firmly woven fabrics, knits, leathers, and synthetic suedes. Pin facing in place behind buttonhole, then stitch in the ditch on right side of garment around buttonhole rectangle (5). On the facing side, trim away fabric close to stitching (6).

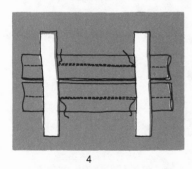
4

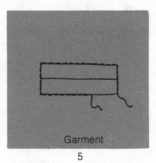
Garment
5

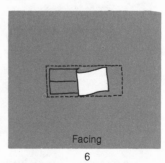
Facing
6

A special tip: To save you time when marking buttonholes, purchase the same size buttons as recommended on your pattern envelope. Your pattern pieces are already marked with the proper buttonhole position and length for this size button.

BUTTONS: Buttons can be stitched quickly and securely by machine, if you have a zigzag stitch. Hold button in place with tape. Set width of zigzag to align with buttonholes and change stitch length to 0. Place a thick needle or toothpick on top of button to create a thread shank as you stitch. Pull threads to underside of button, and twist tightly around the stitches to form the shank.

OTHER OPTIONS: Here are some other fastening ideas to substitute for buttonholes and buttons.

For easy-to-make fabric loops, cut a bias strip four times the desired finished width. Fold edges to center of strip, fold strip in half, and edgestitch (1). Or use narrow braid, cording, or ribbon for extra easy loops.

With casual shirts and jackets, consider using plain or decorative snap fasteners that can be applied with special pliers or applicators. Position fasteners at button and buttonhole markings on garment (2). Hook and loop fasteners can be machine-stitched to fabric, replacing snaps, hooks and eyes, or buttonholes. You can conceal the stitching on the outside of your garment with a button (3).

Or fasten a closure with fabric or grosgrain ribbon ties. Make fabric ties same as for fabric loops, except turn in one end when folding fabric. To attach ties, place raw edge over marking, stitch, and trim. Turn tie back over raw edge and stitch again through all layers. Cut ribbon ends diagonally or notch to prevent raveling (4).

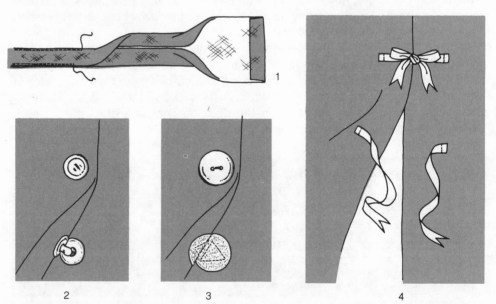

For a waistband, use a large hook-and-eye closure instead of several tiny hooks and eyes. Some types can be hammered onto the fabric before the waistband is completed.

Ready-made fasteners, such as frogs, toggles and loops, and special buckles, are both decorative and fun to use.

Hems

The final finishing detail of a garment is usually the hem. Take a tip from designers and utilize new methods of hemstitching for easy and decorative results. For an invisible hem, fusible webs will hold fabric layers together with neither machine nor hand stitches. So if you are eager to complete your garment, just machine-stitch or fuse the hem in place, and you're ready to go!

Topstitching can be used to finish the hem and trim the garment at the same time. Use one, two, or more rows of stitches, taking care to keep them straight and parallel. If other areas of your garment are topstitched, the hem should be topstitched the same distance from the edge. Or you can duplicate a banded effect at the hemline to match a banded edge around the neckline or front of your garment. Finish by pinking close to the stitching.

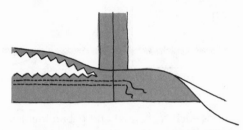

Narrow hems are ideal for sheer and lightweight fabrics. For woven fabrics, turn up ⅜″ hem, fold in raw edge, and stitch. For knits, the hem can be stitched single thickness and then trimmed close to the stitching (1). Or you can use a special hemming foot that folds and stitches the hem in one operation. For best results, prefold an inch or so of your fabric so it will feed evenly into the foot (2).

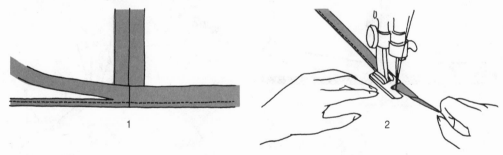

Mediumweight fabrics can be blindstitched by machine for a quick, invisible hem if your machine has the special stitch. Press up hem and turn under raw edge, if necessary. Fold back garment ¼″ below hem edge. Align stitches so that straight stitches fall on the hem allowance and the single zigzag stitch just catches the garment along the folded edge. Press hemline flat.

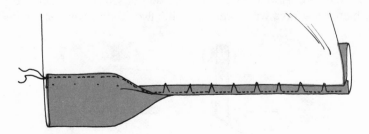

The blindstitch can also be used to create a shell edge on a hem. Trim hem allowance to ½″ and fold under. Stitch along folded edge so that the zigzag stitch forms over the fold and scallops the edge.

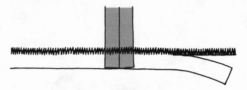

Other decorative hems, some created by designers, can also be done by machine. Jersey and double knits can be finished with a zigzag stitch. Sew along hemline with a small, narrow zigzag, then trim away hem allowance as close to the stitches as possible.

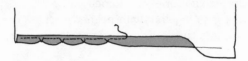

With mediumweight fabrics such as flannel and gabardine, try using a satin edge finish. Fold up hem and sew a row of narrow zigzag stitches (often called satin stitches) along the folded edge. Repeat with a second row on top of the first; trim away fabric close to stitching (1). Lightweight stretchable knits can have a special rippled or "lettuce" edge finish. Trim hem allowance to ½″ and press up hem. Stitch along folded edge with a zigzag satin stitch, stretching fabric as you sew (2). Do not use if knit runs easily.

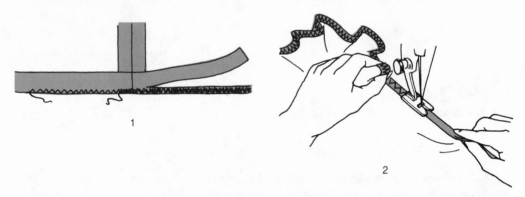

Fusing is one of the fastest ways to complete a hem. Always mark, trim, and press up hem before fusing. Place fusible web about ¼″ below cut edge to help eliminate hem outline from showing on right side of garment and to prevent any web from coming into contact with iron soleplate. Also, cut web on each side of seam allowance for a smoother finish. To alter hem, press area with steam until the two fabric layers can be gently pulled apart.

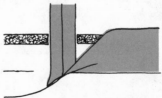

Tailoring

Tailoring is certainly not a fast or easy method of clothing construction. Yet there are many shortcuts for underlining, interfacing, padstitching, and lining that make tailoring less complicated and time-consuming. Professional results are still the goal in Very Easy Vogue tailoring, with machine stitching and fusing replacing traditional hand sewing wherever possible.

UNDERLINING: When stitching underlining and fabric sections together, zigzag along outer edge of fabrics to finish seam allowances at the same time .

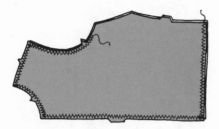

SEW-IN INTERFACING: Padstitch collars and lapels by machine rather than by hand. For collar, machine-baste interfacing to wrong side of undercollar ½″ from edge; trim close to stitching. Using regular stitch and matching thread, padstitch stand of undercollar. Stitch first along roll line and then stitch parallel rows ¼″ apart from roll line to neck seamline. For rest of collar, begin at center back and stitch toward collar seamline following grainline. Continue stitching parallel lines ½″ to ¾″ apart, pivoting near seamline and roll line as shown (1). Press with steam to shape.

For lapels, machine-baste interfacing in place, as for collars. Stitch parallel rows of padstitching from top of lapel down to seamline, starting near roll line. For extra body in lapel point, space rows more closely together. Roll line can be taped by zigzag stitching twill tape in place; see Menswear page 501. Shape lapels by steam-pressing over a pressing ham or tightly rolled towel (2).

1

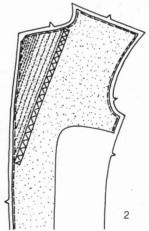

2

For hemlines, you can machine-stitch interfacing to hem allowance instead of catch-stitching by hand to wrong side of garment—a real timesaver!

FUSIBLE INTERFACING: Fusible interfacings have made tailoring easier than ever before. No catchstitching, no padstitching—just fuse interfacing to fabric. With the introduction of many different types and weights of fusible interfacings, you can achieve the exact amount of shaping desired. For collars, trim seam allowances and points of interfacing before fusing. For extra shaping in collar stand, cut a second piece of interfacing to fit between roll line and neck seamline, and fuse in place on top of first. Collar points can also be weighted with a triangular-shaped piece of additonal interfacing (1). Steam-press collar to shape.

For lapels, trim seam allowances and points before fusing. Lapel point can be weighted with another piece of interfacing just as for collar points. This will help to make the lapels lie smoothly against the garment (2). To tape roll line, zigzag stitch twill tape to garment; see page 501.

For hemlines, fuse interfacing directly to wrong side of garment, cutting at seamlines and fusing behind seam allowances (3). Or you can fuse the interfacing to the hem allowance.

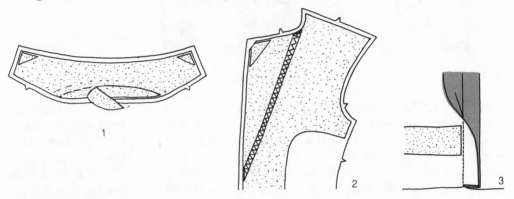

LINING: To insert a lining by machine, complete garment but do not tack facings to shoulders. Stitch lining pieces together, set in sleeves, and staystitch around curved neckline; clip to staystitching. With right sides together, pin lining to facings, matching center backs and shoulder seams. Starting 3″ above lower edge, stitch from lining side around neckline, ending 3″ from opposite lower edge. Press seam allowances toward lining and turn garment right side out. Tack lining to garment at underarm seams. Hem lining at sleeve and lower edge of garment by hand or use machine blindstitch; slipstitch front corners in place.

For an even faster finish, eliminate the lining. To finish the inside of your garment, bind seam allowances with double-fold bias tape or lace binding; or turn the seam allowances under and stitch; or lap narrow lace or trim over the raw edges and stitch.

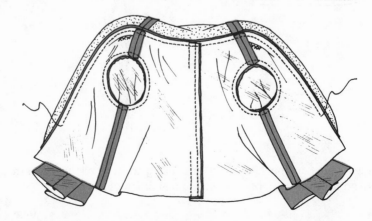

8

Impeccable Tailoring

Creative Tailoring

If you want to make a tailored garment, be prepared to spend a reasonable amount of time and effort. ***Tailoring*** by its very nature is synonymous with difficulty to some people—enough so that they are fearful of trying it themselves. Actually, tailoring is simply the additional pressing and hand-sewing techniques required to shape and stabilize the fabric to retain the precise look intended by the designer.

A tailored garment is molded and shaped by pressing and sewing with the aid of supporting inner fabrics and specialized hand stitches. Tailoring is not difficult once you realize there are no shortcuts to a professional finish. Develop good habits now and they will remain with you to polish every succeeding project.

Choose a style that will not go too far beyond your previous sewing experience, but also try to select one that will give you a real appreciation of what tailoring techniques actually add to a garment. Attempt to make yours a learning experience as well as an enjoyable challenge. If you already have some experience in the fine art of tailoring, treat any familiar information as a refresher course to recall important basic methods.

Tailoring can be divided into two categories by the degree of tailoring required. First there are tailored wool suits or coats that require special pressing and shaping techniques and special handling of the underlining, interfacing, and seams. The second category consists of garments that require tailoring techniques in certain areas, such as the collar and lapels of a soft dress, and of fabrics which require tailoring to achieve the proper molded look, such as limp, loosely woven, dressy, or washable fabrics. To be creatively tailored, garments of either type should have all these identifying characteristics:

☐ Pattern and fabric have been chosen to compliment your figure.

☐ Garment has smooth lines without wrinkles or sagging, and is molded to retain its shape without being stiff and uncomfortable.

☐ Buttons, flaps, pockets, and cuffs are positioned properly and are in the right proportion for the wearer.

☐ Collar rolls smoothly and evenly without seams showing at the outer edge and sits softly on garment without curling.

☐ All edges are pressed into soft or crisp edges as planned by the designer with seams at facing edges invisible.

☐ Hems are invisible with just the right amount of pressing.

☐ Lining does not pull or interfere with the hang of garment.

Tailoring will require some special equipment in addition to that needed for dressmaking. These tools, most of them pressing aids, will help to give you a better-looking garment: tailor's ham or cushion, seam or sleeve roll, point presser or tailor's board, pounding block or clapper, pressing mitt, pressing pad, pressing cloths, sleeve board, pointer and creaser, needleboard, and silk thread for basting.

When you approach tailoring, your preliminary decisions are the most important—style and fabric. For your first tailoring project, choose a style with basic lines that are flattering to your figure. To show off your skill, your garment should show fashion awareness as well as a long life.

All Vogue patterns clearly state on the back of the pattern envelope what type of fabric may be used for each design along with all pertinent buying information. Purchase all notions and findings (dressmaker's tools) as suggested, to expedite your tailoring project once it is started. Choose a fabric that can withstand standard wearing and cleaning. All your materials, inside and out, should help maintain the built-in shaping of tailoring.

Vital Preparation

First prepare your fabric. Preshrink all underlining, interfacing, tape, and other notions that will be used in your tailored garment, as the great amount of steam used in tailoring will affect all fabrics and findings.

Make any adjustments or alterations in your pattern. You may wish to make the jacket or coat shell first in muslin. Jacket patterns allow an additional amount of wearing ease at the circumference of the bust, waist, and hip, plus style ease when needed. This will provide ample room for your jacket to move easily over a dress or blouse and skirt. Coats also have an additional amount of wearing ease so you have ample room to wear a suit underneath. Coat sleeves are made large enough to be worn over a jacket. Two notes of caution, however: first, do not confuse the top of a two-piece garment with a jacket, as these tops are made with the same measurements and ease as a one-piece dress; and second, you cannot wear a coat over a jacket that is a cutoff version of the same pattern.

CUTTING AND MARKING: Always cut your fashion fabric first and *cut the seam allowance wider* than marked on the pattern. They should be at least 1″ wide on all edges that may require fitting over the bust, waist, and hip area of the garment, and on sleeve underarm seams, outer edges of upper collar, and lapel facings. Transfer all center markings before removing the pattern tissue.

Next, cut your underlining fabric, widening the seam allowances as for your fashion fabric. Transfer all seamlines, construction lines, grainlines, and symbols to your underlining with a tracing wheel and dressmaker's tracing paper.

Refer to Interfacing, page 422, before cutting your interfacing. Cut out the given lining pieces, using wide seam allowances as for your fashion fabric. Also refer to Skirt Lining, page 421, if your pattern does not include one. With your cutting completed and all fabric pieces stored on a flat surface, you are ready to do your first sewing.

BASTING: Pin the underlining to all of the fabric pieces, matching center lines and grainlines; review the marking section, page 149, and baste.

Some garment areas will require special attention as you baste to maintain their proper contour. Shape the undercollar, placing the underlining uppermost (1). The fashion fabric should be uppermost while you are shaping the upper collar (2) and sleeves (3).

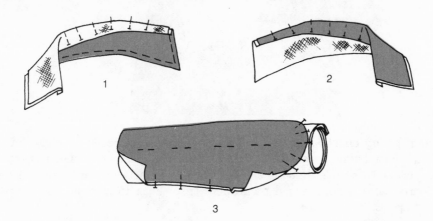

Turn jacket lapels along roll line as you baste, keeping the underlining uppermost.

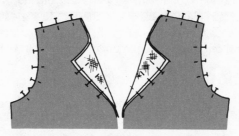

If your garment piece contains pleats, fold them, basting as you do to ensure smooth layering. Baste along foldline and roll lines, then turn fashion fabric along these markings in the direction they will fall.

Finally, baste along your traced seamlines. You will refer to these seamlines constantly during fitting. Then thread-trace along the lengthwise and crosswise grain of your fashion fabric on all major pieces. These markings will also be used as fitting guides.

First Stage: The Skirt

Since all tailored garments must be fit to move easily over one another, the skirt is the first unit to be constructed. Before you begin the actual construction, make a waistline stay to support the fabric during fitting. Cut a strip of 1″ wide grosgrain ribbon your waist measurement plus 2″. Position it around your waist, allowing ½″ wearing ease; pin. Mark closing and centers.

You should prepare the skirt for fitting by first attaching the underlining; then, basting darts and pleats; flatten with fingertips. Baste seams or pin closely along the seamlines. Sew ease or gathering threads by hand. Lap skirt over waistline stay, matching centers, and adjust the ease or gathers. Pin and baste the waistline seam of the skirt along the edge of the stay.

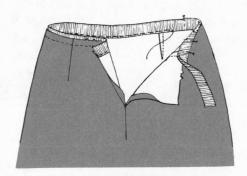

Important fitting checkpoint: Try on skirt and position correctly on body. Fit skirt according to First Fitting, page 121. Transfer any new seamlines, dartlines, etc. to underlining with tailor's chalk. Rebaste any adjustments. Remove waistline stay. Stitch any seams or darts that were not changed; press open. Try on again to check fit. Stitch together permanently; press. Insert zipper.

SKIRT LINING: The lining is constructed very much like the skirt. Most patterns do not include separate pattern pieces for a skirt lining; therefore, cut your lining from the skirt pattern pieces, allowing the same width seam allowances. To reduce bulk in a gathered or pleated skirt, cut your lining from a straight or A-line skirt pattern. Then baste the lining together as for the skirt, following the same alterations and leaving the appropriate seam open for the zipper. Pin lining to the skirt at the upper edge, wrong sides together; ease skirt to fit lining if necessary. Pin and baste attached skirt and lining to the waistline stay as before (1).

Important fitting checkpoint: Try on skirt and lining, positioning them correctly. Lining should hang free of skirt without bubbles or wrinkles in lining, or binding, or pulling in skirt. As with all circumferences, the outer layer (skirt) should be slightly larger than the inner layer (lining) for both layers to work together. Make any alterations by changing each seam minutely. A real problem will occur if the lining is considerably smaller than the skirt; it will be uncomfortable, the lining will wear out before the skirt due to strain, and you will not be able to complete the lining satisfactorily. When you have eliminated all fitting problems, stitch lining sections together.

Determine at this time whether you will hem your skirt and lining together or separately. If you are using a soft lining fabric, the two should be hemmed together; if you are using a crisp lining, they may be hemmed either way. The seam allowances will need to be finished only if your fabric is exceptionally ravelly or the hems are done separately.

Pin the skirt and lining together along the upper edge, slipstitch lining to zipper tape, and baste upper edges together. Pin hems to an approximate length, making the lining ½″ shorter than skirt (2). The skirt hems should not be completed until you are prepared to sew the hem of the jacket or coat. The two hems must be in proportion to one another if you wish to achieve the most attractive results.

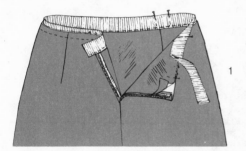 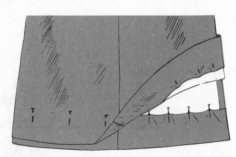

WAISTBAND: The final step is to attach the waistband. This permanently joins the skirt and lining at the waist. Use the waistband construction most suitable to your fabric (pages 307 and 308), adjusting it to your measurement. For a thick or bulky fabric, you may have to allow up to ½″ more in the circumference of the waistband. Attach waistband and fasten with hooks and eyes.

Tailoring Challenge: Jacket or Coat

The construction of a jacket or coat is the same in most cases; exceptions will be noted as they occur.

Construction Procedure

The first step is to construct and fit the *shell* of your garment, which consists of the front and back pieces only. Follow same procedure as for the skirt: prepare and attach underlining, baste and press darts, add ease or gathering threads by hand, and pin or baste sections together. Flatten seams with fingertips or creaser.

Important fitting checkpoint: Try on the garment shell over the skirt. Match the center front markings and pin. Position it correctly on your body. After fitting, transfer any new seamlines, dart lines, etc., to underlining. Stitch and press any darts and seams that were not changed. Baste along any new construction lines and flatten seams. Try garment shell on again with the skirt to check adjustments. Remember to allow enough room in a jacket for movement over a blouse or dress, and enough in a coat for over a jacket.

Stitch the shell together permanently, using your pattern's sewing guide for basic construction procedures. Press any remaining darts and seams.

BOUND BUTTONHOLES: To select the type of buttonhole you prefer, refer to the buttonhole section, pages 313 to 320, and read thoroughly. Respace buttonhole markings evenly if you have made any alterations. For man-tailored garments, you may wish to make corded keyhole buttonholes just before completing the garment.

Interfacing for Shaping

The degree of built-in shaping that highlights the tailored garment is dependent upon the proper use of interfacing. It must support the shape and withstand numerous wearings and cleanings without overwhelming the fabric's draping qualities. Interfacing also protects your fashion fabric from ridges being formed at seam allowances and darts during cleaning and pressing. If you are in doubt as to the appropriate weight and type of interfacing for your fabric, refer to the chart on pages 163 to 167.

Lighter-weight interfacings, which have relatively little bulk, can be sewn into the garment seams, and their seam allowances trimmed away close to the stitching.

Heavier-weight interfacings, including hair canvases, are more rigid and should not be caught into the garment seams. Instead, all of the seam allowances except for the armhole are cut off before the interfacing is applied. Then the interfacing is catchstitched to the garment along the seamlines. The interfacing is stitched into the armhole seam, which is not pressed open, to give further support to the shoulder area. The following tailoring techniques will illustrate this catchstitch procedure.

ADAPTING PIECES: Interfacing is necessary for support around the neck, shoulder, front, and armhole edges. If interfacing pattern pieces are not available, you will need to adapt your existing pattern pieces. Except for armholes, eliminate all seam allowances, including style seaming details. Pin all front pattern pieces together to act as a unit. To draw your interfacing pattern, use a piece of tissue paper large enough to cover the desired interfaced area. Make the inner shaped edge ½″ wider than the width of the front facing and draw a curved line from it across front, ending 2″ below armhole seamline (1). For the back section, pin the pattern pieces together. Place tissue paper over them and draw pattern, starting 2″ below the armhole and making it about 5″ deep in the center back (2).

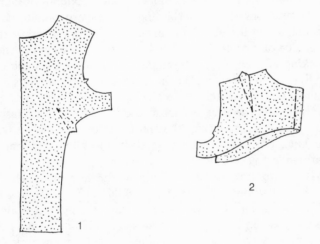

DARTS: There are three ways to make darts in interfacing. The first two are to be used when darts do not correspond exactly to the garment darts. (They can also be used for lightweight interfacing when darts do correspond.) The third is best suited for darts that do correspond to those of the garment.

First method: trim along dart lines (1). Bring cut edges together, center a strip of underlining or ribbon seam binding over the edges, and stitch securely (2).

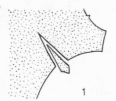
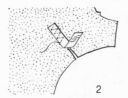

Second method: slash through the center of dart lines (3). Lap edges, matching dart lines, and stitch together; securely reinforce the point with additional stitches (4).

Third method: simply trim darts away along dart lines (5). Pin interfacing to garment and pull garment dart through cut edges; catchstitch edges to underlining (6).

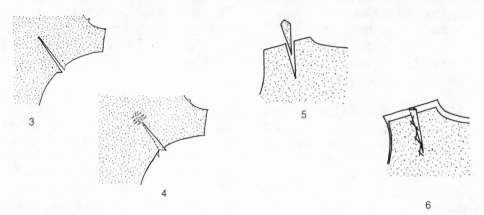

HAND STITCHES FOR TAILORED GARMENTS:
HAND STITCHES FOR TAILORED GARMENTS: In order to ensure that all layers of fabric will be stabilized, you will need to master two hand stitches. The firmness built in by these stitches will enable the layers to move as one through repeated wearing and dry cleaning. Both are variations of diagonal basting. Use a sharp needle and matching thread, coating a single unknotted thread with beeswax to eliminate possible snarls. Secure the thread end at the edge of the interfacing with backstitches; work in direction of the grain.

Diagonal Tacking is used to attach interfacing to the underlining only. Take a tiny horizontal stitch through interfacing, catching a thread or two of underlining; repeat directly below, placing stitches approximately ¾″ to 1½″ apart and forming a diagonal stitch on the interfacing side. Keep stitches long and loose and do not catch the fashion fabric as you sew (1). Cover surface of interfacing, shaping fabric as you sew to retain the garment contour. If you have not used underlining, omit this stitch and catchstitch edges of interfacing to garment along seamlines.

Padstitching is used to mold and control undercollars and lapels (whether underlined or not) by actually sewing in the shape. It is done exactly like diagonal tacking except that you sew through all layers, catching only a thread or two of the fashion fabric, and holding the fabric in the desired position as you sew. Make stitches ¼″ to ½″ apart (2). Practice first on scraps of your fabric layers to get the feel of manipulating your fabric.

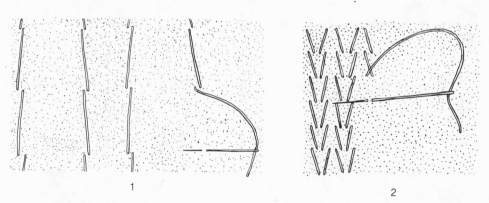

ATTACHING INTERFACING: You must first make sure the interfacing and garment shell will relate well to one another. Pin the two layers together, placing front, neck, and side edges along seamlines, and match armhole seamlines. Pin the interfacing to the garment and then baste shell along the center markings or seams only.

Important fitting checkpoint: Try on garment shell. If bubbles or ridges form in either interfacing or shell, they are not molding as one. If so, remove pins. With the right side of your shell uppermost, place both layers over a rounded surface similar to your body contour. Smooth the shell over the interfacing (with the grain as you did for the underlining), and pin where it falls inside the seamlines. Repin along foldlines and raw edges. Also make sure your lapels will roll smoothly; turn interfacing to outside along proposed roll, and pin along roll line and edges of interfacing as it falls in place (1). The interfacing should now relate to your garment shell and your body contour.

After any necessary adjustments and repinning, pin the interfacing securely on the inside. Examine interfacing edges along the seamline. They should be a scant ⅛'' short of the seamline. If necessary, trim interfacing so it will not bubble when seams are pressed open or encased.

Baste interfacing to front along all edges. Sew it to the underlining along hemlines and any foldlines with long running stitches, and along the inner curved edge with catchstitches Cut out rectangular openings in the interfacing exactly behind each buttonhole. Pull raw edges of bound buttonholes through the cut openings in the interfacing(1).

Now attach the front interfacing to your underlining with diagonal tacking. If you are not using underlining, sew the interfacing edges to the seamlines with catchstitches and along the foldlines and hemlines with long running stitches (2).

For back interfacing, cut away shoulder darts along the stitching lines. Pull garment dart through cut edges; catchstitch edges to underlining along dart seamline. Baste neck, shoulder, and side edges in place and baste armhole edges together, retaining the garment's shape as you work. Catchstitch sides. Attach interfacing to underlining with diagonal tacking, or catchstitch the edges to the seamlines as you did for the front interfacing (3).

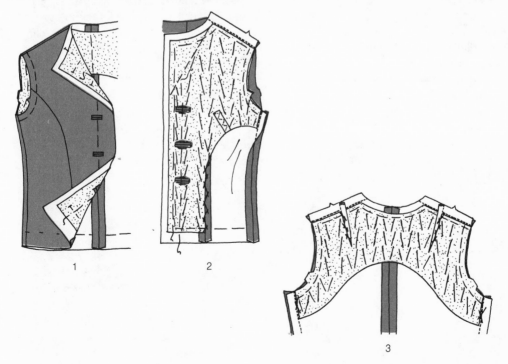

1   2

3

Important fitting checkpoint: Try on your garment shell and evaluate your work so far. If you notice a slight droop around the back of the armhole between the seam and shoulder blade or a slight indentation on the front between the armhole seamline and the apex of the bust, you need padding to get that impeccably tailored look.

TAILOR'S PADDING: Cut another layer of interfacing the width of the shoulder seamline less ½", using armhole shape on one edge and a curved shape on the remaining edges to extend to ½" beyond the end of the problem area. Then cut a piece of lamb's wool or heavy cotton flannel ½" less than the interfacing piece on all edges. To attach padding to garment back, sew lamb's wool to interfacing with long running stitches along all edges. Use diagonal tacking to hold the center area in place. Now place the additional interfacing layer over the lamb's wool and attach it to the main interfacing in same way (1). Attach the padding to the garment front section in the same manner (2).

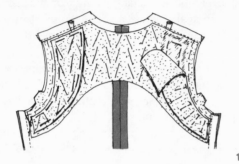

1

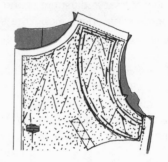

2

Undercollar and Lapels

Since many collar styles can be used on a tailored garment, turn to the collar section and review the introduction and the construction most closely related to your garment.

INTERFACING: To prepare interfacing for collar, trim away all seam allowances except the center back seam, if applicable (1). The interfacing sections can be joined in two ways for the center back seam. For the first method, you can lap the ends, matching seamlines, and stitch; trim both seam allowances close to stitching (2). For the second method, trim away center back seam allowances. Match edges, place a strip of underlining or seam binding over them, and stitch securely (3).

Then center the interfacing over the undercollar between the outer seamlines. Pin in place *along the neck seamline.* Shape the pieces as they will be worn. Make sure the interfacing is a scant ⅛" short of the seamline. If not, trim the interfacing so it will not bubble later when seams are pressed open or encased (4). Catchstitch the edges to the undercollar. Staystitch the neck edge if you haven't already done so.

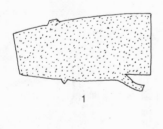

1

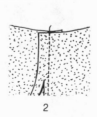

2

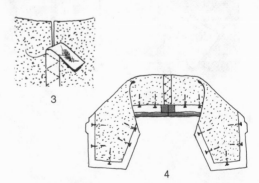

3

4

FIT AND SHAPE: Lap and pin undercollar neck edge over garment neck edge; match seamlines and markings. (If extended facings are to be used, they should be turned back at foldline, wrong sides together, and basted along neck edge at this time.) Baste collar in place, clipping the neck edge where necessary to lay flat.

Important fitting checkpoint: Try on garment or put it on a dress form to establish roll on collar and lapels. Lap and pin right front over left, matching centers and buttonhole markings. Begin rolling lapels at top buttonhole markings. The collar should lay as close to the neck as shown on the pattern illustration without riding high or low. The roll should be smooth, even, and unbroken from front to back. Be sure points of collar and lapels lie symmetrically against the garment.

The outer seamline of the collar should cover the back neck seamline. Adjust collar at the neck seamline until all features are correct. Transfer any seamline adjustments to both collar and lapels. Pin along roll line on both collar and lapels. This roll is very important in determining the finished shape. Thread-trace roll lines on collar and lapels and remove collar.

STABILIZE THE ROLL: Pin the undercollar to a tailor's ham. Using steam, hold iron over roll, never resting it on the fabric. Work from center back to center front, shaping each half separately but identically along your established roll. Never press the roll into a crease; use your finger to shape the roll. Allow undercollar to dry thoroughly. Now shape lapels in the same manner and allow to dry.

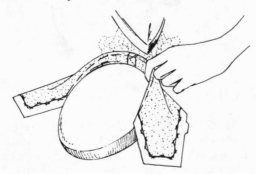

PADSTITCH UNDERCOLLAR: The area between the neck seamline and the roll line (called the *stand*) must have small padstitches placed close together—¼'' or less—to stabilize the stand. Hold the undercollar over your finger in the shaped position. Padstitch heavily from the neck edge to the thread-traced roll line; work along either the straight or crosswise grain (1). When you have completed the stand area, use larger stitches (about ¾'' apart) to padstitch the remainder of the undercollar (2).

To blend the pad stitches into the undercollar, it must be pressed carefully. With the fashion fabric side up, press the outer curved area, placing a damp press cloth over the fabric. Press to the roll only (3). Do the same along the stand, always retaining the roll, and allow to dry thoroughly.

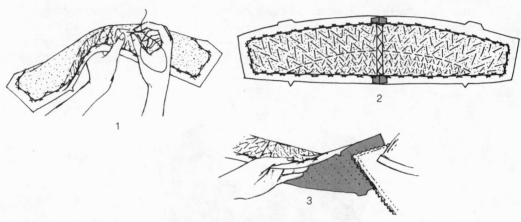

PADSTITCH LAPELS: Start at roll line and fill in area between thread tracing and seamlines, spacing stitches about ½'' apart. Press the lapel area as for the undercollar and allow to dry.

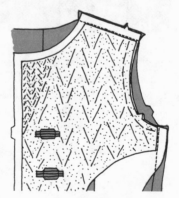

Taping for Stability

According to traditional tailoring techniques, you should tape edges that will receive strain during wear and cleaning. Tape is especially needed along the front edge of your garment, around the neck seam, and on lapels because these areas have a tendency to pull or stretch out of shape. You may wish to tape other areas that might "give" with wear, such as shoulder or armhole seams, and foldlines of a seam pocket or vent openings.

Ribbon seam binding lends itself well to taping: it is thin, firmly woven, and usually preshrunk. Cotton twill tape, ¼'' wide, is often used; be sure it has been preshrunk.

To apply seam binding, place it ⅛'' over seamline (or foldline for an extended facing) with the larger portion within the garment area. This automatically grades the binding when the seam is completed. Baste the edge that will be caught in the seam and sew the inner edge to the interfacing with diagonal tacking. Make the stitches about ½'' apart and catch a few threads of the interfacing with each stitch (1). Twill tape is applied in the same manner. Place one edge over the seamline just enough to be caught in the seam (2).

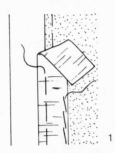

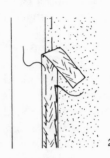

Begin by placing the tape along the front shoulder edge, extending it slightly beyond neck and armhole seamlines. Sew it to the seam along stitching with catchstitches. Sew the inner edge to the interfacing with diagonal tacking. Then tape front edges, extending tape slightly beyond the neck seamline and hemline. For lapel area, the tape must be placed from the shoulder seamlines to the point where the lapel begins to roll; placing tape just along roll line of lapel will not give enough support. Secure both edges to interfacing with diagonal tacking (3).

To tape foldlines, position tape the same as for a seamline; secure both edges by sewing it to interfacing along foldline with long running stitches and along the remaining edge with diagonal tacking.

To tape curved edges such as neck and armholes, seam binding is the best choice. Twill tape will add bulk to the seam, as it tends to roll when stitched in a curved seam. Make scant ¼'' clips at even intervals, place unclipped edge ⅛'' over seamline, and baste. Sew clipped edges to interfacing with long diagonal tacking stitches, placing the long stitch over the clipped edges (4). After mastering the techniques of taping, you may want to try a quicker method. If you are sure that your garment fits well, you may eliminate some handwork by machine-stitching tape to the interfacing before it is attached to your garment. Make sure the tape extends a generous ⅛'' beyond the trimmed edge of the interfacing so the interfacing will not catch in the seam.

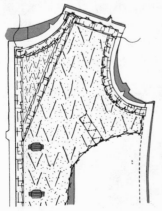

Collar and Facings

When you have completed taping, return to your collar. First pin undercollar to garment once again and check for all small, last-minute adjustments that may be needed.

PREPARE UPPER COLLAR: The upper collar will need additional handling to make sure it is large enough to hide the outer seam when the collar is completed. Make a minute tuck at the center of upper collar neck seamline, letting it taper to nothing at other edge. When released, it will automatically allow just enough fabric for you to favor the outer edge easily so any seams will fall on the undercollar side. Then pin upper collar to undercollar along neck edge, matching seamlines (1). Now shape collar as it will be worn with upper collar on top. Pin outer edges in place as they fall. To baste upper and undercollar together, follow seamline you thread traced on the undercollar previously (page 427). This maneuver will result in narrower seam allowances on your upper collar (2).

Stitch the collar sections together from the undercollar side, stitching along the thread-traced seamline. Use small stitches at points and end stitching ⅝″ from neck edge. Trim, grade, and notch or clip seams as needed. Press seams open on point presser for easier turning. See Seams at Finished Edges on page 346 of the pressing section. Turn the collar and tailor-baste along the outer edges, using silk thread. Favor the upper collar at its outer edges so that the seam is on the undercollar side as you baste (3).

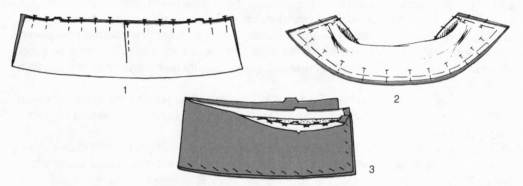

Press, using a damp press cloth to create a lot of steam. Then use a pounder or clapper to shape the edge to the desired effect (crisp or slightly rolled, depending on the style of your garment). Work with your fingers and the pounder to avoid shine or overpressing and allow to dry thoroughly. Staystitch the neck edges of the garment and facing pieces if you haven't already done so.

ATTACH COLLAR AND FACING: Pin undercollar to garment between markings (where collar ends and lapels begin). Baste, clipping garment seam allowance as necessary, and then stitch. Stitch neck and front facings together; press. Clipping facing seam allowance as necessary, pin, baste, and stitch upper collar to facing between markings

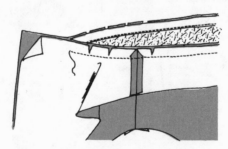

Make a minute pin tuck on lapel/facing, so you will have enough fabric to favor the lapel seam when garment is turned to right side (raw edges will not be even at this point). Pin the facing to the garment (1).

Baste facing to garment, following garment seamlines. Start stitching from the garment side where garment meets collar in order to eliminate bubbles that sometimes occur where the collar meets the lapels. (For bulky or heavy fabrics you may not be able to start exactly at the markings; leave thread ends long enough that you can complete that area by hand later.) Reinforce points and continue around lapel/facing. Clip seam at end of collar to stitching. Trim and grade lapel facing seams as needed. Trim only upper collar and facing neck seam, leaving the garment and undercollar seam ⅝". Clip both neck seams (2).

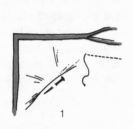

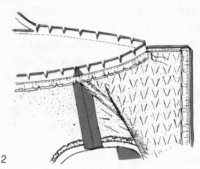

Press facing seams and both collar neck seams open on a point presser. Turn facing. Using silk thread, tailor-baste facing edges for pressing to within 5" to 6" of lower edge. Favor the lapels at the outer edge so the seam is on the undercollar and garment side; below the point where the lapel begins to roll, favor the garment so the seam is on the facing side. Press these edges with a damp press cloth, using a pounder to achieve the desired effect. Retain basting.

Try on jacket and reestablish roll. Remove jacket and pin about ¾" above the neck seam to hold the layers in place. Lift up facing and sew the neck seams together with long, loose stitches in a zigzag pattern, being very careful *not to force the seams together* if they don't meet. This holds the upper collar in place so it will not twist or pull during wearing or cleaning. Retain pins in facing.

At this time you should decide how to finish the underside of the bound buttonholes. The couture method, page 448, must be done at this time. The conventional methods, page 316, can be done before the buttons are attached. Sew inner edge of facing in place with long running stitches to within 4" to 6" of lower edge.

Pockets, Flaps, and Welts

Your most important consideration will be placement. Remember to reposition any pocket, flap, or welt placement lines if you have altered your pattern. There is nothing more frustrating than to end up with a beautifully made pocket that is too close to the jacket hem to be usable because the hem had to be sewn over it.

Pockets can be classified into two groups—utilitarian and decorative. Utilitarian pockets should be at a comfortable height for use, while decorative pockets should be placed as featured in the design. Both should add a balanced look to the total silhouette. To make sure that the pocket, flap, or welt placement is right for your garment, take the exposed portion and turn in the seam allowances along the seamline to simulate the finished item. Pin up garment hem along proposed hemline, then pin pockets, flaps, or welts to garment at placement lines. Try on garment (include skirt with jacket) and check position.

Experiment with the placement and size until you achieve the desired effect. Carefully analyze the position of the pockets, flaps, or welts in relation to the center front marking, and be sure they end an equal distance from the center marking and the lower edge of the garment. Transfer any necessary adjustments to the garment and individual pieces. You are then ready to construct and apply your pockets, flaps, or welts; refer to the instructions on pages 294 to 303 and choose the method that best suits your needs.

Sleeves

Tailored sleeves are basically the same as any other sleeve. The two-piece set-in sleeve is considered the classic tailored sleeve when its hem is interfaced appropriately to retain the shape. Since a poorly executed set-in sleeve will mar the appearance of a tailored garment, it would be wise to take the time right now to review all sections that will help you get a perfectly fitting sleeve. Then you will be able to insert your sleeve quickly, neatly, and easily. Turn to pages 92 to 95, 123 and 124, and 273 to 279.

Since the major alterations have already been done, your problem now will be adapting the fabric to your needs. Add the sleeve cap ease threads, using the stitch length appropriate for the fabric, and break the stitching at the seam so that you do not easestitch over the seam allowances. For extremely heavy fabric, add the ease threads by hand. Pull up ease threads the desired amount and secure them for fitting. Do not shrink the sleeve cap at this time. Baste the sleeve seams along the seamline, right sides together, and press seams open with fingertips or lightly with an iron so you do not leave an impression. Then baste the sleeve in the armhole.

Important fitting checkpoint: Try on garment with skirt to evaluate the sleeve lengths with the sleeve hems pinned in place. Allow enough room in a jacket sleeve to move freely over a long dress sleeve. Coat sleeves should be full enough to fit over a jacket sleeve. Place shoulder pads on shoulders if the sleeve needs support. Check sleeve lengths again. Stylized sleeve hems require careful planning ***before*** cutting so you will have only minute adjustments.

Check grainlines. Make any necessary adjustments and mark fabrics. Remove sleeve. To support heavy fabrics or to help retain the shape for loosely woven fabrics, apply tape to seams before stitching. If sleeve has a plain hem, stitch seams; press open, using sleeve board. If the sleeve has a vent opening or other stylized hem, stitch the seams necessary to complete hem.

SLEEVE HEMS: Interfacing applied correctly will protect your fabric so the imprints of hem and seam allowances will not show through to the outside during wearing, cleaning, or pressing. Choose an appropriate interfacing that will hold the curved line of the sleeve hem without "breaking."

Cut bias strips of interfacing equal in length to the circumference of the hem (allow additional fabric for lapping ends on a continuous sleeve hem) and equal in width to the depth of hem plus 1⅜".

Place one edge of interfacing ⅝" below hemline in hem area with the greater portion on the garment side; pin. For heavy or bulky fabrics, slash through interfacing along seamlines and tuck ends under seam allowances to prevent any imprint of the seam allowances. Sew interfacing to underlining along hemline with long running stitches and along the upper edge and ends with long catchstitches. (1).

For hems that will be topstitched, cut interfacing ¾" wider than the hem depth and place one edge along the hemline. Baste hemline and foldline edges in place; catchstitch all other edges.

If you are not using underlining, the interfacing should still be attached in the same manner; be careful to catch only a thread of your fashion fabric so the stitches will not show on the right side of the fabric.

For a vent opening, cut a strip of straight-grain interfacing the length of opening plus ⅝" to extend beyond hemline, and wide enough to extend ½" beyond the end of the buttonhole on one side and ⅝" beyond foldline on the other. Place interfacing over vent buttonhole markings with one edge and end extending over foldline and hemline. Sew it to underlining along foldline and hemline with long running stitches and along upper end and edge with long catchstitches. Make bound buttonholes. (Make buttonholes through only the lightest weight interfacing; otherwise, apply interfacing after buttonholes are made.)

When interfacing is completed, pin hem in place and baste close to fold. (For a vent opening, the layers need to be graded to avoid ridges where several edges fall in the same place.) Trim away ⅝" from hem allowance edge of vent facing, ending at foldline. Sew hem to interfacing with long running stitches (2). For heavy or bulky fabric, blindstitch the hem in place. Stitch any remaining seams as directed in sewing guide; press. Do the same for the vent opening (3). Press hem over a sleeve board, using pounder or clapper and steam to get the desired edge.

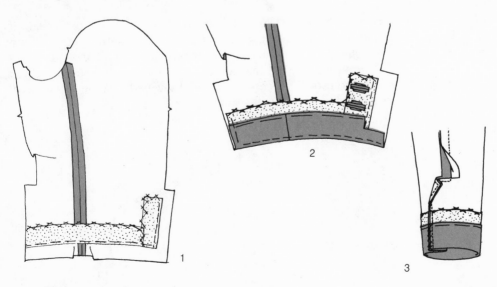

INSERT SLEEVE: Pin sleeve to garment. Adjust ease and baste. ***Important fitting checkpoint:*** Check position of armhole seam and ease distribution. Remove sleeve and shrink out fullness. Rebaste sleeve into armhole and then stitch. Between notches, add a second row of stitching over the first for reinforcement. Trim seam allowance to ¼″ between notches.

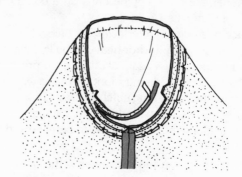

SLEEVE HEADING: This is used to support the weight of the sleeve cap fabric so it will not collapse. For padding, cut one bias rectangle of lamb's wool, polyester fleece, or heavy flannel, 3″ wide and 4″ to 6″ long for each armhole. Make a 1″ fold on one long edge. Slipstitch folded edge of padding along seam at cap of sleeve.

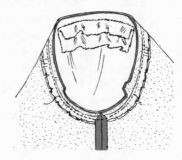

SHOULDER PADS: Use these to help maintain the shape of the shoulder line if needed. Be careful not to use too thick a pad, or it will distort the natural shape of the garment. Strive for a soft, fluid line rather than a rigid, raised shoulder. Try on jacket for exact pad placement. Pin pad securely on one side of the seam from the outside. Open out any facings at shoulders to avoid unnecessary bulk and sew pads to seam allowances. For directions on making shoulder pads, see the Couture section page 447.

Final Fitting

Now it is time to determine the hem lengths for all the pieces of your tailored garment to ensure they are in proportion to one another. For help when measuring the hems, refer to page 338.

Important fitting checkpoint: Try on garment and skirt with the hems pinned in place. Wear the appropriate undergarments, shoes, and accessories. Lap fronts, matching centers, and pin. Be sure garments drape naturally and comfortably. Mark any necessary hem adjustments with thread tracing.

The right front must lap over the left front, concealing its lower edge. The inner folds of pleats should not show, nor should the underlap of a vent. Check your button placement markings once more for accuracy. Do you need a strategically placed snap, hook, or inner button to support the left front? Adjust any area that may need a final pinch of fabric removed or let out a bit. It is now the time to complete your hems.

Hems, Vents, and Pleats

You have already hemmed your sleeve successfully, so you are well on the way to finishing all of your hemming details. Work with the bulk of your garment on a table to avoid unnecessary wrinkles as you hem. Since you have already chosen the interfacing fabric for the sleeve hem, you should use the same type for the jacket hem.

Cut bias strips for the circumference of the hem and 1⅜" wider than the hem. Open out facings. Pin interfacing to garment with one edge ⅝" below hemline and lap ends over front interfacing. Trim and catchstitch ends to front interfacing. Then attach to garment hem as for sleeves (1).

For heavy or bulky fabrics, slash strip where it falls over seams and tuck edges under seam allowances. For a shaped or eased hem, preshape interfacing to fit contour of garment before applying.

Turn up garment along hemline and baste close to the fold; use silk thread (2). If necessary, add ease thread to hem edge before pinning it to interfacing.

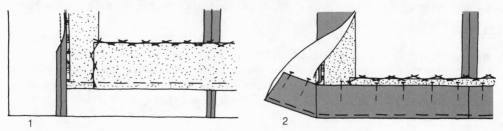

SMOOTH CORNERS: There are several ways to handle corners; select the one best suited for your fabric, design, and individual needs. The first, while probably the quickest and most popular method because the garment hem **can be lengthened** at a later time if necessary, does not give the best results for bulky fabrics. Prepare the hem as on previous page. The facing hem should taper up slightly, so it will not show on the outside. Trim ⅝″ away from end of hem between top and basting. Then trim ⅝″ from top of hem to seam or foldline. Sew the hem to the interfacing with long running stitches or blindstitch in place for bulky fabrics (1). Press the hem, using steam and pounder or clapper to get the desired edge.

The completion of this type of corner depends upon your fabric. For lightweight fabrics, make a ¼″ clip at the top of the hem and turn it in below the clip; pin (2). Slipstitch the facing below the clip and across the lower edge (3). For heavier fabrics, turn back the facing at the lower edge; blindstitch loosely to hem (4). Sew the raw edge of the facing securely to hem with hemming stitches (5). For both, sew remainder of facing in place above hem. Press, being careful to avoid shine on your fabric.

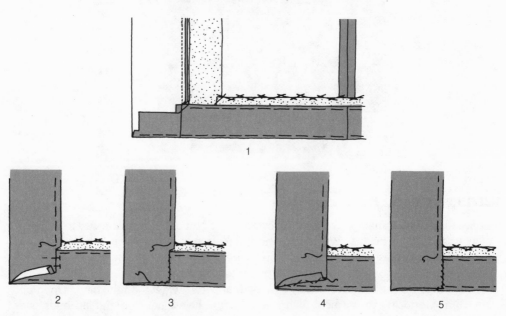

This alternate method will give you a flatter hem for bulky fabrics, but the hem **cannot be lengthened** later. Prepare hem as on previous page. Mark where facing edge will fall on hem. Open out facing. This method requires staggered trimming. First trim facing hem to ⅝″, ending at seam or foldline. Then measure ½″ from the marking toward the facing, and slash hem at this point to within 1″ of hemline. From this point, trim across hem to seam or foldline. Clip alongside seam to first trimming line. Secure the trimmed edges with long, loose catchstitches (6). Sew hem in place and press, using steam and pounder or clapper to get desired edge. Turn facing to inside; press. Slipstitch lower edge together (7). Finish raw edge of facing with hemming stitch; press (8).

Excess fabric or extremely curved hems may be a problem also. Some openings work well with mitered corners, page 234. For handling an extremely curved hem, see page 451 of the couture technique section.

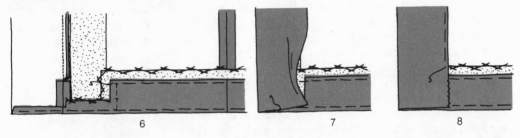

6   7   8

VENT or **PLEAT OPENINGS:** Jacket and coat vents or pleats differ only in length from those found in a sleeve hem. End the interfacing at the seamlines or extend it ⅝″ beyond the foldlines, interfacing the outer layer the same as you would the hem. Be sure to support the foldlines with tape to stay the fabric (1). Use your sewing guide for the basic construction. Choose the corner finish appropriate for your fabric from the opposite page.

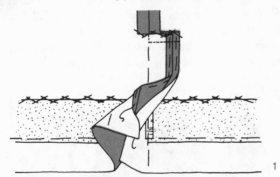

1

SKIRT HEM: If you are making a skirt as part of an ensemble, complete the hem and the lining hem at the same time as the jacket.

An Ultimate Pressing

Place the garment on a dress form or a well-padded hanger suspended from a wire so you can work around it. Look your garment over well—front, back, sleeves, collar, and pockets. Are there any creases or wrinkles that may need to be eliminated? Remember, once you have attached the lining there is little you can do to press some areas well. Use your press mitt and press cloth, or use the dress form as a pressing aid. Allow your garment to dry thoroughly on the dress form or hanger with the garment hanging free and the openings pinned in the proper position. Pad sleeves, collars, or other areas with tissue paper to help retain their shape.

Lining as a Finale

Lining a garment is the final construction step in tailoring. Lining fabric should complement fashion fabric in weight, wearability, and cleaning requirements. Be sure interior construction does not show through the lining. A smooth-fitting lining is absolutely essential for professional results and will greatly influence the total look.

The lining is the last layer to be applied. It demands the same careful attention to construction and detail as your actual garment shell. A lined garment must slide easily over another garment. Pleats and wearing ease should be placed where the garment must give with body movement at center back, above and below waistline, bust area, hem edges of sleeves, and hem of garment. Center back pleat should be ½" to 1" deep from neck to hem. Adjust the pattern before cutting to allow for pleats or wearing ease if necessary. If warmth is a factor in the garment you are making, refer to Interlining, page 442, before you stitch the lining together.

CONSTRUCTION: Baste darts and seams together. Make the same seam adjustments as you did for your garment. Press seams, darts, and pleats with fingers or crease.

Slip lining into garment, wrong sides together. Lap lining over facings and pin or baste, matching seamlines around front, shoulder, neck, and armholes.

Important fitting checkpoint: Try on and test lining to make sure it does not interfere with the garment. Look for excessive wrinkles. The inner circumference of your lining should be just like the inner measurements of a cylinder, smooth and slightly smaller than the outside. Adjust lining, fitting as necessary. Mark any adjustments. Stitch only underarm bust darts. All waistline or shoulder darts, pleats, and tucks should be basted first, then anchored in place from right side of fabric with cross-stitches through all thicknesses. Place cross-stitches at neck, waist, and lower edges of back pleats. Stitch all major seams except shoulder seams. Press, using steam sparingly. Staystitch front, back shoulder, and neck edges, and across underarm between the notches. Turn in front, back shoulder, and neck edges along seamline. Baste, clipping or notching seam allowances so they will lie flat. Do not press edges.

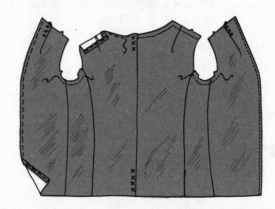

INSERTION: Work from center back to front opening edges. Pin lining to garment, matching center back. Then, matching any back seams first, sew the seam allowances together loosely by hand with long running stitches, ending the sewing 6" from lower edge. Sew any side or side front seam allowances together in the same manner. Now pin armhole, front shoulder, and front edges of lining in place. Sew front shoulders to back seam allowance with long running stitches (1). Slipstitch front turned-in edge to facing, ending 4″ to 6″ from lower edge. Place stitches about ⅛″ apart and secure with backstitches at 3″ to 4″ intervals. Next, pin back shoulder and neck edges in place and slipstitch them to front lining at shoulders and to the back neck facing. Baste armhole edges together alongside seamline in seam allowance. Clip underarm of lining between notches every ½″ (2). For vent openings, attach lining as directed on sewing guide.

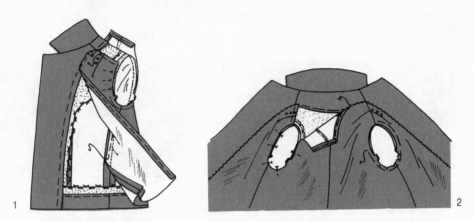

In man-tailored garments, the garment sleeves may not be sewn into the armholes until after this phase of the lining is completed. Then sleeve is sewn into armhole through all thicknesses. The sleeve lining is completed in the regular way.

Lining Hem

Now that the lining shell has been carefully sewn in place along facing and shoulder edges, you have only the lining hem to do. If you follow carefully the methods of handling your lining hem, you will have a better-fitting garment and the lining will not overwhelm the fashion fabric, causing pulling or distortion at the hem edges.

ANCHOR LINING: Work with garment on a dress form or on a padded hanger attached to a wire suspended from ceiling so you can work around the garment. This way the lining will drape well with the garment. From the outside, pin the lining to the garment 4″ to 8″ above hem, placing pins at right angles and at 2″ to 3″ intervals.

ATTACHED HEM: Begin by trimming the lining even with garment edge (1). Then add an ease thread ¼" from raw edge of the lining if the hem requires it. On the outside, make a ¼" wide tuck across the lining below the pin line, placing the pins parallel to the fold. Now turn in the raw edge ¼" and pin to hem where it falls (2). Slipstitch entire lower edge of lining to garment hem.

Remove pins from tuck. The lining will now smoothly fall down over the hem, forming a soft fold (3). Steam and pat into place with pounder. This fold allows for body movement and stretching during wearing without putting strain on garment hem. Slipstitch remaining turned-in-edges of lining to facings or any vent opening, continuing to edge of fold (4).

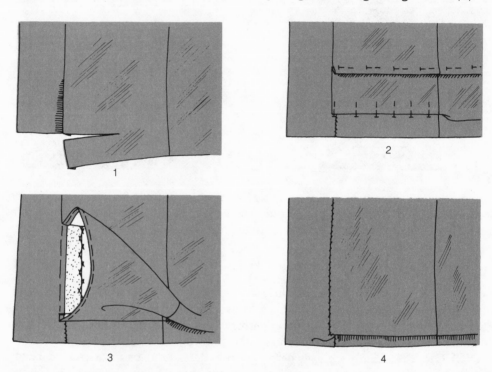

FREE HANGING HEM: Pin lower edges of garment and lining together as shown. Then turn up lining hem so the lining is ½" shorter than the garment and baste close to the fold. Now measure the depth of the lining hem and trim evenly if necessary. Use appropriate finish and method to complete lining hem. Press lightly (1). Slipstitch remaining turned-in lining edges to facing and hem or any vent openings (2). Sew lining hem to garment hem with 1" French tacks at seams (3).

Some garments will require a combination of these two methods of hemming a lining, such as a coat with a full pleat in the back. The front of the lining would be attached and the back would hang free to allow the pleat to drape naturally.

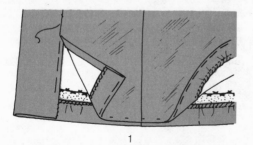

Sleeve Lining

This step will require additional molding. Baste seams and darts and adjust ease if necessary. Finger press seams. Wrong sides together, baste lining sleeves into armhole of garment lining along seamline, lapping edges and adjusting sleeve cap ease.

Important fitting checkpoint: Try on garment. Check fit of sleeve lining. Examine garment sleeve for wrinkles or bubbles. Shape sleeve cap lining inside garment. Mark adjustments on cap and seams; baste.

Stitch basted sleeve lining sections together and press seams open. Add new ease threads if sleeve cap was adjusted. Shrink out excess ease now, since this will be the last time you should press this part of the garment. Staystitch underarm between notches. Turn in armhole along seamline and baste; clip to stitching, if necessary, so underarm seam allowance will lie flat.

With wrong sides together, sew lining seam allowances to garment seam allowances with long, loose running stitches, starting and ending 4″ from each end (1). Turn lining back over garment sleeve (2). Pin sleeve in armhole, matching seamlines and markings. Adjust ease and slipstitch, placing stitches ⅛″ apart and backstitching at 1″ intervals (3).

With garment on dress form or padded hanger, complete sleeve lining hem. Anchor hem first with pins as you did for the garment and then complete, using the attached hem method on page 440. You need the fold at the lower edge of the lining hem for movement and strain the same as you do in a garment hem (4).

Press all lining edges, using a light touch. Steam front and neck edges, patting lightly. Do the same for the fold formed at lower edge of an attached lining.

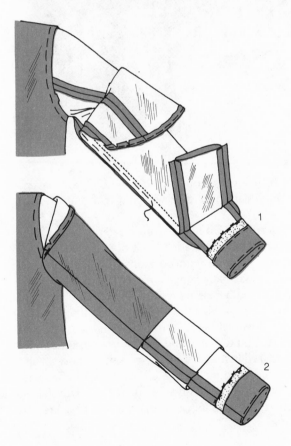

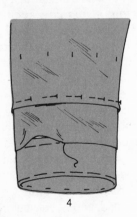

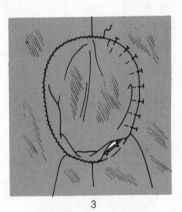

Interlining

A fourth layer of fabric called interlining can be added to your garment for warmth. For information about types and selection of interlinings, see page 159. Be sure to take interlining into consideration when fitting your garment, as it will use up needed wearing ease.

The easiest way to interline is to sew it as one with the lining. Cut interlining from lining pieces, omitting the back pleat. Cross-stitch the lining back pleat in place. Then baste the interlining and lining pieces together. Stitch darts and seams; slash darts and press open; trim interlining close to stitching. After staystitching front, shoulder, and neck edges, trim away interlining close to stitching. Attach the lining in the usual manner(1).

Final Touches

Now is the time to put all the small finishing touches on your garment. If you haven't already done so, finish the back of your bound buttonholes or add your machine or hand-worked buttonholes and attach your buttons.

Important fitting checkpoint: Try on garment. Does the front opening need a little support? Perhaps you will need a covered snap to hold the left front of a double-breasted garment in place(2). Check your convertible collar in both positions. To hold the lapel closed on a cold day, add a tiny thread eye on one lapel edge and a nearly invisible covered hook under the collar (3). Give the entire garment a detailed examination to double-check your workmanship. Did you miss a basting thread peeking out from a seam? If so, remove it with tweezers. You now have a garment which will retain through many cleanings and wearings the image you so carefully created. You will also find that as you become more experienced, many of the procedures emphasized in this chapter will become almost second nature to you. Some steps along the way can even be eliminated; once you know what changes needed to be made to fit your first tailored item, these changes can be transferred to each succeeding garment. Congratulations are definitely in order, for you have created a one-of-a-kind, impeccably tailored garment.

9

The Custom
Touch

Couture Techniques

What transforms a dress into The Dress, immediately marks it with true quality and exquisite taste? Fashion is truly a splendid example of the axiom, "little things make a difference," for it is the little, but far from insignificant, finishing techniques known and followed by the world's most famous designers that will make the transformation work for you. This collection of couture techniques has been gathered for you from the greatest European and American houses of haute couture. They are dedicated to you, the Vogue woman, who delights in making and wearing clothes finished with the infinite touches of a couturier. They are the simple yet irresistible means of putting your signature on everything you sew.

Hidden Details

Most of these techniques are for the inside of the garment and may never be seen by others. Don't, however, let yourself be beguiled into believing that makes them in any way unworthy of the extra time and effort involved. There is nothing mysterious or awesome about any of these methods; without exception, they are actually quite simple and easy to do. And always remember that it is often the hidden details that are the true mark of quality. You cannot help but feel a personal sense of pride each time you see the inside of your professionally finished garment. And, of course, wearing lovely things next to your skin is like wearing exquisite lingerie; it envelops you with a priceless feeling of luxury.

In addition to giving your garments the fine finishing and beautiful detailing that are the mark of a couturier, these "extra somethings" above and beyond the actual construction also increase comfort, convenience, fit, and wearability. Using these techniques, you will always know that your garment will close neatly and easily; that everything you sew will hang and drape beautifully; that your garments will retain their precisely controlled shape; that you never need be embarrassed by the appearance of an open jacket or a dress on a hanger; and that you will be as proud of your creation on the tenth wearing as you were on the first.

Create your garments with the elegant expertise admired by all who appreciate the beauty and quality of the very finest couture. Then you will find that your wardrobe will help to give you the poise and assurance that comes with always being fashion-right.

The Inside Story

Lining and underlining are the hidden components of fine dressmaking that, although not immediately visible, are always reflected in the finished effect of your garment. Not only do they assist in creating and retaining the shape of your creations, but also give them a more luxurious look and feel. They are a "must" in all couture garments, and should be in yours as well.

UNDERLINING: If you intend to construct a garment in the manner of the fine designers, follow their example by **mounting** or underlining your garments to give it beautifully controlled shape and body. As an added bonus, underlining will prevent over-handling by keeping your handwork and markings from showing on the right side. Remember, however, that each and every construction mark must be transferred to the underlining, especially the seamlines and grainlines. This extra effort will provide you with a more faithful representation of the design lines and an accurate reference line for any necessary alterations. See pages 153 and 154 for further information and specific instructions.

LINING: Jackets and coats naturally require a lining to conceal their exposed inner construction, and your pattern instructions provide all the necessary guidance for these garments. But what about those other garments whose construction does not call for lining? This simple addition increases the comfort, durability, and aesthetic appeal of any garment and is really quite easy to do.

Cut lining from major garment pattern pieces and construct in same manner as garment, leaving appropriate seams open for closures. (For gathered or pleated skirts, cut your lining from a straight or A-line skirt pattern to reduce bulk.)

Baste the lining to the garment along the seamlines of the raw edges, treating the two layers as one. Turn under and slipstitch the lining edge to zipper tape (1). Apply either the facings (for dresses) or waistband (for pants or skirts). Blindstitch the facing edges to the lining. Refer to the tailoring section for further information.

Consider "show" value when lining your creations. Rather than discarding scarves that have already seen service in your wardrobe, use them to line a jacket. Use a large designer scarf with the famous signature at the lower front edge, then line the back and sleeves with color-matched crepe. You can also add impact to a lining by using a print, plaid, or contrasting color—perhaps lightweight remnants left over from a previous garment. There is no rule, written or unwritten, which says linings must be drab or inconspicuous. Just be sure your lining doesn't show through your garment fabric.

The Shapekeepers

Here are some additional couture touches to help you master the art of controlled shape. Use them to achieve that air of confidence that comes from the assurance that your garment is always hanging straight, draping beautifully, and not in constant need of adjusting to keep it from shifting.

CAMISOLES: Camisoles support skirts or portions of skirts to allow free swing to the design of the garment bodice. Use underlining or a lightweight taffeta for a camisole in order to keep fabric thickness to a minimum (1).

INSIDE WAIST STAY: This stay is suggested for stretchy fabrics, sheath or princess styles, or when skirt is heavier than bodice. Cut strip of ½" to 1" wide grosgrain ribbon to fit waist, adding 1" for finishing ends. Turn ends back and stitch. Sew hooks and eyes to ends, extending loops over edge. Tack stay at seams and darts, leaving at least 2" free on sides of zipper (2).

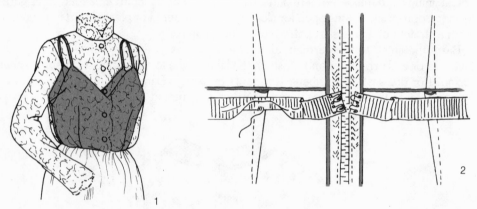

LINGERIE STRAP GUARDS: To prevent shoulder seams from shifting and keep lingerie straps from showing, use about 1½" of seam binding or a thread chain (page 324). Sew one end to shoulder seam near armhole. Sew a ball snap to free end of guard and a socket snap toward neck edge of garment.

FOUNDATION SUPPORTS: Make your foundation supports requiring feather boning from mediumweight taffeta or underlining fabric. The support takes the place of your undergarment and must, therefore, be made of materials sturdy enough to shape your body and to hold up the outer garment. Foundation supports are found most often in evening clothes, where underclothing could add bulk or detract from the sleek, smooth fit of the garment.

BONING: Boning is used to stiffen, mold, and maintain shape in garments such as strapless gowns, lingerie, and swimwear. Made of a firm but flexible nylon or other synthetic, it is usually covered with fabric for easy sewing by hand or machine. It is available by the yard or in prepackaged strips.

FABRIC STAYS: Fabric stays are made to control the fullness of an area of the garment and can be used effectively in skirts, bodices, or sleeves. They are constructed from lightweight lining or underlining fabric to make them invisible from the right side of the garment, but they must be firmly woven to retain the shape and drape as a stay is intended to do.

SHOULDER PADS: Shoulder pads can provide a smooth foundation from which the garment falls, camouflage round or sloping shoulders, or accentuate a broader-shoulder look in fashion.

Shoulder pads can be made of graduated layers of interfacing, polyester fleece, or foam rubber. Thickness can vary from ⅛″ to 1″. The designer's recommendations for shoulder pads are listed on the back of your pattern envelope. Thin pads are usually covered with a lining fabric for use in dresses and blouses. Thicker pads are used for jackets, suits, and coats. Choose wide pads to fill in the hollow between the shoulder and bustline.

Cut pads in a semicircular shape with a flat edge on one side approximately 8″ to 9″ long and a curved edge on the other. Pads should be approximately 3½″ to 4½″ wide at the shoulder seam. Cut one or more layers in decreasing size and tack the layers loosely together by hand. Using steam, press the pad over a tailor's ham, shaping it to fit easily into the armhole. Center pad at the shoulder seam, extending ⅜″ beyond the armhole seam; pin. Try on garment and make any necessary adjustments in size and placement. Sew pads to seam allowances.

WEIGHTS: Weights are used to preserve the design lines of a garment and to prevent it from shifting during wear. They are normally used to ensure the proper drape of a cowl neckline or to make a hem fall evenly. Select type and size by your fabric and desired use.

Flat Circular Weights, used in necklines and pleats, are enclosed in a pouch (1). Cut an underlining strip long enough to fold around weight, or allow extra fabric for a hanging mount. Stitch ¼″ seams, turn, and insert weight. Pin in place and try on garment. Attach pouch with a French tack, or whipstitch through the extra fabric.

Lead Weight Strips consist of lead pellets enclosed in a fabric casing. Place them inside the hem of your garment as it is being placed into position so they will fall directly into the fold of the hemline (2). Begin and end the strip at the edge of your front facings, and tack the casing to the underlining with long running stitches. Never let the iron rest on your hem, as the weights will leave a noticeable impression.

Chain Weights are most frequently used in tailoring. They add the necessary weight to a coat or jacket hem and provide an attractive finish as well. Tack the chain directly below your lining, tucking the ends of the chain under the facing (3).

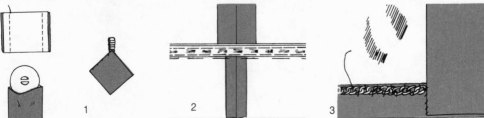

The Finest Fastenings

The master seamstress leaves nothing to chance. She will expertly insert a zipper by hand. She will not let the metallic glint of a snap or hook mar the look of her exquisitely finished garment, or an open jacket reveal any but the most perfect buttons and buttonholes. Follow these tips to make your closures as functional and yet unobtrusive as possible.

HAND APPLICATION OF A ZIPPER: Applying a zipper by hand is a custom technique. It is especially desirable on fine woolens, silks, and linens as well as on delicate and hard-to-handle fabrics. Follow the directions given for zipper placement in either the lapped or centered applications. Then use a tiny prickstitch (page 200) to complete the final stitiching. Always sew with a fine needle and use a double strand of regular thread coated with beeswax for normal use, silk thread to match fabrics with sheen, or topstitching and buttonhole twist thread for added durability.

Use the prickstitch for the entire length of the zipper, always stitching from the bottom of the zipper to the top (1). There will be a space between the top stitches, but the understitches will be long and overlap to provide necessary strength. If your fabric is heavy, you may wish to make a second set of stitches, placing them between the first stitches for added strength.

ZIPPER UNDERLAY: To protect your skin and undergarments, place a piece of grosgrain ribbon (at least one inch longer than the opening) over the teeth. Hem the upper edge of the ribbon, ending the ribbon at the slider. Sew the long edge to one seam allowance of the opening with a backstitch. Catchstitch the lower end to the seam allowances. Fasten with a tiny snap (2).

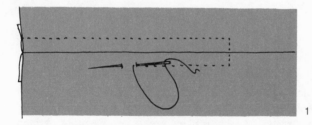
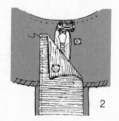

BOUND BUTTONHOLES: Long recognized as a couturier exclusive, beautifully worked buttonholes should become part of your own sewing repertoire. In the buttonhole section we gave you the construction methods. To complete the buttonhole as the great designers suggest, transfer the buttonhole markings to the facing and cleanly finish the facing with an organza patch, as directed for the garment in the organza patch method, page 318. Slipstitch facing to buttonhole for a professionally executed finish.

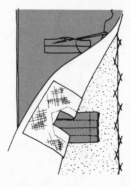

EXTENDED SNAPS: To fasten a collar or stand-up neckline with snaps, sew the ball section in position on the inside of the neckline or collar. Secure the socket section on the opposite side through only one hole, extending it from the edge as you would a hook (1). If your snaps might show, cover them as described above.

HANGING SNAPS: To fasten a neckline with snaps above a zipper, sew the socket section in position on the inside of the neckline. Attach the ball section on the opposite side by forming a thread loop using the blanket stitch, as described on page 324 (2).

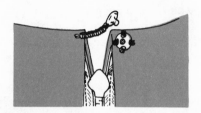

COVERED SNAPS: For inconspicuous snaps, cover them with underlining or lining fabric. Cut two fabric circles about twice the diameter of the snap. Take a running stitch around edge of each circle. Place a snap section face down on each. Work ball of snap through center of fabric circle, snapping both sections several times to spread fabric apart. Draw up threads and fasten each section securely (3).

COVERED HOOK AND EYE: Make your hooks and eyes blend visually into your garment by covering them with a double strand of matching thread. Work from right to left, placing blanket stitches (page 203) very close together until the metal is completely covered. For larger hooks, use topstitching and buttonhole twist thread for quick and sturdy coverage (4).

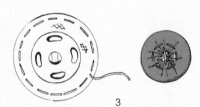

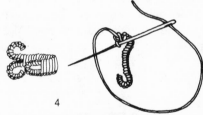

FINISHING BUTTONS: If you wish to cover the wrong side of a covered ring button (page 327), cut a circle of fabric the size of the inner diameter of the ring plus ¼″. Sew a gathering line around edge and adjust the gathers. Slipstitch to back of button (5).

COVERED BUTTONS: Individually decorated buttons can match or contrast with a garment. When using a small-scale print, center the motif on the button (6). Underline lace or eyelet with a matching or contrasting fabric (7). Use embroidery to monogram an initial, outline a motif, or stitch a simple design directly on the face of the button (8). Or stitch small beads to buttons for a sparkling effect (9).

THE CUSTOM TOUCH   449

The Finishing Touches

The first things to catch your eye when you look at the inside of a couture garment are the beautifully finished seams and hems. It takes very little extra effort to impart the same custom touch and fine workmanship to your own garments.

LACE AND TRIMS: Lace can be an attractive and sturdy substitute for seam binding on your hems and facing edges, or you may wish to tack it on coats or jackets along the edge where the lining meets the facings. Select narrow, flexible lace for curves, and stretch lace for stretchy fabrics. Other trims (such as ribbon, braid, or rickrack) can also be very effective as long as they are relatively lightweight and flexible.

HONG KONG FINISH: This classic finish is used on underlined garments and is actually quite easy to do. Use 1″ wide bias strips of your underlining or lining fabric, or press open double-fold bias tape. Matching edges, and using small stitches, stitch the bias strip to the garment raw edge in a ¼″ seam (1). Turn bias to inside over seam. Stitch along line where binding and garment meet on the right side to catch bottom edge of binding and completely enclose the raw edge (2).

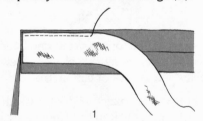

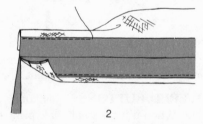

1

2

MACHINE-STITCHED HEMS: Some designers are featuring machine-stitched edges and hems on their couture garments, reflecting their innovative ideas and new techniques. For both woven and knitted fabrics, hems can be topstitched with one or two rows of stitching ¼″ apart. Or a row of zigzag stitching can be placed along the foldline of the hem, then the fabric trimmed away close to the stitching.

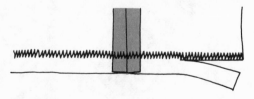

HAND-ROLLED NARROW HEMS: Use this hem to finish sheers, scarves, and lingerie. There are two popular methods, both time-consuming but well worth the effort. For the first technique, machine-stitch ¼″ from raw edge; trim close to stitching. Roll approximately ⅛″ of edge between thumb and forefinger, concealing stitching. Stabilize roll with third and fourth finger and slipstitch, taking a single thread at each stitch (1).

For the second method, stitch and trim as above. Turn edge about ⅛″ and crease sharply. Pick up a thread along crease and carry thread over to raw edge diagonally and pick up a thread alongside the raw edge. Work in a zigzag pattern, making stitches ¼″ apart. Repeat process for about 1″, then pull thread to tighten stitches to create the roll (2).

1   2

SOFT HEM: A couturier rarely intends that the hem of a garment be pressed knife-sharp. The most common method is to simply interface the hem as directed on page 341.

Another method, used especially in very soft fabrics, is to insert additional padding along the hemline. First apply the interfacing; then, before completing the hem, place a 1″ wide strip of lamb's wool, polyester fleece, cotton flannel, or soft cable cord on top of the interfacing at the hemline. Place approximately ⅓ of the strip below the hemline and ⅔ above it so that all the edges will be graded when the hem is turned. Sew to interfacing along hemline; use long running stitches for strips or long loose catchstitches for cord.

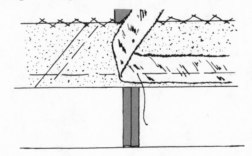

EXTREMELY CURVED HEMS: Some garments are so designed that the hem may have excess fabric or the hem edge circumference is not as wide as that of the garment. In such instances, the hem must be slashed at evenly spaced intervals, no deeper than 1″ from the fold. As you adapt the hem, keep the garment free while sewing. To eliminate excess fabric, cut out narrow wedges and bring cut edges together. Hemstitch them shut. To add width to hem, insert small wedges of fabric and hemstitch them into place.

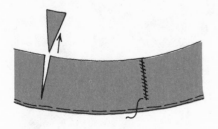

HORSEHAIR BRAID: This hem finish is most often used on full-length gowns, where extra stiffness is required in the hem without extra weight. Carefully mark the hemline. Steam braid to eliminate creases. The cut ends of the braid are very prickly and will require special treatment. To join them, lap ends ¾'' and enclose both sides of braid with a fabric strip applied with a double line of stitching around all edges.

For a narrow braid, trim the hem allowance to ½''. Place the braid on the right side of your fabric and match the edges. Stitch the braid and the hem allowance in a ¼'' seam (1). Turn the braid up along the hemline. Baste close to the fold and complete the hem (2).

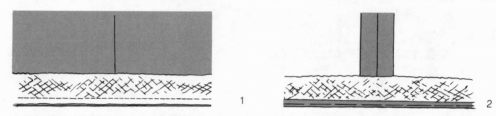

Wide braid usually has one prethreaded edge for easing; if not, run a gathering stitch along one edge. Place unthreaded edge along hemline; baste. Turn up and baste hem to check hemline. Sew basted edge of braid to underlining with long hemming stitch. Draw gathering thread to ease fullness on free edge. Sew this edge to underlining with long running stitches. Turn and complete hem (3).

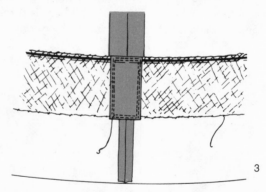

LABELS: For a custom touch, sew a label into your completed garment using small catchstitches or an embroidery stitch. Designer labels for Vogue patterns are available at the pattern counter. Personal labels can also be purchased or specially ordered.

Creative Trims

Trims can add a new and exciting dimension to everything you sew. Apply them always with a tasteful hand, but don't let yourself be inhibited by traditional ideas. Use braid to outline design details as well as to finish the raw edges of a garment. Lace and ruffles always lend a romantic mood to an evening gown, but they also can add a subtle feminine touch to tweeds. The many decorative stitches, from topstitching to trapunto, can add crisp detailing or soft elegance.

Your trims should always be an integral part of your garment, coordinating with your design and fabric. Lavish beading, for example, would not only be inappropriate on a casual or tailored garment, but could possibly distract from an ornate brocade gown as well. A fashion rule of thumb is to coordinate elaborate trims with simple garments, simple trims with elaborate garments. Follow the lines of your garment or add lines to a simple style, but do not let your trimming destroy the balance of your garment by markedly interfering with the basic design. Permit your trims to enhance aesthetically and yet relate structurally by realizing their role in a total design concept.

And, as with everything you sew, relate the trim to yourself and your needs. If you love the rich look of quilting but fear the extra bulk on your frame, why not use it on just a collar or pockets? If you want your new creation for both daytime and evening wear, lace may be a better choice than beading.

If you can't find the perfect trimming in your fabric or notions departments, turn to the upholstery, drapery, or interior decorating departments. They often carry some stunning trims intended for use on furniture or draperies. Don't let this discourage you; they will work beautifully on your garments as well.

Even though there is a bewildering variety of trims, generally only two procedures are used for their application. They are either incorporated during the actual construction, or they are applied after the garment is completed. Always keep the method of application in mind while selecting your trim; don't wait until your garment is finished to discover that the trim should have been inserted during construction.

Armed with your good style sense, let your fancy lead the way. Change the look of last season's creation, give impact to a simple garment, or add the perfect finishing touch to a new dress—with trims, the mark of the creative seamstress.

Braid and Bands

If it's variety you're looking for, take a long look at braid and bands, which range from simple rickrack to gala beaded bands. Included in the galaxy of trims are embroidered bands, braid, lace, sequined bands, purchased fringe, and ribbon—all of them banded trims, in spite of their seeming diversity. Add the many possibilities in use and placement, and the variety totals great fashion excitement.

Whatever type of band you are using, be sure to mark accurately and measure frequently. Select an inconspicuous location to begin and end your application. Machine application, which produces a more casual appearance, is a rapid means of applying trim and may be necessary if the garment requires a very sturdy finish. Hand application with tiny invisible slipstitches will be strong enough to withstand the usual wear and cleaning and will allow increased control, a greater degree of manipulation, and a finer finish.

There are two basic methods of applying braid and bands. The most common method, direct application, is generally done after your garment is completed. Simply pin or baste the trim in place and apply by machine or hand. The second method, inset application, encloses one or both raw edges by sandwiching the trim between two fabric layers (such as the garment and a shaped or bias facing) and must be done during construction.

FLAT BRAID: Generally used to create a border effect or to highlight a specific garment area. Let braid add a touch of fashion or splash of color anywhere, from neckline to hemline. It is available in a wide range of colors, materials, weaves, and widths, making possible any number of effects. Do not always limit yourself to only one row or one shade; braids are often best in combination.

Pin or baste to the garment and apply by hand or machine. Stitch along both edges; do not pull the threads too tight or puckers will appear. Turn the ends in ¼″ before sewing, overcasting them first if they tend to ravel (1).

SOUTACHE OR NARROW BIAS BRAID: Use this popular trim to outline a design with tracery or to emphasize an overall silhouette within a garment. Soutache is often used for a Spanish look on a jacket or dress.

Mark the design with chalk or thread tracing and pin the soutache in place. Ease the braid around corners; they will be slightly rounded, as soutache does not lend itself to sharp corners. Apply by hand with small, invisible stitches or, to apply by machine, baste in position and use a zipper foot (2).

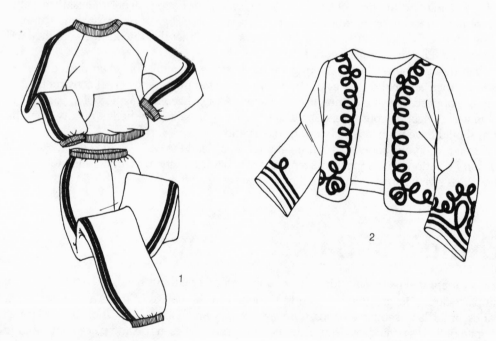

FOLD-OVER BRAID: Designed to trim garment edges, fold-over braid can also be utilitarian when used to finish raw edges such as a neckline or hemline.

Most braids are folded slightly off center, with the top side slightly narrower than the other to ensure catching the underside when stitching. For smooth application, shape the braid with a steam iron to achieve curves similar to those of your garment edge. For better control and a finer finish, apply the braid by hand. However, if you need an especially durable application, apply the braid by machine.

For a machine method with a minimum of visible stitching, first sew the upper half of the braid by hand. Then stitch on the right side of the garment with a zipper foot, as close as possible to the braid, to catch the bottom half. Baste the bottom half first if necessary to maintain control (1).

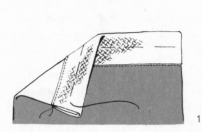

RICKRACK: There is such a large variety of sizes and materials available in rickrack—from baby rickrack to jumbo; from polyester to wool, to metallic—that you need not be traditional nor limited in your applications.

The zigzag shape makes rickrack very flexible for use around curves and corners. If you are using it on a corner, arrange the trim so an outside point is at the most conspicuous corner. Rickrack is often used at garment edges, exposing only the points after stitching; apply the trim by the inset method or machine-stitch along the edge of your garment with matching thread to secure the trim. Apply it within garment lines with a single line of machine stitching down the center or tiny handstitches at each point (1).

OTHER BANDED TRIMS: Embroidered bands and ribbons are available in any number of colors, patterns, and widths. Combine them with ruffles for ultrafrilly appeal, or use the provincial patterns for a charming Tyrolean look. For a touch of opulence, try tapestry or metallic embroidered bands on evening clothes. Combine ribbon with other trims, or team it with a matching bow. Apply these trims in the same manner as you would any banded trim. Special hints on beaded or sequined bands, purchased fringe, and flat lace are given on the following pages (2).

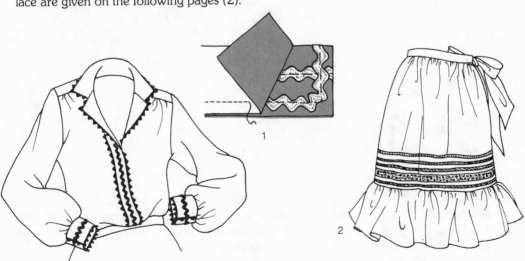

Fringe

Whatever the current trend, fringe and its related trims will always be present on the fashion scene. Purchased or made in a variety of materials and lengths, fringe has almost limitless uses for everything from clothes to home furnishings. Add rayon fringe to a shiny fabric for a slinky effect, or several rows of wool fringe in various shades to accent the subtle colorings of a tweed. Mix fringe and tassels; combine different shades or outright contrasting colors. And remember that two rows—or three or four—are usually better than one. Easy to make or apply, fringe can create a multitude of effects.

KNOTTED FRINGE: Give your garments a mobile finish with knotted fringe. You may make it in any color and in a variety of yarns—wool, rayon, metallic threads. It works beautifully on the finished edge of any medium to loosely woven fabric. Experiment to determine the most appealing look; try several lengths, adjust the number of strands of yarn, change the distance between the groups, add more sets of knots. Generally, the fuller your fringe, the richer it will look.

Cut a cardboard strip the depth of the intended finished fringe plus ½" for each knot. Use the cardboard as a base and wrap your yarn around it. Cut through several strands at one end (1). With a stiletto or fine knitting needle, make a small hole about ½" from the finished edge of your garment and insert a crochet hook into the hole from the wrong side. Center the strands over the hook and pull them partially back through the hole. This will form a loop on the wrong side. Next, work the ends through the loop formed by the hook and pull the ends to tighten. Continue this process along the entire length of the edge. A second set of knots may be made by joining two halves of adjacent tassels with a single loop knot as shown (2). If you have made your strands long enough, several sets of knots may be made for an even more intricate, lacy appearance.

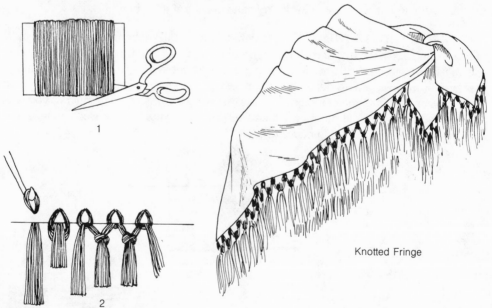

Knotted Fringe

PURCHASED FRINGE: Available in a vast assortment of materials, colors, and styles, all varieties of purchased fringe have a flexible braid heading for attaching the fringe. Just sew this heading to your fabric. Apply with an insert application or with a direct application using either a single row of matching stitching or invisible hand stitches.

SELF-FRINGE: This is a quick, easy trim that is a perfect match every time. It is particularly suited for soft, thick, heavy, or nubby fabrics. Do not feel you must limit your fringing to woolens, however, as most woven fabrics can be fringed with success; experiment first with a small scrap.

First straighten your fabric ends by cutting across the width along the grainline. Determine the desired depth of your fringe and pull out a crosswise thread from within the fabric to act as a guide. With small stitches, make a line of machine stitching along the pulled thread to anchor the fringe. Then remove all the threads beneath the stitching one at a time, always pulling them in the same direction.

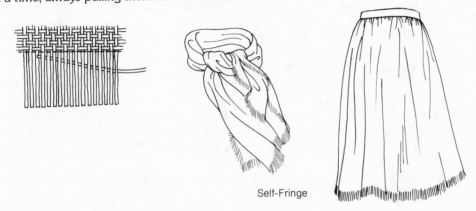

Self-Fringe

TASSELS: These are made in a manner similar to knotted fringe. Again cut a strip of cardboard the desired depth of the tassel to use as a base. Thread a needle with a double strand of your yarn and place strands at top of cardboard with the needle hanging at side. Wind your yarn around the cardboard and the strand of yarn until the proper fullness of the tassel has been achieved. Then tie your threaded strands very securely at the top and remove the cardboard (1). Wind the strand about ½" from top around the upper end several times; slip needle underneath the wound portion and bring out at top of tassel (2). Cut the lower loops and attach the tassel to your garment.

POM-POMS: The same operations are required for pom-poms and tassels except that pom-poms should be very, very full and have less depth. First, cut a strip of cardboard the desired depth. Then, using the cardboard as a base, put a separate strand at the top and wind the yarn around the cardboard. Securely tie the separate strand and cut across the other end (3). Remove the cardboard. Shake pom-pom gently to make a soft fluffy ball. To make a really full and lush pom-pom, repeat winding process. Then slip one wound cluster inside the other and tie the two together at the center, forming a cross. Cut all the ends and spread the strands to form a ball. For both methods, trim the strands of your pom-poms into perfect spheres (4).

1   2

3   4

Lace and Ruffles

So romantic, so fanciful, nothing can be more eye-catching than the perfect lace trim. Imagine the wistful beauty of delicate Val edging for a ruffled collar and cuffs or the effect of heavy Cluny lace for a bodice insertion. Add lace to a velvet jacket for a choir-boy or Edwardian look. Combine laces with each other or with other trims—just think of all the possibilities.

Many charming varieties of lace trims have been produced commercially. Cotton, nylon, acetate, and wool are used, singly or in blends, to make flat lace or pleated, gathered, and ruffled versions. Many lace trims are re-embroidered, giving them an added dimension. The inherent fragility of lace calls for handling its open constructions with special care. Let the fiber content and the openness of the lace guide you in deciding between hand or machine application plus any necessary ironing and washing procedures.

Here are a few techniques you will find helpful in working with lace. If you apply your lace trim by machine, you may find an edge stitcher or hemmer foot attachment useful. To miter corners, pin the lace around the corner, folding it to form a miter. Whipstitch or zigzag along the fold and cut away excess (1). If you plan to attach one trim to another at a corner, gather the outside band at the corner so it will lie flat (2). (See Mitering, page 233, for additional information.)

If the ends will be left hanging free, finish them by making a narrow rolled hem (3).

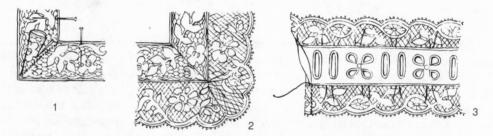

When the ends are to be joined, make a French seam. First stitch the ends of the lace wrong sides together in a scant ⅛″ seam. Then crease along the seam, bringing right sides together, and stitch ⅛″ from the seam, encasing the raw edges (4).

The couturier method of joining lace ends is to appliqué along a motif. To appliqué by hand, lap the ends and trim around a motif on the upper layer. Whipstitch around the motif to join it to the under layer (5). Trim away the excess lace on the under layer. To appliqué by machine, lap the ends, sew around the motif with a fine zigzag stitch, and trim the excess lace on both layers close to the stitching.

FLAT LACE: A type of banded trim, flat lace is applied basically as directed in the introduction to Braid and Bands on page 453. While the insert method is exactly the same, there are a few differences in the direct method due to the unique qualities of lace.

There are several methods for a direct application. To apply to a finished edge, whipstitch through both garment and lace (1). If the edge is raw, trim garment seam allowance to ¼'' and make a rolled hem. Whipstitch lace to edge of hem (2).

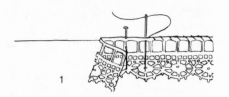

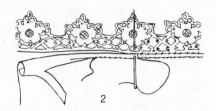

To apply lace within the garment lines, stitch straight edges by machine or hand. Scalloped edges are preferably sewn by hand with small invisible stitches or appliquéd to the garment as directed for joining ends (3).

Another method, insertion, is particularly suited to the open nature of lace, as the fabric beneath is trimmed away. For lace with straight edges, baste in place and cut through fabric halfway between basting lines. Trim fabric to ¼'', overcast, and press toward garment; topstitch from right side through all layers (4). Another method is to topstitch along edges, trim closely, and overcast as shown (5). For randomly scalloped lace, baste in place and hem closely round motif along edges. Trim fabric closely and overcast raw edges.

Another variety of insertion that produces delightful results, but can be rather time consuming, is joining lace to fabric or other lace bands (much like a Mexican wedding dress). Press under edges of fabric strips, then stitch as above.

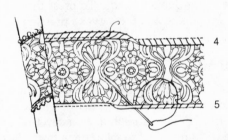

GATHERED LACE OR RUFFLES: You may purchase lace trims preruffled or gather your own. To make a lace ruffle, you will need a piece of lace 2 to 3 times the finished length, depending on the desired fullness. Gather the lace by hand or machine by taking long stitches close to the straight edge of the lace, and distribute gathers evenly. Use two rows of stitching if lace is 3'' or wider (1). With Val lace, just draw up the heavy thread running along the straight edge to gather (2).

You may inset your ruffle or apply it with a direct application as you would for flat lace. Your gathering should be matched to the garment seamline when joining it to a raw edge, with or without a facing. Baste in place, and stitch by hand or machine.

Don't overlook the wide variety of ruffles made in other fabrics. Ready-made ruffling can be purchased in a variety of fabrics, widths, and types. You can also make your own ruffles out of fabric and treat them in the same manner as lace ruffles. (See pages 229 to 232.)

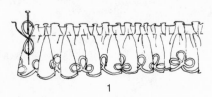

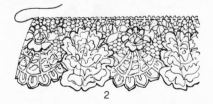

Beading

What can be more glamorous than a dress shimmering with the glitter of beading? Or top off your gown or cocktail dress with a jacket outlined with beaded tracery. The jeweled look is one you can always count on, for its appeal is perennial.

For more casual garments, select natural or colored beads of wood or clay, or the authentic look of multicolored Indian beads.

Beading is often a painstaking procedure, but one in which your patience is sure to be greatly rewarded. Following are some suggestions that will make your beading proceed faster and easier. You will, naturally, need a design. Outline a design in a printed fabric, trace one from another source, or create your own. When you have decided upon a design, transfer it to your garment with chalk and thread tracing.

Although beading is usually applied to a completed garment, you may wish to add an overall beading design in the process of construction. Cut out the garment section and back with a lightweight underlining. Mark all construction lines and transfer your beading pattern. Make sure that any fitting adjustments have already been made so that the beading will not interfere during construction. Stitch all seams with a zipper foot.

Use an embroidery hoop to hold the fabric taut for small motifs, and select a fine or special beading needle that will slip easily through the holes of the beads. Use matching thread coated with beeswax or transparent nylon thread. Keep your thread relatively short; a longer thread will tend to get tangled or knotted. Don't pull your stitches too tight or your fabric will pucker. Be careful when pressing; placing a hot iron on your beading may melt, scratch, or dull the beads. To press the garment around the beading, use a press cloth on the wrong side and press over a pressing pad or Turkish towel; avoid touching the beading.

Beads

You can attach your beads singly, in groups, or in a long strand. If you desire scattered beads, you will need to sew them individually (1). Start from the wrong side and use a backstitch. For a straight line of several beads, take several beads on the thread at a time and use a modified running stitch from cluster to cluster (2). The number of beads you will be able to string at one time depends primarily on the size and weight of the bead; experiment on a scrap first to find out how many you can string without the cluster drooping. For curves, you will have to reduce the number of beads on each stitch, perhaps even sewing them individually on a sharp curve or with large beads. Use a double thread coated with beeswax or nylon thread when sewing beads in clusters. If you are applying prestrung beads, sew over the threads between beads at intervals (3).

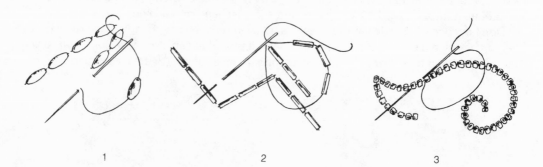

1   2   3

Bead Loops or Fringe dripping from a garment edge or within the garment lines for a scalloped effect is a look that is always elegant. Use nylon or a double strand of cotton thread coated with beeswax to prevent breaking. Count number of beads on each strand to maintain uniformity.

For loops, pull the needle through from the wrong side, string several beads, and return the needle to the wrong side. Secure each loop singly for added security (4).

Do not pull the loops too tightly or they will appear stiff and rigid. For fringe, string smaller beads, a large bead, and an anchor bead, if necessary; return needle through the same or another series of small beads (5).

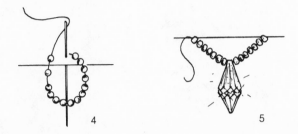

Prebeaded Bands and Appliqué are basted and then sewn. Ease the trim around curves as you baste. Sew with invisible slipstitches through the backing. To finish the ends, remove several beads from the backing, turn it under, and slipstitch securely in place. Be sure to firmly secure the last bead to prevent losing beads.

Sequins

Sequins can also be applied several ways. Apply single sequins with a backstitch from center hole to edge. For a finer finish, apply with a small coordinated bead. Bring the needle up through the hole, string a bead, and return through the hole (1). For sequin rows, bring needle through hole and take a backstitch over to edge. Bring needle forward in position for the next one, which will overlap the last and conceal the thread (2). Pre-strung sequins are applied in the same manner as prestrung beads.

Paillettes, while larger than sequins, are applied in basically the same manner. The hole is located at the edge rather than in the middle. They may be applied with a backstitch from hole to edge, or with a bead. Rows are applied like sequin rows or individually if they are very large (3).

Sequin Bands and Appliqué can also be purchased. These trims generally have a series of thread chains or an elastic backing to act as a flexible foundation. Invisibly tack these strands to your garment. If you are using clusters, snip away the threads between the motifs and anchor the thread ends with a knot, clear nail polish, or glue to prevent raveling. Fold transparent tape over the cut ends to avoid unnecessary loss of sequins.

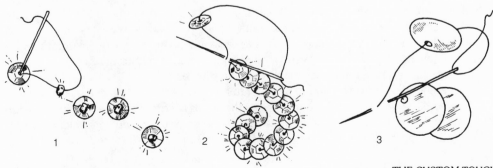

Feathers and Fur

Trimming with feathers or fur is a glamorous finale to any garment. Each has been adorning clothes for centuries, yet over the years neither one has lost its lush hypnotic appeal. Add a fur collar to a tweed coat and see how beautifully it frames your face. A full flourish of feathers at your hemline or an unexpected burst at the edge of a sleeve or neckline can be sensational. Don't be skimpy—use rows and rows for a lavish effect. Whatever you do with feathers and furs, don't overlook them!

FEATHERS: Feathers are usually purchased in strips. The most common application is to sew an overhand stitch through the fabric edge and over the cord-like base of the trim. Keep the stitches fairly loose and far apart, but firm enough to support the trim. Conceal the threads and refresh the feathers by using a large blunt needle to work out each vane from underneath stitches.

To facilitate the removal of the feathers for cleaning, attach small thread loops to your garment edge. They should be several inches apart and large enough to accommodate the width of the trim. Then you can simply pass the feather strip through the loops as you would a belt. Close the ends of the strip with whipstitches and work out each vane from underneath the loops (1).

FUR: These trims are available in a variety of furs and in many widths and lengths. Usually in straight strips, some are already shaped for you to use on collars or lapels. The majority of fur trims are already neatly backed with lining fabric or grosgrain fabric. Therefore, joining the fur to your garment edge is just a simple matter of sewing the backing to the garment with firm but unnoticeable running stitches.

For cleaning ease, however, you may prefer to apply your trim by attaching large covered snaps to both the garment and the fur. Space the snaps according to the weight and width of the trim. Then you can merely snap the fur on and off at your own convenience (2).

For further information on the handling of fur, turn to pages 379 to 382.

Stitchery

The efficiency of the sewing machine has taken away the drudgery of hand sewing, but don't let it take away the enjoyable decorative role of hand sewing as well. Who would care to do without the marvelous custom effect of saddle stitching, or the richly seamed look of its machine-sewn version, topstitching? Decorative tacks can certainly add to a finely tailored appearance. If you have been limiting embroidery to tablecloths and pillowcases, you've been overlooking some great fashion ideas. A personal monogram can always add distinction to any garment. Embroidery floss, topstitching, and buttonhole twist thread, and yarn can be used to sew your finishing details. Just think of the wonderful fashion effects you can gain with a needle and thread and a small amount of time!

TOPSTITCHING: The most popular form of fashion stitchery, topstitching emphasizes the structural lines of your garment while working to keep the seams and edges flat and crisp. Although done by machine, it gives the same detailed look as fine hand sewing. Don't forget that it is often a construction procedure as well in such features as pockets, pleats, and man-tailored shirts.

The stitching can be done after the garment is completed, but it is often necessary or easier to stitch individual or large areas during construction. Make any fitting adjustments *before* you topstitch seams.

Use topstitching and buttonhole twist thread in the needle, and either topstitching thread or regular sewing thread in the bobbin. Use a size 14 or 16 needle, and 6 to 8 stitches per inch. You will probably have to adjust your machine tension before stitching; experiment first on scrap layers of your fabric and underlining. Stitch carefully, using a guide, such as the edge of the presser foot. Be particularly cautious at curves and pivot the fabric at corners; mark these tricky areas with thread tracing before stitching. Stitch two lines very close together on heavy fabrics. Leave thread ends long enough to be worked to the wrong side with a needle and tied.

SADDLE STITCH: This is a trimming stitch which, used with discretion, can be a charming subtle touch. The simplest of all stitchery techniques, it is usually added to a completed garment. Use topstitching and buttonhole twist thread, embroidery floss, or yarn—preferably in a contrasting color—and simply make continuous running stitches, evenly spaced and at least ¼" long.

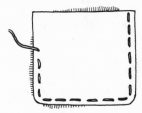

DECORATIVE TACKS: These are used on pockets and pleats on tailored clothes. First mark triangular shape. Secure thread for tack with small backstitches.

For the *Arrowhead Tack,* bring needle out at A and take a small horizontal stitch at B. Insert the needle at C and bring it out again just inside A. Continue until the entire tack is filled in (1).

For the *Crow's Foot Tack,* bring needle out at A and take a small horizontal stitch at B. Then make a small diagonal stitch at C and then across base to A. Continue until the entire tack is filled in (2).

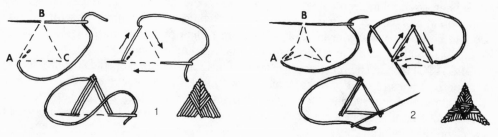

EMBROIDERY: Once confined to home furnishings, embroidery has become an indispensable addition to many good-looking clothes. Mark your design with thread tracing or chalk, and use three or six strands of embroidery floss, yarn, or one of the heavier decorative threads, depending on desired effect. Several designs can be sewn with zigzag or special machine attachments; refer to your manual for instructions.

The *Outline Stitch,* a slanting backstitch, is worked from the left to the right in a single line. Each stitch is followed by a short backstitch back to the right side very close to the previous stitch (1).

For the *Satin Stitch,* work close parallel stitches over an area padded first with tiny running stitches. For straight lines, the stitch is done on a slant; for curved lines, place the threads closer together on the inside of a curve, further apart on the outside (2).

For the *Cross-Stitch,* bring needle out at 1, cross over and take a stitch from 2 to 3, and then cross over and take a stitch from 4 to 5. Continue these diagonal stitches in same direction. Next, working in opposite direction, cross each stitch, keeping points together (3).

For the *Herringbone Stitch,* bring the needle out at 1, cross over and take a stitch from 2 to 3. Cross over again, taking a stitch from 4 to 5. Repeat to finish row (4).

For the *Blanket Stitch,* work from left to right between two lines. Bring needle up on lower line and hold thread down, insert needle a little to right on upper line, and bring up directly below on lower line. Draw needle through the loop formed and pull thread taut (5).

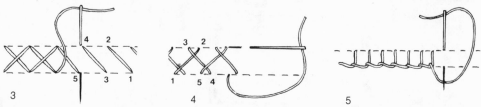

The Creative Touch of Trims

Creative trims can add a distinctive personal statement to any garment. From rows of topstitching outlining a coat to jeweled appliqués gracing a gown, trims can express your originality and creativity. Trims create a dramatic focal point of glitter and shine . . . add a dainty detail of delicate lace or embroidery . . . form a tailored accent of braid or stitchery. Trims should always enhance the fabric, the design, and you.

Use braid to accent an edge or outline a design within a garment. Create texture with self-fringe at a hem or fagoting around a bodice. To add drama, highlight a fabric with topstitching, embroidery, quilting, or trapunto—all easy to do with machine stitching.

Lace can trim a neckline, bodice, sleeve, or hem. Colorful appliqués add fun and enchantment for young and old. Bright rickrack and braid form eye-catching designs. Decorative hand sewing becomes the focal point of a smocked bodice or an embroidered gift for someone special.

Fashions
for Men

Men's fashions are changing rapidly to suit individual life-styles. Wardrobes must be coordinated to fit the occasion and to meet the needs of the man. The classic suit or a more casual jacket can be tailored to perfection by hand or machine. Add a shirt—softly styled for casual wear, or crisply accented for the business day. Mix and match colors and fabrics for greater wardrobe versatility.

Carefree casuals range from shirts to pants to swimwear. Whether a participant or a spectator, a man can achieve both comfort and flair in his selection of casual clothes.

The **Featherstitch** is a variation of the blanket stitch. The pattern depends upon the location of each consecutive stitch. For an alternating design, draw two guidelines. Make individual stitches ¼" from each other diagonally, holding thread to left (6). For a single line, make each slanted stitch ¼" directly from preceding one (7).

The **Fly Stitch** is another type of blanket stitch. Bring thread out at 1 and work from left to right. Hold the thread down and stitch from 2 to 3. Take a small stitch at 3 to secure the loop. Return to higher point for next V (8).

To make the **Chainstitch,** bring the needle to the right side, holding thread down while taking next stitch. As needle crosses over thread, it will form a loop (9).

The **Lazy Daisy Stitch** is an elongated, detached version of the chain stitch, grouped to form a daisy. Begin at the center of your flower, and return the needle to the pivot point after taking each stitch (10).

The **French Knot** is made by twisting thread around a needle. Bring needle to the right side, hold thread taut, and twist needle so thread loops around it three or four times. Return needle to wrong side, very close to the point where it emerged, and pull thread through loops and fabric until a small knot remains (11).

MONOGRAMS: A monogram is a simple embroidered way to personalize almost anything you make. Stamp your initials and even your name in all kinds of expected or unexpected places. You may purchase an iron-on transfer pattern or find your own. Unusual letters in magazines or newspapers might appeal to you. Or, most personal of all, use your own handwriting as a guide. Don't limit yourself to capital letters; small letters will often combine to make very attractive and unusual monograms.

Cut out your pattern in paper and pin it to your garment to determine placement. **Lightly** trace around it with chalk or pencil and outline the design with thread tracing. Follow manufacturer's guide for iron-on transfers.

Use an embroidery hoop to hold your fabric taut. If your fabric is soft or loosely woven, apply a backing of a lightweight fabric under the design before stitching; trim excess when completed. The satin stitch is the traditional monogramming stitch, but you may use other embroidery stitches as well. Monogram by hand, or refer to your sewing machine manual for machine embroidery.

Fabric Trims

Are you wondering what to do with all those leftover pieces of fabric that are too small for a garment but too lovely to throw away? Here is your answer, and a way to embellish your other garments as well. Use those scraps, or newly purchased fabric if you wish, to create appliqués or patchwork. Appliqué can add great charm to a simple garment. It can create any fashion mood you wish—gay when in bright print on a solid or contrasting print, elegant when in antique satin on brocade, and so on. And don't overlook the great variety of purchased appliqués. As for patchwork, imagine the admiring looks you would attract in an evening skirt done in a patchwork of shimmering fabrics, or a pert vest made in squares of brilliant prints. Virtually any fabric can be used for either appliqué or patchwork, so the possible combinations are almost endless.

PATCHWORK: You can make your patchwork out of any fabric that will not ravel easily and is not excessively bulky. All the fabric patches should preferably be of relatively equal weight. Decide what shape you want your patches. Make a pattern out of heavy paper the size of the finished patch plus seam allowances of ½″ to ⅝″. Cut patches on the straight grain and in substantial numbers before stitching any together.

Arrange a number of patches (enough for two or three horizontal rows) on a flat surface until you achieve an attractive combination. Pin together in strips. Stitch, using allotted seam allowances. Stitch the patches together in horizontal rows the width of the pattern piece. Press all seams open on each strip before joining to another strip. Then stitch the horizontal rows together with long seams. Repeat this procedure for the desired length of the pattern piece. When the patchwork is large enough to accommodate your pattern pieces, pin and cut them as with regular fabric.

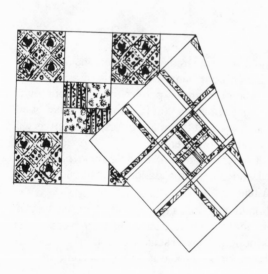

APPLIQUÉ: This trim consists of a separate piece of fabric applied as a decoration to a larger background. You may purchase the appliqué or make your own by cutting out a motif in your fabric or creating your own design. Avoid fabrics which ravel easily. Prints, contrasting solids, or fabrics with a definite texture lend themselves to appliqué.

For **hand appliqué,** transfer design to appliqué fabric and stitch close to outline. Trim excess ⅛" outside stitching. Baste to garment. Attach with a small blanket stitch around edges, using matching or contrasting thread (1). If you prefer, turn and press the raw edges to wrong side along machine stitching and sew to garment with invisible slipstitches (2).

If fabric does not ravel (e.g., felt), eliminate stitching and cut directly on the design outline; sew with hemming or blanket stitches.

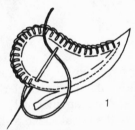 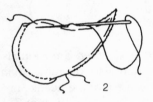

1   2

For **machine appliqué,** cut appliqué with a 1" seam allowance. Back with a lightweight yet stiff backing (such as organdy), then pin to garment and baste. Match thread to appliqué and attach with a close zigzag stitch, stitching slowly. If several appliqués are overlapped, do not stitch portions that will be covered; previous stitching lines may show through or cause your sewing machine to jam. Trim away any excess fabric, keeping the fabric flat on the table and the scissor blades close to the stitching line.

Decorative Surfaces

You can use quilting or smocking to add surface interest to any garment. Let your fabric become its own trim! Both quilting and smocking are probably familiar to you, but remember that in fashion the trick to turning heads is to use the familiar in an unusual way. Try working with silk, wool, velvet, crepe, or brilliant prints. Instead of overall quilting, add it to just the cuffs and lapels of a suit or the collar of a simple dress. Don't limit the soft touch of smocking to bodices; let it make a fluid statement on the hip yoke of a swing skirt.

SMOCKING: The softness of smocking is achieved by accordion-like folds created by stitches taken on the right side of the fabric. Use six strands of embroidery floss, following either small dots transferred to your fabric or the checks in a gingham plaid as a stitching guide. If you would like the look of smocking on areas which require considerable "give," refer to Elasticized Shirring, page 228.

Honeycomb or Seed Stitch Smocking is the most popular smocking pattern. Bring your needle to the right side at 1. Take a small stitch at 2 and another at 1. Pull the thread taut. Re-insert the needle through the fabric at 2 and bring the needle up at 3. Repeat earlier procedure at 3 and 4 and again at 5 and 6. Continue until design is completed.

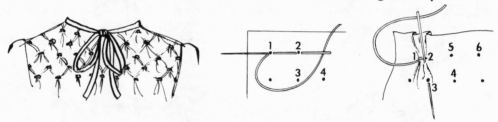

Diamond or Chevron Smocking is similar to the honeycomb, but the thread is on top of the fabric from row to row rather than underneath. Bring the needle to the right side at 1. With the thread above the needle, take a small stitch at 2 and another at 1. Draw stitches together tightly, and take stitch at 3. With thread below the needle, take a stitch at 4 and again pull tight. Take a stitch at 5 and with thread above the needle, take a stitch at 6. Draw the two together tightly. Continue, alternating from row to row.

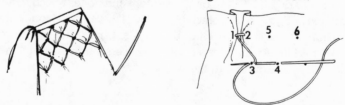

Cable Stitch Smocking is yet another variation. Bring the needle to right side at 1, placing the thread above the needle. Now insert the needle through the fabric under 2 and draw up the thread. Hold the thread below the needle and make a second stitch at 3. Again reverse the position of the thread by holding it above the needle for a stitch at 4. Draw up the thread. Complete the row and continue in this manner.

QUILTING: The richly textured look of quilting is created by stitching through two or more layers of fabric in a design or pattern. You may purchase prequilted fabrics or make your own for a custom look. A layer of light padding—polyester fleece, outing flannel, cotton wadding, or very thin foam rubber—is joined to your fabric to produce the raised effect. Back wadding or foam rubber with batiste or voile before quilting to increase durability. Use an underlining fabric for a backing on unlined garments or for an even more durable finish. Experiment on a sample of your fabric layers to determine the proper tension, pressure, and stitch length. Use matching or contrasting thread, or topstitching and buttonhole twist thread for a pronounced stitching line. A quilting attachment is very useful. Complete your quilting before cutting out garment sections, as quilting will reduce the size of the fabric.

Pin the padding (and backing, if used) to your fabric, wrong sides together; baste around the edges and along the lengthwise grain at 2″ intervals to prevent shifting. Transfer quilting lines to the right side with chalk and/or thread tracing. Mark all lines for irregular design, or one line to follow with quilting foot for diamond design. If quilting a design in the print of your fabric, use that as your stitching guide. Then carefully stitch along markings on right side. When quilting is completed, cut out your garment sections. To reduce bulk in seams, pull or trim away padding from fabric in seam allowances. Do the same to darts, or slash and press open.

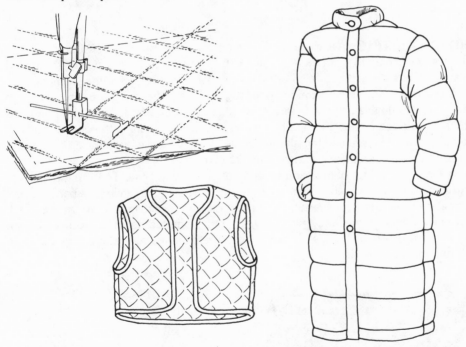

TRAPUNTO: A form of quilting in which the background is left unpadded and only the design stands out in relief, trapunto is done after a garment section is cut out. The design is backed with a soft fabric (such as organdy) and padded with strands of yarn. Choose a design, determine its placement, and transfer it to the right side of your fabric with chalk or thread tracing. Baste the backing to the wrong side in the desired location. On right side, stitch along the pattern with small stitches; tie the thread ends on the wrong side.

To pad the design, thread strands of matching yarn through a blunt needle. Insert the needle through the backing, and carry the yarn between the fabric and backing from one stitching line to the other. Clip the ends of the yarn close to the stitching. Pass the needle as far as possible before bringing it up, and do not pull tightly. For large areas or angles and sharp curves, bring the needle out and back through the backing. When changing directions, leave some slack to fill out the angle. Continue until the entire area is padded. Slightly stretch the fabric around each section of the pattern to make the tiny yarn ends recede into backing. Press lightly on the wrong side over a Turkish towel or pressing pad.

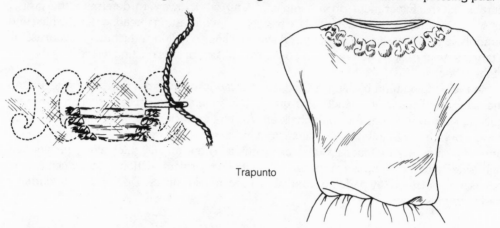

Trapunto

CORDED QUILTING: A variation of trapunto, corded quilting consists of several parallel rows of stitching that are then padded with strands of yarn. The quilting is applied to a garment area, such as a neckband or hemband, before it is joined to the garment.

Stitch the band sections together along one long edge or fold a one-piece band along the foldline to create a double layer of fabric. If one end of the band will not be enclosed in a seam, fold the end seam allowances to the wrong side before stitching the quilting lines. If several sections must be seamed together to create the band, leave open the inside portion of one seam to create an opening for inserting the yarn.

Baste the long raw edges of the band together along the seamline. To form the quilting, stitch through both layers of fabric in parallel lines spaced approximately ½″ apart. To pad design, thread several strands of yarn between the stitching lines to create the corded effect.

Baste along the seamline and trim the yarn out from the seam allowances before stitching ends into a seam. If ends are not to be enclosed in a seam, trim excess yarn and slipstitch the opening closed.

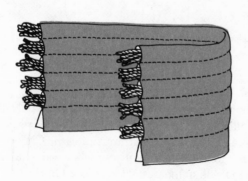

10

An Approach to Men's Fashion

Creating Fashion
for Men

Home sewing is joining the menswear revolution. One of the most satisfying as well as one of the most creative endeavors, men's fashions today are vibrantly entwined with style and design. Fashion individuality almost demands custom-made clothes, and sewing them yourself is one of the best and most personal means of acquisition.

Here in chapter 10 the tailoring and fitting of men's clothing will be discussed only as the techniques involved differ from those used in constructing women's garments. These variations occur simply because men and women are built differently, and their clothes must be, too. There are no special tricks in making men's clothes—just adaptations of dressmaking methods. You will see that some tailoring of a man's jacket is similar to that of a woman's. Put aside your fears, and involve yourself in creating men's clothes—the rewards will be worth it!

Contemporary Design

Patterns and fabrics for men's wardrobes are continually expanding, as are the numbers of people who sew menswear. Fabrics that are suitable for shirts, casual wear, and classic suits are becoming accessible to the home sewer as well as the professional tailor. With a little imagination, you can produce beautifully tapered shirts in unique fabrics, then combine them with smartly tailored suits in nonconventional or classic fabrics to put your creation in the winner's circle. Apply the same creativity for sports clothes and leisure wear, using perennially favorite fabrics, or the newly popular ones.

The variety of available pattern styles with the expansive array of fabrics on the market, will encompass the tastes of every man. The fashion statement made by sewing menswear can express everything for today's man through his manner of dress, whether exciting or subdued, colorful or quiet. The choice and the satisfaction of creative sewing make menswear great and rewarding fun.

Couture For Men

To complement the great new swing toward sewing for men, Vogue Patterns offers top fashions for men created by some of today's foremost designers. These patterns afford many possibilities for a man's individual fashion preferences, as they are both versatile and classic. Each pattern brings you the best in contemporary men's fashion.

Bill Blass, an American whose first designs were for women, carries his characteristic clean lines into his designs for men—magnificently tailored garments are emphasized with the trim lines. Givenchy and Christian Dior, both originally designers of women's clothing, offer elegantly styled menswear patterns. Their French haute couture background is revealed in the superb cut of their clothes and the craft in their workmanship. While style lines or details may appear more complex in these designer patterns, their construction really only involves combinations of the sewing techniques used in all Vogue patterns.

You will find that the designer patterns are no more difficult to construct than other patterns. What makes the designer patterns special is their unique styling, not their

construction techniques. As in all your other sewing, you can adapt your own sewing methods and simplify procedures in making men's designer fashions. The results, however, will be no ordinary garment, but the ultimate in quality design and appearance.

Vogue Patterns' Own Designers

Included in Vogue Patterns' menswear collection are our own designs for men. Vogue Patterns' designers have created a series of well-styled garments to complete the range of men's fashions available in patterns. Sport clothes, suits, leisurewear, and sleepwear patterns make it possible to sew a complete wardrobe for a man. Along with the varied styles, the patterns are adaptable, too; a suit can be made in wool flannel or double knit for office wear, then in velvet for evening wear. The shirt and tie have developed new personalities—the shirt collar now takes many shapes—from round to pointed, from standing band to buttoned-down. Sportswear patterns allow for a great deal of creativity with separates—shirts, pants, tennis outfits, etc.—sometimes incorporating the newest trim ideas such as rib knit bands or colorful zippers. Or a robe can be made in brocade for lounging and in terry cloth for after-shower. Vogue patterns cover every fashion need—our designers keep abreast of the new trends appearing on the fashion horizon and create timely new designs, incorporating new fabrics, notions, and trims—utilizing familiar construction techniques.

Very Easy Vogue

Very Easy Vogue patterns are also available for men, ranging from jackets and pants to shirts and easy-fitting tops. These patterns have been designed with a minimum number of pattern pieces and feature easy construction techniques. Jackets can be unlined or constructed with only a partial lining. The jackets, shirts, and tops are either loose fitting or semifitted, requiring less attention to fitting details.

On the pattern envelope, recommendations are given for fabrics that are considered easy to sew, yet enable you to create contemporary designs in today's fabrics. Very Easy Vogue patterns for men, though easy to sew, still offer the same Vogue look in fashion!

Fabric Spectrum

The right fabric is what really "makes" your menswear project. In choosing fabric, follow the suggestions on the pattern envelope back, but don't hesitate to make your own substitutions. Refer to pages 30 to 47 for a discussion of fabric structure and properties if you need some guidance. Then, take some time to organize your thoughts so you know what you **do not** want and what your budget limitations are—your trip to buy fabric is assured of success rather than confusion.

Your Fabric Choice

The final fabric choice is yours: select problem-free fabrics, or accept the challenge of special fabrics with surface interests. Match fabric to your tastes, life style, and the pattern design, and you are well on the road to success.

A chic shirt in crisp cotton blends or body-hugging synthetics can be made of many fabrics—knits, broadcloth, muslin, voile, gingham, lightweight corduroy, or wool flannel. Then add intrigue with geometrics, prints, plaids, and stripes, and you are creating an individualistic shirt. For the man who asks more of fashion, make a leather shirt or a luxurious shirt in silk, satin, or crepe for a custom touch. If easy-care properties such as permanent press are important in your selection, be sure to read the fabric label carefully.

Pants fabric should have body so that it wears well and will retain its shape. Test the fabric before you buy—crush it in your hands to see if it springs back into form. Many traditional fabrics like chino, sailcloth, twills, denim, and poplin are now treated with a wrinkle-resistant finish to keep them fresh-looking. A printed or plain pinwale corduroy can be both fashionable and durable. Double knits are extremely comfortable, and can be solid-colored or have multicolor jacquard design. Lighweight or mediumweight wools such as flannel and gabardine are both warm and attractive—a fine tartan plaid can look sensational. Experimenters may wish to make pants from leather or synthetic suede.

Suits for every occasion tell a different fabric story. A tailored jacket should be made from a malleable fabric that has enough body to keep its shape—a fabric that is pliant, yet sturdy. For these requirements, wool is the best material; it is the easiest to shape for tailor-perfect collar and lapels, it drapes well, and it is always in fashion. However, if you prefer an easy-care fabric for suits, double knits are recommended, and are available in subtle plaids and stripes especially designed for menswear. A tailored jacket is not meant to be washed, however; if this is desirable, remember to modify the inner construction and to use washable and preshrunk fabric, interfacings, and lining.

Other possible suit fabrics include denim, corduroy, seersucker, and linen, in prints, solids, stripes, plaids. Avoid sheer, soft fabrics because you will not be able to build in the foundation that jackets require.

For something truly special, a velvet suit in a deep, rich color with a satin cummerbund would be ideal, or a jacket in brocade with lapels and pants in velvet. For sportswear, try trimming a wool jacket with a leather upper collar, pocket flaps, and elbow patches; and adding leather piping, pocket welts, or belt loops to the pants. Pick out a zingy Madras plaid to accent a spectacular weekend wardrobe.

Sports and leisurewear fabrics for swimsuits, tennis outfits, and lightweight jackets are generally cottons and synthetics—either knitted or woven. Sports jackets can be made from duck, sailcloth, canvas, and denim. Use quilted synthetic fabric for a ski jacket, and lightweight to mediumweight washable wools for attractive battle or bush jackets or baseball jackets.

Pajamas and robes are easy, practical garments to sew. For pajamas, fabrics should be soft, washable materials such as surah, broadcloth, pima, or lightweight stable knits in any attractive color or print. Fabric for a robe can be almost anything, depending on when and how a robe will be worn. An after-shower or swim robe would be ideal in terry cloth or velour. For lounging, try lightweight wools or double knits. For leisure in luxury, think in terms of velvet, brocade, or heavy silk.

Vests, ties, and ascots are accessories that stylize and individualize a man's appearance, and should be coordinated with his taste and wardrobe. Use an interesting fabric to complement a favorite outfit—wool, corduroy, linen, velvet, brocade, and double knits are possibilities for vests. Ties and ascots can be made in any fabric that is not extremely bulky, heavyweight, or rigid.

Achieving a Custom Fit

Accurate measurements are needed for a tailor-perfect fit. The stance of the man being measured should be natural; keep away from mirrors that inspire the assumption of an ideal figure—one that is too erect and with taut, rather than relaxed, muscles will cause the garment to fit improperly with normal stance. Follow the guidelines as illustrated, applying the appropriate measurements to your particular sewing project.

Measuring for Pattern Size

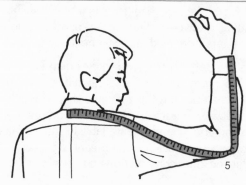

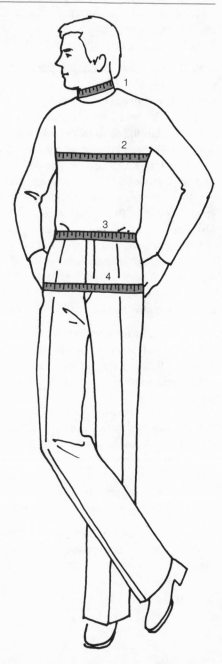

Shirt patterns with classic collars are purchased by neck size; other shirt patterns are selected according to chest size. Pants patterns are purchased by waist and hip (seat) size. Jacket and suit patterns are sold by chest size only. Casual wear such as robes are available in sizes small, medium, large, and extra large, corresponding to chest size.

Neckband: Measure around the full neck for neckband size, plus ½″ for wearing ease (1).

Chest: Place the tape under the arms around the fullest part of the chest (2).

Waist: While a man usually has a definite waist, he must indicate where he likes to wear his pants, which is where the waist measurement should be taken. Tie a string around this established point for the waist (even though this measurement is essentially one of personal preference). Measure the body at the string (3).

Hip (seat): Position the tape around the fullest part of the hips (4).

Shirt Sleeve Length: Bend arm up; place tape measure at base of neck. Run tape from center back to elbow, across elbow crook and up over the wrist bone (5).

Measuring for Custom Fit

After you have purchased a pattern in the correct size, a few more localized measurements are needed for precision fit. Vogue patterns are designed for a man of average height, 5'10'', corresponding to a "regular" in ready-to-wear.

Several measurements are needed to customize a shirt—the correct sleeve length for a classic shirt (see opposite page), arm circumference and length measurements for fitted sleeves. Waist, chest, and length measurements must be considered for both types. Pants may need to be adjusted for the correct crotch length and leg length.

Jackets are fitted according to the shoulder area (as opposed to the bust area for women); therefore the neck, shoulder, and arm measurement are necessary. The center lengths and the back width are also important for jackets.

High Hip: Measure at the top of the hip bones (6).

Thigh: Just under the crotch, measure the fullest part of the thigh (7).

Knee: Take measurement around the leg at the knee (8).

Outseam (side length): Measure from the waist (see measurement #3) to the top of the shoe heel (9).

Inseam: Take measurement over pants; position crotch correctly on body. Measure along inseam between crotch seam and shoe heel top (10).

Neck: Measure at base of neck (11).

Shoulder: Measure from the base of neck to top of the arm hinge (12).

Center Front Length: Measure from base of neck down the center of the chest to established waist (13).

Arm Length: Measure from arm hinge to elbow, and then from elbow to wrist bone. Record both measurements (14).

Arm Circumference: Measure bicep at the fullest part (15), and wrist at the bone (16).

Center Back: Measure from the base of neck down center back to the established waist (17).

Back Width: Measure straight across the back, over the shoulder blades, from arm hinge to arm hinge (18).

Crotch Length: Sit erect on a hard, flat chair. With a ruler, measure from waist to chair seat.

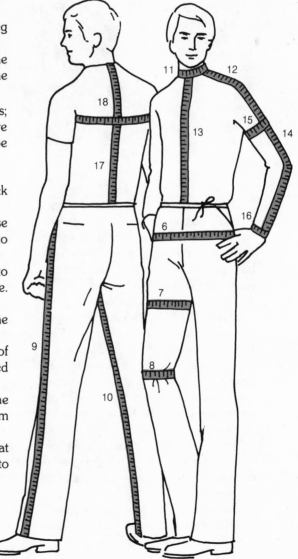

Pattern Selection

Now that you have exact body measurements you must select the correct pattern size. Size charts are on the pattern envelope and in the pattern catalogue. Select pattern size by matching the actual body measurements as closely as possible to a size on the chart.

Men's patterns are sized for men of average build about 5'10'' without shoes.

Sizes	34		36		38		40		42		44		46		48	
	in.	cm.	in.	cm.	in.	cm.	in.	cm.	in.	cm.	in.	cm.	in.	cm.	in.	cm.
Chest	34	87	36	92	38	97	40	102	42	107	44	112	46	117	48	122
Waist	28	71	30	76	32	81	34	87	36	92	39	99	42	107	44	112
Hip (Seat)	35	89	37	94	39	99	41	104	43	109	45	114	47	119	49	124
Neckband	14	35.5	14½	37	15	38	15½	39.5	16	40.5	16½	42	17	43.5	17½	44.5
Shirt Sleeve	32	81	32	81	33	84	33	84	34	87	34	87	35	89	35	89

Classic shirts are purchased by neckband size. When purchasing a **shirt** or **jacket** by chest measurement, those who fall between two sizes must consider their build. A thin, small-boned physique should choose the smaller size, while a large-boned, ample physique will require the larger size. **Pants** have accommodations for this situation—a wider center back seam allowance—so the pants can be fitted for the in-between size. When pattern types are grouped (such as a jacket or shirt with pants), choose size by chest measurement and adjust pants, if necessary.

UNDERSTANDING EASE: Vogue patterns for men, just as for women, have a certain amount of ease built into them. *Wearing ease* allows for body movement and comfort. *Design ease* is additional fullness added by the designer to obtain a certain fashion look. (See page 63.) Classic shirt patterns have both wearing and design ease; body-fitting shirts have only wearing ease. Pants patterns have only wearing ease through waist and seat area; however, some styles with pleats and wider legs may have design ease too. Jackets may have both wearing and design ease and are designed to fit over a shirt and vest.

Thus the actual measurement of the pattern piece will be larger than the body measurement for which it is designed. The description on the pattern envelope and in the catalogue—loose-fitting, semifitted, close-fitting—is your guide to the amount of ease in the pattern.

The pattern envelope should be read carefully, for in addition to listing the standard measurements it has all the vital information concerning required yardage, notions, and findings.

Adjustments for a Better Fit

Tailor-perfect fit should be your goal in creating menswear fashion. If figure flaws cause wrinkles and pulls of excess fabric in ready-to-wear garments, the same thing will happen with a garment sewn from a pattern that has not been adjusted from statistical pattern measurements to the actual body measurements.

To determine whether flat pattern adjustments are needed, compare the standard body measurements given on the previous page and those found on the back of the pattern envelope with the actual body measurements. Review Flat Pattern Adjustments, pages 78 to 83, on how to adjust pattern lengths and circumferences. Many men's figure needs create the same fitting problems as for women.

Length Adjustments

Bring the vertical length of the garment areas in line with the measurements you have taken. There are many combinations that may be required—a tall man may have short arms and a high waist, while a short man may have long legs with a low waist—few people match the pattern's statistical measurements exactly. Build length into pattern before cutting your fashion fabric to achieve a better fit.

SHIRTS: Properly adjusted sleeve length is very important for any shirt. A loose sleeve with a cuff has a single set of adjustment lines while a more fitted sleeve has two, one above and one below the elbow. The shirt body has only one set of adjustment lines so decide where the shirttail should end. Be sure to adjust the length of any bands, facings, or other related pieces.

JACKETS: Proportion is most important—a classic jacket should cover the seat, ending where the legs join the buttocks—the jacket waist should fall at established waist. The lapel length is crucial (use measurement #13, page 477, to correct). Usually a tall man will need length in this area while a short man may need the length reduced. Even a regular height (5'10") may need adjustments to bring the pattern in line with his body. Lengthen or shorten the jacket above and/or below the waist as needed. If you do not find adjustment lines on the pattern where you need them (i.e., about 2" above the top buttonhole for a lapel adjustment), draw a line at right angle to grainline; adjust the length accordingly. If necessary, shift pocket placement lines to complement the proportions after adjusting length below waist. Make the same changes in lining, interfacing, and facing pieces.

Too Short   Too Long   Correct   Too Short   Too Long   Correct

PANTS: Your actual measurements for the outseam (measurement #9) and the inseam (measurement #10), when taken as directed on page 477, are used for pants length adjustments. The inseam indicates the length of the leg while the outseam indicates rise (called crotch depth in women's pants).

For length adjustment, first measure the **front pattern piece** along the inseam seamline between the crotch seamline and the hemline (1). Then measure the pattern along the outseam from the top seamline of the waistband to the hemline; include any pocket pieces that may affect the outseam length and exclude seam allowances (2). Note: Men's classic pants are worn with top of the waistband at his established waist.

Lengthen or shorten the pant leg as needed, until the **inseam** is the correct length. (This adjustment is not shown.) If an adjustment line is not given, draw a line perpendicular to the grainline in the knee area. Now, any difference between the pattern measurement indicates that the **pants rise** needs adjusting. Lengthen or shorten the rise as indicated, until the **outseam** is the correct length (3).

Caution: Make sure front pattern piece adjustment lines are placed above the fly symbol—to adjust below may distort fit or make opening unusable. For pattern pieces without adjustment lines, draw them in at right angles to grainline well above the fly symbol. If adjustments interfere with a pocket, reposition symbols or adjust extensions maintaining the original opening length. Make equal changes in **back pattern piece.**

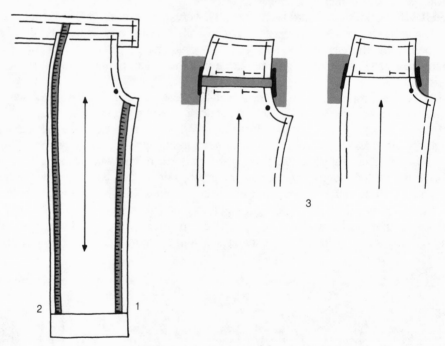

3

Circumference Adjustments

To establish a need for circumference adjustment, analyze each garment: for a **shirt** or **jacket** the waist circumference is usually the only flat adjustment needed. See pages 81 to 83 for reducing and enlarging waist and hip. **Pants** patterns usually give a wider center back seam allowance, allowing you to adjust the waist and seat when fitting. If it is not included, see page 114 for the waist circumference adjustment. Other fitting problems should be worked out in muslin. See next section on alterations.

Alterations for a Custom Fit

While flat pattern adjustments allowed you to make the pattern statistically accurate for your fitting needs, they cannot accommodate figure flaws due to posture, excess weight, or bone structure. These significant personal alterations **must** be worked out in a fitting muslin and should not be confused with minor fitting changes (see pages 121 to 124). The problem of an excessively large or small garment must be eliminated in muslin, with the same amount of change made in *every* garment you sew.

Making a Muslin

If this is your first venture into sewing menswear, *take the time to make a muslin fitting garment* to ensure a custom fit *before* cutting the fashion fabric. Select classic styles: the traditional shirt with collar, neckband, and yoke; straight-legged pants with regular width waistband and an inseam side pocket; a two-buttoned jacket with moderate lapels and natural shoulders. Choose a good quality muslin—lightweight for a shirt and medium-to-heavy weight for pants or jacket. If balancing the grain is part of the fitting problem, use a cotton with a woven stripe. *Never* use permanent-press fabrics as the grain cannot be straightened.

Be sure fabric is grain perfect (see pages 131 and 132) before cutting, and use your *adjusted pattern*. For shirts, cut all pieces, except pockets; for pants, eliminate pockets if possible; for jackets, eliminate pockets, facings, and upper collar.

Use tracing wheel and dressmaker's carbon; trace all seamlines and symbols so changes will be obvious. Mark lengthwise and crosswise grains on the right side of the fabric. Sew with machine basting for easier fitting changes. Pin the hem.

Test for wearing ease while sitting, moving, stretching, and bending. The garment should balance on the body; lengthwise seams and grain markings should hang straight and perpendicular to the floor. Crosswise grain markings and seams should be parallel to the floor and perpendicular to lengthwise markings.

Shirts: Neckband should be comfortable, neither binding nor loose. Sleeves should have ample length when cuff is closed. Shirttail should stay securely tucked into the trousers, with adequate wearing ease over waist and hip.

Pants: The top of the waistband should fall on the established waist; the crotch seam should not bind or hang too low. The legs and seat should be wrinkle-free.

Jackets should not wrinkle or pull. The shoulder seam should lie straight, directly on top of the shoulder, and extend from the base of the neck to the top of the shoulder bone. The shoulder area and sleeve should fit and mold smoothly with the elbow at the center of the sleeve's fullness. The undercollar should hug the neck in back and the outer edge should just cover the neck seam. The notch area of the lapels should be symmetrical on the body; the lapels should roll smoothly from the top buttonhole. The waist area should be smooth; vents should hang straight without spreading or overlapping.

IMPORTANT ANALYSIS: As you analyze your muslin fitting garment you may still see areas that need to be changed for a tailor-perfect fit. This is the time to fit the muslin to add the necessary ease, or eliminate excess fabric for your personal needs.

ALTERING SHIRTS AND JACKETS: Figure flaws and personal preference will allow you to try your hand at custom fitting. Should you need to alter a shirt, make the same amount of change in a jacket. The classic collar and neckband are not usually altered, but for extremely disproportionate neck circumferences it may be necessary (see page 86). For shoulder problems, apply the techniques found on pages 88 to 90. Chest and back flaws will be apparent in body-fitting clothes (see pages 100 to 103). A fitted sleeve may need altering (see pages 92 to 95) though classic sleeves usually do not.

ALTERING PANTS: Tailor-fitting pants depend on personal preference, body contours, and stance. Men often have fitting problems due to posture and excess weight. Refer to page 102 (fitted skirt) to correct for a swayback, page 120 (flat buttocks) for a flat seat.

Special Alterations

There are four figure flaws that seem to be unique to men that require alterations not covered on pages 86 to 120. The first two are caused by excess weight and cause fitting problems in shirts, pants, and jackets. Adjustments made before cutting will not give you girth in the right place to fit correctly. The *bay window* is created by excess flesh through the midriff area. This protrusion will cause the shirt or jacket front to ride up, pull side seams, and strain buttoned closures. In pants, it forces the waistband down across the front as the center front length is too short to cover the extra flesh. Outseams pull forward, and the inseams are strained and wrinkled. The *bulging hips* are created by fleshy pads settling on the side hips, making the body very broad at this area. These pads cause the shirt or jacket to ride up over hips, resulting in pulling, straining, and an uneven hem. In pants, wrinkles and straining are evident through hip area, pulling the outseams, while the inseams are strained, causing wrinkles.

The other two are caused by posture or bone structure and create a significant problem when fitting pants. The *forward hip stance* is evident when the abdomen and hips are thrown forward, causing a swayed back and the chest to appear sunken. "Horseshoe" wrinkles form under the buttocks and pants hit back of legs below knees. The *backward hip stance* is apparent when the hips are thrown high and toward the back. This pulls the pants front down, causing wrinkles as the center back length is too short, thus straining the inseam. The pants cling to the legs below the knees.

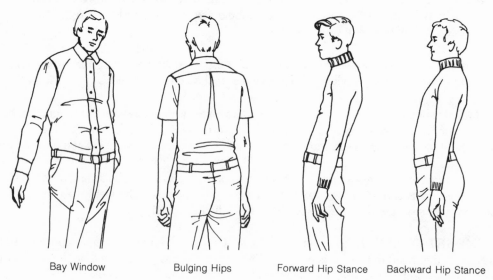

Bay Window   Bulging Hips   Forward Hip Stance   Backward Hip Stance

Caution: Test these alterations by correcting your fitting muslin as indicated by the pattern pieces before cutting into your fashion fabric. Jacket pattern pieces are not shown; make the same alterations needed for a shirt.

BAY WINDOW: To correct *shirt* when 2″ or less is needed, slash front to point opposite armhole and spread amount needed. Form a pleat from slash to side edge. For more than 2″, also add to the side seam of front and back.

To correct *pants*, increase the center front length and add to the front inseam until the pants hang straight. Reshape any darts or pleats to fit contour.

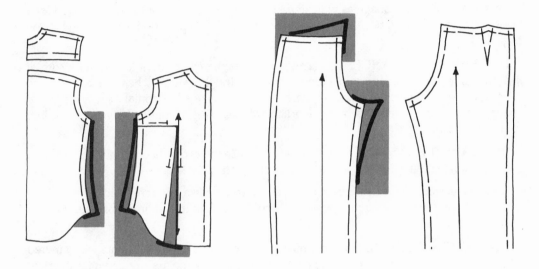

BULGING HIPS: To correct *shirt*, slash front and back to a point just below the armhole and near the side seams. Spread as needed, making equal changes on front and back.

To correct *pants*, increase outseam length and add to the side edges of the front and back until you have the necessary girth. Then add to the inseams until pants hang straight. Shape darts to fit contour, adding darts if necessary.

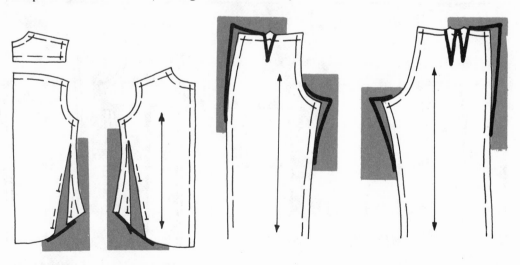

Pants should be wrinkle-free—contrary to popular belief, you do not need excess fabric between the seat and the knee for sitting. Work out these wrinkles in a muslin—once mastered, you can transfer this knowledge to every pair of pants you make. Be aware of overfitting—this will make it virtually impossible to have them wrinkle-free. Make a horizontal tuck across the back of the leg, just under the seat, to remove excess fabric, continuing the tuck across the front, tapering to nothing at the inseam. Restitch the inseam in your muslin pants, stretching the back inseam edge to fit.

Transfer alterations to pattern pieces as shown in the two alterations—forward hip stance and backward hip stance.

Correct grainline and shape as indicated. This may be the only alteration you need for a tailor-perfect fit, or it may be needed with the corrections for bay window or bulging hips on page 483.

FORWARD HIP STANCE: To correct, decrease the center back length, the width at the seat curve, and the inseam until the pants hang straight (see sketches above).

For more extreme wrinkles between seat and knee, make a horizontal tuck as explained above and shown on the accompanying illustrations. Test in muslin **before** cutting into your fashion fabric.

BACKWARD HIP STANCE: To correct, increase the center back length, the width at the seat curve, and the inseam until the pants hang straight.

For more extreme wrinkling between seat and knee, make a horizontal tuck as explained above and shown on the accompanying illustrations. Test in muslin **before** cutting into your fashion fabric.

COMFORT ALTERATION (sometimes called left dress): In fitted pants with tapered legs, men may need extra fabric in the left leg for comfort (some may require it for the right leg). Make this provision when cutting out the pants; allow ¼″ to ¾″ as indicated at the crotch point for both the left and right front. Then cut along the cutting line for the right leg, retaining the extra fabric for the left leg. Naturally, this procedure is reversed if the additional fullness is needed on the right.

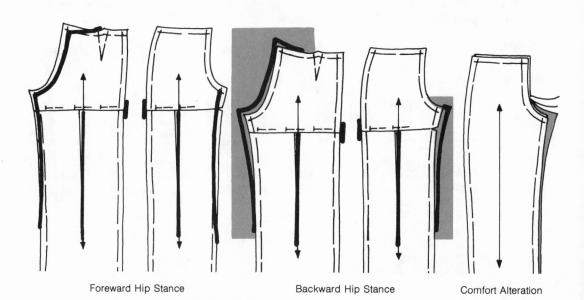

Foreward Hip Stance   Backward Hip Stance   Comfort Alteration

Tapering Menswear

For a sleek, trim fit, men have had their ready-to-wear shirts and pants "tailored" by the experts. Now you can do the same—make the provisions on the pattern before cutting out your fashion or do it at the fitting stage.

A natty look starts with a body-fitting shirt—do not over-fit. To remove excess fabric, add double-pointed contour darts (page 217) in front and back. At seams, decrease waist and hips. Divide the amount to be reduced evenly between darts and seams. Transfer fitting needs to pattern pieces as shown.

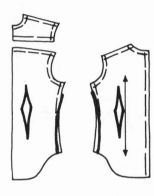

Since the revolution in men's clothing is upon us, pants can be worn exactly as the man decrees; for a trim fit, there are two ways to remove the unwanted excess fabric.

BACK-FITTED CONTOURING: This technique creates ultratight-fitting pants—do not over-fit. Turn the back crease into a fitted seam from waist to hem. Baste, keeping fold on straight grain if possible, and test; seam will vary in depth. Transfer to pattern piece (1).

TAPERED PANT LEGS: Turn straight-legged pants into slim-fitting ones—do not overfit. First, mark the knee level on each leg, then divide the amount to be reduced evenly between the inseam and the outseam. Decrease as indicated above and below the knee. For bell-bottoms, taper gradually from the knee to the original width at the hem. Transfer fitting needs to front and back pattern pieces as shown for the back (2).

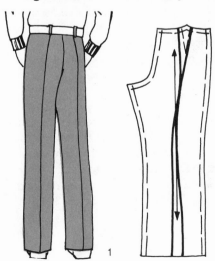
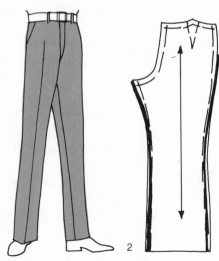

Menswear Sewing: Pure and Simple

The keen interest in sewing menswear today is due to the dynamic fashions available. No longer is each man a near carbon copy of the other; they can have individuality in the creation of their wardrobe by sewing at home. Vogue Patterns has answered this need with styles that can be sewn in the newest fabrics. Some are easy to sew and quick to complete. Others will require more time to achieve professional results. The actual construction methods for menswear are basically the same ones used in women's garments. However, the difference between the two is *where* and in *what order* certain construction techniques are employed. Throughout history, the tailor has always plied his trade with care and, we may add, some secrecy. Therefore, an exhaustive search into menswear sewing techniques has been made to present here what are the most important facets of sewing men's garments. Also, in certain cases the techniques were modified to make them more understandable and applicable to home sewing.

Adapt Your Knowledge

If you can sew, you can sew menswear. Use your basic know-how to widen your sewing experience by making a man's garment. Couple your pattern's instruction sheet with the ideas given here to create, without difficulty, a beautiful garment. Little sewing tricks, such as how to match plaids and how to press, are just as vital for menswear as they are for sewing any garment. Your repertoire of sewing techniques will be valuable.

Shirts, jackets, and pants are discussed with the purpose of augmenting your pattern sewing guide. The directions given here should aid you in taking your garments one step farther as you consider your fabric choice. Synthetic fabrics do not always "shrink" as well as natural fiber fabrics when making a seam with ease, and some permanent-press fabrics look puckered and wrinkled after laundering when topstitching is used for seam finishes and as trim for pockets, bands, or cuffs. The special tips suggested in the chapter will aid you to make well-tailored garments. Other men's clothes—robes, vests, ties, and ascots—utilize sewing methods already presented in other chapters, so they need no further enlightenment here. Your pattern sewing guide supplies basic construction techniques which, for these garments, are methods universally used in both men's and women's wear.

Organize

Think about your garment before you start to sew. Review the instruction sheet in conjunction with this chapter to see how you will proceed—try to get a clear picture of how the garment goes together before you start. This will aid you in understanding why certain particulars of construction are present, as well as enabling you to substitute other ways of construction. Organize your project so that you can select the most appropriate methods for your fabric and allow yourself to be more creative. There are no secrets here, so proceed!

Seams and Stitches

The flat-fell seam is most commonly associated with menswear, providing a strong, self-finished seam. The fell can be made on the outside of the garment by placing the wrong sides of the fabric together, or on the wrong side by placing the right sides together. Stitch a plain seam, press it toward one side, and trim the lower seam allowance to ⅛″. Turn under the edge of the other seam allowance ¼″ and stitch close to folded edge (1).

A double welt seam, which simulates a flat-fell seam, can be made by stitching a plain seam and pressing the seam allowances in one direction. Stitch close to seam, then again ¼″ to ⅜″ away (2).

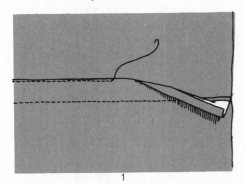
1

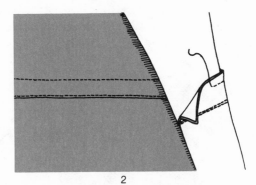
2

For permanent-press fabrics, use a plain seam and finish the seam with zigzag stitching, pinking, overcasting, or turning the edges under and stitching. For most knit fabrics, the seam allowances do not have to be finished. However, for lightweight knits whose edges tend to curl, double-stitch the seams by placing a second row of stitching ⅛″ from the first. Trim seam allowance close to stitching and press seam to one side. See section on Seams and Seam Finishes, pages 210 to 214.

With some fabrics, it may be necessary to reinforce the seams in areas of the garment that will receive extra stress (such as shoulder or crotch) by using a second row of stitching or by taping the seam (see page 209).

Many menswear patterns include topstitching and edgestitching. Use the edge of your presser foot, needle plate markings, or tape as a guide for accurate, straight stitching.

Make A Shirt

When making a shirt, think first of the fabric and its care; then choose the construction method that is most appropriate.

The traditional technique for constructing a shirt—using flat-felled seams and a faced yoke—ensures that no raw edges are exposed anywhere in the shirt. However, some permanent-press fabrics with topstitched bands and flat-felled seams look wrinkled after laundering. If your fabric needs support, use lightweight, preshrunk interfacing.

OPENINGS: The familiar band opening is most often used with traditional fabrics, and a self-faced opening is usually found on permanent-press and knit fabrics. However, today men's shirts employ many opening variations and a wide range of closures. When you start sewing, remember, men's shirt closures lap **left over right.**

Band: To make, turn in the **right** front along the foldline; press. Turn in the raw edge ¼″ and edgestitch inner fold through all thicknesses (1). For the **left** front, interface if desired; then place the right side of the band to the wrong side of the shirt; stitch in a ¼″ seam and press open. Fold in remaining raw edge on seamline; turn band to outside (over seam) along foldline; baste and press. Topstitch ¼″ from both long folded edges (2).

Extended Facing: If possible, cut the front edge on a selvage to eliminate finishing. If fabric needs support, cut interfacing the facing width. Place it on the facing and baste along the foldline; secure outer edge by stitching ¼″ from the selvage or clean-finish the raw edges together (3). Next, turn in front edges along foldline; press. Baste in place at neck and hem edges (4). When interfacing is used, the buttonholes and buttons will hold it in place adequately.

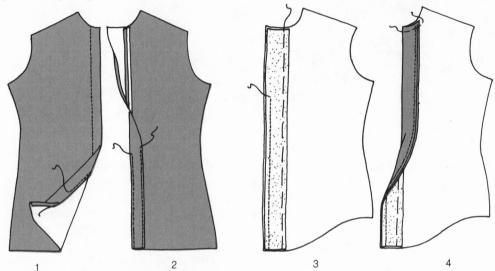

BACK FULLNESS: To add pleats or gathers in the shirt back, simply lay the "place on fold" line 1″ to 1½″ from the fabric fold when laying out the pattern. The fullness added can be inverted (1) or box pleat (2) at center back; a box or single pleat over the shoulder blade (3); or gathers (4).

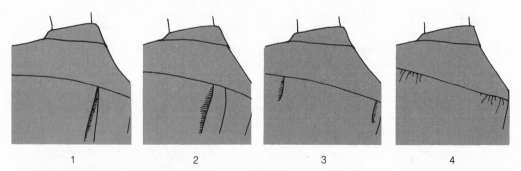

YOKE CONSTRUCTION: Light and mediumweight fashion fabrics can be self-faced. Heavyweight fabrics may cause bulk, so face the yoke with a durable, lightweight fabric. Stretchy fabrics may need the support of interfacing.

Pin one yoke section to shirt; baste. Use the remaining yoke section (lining or self-fabrics) as a facing, pinning the right side of the facing to the wrong side of the shirt back. Stitch seam through all three layers; trim and grade seams. Press yoke and facing over seam; edgestitch through all thicknesses (1). Next, pin and stitch right side of the yoke facing to wrong side of shirt fronts; trim and grade seam and press. Pin yoke in place over seam and edgestitch through all thicknesses (2). Staystitch neck edge.

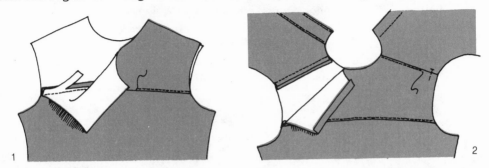

COLLAR CONSTRUCTION: The shape and style should be flattering. If you cannot find the desired shape, experiment, making a **_test collar_** first before cutting your fashion fabric.

If the fabric is heavy or bulky, shape collar as shown for the rolled collar, pages 260 and 261, before attaching it. When the collar is joined to the shirt and facings in separate seams, such as the notched collar, pages 262 and 263, it, too, needs shaping. **_Collar Stays_** give support to the collar points and can be easily removable. Make a buttonhole (slightly wider than the stay width) on the undercollar before it is interfaced (1). Then baste interfacing in place and make a pocket for the stay between the layers with two long rows of stitching and short one above the buttonhole (2). Prepare collar and attach. Insert stay when shirt is completed (3).

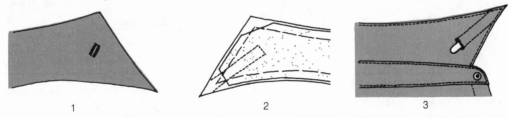

Classic Shirt Collar: Complete step 1 for collar with stand, page 269. To attach men's shirt collars, which are applied entirely by machine, stitch noninterfaced band to the inside of the shirt, clipping shirt neck edge if necessary (4). Trim, grade, and clip seam allowances. Pull collar and band up, then press seam toward band. Turn in remaining free edge of the band and pin over the seam. Edgestitch through all thicknesses (5).

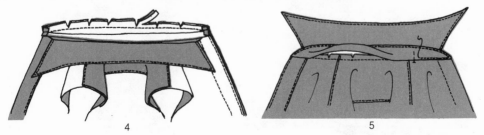

THE MASCULINE SLEEVE: Use flat-felled seams for traditional fabrics and a clean-finished plain seam for permanent-press and knit fabrics. For a flat-felled seam in a heavy fabric, cut wider seam allowances on one edge. If there is too much fullness in the sleeve cap, remove excess ease, following instructions on page 93.

Complete *sleeve plackets* before the sleeve is set in. Be sure that one sleeve opens on the *right* and the other on the *left.* Use the classic men's shirt sleeve placket, or substitute the faced placket or the continuous bound placket, pages 284 and 285.

Flat-fell Insertion: Flat-fell seams can be made from the *outside* or the *inside.* The method shown is made from the outside. Narrow-hem the shirttails first. Pin sleeve to shirt, wrong sides together, matching markings; adjust ease; complete the flat-fell seam (1). Join sleeve edges and shirt sides in a continuous seam (2).

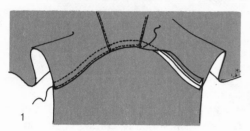 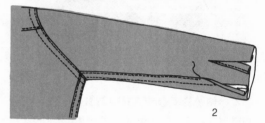

Clean-finish Insertion: With right sides together, pin the sleeve in the armhole; adjust ease. Stitch in a plain seam; stitch again ¼″ away, using a straight or zigzag stitch. Trim close to stitching (3). With a straight stitch, overcast raw edge. Stitch the sleeve and side seam in one continuous seam and clean-finish same as armhole (4).

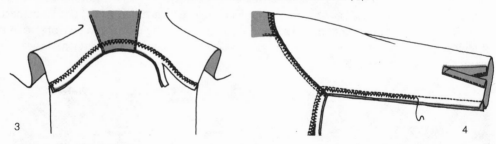

SLEEVE FINISHES: The classic shirt sleeve cuff or the French cuff, page 290, are still the most widely used cuff. A plain hem may require interfacing, or you may want to use a bias or shaped facing as a sleeve finish.

Try a *self-finishing hem* that looks like a stitched band. Allow ½″ extra to the sleeve hemline when cutting. Make hem before sleeve is completed—fold hem allowance up along hemline and press. Now turn the folded edge up to enclose the raw hem edge and press. From the outside, stitch ¼″ from the last fold through all thicknesses; press hem down and tuck up. Insert sleeve.

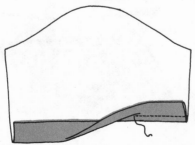 

POCKET: Both decorative and functional pockets are easy to construct. See pages 294 to 303 for the various techniques. Pin pockets in place to check the position—they should be straight and parallel to the center front.

SHIRTTAIL HEMS and FINISHES: A smooth hem, well-made buttonholes, and correctly positioned buttons are marks of a beautifully tailored shirt.

Shirttail Hems: Narrow hems are the most common, but vents and wider hems in the shirttail may be used. Machine-stitched hems are the most practical finish for shirts—use matching thread and 10 to 12 stitches to the inch.

Buttonholes and Buttons: Machine-worked or hand-worked buttonholes, pages 320 and 321, are placed vertically on the front opening (with the exception of the neckband) and evenly spaced to accommodate points of strain. Mark and make the neckband buttonhole and button carefully to avoid gaping. For a button-down collar, anchor it with button and buttonhole at center back (horizontal) and on each point where it falls on the shirt front (vertical). For two-button cuffs, make horizontal buttonholes, moving the lower one in about ¼'' for a better fit. For French cuffs, make four horizontal buttonholes.

Tailoring Tips for Pants

A quality pair of pants must combine perfect fit and durability—follow these construction tips from the best tailors to achieve your goal. Pants are one of the easiest garments to sew, but are the hardest to fit. You may wish to work out your fitting needs in a muslin (see pages 481 and 482). The few hours used to make a muslin will return double-fold—your sewing time will be cut considerably and every pair of pants will fit perfectly.

Basic Construction Procedures

Take some of the frustration out of pants construction by working as much on the flat as possible. These pointers will allow you to proceed faster.

POCKETS: Be sure to use strong, tightly woven cotton poplin or blend for pockets—avoid traditional lining fabrics as they may not withstand the rigorous use. Add pockets to pants back and front; then stitch the outseam (inserting any pocket). Follow your pattern's sewing guide for pocket placement and basic construction.

Instead of French seamed pocket edges, you can stitch pockets right sides together along the ⅝'' seamline then zigzag ¼'' away. Trim close to the zigzagging (1). Or, trim seam allowance to ¼''; bind the raw edge with double-fold bias binding or bias hem tape (2). Remember, pockets must be sturdy and last the life of the garment.

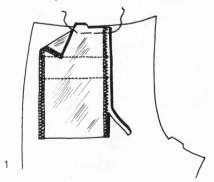

FLY FRONT PLACKET: Stitch front sections together along center front seam between symbols; clip to stitching below extensions. Finish outer edge of left front extension.

Turn in both front extensions along the foldlines and baste close to the folds. Pin or baste the closed zipper under the right front opening edge, with the teeth close to the basted edge and the bottom stop at the bottom of the opening. (Note: Zipper will extend above the opening.) Lap the left front opening edge over the right front, matching the center front markings, and baste it in place (1).

With the left front extension opened out, baste the zipper tape to it, being careful not to catch the front of the garment. Stitch the zipper in place close to the teeth (2). Then turn the left extension back and baste it to the garment across the upper edge.

Stitch fly to lining along unnotched edge; trim, turn, and press. Baste raw edges together. On the inside, baste the fly to the right front extension over the zipper. Make sure the raw edges are even and the lining faces the inside. Stitch seam, ending at marking, keeping the front of the garment free. Finish raw edges (3). Baste upper edge of fly to right front.

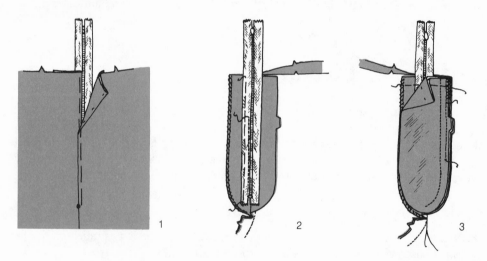

Remove center front basting. Stitch right front opening edge close to the zipper teeth, keeping left front free (4).

On the outside, lap left front over right, matching centers, and baste in place. Stitch left front along the stitching line, keeping fly free (5).

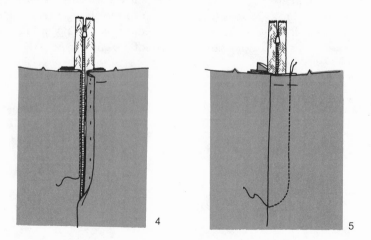

WAISTBAND: The waistband for men's pants is cut in two sections, one for each side of the body. Each section is stitched to the corresponding pants section, then the back seam of both pants and waistband is stitched in one continuous seam. This allows for easy alterations in the future.

Many patterns include instructions for making a self-faced waistband reinforced with interfacing and tape. However, for a professionally made waistband using a separate facing, follow the instructions below. The facing can be made of a tightly woven, lightweight fabric, such as cotton twill, or you can use a purchased waistband facing. For interfacing, use buckram or a very heavy, nonfusible hair canvas.

Because the fly lining must be attached *after* the waistband is sewn, the fly front zipper application is different from the technique on the preceding page.

Do not stitch inseam or crotch seam at this time.

Fly: Turn under right front seam allowances ⅜'', clipping to fold at symbol; baste and press. If your pattern does not include a crotch shield (see page 495), you will have to reinforce the inseam leg area. For leg reinforcements, cut two sections of pocket fabric as indicated, using pants front as a guide. Baste in place and overcast the raw edges together (1). Interface left fly, if desired, and clean-finish the outer edge; stitch to the left front, ending at symbol. Clip pants to symbol; press seam toward facing; and understitch (2). Turn to inside; press.

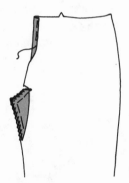
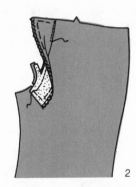

1

2

Place closed zipper face up along the turned-in edge with zipper stop ¼'' above symbol; baste. Bring left front over zipper, matching centers; baste (3). (Note: Zipper may extend above opening.) On inside, open out left fly; baste zipper in place, keeping garment free. Stitch zipper to left fly, close to teeth, and again at tape edge (4). Release basting. Interface right fly, if desired. On inside, place fly over zipper, with raw edges even; pin. On outside, open zipper, baste through all thicknesses, keeping right front free (5).

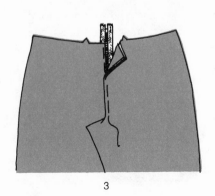
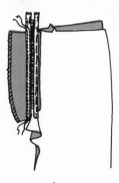
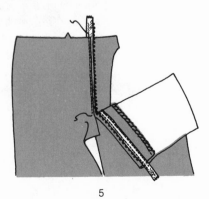

3

4

5

Waistband: Follow these instructions for a professionally made 1½'' wide waistband (a purchased waistband facing may be used). To adapt waistband, extend left front about 2½'' beyond the center front seamline. For a self-faced waistband, make a ⅝'' seam allowance beyond the foldline on the unnotched edges. To make facing, fold fabric on the true bias. Cut 1½'' wide folded bias strip the length of each waistband, plus 2'' for a pleat, and two single-layer bias strips 1⅝'' wide and the length of each waistband.

Stitch waistband to pants right and left half, matching symbols, and opening out left facing. Trim seam to ⅜''; press open. Cut off excess zipper tape (1).

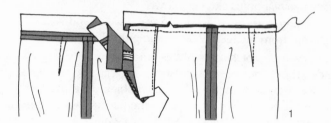

Pin two single, bias layers to each waistband section, ending facing at ***right*** waistband center front and 1'' beyond zipper seam on ***left*** waistband. Baste in place using a ¼'' seam. Cut a straight-grain strip of interfacing 3½'' wide and the waistband length. Fold in half lengthwise; press. Place interfacing over the basted seam, with one end at center front and back edges even, with raw edges extending ¼'' over basted seam. Stitch facing strips and interfacing to waistband sections through all thicknesses along basted seam (2).

Keeping interfacing free, pin the raw edges of the folded bias strip to the facing strips already attached, forming 1'' deep pleats over each outseam; stitch in a ⅝'' seam (3).

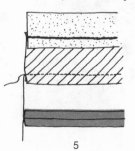

Turn waistband to inside ⅜'' from seam; turn facing and interfacing down. Press first facing seam allowances down, the second seam allowances up (4). Facing is anchored when belt loops are added.

To apply purchased facing, adapt waistband pieces and face each section between the areas suggested above. Keeping interfacing free, pin facing to the waistband sections, using a ¼'' seam allowance on the waistband (5). Reposition interfacing; turn waistband to inside ⅜'' above seam, facing down. Press. To complete waistband and fly, see next page.

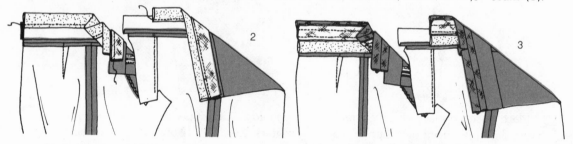

Complete fly and waistband: If necessary, adapt **right** fly facing or lining, adding the width of the waistband plus ⅝″ to the upper edge and a 2″–3″ long extension, about 1¼″ wide to the lower edge for crotch reinforcement. Cut from pocket fabric, making it double; fold in half lengthwise or stitch the long edges together. Keeping the raw edges even, stitch the lining to the right fly across the top of the waistband, continuing down the side edge to the symbol. Trim and grade seam (1). Turn to the inside; press. Stitch inseam, and then crotch seam between facing edge and front symbols (not shown). On the outside, position extension over front crotch curve, turning in the end ½″ at the inseam; baste free edges in place. From outside, stitch zipper in place, permanently catching lining in stitching; start at waistband seam and end at crotch seam (2). On the inside, stitch edges of crotch reinforcement to seam allowances only; keep pants free (3).

 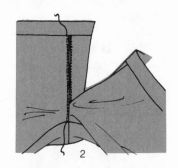 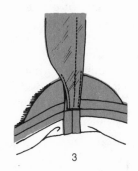

Press center back seam open for about 10″ and turn in ends of facing diagonally; press (4). Turn facing to the inside and tack facing to back seam. Turn left fly and waistband to inside; slipstitch waistband edges together (5). On the outside stitch along stitching line to hold left fly facing in place, forming a triangle at the end for reinforcement (6).

Prepare belt loops, page 312, substituting two rows of machine stitching for slipstitching. Add the belt loops by machine as shown (7). Fasten opening with appropriate closures.

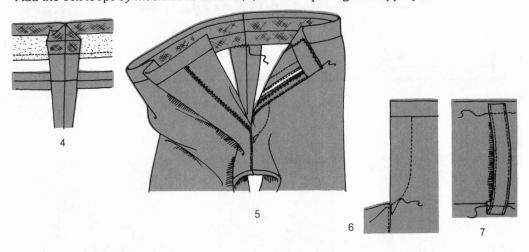

Crotch shield: Some pants will not require leg reinforcements (see page 493) because the pattern includes a crotch shield. Seam crotch shield sections, then stitch the two fabric layers together, leaving an opening. Trim, turn, press, and slipstitch opening. On inside, pin crotch shield to pants; turn crotch seam to one side and blindstitch shield to pants along seam. Tack at inner leg seams.

HEMS AND CUFFS: Smooth, even **hems** on pants are the result of careful work. Match the method to the fabric; for example, knits and lightweight fabrics may need interfaced hems. Refer to pages 338 to 341 and choose the hemming procedure most suitable.

Pants with flat, sharp-looking **cuffs** look especially well-tailored. If your pattern does not have cuffs, establish the outseam length (page 477), then allow twice the desired cuff width, retaining a 1″ hem. The trick for perfect cuffs is to make the upper edge a bit wider than pants leg, so the pants legs do not wrinkle. Interface cuffs in fabrics such as knits to prevent them from collapsing. Cut bias strips the cuff width plus 1¼″; center strips over the outer cuff layer and baste. Machine-stitch interfacing in place a scant ⅛″ above the foldline and below the hemline. Stitch the leg seam; taper in from the knee to the hemline, reducing the circumference of the lower edge. Then taper stitching back to the seamline at the cuff foldline. Taper stitching in again to second hemline, then back to seamline at bottom edge. Press seams open, clipping if necessary (1). Finish the raw edge with a zigzag or overcast stitch. Turn cuff inside along the foldline. Baste close to the fold (2). Roll the folded edge to the outside, forming the cuff. Baste through all thicknesses to hold the roll in place (3). On the inside, blindstitch hem edge to pants (4).

Press carefully, forming crease. Then secure the cuffs to the pants with French tacks at the seams (5) or stitch on the outside directly in the seams (6).

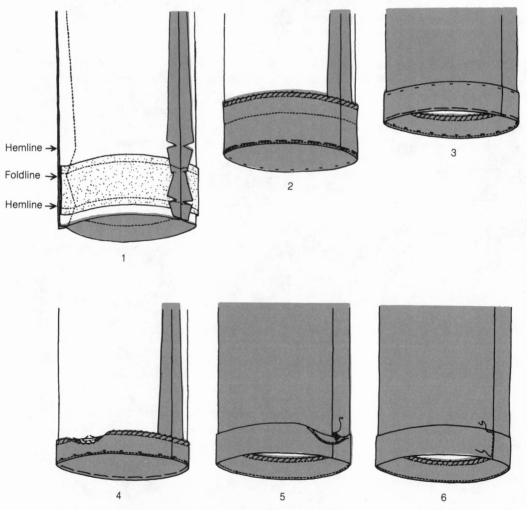

Hemline →
Foldline →
Hemline →

1

2

3

4

5

6

Tailoring a Man's Jacket

Your good sewing techniques will set the stage for a great-looking man's jacket. Make any necessary adjustments on the jacket pattern. You may wish to make a muslin fitting garment, as reputable tailors do, to work out any fitting problems. See pages 481 and 482.

First we will consider a hand-tailored jacket with modifications, then you will find machine techniques for fully washable jackets. Because the majority of tailoring techniques of menswear are the same as for women's wear, review the section on tailoring, pages 422 to 442.

A Hand-Tailored Jacket

A tailor-perfect jacket starts with the shell and the inner materials—the built-in support of interfacing, tape, shoulder pads, and tailor padding. Remember, jackets with this construction are meant to be dry-cleaned only.

INTERFACING: Match the interfacing's weight and care to the fashion fabric. Interface jacket front as indicated by your pattern—make any darts in the interfacing (pages 423 and 424). Many patterns include one or more additional front interfacing pieces, used to round out the hollow in the front of a man's shoulder. These chest pieces can be attached to the front interfacing with catchstitches and then padstitched lightly through all thicknesses (1).

Important Fitting Checkpoint: Baste darts and seams in jacket front and finger press. Pin interfacing in place; baste along center front and lapel roll line. Baste the jacket shell together. Try on with shoulder pads; make sure interfacing and fabric are molding as one, and that the jacket falls smoothly across the shoulders, chest, and back. Check pocket position; mark changes. Release basting.

Stitch and press seams or darts in jacket front and make all pockets (pages 425 and 426). Pin interfacing to wrong side of front. Baste around edges and along roll line, but keep lapel edges free (2).

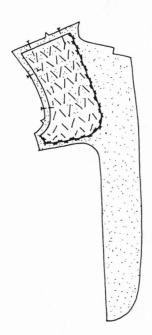

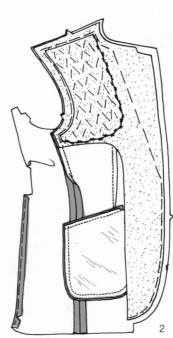

TAPING: Preshrink twill tape. Use ½″ wide for lapels and straight edges and ¼″ inch wide for armholes and neck curves. The tape on the lapel roll line, called the *bridle,* holds lapel closer to the body and prevents stretching. Cut tape according to pattern guide or to the length of the lapel line minus ⅜″. Pin securely, distributing fullness evenly. Diagonal tack both edges of bridle to interfacing. Shape lapel over hand and padstitch lightly from roll line to outer edge through all thicknesses. Press to set padstitches (see page 428). Next, tape shoulder and front edges. When taping front edges, make the tape ⅜″ shorter below the waist and ease jacket to tape (jacket will lie closer to the body). Interfacing should not be caught in the seam. Sew inner edge to interfacing with long running stitches. Catchstitch outer edge in place.

Stitch jacket shell together, with any fitting changes. If vents need extra support, see page 435. Staystitch neck through lapel markings; then tape neck and armhole edge.

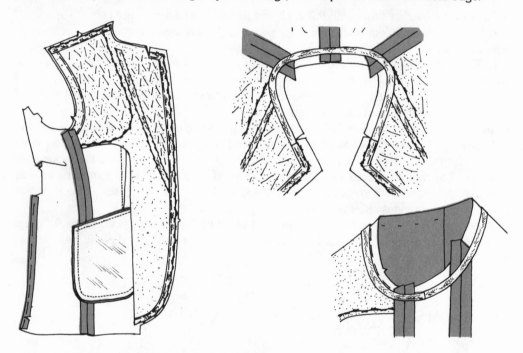

PREPARE UNDERCOLLAR: The steps for the undercollar will depend on the type of fabric—tailors use a French melton, or you can substitute felt. Otherwise, use your fashion fabric. Stitch, trim, and press any center back seam; join interfacing at center back (page 426). Pin interfacing to the undercollar along neck edges. Backstitch interfacing to the undercollar along roll line to prevent stretching. Over a tailor's ham, form a sharp crease along the roll line; a pounder and steam may be used (1).

Padstitch the stand from neck edge to roll line (see page 428), but *do not* padstitch remainder of undercollar as instructed for women. Instead, start at the center back and work rows from the roll line to the outer edge, fanning the rows to the points (2). Trim away interfacing if it is seen from the outside. Press undercollar to set padstitches. Allow it to dry.

ATTACH UNDERCOLLAR: Baste undercollar to jacket, matching symbols, placing neck edge along jacket neck seamline or as indicated by pattern. Sew undercollar to jacket with felling stitch, clipping jacket neck edge to staystitching if necessary (1).

Felling Stitch: This is a hand stitch used by tailors to ensure a flat seam when using a raw edge. Make a vertical stitch over the raw edge inserting the needle at the angle indicated to start the next stitch. Make stitches about $\frac{3}{16}''$ long and $\frac{1}{8}''$ apart (2).

Important Fitting Checkpoint: Try on jacket, matching centers and button markings; lap *left* over right and pin. The collar should be high in the back; the outer edge of the undercollar should cover the neck seam and hug the shirt collar smoothly. To make undercollar and lapels lie correctly, stretch the outer edge of the undercollar, working each side from the center back to the corner as shown (3). Crease lapel roll for about 1″ where it meets the undercollar roll. This will help you set the perfect foundation for upper collar and lapels. *Do not* proceed until you have a perfectly set undercollar and lapels, with smooth, unbroken roll and symmetrical notch placement. Make any changes needed.

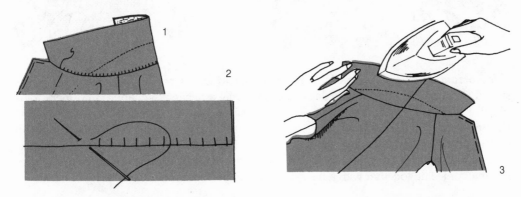

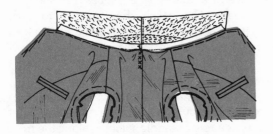

LAPEL AND UPPER COLLAR: First, stitch *front facings to front lining sections*, ending at symbol near hem edge (or about 4″ above hem); construct the inside pocket before continuing. Then assemble the remainder of the lining, with the exception of the sleeves; staystitch lining neck edges. Next, join the facing and lining unit to the jacket front, making a minute pin tuck in the lapel area as explained on page 431, before stitching seam. Press seam open over point presser, trim, grade, clip, and notch seam allowances. Turn facing and lining right sides out, tailor baste, and press finished edges only.

Now, shape the facing over the lapels and pin near seamline. Turn in the neck edge where it falls and turn in lining along seamline, clipping where necessary. Baste and pin folded edge in place (1).

Reinforce neck edge of upper collar through shoulder markings. Then place it over the undercollar, wrong sides together, matching neck seamline; pin. Smooth stand and pin along roll, tailor-baste. Now shape upper collar over outer area; pin and baste (2).

For **loose** or **thin** fabrics, enclose raw edges of undercollar with seam allowances of upper collar; baste close to fold. Miter corners and trim to reduce bulk, and trim edges evenly; baste and press. Secure with felling stitch (3).

For **thick** or **firm** fabrics, felt, or French melton, turn in outer edges and ends so they extend a scant ⅛″ beyond the undercollar; baste close to fold. Remove upper collar, press edges; miter and trim corners to reduce bulk. Repin upper collar into position; baste along stand and the outer edges. Sew collars together with felling stitches (4).

For both methods, the next step is to complete the **gorge line** (the seam where the upper collar meets the lapels). Turn collar in to meet edge of lapel; pin, then baste.

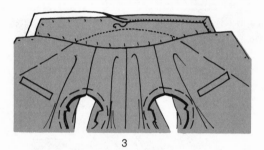

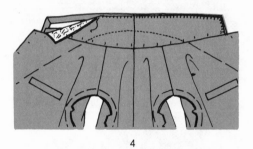

3

4

Important Fitting Checkpoint: Try on jacket to check gorge line; collar and lapels should lie smoothly without wrinkles or bubbles. Make necessary changes and mark folds of collar and lapel where they meet. Trim lapel seam allowance to ¼″; turn in and baste. Next clip upper collar neck edge to shoulder marking and blindstitch back neck edge to jacket. Then trim collar seam allowance to ¼″ (5). Now form the gorge line carefully, turning under the collar seam allowance so it meets exactly the folded edge of the lapel; sew the gorge line together with a backstitch (6). Slipstitch neck edge of lining in place.

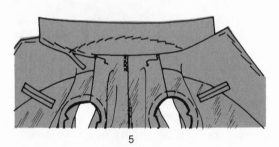

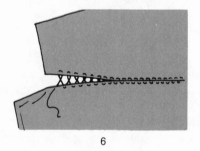

5

6

SLEEVES: Review pages 432 and 433 for pointers on sleeve finishes.

Important Fitting Checkpoint: Baste sleeve into armhole and fit before inserting permanently, as instructed on page 434. Insert sleeve padding and try on jacket, positioning shoulder pads correctly; the edge of the shoulder pad should line up with the armhole seam allowance edges. Pin pad in place from the outside. **Never** trim shoulder pads to conform with the seam allowance edges. Catchstitch shoulder pad to front interfacing and sew the armhole edge securely to the seam allowances. Then baste lining in armhole, forming a pleat at each side of the shoulder seam to eliminate excess fabric. Insert sleeve lining as shown on page 441.

HEMS: Make jacket and lining hems following instructions on pages 436 to 441.

FINISHING: Make keyhole buttonholes on the **left jacket front**, cording them for a tailored touch. (See page 321.) Sew on buttons. As a couture touch you may want to put decorative tacks at the ends of the pockets or work a row of saddle stitching along the front edges and collar.

A Machine-Tailored Jacket

The following tips will help create a durable, washable jacket. This **unstructured** construction will save time—shaping materials are handled differently to withstand laundering; machine methods are substituted for hand-sewing wherever possible—and can be used for fabrics that require dry cleaning, too. Remember that every item—notions, interfacings, lining—must be washable and require the same care as your fashion fabric. Any jacket pattern can be adapted to this easier way of construction.

INNER CONSTRUCTION: For speed, interface the jacket front and collar with one of the fusible interfacings (see below). For lighter-weight, nonfusible interfacings that you want to catch in the seams, add ⅝″ seam allowances to the front and neck edges of the front interfacing if they were eliminated in the pattern—it will be held down by the buttonholes and buttons.

Padstitching can be done entirely by machine, using a straight or zigzag stitch (see next page). The bridle can also be attached by machine—substitute a row of machine stitching for the diagonal tacking. Stitch through all thicknesses along the edge next to the lapel roll line. The front edges can be taped by using a straight or zigzag machine stitch.

LINING: Consider the time spent constructing a lining versus clean-finishing each exposed seam, or facing and hem edges. For **lining**, stitch front facing and front lining section together to within 4″ to 6″ of lower edge. Add a patch pocket, if desired, then complete lining. Stitch back pleat for 2″ at neck and waist; insert sleeve by machine. For an **unlined** jacket, purchase extra fabric. Cut two additional fronts, instead of using the front facing piece, to cover the front interfacing and shoulder pads; make a self-fabric cover for the back of the shoulder pads. Finish the exposed seam allowances, facing, and hem edges with machine zigzag stitching or by binding the edges with double-fold bias tape. Flat-fell, welt, and double-welt seams (pages 212 and 213) are three self-finishing seams that are often used in menswear. Many firmly woven or knitted fabrics may need only topstitched seams for a durable finish.

FUSING INTERFACING: On front interfacing, trim away all seam allowances except at armhole. Trim diagonally across tip of lapel point to eliminate bulk. Fuse interfacing in place, following manufacturer's instructions.

To give added weight to the lapel point so it will lie flat against the jacket, cut another piece of interfacing the shape of the lapel point. Trim away seam allowances and tip of point and fuse on top of first layer (1).

For collar, trim away all seam allowances on interfacing and fuse to undercollar. To reinforce collar stand, cut a second layer of interfacing to fit from roll neck line to neck seam and fuse on top of first layer (2).

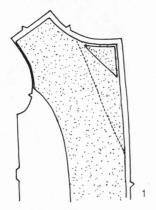

1

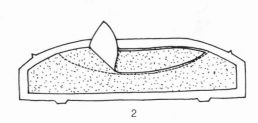

2

PADSTITCHING BY MACHINE: To stabilize the undercollar and interfacing, substitute a row of machine stitches for the back stitches along the roll line, page 498, then shape as directed. Replace padstitching with machine stitches, ending stitches at seamlines as shown.

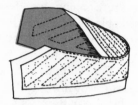

CONSTRUCTING COLLAR AND LAPELS: This technique works equally well on all fabric weights, but *you must add a ⅝'' seam allowance to all edges of the undercollar* if it has been eliminated for hand-tailoring by the pattern.

First staystitch the jacket neck edge. Then pin the undercollar to the jacket, clipping jacket neck edge as needed. Stitch neck seam between the symbols. Trim seam allowances to ¼''; press open (1). Now stitch the upper collar to the facing/lining unit or facing unit in the same manner as for the undercollar. Do not trim seam; press it open (2).

With right sides together, pin the facing/collar unit to the jacket matching neck seamlines; baste neck edges together. Now fit the jacket *wrong side out* so the upper collar is on top and the front facing edges are next to the body. Shape upper collar and lapel facing over the undercollar and jacket lapels, maintaining shape of undercollar and lapel roll. Pin collar, lapel, and front edges together as they fall; the undercollar and garment lapel edges may extend beyond upper collar and lapel edges (3).

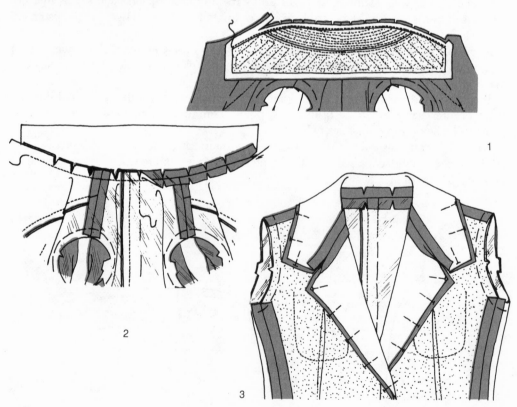

Stitch collar edges together between markings along undercollar seamline, stretching or easing (keep neck seam allowances free). Now stitch facing to garment between marking using garment seamlines. Trim, grade, clip, or notch seam (4). Remove neck basting and turn garment right side out. Press edges, favoring upper collar and lapel to end of roll; then favor jacket below. Topstitch ¼'' from front, lapel, and collar edges to hold them in place.

Complete *sleeves* including the hem. To insert sleeves and place shoulder pads, see page 434. Sew shoulder pads securely to the front interfacing and the armhole seam allowances.

For a lined jacket, match neck seams and stitch in seam between shoulder. Hold the armholes in place with a prickstitch (page 200) making tiny stitches about ½'' apart in the seam (5).

For an unlined jacket, turn in neck edges ⅝'' and sew to jacket by hand or machine. Anchor shoulder and side edges of front facing to the back seam allowances *only* by hand or machine. Then clean-finish armhole seam (6).

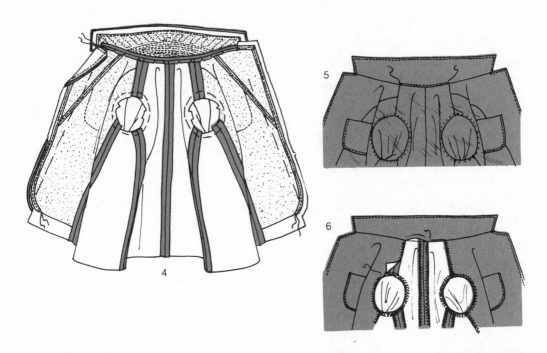

Note: There are other collar methods that will work equally well for an unstructured jacket that will look well after laundering. (See pages 260 to 263.) The rolled collar works well for thin, lightweight fabrics. But do not use it for heavier or bulky fabrics as the collar will be sandwiched between jacket and facing, forcing the seam allowances in one direction. This may cause an unsightly ridge on the gorge line. The notched collar may be used for any fabric weight. The tailored collar techniques (pages 426 to 431) are especially good for mediumweight, heavyweight, or bulky fabrics.

FINISHING: Complete the jacket hems, finishing corners as suggested on pages 436 and 437. Complete lining hem by the free-hanging method (page 440) for easier pressing. Make hand- or machine-worked keyhole buttonholes (pages 320 and 321) in the *left front* and sew buttons securely to the *right front*. Now a final pressing is in order. With your jacket completed in record time, you should be happy; the jacket will be able to withstand rigorous wear and give you many hours of pleasure.

Index

d